FOREBODINGS

CONQUERORS OF K'TARA
BOOK 1

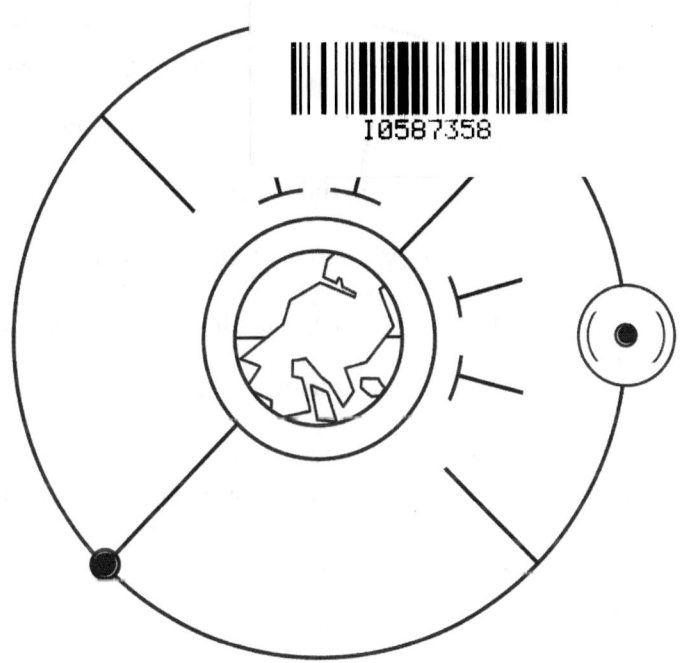

I0587358

L.A. DI PAOLO

To my parents.

Ai miei genitori.

ACKNOWLEDGEMENTS

As is the case for others who have attempted and done what I have done here, the coming of this novel would not have been possible without a number of people who encouraged me and supported me throughout.

The first I must thank are my children: Sofia for her helpful comments even though she was only thirteen when I finalized the manuscript; Joseph for his invaluable input into the biological and astronomical settings of the novel; Tristan for reading the entire first draft, being my number one fan, and giving me priceless ideas for various scenes and character names. I also wish to thank my brother, Pat, for reading my final draft and giving me useful advice about format and structure to improve the reading experience, and his wife, Mariève, for doing what no other could have done: help me describe the novel verbally and with confidence. My warmest thanks also go to my sister, Vicky, and my parents, Pasquale and Filomena, for reviewing my author's web site and giving me their thoughts on its contents, as well as to my good friend Nathalie Marquis Rosati who provided many corrections and unmistakable encouragement with her funny and honest reactions, and to everyone else who supported me in their own way along the way.

I wish to thank, as well, Michele (pronounced Meekeleh) Parisi, the young Italian illustrator who gave life to the images I had in my mind, and Guylaine Audette for her part in creating a wonderful cover.

And lastly, I must not forget to thank Samantha George, who – although she was only a high school junior when I hired her – edited and critiqued my manuscript as well as any professional editor or reviewer could have done.

Table of Contents

To my readers: If you find errors in the book – which can remain despite the thorough editing process – you may email them to me through my website's contact form (at https//ladipaolo.net) and run a chance to win a free copy of a new edition of Book 1 or a free copy of Book 2 upon their release.

Note about this edition: Aside from the usual typographical and syntactic corrections, several scenes were revised to enhance the quality of the text as well as to remove unnecessary material from them, which slowed the action at inappropriate times. Most importantly, a few names were changed: Rania Lux Baiula became Tania Lux Baiula.

"It will come to be that the truth about the past and the fears about a future yet-to-be-etched will have crushed a people. Yet, it will also come to pass that from their ashes, a new order will emerge, and a new song will rise."

I THE BOLINGARS

Toras's sudden screams shattered the dead calm of the midday hours. His skin was being split open and burned by the unforgiving rays of the twin suns which cared not who their victim was, or why Toras had lain there as they reached toward the zenith of their daily journey through the K'Taran sky.

But today was not the day the young Human would let the suns have his flesh. Screaming from the pain, heart racing from panic, mind numb from the heat, and his legs still unsteady, Toras shot-up despite it all and ran toward the woods as fast as he could.

Toras felt an immediate sense of relief upon entering the woods which enveloped him with cool, moist air. He looked down at himself and shook his head when he saw his skin covered with old, dried blood and dirt surrounding numerous, fresh blistering lesions on his limbs. He also felt throbbing wounds on his face. He realized that unless he washed and dressed his wounds quickly, they would surely become infected in this cool and humid environment, and he did not have the energy to fight an infection now.

Toras should have known better than to sleep out in the open, and he berated himself for it. But the exhaustion of the last few days had finally caught up with him, and upon landing in the middle of that clearing the night before, he had just thrown himself down onto the ground and drifted off into a deep sleep, trusting that he would wake before the suns reached their apex the following day. Unfortunately for him, he had not; the suns had begun to do their work and the storm, which always followed, could be seen in the distance approaching quickly.

Toras groaned as the novelty of the coolness passed and the pain resurfaced with renewed vigor. He shook his head and said aloud, "I need to clean all this, and bandage it…quickly."

Responding to a sudden realization, he said "Where's Scorch? Scorch!"

Some ten meters behind him, a curled-up form raised its head abruptly. When Toras shouted his name again, the proud creature stood on his four muscular limbs and stretched his leathery wings

1

while sending a screech filled with concern, and then started toward his master with a quickening pace.

When Toras saw the animal, it was with joy he said, "Scorch! For a moment, I thought you'd left me."

Scorch released short, tremulous rumbles which accompanied the furious beating of his hindwings against his forewings. He backed away, resenting his master's insinuations.

Toras said in between groans "Come on, Scorch! I need the saddle…which I left on your back last night. I'm really sorry for that."

Scorch sent an accusatory screech this time, but then approached his master to let him take the saddle. Toras thanked the animal with a pat on his smooth, ridged beak, grateful for having such a dependable companion. In fact, Scorch was his most loyal friend, taking him across fields and mountain tops, or unending miles of deadly waters, by day and by night, and in peacetime as in wartime without ever complaining. It was perhaps the fact that furan and prince had quite literally grown up side by side that bound them to one another so strongly, even more so than the utility provided by the furan to his master, or the food the latter provided in exchange.

As soon as the saddle was off, Scorch arched his back and made a strange moaning sound. Just then, Toras's wounds fulminated with pain again, and he screamed. Scorch turned to his master with a worried look.

Toras said "I really need to take care of these wounds, Scorch…which means I first need to wash myself."

Toras continued, "If I'm not mistaken, Aquilaqua [1] is about three hundred meters west of us, across the woods."

Scorch nodded with the typical up-and-down motion of his head. Toras looked at him, wondering whether it would be fair to put the saddle back on him. But though he would have preferred to do just that, he decided to carry it instead. After all, this situation was entirely his fault. So, he picked up his burden, motioned Scorch to follow, and got going.

Ten minutes and a few more growls and curses later, Toras and Scorch stepped onto a pebbly beach. In front of them, a stream gurgled and splashed as it flowed over and between stones and

---

[1] Aquilaqua: meaning "Water of the Aquilians."

boulders. Toras noticed a wide, calm pool, which looked like a good place to clean his body, not too far upstream of the rapids. He walked to it with an urgent pace, looking forward to finally washing and treating his wounds – and doing it before the storm hit. Having placed the saddle on a large dry boulder, he proceeded to undress, throwing his heavily soiled and bloodstained clothes onto the pebbly beach, and dove in. The prince swam to a sandbar, then stood and began gently rubbing and cleaning the fresh wounds, groaning every so often, while scrubbing the rest to remove the dirt and the old, dried blood.

Toras drew back in disgust when he noticed patches encrusted with a greenish cruor – the blood of the foul things that had attacked them the other night. The memory of the *gnarlers* – that's what he had decided to call them – assailed him suddenly and sent tremors through his body. The simple thought of them – the most grotesque and vile things he had ever faced – revived a fear in him which made him very uncomfortable, and he shook his head to try and dispel the memory. The trick worked, if only for a moment, because as the foreign matter softened and washed away, an acrid smell invaded his nostrils and brought back memories of the foul creatures ripping through his men.

Toras grunted, and started rubbing harder and faster, eliciting new groans each time he got too close to a blister. When the water had eventually taken away all the impurity, diluting it until it was no more, his mind found some calm again and Toras turned on his back and just floated there for a while, letting the coolness of the water soothe his tired muscles. But, as he looked toward the sky, a dark cloud arriving in advance of the storm sent some strange shadows through the trees' branches which – combined with an unexpected, innocent screech from Scorch – brought back even more chilling memories, those of an impossible creature he had met recently, a terrible creature from the past known as *the Serpent*, though to most who saw it, it only looked like an abnormally large rokon [2]. It was the encounter with this creature which had launched Toras on his deadly journey. The memory of the Serpent's blood-curdling screeches reverberated through Toras's bones and muscles just as the

---

[2] A large reptilian flying predator from Mo'Tarkoth, a land to the north of the continent of Aquinos.

river swelled from an onrush of dangerous-looking waves, causing the prince to panic momentarily and to choke as water splashed into his nose.

Worried for his master, Scorch moved to jump into the water, but Toras stopped him with a shout as he began swimming back. Fortunately, the shore was only a few meters away, and despite the quickening flow, Toras got out safely.

When he walked out of the water, Scorch approached him and nudged him with his beak – his dark eyes worried again.

"I just had some unwelcome memories when you –" Toras was about to blame the furan for what happened, but he caught himself and said, "when the water rushed me, and I panicked for a moment. But thanks for your concern."

The furan replied with a deep purr and a nod, understanding from his master's tone and words that he was well, if in a bad mood.

"I think we should find somewhere safe to wait for the storm to pass. Come Scorch."

Toras hurried to his saddlebag, put on some clean clothes, stuffed the dirty ones in, winced as he put the saddle on his shoulder, and ran into the forest, with Scorch behind him.

After a few minutes, he found a large boulder which created a sort of cave, and they took cover underneath it just when the storm's winds, which ripped across the land as the Bolingars [3] neared their end, tore a branch from a nearby tree. Fortunately for Toras and Scorch, today's Bolingars were not as bad as they would be in another few days when they'd be right in the middle of the next Bolingar Fourth [4].

Toras now did his best to dry his skin and dress his wounds, though the wind and dust made the latter somewhat difficult. As he applied the last bandage, he shook his head and said to himself "Damned stupid, is what I am. It might have been a fitting end for

---

[3] The Bolingars were the hottest hours of the K'Taran day, when the Blue Sun and Red Sun stood side by side, two fourths every month. The term Bolingars was an Alvinorian deformation of "Boiling Hours". The Bolingars were accompanied by fierce storms.

[4] A Bolingar Fourth was a fourth during which the two suns were side-by-side. Bolingar Fourths alternated with the In-Between Fourths during which the suns overlapped, with the smaller Blue sun or the larger Red sun in front; these fourths were cooler than the Bolingar Fourths.

me to just die out there, turned to ashes by the suns, after all the men who lost their lives because of me this past fourth [5]!"

Toras spent some time thinking about all that had passed of late. After half an hour, when the winds quieted, Toras heard his stomach rumble a complaint. But he and Scorch needed to resume their journey, so they would have to satisfy their hunger with some dried mound grubs until they reached their destination.

The prince was on his way to Furan City, the capital of Alvinoria, to rejoin his eldest brother and father, and he still had some twenty hours to go. Fifteen days earlier, following the battle with the Serpent, he and thirty of his and his brother's guardians had left the fortress at Horn's Pass and flown south to look for the high king who had been missing. Toras had found his father, but most of the men who had accompanied him were now dead. Indeed, the day after leaving the fortress, the prince lost the first ten men when they made a detour to go defend the inhabitants of a village against the same rokon – or Serpent, or whatever it was – that had already attacked the fortress. A little later, due to a bad decision on his part – a very bad decision, which still knotted his stomach every time he thought about it – he lost another nine. And on the way back, after having found his father, another four men died at the hands of the vile *gnarlers*. Only three men survived now, in addition to Toras.

The king, Toras hoped, was continuing safely toward Furan City. Indeed, when the *gnarlers* attacked them, Toras begged his father to ride on toward the capital, while promising to catch up with him as soon as he and the men had dispatched the vile things. The king had resisted such an insulting request at first, but staying would have been foolish given that he was not dressed for combat, and that the company was being assailed by an unknown foe which had already killed a man and half of their mounts. So, with great reluctance, the king agreed to leave.

Aside from the grief that the loss of so many men still caused him, the equally large loss of furans angered and saddened Toras; they had not asked to be there, to die in incomprehensible agony. And yet, death had claimed them, as it had most of his and his brother's men.

---

[5] A fourth was an 8-day period. The Alvinorian calendar had four fourths in a month, and ten months in a year. The fourths were based on the suns' cycle of rotation around each other, which lasted 32 days.

The prince simply could not understand what was happening. He had never seen these creatures before and had only heard of one of them in stories people told each other around fires. All had had the same questions: *Where are these things coming from? Why are they here?* A rokon which was not a rokon and which the Sisterhood referred to as "the Serpent", and obscene creatures the guardians had had no name for until Toras had given them one. This had shaken the prince to the core of his bones, a sensation he had rarely felt. Only when he was ten, and had fallen off Scorch, had Toras ever felt such fear. Questions upon questions piled atop each other, none of which he had answers for.

The only survivors of Toras's doomed company were one of his brother's men, as well as his primus [6] and one of his guardians. But given that their furans were dead, and that they were in no state to travel anyway, he had been forced to leave them behind at the southern end of the Colossi's Peaks, two mornings ago. Primus Kendor had a festering wound on his torso, to which Toras had applied most of the salve a Lux Baiula [7] had given him, hoping it would help heal the officer more quickly. The prince wasn't sure, though, if the woman's medicine was made for this type of wound. As for the other two men, they had several deep wounds and had been floored by a terrible fever; Toras and Kendor had done their best to sew and cauterize the gashes. As for himself, the prince had had his right arm cut by a *gnarler's* claw. However, and fortunately for him, the cut had been shallow, and his Halfling blood had been able to neutralize the venom.

After he swallowed the last of the dried mound grubs, Toras got up and prepared Scorch for departure. As he did so, he wondered whether the men were still alive; he hoped they were. In fact, he prayed they were, despite his agnosticism. Having checked the cinches one last time and finding them properly tightened, Toras hopped on Scorch, and without any visible cues, the furan took off.

---

[6] Primus was the highest rank in the Black Guard, after that of Lord Commander. In the Royal Guard, the rank of Primus followed that of High Captain and of High Lord Commander. A Primus's insignia consisted of a blue sun on red, and a red sun on blue, within a tall rectangle formed by blue and red embroidery.

[7] Lux Baiula: Bearer of Light, a member of the Sisterhood of the Light.

The wind felt good on Toras's skin. He still winced every so often, but the pain was tolerable now. Twenty more hours to go, two days at most – less if Scorch could manage it.

II THE SERPENT

Toras had first met the Serpent at his fortress, the night before the Celebration of the Colossi, when it came looking for something…or someone. The howlers [8] must have sensed its approach that evening because their low, continuous howls had pervaded the stronghold and nearby village of Horn's Pass. Some people simply believed that a very bad storm was coming, which would be a real shame with the festivities about to begin – they thought. However, there were those – the superstitious kind – who believed that something bad, perhaps evil, was approaching; they would be right, this time.

Despite the howlers, Toras and his brother Aithen were trying to relax in the dining hall. They had spent the day coordinating and helping with the arrangements to celebrate the liberation of the fortification by the Colossi during the Trionian War four hundred and sixty-seven years before, in 1333 CE. The most difficult part of the preparations was certainly the recreation of the battle scene in the village of Horn's Pass, just a kilometer south of the fortress. There, statues of the Rokothians and Zebulonians with wicked looks on their stone faces, of the glorified Colossi and Kynarians, and of Humans with their wondrous furans had been taken out of the barns and placed around the town green to represent the battle scene.

This was definitely hard work, especially with the statues of the Colossi weighing almost a ton each, but the men had performed it in song, sweating rivers all the while, as they did every year. The women, in the meantime, had busied themselves mending old costumes or sewing new ones similar to those worn by the Alvinorians and their allies during that war, as well as tired themselves butchering bleaters and cacklers for the feast. As for the kids, they had been left to their own devices to amuse themselves as they wished, running around, playing games of stones, or getting into one or another mischief. All in all, it had been a good and rewarding day, especially once all the statues had been set, and the brothers,

---

[8] Howler: Large, domesticated predatory Flyer used by Humans to guard their property as well as for their companionship.

heirs to the throne of Alvinor, were quite satisfied despite their fatigue.

Toras and his brother were the sons of High King Octavius I of House Coriolis, King of Alvinoria, and Overlord of the lands of Jarah, Pargah and Yerlah, and of Lady Darya of Laranir, a Kynarian noblewoman and priestess. They were thus Halflings.

Physically, both princes, and their younger brother Ori, exhibited a mixture of traits. From their Kynarian ancestry, they got height and a lean yet muscular build, a thin straight nose, and pale brown skin. From their Human ancestry, they received black hair and a hairy face. But their most distinctive traits were the green eyes and eyebrows they received from their Coriolan lineage.

Despite their shared features, though, the two brothers were easily distinguishable from one another: the younger Toras had a squarer face as well as thicker bones and a heavier musculature owed to his more physically-active lifestyle, whereas Aithen sported a thinner build and smoother hands given that he spent much more time overseeing the army than in the field with the soldiers. The brothers' mix of features combined to create figures which generally pleased Human girls, though not their Kynarian counterparts, and Toras often wondered why the latter appeared to disapprove of him and his brothers when they visited Kynaria.

Now, though the princes shared a physical resemblance, they were nothing alike temperamentally. Indeed, while Aithen was a thinker and strategist, his brother was a doer and sharp tactician. Toras also had a more difficult time than Aithen managing the conflict between their introverted Kynarian nature and their fierce and extraverted Human disposition, a difficulty which resulted in a volatile temperament that often troubled those who did not know him.

Notwithstanding his shortcomings, though, Toras was, at only twenty-two years of age, Lord Commander of the fortress at Horn's Pass, which served as a barrier between Rokoth, to the west, and Lower Alvinor, to the east, where the capital city of his father's kingdom was located. The prince defended the pass with a force of one thousand men, known as the Black Guard, a guard which was – in the eyes of its members and even of some outsiders – as formidable as the Royal Guard itself, despite its smaller size. Whether this was true or not, it was the source of continuous friction between the two guards despite, or perhaps because of the princes' kinship.

But there was one period of the year during which the members of the Royal and the Black guards enjoyed and even sought each other's company, and that was during the five days of the Celebration of the Colossi. And this year had been no different with men of both guards laboring together and challenging each other with wide grins and good-hearted laughs – for the most part – all throughout the preparations.

Some forty minutes before the Red Sun set, as the soldiers were sitting for the night's pre-feast meal, and as Toras was pouring some more wine into his brother's cup, a jarring screech came from the west and startled everyone in and around the fortress. This screech was followed by several more ear-piercing cries, which alarmed everyone, and people looked up in the beginning darkness, wondering what was coming.

The princes put down their wine cups and ran toward the wide balcony that extended from the fortress's dining hall. From there, they could only see the jagged cliffs of the mountain upon which the shrieks continued to reverberate. Aithen, perhaps responding to an instinct, said with some urgency in his voice, "Toras, I think we should put the guardians on alert."

Toras gave him a questioning look and said, "You're worried too? What with the howlers baying so strangely this past hour, and now these screeches? They sound like the shrieks of a rokon, but no rokon I've met has ever made me nervous, though I do hate them, and I've dealt with my share of them coming through the Pass."

"I do not think it's a rokon, Toras. And I do not know why, but there is something about these screeches that sounds wrong."

Toras nodded in agreement and called the guardians posted at the entrance of the dining hall.

Two young men, with barely any facial hair, came in to take their commander's orders. The assignment of such young men to guard the prince was a sign of the peaceful times. But Aithen remembered that more seasoned soldiers had been posted there before.

Addressing the taller of the two guardians, Toras said, "Parthos, please ask Primus Kendor as well as High Captain Harlion to put the men on alert. The High Lord Commander and I will be out in a few moments."

11

As the young soldiers stepped out, a stunning woman appeared in the hall. She had long, wavy reddish hair and deep blue eyes. A purple cloak hung over her shoulders, covering a dark blue dress tied at the waist by a vivid purple sash with a piece of a red sash sewed onto it; the colors of her attire seemed to be made to daze and command the attention of people. The woman also had the allure of a person used to giving orders with her narrowly-spaced, high-arching eyebrows, and firm straight lips.

The woman was Elyana Lux Baiula, advisor to the high king and a member of a powerful and ancient Order, known as *Lucis Sororum Societas*, or Order of the Sisters of the Light. Its members, known as *Lux Baiulae,* were gifted with a biology that gave them abilities well beyond those of ordinary people, some of whom looked at them in awe, while the rest looked at them with a deep distrust. The Order's head, known as *Magna Mater* [9], was the next most powerful – if not the most powerful – leader in the civilized parts of Terrae Regis.

The woman entered Toras's chambers without invitation, stopped in front of the princes and said, "Aithen, Toras, you must let me handle this!"

Toras started, "What–!"

"You have no idea what is coming, and I have no time to explain. Do not try to argue with me, Toras. Follow me; we need to organize the defenses."

The princes eyed each other uneasily. Toras shook his head and caught up with the Lux Baiula who was already a few steps ahead of them.

"Elyana, what's going on? It's not a rokon coming, *is it?*"

Without breaking her stride, the woman made to answer but then told the prince to just follow.

With an indignant tone, Toras said, "Elyana, I'm Lord Commander of this fortress, and I need to know–"

The Lux Baiula paused for a brief moment, and looked the prince straight in the eyes, "Toras, you are right. But something is coming which may very well destroy us all, so our priority is to get the fortress ready."

"*My* priority will be to get the fortress ready once *I* know what is going on!"

---

[9] Magna Mater: Great Mother.

12

With a grim look on her face, Elyana replied calmly, "Toras, you will not be able to defend the fortress against this – if I'm right. I will explain everything once the men are assembled."

And with that, Elyana resumed her frenetic pace down the hallway.

Toras looked back at his approaching brother, shook his head again and ran after Elyana.

As they came down the large black steps of the hold, on either side of the Lux Baiula, the princes noticed the confused looks of the civilians, and the purposeful motions of the soldiers as they got their weapons ready and moved to their assigned posts under their commanders' barks, despite their own misgivings.

When he noticed the princes come down, Primus Kendor started toward them, but Elyana Lux Baiula held up her hand, stopping the officer in his tracks. When she reached the bottom of the steps, she proceeded to call the princes' respective ranking officers to herself. The men walked over with questioning frowns, but with calm and assurance, hiding the inner worries spurred by the Lux Baiula's taking of command. Something terrible must be approaching. But what could it be? The cries were those of a rokon, weren't they?

"High Captain Harlion, Primus Kendor, you will follow my orders. Please assemble your men immediately."

When the men hesitated, Toras and Aithen nodded their heads. The officers gave a nod in return and did as the Lux Baiula requested.

It took the soldiers a few minutes to come together in the fortress's plaza. Once gathered, the Lux Baiula wasted no time and gave all a description of the physical attributes of what they were going to face. Incomprehension flooded the men's faces. All the members of the Black Guard had seen rokons before, as had many of Aithen's Guard, and no rokon had been as large as what the Lux Baiula had just described. Moreover, the rokons they had encountered had never been the cause of such high alarm that two guard units had needed to be mobilized to defend against it.

Although he too was worried about this approaching rokon, something nagged at the younger prince. So, he approached the Lux Baiula and asked quietly, "Elyana, how can you know the physical characteristics of this rokon? It's still kilometers away, and I know you *cannot* see things from a distance. There's something else you're not telling us."

13

Just then, another hair-raising screech pierced the darkening skies, as if to reinforce the prince's statement. The few civilians in the fortress, standing huddled to the side of the soldiers, jumped out of their skins, while the soldiers remained outwardly calm but were starting to wonder whether the Lux Baiula might not be rightly concerned.

Elyana knew Toras was right to demand to know more, so she motioned the high prince and the two captains over and began, "My Princes, captains, listen closely, and do not repeat any of what I am about to tell you to anyone else; I do not want to paralyze your men or the civilians with thoughts of the supernatural. I am telling *you* because you should all be able to handle the truth, and having the information will help you stay safer. But there is no time for questions, so you will need to simply trust what I say, and then do as I ask."

The four men nodded, more or less reluctantly, and Elyana proceeded to tell them what she knew of the *Serpent* – the name by which the supernatural rokon approaching the fortress was known in the Sisterhood. She told them of the legends, and the facts both, because she needed to make certain that they were ready to face the reality of it, as well as control what their imaginations might invent once they saw the creature. All four men stared at the Lux Baiula in disbelief, shocked and muted, but for various reasons: Toras and Kendor couldn't believe such a thing really existed, while Aithen and Harlion couldn't believe such a thing could have come back.

The Serpent was supposed to have died some six hundred years ago, at the end of the Dark Battle, which meant that most humanoids only knew of it as a mythical monster – a terrible, frightful creature mothers told their children about to convince them to go to sleep when they argued. But the Lux Baiulae, and those few who were taught history by them, knew the Serpent to have been a real creature, one which had ravaged humanity in the service of an even greater evil, before it finally came to its end.

The various books in the Sisterhood's library described the Serpent more or less consistently. The most detailed accounts had been pieced together by chance and science, and described the Serpent as measuring a good ten meters from wingtip to wingtip. It had five-centimeter long [10], razor-sharp, forward-facing teeth covering the whole of its body – teeth with which it ripped the flesh of its victims. The snout had two frighteningly long fangs, and, based on wound and cadaver analysis, it also had solid, sharp edges with which is crushed its prey's bones behind the fangs. All scholarly authors agreed that the Serpent fed on humanoids as well as on the occasional furan, while lay authors often described the creature as feeding exclusively on beautiful but impure maidens – or on disobedient children.

The most closely-guarded books of the Sisterhood also told of some unnatural abilities the Serpent seemed to possess. By some accounts, the creature had the ability to kill a humanoid by tearing away his or her soul, which soul could be seen resisting with terror, fighting to remain within its body. But the evidence accumulated by the Sisterhood's scholars presented a somewhat different reality, having more to do with some kind of energy that the Serpent used to attack its victim's brain and caused it to quite literally fry. This cooking of the brain led to the release of smoke and ashes, which the uneducated interpreted as the soul being pulled out through the victim's shrinking eyes. A few decades after the Dark Battle, a humorous scholar even coined a phrase for these attacks: Dark Energy Brain Surge Attack, or DEBSA. Despite the neat, natural explanation though, the supernatural beliefs about the Serpent had persisted in many circles because no one in the Sisterhood had been able to recreate the process, given that Lux Baiulae were barred from intentionally killing eyed organisms for experimental purposes.

When the Lux Baiula was done describing the Serpent, the four men just continued to stare at her in disbelief. The princes were the first to shake themselves out of their shock, and asked almost as one, "What do you wish us to do, Lux Baiula?"

Elyana gave the princes what seemed to be a smile of gratitude, and replied, "High Captain, Primus, I need you to gather all the villagers within the fortress. Ask the men among the civilians to arm themselves, and have everyone else sent into the mountain. I need all the defenders – soldiers and civilians alike – at the ready within twenty minutes. Most importantly, instruct everyone to remain within three hundred meters of the central fountain. Aside from this,

---

[10] 5 centimeters is approximately 2 inches.

15

you may organize the various corps of the two Guards, as well as the civilians, as you see fit to defend against aerial attack...and have the tall lanterns around the fortress lit so that we may better see our foe."

The captains nodded and were about to execute the Lux Baiula's orders, when Elyana asked, "Furans and vorans [11] are in their night stables, I assume?"

The night stables were stables built into the mountain itself. The Black Guard kept its mounts there at night to protect them from theft as well as from predators which might want to prey on the vorans.

Primus Kendor replied affirmatively.

"Good. You must know that I will not be able to assist in the offense as I will be solely focused on protecting the defenders, and the princes in particular. To do that, I will establish a nebula [12] over the fortress to shield everyone from the Serpent's mental attacks," and in a rare moment of public self-doubt she added, "At least I hope I can make this Binding work."

That caused the princes and the captains alike to eye each other nervously.

"You must also know that I will not be able to protect anyone from physical harm, except the princes whom I will cover with Bound Shields [14]."

Kendor, always questioning things, like his commander, asked, "Lux Baiula. Why the three-hundred-meter radius around the fountain?"

"Simply because that is as far as I may be able to extend the nebula, Primus."

The officer nodded.

---

[11] Voran: A tall, domesticated three-toed herbivore, one of the many Trumpeter species, used for pulling carts or riding. Vorans had very beautiful trumpet-like calls.

[12] Nebula - A field of energy generated by some Lux Baiulae which could shield people from certain harmful cerebral waves; also known as a disruption field.

[13] The night stables were stables built into the mountain itself. The Black Guard kept its mounts there at night to protect them from theft as well as from predators which might want to prey on the vorans.

[14] Bound Shield: An electromagnetic shield generated using the Bind, and which repelled physical objects.

Harlion asked, "Is that all, Lux Baiula?"

"It is, except for this: your men may see things tonight which they will not comprehend. It will therefore be important for the two of you to keep moving around the fortress to maintain your men's spirits. You are seasoned officers, and I trust you can keep your doubts in check to preserve order even in the most desperate of situations."

The captains nodded crisply to acknowledge her trust and went to do as commanded.

Meanwhile, Elyana gave the royal brothers some advice too, "As for you, my Princes, I would prefer you remained in one spot as it would be easier for me to keep you shielded that way. But the villagers will need reassurance too, and I do not believe they will respond to the military commanders as well as they will to you, so it would be helpful for you to go around the fortress to strengthen their courage when it starts failing. Just be careful, and do not let anything you see startle you; it would not help boost anyone's confidence. Most importantly, be sure to stay within three hundred meters of the fountain!" Then, she added with a finger on her red lip, as if speaking to herself, "In fact, it would be helpful if the limit could be delineated on the ground."

Toras replied, "I will see to it that the safe zone is clearly marked, Elyana."

"Very well, thank you Toras. And be careful, both of you."

With that, Aithen and Toras left to see to the organization of the villagers who had started flocking into the citadel at the sound of the alarm.

Elyana looked toward the soldiers and noticed the questions on the men's faces as their officers transmitted her orders. It was clear they did not know what it was that she expected from her tactic, but they obeyed their officers anyway. Satisfied, Elyana walked toward the central fountain. Standing next to it, she would be completely exposed, but from that position, she would be able to cover most of the fortress with an invisible nebula – if she was able to generate it. Indeed, she had never done it before, but the Binding came to her along with the memories of the Serpent, when she first recognized its cry. This knowledge was the result of the Memory Transfer she had received soon after becoming a Lux Baiula, an age ago it seemed. But she hoped against hope that the disruption field would be able to save the defenders from the horrible brain attack the Serpent was known to have used on its victims so long ago.

These memories also told her that many would die tonight. Yet, what other choice did she have? Perhaps, she thought, if the Serpent attempted to attack *her* with the DEBSA – how strange that Sisters from so long ago had already learned to coin acronyms – she might know what Binding it was using and might then be able to create a more effective shield against it, if she survived the attack herself.

If the Serpent attacks me, I will *survive, and I* will *protect the princes and the men.*

Even if her nebula worked though, she could not keep the defenders from being terribly wounded or swooped up by the Serpent, unless she killed it, which was unlikely even for a Sister of her strength. She knew her energy would be strained beyond anything she had experienced in a long time because of the need to shield the fortress with the disruption field, while simultaneously protecting Aithen and Toras with a Bound Shield, even as they moved about the compound.

I wish there existed a way to give them the knowledge of the commanders who fought the Serpent in the Dark Battle. But K'Tara help them, *the princes and their officers are just going to have to rely on their skills and present experience to fend-off the creature.*

* * *

That night, then, all the men able to fight – civilians and soldiers alike – took part in defending the fortress and the village of Horn's Pass that lay just outside the stronghold. About two thirds of the defenders were soldiers, and the rest were blacksmiths, farriers, peddlers, farmers, and other civilians. Fortunately, most had some experience with bows as they used them to hunt or to protect their herds or flocks from wild furans, as well as from the occasional rokon and other predators that roamed these wild regions of the kingdom.

As for the rest, women and children and all those unable to fight, they had been taken by the village healers into the caves of the great fortification, which had been built out of the mountain itself. The caves smelled strongly of vorans and furans, which brought a grimace on the healers' faces as they pressed people forward. Some people complained about having been forced to abandon the cooking

18

food, which everyone, including the guardians, had planned to enjoy together after the long and tiring day. Fortunately, there was food aplenty in the caverns – though it may not be fresh and warm – and there was more water than could be drunk thanks to the underground river which ran through the caves, so the complaints eventually subsided, especially when the creature's cries increased in intensity.

Just before the Serpent arrived, Elyana – who had spent the last few minutes stilling her thoughts against the knowledge that many would die that night – clapped her hands and caused an unnaturally loud sound to reverberate throughout the citadel. Everyone turned toward her as if by force, and with a voice that carried just as unnaturally as had the sound of the clap, she gave the men her final advice. She urged the defenders to remain calm despite the great fear they might feel, and to focus on hitting the Serpent's head and wings, always the weakest points on a well-armored, flying creature. The soldiers nodded, while the civilians stood there nervously, either tapping fingers on weapons or eyeing each other with fear. Dread permeated the fortress as if it were a physical thing.

Then it came. Many men simply froze, surprised and shocked at the sight of the gigantic lizard, while many of the younger ones could be seen turning toward their princes as if to ask, "How are we supposed to fight this?" Elyana also saw what seemed to be defiance in some men's expressions. They appeared to be thinking *"Come, come you wretched thing! I don't know what you want with us, but I'll fight you to the death!"*

But the shrieks, the shrieks were now so loud and penetrating that they were even heard by those hiding deep within the caves. Babes started crying to the top of their lungs, and their mothers could do nothing except huddle them closer, while trying to contain their own desperate fears that they were all going to die. Many, especially the older women, dropped to their knees and started praying to the Originator and the Founders.

Along the citadel's walls, a few villagers – unable to wait for the officers' signal and fearing that if they waited a moment longer they would die – released the first arrows on the Serpent. The creature responded at once with an angry shriek, diving toward the peasants who had shot those arrows. Seeing this, Harlion and Kendor gave the archers the order to shoot.

19

In the beginning, no one succeeded in lodging any projectile in the furious lizard. The civilians, spread among the soldiers, did their best to hit the Serpent, but their fear and the resulting tremors sent the arrows meters from their target. The soldiers also missed the Serpent initially, unused as they were to the deflecting winds it created with its wings.

But the guardians, split into archers and lancers, with the latter arranged along the high walls and the former along the lower ramparts, were better disciplined and equipped, and quicker to adjust their techniques, and they began hitting the Serpent. There were no shouts of joy, however. Instead, they stared with incredulity as the arrows simply fell to the ground after hitting the Serpent's body.

Toras was just as shocked. The guardian next to him said "This is no ordinary rokon, Lord Commander, on my life it isn't."

Elyana, not wanting to weaken the nebula or the Bound Shields around the princes, resisted the urge to support the defenders with her own attacks.

After a few more, unlucky volleys by archers and lancers, the high prince was finally able to pierce the Serpent's wings with an arrow each. The men shouted with joy. Seeing his brother not too far from him, Aithen shouted "The first true hit, Toras!"

Was Aithen mocking him? Toras just about hit the creature in the right eye, but it ricocheted off the scales just behind it; Toras looked at Aithen, infuriated at having missed, especially after his brother had had a successful hit.

A moment later, though, Toras succeeded as well, putting an arrow through the Serpent's left wing. Even a few soldiers got their lances to successfully pierce the Serpent's limbs, tearing through the right wing again. The Serpent's flight suddenly became jerky, and it gave an angry screech.

With all these wounds, the men were sure the rokon would slow down, but the lizard just shot itself upward, and then glided upon the winds for a minute. Could it be mending itself with some unnatural power? Toras and Aithen gave each other worried looks, refusing to acknowledge what they knew they must both be thinking.

Then the Serpent resumed its attack, taking several lives as it smashed into the citadel's walls, sending men crashing to their deaths below. As Elyana had predicted, the fighters' courage – especially that of the civilian defenders – began to fail in the face of

20

such an unstoppable foe. So, Aithen decided that it was time he and his brother go around the fortress to shore up the men's resolution. He called Toras and motioned with his head toward some farmers who had dropped their weapons despondently. Toras nodded and went to them, but not before yelling at his men to keep shooting at the creature, and yelling at the squires to refill the quivers.

As Aithen came to a middle-aged villager and what must have been his three teenage boys – all sitting with their backs to the wall and looking forlorn – he felt some anger well up within him. Here was a man who, because of his own fear and doubts, was now keeping three others from fighting! Aithen went down on his haunches to be at a level with the peasant, and said, "Good man, I need you to keep fighting. I need you all to keep fighting. I know it seems bad, but –"

The graying villager suddenly raised his head and asked angrily how they were expected to fight this monster. But when he saw the prince's surprise and disappointment, he felt deeply embarrassed, and apologized, promising to try.

Aithen helped the man to his feet, and that simple act gave the peasant more courage than words. He picked up his bow, called his sons, and all four returned to their posts more resolute than before. The prince continued his round, encouraged by this small success.

***

Elyana, alone in the center of it all, her face illuminated by the torches surrounding the fountain, could be seen sweating and exhausting herself to maintain the nebula above the fortress, as well as the shields around the princes. It seemed that the disruption field was working as she hadn't yet noticed anyone keel over inexplicably, or anyone falling to his knees in prayer at the sight of a "spirit" leaving his neighbor's body. As for the Bound Shields, they had already saved the princes' lives a few times, deflecting large, skull-crushing fragments of stone that the Serpent had torn from the fortress's ramparts. Aithen and Harlion turned her way every so often, wondering how much longer she could hold the shields.

Another hour passed, with hits and misses, but despite the best everyone did, despite the numerous wounds that had been inflicted on the Serpent, it could not be stopped, least of all killed. Every so

21

often, it would fly to the top of the cliff facing the citadel, and rest. Every time it did that, Aithen stopped, breathed a couple of slow breaths, aimed for the head and shot an arrow. The prince should have been able to hit the mark, but each time the Serpent moved its head just before the projectile hit. It was as if it knew Aithen had released an arrow. All the prince could do was growl in anger. After a few moments of rest, the Serpent would descend again to continue its attack with renewed fury.

By now, the creature had completely destroyed the outer northwestern tower of the fortress; three sweeps by it, hitting it with its tail as if with a gigantic sledgehammer, were enough to destroy it and send a dozen men to their deaths. Parts of the village were also ablaze after the Serpent tore through some homes where lanterns had been left burning. The animals – bellowers, bleaters, and trumpeters [15], as well as the howlers – were either dead, dying, or had gotten away. It was a good thing that the Guards' mounts were stabled within the protective walls of the mountain or they probably would have suffered the same fate as that of the villagers' animals.

To everyone's surprise, the Serpent suddenly let out a cry of pain and was seen tumbling toward the ground. Men on the inner ring of the northern wall cheered and shouted compliments. One of them had put a long arrow right next to the Serpent's wing joint. But as unexpectedly as it had tumbled, it rose back up, having pulled the arrow out of its limb, and it attacked the fortress with even more anger and viciousness. It descended on five men, four soldiers and a villager, and tore them to shreds with a spiraling motion. One of the men was hooked by the teeth on the Serpent's chest so deeply that he got stuck to it, causing the Serpent to jerk and slow down. The *thing* shook itself violently, unhooking the body and hurling it to the ground right next to Elyana. Blood and flesh splattered onto her; if she felt revulsion, the woman did not show it.

The rokon now flew up the cliff and stopped on a ledge to rest another moment. When it descended, it let out a screech so violent and deafening that many men fell to their knees from sheer pain and

---

[15] Bleaters were milk-producing land flyers, having lost the ability to fly during the course of their evolution; bellowers were large herbivorous, furred animals from which coonay, an edible substance, could be obtained; trumpeters were three-toed herbivores, recognized by their trumpet-like calls.

started to weep like children. Few were those who had ever faced anything remotely like this before.

Elyana, seeing the desperate situation, felt anger well-up inside of her. Questions and thoughts flooded her mind *Why is this abomination here!? What does it want? I need to put an end to this or else we will all be annihilated before the highnight comes. But I am so tired. Still, I must hold on. I* cannot *let it win, and I must protect the princes...I* must *hold on...* The Light Bearer finally decided that it was time to take some risks and begin attacking the Serpent. Yet, if she did, she would likely weaken the nebula and Bound Shields. Hoping to prevent them from completely dissolving, she focused on her metabolism and accumulated a quantity of sweet salt around the centers in her body that sustained the shields. That done, she took a deep breath and started drawing to herself the atoms from the air around her to form them into a dense, javelin-like firebolt. Men turned around and gazed in awe at the apparition of the bright, dangerous-looking form in front of the Lux Baiula.

Elyana launched the projectile. The firebolt jolted toward its target with a burning hiss. To everyone except Elyana and the princes who also had enhanced vision, the bolt was there instantly. But regardless of the apparent duration of the bolt's flight, the result was clear to everyone who saw it vanish the moment it hit the Serpent.

Elyana's heart almost sank when she saw several men suddenly drop to their knees, without apparent cause. She realized then that her fears had come true, that the nebula had indeed weakened when she shifted her focus.

Men screamed to the top of their lungs, with their hands on their temples and in total terror, trying to resist something unseen. Fortunately for them, some might say, the agony did not last long, and after a few moments the poor men fell over completely, dead. Those standing next to them were gripped by a fear unlike any they had every felt before and froze where they stood, forgetting even the Serpent.

Elyana reinforced the nebula a little more, and then refocused her mind on the Serpent, despite something inside her knowing that she had just made a grave mistake and men were dying a horrible death because of it. *So long as it doesn't take the princes,* she thought. She formed new firebolts, and launched them on the Serpent, ignoring

23

the death and the sense of doom that hung around her. But the bound-bolts just continued to vanish the moment they touched the creature.

So, Elyana began launching enormous firewhorls, which she filled with flammable matter she picked up from ground. The flames surrounded the Serpent completely. This time, the Serpent let out cries of pain, as the scorching particles of debris cut and seared its skin. Cheers rose from the fortress's defenders in response to Elyana's first successful strike and the pause it caused in the Serpent's attacks. Elyana, herself, felt a tiny sense of hope arising within her. But the Serpent healed its wounds the moment Elyana stopped hitting it to catch her breath, and it resumed its attacks, this time spiraling through a dozen unprotected civilians and tearing them to shreds.

Elyana became desperate at the sight of her failure, and against her better judgement and despite the danger to herself, she decided to gather as much energy as she could handle, wishing only to blast the Serpent to the Netherworlds. As the flow of energy increased, her hair stuck out from her head and her face became as hard as marble. The woman became luminous as a faint bluish glow started radiating from her body. Soldiers and civilians turned toward her, mesmerized by what they were seeing, whether they had seen it before, or not.

But just when she was ready to unleash a colossal thunder-strike, a weapon of the Bind rarely used in battle because of the difficulty one had in aiming it accurately, the Serpent stopped itself in midair, turned toward the Lux Baiula, and fixed its gaze straight upon her. Arrows and lances stopped flying and all in the fortress, including Toras and Aithen stood transfixed. It was as if something momentous was about to happen; none dared speak, none dared ask a question and none moved – even the Red Sun seemed to have stopped descending to illuminate this crucial moment – but not a minute later, they saw the Lux Baiula falter in the middle of the plaza as an inconceivable amount of energy rushed from her, like water through a broken dam, and blasted the mountain wall. Rock shattered over a stretch at least thirty meters wide and blocks of stone came crashing down within as well as without the fortress. Dozens of men were hit by the stone and several were crushed where they stood.

The princes, who were standing next to each other, saw an enormous rock racing toward them, while another large stone sped toward Elyana. Toras and Aithen jumped back reflexively and fell, and at that moment they knew they would die. But the rock shattered two meters above them, stopped by the Bound Shields, which were evidently and fortunately for them, still holding.

As for the Lux Baiula, she was on the ground, wounded by a piece of rock which had hit her right leg. Nevertheless, she got back on her feet, and paused a moment to think. As no ideas came, she restored the nebula, and with another brain-draining effort, pulled moisture out of the ground to flood the citadel with a thick fog, hoping that it would give her a few minutes to regain her composure and think about her options. To Elyana's immense relief, she heard the beat of the Serpent's wings and the sound of its screeches grow distant as it flew back to the top of the cliff.

Taking a welcome breath, a breath she had been holding for far too long it seemed, the Lux Baiula pushed away the desperation that had gotten the better of her earlier, and started running through countless tactics, looking for something that would keep the defenders safe while she *tried* to bring the Serpent down. But not even her Transferred Memories offered any useful solutions.

While Elyana racked her brains for something, some course of action that would allow them to defeat the Serpent, Harlion was running as fast as he could, bumping into men because of the fog, and jumping over them at the last moment or pushing them out of his way to get to the princes. Aithen, his blood drained from the near miss, was helping his brother get up when the high captain arrived, panting.

Breathing heavily, Harlion said, "My lords, I thought that was the end of you."

Aithen replied, "We are fine, Harlion, but what of Elyana?"

"Well, I saw her still standing near the central fountain just before this strange fog blanketed the fortress, and the *Originator burn me* if I know how she hasn't collapsed yet. But Your Highness, from the look of her, I know the Lux Baiula won't be able to sustain her efforts much longer, and our arrows and lances are of no use against the Serpent. We need something else!"

Aithen nodded his grim agreement and asked, "What do you propose, Captain?"

"My Prince, I would like to take some of our men to the inner southeastern tower." Aithen was about to respond but let him continue.

"I know the tower is beyond the reach of the nebula, my Prince, but from there, we'll be able to use the arbalests and hopefully kill this wretched thing as you and I did the varagoths [16] so long ago. That is, as long as this fog lifts."

Toras gave the officer a dubious look and said, "High Captain, those arbalests have not been used in ages, and I doubt there remains anyone who –"

"I'm sorry Lord Commander, but *I* do have men here who can operate the weapons."

Toras frowned and was about to reply when a young squire arrived, panting.

Addressing himself to Aithen, he said, "My Prince, I have an urgent message from the Lux Baiula."

Aithen asked more brusquely than he intended, "Well, what is it, Kil?"

Kildare was the prince's squire. He was a young Human of eighteen, the son of a minor lord northwest of the capital.

Kildare straightened and replied, "The Lux Baiula wishes me to inform you that she has created this fog so that she may rest a few minutes and give us a chance to reorganize our defenses. She said that arrows and lances will not do anymore, but neither will her…*Bindings*. She suggests we use the…"

Toras cut him off, said, "The arbalests? How would she think of *them*?"

The messenger raised his brows and shrugged his shoulders.

Toras continued, "Well, no matter. High Captain Harlion has just had the same thought." Then, turning to the captain, he said, "Very well, Captain. It appears the arbalests are it. How can I help?"

"I need the varagoth nets, and bolts for the arbalests."

"We have both, Captain. The net is in the armory, and the bolts are already by the arbalests. I will have someone bring the net; but it's heavy. My men will need a few minutes."

---

[16] Varagoths were large carnivorous beasts, some seven meters long from head to tail, and three meters high at the shoulder. They had six long horns on the forehead as well as two long canines. Their body was muscular, and their leather so thick simple arrows could not pierce it.

"Thank you, Lord Commander. I have someone who can carry two nets while sprinting up the tower. If you don't mind, I'll send him to fetch what you have."

Toras blinked in wonder. Varagoth nets weighed near one hundred and fifty pounds each! How can a man carry two up a hundred stairs? But he said, "Very well. Anything else?"

"Yes. I need the Lux Baiula to draw the Serpent's attention such that it presents its belly or flank to us right before we release the bolt. I will give her this signal when we are ready." Harlion made a sign with his arm.

Aithen replied, "I will have Kil take the message back to her, Captain."

Aithen continued, "Be careful, my friend. And at the first sign of trouble, get out of the tower with your men and return to the safe zone."

The high captain gave both princes a nod, as well as a courageous but knowing smile and left as fast as he had come.

Aithen followed him with his eyes until the fog swallowed him, which was but a few paces away. He felt pride at having such a brave and wise man by his side, and he hoped Harlion's plan would work and that the man would not fall prey to the Serpent.

Toras still had a doubting frown on his face, but it seemed High Captain Harlion knew what he was doing, so he decided to trust the old soldier and turned his attention to his own men after giving his brother a parting sign.

Having watched Toras disappear in the fog, Aithen turned to Kildare, who was still waiting for the reply, and said, "Kil, run back to Elyana to let her know I've gotten her message, and that I need her to lift the fog in ten minutes, at which point she should watch for the high captain's signal. The captain will be in the inner southeastern tower. Tell her that when she sees this signal," and Aithen repeated Harlion's gesture, "she is to distract the rokon such that it presents its belly or flank to the tower. That is all, now go!"

The squire saluted and ran to relay the prince's instructions to Elyana.

Meanwhile, Harlion was gathering his men, his heart pumping hard from the frenetic running. Because of the fog, he accidentally knocked over a few men, the last of whom was one of his officers,

Secundus [17]Loris, cousin to the princes. The man began to curse but excused himself when he realized who had bumped him.

With obvious urgency in his tone, Harlion said, "My apologies Secundus, but where are the twins?!"

"On the second level, Captain, toward the southern end of the inner wall," replied the officer, pointing toward the location of the men, though there was nothing to see through the dense mist.

"Perfect!" was all that Harlion said, as he resumed his breakneck race across the fortress to gather his men. The twins, Mekiir and Kemiir, were from Upper Alvinor. They weren't tall fellows, but they had a frightening musculature which Harlion was going to put to proper use now. As soon as their commander arrived and asked them to follow, they turned around, picked up their lances and started after Harlion who was already running to get a third man on the northwestern side of the inner wall.

Urlis was from Shadin City. He also boasted a musculature as frightening as that of the twins, but to the contrary of the brothers, he was also a very tall fellow. And most of all, he was experienced with nets that required five ordinary men to handle and cast, having grown-up on fishing ships to help his father hunt sea leviathans, creatures eight to ten times larger than the Serpent.

"Urlis, I need you to get the varagoth net and carry it to the inner southeastern tower. Secundus Loris will show you where it is. You will load it onto an arbalest and use it to capture the beast if we can't kill it. Hurry!"

Urlis responded only with a vicious twinkle in his eye and left to find Secundus Loris.

Harlion then sprinted to the tower with the twins. *We have to be there on time. We have to make it. The Lux Baiula will probably not hold on much longer, and we must find a way to destroy that wretched creature before she's completely drained and falls down unconscious or dead, because if that happens, we are all doomed.*

It took Harlion and the twins two minutes to cover the five hundred meters between the northwestern wall and the top of the southeastern tower, which was a real feat for the aging captain. In fact, the man felt a sudden and brief pain in his chest when they

---

[17] Secundus was the lowest commissioned rank within the Guards. A Secundus's insignia consisted of a blue sun on red, and a red sun on blue, within a tall rectangle formed by white embroidery.

reached the top of the tower, and for a moment, he wondered whether his heart might not take him before the Serpent did.

However, the soldier in him immediately returned his attention to the task at hand, and he said, "Mekiir, Kemiir, I need you because you are two of the few men who can still use these massive crossbows."

The brothers looked at the weapons on their right: unlike the usual portable arbalests, these were mounted on a pivoting base. They measured three meters long and their arms were almost two meters wide. They were used only against the varagoths, but this large predator species had disappeared from the area fifteen years ago already and thus, none of the guardians currently assigned to the fortress had had experience with the weapon. The twins, however, had made a specialty of hunting varagoths since the age of sixteen, and continued to do so each year. Indeed, Harlion sent them throughout the kingdom for a month each autumn to hunt this carnivore, which was unfortunately incompatible with Humans. A mischievous smile painted the faces of the twins when they looked at each other.

Harlion continued, "My hope is that these bolts will be able to pierce the rokon's hide, even at its thickest, around the belly and chest. To help you, the Lux Baiula will try to cause the rokon to present its flank or belly before you release the bolts."

The brothers nodded.

Just now, Urlis arrived with the huge and heavy net, barely panting or sweating. The twins looked at the tall man with envious eyes.

Harlion nodded and said, "Get to your posts men, and let's bring that creation of hell down!"

The three guardians were at their posts in a flash, Kemiir and Mekiir taking the left and right arbalests and Urlis taking the middle one. As the men began loading their weapons, they wondered if the machines would function properly because it was obvious from the difficulty they had in cocking them that they had not been adjusted or oiled in over a decade.

Once all were done cocking their weapons, the brothers with heavy, barbed projectiles, and the fisher's son with a varagoth net, they looked to their captain to signal their readiness and waited anxiously for the fog to lift and the creature to come.

Harlion closed his eyes a moment and felt that the ten minutes to Elyana lifting the fog had almost passed. The ability to tell time was something all officers had to learn but which not all mastered – Harlion did. Keeping his eyes closed, he said "Be ready", and then he started counting down quietly: "7, 6, 5, 4, 3, 2, 1." The fog lifted as soon as he said "one", as if he had commanded it.

That startled the soldiers a little, because even though they knew officers were expected to develop the skill to tell time – or were they born with it? – the sudden disappearance of the fog seemed to have been caused by him. But they knew better, and they turned their attention to the top of the cliff, where the rokon still perched, and they wondered when it would descend again.

It was not long before the Serpent answered their question and sped toward the fortress. Seeing the creature apparently fully restored, Mekiir's and Kemiir's hearts started skipping beats, and they said quick prayers, hoping the Founders would give them some assistance so that they wouldn't be forced to join their ancestors just yet. Their hands tightened on the arbalests, and their eyes now saw nothing else but their target.

As one, the twins shouted, "Come on, come on you damned beast! Let's finish this!"

Not a moment later, the unnatural lizard turned toward the tower, screeching and crying. When the Serpent was within fifty meters of the structure, Harlion gave the Lux Baiula the signal. Elyana receded into the Bind and called the Serpent toward her as forcefully as she could, causing it to veer west and expose its belly. At that moment, Harlion gave the twins the order to release, and the deadly javelins sprang forth and pierced the air, as if they had waited for ages for just this moment – and everyone held their breath.

However, the Founders must have found the prayers lacking because at the very last moment, the Serpent made a tight loop and dodged the bolts. The brothers fumed and cursed at the Serpent.

The captain, noticing the Serpent's sudden change of direction and realizing it intended to ram the tower, yelled, "Urlis, ready yourself! Mekiir, Kemiir, hurry! Reload, and release again!"

The twins rushed to reload their weapons.

Mekiir yelled angrily, "Damnation! Damned be the Founders! My arbalest is stuck!"

The captain punched the wall, and asked, "Kemiir, are *you* ready?"

Fortunately, Kemiir nodded that he was, and Harlion made another sign for Elyana, immediately followed by an order for Kemiir to release.

Kemiir let go, and for a moment that seemed to last forever, he prayed he would hit the creature. But the bolt missed again. The Serpent had stopped too early, launching itself upward just before the weapon could hit, and the projectile continued until it hit the ground and lodged itself just a few meters from where Elyana stood.

Elyana thought: *How many more times are flesh and rock and projectiles going to land next to me?* whereas Kemiir covered his face and shook his head, thinking of what had almost happened.

Urlis had been silent all this time, but just now yelled angrily that he could do it, he could hit the beast and asked to take Mekiir's or Kemiir's place.

Harlion shook his head and said in a dejected voice, "No, better try –" As he spoke, the creature turned to come back again. Harlion noticed, and shouted, "The Dark One's in it. Urlis, the net! It's our last chance. Hurry!"

The fisher's son looked his target in the eye and readied himself; he would not miss! Although he wondered if those teeth the creature had all over its body would not simply cut through the net. But he had to hope, and he did, and gave the arbalest one final crank.

Mekiir said, "Come on Urlis, throw!"

The man responded with a calm, "No, not yet."

Kemiir too yelled for their comrade to throw the net, and still, Urlis waited – and Harlion held his breath, trusting the man. But the captain made note in his mind to talk to the twins – if they all survived – about their interference.

The Serpent was now only thirty meters from the tower when the twins made to shout at their comrade again, but Harlion gave them a sudden and severe look, and they bit their tongues instead. Everyone became tense to the point of tearing muscles when the Serpent looked like it was going to hit the tower if Urlis waited any longer. But at that precise moment, captain and twins heard Urlis pull the latch and launch the net, calmly and true. The net enveloped the Serpent, and Urlis shouted with indescribable exhilaration, "Yeah! I got it Capt'n! I got it!"

Harlion thanked the Founders, while Kemiir and Mekiir cursed the fisher's son for giving them ulcers. The men screamed with joy when the thing began to fall. They had done it, and they couldn't believe it – and neither could the rest of the defenders. But the joy was short-lived because the Serpent started to twist its body and tore the net to shreds. It roared madly now, impossibly so, and flew back up straight toward the tower.

With all the force in his lungs, Harlion ordered his men to jump out of the tower, but before they could get out, the Serpent arrived and rammed into the structure. The roof shattered, and stones fell on their heads. A large piece of the collapsed roof cornered Harlion against the wall. But he quickly recovered his senses, heaved himself out from under the stone slab, and got back on his feet to look for his men. His heart sank when, in front of him, he saw Kemiir, dead, his head crushed. For a moment, he couldn't see or hear anything else except the crushed body of his man, and the twitches of his limbs. But his senses returned – an officer was used to death – and he heard Mekiir's and Urlis's cries of agony coming from the right. Two men lived! Harlion rushed to them and pulled them from under the rubble. Urlis was well enough, and he shoved him out the tower. Then he grabbed onto Mekiir and jumped out the tower with him.

Perhaps Mekiir's prayer had finally reached the Founders, because bales of hay received them at the bottom of the tower, just moments before the Serpent rammed into the turret anew, and this time destroyed it completely. Harlion thanked his luck when none of the stones fell toward them.

Meanwhile, the Serpent stopped in mid-air and scanned the rubble with an intense, malicious gaze, and everyone watched the creature, except for Elyana who, for some reason, stared at where the tower had stood with barely hidden shock and alarm. After a moment of paralysis, Elyana came to her senses and noticed the Serpent staring at the rubble. She couldn't see whether any of the men had survived the toppling of the tower, but when the Serpent suddenly shrieked and directed a hateful glare toward the far side of the debris, she knew that someone lived and that she had to do something before the Serpent went down to finish its work. The Lux Baiula decided to remove the Bound Shields from around the princes and to reform a larger one over the wreckage. A moment later, the Serpent slammed into the invisible barrier and was thrown off to the right. Enraged, it flew back toward the center of the fortress, intent on taking revenge. Elyana yelled to Toras to have him send some men to fetch the tower's survivors, after which she quickly restored the Bound Shields around the princes.

Despair returned to everyone's heart when the lizard grabbed six men, despite the hundreds of arrows and lances hitting it – some of which actually pierced its wings – and hurled them to crash on the cliff behind the fortress. Another half hour of deadly battle and continued destruction ensued, following which, the lizard flew to the top of the cliff, appearing to want to rest again. But the creature abruptly came back down, and dove toward Aithen. A futile barrage of arrows and lances formed to prevent the Serpent's descent on the prince; the Serpent either avoided the projectiles entirely, blocked them with its spiraling motions, or accepted the injuries so that it may reach its target.

Believing that the high prince was doomed, everyone yelled for him to retreat from the parapet, but Aithen would not move. Then, when it seemed the Serpent was sure to crash into the prince, the monster veered to the left and grabbed another man. The poor soldier released screams of terror and agony as the creature closed its beak on his hips and flew back up.

The Serpent did not go very far though, and instead stopped a short distance above the fortress, and turned to face it. Horror paralyzed everyone when the Serpent flipped the still agonizing man in the air, caught him again, and swallowed him whole before finally turning to the northwest and leaving as it had come. As it did, it thrashed its tail along the walls of the mountain in a final fit of fury, and its screeches – deeper than they had been because of its constricted airways – diminished as it disappeared.

At first, no one understood what had happened, why the thing had just turned and left. But after a few minutes of hearing no more of the creature's screeches, the fighters fell on their knees and prayed, or simply thanked the Founders or K'Tara itself – depending on their beliefs – for saving their lives. Soon, however, men started asking questions and voicing their worst fears, the civilians more strongly than the guardians: What was that lizard? Not a rokon, surely. A creature straight from the Nethers, yes! Come to destroy humanity. No, the princes. No, it had been called forth by the Lux Baiula! And emotions flared when no satisfying answers came from the princes, who did the best they could to reassure everyone without revealing the truth or seeming to hide anything. When calm eventually returned, the princes and their officers moved on to the task of assessing the damage.

The destruction was extensive: virtually every home in the village had been rendered to mere stones and broken planks, while the fortress had suffered much structural damage. Three of the towers had huge gaps in them where the walls had been shattered, while the fourth – the one from which Harlion and his men had hoped to bring down the Serpent - was completely destroyed. Several of the taller structures had been damaged as well. It was a fortunate thing that the fortress had been built with the help of Lux Baiulae who had used the Bind to harden the granite and fuse together the already large blocks of the stone; without this, the entire stronghold might have laid in ruins. Even so, the mere fact that the Serpent had brought down a tower and caused damage to other parts of the fortress worried many, especially Elyana – in fact, this sickened her almost more so than the deaths and the injuries. The Sisterhood's Stone Workings were supposed to be eternal, and so the structures built with them! Elyana did not dare think of the implications.

As far as the men were concerned, a large number had been wounded, especially the villagers, and some forty had been killed, again, mostly villagers. One of the dead was the princes' cousin Loris, a brave man and secundus in the Royal Guard. Aithen would need to inform his uncle. But for now, he needed to help his brother see to the injured, to *all* the dead and to the now homeless villagers.

Toras gave orders to get the healers and tell them that the Lux Baiula was going to help with the wounded, *civilians included*, just to be sure they did not cause an unnecessary scene when they saw her minister to a villager. He also gave orders to let the villagers out of the caves, in as orderly a manner as possible, so they may reunite with their dead, or injured, family members.

Primus Kendor and his men did their best to control the outpouring of villagers from the caves, but their arrival in the fortress still caused a terrible ruckus, with women, children, and elders crying for the injured or dead ones. After a couple of hours, though, after the dead had been seen to and prayers told, a semblance of calm returned to the fortress. It was now past the highnight, and linens were being retrieved from the caverns' storage rooms to give to the villagers who would be sleeping on the granite floors of the caves that night – if they could sleep at all.

* * *

As she took care of the wounded, Elyana Lux Baiula repressed the guilt she felt at having caused the death of so many men when she released the nebula, and then again when she lost control of the thunder-strike. But the guilt was there, nevertheless, waiting for a moment of weakness to assail her.

The princes and their officers did their best to stamp down any criticism of the woman, or any nascent anger toward her, and made certain everyone knew that had she not been there, none of the defenders might have survived the Serpent's mental and physical assaults. But, people being as they were, some could not help but assign blame to someone, who, in this case, was the Lux Baiula. In fact, Sisters often took the blame for things they had not caused, simply because they would not spend the energy defending themselves, and rather preferred to remain focused on their duties, regardless of the consequences.

Helping Elyana care for the wounded were the village's two healers, who also acted as medics for the fortress's Guard. Almost every village had one or two of these women, women who had learned about the healing powers of certain plants and insects. Their usual labor was to take care of the injuries and illnesses that their fellow villagers might suffer from every so often. But tonight, the task was quite a bit more challenging.

If one could hear the healers as they prepared some fresh poultice, one would hear them grumble about the Lux Baiula.

The shorter one, named Frelina, whispered, "Why is she here? We don't need her help, by Elande [18]!" She had the look of one who liked to be in charge, but who was never actually given the chance, perhaps because of her attitude.

Karista, the other healer, was a tall, large woman. Some, particularly the children, actually found her intimidating, especially with her hair tied in the back of her neck and pulling her face taut; she was First Healer of Horn's Pass. She replied, "I don't much trust

---

[18] Elande was one of the Founders, Principle of Balance, a creation of early K'Tarans.

her kind neither, and I'm not exactly sure that when they do what they do, they're not puttin' hidden evil things inside the minds of those they help. Once, in a village near Praeghe, a Lux Baiula went to heal a man whose leg had just been crushed by a farmer's cart. The man's leg was healed all right, but during the following days, he began runnin' the streets, saying mad things I daren't repeat. One of the local healers told me that the man had always been a model citizen 'til he was treated by the witch!"

The shorter woman replied with a whispered curse and said, "I don't think they're just stories, Karista. An' have you heard what the soldiers say? That she killed a dozen men?!"

"I have, but the princes say it wasn' her fault, that the rokon deflected her strike. So, for now, I'll let it be. In any case Frelina, we have no choice; there are just too many injured. But if one of our people loses his mind after this, I can promise you *she* will regret it."

"I'm not cert'n I would be so trusting, Karista. She could do somethin' to the men but blame it on the creature."

The First Healer's reply left no doubt as to her view of her own skills, "Believe me, I'll know if she does."

At the western end of the plaza, Elyana walked purposefully, if fitfully, toward Mekiir, the surviving twin. Another guardian was tending his wounds as best he could, while Mekiir did his best to contain his screams. Urlis was sitting nearby, apparently unharmed.

When she arrived, Elyana took a deep breath, put her doubts aside and said with an unusually caring tone, "I believe you are Mekiir?"

With a grimace contorting his face, the soldier nodded yes.

"High Captain Harlion asked me to look at your wounds." Elyana got down on her knees, assessed the man's condition, and then began rubbing his broken leg, as well as his bruised arm and torso. Saborin, Mekiir's companion, looked at the Light Bearer expectantly, hoping to see something magical happen. Mekiir felt his legs, arm, and chest warming up with each pass of the Lux Baiula's touch. The heat spread to his bones, and then he felt pain and his body tensed up.

Elyana now closed her eyes and felt herself reaching inside of Mekiir, opening her mind to the vivid colors caused by the fractured bone in his leg which cut at his muscles and nerves. After homing in on the region of interest, she looked for zones of silence, which were the pieces of crushed bone. Having found them, she formed a resonant beam and sent it in to dissolve the shards. Once the shards were all gone, she paused to think on what to do next. A medic would now have been able to regrow the bone as well as mend the torn muscles, blood vessels and nerve fibers. That was beyond Elyana's skillset. But what she could do was to prime the tissues to heal themselves, so she directed a tight beam of energy in the zones she knew to be zones of growth, and activated the cellular processes required in the healing process. If all went well, and with the help of medics from the capital, Mekiir would be as he was before within a few fourths.

Having taken care of the broken leg, Elyana gave another look at the soldier's right arm and torso, and, seeing that those injuries were only flesh wounds, she decided not to expend her waning reserve of energy on them. So, she removed her hands from Mekiir, sat back, wiped her brow with her handkerchief, and exhaled a long weary breath.

Mekiir still felt the heat in his muscles, but most of the pain was now gone. He wanted to ask what the Lux Baiula had done but kept silent; he just looked at the woman in wonder.

Elyana said, "Your leg is still broken, but you will be all right; your body should take no more than a few fourths to finish the repairs. But you will need to be seen by a medic once you get back in Furan City if you want your tissues to grow straight and strong."

The man nodded.

"I will let your Saborin, here, bandage your leg and dress your chest and arm."

Saborin nodded in appreciation of the Lux Baiula's trust.

Elyana gave him a smile and continued, "I am sorry for your loss, Mekiir. You and your brother were both very brave up there." Then, encompassing all three soldiers with her regretful gaze, she added, "You were all very brave." And with that, she got up and went looking for another man to heal. As Elyana walked, she put her thumb and middle fingers together. She then took several slow, deep breaths and replenished her tired body as much as she could. But she knew she would need some food and rest soon; if she let herself completely deplete her reserves, she would need several fourths to recover, and she could not afford that, not with the Serpent come back to K'Tara.

When the Light Bearer had gone, Saborin asked his companion what had happened and received a very disappointing answer.

37

Mekiir didn't know, except that he didn't feel the excruciating pain anymore, and that he could breathe much more easily, now. Saborin found himself hoping that the next time he would be injured too so he could feel for himself what it was that Lux Baiulae did when they healed someone. But he quickly berated himself as he certainly did not wish to see that infernal beast again.

III BENEATH THE SOUND SHIELD

Dawn was only a few hours away when, seeing that everything was under control, Toras invited his brother to walk with him to his private quarters for some wine. Once there, Toras became visibly shaken. He looked around and saw rubble here and there on the floor of his day room. The physical damage that the fortress had sustained shook Toras. To him, Horn's Pass was a sign of the kingdom's strength.

The younger prince walked toward the large hearth that had just been lit by his housekeeper. Indeed, even though the days could be pleasant and reach fourteen to seventeen stones[19] during the summer months, the nights always grew cold in the Pass, with the temperature frequently going down to a one howler-night[20].

Toras stared blankly into the fire. Aithen approached him. "You look troubled."

"I —" Toras shuddered as the fear he had hidden from his men during the battle resurfaced. "The Serpent — I could feel it trying to tear my mind away. It was even more frightening than the thought of being torn to shreds by it. Didn't you feel it dig into your mind too?"

Aithen shook his head.

Toras continued, "It was horrible! It took every ounce of will I had to not let the men see my panic."

"And why was it here?! Why?! What does it want?!"

His arms crossed, and right hand on his lower lip, Aithen replied, "I wish I knew, Toras," Then, he added, "Father must be told of what's happened here."

Suddenly, Toras's anger flared. "Why isn't he back anyway!? He's been gone for fourths, and still no word from him! He should have been here, yesterday!"

---

[19] One stone was the temperature reached by a liter of near-frozen water in one minute when one burning, 10g (0.3 oz) stone was added to it.

[20] A howler-night was the number of howlers a woodsman would gather around his body to keep warm. The more howlers were needed, the colder the temperature was.

Aithen replied with more force than he intended, "It worries me too, Toras! But it's possible his business in Spiritii retained him longer than expected. There's no need to be so irate about that!" As soon as he said that, Aithen felt embarrassed. He understood his brother's fears – he felt the same way – but he simply did not like emotional outbursts. Still, after a moment, he added, "I'm sorry."

It was perhaps the fact that Aithen was four years older than Toras, along with the fact that he was High Lord Commander of the Royal Guard and first heir to the throne that caused him to view fits of temper as a sign of weakness.

Toras now looked at his brother with a resigned look; his facial expressions could change so suddenly – and his temperament with it. He said, "You're probably right, Aithen. But this is still very unusual for him."

Aithen, who had walked away when Toras became angry, turned and said, "I know." He continued walking away, stopped in front of a desk strewn with documents – reports it seemed. He picked them up, but did not read them and said, "Toras, can you send for Elyana? We need her advice, as well as some answers on what has happened here tonight."

"I'll go get her myself." As Toras walked out of the chamber, an older guardian – the younger men who had been posted there the day before were still recovering – started to follow him, but the prince stopped him with a brusque voice, saying, "Don't. I'll be right back."

"But –"

"I said no, Rathos."

And with that, the prince strode off, his face haggard and anxious, to find the Lux Baiula, uncertain whether her answers would help him find some measure of calm again.

Rathos exchanged worried looks with the other guardian on door duty, and both released a heavy sigh as they watched the prince go.

While Aithen waited for his brother to return, he went through everything he had learned about the Serpent, from his father as well as from the Sisterhood, hoping to make some sense of its presence, here, now. But it was a futile exercise, and it frustrated him. The creature was said to have been destroyed. So, unless the Lux Baiulae who had witnessed its end had lied or had been deceived, how could it be here?! Or perhaps – Aithen thought – Elyana was mistaken and this creature she referred to as the Serpent was not *it*, but only looked

– and behaved – like the Dark Lord's Wings? But who would have created this copy? The Serpent was said to have been created by Noctiferus, himself, out of a young rokon. The logical implications of these scenarios were not ones Aithen dared explore further.

When Toras returned with Elyana, Aithen shook his worries away to greet the Lux Baiula. Toras stood next to her with a much calmer demeanor. Aithen eyed him questioningly, but he could guess what had quieted his brother's mind.

Though Toras had some misgivings about the Sisterhood, he did like Elyana, and had often found himself thinking of her as an older sister while growing up. How could he not? She'd been the king's advisor for more than thirty years now, and had practically lived with them, in the Royal palace, for much of that time.

For sure, Elyana had not been there to entertain the princes, but rather to advise the king and help educate his children. She had done both remarkably well, despite the fact that the younger prince had always preferred physical activity to intellectual studies. In his early years, that had consisted of running around outdoors and chasing whatever creature he could find, while in his adolescent years, his interests had progressed to more strenuous activities such as the martial arts, flying furans in wild formations alongside the Royal Guard's furanback elite, and catching and taming belwohrs. [21]

And Elyana, who had always had a keen sense of what motivates Humans, understood that to educate Toras, she needed to share in his own interests. So, she had taken to sparring with him every so often, which she was quite skilled at given that she had been a Red Sash prior to becoming the high king's advisor. The Lux Baiula's decision had of course shocked many, including the high king and his consort, but her stratagem had worked, and the prince had come to understand the things a person must know to lead others, even if his interpretation of the principles of leadership and government differed somewhat from the king's.

Looking at the Lux Baiula with a thankful smile, Aithen said, "I know you are exhausted, Elyana, but there are a few things Toras and I really need to know, and there are also some decisions we must make before we all retire for whatever remains of the night."

---

[21] Belwohrs were huge carnivorous animals of the Furan Peaks, the size of a battle voran, which often tried fed on young furans and sometimes on Humans.

Elyana nodded her understanding. As she did, a patterned sequence of three knocks came through the door. Toras responded with a "Come in, Lenion."

A short, slightly bulky woman, with a warm smile, walked in with a jar of wine and three cups. The woman was Toras's housekeeper. Looking toward Elyana, the prince said, "Some wine?"

Elyana nodded yes, and Lenion poured each of them a cup. That done, she bowed respectfully toward everyone as she backed away and out of the room.

After taking a sip of the wine and enjoying its aroma for a moment, Aithen said, mostly to himself, "Strange that I should find pleasure in this wine…even after the night we've had. Will any of the civilian survivors find anything to enjoy?"

Toras had been about to take a gulp of the wine himself but stopped his hand. He turned toward Elyana, wondering what she thought of his brother's comment, but he only saw a blank expression on her face.

Aithen noticed the effect of his comment and rushed to add, "I did not mean to suggest that we shouldn't…be having any wine. I'm simply feeling dazed and out of sorts, and guilty thoughts are crossing my mind." Then, with a sudden change of tone and topic, Aithen said, "But, how is the Healing proceeding, Elyana?"

The Lux Baiula did not react with the surprise Toras felt. She said, "As well as can be expected, given the number of injured. But the village healers have some decent remedies for superficial wounds, and their assistance certainly helped me focus whatever energy I had left on the more serious injuries. But, I was unable to do anything meaningful for the men who were aggressed by the Serpent's mental attack – and survived." Elyana paused a moment, and with a grim tone, which seemed filled with her own feelings of guilt, she added, "I think that they might have been better dead."

Hearing the Lux Baiula make such a statement troubled the princes. Aithen objected, "You know what happened wasn't your fault, Elyana."

"Thank you, Aithen, but I have no need for soothing. I made several errors in judgement this night, and it does not matter what ultimately caused the deaths and injuries." After a short pause and a rare sigh, the Sister added, "Your comment about the wine may have been appropriate…for me, at least. Still, thank you both for voicing your support earlier, as I very much doubt that anyone would have let me heal him if not for your intervention."

With a resigned shake of his head, Toras concluded, "Well, as Aithen said, we don't believe you are to blame, Elyana."

Elyana just gave her usual blank stare in response, and said, "One thing which surprised me but comforted me, nevertheless, is the fact that the Serpent did not use its mental attacks on Harlion or his men while they were in the tower."

Aithen said, "I wondered about that too. Could it be that the Serpent was so shocked or irritated by this new attempt to bring it down, that it simply *forgot* to use its mental attacks, as you call them?"

Toras interrupted with a chuckle, "Indeed! It happens to men, too, sometimes, especially the impulsive kind." The comment surprised Aithen and Elyana, but Toras continued, "You've seen it happen, Aithen, when a captain is so shocked by the enemy's tactics that he decides to charge at once, forgetting all about his carefully laid-out plans. Perhaps, it's a weakness we can exploit, if we ever meet the creature again."

Elyana let out a cynical grunt. "I do not know why the Serpent did not use its mental attack on Harlion and his men, as this would have killed them more surely than attempting to topple the tower, but your hypothesis could very well be right, Toras. But I have no memory of such a weakness. Nevertheless, your suggestion is a good one, and I will keep it in mind, as we are certain to see the creature again."

At that, Toras frowned. He then invited his guests to sit on the chairs by the hearth. Toras took the seat next to Elyana, leaving his brother to sit across from them, which, for some reason, irritated Aithen.

After a short silence during which the princes considered Elyana's statement, the high prince cupped his wine goblet with both hands, elbows on knees, and said, "Elyana, we need to understand what happened here tonight, and we need honest answers."

Elyana considered Aithen's request only a moment before deciding that he and his brother had the right to know everything she knew. Indeed, she had been sent to Furan City thirty years earlier to counsel and advise the Crown, and that included the princes when they became of age; that is what she needed to do now. The practice of assigning an advisor to Alvinorian rulers was a requirement of the alliance between the Coriolan dynasty and the Sisterhood, and it had been adhered to by the Order for nearly five hundred years now. And for the most part, the practice had benefitted and continued to benefit both parties, even if there had been advisors who had been kicked out of Furan City after losing the king's, the senate's or the people's confidence.

Lay scholars believed that the Order's oath to protect all life was itself the cause of the distrust some had felt and still felt toward the Sisterhood, given that the protection of *all* life meant that a Sister might – under certain circumstances – decide in favor of non-Humans if she judged that a particular situation would harm the non-Human party more than it would benefit the Humans. But, given that the oath stood at the very core of the Order's identity and behind their every action, it had remained unchanged through the ages, and it continued to feed the fears of the fearful, as well as the cynicism of the cynics.

After setting her wine cup down, and delicately putting a piece of a fleshy, dark purple fruit called sabara into her mouth, Elyana clapped her hands and, using painting motions, surrounded them with a distorting energy field.

The princes had experienced this type of field often, when Elyana created it at their father's request to discuss highly confidential matters. The field was a Sound Shield. Not the only kind, but one easily created by increasing the density of matter along the surfaces of a room, and causing said matter to vibrate in a distorting manner. Anyone outside the shield would only hear muffled voices. The disadvantage of this shield was that it also muffled sound in the other direction.

Elyana said, "What will be said here cannot go beyond these walls, not for a while in any case." The princes nodded their understanding. Elyana continued, "Aithen, do you remember how the last battle against Noctiferus ended?"

Aithen pulled his head back in surprise, but replied, "I do. It has been a long time since you taught me this, but I do remember. K'Tara lost a great number of people – in the tens of thousands if I remember correctly, and your Order lost about half of its Sisters. At the end of the Dark Battle, the Serpent was captured by the Lux Baiulae and

44

Luxori and taken to Aiala'Rhi's [22] temple where the Originator took possession of it. Aiala'Rhi, herself, is said to have captured Noctiferus whom she presented in chains to the assembled K'Tarans. The removal of the Serpent and of Noctiferus allowed Emperor Flavius the First, along with what remained of your Order and the Luxori, to eradicate the then leaderless forces that had served Noctiferus, although some remnants were said to have escaped to the recesses of our orb. It is also written that Noctiferus was stripped of all powers and taken to some remote corner of our universe, to remain there imprisoned on some unknown world. As for the Serpent, there exist eye witness accounts about its destruction by Aiala'Rhi."

Toras asked, "How can the Serpent be here, then, if it was terminated?"

Elyana replied, "I do not know, but it *is* nevertheless. It was either resurrected, or the accounts of its destruction are false. Either way, it is here now, and it is searching for something." The Sister hesitated a moment before continuing, a very unusual thing for a Lux Baiula. Elyana, especially, was a very confident woman and said things as they were, but now, an imperceptible tremor coursed through her. The princes eyed each other worryingly and looked back at her questioningly. Elyana exhaled with continued hesitation, "While I shielded us from the Serpent...I heard it talking to me. I was shaken by that, and you saw the result of it when I unleashed the thunderstrike on the mountainside. It repeated something in the Ancient Tongue, over and over: *"Finis adest. Sequimini aut morimini!"* meaning –"

"I know," said Aithen, with fear in his voice, "The end is here, and you will follow or perish! ""

Dread, deep and unsettling, marred the brothers' faces.

Elyana tried to lighten the mood by remarking on Aithen's translation, "Your knowledge of the Ancient Tongue has much improved, my Prince."

The high prince shrugged his shoulders, not caring much for praise at the moment. Instead, he asked, "Will you inform the Magna Mater of this?"

---

[22] Aiala (or Aiala'Rhi) was the Originator, the first Founder, and creator of all things in the Rhiian religion.

45

"Indeed, I will. As soon as possible. The creature's return is a threat to–"

Toras suddenly interrupted the Lux Baiula, shouting, "But what is the meaning of the Serpent's words, Elyana. *The end*? The end of what? And *follow* who?!"

The Lux Baiula was about to berate the young prince for his impatience, but she let out a wearied sigh and said, "I know no more of the meaning of its words than I do of its reappearance. But its mere presence here is a sufficient threat to all of K'Tara, as I was going to say when you interrupted me...my Prince."

The scolding caused Toras to stand abruptly, raise his arms in frustration, and turn toward the Lux Baiula with visibly tense features. "I'm sorry, Elyana. But you know how my mind races in the face of danger, until I've understood it." To prove his point, Toras started pacing in the small space between the chairs, annoying Aithen.

Elyana regarded the prince knowingly, "What else is sprinting through your mind, Toras?

"I'm thinking that we need to find Father, and alert Mother!"

Elyana replied, "A sensible point, my Prince, and I will see to it that a message reaches the Lady Darya. But since it will need to pass through Kynaria's Ruling Seat, I will not be able to reveal much in it. As for your father, he should indeed be brought back as quickly as possible."

Toras, always prompt for action, immediately offered to do it, "I'll go get him. I and my winged Guard know the land between here and the plains to the north of Spiritii better than you or the Royal Guard do, Aithen." The high prince's annoyance turned to irritation, but before he could say anything, Toras asked him, "He's escorted by the usual five [23], I assume?"

"Yes, he is. But, Toras, it is *my* duty and responsibility to bring back Father, and the Royal Guard is more than capable–"

"My Lords," said Elyana, stopping the beginning argument between the brothers, "in the present situation, I do believe it would be wiser for Toras to go south and bring back the high king, given that Aithen will need to see to the relocation of Horn's Pass's

---

[23] The king's personal guard was composed of Primus Julian, Jashan, Almiar, Kiron, and Merr, all young but highly experienced guards.

population, address the Senate about it, as well as bring the Union's Council together to prepare the kingdom against a repetition of what happened here."

The enumeration of all the things Aithen would need to do because of the Serpent's attack deflated him, and he said, "Very well. Elyana is right. Go. But take fifteen of my guardians as well."

Toras nodded his thanks and said, "Your fifteen and fifteen of my best flyers. We'll leave at the break of dawn – that'll give us a couple of hours to rest. I know I need it. Anyway, we'll find Father and be back with him before you reach Furan City."

A sigh was all Aithen gave in response. He knew Elyana was right about this. He just wished he had realized it, himself. He also did not look forward to dealing with politicians.

Elyana added, "I will *also* try to find the king – through the Bind. Should I locate him, I will have a message brought to him by the nearest Sister to inform him of your coming, my Prince."

"Thank you."

"Also, Toras, remember that what we have discussed here must be kept quiet – for now."

Toras nodded his understanding. He then approached his brother, put his hands on Aithen's arms and said goodbye with a look filled with a mix of fear and hope. Toras had always been very expressive, while his brother, on the other hand, would have been content with a simple farewell – an attitude which often frustrated the other members of the royal family. In any case, after Aithen returned his goodbyes with a grunt, Toras left, anxious to get things ready for departure – and to get some sleep. As he stepped out of the room, he felt the strange rumble on his eardrums caused by the Sound Shield's energy field, as well as the muffling of Aithen's and Elyana's voices. He thought: *I really wish I could learn to do that.*

***

After Toras had gone, Aithen said, "I just had a thought, Elyana. It is very likely that some peddler who was at Horn's Pass when the Serpent attacked is already on his way to the City to spread the news about it, unless he's among the dead or the injured."

Elyana nodded in agreement.

Aithen asked, "Can you send a message to Irania Lux Baiula through the Bind? We should ask her to intercept anyone coming

47

from Horn's Pass to make certain they do not spread rumors. We should also ask her to visit First Senator Leo to inform him of the situation in case rumors *do* start spreading despite her efforts."

"I agree. We must avoid the spread of tales regarding the nature of the rokon at all costs, or the situation will quickly get out of hand. If it means replacing some memories, Tania Lux Baiula will do it."

This made Aithen shudder. Erasing memories was not very well viewed. Then, he remembered his younger brother and said urgently, "We need to send someone to Ori too. I *definitely* don't want him to hear rumors of death!"

"You are right. I could have Tania go see him. I think he has a liking for her. She will need to tell him that a *rokon* attacked Horn's Pass, mind you, but most importantly, she can reassure him that you and Toras are both well."

Aithen nodded his thanks. Elyana continued, "As I said earlier, you will also need to convene a meeting of the Union Council to plan the defense of their lands and peoples, should the Serpent decide to attack them too."

The high prince heaved a heavy sigh.

Elyana let a moment pass, then continued, "I know you do not look forward to that – politics is not to your liking, but rational response to threats *is*, even if we have not seen much conflict in a while. This ability of yours, to reason through things even while chaos festers around you, is what your father's vassals and subjects will need from you – until his return."

Aithen let out another sigh.

"But, of course, I will be at your side, to assist you through these meetings."

Aithen thought about that a moment. Did he want the Purple Sash, his father's advisor, by his side, reading people's emotions for him to make sure he did not make mistakes in his responses to the senators, or to the landholders? As bad as the idea seemed, he decided that he did not. He said, "I am sorry, Elyana. I need to do this by myself. But I will still welcome your counsel on the road to Furan City."

Elyana nodded, feeling a strange sense of pride in the prince as she thought about how he had handled himself during the attack, and about what he might be called to do in following fourths and months.

She said, "I must say that it was...nice to see how you kept your wits through the attack; they will be essential to you, and to those who depend on you, including your father. And if – and I am saying *if* – we should not find the king, or we should find him incapacitated, your wits will serve you well given that you will need to become much sooner the leader that he has raised you to be."

Aithen looked at her with conflicted emotions. On the one hand, he did not dare think of needing to take over his father's mantle; Octavius lived, and they would find him, period! Nor did he know whether he was ready to take the reins of the kingdom, despite having been trained and educated by the best to do just that, some day. But he did not wish the crown, not now, not like this.

On the other hand, Aithen was touched by Elyana's praise, and by her hesitation in giving it. It was almost as if she were hiding some feeling she had for him. This thought stirred Aithen's own nascent feelings for her, feelings he had not yet learned to deal with. In fact, they made him right uncomfortable. Elyana was a beautiful woman despite the fact she was decades older than him. Indeed, she did not look a year older than himself with her firm and supple pink skin, long, wavy reddish hair, and the bluest of blue eyes. This, combined with the woman's remarkable intellect, made the prince desire Elyana's company more and more each day.

While the prince battled with his budding feelings for the woman, the Lux Baiula was processing her motives for speaking as she did when she praised the prince. But unlike Aithen, she did not wrap her reactions in emotional thoughts, but rather in rational ones, although one might wonder at that if one heard the debate she was having with herself: *He is a good leader, and he is an exceptionally intelligent man. I don't know why you hesitated, Elyana! Founder, I could whip myself for it!*

Finally noticing the awkward silence, Elyana said out loud, "I will retire to my rooms now and contact the Magna Mater. I must inform her of what has happened here...and who knows, she might be able to shed some light on all of this." With that, she gave Aithen a slight nod, dropped the Sound Shield, and left the room.

Aithen followed her with thankful and wistful eyes, and a silent sigh escaped him as one of his own guardians, who had taken the place of Toras's guardians, shut the door behind her.

IV RIDE TO THE LAKE OF SHADOWS

Before the light of the Blue Sun lit the morning, Toras, Kendor, and fourteen of their best men, as well as fourteen men from the Royal Guard and their commander, Secundus Jamir, were ready to go. Toras had had a short and fitful sleep, as had Kendor, but short nights were nothing new to seasoned soldiers, and so, aside from being grumpy, all were alert and ready to go.

The prince, his officers as well as Secundus Jamir had just finished discussing the route they should take to get to Spiritii and had finally decided to fly along the eastern edge of the Furan Peaks. That would allow them to make an overnight stop at an outpost at the foot of the southernmost end of the Furan Peaks, next to a body of water known as Mountain Lake. Half a dozen of Toras's men took yearly turns there to relay messages to the Fortress in case of danger or need in the region. From Mountain Lake, the prince's company would need another three days or so to make it to the flatland between the Colossi's Peaks and Spiritii.

Primus Kendor had argued for flying nearer the top of the peaks given that furans fared better in the cool air of the mountains when crossing great distances, but the constant storms over the mountains at this time of year concerned Toras, and he decided against such a course, opting instead to fly along the foot of the mountain ridge. This option too, however, bore its risks, such as the biters which swarmed the humid lowlands along the foot of the Peaks. Some species of biters, in fact, could tear pieces of flesh from the bellies and napes of Humans and furans, leaving holes the size of a pinhead that bled a long while. These wounds invariably became infected, and certain infections were fatal.

Well, thought Toras, *as long as we don't fly too close to the ground, we should be okay.*

After all, he and his men were familiar with this terrain. The only real risk was crossing the prairie between the mountains and Spiritii, because the region was infested with *wrigglers*, an insect which came out at night in swarms of tens of thousands to attack any warm-blooded animal unfortunate enough to cross that area or stop in the otherwise lush and inviting prairie. It was said that being caught on

51

those plains after dusk was pure suicide. Indeed, according to the rare survivors' accounts, the vile insects could eat away a Human's flesh in a matter of minutes. No one had yet tried to capture specimens of the insects to verify the survivors' claims – not even the Sisterhood. But there was enough evidence about the dangers of that prairie for the wise traveler to steer away from it entirely. Toras assured his brother and Elyana, who had become concerned about his planned itinerary, that he would avoid halting in the prairie at night.

The prince was now looking at the men while he rubbed his furan's head with gentle motions. The soldiers had finished packing all the essentials, as well as finished saddling their mounts, and it had seemed to Toras that they had done it with unusual spryness given their exhaustion. Perhaps, thought the prince, they were anxious to get away from the fortress and see better skies. Or perhaps Elyana had visited them all last night and taken away their fatigue. Either way, he was grateful for their promptness because he was just as anxious to get going.

He wondered if the animals, stamping their paws and snorting nervously, felt the same way. But they were probably just responding to the agitation around them. For sure, furans had an intelligence unlike that of any other animal species. They lived in structured societies, communicated complex thoughts to each other which they used to organize their hunts, and certainly understood humanoid languages as well as sign language. Unfortunately, their squawks and purrs were not easily understood by humanoids, though soldiers learned to recognize some of their vocalizations as well as the motions furans made with their heads and paws, and Kynarians were able to read their thoughts through the Bind. Unfortunately for Toras, the beast-reading skill was not one he had, despite being half-blood. Still, he could understand their vocalizations better than most, and he took pride in it. As he watched the furans squawk at each other, another question crossed Toras's mind. Would it have helped if they had used the furans to fight the Serpent? Probably not, he concluded, as that would have placed the furanteams outside the Lux Baiula's nebula. And yet, the Serpent had not directed its mental attack on Harlion or his men while they were in the tower. Perhaps. Perhaps.

The prince also wondered at the difference between his men and the Royal Guardians. Indeed, the latter were dressed in pressed golden uniforms, despite the previous night's battle, and carried spears and swords, while the former wore their usually stark black uniforms, which were more gray than black this morning, and they bore daggers as well as Alnoor longbows and yerlayan arrows for weapons.

Alnoor longbows were the most prized bows in all of Terrae Regis. They were made of the branches of a unique tree, the Alnoor, found only in the woods adjoining the Colossi's forest. Their fibers were long and resilient but highly resistant, which made for a bow that could project arrows at distances well over one thousand meters. Of course, Humans could not distinguish things that far, and so they rarely used the wood for their own bows, but Toras, whose Kynarian eyesight enabled him to mark a target eight hundred meters away, did use the Alnoor longbow. He had also had the bow modified so that his soldiers could make good use of it too. The modifications allowed them to adjust the bow's tension according to the distance and size of the target. These technical modifications coupled with rigorous training had turned the guardians of the Black Guard into the most feared archers in all of Terrae Regis, second only to their Kynarian counterparts.

Just now, Primus Kendor approached the prince with a harrumph, "Lord Commander, the company is ready to depart. We are only waiting for your order to do so."

Toras pulled himself out of his thoughts and nodded his order to Kendor. With that, the stocky, square-faced officer walked to Secundus Jamir with an eager step and communicated the Lord Commander's order. Within a mere twenty seconds, all soldiers had mounted their winged steeds.

Just when Toras was about to give Scorch his cue, his brother appeared on the dining room's balcony. The young prince nodded toward his elder brother who responded in kind. He then gave Scorch a verbal cue, and the animal launched himself into the air with an excited screech, which was repeated by the furans of the Black Guard, which included two pack furans. A moment later, the screech was picked up by the Royal Guardians' mounts.

Aithen watched the furan-backed company with a mixture of apprehension and jealousy as they faded away. He then sighed and walked back into the dining room to break his fast and start making his own preparations for departure.

At the end of the first day, having flown without rest since leaving, except during the two Bolingar hours around Highsun, the company stopped by a copse of trees in the middle of a prairie nestled between the north and south branches of the Great Torrent River. The prairie was splashed with sky blue, orange and purplish-pink flowers that lit the field in these waning hours. Toras would have normally circled the area a while before setting down, simply to enjoy the spectacle, but not tonight; the men needed to rest, and so did he.

After unsaddling their mounts, the men sent a pair of them to fetch some game. The idea of a nice bleater after what they had endured the previous night should have made the men sing with anticipation. But not tonight. Not even the sight of the furans' catch, or the cooking of it, which released pleasant smells in the air, or the eating of the tender meat caused the men to sing. Instead, the conversation quickly turned to the rokon and to speculation about its true nature, as well as to remembering their lost comrades. The men did try to speak of more joyous things, but they simply couldn't. Even Toras, who often entertained his men with one story or another, couldn't liven up the mood.

So, when the moon was halfway to its highest point, and stomachs had been quieted, the men laid down their blankets around the fire and went to sleep. But sleep came with difficulty to most men, and the sentries, hearing the frightful sounds emanating from those who did find it, wondered if it might not be better to stay at their posts until morning. Fortunately, the night terrors eventually gave way to the deep sleep welcomed by all tired soldiers. And it was a good thing, for only then did the Lord Commander let his mind drift away into slumber.

The next day, the furans' murmurs – a soft sound they made to greet each other when the Blue Sun was the first to rise in the morning – awakened the men. To everyone's surprise, their mood was better. The flowers, which had been colored in blue, purple, and orange hues the night before, were now all white and yellow, and released a fragrance that put smiles on the grouchiest of the soldiers. Even Toras caught himself smiling while taking a deep breath. Perhaps Elyana had been wrong and the creature that had attacked Horn's Pass was just a rokon; unusually large, but still only a rokon.

At least, that was the thought that these heavenly surroundings put in his mind. But he knew better, and the smile faded – if slowly.

Before breaking camp, the men chewed on some of the left-over meat from the previous night; its taste was a little off – being cold – but the meat still satisfied the soldiers' appetite. Thirty minutes later, the company was back in the air.

The day would have been uneventful, if not for the ruckus caused by a flock of Horned Honkers anxious to find cover before the Bolingars, and the repeated ruckus when Toras and his men decided to take cover under the same copse of trees as the Honkers for lack of other suitable shelter nearby. The soldiers would have preferred to shoo the flyers away, but Honkers were one of the few large flyer families without Sunshields [24] and chasing them away would have been the same as sending them to their deaths for indeed – out in the open – most creatures without a Sunshield died from the heat, and any creature foolish enough to stay in the open, even with a Sunshield, risked serious injury if not death, from the Bolingar storm. So, the soldiers made do with the noisy sheltermates. In fact, the Bolingars made temporary sheltermates of many creatures. This often led to strange assemblages of predators and preys, segregated but near each other nevertheless, eyeing each other calmly in the first hour but with increasing tension as the Bolingars' final minutes approached, until the preys dashed away in a mad escape the moment they felt the predators' muscles twitch.

When the Bolingars passed, the Honkers honked fearfully toward the furans to keep them away, exited the shelter, and then took to the air just as raucously as they had landed. Needless to say, furans and Humans alike were pleased to be rid of the noisy animals. A few minutes later, the company resumed its own flight.

Just before the Red Sun set that day, Toras found what he was looking for through the intense golden rays. He called to Kendor, who was flying some ten meters to his right, and pointed to the lake beneath them; at the western tip of it, the Mountain Lake outpost stood like a beacon. Kendor made a sign of the head and blew his horn to call the furanteams to attention. He then blew of his horn louder and longer so that the out-posted men might hear.

---

[24] 'Sunshield' referred to the covering membranes or chemical mechanisms, which animals that could not hide from the suns at midday, deployed over their bodies in order to protect themselves.

On land, one of the soldiers heard the horn, and shouted to alert his sergeant. The sergeant came out of a largish barrack, pulled out his looking glass, and quickly put it to his eye to see who might be arriving. When he recognized the riders at the front, he yelled for one of his men to bring him the flag. A soldier named Curos handed the Alvinorian flag to his officer. As soon as the man had it, he waved it to inform the incoming party that they were permitted to descend. Kendor waved back and looked to his commander who immediately raised a hand to signal the furanteams. Toras and his men dropped first, followed by the members of the Royal Guard and the two pack furans. The teams touched ground a minute later.

Sergeant Tamas walked toward his commander with a lively step and a wide smile. "Lord Commander, welcome! I was not expecting your coming. In any case, you will find the outpost in perfect order," continued the proud soldier.

The prince barked a laugh and said, "I'm sure your outpost *is* in perfect order, sergeant. But, as you can imagine, I am not here on an inspection tour. We're on our way to Spiritii and need to stop here for the night."

The sergeant gave his commander a questioning look, to which Toras replied, "We're flying with men from my brother's guard…on special assignment."

The middle-aged Tamas frowned as if skeptical. But he knew it wouldn't be proper to question his commander, and let his doubts be. Instead, he said, "But, you and the men must be hungry, Lord Commander. I'll send the furans out to find us some tender game." And the sergeant turned around and yelled, "Curos! Release our hunters to find us some nice grazers. And be sure they bring back the tenderest meat only!" And he laughed a joyous laugh.

That warm welcome brought another smile to Toras's face and he tapped the officer on the shoulder as he said, "Sergeant, Scorch will join your furans; as you know, he enjoys hunting and though we've been flying since morning, I'm sure he has enough energy to bring back a belwohr!"

"Certainly, my Lord. And I will have one of my guardians bring out some shellies [25] for the other furans; they can start with that until the hunters are back with fresh meat."

---

[25] Shellie: Small invertebrate creature with a thin shell on its back.

The sergeant shouted these other orders to a young recruit who was being introduced to Toras's men by his companions. Without a moment's hesitation or a hint of annoyance, the man turned, acknowledged the order, and went to do as ordered.

Embracing the sergeant with an ever-widening smile, Toras found himself thinking that he really liked this Tamas. Looking at him, one would not suspect him to be of such a jovial nature. For one, the man was built like a belwohr. He was not very tall, but he was stocky, with trunks for legs and ropy arms, and hands that could crush a stone mug. In fact, sergeant Tamas had been the victor of the celebratory combat games that marked the yearly return of out-posted men for the sixth year in a row now. But for all his frightening appearance, he was a most jovial fellow.

Toras turned from the sergeant when he heard men laughing. It appeared his soldiers and those from the outpost, most of whom knew each other well, were now making fun of each other's condition.

The prince thought: *That's good. I'm glad they've found something to laugh about.* But he frowned when he noticed Jamir and his lot keeping to themselves. He knew they likely did not know anyone at the outpost, but he suspected that some of them, such as Jamir himself, did not think too highly of these "bags," as city soldiers were wont to call them, and were more than content to stay away.

Some of the furans knew each other too, and the "locals" greeted the approaching "visitors", led by one of the out-posted men, with short, repeated, tremulous chirps. Next to the paddock, Curos was giving the assembled hunters – ten of them, including Scorch – the command to return with food with a sign of the hand toward his mouth, followed by his finger pointing at them, and finally by both hands moving down from the sides of his chest toward the ground which was the sign for people. The animals nodded as they let out an excited cry. They then started flapping their powerful wings and were aloft a moment later. The furans would find food for themselves, which they would carry between their paws, as well as food for the soldiers, which they would carry with their beaks.

Three soldiers – the Falirin twins from Toras's unit as well as a man from the outpost – now set out to prepare a fire with which to warm themselves and cook the meat when it arrived. They walked toward the back of the barracks where the logs and dry branches for kindle were neatly stacked. Once there, the local guardian, a slender but ropy, dark-eyed and dark-haired fellow in his mid-twenties named Hanne, eyed the large logs tauntingly. The twins, also in their twenties and good friends of the former, knew at once what Hanne meant with his provocative grin. They looked at each other with anticipation and promptly accepted the challenge. Upon Hanne's signal, each man rushed to grab five large logs, and then ran toward the fire pit as fast as he could. Hanne won, as he expected, but he grabbed Falor and Felor and gave both a good-natured slap on the shoulders. The men then got back to their task, lighting the fire, and placing the spits atop the flames to sterilize them.

Meanwhile, the rest of the men from both guards saw to their furans, unsaddling, brushing, and checking them for back sores. That done, they setup the prince's tent as well as the common tent for themselves.

Half-an-hour later, the hunters returned with a grazer and a large fish each. The furans dropped their catch in front of Curos, the furan-keeper, except for Scorch who landed in front of his own master to drop his catch. Toras thanked him but sent him back to Curos with his prey. Scorch went, although he seemed a little irritated. Once Curos had each furan's catch in front of himself, he thanked the animals, accompanying words with gestures as he always did, after which he had the cook and his assistants take the grazers away.

Curos then let the hunters into the paddock with the other furans, and with the help of another soldier, cut-up the fish in sufficient pieces to give each furan his share, including those who had not hunted.

In front of the fire pit, Hanne and the twins thanked the grazers for giving their flesh and went on to prepare them for cooking, returning the skin and inedible parts to the furans. Thirty minutes later, the food was ready, and Hanne called everyone to sit and eat. Toras, seeing that the men were looking to segregate themselves by Guard, called on Secundus Jamir and invited the officer to sit by him and Kendor. Jamir accepted the invitation, if begrudgingly, but this nevertheless forced some mixing. And it was good because once the eating and drinking started, the story-telling and singing followed, and the Royals – seeing their peers so joyous – joined in the reveling too.

This was a pleasant surprise to Secundus Jamir who glanced at the prince and nodded in appreciation of the Lord Commander's invitation. Toras smiled in return and then turned to look at the sky. In the distance, he saw a pride of wild furans flying over the valley between the Furan Peaks and the Colossi's Peaks. They looked small from here, but the reflections of the setting Red Sun on their bellies and wings still brought another smile to Toras.

There were three known species of furans on K'Tara. The smallest species, known as the Green Furan, had an average wingspan of two meters, and with its mild character it made a good pet when Humans were able to capture a young one. The White Furan was a larger species; it had an average wingspan of two and a half meters. It was a territorial species, with the males often fighting each other to the death, and could not be tamed. The largest of all furans – the species from which the Royal furans were selected and bred was known as the Black Furan and had an average wingspan of four meters. Its size, fierceness and carnivorous nature should have made it incompatible with humanoids, but Black Furans fortunately disliked their flesh. Instead, the species preyed upon some of the quadrupeds that inhabited the slopes of the Furan Peaks as well as on the larger species of fish in the surrounding bodies of water. The Black Furan was long-lived, reaching seventy or eighty years of age. Because of its longevity, the bond it formed with its master could be very strong indeed, if it was treated with respect, and if the initial bonding was properly done. But most of all, the Black Furan was a highly intelligent creature, with a complex social structure and language which, when harnessed properly, were two very useful traits to humanoids.

Just as Toras let out a silent sigh in response to the spectacle offered by the wild furans, one of the outpost's soldiers – a tall and muscular man despite his old age – approached Sergeant Tamas.

He said, "Sergeant, there's someone coming who seems to be running his voran to death."

Tamas stood and looked down the hill to the east. "Hum, with the Red Sun almost set, it is hard to tell who might be coming. Why don't you go meet him at the top of the hill, Elmanon?"

"As you wish, Sergeant."

Elmanon went and put himself across the narrow road which led to the outpost. The rider was now but a short distance from Elmanon, and the soldier recognized him for a messenger with his flat, red and black-striped, narrow-brimmed hat. Elmanon raised an arm to force the man to stop his voran.

The rider halted his voran some three meters from the old soldier but did not step down. Elmanon did not ask any questions and watched the man with a borrowed air of authority for a moment. Meanwhile, rider and voran tried to catch their breaths, which they seemed to have been holding for far too long. Finally, Elmanon inquired about the man's business, and the rider – still gasping for air – replied that he had an urgent message for the post's commander. But Elmanon merely signaled the messenger to come down. The rider was about to complain, but he did not wish to anger the soldier, so he did as ordered.

The rider was a short, stocky man, with a peculiar accent and an even stranger beard, which was split and pulled back to wrap around the man's ears.

Not understanding the soldier's lack of urgency, the messenger shouted, "I've travelled one hundred n' sixty kilometers to get here, guardian, and it's urgent I see the post's commander, now!"

But Elmanon was not one to relinquish an opportunity to exert authority over others, and so he continued to test the newcomer. "And what's this place you've travelled from, messenger?!"

The poor man let out an exasperated sigh and replied, "It's a village 'long the eastern coast named Galior, and if your post doesn't bring it help soon, it is likely all my people will be dead by the time I return. Please let me see your commander."

Elmanon raised a doubting eyebrow, but the messenger *had* ridden his voran like a madman, and now he was begging, so perhaps he was telling the truth. The old soldier beckoned the messenger to follow him, and they started toward the camp. The stranger followed with anxious motions, adjusting his hat and dusting his pantaloons repeatedly, wishing the soldier would walk a little faster.

By the fire, men still sat, finishing their meals or drinking a final mug of Breminese beer. Toras and the officers wondered why the newcomer was so agitated, and they watched him with either questioning or worried eyes. Sergeant Tamas excused himself and walked toward the approaching men to find out what catastrophe had brought the messenger to the outpost.

As the three got closer to each other, Elmanon quickened his step. Upon reaching his commander, the old soldier promptly relayed the messenger's request. Tamas acknowledged the man who stood behind Elmanon and realized from the visitor's exasperated appearance that the soldier must have caused it, so he quickly thanked the guardian, and ordered him to see to the voran's needs. Elmanon obeyed, but not before shooting a displeased grin at the messenger and drawing an annoyed sigh from Tamas who had noticed the soldier's expression.

As Elmanon left with the voran, Tamas approached the newcomer and said, "My apologies for my man's behavior, messenger. He enjoys intimidating people when he gets a chance – a habit I haven't been able to rid him of."

The man made an uncertain nod.

"Now, what brings you here, messenger?"

Words rushed out of the man's mouth like water from a broken damn, forcing Tamas to slow him down more than once, especially when the messenger mentioned some unknown "evil creature."

When the messenger was done, Tamas shook an incredulous face and said, "All right. I think you had better repeat this to my commander. Follow me and remove your hat."

The man obeyed but did not understand why he should remove his hat; as far as he knew, one only did that in front of a noble. But he did as ordered and followed the sergeant.

Upon reaching Toras, who was speaking with his primus, Tamas leaned toward him and said, "Apologies Lord Commander. A messenger from…Galior," Tamas looked back at the man to make sure he remembered the name of the village correctly, "a small village along the coast. He has some rather incredible news, and I'm not sure what to make of them, but he came here to ask for our support."

"Well, let him step forward, sergeant."

Tamas turned around and said, "Come forward man, and make your case to our Lord Commander."

The short man looked suddenly nervous. He was not certain what titles identified whom in the kingdom's army, as he had never before dealt with any of its superior officers, but a "Lord" was going to be someone fairly high in the hierarchy, in any case. As he approached

61

and looked timidly to see who it was he would be speaking with, he turned his hat nervously in his hands.

"Well, what is it my good man?"

"Sorry m'lord, 've been sent here to ask for hel–" The messenger suddenly took a step back and bowed low, very low, and looked to the ground. He might not be a worldly man, but he surely could recognize members of the royal family given that every town and village had a painting of them hanging in their mayories. The man was taken aback by the presence of the younger prince right here, in front of him. After a few moments, he straightened himself, but kept his eyes on the ground, hat in hands, and rushed to introduce himself as Grom of Galior.

The prince said, "No need to look down, Master Grom. What is threatening your village?"

The messenger thanked the prince for his permission to look up but raised his head only slightly and proceeded to answer the prince's question. "M' Prince, a beast we never seen b'fore has been attacking villages on the coast, and it has killed many 'lready. Yest'day, it 'ttacked a village just twenty kilometers from ours. The mayor thought it'd probably attack us next. He sent me to get help before it's too late f'r us too."

The prince's reaction surprised all those who did not know him well when he growled, "Aghrrrrr! Damn it! Why now?!? Why?!"

Grom backed away, thinking he had angered the prince.

Noticing the messenger's reaction, Toras quickly calmed himself. "I'm sorry, Master Grom; Horn's Pass was attacked last night, and I'm quite sure it was the very same…creature you mention – a large rokon."

Still looking half-way down, Grom replied, "'m sorry, m' Prince. But it can't be a rokon. Surviv'rs have spoken of people dying in ways no rokon kills."

Well, thought Toras, *it appears it's going to be very hard to keep the lid on the true nature of our foe. And I wish we could tell the truth, but I will respect Elyana's request. I guess all I can do for now is give non-committal answers to everyone.*

Toras said, "Master Grom, fear can cause us to see a ghost where a shadow has passed."

The messenger looked terribly contrite, as if he had just attempted to insult the prince's intelligence. He backed away and apologized for his ignorance.

"There's no need to feel so ashamed, Master Grom. Just don't spread any rumors; it isn't wise to do, especially not of a messenger. In any case, your mayor's request for support will be answered. Please give us a moment to confer."

Grom was more than happy to give the prince time to consult with his officers in private – and to have some time for himself to recover some dignity – so he bowed anew and went toward his voran, which had been tied next to the furan paddock.

Kendor spoke first. "Lord Commander, I say we split up. I know our orders, but it is the right thing to do. A third of us can go to Galior and the rest continue with you to Spiritii."

Jamir was shocked by the suggestion and said, "We can't do that!"

"You'd rather let another whole village be massacred?" replied Kendor with some heat in his voice already. "Sergeant Tamas and his men can't possibly take care of that thing on their own!"

With slight but definite mockery in his tone, Jamir said, "Our orders are to bring back the high king, *Primus* Kendor."

Kendor had to keep himself from hitting the idiot, but he stayed his hand and gave Jamir a look that would surely have slain him, if looks could kill. Toras cursed the Royal beneath his breath. He frankly did not know what made some Royals so prejudiced toward the Black Guard; certainly not his brother or Harlion. Both had served in the Black Guard and respected it. Was it jealousy that caused these men to be so ill-disposed toward them? Or just anger at being subordinated to a man other than an officer of the Royal Guard? Either way, this Jamir certainly did not realize that his lack of respect for a man of the Black Guard ultimately insulted him, its commander, and under any other circumstances, Toras would have given the man a stern reprimand. But not today. There were other, more urgent matters to deal with now. Still, he promised himself he would speak to his brother about some of his men's attitude.

As he brought his focus back on the situation at hand, Toras noticed that Kendor and Jamir were waiting on him – rather impatiently – to make his own opinion known. So, Toras made a quick sign of his hand to stop the men from uttering any other

63

complaint, and said, "Primus Kendor, I want you to take five of our men, as well as another five of Secundus Jamir's and go to Galior."

Jamir started saying, "I must obj–" But Toras stopped him with an angry look, the same look the king always used when his sons or another man irritated him. That stopped the officer in his tracks.

Toras said, "Secundus! Defenseless people need our help, so we'll provide it. And since it is also the responsibility of the Royal Guard to see to the defense of the kingdom's subjects, I am sending some of your men along with mine."

The officer stood there like a mute, with a startled look and injured pride. Well, there was nothing Toras could do about that. The man had asked for it.

The Lord Commander continued. "Primus, you have your orders. Secundus Jamir, please select five men to go with Primus Kendor."

Both men nodded in turn, one with satisfaction on his face and the other with a blank stare which turned to surprise when Toras added, "And Secundus, I will need you to act as my second in command until Primus Kendor returns."

Jamir looked totally puzzled by the high prince's brother. Aside from the well-deserved praises for the younger prince's fighting skills, Jamir had heard mostly negative things about his tempter and his frequently brash decisions. But this way he had to embarrass people one moment, and grant them his trust in the next, confused him thoroughly.

Toras continued, "Primus, if you cannot kill the Serpent – which is likely – try to coax it away from the village at the very least." Then he added, more as a statement than a question, "You know the risks?"

The soldier looked at him with a grimace which meant he knew very well what the risks were.

"Good luck, my friend, and may your body be worthy."

The men shook arms, and Kendor informed Grom they would be leaving for Galior in a few minutes. Toras saw Grom's relief. But the prince, himself, felt like his task just got that much more complicated and desperate. Toras also noticed the agitation of the men who were told they would be departing for Galior shortly. Sudden changes in plans were never received as a good sign. The out-posted men and their sergeant helped Primus Kendor and his detachment get ready for departure, wondering all the while what-in-Dark-One's-Pit this talk of a rokon causing such destruction was all about.

Just now, Toras invited the officers to his tent to discuss the tactics for the Galior detachment. As soon as they were all gathered and Toras was about to begin, Secundus Jamir interrupted him – politely – to suggest that the prince should send a message to his brother to inform him of the change in plans and consequent splitting of the company, which caused Toras to release another growl, startling everyone within as well as without the tent.

It was not Jamir that had angered him, but rather the reminder that not everyone was going to defend Galior. *Why should I, or anyone else, stay here to sip tea, drink beer, or sleep, when the others will likely be facing the Serpent in less than an hour!? Why!?*

The desire to go to Galior and fight with his men was stronger than his duty to find the king. He *needed* to go to Galior. The situation there was simply too grave for him to let his men risk their lives while he went on safely. His father was important, but he was protected by some of the best men in the kingdom, and he was probably fine, wherever he was.

As these thoughts battled in his mind, the prince grew angrier and angrier, and Jamir took a step backward – just in case. Suddenly, Toras slammed his fist into the central pole of his tent with all his force, causing it to crack with a terrible noise – and the roof came down. In his rage, Toras pulled at the canvas, causing the rest of the tent to collapse. All the men could do was duck, to protect themselves from the falling poles.

Secundus Jamir – like the other men – was down on his knees, covered by canvas, and shaking his head. *So, this is what they mean by the prince being unpredictable and as dangerous as a raging Belwohr.* Just then, the officer heard the prince still growling not too far to his left. With a sigh, he unsheathed his longblade and started ripping the canvas to try and reach the prince. But it was no easy going with the many layers of material, and the poles crisscrossed as they were. Still, he did progress and a moment later, he found himself next to Kendor, who was also trying to reach the prince. Jamir thought the man would look embarrassed, but instead, he raised shoulders and brows in a sign of resignation to his commander's nature. Both men now shouted and asked the prince if he was ok.

The prince growled the reply, "Of course, I'm ok. Why wouldn't I be?!"

Jamir had to hold back a laugh as he looked at Kendor who was shaking his head. Kendor said, "My Prince, please move back. We are going to rip the canvas on this side."

A moment later, the prince emerged from the debris, followed by the two officers. They walked out in front of bewildered men who had taken up arms, fearing that something or someone was attacking the prince.

A soldier asked, "Lord Commander, are you all right?"

Toras paused a moment but did not reply. He simply looked at the man with a clenched jaw, irritated that the soldier would ask him the same question about his condition. The soldier stepped back and mumbled an apology.

Toras resumed his furious walk and strode to the paddock to retrieve Scorch and prepare him for departure.

"Scorch, come here!"

Toras saw Scorch raise his head at the back of the paddock, but the furan made no move to approach. Toras called his name again, or rather yelled it again, and this time Scorch responded with a soft growl as he bobbed his head in refusal.

Toras was about to yell again, when he realized what was happening and said to himself, "Right. You're certainly not the one who deserves my anger. In fact, I'm sure that if it were up to you, we'd already be in Galior."

Toras called him again, but the furan still refused to go, until the prince realized he needed to take a deep breath, calm down and apologize. The furan accepted the apology with a reproachful purr, but finally approached his master who took him out of the paddock to saddle him.

By the crumbled tent, the soldiers had gathered around their captains. Those who did not know the Lord Commander personally wondered whether the man had gone mad. But Toras's men realized this was "simply" going to be another one of those days, or rather, nights. Grom asked a tall and wiry soldier near him whether the prince had lost it.

The soldier replied with an honest, "Nope, he just can't let his men put themselves in danger without him."

As for Kendor, he could guess what was going through the prince's mind, as well as what was going to happen next. So, he just waited with the soldiers, and reassured those who needed reassuring – especially the members of the Royal Guard. It did not take long before the prince's command rumbled through the camp.

"Primus Kendor, Secundus Jamir, get the men ready. We're all going to Galior! And I don't want to hear any argument or complaint!" Then, turning to Tamas, who had come to find him, he said, "Sergeant! Please send a messenger to the east to find my brother and inform him of what is happening here. The caravan is probably somewhere on the Capital Road by now."

So it was that Lord Commander Toras and his detachment made a fateful detour to Galior.

V THE RELOCATION OF HORN'S PASS'S PEOPLE

A few hours after Toras and his band had left Horn's Pass, Aithen, his guardians, and Elyana started organizing the population for the departure. The Black Guard – responsible for the defense of the Pass – as well as several carpenters and masons, and the head of each household were going to remain behind to rebuild the village and repair the fortress. The fortress's servants were also going to remain behind to tend to the cooking and other needs of the guard, as were the healers.

In a few days, Sisters would arrive, at Elyana's request, to assist in the repair of the fortress. Indeed, Yellow Sashes were skilled in using the Bind to strengthen stone, and this strengthening was a necessity given that the fortress was all that stood between the enemy nation of Rokoth in the west, and Lower Alvinor in the east, where the Coriolan capital was located.

By the end of the day, carts were ready and loaded, all necessary provisions for the journey gathered, and final instructions had been left with Secundus Sheffar. Those who could sleep gathered under tents or in their wagons. Those who could not find sleep huddled around fires to wait for the morning, singing some old songs about death and love.

When the Blue Sun rose, most villagers were already awake, waiting anxiously for departure. Men, women, and children were breaking fast, eating bread dipped in oil, if they had oil, and cooked fresh blood from their bellowers which they obtained by slitting the skin on their necks; otherwise, they had water or wine. At about Six Hours and Thirty Minutes after Highnight, High Lord Commander Aithen ordered the bugler to sound the horn.

The hearts of the civilians skipped a beat at hearing the horn, and, willingly or unwillingly, the adults readied themselves, their kids, and their carts, as well as harnessed and hooked their vorans or bellowers. Families had been authorized to bring the animals which were going to pull their carts, as well as their howlers, if they had any. The rest, they had to leave behind. Each family had also packed a sack of dried food per adult and half a sack per child or senior, as well as a barrel of water. That would have to suffice until they reached Furan City. Once there, each family would be provided with shelter, and one adult per household would be given work to sustain his or her family until everyone could return to Horn's Pass.

As for the guardians, they moved to their assigned positions with disciplined organization and without much trepidation. Five of the fifteen guardians were on voranback to see to the orderly progression of the caravan, while their furans would fly freely alongside the other ten guardians who were on furanback. The furanteams were going to be scouting the land – and the air – to help ensure the safety of the caravan. Aithen himself was going to make the trip on voranback so that he may discuss matters with Elyana Lux Baiula as well as with his captains during the journey to the capital. His own furan, Xyre, was free to fly with the other riderless furans, or to walk alongside Aithen's voran.

If any of Aithen's guardians or officers felt any anxiety at the thought of bringing such a large number of refugees to the capital, they did not show it.

The prince, sitting comfortably astride his voran, looked at his furan, who was already in the air, and sighed. Xyre was a remarkable animal. At twenty-seven years of age, he was an experienced and reliable furan, cautious but courageous nevertheless, unlike Scorch who tended to take too much risk – like his master. Xyre's reliability was a trait Aithen admired above all else, one which he exhibited regardless of his condition and regardless of the difficulties facing him. That the animal belonged to Aithen was no mere chance either; the royal family had first right to the best capture during the decennial hunts. The other furans – not at all lame themselves – were typically divided amongst the winged divisions of the Royal and the Black Guards.

Some twenty minutes after the trumpet first sounded, the caravan was ready to depart. Aithen signaled the bugler again, and the young lad blew the trumpet once more, loud and clear, to call the caravan into motion. Thus, it started on its way to a place most civilians knew not, except through the stories told by merchants and soldiers. Many Horn's Passers felt a kind of excitement at the idea of going to Furan City, the city of Kings and Emperors, a place of dreams for those who had never seen it, and of the greatest beauty for those who had. But despite the excitement, the feeling of loss was in most

70

everyone's expression, and it remained for a while as they whipped their animals into motion to begin their march toward the safety of the unfamiliar capital.

The road between Horn's Pass and Furan City was one of the rare graveled roads crossing the kingdom, which meant that, despite the fact that the trip was going to be a slow one with ninety-five carts in the caravan, it was still going to be a relatively comfortable one for the cart riders.

A few young boys chose to ride the animals pulling their parents' wagons, while many of the older kids – already over the fears of the previous day, or perhaps trying to forget – decided to run alongside the carts and fool around, rather than stay with their grieving families any longer.

After a couple of hours, though, the general mood started to lighten-up almost magically. Indeed, the Capital Road was now within fifty kilometers of the northern coast, and the joyful songs of the Chirpers in this area, along with the warm breeze which began to fill the air with the fragrance of the Lonem tree, helped lift-up the spirit of most, if not of everyone.

The Lonem tree, which grew in stands of ten to fifteen trees in this region, was a needled tree of gigantic proportions. The largest of them could reach a height of one hundred meters and boast a trunk nine meters wide. The oldest among them, known as *Adagnitius*, had witnessed the rise and fall of the Coriolan Empire, the foundation of the Order of the Sisters of the Light, the terrible years of the Dark Battle, and the emergence of a virus which exterminated the Luxori. Adagnitius was revered by the locals who were members of an occult but harmless sect that lived within the trees. Indeed, these people, known simply as Tree-Dwellers, believed that because of the trees' extreme age and size, the plants carried the accumulated knowledge of all that they had experienced since their germination, years to centuries to ages ago, and that the trees could transfer this knowledge to those living within their trunks. The leader of the cult, the Living Branch, was the foremost recipient of such knowledge, and lived within the great Adagnitius himself.

As the caravan passed the nearest copse, which stood some one hundred meters away, Tree-Dwellers stepped out of their ligneous abodes, like curious creatures, to gape at the long line of wagons and at the wondrous furanteams flying high above the caravan. The Horn's Passers looked back with even greater curiosity.

Just now, a sturdy old woman holding a long, bright orange staff, stepped out of the nearest tree. After she cleared the tree, she stopped and planted her staff squarely on the ground, causing a loud reverberation to reach the caravan and startling many.

Without even turning to see what had caused the sound, Aithen said, "The Living Branch. I should have expected this."

Harlion, riding on the prince's left, said, "Someone should probably go give her some explanation for this."

Aithen confirmed his captain's suggestion and turned to Elyana, who replied, "I will go. She will receive me better than she will one of your officers, my Prince."

Aithen replied with a candid smile, "She will, will she?"

Elyana responded with a simple nod and a similar smile.

The prince watched the woman gracefully dismount her voran, and he continued to follow her with desirous eyes as she walked toward the Living Branch, responding only distantly to some comment Harlion was making about the cultists. Aithen shook his head as an intense and unexpected image suddenly crossed his mind, and he asked his captain for an update on his estimated arrival in the capital to steer his attention away from the Lux Baiula.

When Elyana reached the Living Branch, the two tipped their heads respectfully toward each other, and then conferred quietly for a few minutes. Every so often, the old woman looked toward the caravan with concerned eyes and then toward the prince with a weighing gaze. Elyana finally gave the Living Branch another respectful nod and returned to the caravan.

As the Lux Baiula got back on her voran, Aithen scratched his arm awkwardly and said, "Well?"

"Well indeed. We can resume our travel."

Aithen looked back at the Lux Baiula with half a frown and said, "Elyana, please."

"Yes, Aithen. I mean that the Living Branch accepted my explanations though I am not certain she necessarily believes them given that rokons do come this far every so often and that they have never been the cause of a displacement such as this. Either way, no rumors will be spreading from here; as you know, Tree-Dwellers do not travel beyond their territory and those who come here only learn what the Tree-Dwellers have directly learned from the trees, and fortunately for us, the trees have not seen the Serpent."

Aithen snorted and replied, "Thank you Elyana. I appreciate your taking care of this, though I doubt the trees would care one way or another, even if the Serpent decided to…shit on them as it passed."

The Lux Baiula blinked in shock, but recovered quickly and said, "Now my Prince, you do not know that for a fact. But you are welcome."

It was now the prince's turn to stare back with wide eyes. His captain, who had listened to this exchange with some interest, barked a genuine laugh and said, "Well, I will not pretend to understand what is passing between the two of you, my Prince, but the Lux Baiula has a point." And the man laughed another heartfelt laugh.

The prince, feeling a little miffed, decided to ignore the comment and gave the order to resume the march, shaking his head and snorting quietly to himself every so often, as he thought of the strangely irritating, yet stirring exchange between him and Elyana.

As the objects of everyone's curiosity disappeared in the distance, the general mood – stirred by both the lingering fragrance of the trees and the warm breeze – returned to one of delight.

The prince's mind, however, soon went back to gloomy thoughts despite the beauty and life that surrounded the caravan, and despite the pleasant sound of Elyana's voice as she conversed quietly with Harlion. The significance of the recent events, the need to make sense of it all, and the responsibilities which now weighed on him churned his brains.

If what Elyana believes is true, we are all doomed. How can we hope to fight the Serpent and whatever else may soon join it? Who remains today with the knowledge to defeat such things? How am I going to answer the onslaught of questions that is sure to come from the members of the Union's Council? And the City's senators will certainly stand bewildered when they see me arrive with eight hundred and thirty-nine men, women and children…And why do I keep thinking about her and feeling like a fool in front of her? I don't have the time to be distracted by these feelings *now!*

Thus went Aithen's thoughts, all the rest of the day. He also wondered how his father and mother would react if they knew his eyes were setting on a Lux Baiula. Octavius and Darya had begun to pressure him recently into settling on a good party to marry, although he had just barely completed the first eighth of the long life he expected to have. Aithen could not understand why they would want to see him betrothed so young given that if he had a child at this age, his son would be an old man before he ever sat on the throne.

One thing he did suspect, though, was that if they knew his eyes were setting on a Lux Baiula, they would likely object. Indeed, upon becoming a full Sister, a woman had to relinquish all titles to any and all property, which meant that such a union would bring no financial advantage to the throne. Moreover, although Sisters were allowed to marry, it occurred only very rarely, and none had ever married a man with any amount of power or wealth, as this was frowned upon by the Sisterhood who believed that such a marriage would cause a Lux Baiula to lose her objectivity in the use of her powers. These thoughts only strengthened Aithen's resolve to resist his nascent feelings for the woman.

When midday approached and the heat of the Bolingars started to become dangerous, Aithen ordered a halt, and the caravan moved into a field by the road. People immediately pulled reflective canvases over their carts, while the members of the prince's party sheltered themselves in a few, similarly reflective, large tents. Vorans and other trumpeters were also covered with thin but tough, light-reflecting sheets, whereas bellowers and furans were left as they were: indeed, the former shed their outer layers of skin to cover themselves in strong, sheet-like cocoons during the Bolingars, while the latter simply veiled their heads with their wings and let the iridescent skin of their four wings keep their bodies cool and protect them from flying debris during the wind storm that followed the Bolingars. Fortunately for the caravan, the Bolingar winds were not as strong near the northern coast of Alvinoria, and although the debris could tear thin fabric or skin, it would not break bones or carts.

The vast majority of land creatures – humanoids included, unless they had access to some cooling technology – spent the Bolingars in a forced slumber, a slumber brought on by the intense heat which exhausted the body and numbed the brain. Only a very few species of flying lizards, which had the ability to spray themselves with a continuous mist of water even while flying, remained active during those deadly hours.

When, a couple of hours later, the winds quieted, and the bellowers bellowed and started shedding their cocoons, everyone awoke. The trumpeters, vorans included, were promptly uncovered, tents packed, and the roofs from some of the carts retracted, while the furans unfolded their wings and stretched their legs with long, soft screeches.

After checking their possessions for damage, and clearing debris from their immediate surroundings and carts, most families prepared a cold mid-afternoon meal composed of whatever dried fruit, bread, or cheese they had. Those with a mooer, however, prepared a low burning fire and sent the kids to the animal to collect the remaining sheets of cocoon before they all fell onto the ground. The cocoon sheets were then carefully crumbled into a pot and cooked at low heat until caramelized. People called this substance "coonay, " and they spread it over bread or used it to dip dried fruit in. But this was not a food which townsfolk enjoyed, and most guardians in the company – given that they came from families of decent means – frowned at the sight and smell of the stuff. But a few of the guardians did have humbler origins, and they eyed the peasants with envy, hoping that one family or another might share some coonay, which they did, and the guardians accepted it gratefully despite their comrades' disgusted looks.

An hour later, the trumpet sounded again, and the caravan resumed its long march toward the capital, causing tremors in the ground. The air was filled with the ground's reverberations, the shouts of men and women exhorting their animals forward, and the sound of whips hitting the leathers of vorans, as well as hitting the now fresh – and thus more sensitive – leathers of the bellowers which responded much more spryly because of it. Near the back of the convoy, some young men started a fight after their families' carts almost collided, adding their shouts to the cacophony. But eventually, the noise of the myriad wheels crunching the gravel muffled all else and settled over the convoy.

In front of the forever stretching line of carts, Aithen and Elyana spoke of what he would need to do once in the city: his first task would be to meet with the City's Senate to discuss his plan for the refugees; he would then have to meet with the Union's Council to have everyone put their respective cities and villages on guard. His final task, one which Elyana had strongly recommended but which Aithen had argued against as long as he could, would be a most unpleasant one. He would need to meet with Galadrin, First Cleric of the Order of Aiala, to ensure that the Order did not spread unwanted, supernatural rumors about the attack at Horn's Pass, which it was wont to do whenever an unexplainable event occurred.

Aithen often wondered why the Order of Aiala was so different from that of Elande, a religious order with more rational beliefs – if it could be said that religious beliefs were ever rational. The answer, according to Octavius, was that the former had political ambitions which the latter did not. Given his dislike of both politics and religion, there was little hope Aithen would ever enjoy his interactions with First Cleric Galadrin. But the cleric's worldview and motivations were not really the reasons for the prince's dislike of the man. No, the true reason was the man's fanaticism, a fanaticism all too visible on his burnt and intentionally scarred face. Indeed, the burning of a person's face – a sign of their submission to Aiala – was a prerequisite to their admission in the Order. The burning was repeated as the member achieved ever higher levels of *submission and purity*. Galadrin's had been burned more often than any of his predecessors and his appearance rightly disgusted and disturbed Aithen who could not understand how a group with such beliefs and practices could exist at all. But the prince knew that his personal feelings were irrelevant when matters of state were concerned, and so, he would meet with the First Cleric, as Elyana recommended it.

A more difficult matter the prince and Lux Baiula discussed at length was whether to tell senators, lords, and clerics about the true nature of the rokon. Elyana maintained that it was unwise to do so before both Urbs Lucis and the Crown had agreed on a response. But Aithen insisted that the truth must be told unless another truth take shape on its own, one which would help neither the Crown nor the Sisterhood. In the end though, the Lux Baiula had the stronger argument, and the prince agreed, albeit reluctantly, to keep the rokon's true nature quiet for now. In any case, there were too many things they did not understand yet, and Aithen agreed it was best to keep the entire matter to a restricted few.

The rest of the day went smoothly, except for a ten-year old child getting hurt under the wheels of his parents' cart. Fortunately for the boy, one of Aithen's guardians – who happened to be riding nearby and had some training in emergency field procedures – had responded at once and tied a tourniquet around the boy's crushed calf to stop the bleeding. The guardian had then sent one of his comrades inform the prince of the injury. A few minutes later, the prince arrived with Elyana. The boy's parents were fearful at first, thinking they had angered the prince for delaying the caravan. But once Aithen explained why he had come, they felt embarrassed and asked the prince for his forgiveness. Needless to say, all in the caravan later learned of the prince's attitude toward his people.

Aithen spoke with the boy's parents a little while longer to ask if they would accept Elyana's help. Typically, treating the ill and the injured – whether Human or animal – was a village healer's responsibility. But both healers had remained in Horn's Pass, and although Peter, Aithen's guardian, had done a decent job at stopping the bleeding, the boy's injury still needed some attention. The man and woman were unsure; it was obvious they had the same all-too-common, and specious biases against Lux Baiulae. What was more, the prince had informed them that she was not a medic, but that all Lux Baiulae were trained in emergency procedures, and Elyana Lux Baiula would therefore be able to help speed-up the boy's recovery – if not heal him completely. After much nervous nail-biting, the parents finally agreed to let the Lux Baiula treat their son.

Elyana approached the boy who was now lying down in the back of the cart, crying. She hid well her own uneasiness at the thought of having to examine and heal a civilian. Sure, she had treated injured defenders at Horn's Pass, but she had had no choice there. This was different: Aithen's guardian had already stopped the bleeding, and she knew well that the civilians still distrusted her, even though she had helped many who were now in this caravan. Having decided to help, she put on a genuine smile, and asked, "What is your name, boy?"

Seeing this powerful and oh-so-beautiful woman address him, the freckled, red-haired boy drew back his tears and withheld a pained grunt – he would not let her think he was weak – and he said, "M'name's Martius, Ma'am."

"Martius. That is a very nice name. Do you know how lucky you are?"

"'am lucky?"

"Of course. What other boy will be able to tell his friends the prince brought him a Lux Baiula to heal him?"

The boy grinned despite the pain and relaxed noticeably.

Aithen watched Elyana, amazed. He had never seen her interact in this way with a child, though he did remember her giving him and his brother lessons when they were kids, and she did smile like this at them. This line of thought made him suddenly uncomfortable, though, so he dismissed it as he shook his head slightly and refocused on the boy. *I hate these differences in age!*

Elyana said to the boy, "I am going to touch you now, so I can understand the extent of your injury. I'll do my best not to hurt you but tell me if it does. I will then take another minute to probe you. You should not feel that at all."

"Probe me?"

"Yes, I will use the Bind – you've heard of that, yes?" The boy nodded. "I will use the Bind to look inside your body, inside your leg. Do you trust me?"

The boy looked at his parents, bleatishly. His parents looked at each other, then at the prince, and finally back at the boy with a nod. If the prince trusted her, they would too.

Before she started, Elyana turned her head slightly toward the kid's parents and said, "As the prince has told you, I am not a medic, but I will be able to stop any internal bleeding and begin mending the bones. Once we reach Furan City, you should take your son to one of our medics who will complete the healing. If you do that, he will be able to walk and run, as before."

The boy's parents, not knowing how to address a Lux Baiula or how to thank her, turned to each other as if to ask the other to respond. A moment later, the husband replied for both, "We will, Ma'am...Lush Baiula. Thank you."

With that Elyana proceeded to check the leg. The boy did wince every so often, and Elyana pretended not to notice. She lifted the bandage the guardian had put around it and saw that the bleeding resumed when she loosened the tourniquet.

Without looking up, she said to the soldier, "Guardian, you are a medicus militum [26], I assume?"

"Not quite yet, Lux Baiula. My insignia got damaged during the battle against the...rokon, so it does look like that of a full medicus

---

[26] Medicus Militum: Military medic.

militum, now. But 'am only a student of the art. Even so, 'am willing to help, as I can."

"Good, that is all I need. Please retighten the tourniquet and be ready to slowly loosen it when I tell you."

The apprentice medic did as requested, and Elyana got on with her task. After a minute of probing, a minute during which the boy and his parents wondered what, if anything, was happening, she knew what she had to do. Addressing everyone but looking at the boy, she told them what she had found and what she was going to do in terms they could understand. They agreed, and Elyana began the healing process.

After ten minutes of sending vibrations into the boy's leg to prompt his immune system to suture the blood vessels and to begin fusing the bone, the boy wincing, the parents holding each other's hands tense with worry, and Elyana giving instructions to the apprentice military medic to hold their patient still – ten minutes during which Martius had watched intently, wincing every so often but less and less frequently as the minutes passed, all the while wondering what the woman was doing to his flesh – Elyana finally sat on the cart next to the boy, wiped her brow and said, "I have done what I could. How do you feel Martius?"

"Feels…good? Can I move m'leg?"

"No. I suggest you let it rest for the day, and then, only walk on it. No running until you have seen the medics in Furan City. Can you do that?"

With a wide grin, the boy replied, "Yes, I can, ma'am…Lux Baiula." The boy beamed, apparently proud to have pronounced the strange title properly.

Elyana smiled in return and said, "Very well young man. Guardian Peter, here, will come back tonight to change your bandage, and continue doing that daily until the scars are fully formed and dry."

At that, the boy looked somewhat saddened and Elyana quickly added, "I promise to come back too, to see how you are doing, and make certain our young medic does a proper job."

Another wide smile, which warmed Elyana's heart, appeared on the boy's face. She turned away to prevent her emotions from overwhelming her and approached Aithen.

Aithen said to the parents, "We will leave you now, but your boy will be fine."

The mother replied, with hands clasped in prayerful thanks, and tears in her eyes. "Ooh, thank you, my Prince. Thank you. And thank you too…Lux Baiula…you are not at all as they say your kind is."

"You are welcome, mistress…?"

"I am Sharan, Lux Baiula."

"You are welcome, mistress Sharan. And I am glad you feel that way. You will find that…my kind…are actually good people, but it is a simple fact of life that when one does not know another, it is quite difficult for trust to develop."

Elyana thanked the guardian for his assistance, and then she and Aithen climbed onto their vorans to return to the front of the caravan to resume the march toward the capital.

As they rode, Aithen glanced at Elyana and said hesitatingly, "You were truly amazing, Elyana. The way you interacted with the boy, and with his parents…I didn't know this other side of you. You've always been so formal, for as long as I can remember."

"That is because I have always been around you in an official capacity. And you and your brother were not regular child–" Elyana stopped herself when she noticed Aithen's jaw clenching. "Well, you know what I mean."

"I suppose I do. But, well, anyway, you did a good job. Thank you…for taking care of the boy."

Suddenly, Elyana laughed. She laughed a beautiful, childish laugh, and then stopped herself, seemingly feeling guilty. She then shook her head as if upset with herself, thanked Aithen for his comment, kicked her voran and rode on.

It was just as well, thought Aithen, because his cheeks had flushed from embarrassment. *I'm a prince? Heir to House Coriolis?! I'm a fool, that's what I am!* Aithen did not try to catch up to Elyana, but he did give his voran a slight kick to speed him up a little. When he got to the front of the line, he went to Harlion, ordered the caravan forward again, and stayed next to his captain until he forgot his embarrassment.

As was expected, the Lux Baiula's success in healing the boy sent rumors spreading all through the caravan, and this, along with the prince's own caring actions toward the child, kept people talking with hope for the rest of the day, although a few did continue to distrust the Lux Baiula, saying that the kid's parents would regret it when they woke one morning and found their child babbling nonsense.

By the time the suns began to descend, Aithen had forgotten his earlier embarrassment, and he was now riding next Elyana. "This looks like a good spot to make camp, and I think the people will be grateful to stop early after the long and sweltering day we've had."

Elyana said, "I would welcome it as well. I need to stretch my legs and put some food in my stomach."

"Well then." Aithen waved High Captain Harlion over.

"Lord Commander?"

"My friend, we will rest here tonight. The journey has been long enough on this first day."

"Hum, I would recommend continuing a little longer, since the suns won't be set for another three hours or so."

"Thank you, but I prefer to stop now. It will allow the children to burn some of their stored energy before bedtime. Order the caravan stopped and have the villagers' carts assembled in a circle with our own tents placed around the villagers."

Harlion did not argue, though he thought the prince's concerns a little strange, and he left to see to his duties with a "Yes, my Prince."

With Harlion gone, Aithen shouted, "Kildare!"

"Yes, my Lord?"

"We are halting here for the night. Have the cook prepare a meal for Elyana Lux Baiula, High Captain Harlion, and me; we will eat in my tent once it is set up."

"Certainly, my Prince. Should I also have some wine brought over?"

"Yes, I think that will be welcome. Please take care of Magnus afterwards, as well."

"Yes, my Lord." The prince's squire left with a bow.

Magnus, Aithen's voran, was a remarkable destrier, though there were more striking ones in the Royal Guard. But that was of little concern to the prince whose primary mount was his furan, and who only cared that his voran be sound, and obedient, which Magnus certainly was.

Magnus's most striking features were perhaps his black-red coat, his dark red mane which encircled his neck, and his tail which contained a mix of black and dark red strands. The voran was tall with his withers standing at seventeen hands, but he was not as imposing as Harlion's battle voran which was not only tall, but also thick-boned. But what Aithen appreciated most in Magnus was his calm temperament, a calm he maintained no matter what he found in front of himself, very much like Xyre.

After dismounting his voran, Aithen started to pet him as he looked toward his captain. The man was giving orders to soldiers who responded promptly and cheerfully. The prince nodded in satisfaction. He had a very good and loyal man in Harlion. The officer had been in the service of the Crown, in one capacity or another, for some three decades now, and had served as one of the prince's mentors during the past eleven years, instructing him in the arts of war and leadership. This last was an area of study both Octavius and Harlion deemed essential to the Crown Prince's education, and Harlion had therefore spent much time instructing Aithen and discussing with him interactions with – and responses to men who were expected to give their lives for their commander, the high king, and the kingdom.

When Aithen was finally given the command of the Royal Guard, it had been an easy decision for him to retain Harlion as his first officer. The man had continued to prove to be an invaluable asset, even when the prince ignored his advice, which happened every so often. But Harlion was a strict, disciplined man, extremely respectful of the chain of command, and once the prince made a decision, the officer did his best to execute his orders successfully. And thanks to Harlion – though others might say that the prince underestimated his own skills – Aithen had not suffered a single defeat yet. Yes, the man was an invaluable asset, and a good friend.

***

Primus Kendor – who was stepping off his furan – suddenly tensed-up and said, "My Lord, did you hear that screech?"

With a grim look on his face, Toras replied, "Yes, I did."

By now, the night was dark, with only feeble light coming from the waning moon, Alba. But the looks on the men's faces were perhaps all the more striking for it, and those looks said that they were not eager to confront the Serpent again, though they had expected it when leaving the outpost. The fact was, the men were exhausted, as were the furans given the three hours it had taken them to get to Galior.

Just now, Kendor shouted, "Guardians! Stop wasting time and water your mounts. It's the least we can do for them, now."

Everyone obeyed – even the Royals. Toras nodded to himself and gave Scorch as large a drink of water as he could spare. A few meters from him, Grom moaned and began to scream at the thought that the beast was already there.

Toras said, "Master Grom, control yourself!"

"My-my app-pap-pologies my Lord, I can't help it. My-my-my family is there. What is going to happen to them?!"

Toras could smell the man's fear and decided against answering his question. He wondered, too, how a man with a stutter could be a messenger. But this stammer was obviously the result of his fear, and it was likely he didn't have cause to fear for his life or for that of this family when he delivered messages.

The man must have realized that his question to the prince was not going to receive an answer, and so he asked another, "My-my-my Lord, do-do you have a plan?"

Toras sighed heavily and said, "Not yet, Master Grom. I first need you to give us a description of the layout of Galior and note where your people might be hiding. Can you do that?"

Grom nodded and gave Toras and his men a description of the village as concisely as he could, given his continued stuttering, indicating the locations of the safehouse, the mayor's home, and the wine cellars – all places where the villagers might be hiding. As soon as he was done, Grom asked to be excused so he could go down to the village to try and find his family. The prince let him go, though he had no idea how the man would be of any help to anyone.

Toras watched the man go for a moment, tripping on branches and stones as he raced down the steep hill. Toras sighed, then lifted his head as an immense shadow crossed Alba. *I don't want to be beneath it,* thought Toras, and he walked to the officers to form a plan of attack, extricating himself from the gloomy shadow.

The prince was relieved to hear Secundus Jamir willingly offer a few promising ideas along with Kendor. Once the plan was formed, men got onto their furans and spurred them into an arduous climb up the mountain, loping toward a cliff overlooking the eastern side of the village. From there, the prince and the officers hoped to surprise the monster.

As the minutes passed, the creature's shrieks became louder and more frequent, and the screams of terrified Humans started to reach the men's ears as well.

Near the top of the cliff, the company found the clearing they had been searching for. They approached the edge of the bluff, sticking to the tree line for as long as possible. And then they saw it, attacking the village with the same fury it had used at Horn's Pass, except that this time, no fortification resisted its poundings, and no Lux Baiula or guardians kept it at bay. The few defenders there were could do no more than irritate the creature, like biters annoying a man.

The men looked at each other, some with anxious anticipation, others with a tinge of fear in the whites of their eyes. Toras and Kendor merely nodded to each other with the resolution of men used to doing what needed to be done, their emotions stashed away somewhere else.

The prince turned to the men and said with a calm and confident front, "This is it, guardians. And you can see now why I brought us here. There are people down there unable to defend themselves, and they are dying. We will do what we know to do to give them a chance. From this moment until the moment we pounce on that damned creature, keep your thoughts and fears as quiet as possible. In fact, do not think at all; just follow and do. Thinking will only delay your responses and weaken your resolve."

A young soldier from Jamir's company asked with some embarrassment in his tone, "Pardon Lord Commander, but I heard some guardians back at the fortress say that this rokon can read our thoughts and…fry brains from a distance. Is that why you are telling us to shut our minds?" The other soldiers looked horrified, and Secundus Jamir was about to scold the guardian, but the prince stayed him with his hand.

I really wish we didn't have to keep up this lie. And I wish I had Father's or Aithen's skill to twist things around…And me standing here without responding is probably not helping. Toras took a deep breath to dampen the irritation he felt at being asked this question, and answered, "No guardian, that is not why. The reason is that attacking the rokon with our furans flying at breakneck speeds, and having to respond instantly to the creature's counterattacks, none of it can be done if you have to think about it; you and your furan will both be dead before your brain can analyze or decide anything." *There, I said a truth. Maybe I am more like Aithen and Father than I think I am.*

Everyone turned a glaring, impatient eye toward the soldier, until the young man finally apologized for his stupidity, took a step back and stood at attention, ready to do as the prince commanded.

"Good. If anyone else has any doubt about what we are going to do here, say so now, and you can stay behind to take care of the wounded when we're finished."

All the men stood at attention as one to show their readiness to follow the prince. Kendor, Jamir and the prince regarded each other with resolute nods, hiding their well-founded fears so that their men might fight with some hope of success.

From their vantage point, the troop could see the many houses already afire – probably the result of shattered lanterns or red-hot logs being blown wide by the rokon's destructive fly-bys. The flames had a fierceness which was lessened only by what they revealed: dozens of men, women and children laying on the ground dead, screaming in pain, or simply staring toward the sky before falling over.

Toras said, "All right. Ready to get this wretched beast away from here?"

Everyone nodded.

"Let's go then, and may our bodies be worthy!"

Whatever fear anyone felt, they now locked it up as well as they could, and they focused on the battle plan as they mounted their furans. Kendor and his nine men were first to take flight, positioning themselves to the west of the Serpent. Jamir and another nine flew to the north, and Toras was going to drop with the rest dead center on the Serpent. Each officer was to position his furanteams about one hundred meters above the Serpent, and attack with longbows at Toras's signal. If they could hit the Serpent and slow it down a little, the company would then switch to lances as these would cause more damage.

But before they could even begin their assault, the Serpent turned of a sudden, and flew with rage toward Toras's team. The prince tried to call his men back, but it was already too late, and the beast rammed into three furanteams. Guardians and furans dropped to the ground instantly. When the sickening sound of shattering bones reached the others, they realized that few would survive this night.

VI ARRIVAL OF A ZEBULONIAN

Aithen was sitting around one of the fires that had been lit up for the evening meal. The fire was small, to minimize the heat it produced given that the temperature was still fairly high at this hour of the day. Officers and guardians sat around the fire with Aithen, along with a few civilians. Indeed, the villagers had been told that they were welcome to join the prince or his guardians around their pits this evening, to give them a chance to enjoy some singing and storytelling while the meal was prepared by Aithen's cooks. Some Horn's Passers did do so, although only a few chose to sit around the prince's fire. Indeed, the prince might be a brother to the fortress's lord commander, but he was still the kingdom's heir and most villagers felt too intimidated by him despite the care he had shown earlier in the day with the injured boy. The few who had decided to sit around the prince's pit had done so only because they knew a few of the guardians sitting there. Nevertheless, an old man – the village's librarian, as incredible as that was – did take a seat right next to Aithen, and the prince was pleasantly surprised to find that he enjoyed Master Longbrows' company. So, they talked a while about topics as varied as rural life, history, and philosophy, and just when the librarian began to question the prince about the very peculiar rokon that had attacked Horn's Pass, Harlion arrived and saved him.

"High Lord Commander, my apologies for interrupting you."

"That is fine, High Captain, the librarian and I can always resume our conversation later. What is it?"

Harlion reacted with some surprise at hearing the title the prince had used to refer to the old man but decided he must have misheard and proceeded to give his message to Aithen, "There is a man who just arrived in the camp and wishes to be granted an audience with you. He was actually hoping to speak with the king, but in his majesty's absence, the stranger now wishes to speak with you. He claims he has news of vital importance to the kingdom."

Aithen showed some surprise at that and asked, "Why would he come look for the king here?"

Harlion's expression said he did not know the answer to that question.

Aithen frowned and said, "What is this man's name?"

With some embarrassment, Harlion replied, "My apologies, Commander, but he did not give me his name. I can tell he is not Alvinorian, though."

Hum, this is all very strange. But at least, it will keep me from having to answer Master Longbrows' question. So, let's give this stranger his audience. "Very well…bring him to my tent – I assume the tent is ready?"

The officer nodded affirmatively. He then turned toward the time disc which always stood on a tall pole a few meters from the prince's fire – the center of the camp – and said, "I'll bring him over at Seven Hours after Highsun."

"That should be fine. Make sure you search him! And ask Kil to delay our dinner by an hour."

The captain nodded again and left.

After a minute, the prince stood to make his way to his tent. He appeared lost in some unpleasant thought again, judging by the look on his face. The soldiers saluted him, and the plebes – including Master Longbrows – rose to their feet to bow. Aithen nodded in return and made his way to his pavilion.

The prince's tent was certainly large, but surprisingly modest in decoration; not like the extravagant tents that some pompous leaders liked to have. Externally, its pristine whiteness marked it as the tent of a person of high status, while the high-flying flag of Alvinoria marked the occupant as a member of the royal family. As he approached his tent, Aithen looked at the flag, and sighed quietly, thinking about all that the flag implied. The standard was split into two diagonal parts with the left part depicting a Human male holding a golden manuscript and sitting astride a wondrous furan, and the right panel portraying a Kynarian woman extending her hand to appease a wild furan.

The male figure represented High King Lucius the First, founder of the Coriolan line, first king of the Union comprised of Alvinor, Pargah, Jarah and Yerlah, and tamer of the first black furan. And although Aithen found pride in being a member of the Coriolan dynasty, he was even more amazed by fact that he could trace his ancestry all the way back to the First Age when Emperor Tarchus the Great, the founder of the older Aquinian line of the family, first united Aquinos, Kynaria and Unumia, thereby creating what became known as *Terrae Regis* – the Lands of the King. The great empire did not last, however, and was reduced by two-thirds at the beginning of the Second Age in the year 687, when Kynaria and Unumia obtained their independence from the Aquinian rulers. The Aquinian empire was further diminished when, at the beginning of the Third and Current Age in the year 1333, a war erupted as a result of the murder of Emperor Flavius the Third by a Trionian assassin. This led to the secession of Rokoth followed by that of Trionia, which was renamed Zebulonia by its new ruler, Zebula I. Lucius Coriolis, a nephew of the assassinated Aquinian emperor, took the now much smaller throne of Alvinoria and reigned as King Lucius the First, thereby establishing the Coriolan line. Lucius was later crowned High King of Alvinoria upon publishing the Coriolan Carta [27], and forming the currently-existing Union. Aithen stopped a moment, still a hundred meters from his pavilion. He grumbled suddenly and shook his head.

Father is still alive, and he will return soon! There is no reason for the throne to pass to me, now, or even to wonder whether I have what it takes to rule.

Aithen shook his head again and resumed his walk, turning his attention to the woman on the flag: Lady Liolwyn, the first Kynarian to marry a Human. Her marriage to Lucius the First was the result of an accord to ensure an enduring alliance between the two most enlightened races of K'Tara. Aithen often wondered how anyone could make such a statement when there were lands beyond the seas no Human or Kynarian had ever explored. And he felt quite certain that Zebulonians, Unumians and Rokothians must feel similarly enlightened. Still, regardless of the true motivations, Humans and Kynarians continued to bind themselves to each other through this most unusual marriage. And to be certain that neither race ever

---

[27] The Coriolan Carta was the founding document of the land, written by King Lucius the First in 1334 to ensure that the erosion of the Coriolis holdings would end. The document ensured the protection of the kingdom's peoples from abuse; it gave all subjects two unalienable rights: The right to life and the right to dignity. It also defined the political and commercial relationship between the Coriolan king and his vassals, as well as the powers of the king himself.

became more dominant than the other in the royal bloodline – an event which would likely create social as well as political problems – it was decreed that succeeding male heirs would keep alternating between marrying a Human and marrying a Kynarian. High King Octavius, father to Aithen and Toras, was the fifth generation of that lineage and had married Lady Darya, a Kynarian. Aithen, as heir to the throne, would eventually marry a Human to ensure the maintenance of the proper balance between Kynarian and Human blood in the royal line.

Aithen thought to himself: *I wonder what the Selection Council would say if they knew my eyes are setting on a Lux Baiula. She's Human, so she meets one of their criteria, but something tells me they would oppose such a union anyway. And if they didn't, then Mother and Father would.*

Just now, Aithen passed between the two soldiers posted to guard his pavilion. The guardians saluted but were surprised when all the prince did was grunt and ask for Kildare.

One of the guardians said, "Kil is with the vorans, my Lord. I can get him."

"Please do, Coris; I need him straight away."

The middle-aged guardian – one of four soldiers who took turns guarding the prince or his tent, though the prince did not have an official personal guard – nodded and left to do as ordered. Aithen stepped into the main section of his tent, a relatively large area where the prince held his meetings and took his meals. As he walked in, his gaze fell upon the emblem of House Coriolis on the back wall: a two-headed black furan representing the Coriolan line, with the motto "Permanere Usque ad Finem [28]" inscribed underneath. The prince snorted as he read the motto.

I wonder why Father thinks this a good motto. Sure, it's good to believe we will last until the end, but it also means we believe there will be an end, and that is not something I wish to believe in, especially not now.

Aithen stood there for a moment, just staring at the emblem, then shook his head and said to himself, "What's gotten into me?! I've been brooding since Master Longbrows asked me that question about the –"

---

[28] Permanere Usque ad Finem: To last until the end.

"My Lord?"

"Kil! When did you get in?"

"Just now, my Prince. I'm sorry if I –"

"No, don't worry. I was just talking to myself."

Kildare nodded but his eyes betrayed his concern.

Aithen said, "Don't tell me you too are starting to notice my contractions?"

"I am sorry, my Prince, but you do have a lot on your mind lately. If something were bothering you, it would be no surprise."

That innocent comment from his squire made Aithen's worries dissipate, and he sighed, saying "Indeed, it would not be, Kil. I was just frustrated by the thought that I might have to lie to that old librarian."

"Did he question you about the Serpent?"

"Yes, but Harlion saved me from it when he interrupted me. Anyway, I had you called because someone will be here in…" The prince looked at his time disc, "…in ten minutes, and I am still in my dirty riding clothes. I assume I have a clean uniform?"

Kildare nodded.

"Can you get me one and put it on my bed?"

"Yes, my Prince. I cleaned all your uniforms before we left Horn's Pass. I will get you one straight away."

"Thank you. Nothing excessive, though; my white uniform will do."

Kildare nodded, and went into the prince's sleeping quarters which were located on the right side of the tent, behind two Unumian curtains, to retrieve the requested uniform. The quarters were an immaculate white, without any designs woven into its walls, and without anything but a small yet comfortable bed, a nightstand upon which stood a Living Lamp, a mirror in the corner, and a large coffer containing the prince's clothes. Kildare pulled open one of the trunk's several drawers and grabbed a white uniform. He then looked in the coffer's main section and pulled out a pair of clean boots; he placed the latter next to the bed and laid the uniform on top of it, and then returned to the prince.

"All is ready, my Prince."

"Thank you, Kil. If Harlion should arrive with the visitor, have them wait outside the tent."

When Kil announced the visitor, the prince had just finished tightening the strings of his boots. He had smiled when he noticed them next to his bed. Indeed, he had not realized how dirty his riding boots were until the clean pair that Kil put out for him caused him to look down at the ones on his feet.

Aithen had taken the boy on as squire a year ago, at the king's request, to thank the young man's father for his support in a dispute. He had wild blond hair on his head, the beginning of a mix of blond and black facial hair on his visage. He also had a slender body with strong legs, but arms still in need of development due to the fact that he did not like training with the sword much, but preferred to develop his intellect, and spent much time learning everything there was to know about vorans and furans, as well as about leadership and the arts of war, when not running from one place to another to carry out his master's orders. Aithen was fond of the young man, though he did not like the idea of taking on a squire at first. But Kildare was meticulous, always taking extremely good care of Aithen's riding tack; was always ready and prompt whenever Aithen called; and he did have a bright mind which the prince appreciated most of all, though he wished the boy was not as reserved and shy as he was.

Coming into the main section of his tent, the prince walked intently to the opposite side where a small table with bottles of various alcoholic beverages stood, poured himself a glass of Kynarian liquor, and finally told Kil to let Harlion and the visitor in.

When Harlion walked in with the stranger ahead of him, Aithen wondered if he had seen the captain's expression change from calm to irritated and back to calm. *I must have imagined it.*

Now, Harlion said, "High Lord Commander, this is the man who wishes to speak with you."

"Thank you, Captain, but I would rather the man's face be visible before I welcome him."

At that, Harlion's body tensed up, and he turned toward the visitor to ask that he remove his hood, but the man had already done so.

Aithen and Harlion repressed reactions of shock at the stranger's appearance. This man was definitely *not* an Alvinorian and looked very much like the depictions of Zebulonian males in the history books, except for his refined, self-confident and strangely handsome

94

features. Indeed, the books only showed them as rather brutish-looking creatures. But this man *had* to be a Zebulonian, and he was standing right in front of them. His skin was the color of white nutmilk. His hair, which was shaved on the sides and tied in the back in a long tail, was the color of charcoal with streaks of red throughout. His face was perhaps even more striking with a thin red circle beard and red eyebrows. There was also a red symbol painted in the middle of the man's forehead, the symbol separating eyes that were like black pools within fields of pure white. But, to the contrary of the images in Alvinorian history books, this man's facial features were fine, with his narrow nose, thin lips, and thinly slanted eyes.

A furtive glance passed between Aithen and Harlion, who both wondered how a Zebulonian could be standing there before them. But Aithen also wondered how no one, not even Harlion, had noticed the man's aspect; surely – even with the hood on – someone should have. Aithen would need to speak with Harlion about this, later.

As the awkwardness of the silence finally hit the prince, he said, "So, High Captain Harlion says you have some news of the gravest importance to the well-being of my father's kingdom."

"Indeed, my Prince. I have travelled a long way, hoping to meet with High King Octavius to share this information with him. I first went to Furan City, but I was told by the palace staff that His Majesty was not in the capital. Given the importance of my information, I asked around the capital, and was informed by those who deigned speak with me that the high king would be at Horn's Pass for the yearly celebration. So, I found a merchant who accepted to take me there. When we came across your caravan, the merchant stopped, and I learned that the high king had not been at Horn's Pass, but that you were here, my Prince, and I decided to – how do you say it – try my luck here."

The effort he has expended to have this audience is quite unusual; most people would have waited in Furan City. It might be worthwhile to hear him. And why does his accent surprise me? It sounds very close to a southeastern Alvinorian accent. And his pronunciation, it is that of an educated man...a man whose name I should have been told before he was brought before me. Aithen still couldn't believe Harlion had not asked the man his name before bringing him in, or that he, himself, did not ask the man identify himself immediately. *I think the battle at Horn's Pass may have affected us more than we*

95

know. Aithen let out a silent sigh, and asked for the man's name, causing a slight blush on Harlion's face.

"I beg your pardon my Lord, it was extremely rude of me not to introduce myself straight away. I am Lusk Methrim, Master Healer to Lord Brando of Shadin City where I had been living for the last three years. I came there from Zebulonia after Queen Zebula ordered all healers and students of the Healing Arts to be arrested and taken into the Caves of Death to suppress our revolt against the Queen's Janarae for the centuries of slavery to which they have subjected Zebulonian males. Most members of our guild have died by now, but a number of us were able to break free from our shackles. Some went into hiding; others, such as myself, took their chance crossing the border."

"I hear," said Aithen. "You must have been one of the lucky ones, because the Zebulonian border is extremely well guarded."

The visitor replied with a slight nod.

"And what did you do in Zebulonia?"

"I was Private Healer to Queen Zebula's children, but my position did not save me from the persecution."

Aithen nodded then turned to Harlion and said, "High Captain, you may leave Master Methrim with me. I assume you have searched him?"

"I have, my Prince, and he had no weapons on his body."

"Very well, I will see you again later."

With that, the old soldier stiffened his body, tipped his head and stepped out of the tent. Once he was gone, Aithen sat himself behind his desk and asked his visitor, "So, what is this information you have?"

"High Prince, I've heard that Queen Zebula the Sixth is planning an invasion of Alvinoria."

Aithen did not know how to react to this. Maybe the man was mad. But he did not look like a fool or dress like one. Aithen had to at least try to verify the veracity of this wild claim. *And what if he really is here to relay these rumors to me? What does he hope to gain in exchange for this information?*

The stranger seemed to notice Aithen's reaction and decided to wait a few moments before continuing.

Aithen tapped his fingers on his lips, then asked, "And where did you hear this rumor you speak of, Master Methrim?"

96

"Oh, it is not a rumor, my Prince. I was told by one of my former colleagues, who was one of Zebula's personal clerks. He now makes a living crossing the Shadow Lake to smuggle goods into Alvinoria."

Aithen couldn't help but blink.

"My Lord seems surprised. The border, whether across the mountains or across the lake, is slowly becoming more and more porous, and to more than those escaping the oppressive rule of Queen Zebula."

Why haven't I heard of this? How could my informants not be aware of this?

"Tell me Master Methrim, what do you have to gain from telling me this?"

"I have come to believe that this is a land of opportunity, my Lord; opportunities for all to the contrary of the land where I come from. I do not wish for Queen Zebula's powers to extend any further."

"I can understand that. But what do you expect to gain, personally?"

"I would like to offer High King Octavius my services. You see, I fell out of favor with Lord Brando, after he learned of my dealings with the smugglers. I must add, however, that none were damaging to his interests; I only used those contacts to try and help fellow healers escape. But Lord Brando is one for whom things are either good or bad, and he considered my association with smugglers to be in the bad category. I have heard that the high king is a worldly, highly educated man, and with an appreciation for the subtleties of life."

"That, my father is and has. But I am not certain either he or I would approve of your dealings either. Still, you are being honest. Please continue."

"Lord Brando informed me that my employment would be terminated in one month; that was two fourths ago. I decided to ask for a leave and come to offer my services to the high king in exchange for the information I have."

"The high king does not employ people simply for sharing information."

"I understand, High Prince. But I am Zebulonian, and I could prove highly valuable to the king should my information reveal itself to be true, which I believe it is. The king might need someone who knows the language as well as someone who knows the customs of my country. I am also particularly skilled at healing the psychic wounds that soldiers suffer as a result of the violence they must live through, and this is a very rare skill, even here in Alvinoria. I could serve as Healer in the Royal Guard."

"Interesting, and ambitious. Well, should your information prove to be true, we may indeed come to need someone with your knowledge and skills. But you would need to gain our trust first, and that is *not* something either the high king or I give easily. Given that the king is away at the moment, you must pass the test with me first. I will therefore investigate your claim, and if it is true, I will then introduce you to the high king, so you may share with him what you have shared with me. At that time, you may also petition us both for a position as informant in his court, and as Healer in the Royal Guard, which is under my command. Know that until your claim is proven truthful, the information will remain mere rumor to me."

"I understand, my Prince."

"Good, because I do not tolerate the spread of rumors. You are therefore not to repeat what you've told me to anyone, neither here nor anywhere else in Alvinoria."

This was something Aithen would need to discuss with his father very soon, if it proved to be true – and if they found him. But first, he would need to inform Elyana so that she might have her Sisters in the south investigate the rumors.

"I understand, my Lord. You have my word."

"Something puzzles me, Master Methrim. How is it that you have absolutely no accent? That is, no accent other than that of a Shadiner?"

"I am a very quick learner of languages, my Lord." The man said that very simply and naturally, as if it were nothing out of the ordinary. "Zebulonia itself has two official languages and ten dialects. I can speak the two languages perfectly, and five of the dialects fairly fluently."

Aithen blinked again. He himself knew a few languages and dialects, but a healer? Well, perhaps a Master Healer needing to instruct students from different regions might benefit from knowing multiple languages. He took a moment to consider this and finally decided to learn some more from the man.

"You are a very interesting person, Master Methrim, and you have piqued my curiosity. Tell me, who are these – how did you call them – *Janarae*? I must admit I do not know of them."

"Certainly…" The man seemed to hesitate a moment, as if unsure where to start. "Officially, they are the Queen's soldiers and public administrators. But in the past few years, new knowledge has trickled through the various Knowing Circles. It appears that Queen Zebula I instituted the *Janarae* as a secret medical body soon as she rose to power. It is now believed that their initial purpose was to find a way to propagate the Queen's line without the need for men."

Aithen raised an eyebrow and jerked his head slightly, but no more, though he couldn't believe what he had just heard.

"They do have the ability to affect objects and living things with only a thought," continued the Zebulonian. "They may be similar to your Lux Baiulae in this respect, but that is the extent of the similarity because, to the contrary of the Lux Baiulae, Janarae are wicked creatures." The man took a pause and continued. "Sometime during the long reign of Zebula I, the Janarae must have succeeded at the task under the guidance of her Greatness's Royal Surgeon. This mode of reproduction was then extended to all females of rank in Zebulonia, under Zebula II, including to the *Janarae* themselves who were made to pledge their lives and that of their descendants to the protection of the Crown for the privilege of the transformation and the granting of power and land. This egregious granting of privilege had forced the Janarae out of secrecy, but Zebula II took the opportunity to begin using them to transform the Zebulonian society into a nation *ruled* by women, and for the *sole* benefit of women. This is the society that exists to this day, where men continue to be enslaved and are *produced* for the sole purpose of replenishing the slaves' ranks."

Aithen gave him a quizzical look when he heard the word "produced".

"Males continue to be generated through…copulation, as are plebeian females. Birthing mothers raise their male progeny until adolescence, at which point boys are taken from them and transferred to the Janarae who complete their education and teach them to serve the nobility faithfully and unfailingly for the rest of their lives."

"Huh! You must excuse my reaction, Master Methrim, but this is most shocking, and I do not understand how such things as you described can be. What about this revolt you spoke of when you began? How did it happen?"

Lusk Methrim's face looked contorted by some inner conflict, and Aithen was about to withdraw his request for more information when the man responded, "As I said, my Lord, Zebulonia is a female-dominated society where males are generated only to serve, and where even the highest among us is still a slave or a mere mate. Five years ago, during the yearly *Clean Up*, one of the First Janarae fell to some unknown illness, and in a fit of rage while visiting the town's market, unleashed her powers and killed several dozens of males, young and old. In her madness, she shouted that Zebula II should have eliminated men altogether, instead of enslaving them. Her second-in-command, having heard of this unfortunate event, sent five guardians to escort her back to the Region House. A few hours later, near sundown, she sent the Guard to clean-up the mess. The Janarae left without a word and the plebeians remained mute; the males were too dumbstruck to react, while the women either laughed silent laughs, or hid their own pain and shame in the face of this hideous act."

Aithen could not believe his ears; he felt fascinated by this tale and hungered for more. He asked, "You referred to a yearly "Clean Up." What is that?"

"Ah, the *Clean Up* is the removal of all "disruptive" males from a city, whether they be thugs, wanderers, protestors, or mere servants or mates who had the bad luck to displease their masters. What becomes of them once they are removed, no one knows, but it is suspected that they are taken to the Caves of Death to be disposed of."

Aithen did not make any comments following this last statement by Master Methrim, and the man just waited in silence for a while. Finally, he said, "My Lord?"

Aithen began feeling very uncomfortable while the Zebulonian spoke; something seemed to be irritating him. But what could it be? He thought of just ending the audience, but his curiosity was too great now, and what was more, he understood the importance of having this knowledge – if it was true. So, he cleared his mind and said, "Please continue, Master Methrim. This is certainly the most extraordinary, though troubling bit of history I have heard in a long time."

"Of course, my Prince. After this disaster, feelings of anger began rising among the men of the Knowing Circles, especially among the healers. Ah, the Knowing Circles are what you call societies and guilds and include – in addition to the healers – the philosophers, the tanners, and the stone masons, all working to provide the Queen and her subjects with the things they need. As I was saying, feelings of anger began rising amongst us, and for many days and fourths we formed and reformed plans to free ourselves. Then, the uprising started. Tens of thousands of men led by the Healers' Knowing Circle rebelled and walked to their respective Region House and demanded that the Queen free all men from bondage, threatening to stop using their knowledge for her benefit. There followed months of civil unrest during which healers and their supporters were massacred left and right. In the end, the rebellion failed, but because our craft is a necessity for any society, the remaining healers were captured, sequestered in prison camps, and allowed only to train in the Healing Arts other men handpicked by the Janarae. I, myself, had not taken part in the rebellion, but Zebula became suspicious and imprisoned me all the same."

"That is a very disconcerting story, Master Methrim and it has been a very instructive hour. I believe the high king will be interested in what you report, if I can verify it...you should stay with us until we reach Furan City." Aithen's stomach tied itself in a knot as he said those words, but something he could not pinpoint made him want to trust the man, despite the misgivings he had and was unable to explain. Regardless, he needed to keep the man around in case he learned the Zebulonian was lying, because he would then need to jail him or have the Lux Baiulae *adjust* his memories before he began spreading damaging rumors.

After a moment of silence, the man responded to the prince's invitation and said with a deep bow, "I am here to serve, my Prince."

"Good. Guardian!"

Coris, the same guardian who had fetched Kildare earlier, was still at his post and came in to take the prince's orders. He stared in shock when he saw the stranger's face.

"Please see to it that our visitor has a place for himself in our camp. He will remain with us until we reach the Capital. Place his tent in a location easily accessible as I may be calling on him frequently." The soldier knew what this meant and would place the stranger among the guardians. The Zebulonian made another bow and left with the soldier.

***

While he waited for his advisors, Aithen thought about this Lusk Methrim. *Something makes me want to trust the man, despite the fact that I have only just met him, and despite those most extraordinary revelations he made. But something else about him ties my stomach every so often. I will have to have Harlion investigate him to find out who he really is.*

Just then, Aithen heard footsteps approaching his tent, so he shook himself out of his thoughts, and smoothed his face. Another of the guardians outside his tent came in and informed the prince that High Captain Harlion and Elyana Lux Baiula had arrived for dinner.

"Let them in, Piros."

The guardian turned around and invited Harlion and Elyana to enter.

As soon as she saw the prince, Elyana asked, "Aithen, was that the Zebulonian who just left your tent?"

"So, Harlion has already informed you. Yes, that was him. A most remarkable man, I must say, with some astonishing stories. He gave the name of Lusk Methrim and said he has been living in Shadin City for the past three years. Why do you ask Elyana?"

Elyana did not answer but asked another question. "Will he remain in the camp?"

"Yes. A tent is being prepared for him. Why?"

"Keep him from interacting with anyone, though I would rather he was sent on his way immediately…"

"Elyana, *will* you tell me why you are so concerned?"

Harlion also wondered why the Lux Baiula was so worried about the man. He tried to read her face, but it was still impossible to tell what she was thinking of, even after all the years he had known her. But the Lux Baiula finally gave some explanations.

"I felt vibrations emanating from the man which I have never felt before, and it worries me."

"I must admit that I, too, felt strange sensations while he was here, sensations which made me…uncomfortable. But I didn't think

102

he was causing them. What *did* puzzle me is the fact that Harlion did not ask the man identify himself before bringing him to me," Harlion gave Aithen a hurt look but he did feel embarrassed by this and cursed himself in silence, "and that I let him in without asking for his name straight away."

The prince continued, "Do you know that our history books give a false description of Zebulonians? All images I have seen portray them as quite an ugly people, but this man certainly is not. In fact, I would say he is rather…handsome."

Elyana and Harlion both frowned at that, though Harlion gave his commander a nod of understanding, having seen the man's face too. Aithen shifted defensively under Elyana's continued stare. He said, "It is a mere fact."

Elyana finally shrugged her shoulders and said, "Historians view things through their own eyes, and subjective matters – whether concerning events or people or whatever else – will therefore be colored by their biases. When the descriptions of these matters are recorded long after an event, the risk of introducing one's biases in them is even greater. So, it wouldn't surprise me if historians had incorrectly described Zebulonians as an ugly people."

"Even your own historians? With the benefit of Memory Transfer?"

The question made Elyana surprisingly uncomfortable, and she did not answer. Instead, she sighed and continued with her own questions. "My Prince, did *Master Methrim* give a reason for coming here, on the road between Horn's Pass and Furan City, to request an audience?"

"Elyana –" the prince was about to apologize for his question, but stopped himself, and instead said, "No matter. Yes, he did. He told me he went to Furan City first – which I would like you to verify, Harlion – and when he learned the king was expected at Horn's Pass for the Celebration of the Colossi, he decided to go there, given the urgency of his message, rather than wait in the capital."

Harlion and Elyana asked as one, "And what was this message?"

"He claims that Queen Zebula intends to invade Alvinoria."

Harlion pulled his head back in utter disbelief. As for Elyana, her entire face contracted in a frown.

Harlion blurted, "That is a most extraordinary claim!"

Aithen could not say whether he believed Master Methrim's claim or not, but he knew they needed to investigate it, and he said, "Indeed, Harlion, indeed. And the timing could not have been worse, but we cannot simply dismiss the man's claim. Despite our misgivings, Master Methrim did not appear to be a fool, and he did not give me the impression of having fabricated the story."

After a short pause, Aithen asked, "Elyana, can you have your Eyes and Ears in the south investigate this claim quietly?"

"I can."

Aithen thanked Elyana and turned to Harlion, "High Captain, I need you to have your Frumentarii [29] investigate our guest's past; whatever Lord Brando knows about him, I want to know too. Also, Master Methrim claims there are smugglers along our border with Zebulonia, and that he obtained his information about Zebula's intentions from them." Seeing Harlion's and Elyana's reactions, Aithen said, "I had the same reaction when I heard it from Master Methrim; I thought the border was impassable – but perhaps not. If there exist smugglers along the Sagr, I need the Frumentarii to find them, and confirm our visitor's statements. If Master Methrim is a liar or a fraud, I need to know *that* as soon as–"

As Aithen finished his sentence, two young women and a young man in their late teens, dressed with the mark of House Coriolis on their clothes, came in to serve the food. The girls' dresses were cream white and simple but decorated with the royal crest on the right hip. The boy's pants, just as simple and of the same color, had the crest on the right leg; his shirt was a dark green, with no markings on it.

Hoping to relax the mood a little, the prince said, "Well, let us have dinner. I can smell a good stew, and my stomach is growling."

Aithen invited Elyana and Harlion to sit on the cushioned benches set around the table. Elyana unhooked her purple cape and took the bench to Aithen's left after laying her cloak on the bench's low back. The servants moved carefully between them to set the

---

[29] Frumentarius: A member of the secret service of the kingdom. [Note: The Frumentarii were in fact collectors of wheat in ancient Rome. Because their position put them in frequent contact with roman citizens across the territory, Emperor Hadrian – who was in need of intelligence – eventually recruited them to serve as spies].

utensils, followed by the food and beverage. When done, they bowed deeply to the prince, then to his guests and left the tent.

This was the first real meal the prince and his advisors had had since the night of the attack. The food set before them should have been a pleasant relief for all three. But the companions picked up their spoons with distracted motions, their thoughts crowded with a jumble of catastrophic, unbelievable and nonsensical events.

As he ate, the prince glanced up at the Light Bearer, hoping to read her thoughts on her face, but her expression remained indecipherable to him. Had he been able to read her, he would have noticed her lingering fatigue. Aithen turned his eyes to his captain. The man's emotions and thoughts were much easier to guess, with the way he shook his head every so often, or the angry way he dipped his bread. They had lost many men at Horn's Pass, and Aithen knew the death of Kemiir particularly disturbed Harlion. Aithen felt his stomach growl, and he returned to his meal, though his murky thoughts kept him from truly enjoying the food.

Once they were all done with the stew, Elyana closed her eyes, focused and called the Bind as if with a brush to paint the inside of the tent with densely packed particles until she created the same Sound Shield she had created at Horn's Pass. When she was done, she noticed Aithen and Harlion looking at her. She said, "I think we will be having many, highly confidential discussions in the coming days, and this one in particular, I wish to keep our guest from overhearing."

Harlion looked at Aithen with a questioning look.

Elyana said, "It is possible our visitor is an Alterintrant whose life-force is unknown to me, and if he is, he might be able to listen in on our conversation. My gut tells me to beware of him, and I urge you to be watchful too, Aithen."

"I do not disagree, Elyana, and I am being careful. Is this what you wish to discuss?"

"Our guest, yes, as well as the Serpent. But the Serpent first. As I explained very briefly before its arrival at Horn's Pass, the creature is not one of this world; its body may have been formed here, but its mind was fashioned by something from beyond our skies. As you both know, humanoids first encountered it during the Dark Battle where it served the Dark One. I do not know whether the Serpent has reappeared on its own or whether it has come with its former master, but I, myself, have not felt the Night Bringer." Elyana paused and with notable annoyance in her voice, she said, "However, I have learned since Horn's Pass that others in the Sisterhood have felt a presence which none can yet explain – a presence not of this place. Regardless, whether Noctiferus is here as well, or a new master is directing the Serpent, his presence is a foreboding of dark times."

Harlion started, "I thought Nocti–. I'm sorry, I don't like to pronounce that name. I thought the *Dark One* and all his minions and creatures had disappeared from our world at the end of the Dark Battle. How could any have come back? And why was the Serpent at *Horn's Pass*?"

"As I said to the princes at Horn's Pass, I do not know how it is that the Serpent is here now. This goes against all that we know of the fate of the Fallen Founder and its minions, but we must consider all possibilities. The Sisterhood will find out what it can, and as soon as we have more information, I will share it with you."

Harlion could hardly believe what he was hearing. He had seen all sorts of things in his life and had battled wicked creatures such as tarkans and other things of the underground. Yet, these were all creatures of K'Tara, and as vicious as they were, he *knew* he could fight them. But Noctiferus and the Serpent were another thing entirely. "Elyana Lux Baiula, do you believe we stand a chance if your worst fears come true?"

"Should the Dark One be here as well, then we will fight the mightiest battle any of us alive has fought, no matter what the result may be. You know this to be the only answer I can give, High Captain."

Harlion did his best not to show his embarrassment for the second or third time this night. *What is happening to me?! First, letting a man into the prince's tent without knowing who he is, and then asking a question that only a green recruit would ask!*

Elyana continued, "So, back to our guest who appears to turn men into limpfish! There are two possibilities as to whom or what he is given the vibrations I have sensed from him: he could be a creature of darkness, or a simple Alterintrant with a life-force unknown to our Order. This *is* a possibility given that we know little or nothing of the Zebulonians since they gained their independence an age ago. Either way, he appears to be very engaging, and seems to cause men to lose their wits – even men who should know better." Aithen and

Harlion both gave her a look of indignation, but Elyana continued unperturbed. "We, Lux Baiulae, are fortunately not so easily stupefied, and we have ways to detect what is beneath the surface." This time, Aithen and Harlion shot angry stares at the woman, but she was no more perturbed by these than she was by their earlier glares. "I strongly recommend you have your guardians keep their distance from him, High Captain, and to not let them fraternize with him. As soon as I am finished eating, I will go—"

Elyana stopped speaking when she felt her skin tingle. Someone was crossing the Sound Shield. She turned her head and saw one of the young serving women bring in some cheese. The woman approached her, and Elyana took a piece of cheese with more bread. The prince and his captain gave a small grunt and grabbed some cheese too, thanking the young servant as they did. The prince then nodded to her, and the girl bowed and left the tent.

Aithen, Elyana and Harlion ate quietly and sipped some wine for another little while. Elyana thought about the Zebulonian, wondering if he really could simply be an Alterintrant she was unfamiliar with. Alterintrants were humanoids who could connect with the life-force within the Bind. Those who could only feel it were known as Sensors, while those who could also make use of it were known as Binders. Not all humanoid races, however, had the same range of abilities. Most Kynarian women, for example, were able to enter the minds of non-humanoid life forms, and they had an exceptional ability to *sense* all things carried within the Bind, whereas the ability to connect to the Bind was rare amongst Human females. But while only a minority of Humans could sense the Bind or make use of it, those who did were amongst the most powerful of all Alterintrants. And because their use of the life-force could result in great harm just as easily as in the creation of the greatest works, the Sisterhood and the now defunct Brotherhood were established to control the learning and use of the Sensing and Binding abilities. The Sisterhood continued the practice to this day, and any Human female who was found to have the potential was taken in to be trained.

No other races or species were known to be able to connect to the Bind. But it now appeared that the Zebulonians had developed sensing and binding abilities since their secession from the Coriolan empire. If Master Methrim truly was an Alterintrant, Elyana would need to inform the Magna Mater.

107

After he had his last drop of wine, Aithen asked, "If you are done with the Zebulonian, Elyana, I would like to go back to the threat we *are* already facing."

"I am."

"How should I say this? I am concerned that the one organization that may know, *should know* what is happening, has no idea why the Serpent is here or why they are sensing things they haven't felt in centuries. How will we prepare to defend ourselves with so little information about our enemy?"

Elyana replied, "We know enough to make defensive preparations against the immediate threat. But you are correct, even the oldest among us cannot tell for certain what this is all about…*yet*. We *will* find the answers, though, I am certain of it. A Gathering has been called in Urbs Lucis, one month from now, to do just that. I, myself, will start toward our Order's home as soon as I am done in Furan City."

Aithen and Harlion nodded their heads hesitantly. The prince hoped that Elyana was right. Harlion prayed she was. Soldiers were not supposed to be religious, and most weren't, but at sixty, Harlion was beginning to think that the Founders *were* gods, omnipotent, omniscient and unknowable beings, and not just powerful beings living on some far-off island of K'Tara as some people believed. So, he prayed to Aiala'Rhi, the Originator, to ask that she give the Lux Baiulae the knowledge they needed to help them defeat whatever danger was now threatening them all.

Just now, Elyana took one final bite of cheese, and Aithen found himself noticing the delicate motions of her lips and jaw. How he wished he could act on his growing desire for her. But it would have to wait, what with everything going on. And his parents might disapprove in any case. The thought of his parents brought back to his mind his missing father, and he asked, "Harlion, Elyana, what do we do about my father? We do need to find him. This situation is not acceptable any longer!"

Harlion responded with a sigh and said, "I have dispatched carriers [30] to Spiritii as well as to the surrounding cities, my Prince,

---

[30] A carrier was a small flying animal used to carry messages between cities.

but have yet to receive any encouraging news back. Hopefully, Elyana has had better luck."

Elyana dabbed her lips with the white cloth in front of her and said, "I have not been able to locate him yet, Aithen; I am sorry. I have no choice but to recruit other Sisters in the search, but we will find him..."

Elyana seemed to want to say more, but hesitated and Aithen cocked his head, asking her to complete her thought. Elyana hesitated another moment, then nodded to herself and said, "If I had to surmise, I would say that perhaps the king does not wish to be found."

Aithen's and Harlion's stunned looks prompted Elyana to add, "I know how this sounds. It is nevertheless a possibility we must consider given the circumstances. Firstly, the king did not inform any of us of his final destination; secondly, the last reported sighting of a group of five voranmen, anywhere between here and Spiritii, was over seven days ago; thirdly and finally, my searches in the Bind – which *should* have allowed me to find the king – have proven *just* as fruitless."

Elyana stood, moved toward Harlion, and pulled two metallic cylinders from under her sash. Proffering the blue cylinder to the officer, she said, "High Captain, please have your fastest furanteam deliver this message to Merina Lux Baiula in Melinor," and then tendering the purple cylinder, "and this other message to Mara Lux Baiula in Spiritii. I need to expand my search, and I have hopes that Merina or Mara will succeed where I have failed."

"Of course, Lux Baiula. I assume you wish me to dispatch someone straight away?" asked Harlion as he put down an unfinished piece of bread, wiped his hands and lips, and took the cylinders.

"Yes, thank you, Captain."

"Very well. I will see to it immediately." Harlion then turned to Aithen and asked whether he had any orders.

"Indeed, Captain. I, too, need you to have a guardian deliver a message. Please give me a moment." And Aithen walked to his desk, picked up some paper and pen, and wrote a message which he then put into a golden cylinder. This had a purple band in the middle.

Aithen said, "Have the messenger deliver this to First Senator Leo. I am asking him to convene the Senate and the Landholders in ten days so that I may address each body upon our arrival."

"I assume this means we *have* to arrive no later than that morning. It will be difficult given the size of the caravan, especially if we keep halting this early in the day."

Aithen replied with playful encouragement, "We can use all available hours to travel starting tomorrow, Captain. But yes, we need to be in Furan City no later than that morning, ten days from now. I trust your judgement and leave the logistics to you. If you need to lighten the caravan, you may ask the civilians to abandon everything but the strictly necessary. But let them know that the Crown will reimburse them for their losses. As for this message, make sure the messenger has had his meal and to leave within the hour. Given the time it will take for the missives to reach all major Landholders, and the time for them to get to Furan City, it is best the First Senator receive his instructions as soon as possible."

The high captain nodded and left to carry out his orders.

As his officer crossed the tent flaps, Aithen said, "I will see you in the morning, High Captain."

Harlion paused without turning, nodded again, then disappeared.

Looking at the Lux Baiula, the prince said, "I assume you will go meet with the Zebulonian now, Elyana?"

"Yes, and hopefully, I will return with fewer worries."

"I hope so too. As for myself, I think I will take Xyre and fly to the shore; I need some time to myself, even if it's just an hour, to try and make some sense of everything."

The Lux Baiula seemed a little irritated by Aithen's plan, but she did not express it and simply said, "Then you best go while there is still some light. If all goes well, I will be back here in two hours to brief you." She then clipped her cape on, turned around, removed the Sound Shield, and stepped out through the curtain as Aithen followed her with his eyes.

VII OF RISK AND NECESSITY

Aithen was back from his escape to the shore and had just finished changing when Elyana reentered his quarters. He asked, "How did things go with our guest?" But he did not wait for her reply, and instead went on to say, "I, for one, am glad I took my very short trip to the shore. The ocean is such a sight in these parts, with the corals giving the water over this stretch of the coast amazing hues of pink and purple. I think you might have liked it. Have you ever seen it?"

Elyana shook her head.

"Well, you should someday. And these forty short minutes gave me a chance to calm the firestorm in my brains. With the Serpent, and talk of Noctiferus, and with our Zebulonian neighbor apparently planning an invasion, and with no one knowing where my father is – *and* with the death of my cousin, which I have *intentionally* ignored since Horn's pass – I was feeling overwhelmed. But I feel better now, much better."

Elyana looked annoyed when she spoke. "I'm glad you had a chance to relax, Aithen. But to answer your question, which I thought I was never going to be able to do," and Aithen felt a sudden flash of embarrassment at hearing the accusation, "my meeting with Lusk Methrim of Zebulonia was disappointing, to say the least. I thought that I might be able to tell what he really is by carefully and lightly probing him, but I couldn't even sense the vibrations I felt in him when I first encountered him earlier today." Elyana paused a moment, then added with an unusually emphatic tone, "That is *very* disturbing to me."

Aithen could tell this inability to sense the stranger's vibrations – as Lux Baiulae called the life energy that coursed through every living thing – really upset Elyana, but he didn't say anything; he knew his comments would be of no help to her. Indeed, what did he know of the Sensing and Binding abilities? To him, they seemed almost magical, though he knew they were based on very real properties of the universe.

But Aithen still found himself wishing he *could* comfort Elyana. For some time now, he had been feeling extremely attracted to her,

111

and he was constantly fighting his desire to reveal his sentiments to her, to touch her and feel her. And although he had had close relationships with a few women, none had stirred him the way Elyana did. The Lux Baiula was beautiful – to Aithen at least – with her long, wavy reddish hair, and the fine yet strong features of her face. And she was intelligent and confident – how could he not like her; how could he not *want* her?

However, every time he considered his feelings for the woman, he also chided himself for them. Elyana was much older than he was, even though she looked just his age. He had no idea how old she was, in fact, but she had been advising his father for a little over thirty years already, so she must be fifty at least. How could he envisage wooing a woman decades his senior? But then he encouraged himself, thinking that perhaps it didn't matter. Indeed, given that Lux Baiulae could live some two hundred years, it was possible that they aged very slowly, whereas Halflings like himself matured very rapidly but then lived to be quite old too, so perhaps they were in similar places in terms of physical and mental maturity.

Unfortunately for him, every time he reached a conclusion which seemed to support his interest in the woman despite their age difference, Aithen quickly reminded himself that the king and queen, and the Selection Council, would likely disapprove of their union anyway. And this evening, Aithen had another reason for not giving free reins to his feelings: the possible end of everything they knew. All these thoughts took but a few seconds to run through his mind, but they unsettled him, and he hoped Elyana had not noticed anything.

Elyana had noticed, in fact, and it comforted her to know that she could at least sense the thoughts and emotions of some people, although she wasn't certain how she felt about these budding feelings between her and the prince. She certainly could not give them any breath whatsoever. But for some unknown reason, it pleased her to see him struggle as he did. She remembered, also, how she had teased him quite shamelessly at various points during their journey earlier in the day.

But these thoughts were no thoughts to be had and she kicked them out of her mind and returned to their conversation as naturally as if this interlude of thought had not occurred. She said, "What disturbs me so much, Aithen, is that the vibrations I initially sensed in Master Methrim are not the only thing I am unable to perceive. Indeed, during my thoughtcall with the Magna Mater last night – a very faint thoughtcall because she feared that someone might overhear us although thoughtcalls are nearly impossible to overhear – she informed me that Sisters from *all corners of Terrae Regis* have reported sensing some unknown vibrations, something so dark and malicious, that they fear it might be from...Noctiferus himself." Elyana paused and finished her remark with unusual emphasis, "But I have felt nothing of the sort!"

This sudden inability to sense certain things truly frustrated Elyana. Wasn't she one of the most powerful Lux Baiulae, after all? She wasn't ill, she knew that. She could sense her own vibrations, and she was certain that her metabolism and her nervous system were performing adequately. Perhaps her microbial flora had been affected by the strain of the past two days, and if that was the case, she would have to wait until they got back to Furan City to have it probed and restored by Tania Lux Baiula because this was one procedure which was well beyond her capabilities. But whatever the reason for her problems, she needed them gone, because her Sensing skills were even more important to her than her Binding skills.

Aithen asked, "Elyana, how would your Sisters recognize the vibrations of a Founder who is supposed to have been removed from existence so long ago?"

"None of us lived six hundred years ago, but many of us do bear within ourselves knowledge from that age."

"I know about Memory Transfer, Elyana, and I can understand how a thought or image might be transferred, but the memory of a vibration? How can a feeling, *a sensation* be transferred?"

"It is difficult to explain, but sensations do have a physical place in our memories. That is why a smell or sight may trigger a sensation of fear or pleasure felt in one's youth. The Dark One's vibrations can be similarly recalled by those who have the memory of their feeling transferred to them."

"So, again the same question. What do we do if the Bringer of Darkness – as some believers call him – has truly come back?"

"I do not know, Aithen, but the Order will figure it out." After a pause, she continued, "Magna Mater Krystiana requested that I meet her in the Bind tonight so that we may begin our search for answers in earnest. If we are lucky, we will learn who our enemy truly is;

from the little that we know at this point, it is doubtful our foe is the Serpent alone. Krystiana knows I have not felt the darkness she and others have sensed, but I am the only one she will trust to help her with this search, as well as to shield her while we do so." Then in answer to Aithen's unspoken question, she added, "Other Sisters must not know that the Magna Mater entered the Bind to look for our enemy because there are some in the Light's Assembly who would actively question her leadership if they knew she put both her own life and the Order at risk with what is in all honesty, a reckless plan. But it is the only plan now."

Aithen reflected a moment. Although Elyana and his father had taught him many things about the Bind, they had never helped him develop his Sensing skills, despite his frequent pleas. He thought his father, a strong Sensor himself, would have done it, but alas. And the Sisterhood would not do it without his permission.

All Aithen knew about the Bind was therefore limited to a few generalities and warnings such as that access to the Bind could expand one's understanding of the world and allow the Roamer to experience even more wonderful things than existed in the Outer World. Binding skills could also give one amazing powers, ranging from the very useful ability to heal or influence others, to the incredible ability to project balls of fire against an enemy too powerful to be hurt by common weapons. But, if one were not careful, one could also burn themself to ashes, or forever lose themself in the Bind to experience the most horrible things until madness sapped their life away. There was, in fact, an asylum in Urbs Lucis where those Roamers who never made it out of the Bind were housed and cared for. Because of the risks, and because of Octavius's strong belief that a monarch's power should be based solely on his or her intellectual superiority, the king had always refused to let the Sisterhood train either of his sons, even though Aithen clearly had the atomic predisposition for Sensing, and perhaps even for Binding. And Aithen had always resented him for that. If the king could access the Bind, why couldn't he? Wouldn't such a skill be useful to him as future leader of the kingdom?

The prince said to the Lux Baiula, "Elyana, I will come with you!"

"*What?!*"

"I wish to enter the Bind with you."

The Sister shook her head, then said, raising her voice. "Aithen, are you mad? That is simply not possible, and you know it!"

But Aithen insisted. "I know Lux Baiulae can take victims of rape into the Bind to find their rapists. If an Unsensing can enter the Bind with a Lux Baiula, I am certain you can take me with you."

Elyana put her hand to her forehead, not believing what the prince was asking her to do. "Aithen, you are not trained, and I cannot put your life at risk in this manner."

The prince knew that she was right, but that did not deter him; indeed, he could lead armies to war, putting his life in danger every time. He could battle the Serpent, also putting his life in danger in the doing. How was this any different? Anyway, he felt he had no choice. He responded, "Elyana, K'Tara may soon be facing a new battle against forces unknown to most of us; if there is a chance I might learn something about our enemy – an enemy which my armies might need to battle – then I have a right, a *duty* to come."

"True, I am not trained, but you can take me there. And I know I have the atomic predisposition since my father *is* a Sensor himself." Aithen hesitated, not sure whether he should say what he wanted to say, but he did anyway, almost talking to himself. "I don't know why the Order won't test and train me, but everyone knows I am a Sensor. I, myself, have known since I was twelve."

Aithen continued, looking at Elyana intently, "I *must* come, Elyana."

"Aithen, what you are asking is incredibly dangerous. Even the non-Roamers that we take into the Bind receive a minimum of training so that they don't make a stupid mistake that might endanger them as well as the Lux Baiulae, and I can't train you in only an hour! Moreover, we will not be hunting for a mere humanoid, but for a thing of evil." Shivers went through her body as she said this.

"I must come!"

It was all that Elyana could do to contain herself and not shout, but her anger was audible now. "Aithen, you may be the high king's son, but it does not give you any rights when it comes to matters that concern only the Order."

The prince was a little embarrassed at having forced Elyana to become so angry and decided that it was probably not a good idea to keep arguing with her and simply said with a quiet voice, "I am sorry, Elyana. Surely, you can see that I must do everything that I can to protect our land and people. If there is a chance I might learn something about our enemy by coming with you, I will take the risk."

Elyana looked at him with that stare that made Lux Baiulae so intimidating. Aithen kept his own eyes fixed on her. *How can I bring him? I would be violating the Order's law. Not even Krystiana would be able to stop the punishment that would surely come. And though he does have the ability, he lacks the training. And if I should fail while in the Bind? But he is a man now, with a good head on his shoulders, and he might be right about this. I just hope I do not come to regret it.*

"All right, Aithen. If it must, so be it. You do have certain abilities already, so a quick lesson might be enough to bring you with me, so long as I shield you and you do not do anything stupid. Hopefully, it will not be today that I give my life for yours because as much as I am willing to do so, I would rather live a little longer. Now, let's get on with it; Magna Mater Krystiana will be waiting for me in an hour."

Aithen breathed a sigh relief and gave Elyana a grateful smile. He did not know what he might face in the Bind, and how anything in that ethereal world might endanger his life, but he did know that Elyana would indeed give her own life if it meant saving his – and he did *not* like the thought of that, not because of pride, but because he...well, he just didn't like it. So, he promised himself to not do anything stupid while in there.

Elyana said, "From this point on and until we are back, you will follow my instructions to the letter and without question." Aithen nodded. "If at any point I sense your life is in danger, I will send you a thoughtcall with one word only "*exit!* ""

"Sure. But, I have never...made a thoughtcall. I do not know –"

"Once we are connected, you will be able communicate with me via thoughtcalls. As I was saying, if you hear me send the command, you must fade away from wherever we might be. You must feel yourself back in the tent, back in your body."

Aithen thought: *Reenter my body, it sounds so odd.*

"Yes. I realize how strange that sounds," said Elyana.

Aithen gave a start. How did she do that? So often, it seemed as though she read his mind.

Elyana continued, "But it is how one gets out of the Bind. When one enters the Bind, they leave their body behind. Upon leaving the

Bind, they must reenter their body. So, we will try it once to give you a sense of what I mean. In all truth, I do not know if you will be able to do this by yourself; entering and exiting the Bind are things that require years of training for a Lux Baiula, and not all succeed. This will be like throwing a kid off a raft to teach them to swim. So, I will probably be forced to kick you out of the Bind. Know that if I have to push you out, we will both be in greater danger while I increase my focus on you to get you back here." Aithen looked at her with a question which Elyana anticipated. It seemed that as she readied herself for entering the Bind, her senses were becoming even more perceptive than they usually were. Or perhaps it was the anticipation of the risks she was going to be taking by bringing him into the Bind that heightened her senses. In reply to Aithen's unasked question, Elyana said, "I was able to handle much more at Horn's Pass, such as creating physical shields over you and your brother and protecting everyone from having their brains fried while battling the Serpent because the situation was different: we were in the physical world. Here, one does not need to focus so much on oneself just to remain whole."

Aithen nodded, worried.

"Once we are done with our little exercise, we will reenter the Bind where I will look for Krystiana. I will be spending a good deal of energy to keep you hidden in addition to keeping myself whole, so do not, under any circumstance, respond to her presence. Know that the punishment for taking you with me would be great if she were to find you there, and the Magna Mater could not, nor would she do anything to prevent the penalty. I do not like the fact that I will need to hide you from her, but since I cannot ask either her or the king's permission now, I have no choice but to hide you."

"Once I find Krystiana, she and I will begin looking for the Serpent. There might be others of the evil kind with it, so we must be prepared for that as well. And once we find the Serpent, we will attempt to enter its mind so that we may hear whatever it might be thinking or whatever it might be saying should it be exchanging thoughtcalls with someone or something else." Elyana noticed a sign of alarm in Aithen as soon as she said that but kept on. "It will be a shocking and terrifying experience Aithen, but you will be within me, safer than in the Bind on your own, for certain." Elyana had said all this as matter-of-factly as if she were talking about the weather.

"What do you mean *enter its mind*? I don't understand."

"As you will discover, the Bind is a world unlike any other and gives those who can wield it properly abilities beyond the ordinary ones you know of. One such uncommon ability is that of...forcibly entering another humanoid's mind to look into it and hear and see that person's thoughts, visions, and dreams; only three of us – as far as I know – have that ability. I am one of them, and so are the Magna Mater and the Praefecta Medicas [31]. Women with the skill used to be more common, but the practice has been proscribed, and we no longer teach it – not even for use in criminal investigations – since the now exiled Natalia Lux Baiula forced herself into a student's mind some sixty years ago, causing her great psychological trauma, and doing great damage to the Order." Elyana couldn't help but feel embarrassed at the thought of the woman; she had been a powerful Lux Baiula, and could have done much for the Sisterhood, but alas. Elyana paused a moment, then added, "There are also two men who can so enter the minds of other humanoids, but their secret is not mine to tell."

Aithen raised an eyebrow questioningly, but Elyana preempted him and said, "Don't ask, Aithen."

"In any case, you might think that entering the Serpent's mind would be like entering the mind of any other animal, which the Kynarians can easily do, but the Serpent is unlike any animal, and more like a humanoid, and that is why Magna Mater Krystiana and I must be the ones to do it."

"This is madness, Elyana! You will already face the Sisterhood's wrath just for hunting the Serpent in the Bind; why would you add to it by trying to enter its mind? What *will* they do to you if they find out?"

"I would rather not think of that, Aithen. But we will take all necessary precautions so as not to reveal ourselves to anyone who may be Roaming the Bind tonight."

"I do not like this."

"Entering the Serpent's mind is the only way to learn what it might be planning to do next, Aithen. And maybe we'll be lucky and also learn what the source of the foul presence in the Bind is."

---

[31] Praefecta Medicas: Medical Prefect, Head of the Medics' Assembly.

"Why can't you simply find the Serpent and then listen to its conversations from afar?"

"It does not work that way in the Bind, Aithen. Sound does not travel through the Bind as it does through the air or water."

"It still sounds crazy, crazier than anything even Toras has done."

Elyana breathed a heavy sigh and said, "Aithen, I know what I am doing. I am just not sure I should be doing it with you inside me."

At that, Aithen experienced a faint blush of embarrassment.

As usual, Elyana feigned not to have noticed and continued, but not before repressing her own reaction to what she suspected must have caused the prince to blush. "In any case, there are only three rules you need to know to survive this. One, you stay focused on me; two, you do not, under any circumstance, try to contact those we meet; and three, if I say "Exit", focus on your own body, and return to it. Hopefully, by the end of this, you will have learned what you are coming to learn."

Elyana lowered her eyes and thought to herself: *I really do not know why I'm going ahead with this, but things are what they are.*

If Aithen only knew how uncertain she felt at times despite being a Lux Baiula, he might not be as trusting of her as he was. But Lux Baiulae must never show fear or uncertainty; fright and hesitation must be in others. The power they projected depended on this perhaps even more so than on their Bindings.

Elyana invited Aithen to sit on the soft carpet of his tent, facing her. She then spread her hands and between them there appeared a small sphere that seemed to contain the night sky in it, dark but with millions of dots of light throughout.

"Now, Aithen, place your hands on the sphere, close your eyes, and listen for my heartbeat. Once you have locked onto it, you should hear my thoughtvoice. This sphere will make my connection with you easier and more stable."

Aithen wanted to ask her how the sphere worked, but this wasn't the time, so he kept the question to himself and said, "I am ready."

Elyana instructed Aithen to close his eyes while she did the same. The Prince started to relax as his father had taught him. He counted backwards, to calm his thoughts and zero-in on himself. When he reached 'zero', he entered the expected, deep meditative trance. He became aware of the electrical pulses coursing through his nerves and of his heart's slowing beats. After a moment spent enjoying this

119

state of inner consciousness, he felt for Elyana, called for her. But all he could see was his safe room with its white walls, its large, dark and softly glowing desk, its unending bookshelves, and the large window letting in a warm, soft light. He called for Elyana again, felt for the beating of her heart. Still nothing.

He decided to speak out loud, which risked taking him out of the trance, but he had practiced doing that frequently enough while growing up and if he was careful, he should be able to remain in trance. When he spoke, he told Elyana he could not find her. Elyana replied that he needed to open himself to external Sendings. That sent a virtual shiver through him. Aithen truly hated opening his mind to anything and everything that may enter it, even though he warded himself against the entry of malevolent things, as he had been trained to do. Indeed, the last time he had opened himself to external Sendings – a few years ago now – he had experienced such horrible sensations and thoughts that they had lingered on in his mind even during his waking hours. Since then, he had limited himself to only opening his mind to itself and to his own body when meditating.

Sensing his hesitation, Elyana repeated her instruction, but assured him he would find her, and only her, when he opened himself up.

Aithen responded with a simple "ok", refocused his thoughts and started to open his mind to things external to him. The more his mind disconnected from the here and now – from himself – the more conscious he became of things beyond his five senses. At one point, he felt panic try to pierce through his calm, panic which was surfacing at the thought of being open to external influences. But he quickly repressed it, recovering a deep sense of calm, and began to feel for the Lux Baiula's heartbeat. Just now, his mind perceived a faint sound, a quiet two-tempoed beat. *Elyana.* Aithen had not spoken the word, nor had he thought it; it just appeared in his mind.

A moment or an eternity later, Aithen finally locked onto Elyana's heartbeat. It was calm, it was steady. He sensed his own heart begin to beat in sync with hers until he could no longer tell them apart. Then, very slowly, he began to feel a strange pull on his mind, and although he was tempted to resist it, he let himself go with it as he began to *hear* Elyana in this nonphysical world. *So that's a thoughtvoice!* It was soothing. It was so much better than what he experienced when he met with the Locari. He tried to reach out to her, he thought, *"Elyana, I hear you, do you hear me?"*

"I do, Aithen. Now feel yourself following my thoughtvoice. Feel it surround you."

As Aithen let himself become immersed in Elyana's ethereal voice, he felt the pull on his mind become stronger and stronger until suddenly he had the net impression of sharing a space inside Elyana. He thought, *"Elyana, am I here with you?"*

"You are with me, Aithen. You are in me."

Aithen felt slightly confused, but strangely safe though he received no images, and only darkness surrounded him. He asked, *"Will I not see anything?"*

"You will, as soon as I let it happen. Be ready."

Visual impressions suddenly began seeping through their bond. These impressions quickly resolved themselves into bright, pure white light laced by a mist of myriad tendrils. Aithen could not see Elyana, but he felt her smile. Not even his best dreams or his deepest meditations had ever felt this alive. He felt joy. It was incredible! Amazing!

Aithen could not stop a sudden excitement. He asked, *"What is it that I...or we see?"*

"You see what my mind sees. This shimmering world is created by the interconnected minds of all humanoids. It has no physical location, but it exists around us while there are beings who can think and dream." Sensing another question from Aithen, Elyana added, *"All humanoids release this energy but only the Alterintrants can perceive it, enter it, and use it."*

Aithen was at once amazed and frightened, scared at the thought that he was sharing a space with countless invisible beings, though fear had no hold on him; indeed, he had seen and taken part in many battles, flown Xyre like a madman next to his brother, and had done countless other things that would scare most people.

Elyana felt a tug, *"You have a question?"*

"I do. You said that you need to enter a humanoid's mind to hear its thoughts and see what it sees, but since this place is created by all of our minds, can you not know everyone's thoughts simply by being in here?"

"No. For reasons yet unknown, thoughts are still localized, even in the Bind. Only by entering one's mind can you know what lies in

it. But being out here in the Bind can still provide valuable information. I can know where a person is, and I can sense their emotions. I can also see people interact with each other, if they are Alterintrants."

"Hum, it seems like you can know quite a bit about a person by finding their vibration in the Bind; I think Harlion would love for his Frumentarii to be able to do that."

"Unfortunately, males – except for a few rare ones – are unable to access the Bind anymore. And even if they could, they would not be allowed to use it as they pleased. As I said earlier, entering another's mind is prohibited and not taught, and eavesdropping on people's doings and emotions is also frowned upon by those who believe in the right to privacy. You might not know that there now exists a faction in the Order suggesting that perhaps we should stop teaching women to enter the Bind altogether to protect everyone's privacy."

Aithen felt Elyana's revulsion at the thought. He sent, "That sounds rightly crazy. What would you be if you could no longer enter the Bind?!"

"It is crazy, and it maddens me. But, if we could no longer enter the Bind, we could still use it to conjure things in the Outer World."

"Yes, but you would lose the ability to know so much more than one can know in the outside world! It sickens me, every time I hear of such irrational movements caused by fear and ignorance. And it surprises me that even Sisters may be subject to such irrationality."

"Well, fortunately, they are a small faction, and theirs is not an idiocy whose time has come yet."

Aithen's mind formed a frown. He wanted to tell Elyana that sometimes even minorities could bring about the passage of senseless laws, such as the law against the teaching of the theory of the extraorbital origin of humanoids, but before he could Elyana sent, "Very well, let us continue with our exercise." Just now, Elyana said, "Exit!"

That took Aithen by surprise, but he remembered the Lux Baiula's instructions: when he heard the command, he needed to reenter his body at once. So, he felt for it, and nothing happened; he could not sense it. He felt himself become frustrated, and his mind's form began pulsating more and more strongly as a result.

Elyana did not wait for him to try again. Instead, she sent a forceful, "*Aithen.*" His mind's form immediately resolved itself, like water agitated in a bucket suddenly stills itself to perfect smoothness once the agitation ceases. Elyana then sent, *"Though the order to exit requires an urgent action, you need to be calm while you do it. Now, detach yourself from this place and open your senses to the sounds around the tent, feel your body,* feel *your hands on the sphere."*

For a very brief moment, Aithen felt like arguing her instructions. But he knew Elyana was right, and without further delay he did as she suggested. The vibration that was his mind inside Elyana smiled when he felt his limbs tingle. Was it the sound of footsteps he heard just now? Probably not, given that Elyana had set the Sound Shield. He then started to feel his legs and his feet inside the boots, and his hands on something solid. *What is this? Yes! The sphere.*

"Elyana, I feel it, I feel my body!"

"Excellent. Now feel your mind sinking into it."

The prince tried, but every time he did, he got pulled back in by the Bind. He tried again, and still his hold on his body slipped away. *"Elyana, I can't. I try, but I can't."*

"All right, then. Brace yourself because I am going to have to push you out." Aithen had no idea how he might 'brace himself' and wanted to ask, but not a moment later, he felt the world around him whirl, and he felt pain. *"Pain, my body. Elyana! Ahrrrr! Pain!"* In the Outer World, Aithen's body released actual, audible groans. He tried to resist Elyana's push, but that only made it worse. So, he gave in, and with his last cry, he was back, back in his body, in the Outer World.

He opened his eyes and saw his hands still on the sphere. His face was contorted with pain, a pain that gripped his entire body. *What happened?* "Elyana." No response. He felt strangely empty, no, naked. *I can't feel you anymore.* Still no reply. Just then, another jolt of pain shook him, and he groaned. It was a good thing Elyana had put up a Sound Shield around them, or those cries would surely have alerted the guardians.

He lifted his head, and saw Elyana, her body in front of him. He saw pain in her face, and he started to panic. But just then, Elyana's eyes opened, and she said, "I am glad to see you breathing, even though you are obviously aching quite badly."

"Severely indeed." Aithen suppressed another moan, and looked at Elyana, slightly embarrassed, and upset.

"Do you understand now why this is a bad idea, Aithen?"

Aithen did not respond, except to turn away, clench his teeth, and turn back to look at Elyana with even greater determination.

Elyana nodded silently, then looked at the time disc and said, "It is almost time to meet with the Magna Mater. Let us practice once more before we do."

This time, Aithen did succeed and was able to reintegrate his body without needing to be kicked out the Bind, and that was a good thing because he probably would have had to give up on joining Elyana on her hunt for the Serpent, otherwise.

Elyana gave him a few minutes to recover before reentering the Bind to meet with the Magna Mater. Aithen now looked at her and understood from her expression that she was finally coming to terms with his decision. He gave her a thankful, grateful smile, because despite his authority as prince heir to the throne of Alvinoria, he had no real authority over Elyana, who as citizen of Urbs Lucis – an autonomous city of the kingdom – answered only to the hierarchy of the Lucis Sororum Societas.

Elyana responded to the prince's smile with a grunt and said, "Well, let's get on with it. We have no more time to spare. We will re-enter the Bind now and will not return here until Krystiana and I have found what we are looking for. Are you ready?"

"Yes."

"Close your eyes."

Aithen did so and put his hands back on the sphere sitting between him and Elyana. As he did so, he unintentionally touched Elyana's hands, and felt his heart skip a beat. He moved his hands from hers, ever so slightly, to help his heart slow down. He focused, and quickly returned to the required meditative state. He listened for Elyana's heartbeat again, and in this timeless state, he began to feel the same strange pull on his mind, followed by Elyana's thoughtvoice calling to him. Another flash and he found himself back inside her.

"You are back within me, Aithen. Follow my thoughts. And remember! do not try to reach for, or contact anything you might see while in the Bind. You will not be able to do so as I am shielding you; but you would certainly distract me if you tried, which would be

enough to alert Krystiana – or someone else. Remain calm at all times, and just follow my thoughts. I am going to start to call for the Magna Mater, now."

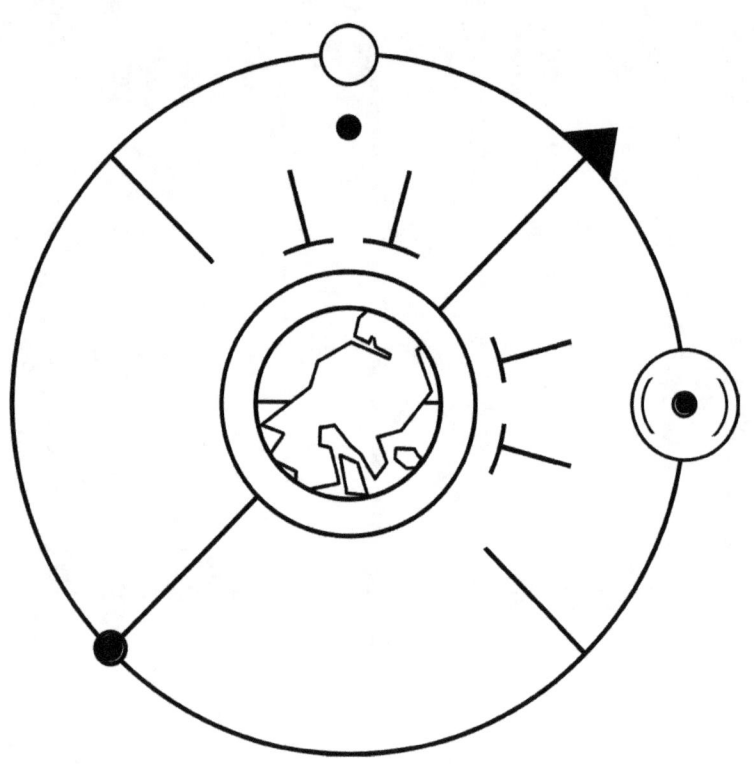

VIII IN THE BIND

"How are the preparations proceeding, Prime Dux?"

The title rankled the tall and imposing Genghis [32]. It reminded him of that stupid ancient language, Latin, which he was beginning to forget after some two thousand four hundred years of life, despite the continuous rejuvenation of his brain.

Genghis was standing by his desk – a desk with only a holoscreen on top of it and a few chairs around it, in this otherwise Spartan office. Only the mementoes of the proconsul's conquests, which sat on the shelves lining the room's glass walls, gave it some personality.

Genghis's response was delivered by a perfectly modulated voice – indeed, he had had his larynx replaced by an electronic module a long time ago already, along with many other parts of his body. He said, "As of a week ago, they were proceeding as planned, Thabo. Andrus3 [33] informed me that almost everything is in place for our arrival in a year's time."

The man called Thabo replied with a good dose of anxiety, "A year. Not too long anymore, and yet far enough for someone to accidentally discover our plans, Prime Dux."

Genghis replied with a careless wave of his hand, "*Even* if Alia were to discover our plans, she could not stop them. In fact, she may very well pass before then."

Thabo reacted with shock and concern, despite his own deep dislike of the ruler – after all, she *was* the creator of everything they now knew, and the one who dragged humanity out of its grave when not the Christian, nor the Hebrew or the Muslim god deigned do so.

Genghis continued with his dismissive tone, "She is old Thabo; I don't even *know* exactly how old – no one does. But what is certain is that her faculties are failing her, and our best technologists are at a loss as to how to prevent further degradations of her brain, let alone restore what she has already lost."

---

[32] Genghis: pronounced "ching-iss."

[33] Andrus3: A META (or medical and tutoring android) of the third generation.

Thabo knew of the other man's deep loathing of the ruler, but his words and tone still scared him, and made the small Thabo look even smaller.

"Don't worry, Thabo. Life will not end with her passing."

The stooping Thabo turned to look out of the room's glassed northern wall, which faced the once glittering, but still grandiose city of New Rome. He did not wish for Genghis to see how troubled he felt.

Standing perfectly erect with hands behind his back and fingers tapping each other, Genghis asked, "What is it, Thabo?"

The man's heart skipped a beat, and he silently berated himself for displaying his emotions so carelessly that the general noticed. He could not tell Genghis how inappropriate his comments regarding their ruler were, so he asked a question he did have on his mind, "Are you certain Andrus3 can deliver, Prime Dux?" Genghis cocked an eyebrow. "I mean, his communications have become erratic, and it is entirely possible he will not survive much longer. In fact, I have difficulty believing he has lasted this long. All other METAs became inoperative within a few hundred years of initial activation, but he has lived for over *two thousand four hundred and fifty years*!"

Genghis raised a curious eyebrow as he moved to wipe some invisible dust from the black onyx surface of his desk, and said, "Yeees, nearly as long as our great ruler, in fact. Isn't it surprising? But he is fine, Thabo, he is fine. The update we sent a few months ago has finally reached him and he is now repairing whatever malfunction affected him. He assured me he will be able to prepare the planet for our arrival. One year, Thabo. One year, and I will change our lives in a way that even Alia has not been able to do for us!"

The small man didn't know whether to smile with hope or shrink in fear. He finally gave the Prime Dux a sheepish smile, and wondered for the thousandth time about the righteousness of what they were planning to do.

***

Aithen saw the shimmering space of the Bind bloom around them. It was magnificent! The experience was like what he felt the first time he flew off on Xyre, only ten times, a hundred times more exhilarating. When the Bind first appeared, he saw that pure white

128

light with its misty tendrils he had come to expect. Now, an incredible pattern of purple, and blue, and yellow hues exploded before him. And although he had no body in this virtual world, his sensations were more intense here than they ever were in the Outer World.

After an unknowable while, Aithen heard Elyana say, *"Hold on."*
He asked, *"What do you mean?"*
"Keep focused on yourself, anchored inside me."
The next moment, his mind was pulled and wound around uncountable shapes. Even though his body was still sitting cross-legged in his tent, it swayed as his mind was pulled again and again, wound around one shape after another. He forced himself to re-center his focus and struggled to do so. When he finally succeeded, he asked Elyana what was happening, why everything swirled. The Lux Baiula replied that she was "simply searching and inspecting." Some of the shapes Aithen saw looked monstrous, while others he recognized as humanoid. Strangely, most of them looked surprisingly …attractive. He wondered why that was and decided he would ask Elyana about it later.

Elyana looped around one last shape, then slowed and stopped. The "slowing down" had felt like nothing he had ever felt before, and it dizzied him even more so than the winding had; not even his furan's sudden stops were this bad. Just now, there appeared in front of him – or Elyana – a humanoid form. It seemed to be near them, and then far from them. Aithen felt a curious apprehension, which he was certain was not coming from him, and yet, he was feeling it. Could it be coming from Elyana? He thought about asking her but decided against it; this wasn't the time. The form in front of them now resolved into a woman's shape and spoke.

"Elyana, it is good to see you."
"It is good to see you, Magna Mater."
Aithen found the constantly shifting distance dizzying.
"I was beginning to fear something had happened to you. At one point I felt your presence, and then, unexpectedly, you disappeared."
"I had to see to some other important matter. But it is all taken care of now, and I should not be disturbed anymore."
Elyana was not lying, but neither was she telling the whole truth. Aithen knew, from having observed it so many times when watching

Elyana or other Lux Baiulae conduct their business, that they often answered questions in this way when they could not tell the truth.

"Very well then; as you are aware, we still know very little about the recent events that have shocked us all. What we do know is that the creature you encountered was indeed the Serpent, and that flying monster is now roaming the lands in search of we do not know what. But as to how it has come back, not even Bilena understands it, and if anyone should know, it is her. She finds this very unsettling, as you can imagine. And then there is the matter of those unusual vibrations a number of us have felt, which worries us even more."

"Have other Sisters aside from the Yellows sensed them?"

"Yes, though not many. But I wish that Sisters of all four Sashes could sense them; they would be safer knowing, especially if those vibrations indicate the return of another one as well," said the Magna Mater, not wishing to name Noctiferus. Then, realizing how Elyana must feel, she added, *"I am sorry, Elyana. I do not understand how it is that you have not been able to sense these vibrations. When you are back in Urbs Lucis, I want you to see Saara, so she may take a look at you."*

"There is no need to feel sorry, Mater. After all, whatever is interfering with my Sensing abilities cannot last forever."

Krystiana nodded and continued, *"So, I was saying that some have sensed this presence, but obviously, everyone is aware of it, and everyone has read the reports regarding the actions of the Serpent. That is enough to worry and puzzle them all. Let us hope we find some answers tonight. And let us hope this roaming session will allow you to recover all your senses because whether you do or not, I will have great need of you to get through the troubles ahead, and it would be better for all if you were in full possession of your abilities. I am thankful, though, that you do not seem to have lost your roaming abilities; these, I cannot do without."*

Elyana nodded. She felt a mix of pride and anger just now, pride in knowing that her friend still needed her, and anger toward her inability to sense this something that might very well be Noctiferus himself.

"All right, enough talk. Let's get to work, Elyana. We will both initiate the search for the servant, but it is best we remain in constant contact. We must establish a mind-tie for that, which will also enable you to shield me in case another of our Sisters should be in the Bind

130

tonight. And who knows, with the mind-tie, should I feel those same vibrations here, it may very well restore your own ability to sense them."

Elyana shuddered a moment, fearing that she might not be able to keep Aithen hidden while her mind was tied to Krystiana's. But Krystiana was her life-long friend and she would not attempt to rummage through Elyana's thoughts. Her friend might still discover the prince in her mind, accidentally, but only if he lost control in there; she hoped he wouldn't.

The lash from Krystiana to establish the mind-tie came without warning. It was an undulating rope of bright blue light, which came with intense violence and swiftly took hold of Elyana's mind. In the physical world, her body jerked in reaction to the assault; if someone entered Aithen's tent just now, they would think Elyana was having a convulsion. Here, in the Bind, the Lux Baiula's image responded violently, distorting itself and sending blinding flashes of light in one direction and then another. A moment later, in this timeless world, a lash raged back from Elyana toward Krystiana; the Magna Mater reacted almost as violently as Elyana had, and her own image lit itself afire.

Both suppressed their cries as best they could, lest they accidentally send a sound to someone else in the Bind – that had been known to happen; when subjected to great pain, a Roamer could accidentally send the thought of the scream to someone they knew. Another violent lash of the rope came from Elyana; Krystiana almost yelled this time, and was about to respond with even greater force, thinking she had seen Elyana grin. *I will have her flogged when we get back to Urbs Lucis.* But the pain flowed over, and she let her ire pass.

The mind-tie was now complete, and both women slowly recovered their composure. In the physical world, they were still trembling; it would be a few minutes before their bodies sat at rest again.

When the encounter with the Magna Mater had begun, Aithen had had to force himself to keep his thoughts quiet, to not even think. But when he saw the lash coming from the Sisterhood's leader, all he could do was stare in amazement at yet another awe-inspiring thing. Elyana didn't *need* to worry about him causing her to lose her concentration, he told himself; all this was so incredible that his

131

thoughts were riveted in place and he could do nothing but stare in wonderment.

He shook his virtual self when he heard Krystiana.

The Magna Mater sent in a sarcastic tone, *"Excellent, I am glad to see you've recovered already."* Elyana grinned, though her brain was on fire. The Magna Mater then sent, *"Let us begin,"* and her image disappeared.

Elyana sent a short but sincere, *"Go safely."*

"And you, Elyana," sent Krystiana.

"I will, and I'll let you know once I find the Serpent."

A distant chuckle returned to Elyana, and then there was a total and absolute silence as all thought exchanges ceased.

Aithen enjoyed the tranquility, more complete than anything he had ever achieved while meditating. When he heard Elyana's voice again, he found himself wishing it had not come so soon. Then, his mind latched on to a confusing feeling, confusing because he recognized the source, even though he had never experienced that sensation before. He sent to Elyana, *"I feel something coming from her – the Magna Mater. How do I know it is from her?"*

"You know because I know, and you sensed my reaction to Krystiana's Sending."

"This is going to be confusing – not knowing if something I sense comes from me or from you."

Aithen sensed a smile from Elyana, and she sent, *"You will get used to it."*

After a moment, she added, *"I will begin my search for the Serpent, now. You have done well up to this point; continue to do as you have. I need not say that we do not wish to reveal ourselves to the creature."*

"Actually, you have *just said it. But I know – I will remain calm, at all times and not reach out to anything or anyone."*

Aithen sensed a short growl coming from Elyana, and she sent, *"There are times I wish I could meet whoever created these silly expressions and tell them how illogical they are."*

Aithen thought about responding, but Elyana began flowing in the space-less world again, and he let his mind quiet and imbibe the sensations. How she could find her direction in here, he hadn't the foggiest idea, but he saw things come and go, changing all the time. Strangely, the search reminded him of when he hunted for belwohrs.

Despite their size, belwohrs were hard to track, and a hunter often spent hours searching for them in the woods that carpeted the bottom half of the Furan Peaks.

Just now, Elyana sent, *"Once I find the creature, I will enter it, but my shield will hide us from its mind. You will be able to hear our target through its own thoughtvoice. It will probably use the Ancient Tongue, but you have some knowledge of it and you should be able to get the gist of what it might say."*

"How can you be so sure you will find it first?"

Aithen sensed a smug smile come from Elyana, and he wondered if her body in the tent was also smiling in this manner. Elyana replied, *"The Magna Mater and I both know I am better than she at this. If it is here, I will find it first."*

The Lux Baiula continued flowing and spinning, reaching for and going past things in this ethereal, timeless world, although the reaching and passing were not as they are in the Outer World: in here, something could be close then far, then close again, ahead or behind. Aithen had the impression that the different apparitions of a form were not all the same. That is, they seemed to excite different senses as they neared them, circled them, and passed them, although he could not tell what senses these might be. Another question he would have to ask Elyana, when he had the chance.

After what seemed like a while or an eternity, they finally came to what looked like a structured place of some sort. Was it a garden? And in it, Aithen saw several forms talking to each other. He asked, *"Who are they?"*

"They are a part of someone's dream. The one to the right must be the dreamer – his form is emitting more energy."

The search continued for another while, and it was quite dizzying, winding 'round shapes every time they got close to one. At times, the forms they saw were just there, surrounded by nothing but the Bind's light. Other times, they were in a place of some sort. He noticed that if a place appeared in the Bind, there was always a humanoid in it.

Finally, all came to a standstill and Aithen felt lightheaded, as when Xyre would drop to the ground at top speed. There was something blurry in front of them, but Elyana looked to her right, toward something else; as the image came into focus, a terrible fear took hold of Aithen. He saw it, the creature they had encountered

133

and battled for their lives not so long ago. It was talking with the form of a Human. This Human was tall and dressed in a dark, blood-red cape. He appeared to be strong, with lean muscles showing on his bare arms. He was also quite handsome, *Like the Zebulonian*, he thought. *Can it be him? No, this man is too pale-skinned.*

Elyana did not respond; she wasn't paying attention to him now. Instead, he heard her speak to the Magna Mater.

"I did find him first, Krystiana."

"Of course! I expected nothing less. In any case, be very careful Elyana," began the Magna Mater, and in a flash, she was there, next to Elyana. *"Neither of us has had any practice in this in a long time, and we definitely have not had any experience entering the mind of the likes of* It!*"*

"I will be careful, Krystiana."

"I will remain here. If anything goes wrong, I will pull you out."

Elyana nodded.

"May your body be worthy," sent Krystiana, even though she knew Elyana never put her fate in the hands of the Founders.

Elyana turned away from her friend then spoke to the prince: *"I suggest you empty yourself of all emotions now; we are going to enter it. And do not resist me in any way."*

Aithen did as he was told, turning to the mind-control exercises his father had taught him while growing up, and forgot all fear, arguments, and questions. The years of training in self-mastery he had received from his father and Harlion, he had received so that he might never give in to his fears, but instead keep his mind and body focused, no matter what, and he had proven to his father and to his mentor many times already that he could do that. But on this night, he might very well strain his capabilities. Still, he was ready. He would not fail – he couldn't.

Aithen noticed something, or rather, the lack of something – Elyana was so calm now, he could barely feel her. His attention turned back to the Serpent, and he wondered how she would enter its mind. It couldn't be anything like when she and the Magna Mater bound each other; that would be like a thief smashing doors while trying to sneak into his victim's home. So how would she do it?

Elyana sent, *"Ready."* This was a statement, not a question, as she prepared to transport them into the beast. Not a moment later, all became blank; all sensation ceased, sound disappeared, and light gave way to darkness. For a moment that must have lasted but a millionth of a second, he wondered what was happening. But he remembered Elyana's instructions, and let go of his thoughts, let go of everything, and the last bit of consciousness went too, and then nothing. Nothing there to even know that anything had ever been there.

Elyana and Aithen were now settled in the deepest recess of the Serpent's mind. Elyana had told him that keeping them hidden within the Serpent was going to require so much energy from her, that they would not be able to stay long, or else. He had wondered about that. Why would energy be needed to perform imaginary actions? She had tried to explain, but it had been beyond his capabilities to grasp.

Elyana sent, *"We are blind for the moment, but we will recover our senses as soon as I release some of the tension on the shield. No matter what happens now, no matter what we may hear or see, remember my instructions. Our lives depend on it. Here we go."*

Not a moment later, a voice came and surrounded them completely and utterly. It was filled with death, and the feeling was as palpable as an object in the physical world. Aithen was at once puzzled and terrified, terrified by the death that surrounded him, but puzzled by his own calm. He found himself thanking his father and captain because without their teachings, he would probably have lost his mind now, and gone running – or rather roaming – like a madman.

The voice he heard now belonged to the Serpent; it was speaking in the Ancient Tongue to its interlocutor. Aithen could see the man better now. He had dark glowing eyes, with thick brows descending at a sharp angle past his eyes, and a narrow, straight nose. His skin seemed to be the color of sand. Aithen wondered why evil beings, whether male or female, always had such attractive looks.

Elyana whispered, *"It is the Umbra, the Shadow."* A faint shudder – which Aithen felt – coursed through her virtual self as she wondered about this new interloper. The Umbra – it had been Noctiferus's lieutenant on K'Tara during the Dark Battle. Elyana wondered if it was hiding somewhere on K'Tara, now. Or did it reach here in its formless body from some far-off dark orb, as gloomy as its soul? Elyana shook these thoughts out of her mind and returned her attention to the Serpent.

135

The Serpent was telling the Umbra about the events at Horn's Pass. It was clearly upset about the unexpected resistance it found there, but what upset it even more was the presence of a Lux Baiula at the fortress. If it hadn't been for her, it said, it probably would have destroyed the whole place despite the fact that the structure had been built with the use of the Bind, and it would have exterminated every single one of those miserable humanoid worms – villagers and guardians alike.

Aithen felt anger stir somewhere within him at hearing those words, but he did not *feel* it really; his emotions remained locked away, and it was just as well.

From their vantage point within the Serpent's mind, Elyana and Aithen could tell that the mentioning of a Lux Baiula had irritated the form facing them from the tension that built-up in its shape as the Serpent told its story. The Umbra sent, *"Stulte! Debes terrorem creare, nec te periclitari!* [34]*"*

The Serpent spoke its reply in Alvinorian; perhaps the Ancient Tongue fatigued it. *"I am not stupid, and I know what I need to do, Umbra. There is no need to remind me –terrorize and keep safe."*

The Umbra, however, continued in the Ancient Tongue, narrowed his vaporous eyes, and asked, *"Invenistine scopos nostros?* [35]*"* to which the Serpent replied that it had not yet been able to locate the men they'd been searching for. That vexed the caped Umbra even more than the Serpent's difficulties with the fortress and the Lux Baiula. He growled, and back-handed the Serpent with a blast of energy. Somehow, Aithen felt a painful sting. He thought about sending Elyana a question but refrained from it. The Serpent backed away from its accomplice and shrieked in response.

The Umbra growled his next question, insisting on an answer, *"Per quartum iam quaesivisti. ubi sunt illi?!* [36]*"*

The Serpent's form vibrated with fearful anticipation of another blow–it did not matter if it searched for a fourth or for a month–it would not be able to find their targets; their vibrations were either shielded or they resided in a shielded location. The Serpent

---

[34] You fool! You must create terror, not endanger yourself!
[35] Have you located our targets?
[36] You have searched for a fourth now. Where are they?

136

responded with a tight voice, made even tighter by the effect that emotions had on form in this ethereal word, *"Nescio.* [37]*"*

Elyana and Aithen wondered who it was that the Dark Lord's Wings and its accomplice were searching for. The Serpent, apparently fearing any more questions on the topic, asked the Umbra if he had been able to recruit anymore humanoids to their cause. After a momentary hesitation during which the Umbra seemed to consider whether to allow the change in topic, he replied smugly that he had indeed been able to bring to their cause a large number of new Human and Rokothian recruits, but sadly, no Kynarians yet.

The Lux Baiula and prince felt a sense of impatient excitement surface from the Serpent when it shouted its next question, causing Aithen and Elyana to fear another blow. *"Sed cur manemus? Nunc debemus copias nostras convocare!* [38]*"*

Surprisingly, the other replied calmly, unruffled, *"Patientes. Mundus erit nostrum, sed primum debemus Sorores et Kynarian perdere.* [39]*"*

The Umbra added, switching to Alvinorian, *"The Kynarians first, and then the wretched Lux Baiulae, as they so stupidly call themselves."*

The Serpent spat its reply, *"The Kynarians, how I despise them."*

Aithen could feel its contempt for them. Something bothered him now – his mother was Kynarian.

The Serpent spoke again, and the prince refocused. It said, *"It will not be an easy thing, eliminating either of them."*

The Umbra replied, *"As a matter of fact, it will not be. When our Master showed me how to create, or rather re-create you, I was pleased. Indeed, even though we were...defeated, six hundred years ago, you had been very useful in sowing confusion and fear, as well as in killing countless numbers of our enemies, and – were it not for some unfortunate developments by the Luxori – I have no doubt we would have crushed the K'Tarans."*

"Today, they are much weaker, but still a significant threat to our aims. I thought that if I could bring you back, this time! we would most certainly defeat them. But I am beginning to wonder how

---

[37] I do not know.

[38] But why are we waiting? We have to assemble our forces now!

[39] Patience. This world will be ours, but we must first destroy the Sisters and the Kynarians.

helpful you will truly be; I suspect something went wrong in the cloning procedure."

The Serpent gave a low, rumbling growl in response. He had never liked the Umbra and had often wished he could simply rip the thing's head off, but alas, that was beyond his powers.

The Umbra interrupted the Serpent's traitorous thoughts, sending, *"If you dislike the sound of these words, I suggest you give me cause to use more flattering ones. Nevertheless, one way or another, the Societas and the Kynarian Order will be eliminated; I have been considering our options for a while now, and I have some ideas which I will share with you if it becomes necessary. Know that to ensure our success, I have also put Vaedrin in play, and he may very well deliver before* you *do."*

The Serpent's form writhed with ire and resentment at the implication, and the tension within its form rattled the space which contained Elyana's and Aithen's vibrations.

The Umbra continued, *"Whether there will be praise or condemnation for you at the end of this enterprise will depend entirely on your part in it."*

Elyana sent an urgent thoughtcall to the Magna Mater, *"Krystiana, do you hear this?"*

Krystiana's distant thoughtvoice came back like a whisper, *"I do, Elyana, and it frightens me –"*

Elyana was about to send a reply, but new feelings of rage swelled within the Serpent in response to the Umbra's insult, and she ended the exchange to reinforce her shield.

But the Umbra seemed to be totally unconcerned about the Serpent's feelings, and he added, *"Before we take any overt action against the Kynarians, I need you to uncover the two Luxori that our Master has sensed, and once you find them, you will bring them to me. I do not care how you do it – you can use the Temptatori if you need to; you know how to find their leader in Kartak – but you will track them down and bring them to me."*

The Serpent growled his response, "I will find them, and I will bring them."

At that moment, fear and dread descended upon Aithen completely. The feeling was so strong that his physical body jerked in the tent, and his heart started pumping hard; if he didn't slow it, his body might sever its connection with his mind, leaving him stuck in the Bind forever. The prince did not know that, but he nevertheless struggled to remain in control, knowing that both his and Elyana's safety were at risk. He asked the Lux Baiula what the Umbra meant. Was one of the Luxori his father? His father wasn't a Luxor – Aithen knew that – but he *was* an Alterintrant. The Sister turned toward him with her mind's eye and answered that they did not know for certain who the Serpent and Umbra were talking about, and urged him to quiet his thoughts, lest they be discovered. Aithen tried, and then heard the Umbra say – his thoughtvoice filled with hatred – *"These two men, I wish I could simply rip their brains from their skulls and their guts from their bellies, and I may, but before I do, they will serve me!"*

The Umbra's hatred filled the Serpent, filled even the Bind. Aithen felt loathing of another kind build within his own mind, and he wished he had a dagger in his hand to rip the Serpent's brain from within and then lunge toward the other to slice his throat. But these creatures' forms were only wisps of energy – nothing a knife could stab. Or could it? If one could die in here, then perhaps an imagined knife could kill one's imagined form, and with it, one's physical body.

Elyana strained to contain her passenger, she sent, *"Aithen, you must control yourself! You can. Should I try and push you out now, we would both be lost."* Worryingly, Aithen did not respond.

The Umbra continued, *"It will take some time to get things ready yet, but once the worst of the Alterintrants are gone, conquering and enslaving the rest will be an easy task, especially for our Master."*

"If *He returns,"* replied the Serpent.

"He will, a year from now. And if He doesn't, why, K'Tara will be mine!"

Elyana felt sudden and irresistible tremors overtake Aithen's mind. Krystiana must have sensed the alarming vibrations and sent a question to the Lux Baiula through their mind-tie. *"Elyana, are you all right?"*

"I am, Magna Mater, I am," replied Elyana, though she was starting to wonder.

Elyana turned her attention back on Aithen and, in what she hoped was a soothing voice, she sent *"Aithen. Focus on me."* But the prince was unresponsive. She realized that she would have to quiet down his mind herself, lest they be discovered, and the latter

139

was not an option. The problem with that was that she would need to turn her attention on the prince and that was a recipe for disaster, but she had no choice; leaving Aithen in his present state meant certain discovery, while turning her focus on him only meant a high probability of discovery, which was better than certainty. Maybe, she thought, if she worked fast enough, the Serpent might not take notice, maybe, but she had doubts. *This is exactly the situation I wanted to avoid when I resisted Aithen's requests to accompany me, and now here we are.*

It took Elyana a split second to make up her mind. As soon as she did, she began sending vibrations, working backwards from the prince's virtual mind to enter his physical brain. She needed to cause his cerebrum to release dousing neurotransmitters, the same ones she caused her own brain to release when she was stressed or anxious. But Aithen's nerve cells refused to respond and Elyana increased the intensity of her Sendings, provoking a burgeoning panic in her own mind. For a brief moment, the prince's body slumped as his cerebrum began releasing calming hormones. Elyana breathed a sigh of relief and was about to stop her Sendings when, suddenly, she felt the Serpent's gaze turn inward; her reaction caused an accidental and large release of stress neurotransmitters in Aithen's brain, and his body jerked and seized in the tent, while panicked discharges began to flare from his mind. Elyana stilled her own reactions, understanding that they would soon join the Black Skies if she didn't get them out of there at once. True to its nature, necessity provided Elyana with the stimulus and the skill she needed to complete the restoration of Aithen's mind, and to call out to the Magna Mater.

"Magna Mater, adiuva me! [40] *"*

That caused an immediate and automatic reaction from Krystiana.

"Elyana, strengthen the shield, now!" sent the Magna Mater.

Elyana had some difficulty re-establishing the shield, and the Serpent now clearly felt the two foreign vibrations tucked in the depths of its own mind. It shrieked, louder than a thousand enraged rokons. The whole Bind reverberated and boomed around them in sonorous waves. Not since the Dark Battle had the Serpent been violated in this way, when a Kynarian had forced herself into its

---

[40] Magna Mater, help me!

140

thoughts. The Serpent's mind now turned upon itself to rip the mortals out and annihilate them. Elyana fought with all her remaining strength to keep the Serpent from reaching that part of itself where she and Aithen were hidden.

Then the whole of the Bind was suddenly ablaze with a tempest of fire that rushed toward the Serpent and its companion. A hell – worse than the one the Serpent came from –sprang forward from Krystiana and drove toward the two. From the middle of the hellfire, a spear of violent red and yellow light appeared. It rushed toward the Serpent at such speed, that the creature had no time to react. The spear bore through the center of the Serpent's image, and the creature let out an impossible shriek, and its form flickered for a moment.

The Serpent's companion was so stunned by what was happening that he had not yet reacted. But just now, he lashed out with his arm; his fingers stretched open with claws ready to rip through whatever was coming. Unfortunately for him, the spear of light continued toward him with such force that he had no more chance to stop it than the Serpent had. His face writhed with hate. As it tore through him, the javelin momentarily decomposed the Umbra's pattern as well.

Just now, Krystiana called to Elyana and asked her to latch onto her vibration. It was time; the Serpent was recovering and Elyana had almost fainted from the massive amounts of energy coming from both Krystiana and the raging Serpent.

Elyana succeeded, barely, in latching onto her friend's vibration and, with the little energy she still had, she turned her mind to an unconscious Aithen and enveloped his form to keep him whole.

When Krystiana seized Elyana from the Serpent's mind and hurled her back out of the Bind, the Lux Baiula lost consciousness too, and it was just as well, because the agony she would have felt otherwise might very well have damaged her permanently.

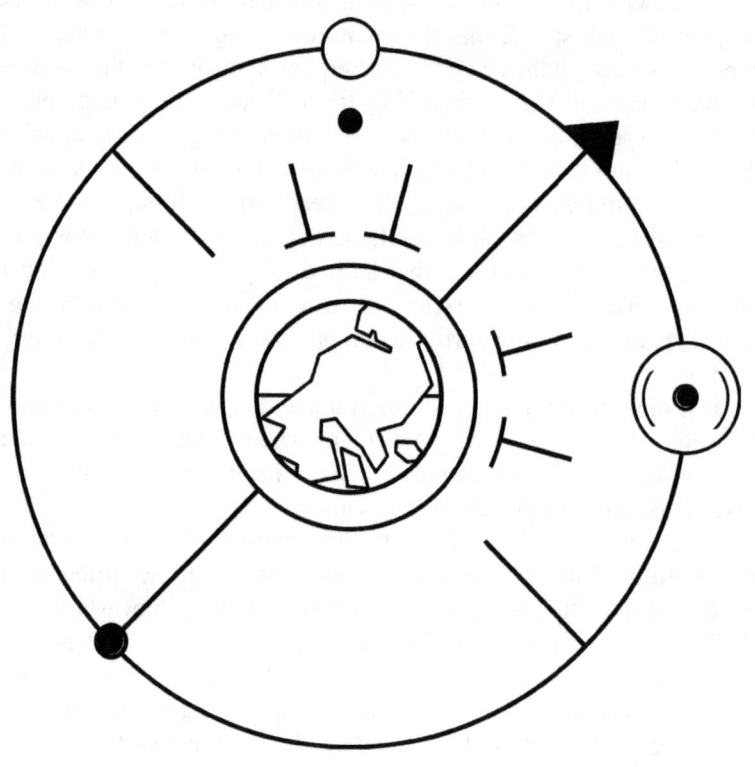

IX GAMES

After throwing Elyana out of the Bind, Krystiana found herself unshielded and completely vulnerable to the Serpent and its companion.

Krystiana saw the Serpent trying to reform its image as it continued to rage.

The Serpent felt as if its mind had been raped. The Human woman would know its wrath and beg for mercy, a mercy which it would not give. After one more crushing, soundless shriek, the Serpent found its form again and turned toward the vulnerable woman with a savage roar that would have shattered Krystiana's eardrums in the Outer World. The Serpent now looked at her with deathly eyes and was about to hurl itself toward the woman, intending only to erase her from existence, when a hand held it back. Standing next to it was the Serpent's coconspirator who had just regained his shape.

The Umbra now presented himself in a black dress and hood instead of his earlier deep red clothing, his dress afire and whipped by an imaginary wind. Underneath the hood, all Krystiana saw were vile eyes, with pupils surrounded by yellow irises. After laughing a laugh filled with hatred, the Umbra spoke to the Magna Mater with a booming voice that seemed to be coming from everywhere at once.

"Well, well, what do we have here, one of those meddling Alterintrant pests? A Lux Baiula, perhaps. And why do I feel like I know you?"

Krystiana felt a sudden, sharp pain as the Umbra's thoughts entered her mind. She raced for an answer to his question and decided to try and fool him, try to keep him from knowing for certain who or what she was – and she needed to get out of the Bind as quickly as possible. She replied, *"You fool! You have no idea who or what I am. And when you do, it will be too late."*

The Umbra seemed upset. What did the woman mean he did not know who she was? As if she could be anything other than a Lux Baiula or a Kynarian!

Krystiana could tell he was trying to hide his uncertainty, but he recovered quickly. *"You make me laugh, woman; it is you who have no idea who you are dealing with. I must say though, that I am very impressed with the courage and strength you displayed earlier to protect your accomplice from certain death. I wonder how she got inside my friend. Regardless, you cannot harm me – or my companion for that matter. I believe you know it as the Serpent – an unkind name, I must say, as my companion is much more than that. But no matter."*

Krystiana listened with a small, insulting smile on her face.

That seemed to irritate rather than scare the man further and his voice boomed around her with renewed intensity. It penetrated her as if it were trying to shatter her courage and resolve, *"I ask again: who are you, and why were you and the other woman here?!"*

Krystiana felt a sudden urge to answer, but she stopped herself, resisting the Umbra's voice inside her, violating her. The Umbra was now definitely annoyed, and he asked again, his voice even more forceful than before. The Magna Mater's mind throbbed with pain, and she felt her form lose its shape under the force of the man's Sendings; if she lost control now, she might never come out of the Bind again. She let out a cry of pain and desperation.

The Umbra yelled, *"You will answer me now!"*

Krystiana gasped when the Umbra's dreadful, burning hand clutched her neck, and she almost lost consciousness from the agony, which was causing her physical body in Urbs Lucis to waver. *I need...to get out...I can't...hold on any longer.*

The Shadow's eyes burned with flashes of rage. How could this puny Human resist him so? He growled and sent *"I've had enough of you; I suggest you pray to your beloved Aiala'Rhi and prepare to die!"* The Umbra clapped his hands, and abruptly, the very fabric of the Bind collapsed around the Magna Mater and very nearly burned her form out of existence.

Her cries were cries of utmost agony; she had no idea one could feel so much pain. But Krystiana, if she was weaker in the Bind than Elyana, was still the second most powerful Lux Baiula in a very long time, and with an incredible effort that buckled her physical body, she forced herself straight and recovered her form. As she did so, the crushing force of the Bind relented, just a bit, and she looked up, her jaw set tight and her eyes, hard.

Watching the woman regain her form and look at them with such nerve unsettled the Serpent. The creature started to tremble from the anger it felt, and it turned toward the Umbra, yelling, *"How can she still live?! She's a mere Human! I'll take care of her!"* But the Umbra barked back that *it* would do no such thing, that *he* was going to finish the woman for good. The Serpent retreated with growing resentment. Umbra or not, the thing had no right to treat the Master's Wings with such disrespect.

As this scene unfolded, Krystiana knew that if she was ever going to exit the Bind sane and safe, this was the time. So, she started to draw as much power as she could manage. Her body burned in her room, while her form in the Bind began glowing. A moment later, just when the two vile creatures turned toward her, she sent an impossible wall of fire roaring in their direction. The blazing torrent crashed on the incredulous pair and blew their forms back, causing the Umbra to release his hold on Krystiana. As soon as she felt the release, the woman hurled herself out.

* * *

A few hours after being ejected from the Bind, Elyana felt the already hot rays of the rising Blue Sun on her skin, and she woke. Her back and shoulders ached from lying on the floor in Aithen's tent all night. A splitting headache caused her to groan, and her groan was quickly replaced by a momentary panic as she remembered what had happened and thought of the Magna Mater.

I have to know if she made it out. Please make it so, Oh Great Founder.

Elyana looked at the prince, his body still sprawled on the floor where he had sat during their Roaming session. He looked so handsome, even covered in sweat, and a shiver ran through her, as her headache forced another groan. *Why am I thinking such things, now? Why at all?*

"Aithen, wake up."

The prince opened his eyes, rubbed them and cringed from the pain in his body.

"Elyana. We are back? What time is it?" He pulled at his shirt, which was stuck to his back and chest from the sweat.

"The Blue Sun is just rising." While forcing back another groan, she said, "I should never have taken you into Bind. If I've ever made an unwise decision – this was it."

145

With an indignant voice, the prince asked, "How can you say that, Elyana?!"

She just looked back with a stony face.

"I am sorry, Elyana. But I am *glad* I came, even with what happened. Would you want me ignorant of what is brewing out there?"

Elyana did not reply.

Aithen continued, "It is one thing to know of evil things through the histories and legends, but it is quite another to be in their presence, or rather, inside of them! All I could feel was death, and hunger for death and evil deeds. All those years of training in self-control made me believe that I was impervious to fear, but I was afraid in there, and I can still feel the dread that the creature's thoughts caused me."

"That does not surprise me."

The prince looked at the Lux Baiula as if to ask something, but hesitated. Elyana looked back unpretentiously and said, "You wish to know whether I, too, was afraid?"

"Well, one does assume a Sister has no fear, just as a peasant soldier assumes regulars are unafraid, and just as my own guardians assume nothing frightens *me*. But –"

"But you are, and you are just good at hiding it. Well, I was afraid too, Aithen, especially when you started losing control. We are alike in that."

"Hmm, I am not so sure. I have never seen you react as I did in there."

"That is because you have never seen me with a sword on my belly or a dagger on my throat."

Aithen snorted playfully and gave Elyana an appreciative nod, thankful for her empathy. Then, feeling painful knots in his back, he stretched forward and complained again.

A thought popped into the Halfling's memory, and he asked, "What about those – what did the Umbra call them – Temptors?"

Elyana corrected him, "Temptatori."

"Right, what are they? I have never heard of them. But I know of Kartak: it is a town filled with every type of scum, from thieves, to poachers, to slave traffickers. Scum!"

"The name is new to me as well. But we should make it a priority to learn everything we can about them very quickly. I do not know if the Order has spies in Kartak – likely not – but I will find out. Either way, this will be a matter better dealt with by the Sisterhood as these Temptatori are most likely Alterintrants."

Aithen felt his head spin. First the Serpent, then Noctiferus, then the Umbra, and now Temptatori! What else was going to pop out of the shadows? Aithen sat himself, clasped his hands on his knees, and shook his head. He said, "This is madness, Elyana. It's just…overwhelming. But you, you and your Sisters are the ones who will be right in the center of it." Aithen looked up, and asked with a deeply worried tone, "Will the Sisterhood even be able to protect *itself* against all these…foes?"

"Do not worry yourself with Sisterhood business, Aithen; we will take care of ourselves."

"Do not worry myself? You can't be serious. We are not talking about Rokothians, or mad Binders, or… or Zebulonians. We are talking about things not of this world!"

"Technically, all of them are of this world, except for the Dark One. And if he *is* involved, then the Serpent, the Umbra, and the Temptatori are in fact under the *influence* of something not of K'Tara. But no one knows for certain yet that the Dark One has returned."

Elyana paused and then repeated, "But we are not weaklings, Aithen, although it is a fact that our Order is much smaller than it once was, and that the loss in numbers has caused a certain loss in skills."

Aithen added, "And you don't have the Luxori to fight alongside you, as during the Dark Battle, although the Umbra seems to think there exist at least two."

"Indeed, no Luxori to help, despite the Umbra's statement. Honestly, I do not know what the Umbra was referring to; perhaps to male Alterintrants – and your father is one – but they do not have the powers, the skills that the Luxori had."

Elyana continued, "Regardless, we can defend ourselves and fight, Aithen. And, thanks to Afanasiia Lux Baiula's discovery during the early years of the Dark Battle, the Sisterhood has been able to conserve much of the knowledge that was acquired during those years, and that will serve us well against these creatures, if they are indeed linked to the Founder."

Hearing that, Aithen felt the same sense of wonderment he did every time Elyana spoke of Memory Transfer. In fact, the thought that these women could carry in their minds the memories of generations of Sisters gave Lux Baiulae an aura of immortality that inspired fear and respect in plebeians and monarchs equally.

Elyana added with great – and perhaps misplaced – conviction, "Anyway, whether our enemy is of this world or not makes no difference. Here, we are all subject to the same laws of physics, and we can work with that."

But the prince did not share that conviction and said, "I guess." After a moment of silence, the prince said urgently, "Elyana, we need to find my father and warn him. I know the Serpent and Umbra named no names, but we cannot take the chance it is him they are after."

With a sigh and a grim look on her face, Elyana replied, "I agree. I will try again tonight to locate the king through the Bind."

"I don't like this, Elyana. I don't like the thought of you going back into the Bind, tonight. Can't you let other Sisters do it? What if the Serpent and Umbra find you in there? You will not escape again!"

Before she could answer, Elyana jerked with alarm. She released the Sound Shield and ran to the opening of the tent. When she pulled the door flaps apart, Aithen's guardians stood at attention. Across from the tent, Elyana saw Lusk Methrim talking to a sergeant as the man inspected the camp. She followed the visitor with her eyes for a few moments. She was sure the Zebulonian had noticed her, but the man continued his chat with the sergeant as the latter inspected a soldier's armor and made a comment about a rust stain. Elyana bit her lip and turned to reenter the tent. As she did so, she noticed the guardians looking at each other, holding back knowing smiles, but they stiffened, embarrassed, when they realized the Lux Baiula was glaring at them.

As Elyana reentered Aithen's tent, he said, "Master Methrim?"

Elyana replied, "The Zebulonian," as she came to a resolution and added, "Aithen, please have your guardians bring him to my tent. I will go there immediately." But before she did, she straightened her dress and then looked around for a mirror to fix her hair. When Elyana turned to Aithen to ask if he had a mirror, the prince responded promptly that he did, then suggested hesitantly that she could enter his private quarter to use it. Elyana thanked him, grateful that she would not be forced to show herself to the entire camp in her present condition after coming out of the prince's tent.

When Elyana came out of Aithen's sleeping quarter, she appeared refreshed and her hair, although not perfectly set, looked as it usually did – from far. Aithen remarked on it, and then informed her that the Zebulonian would be brought to her tent in ten minutes. Elyana thanked the prince for his help and left to ready herself for the visitor.

As he watched Elyana leave, Aithen felt an intense pain wash through his body. He even had to grab the tent flaps to keep from falling backwards. It was a good thing his guardians hadn't seen him wobble that way; they were watching the Lux Baiula leave, as they always did, probably wondering how such power and beauty could be found in one person. Not wanting to risk anyone seeing this temporary weakness, the prince pulled the tent flaps closed, and rested a few more moments before calling in the guardians to instruct them to not disturb him or let anyone in until further notice.

The guardians saluted, stepped out, and Aithen went to his bed to try and rest for an hour.

***

Elyana sat at her desk, a simple, polished table with a few drawers, not too heavy but sturdy enough to sustain the harshness of travel and – most importantly – to provide for a stable writing surface. While she waited for the visitor, Elyana went through everything she knew about the man: he had the looks of a Zebulonian, which he claimed to be; he was apparently a healer, but she had not been able to ascertain that yet; and he had apparently been one of the persecuted, back in Zebulonia, and was ready to sell his services to House Coriolis.

"Elyana Lux Baiula?"

Elyana stood as she replied "Yes?", expecting that the stranger had arrived.

"This is High Captain Harlion. May I enter?"

"Of course, Captain, come in."

Harlion entered with a worried look on his face, stopped at the entrance.

"What is it Captain? You have not brought the Zebulonian."

"No, not yet. He cannot be found, but I have sent two soldiers to look for him. I am here because three guardians have been found irresponsive in their tents. My guardian and medic apprentice Peter has seen them, but he is unable to diagnose their condition, let alone bring them to."

Harlion couldn't tell whether the Lux Baiula was annoyed or troubled by that, but she shook her head before saying with a slightly accusatory tone, "You know I am not a healer, Captain. But I will come see these men."

"Thank you, Lux Baiula. If I had known our trip to Horn's Pass was going turn out the way it did, I *would* have brought a full medic along. Anyway, the unit's sergeant waits outside to tell you what he knows."

"Very well, let us go, Captain."

As they stepped out, the Blue Sun blinded Harlion and Elyana. It was just above the horizon now, facing Elyana's tent. Its intense, bluish rays heated up the young summer day; this was the time of day K'Tarans hated the most because they had no choice but to be active during the overly hot mornings if they wanted to accomplish anything given that the Bolingars already took away a few hours out of each day during which no one could be outdoors. On the other hand, everyone enjoyed the one fourth during each month when the Red sun hid its blue twin and made the days much more tolerable, from dawn till dusk.

Sergeant Leon saluted his commander and gave a respectful nod to the Lux Baiula who immediately questioned him about his *sleeping* men. The sergeant gave a description of his men's activities and meal the night before, and of the condition in which he found them at sunrise.

One thing only alarmed Elyana – the guardians had shared a few drinks with the visitor. They had listened to his stories, and later told him of their nightmares since Horn's Pass.

Elyana said, "Sergeant, lead the way. I need to see your men at once."

With his commander's nod, Sergeant Leon turned and took the group to his men's quarters, passing in front of a row of carts where women were getting breakfast ready. Upon seeing Elyana, many women gave a heartfelt smile and a respectful nod before continuing with their tasks, while others still looked at her with some diffidence.

150

Elyana replied to the first with a smile of her own and gave the others a half nod.

***

The Lux Baiula, High Captain, and sergeant were met by a group of curious guardians standing in front of the tents where their bewitched comrades were still "*sleeping*". Harlion waved the curious away, sending them to back to their morning chores with a growl. Once the area was cleared, he asked Elyana to follow him into one of a dozen tents in the vicinity and ordered sergeant Leon to *keep* the curious away.

Peter, the apprentice medic guardian, was sitting next to the bed with a mystified look on his face. He did not immediately notice the entrance of his commander with the Lux Baiula. When Harlion grunted, the young soldier began to curse, but when he turned his head and saw who stood there, he shut up at once, saluted his commander and nodded to the Lux Baiula, embarrassed. He then apologized unendingly for the inappropriate language.

Harlion stopped him and said, "You are forgiven guardian. Now, how is your comrade?"

"Jurr is as we found 'im, Captain. Like Grael and Loke. Only a poison or venom, or some other substance anyway, could have put 'em in this state, but I can't find any evidence of any such substances having entered their bodies." Peter paused, and after a short silence added, "This is very frustrating, Captain. My skills are of no use here!"

The soldier's tone creased the high captain's forehead, but before he could reply, Elyana said, "I would not be so hard on myself, if I were you, guardian. I know for a fact that what you can do, you do really well. I have no idea whether I will be any more successful than you have been at diagnosing your comrades' condition, but I will try. And if I cannot help, I will contact one of my Sisters of the White Sashate."

"Yes, Lux Baiula. It's just frustrating to not even have an idea about what is affecting 'em."

Elyana gave the medic apprentice an understanding nod and then took his place on the chair next to the bed. The unconscious guardian – a man in his late teens as far as Elyana could tell – lay perfectly still on his cot, with a peaceful expression on his stubbled face.

151

Elyana leaned over and began palpating him. She was not a medic herself, and always felt somewhat apprehensive when she needed to examine a person. But she knew enough to do a basic examination, and to perform basic emergency healing when necessary, although she would not be able to rule out a disease or disorder if she found nothing. This often worried her more than finding something which she could at least alleviate.

The palpations did not reveal anything unusual on the surface: no new wounds, no infection on the old wounds, and no puncture that might indicate an insect's bite. Whatever caused the soldier to enter this state of torpor did not enter his body via his skin – of this, she could be fairly certain. So, Elyana started probing the young soldier with the Bind. She did not detect any unusual molecule in the young man's bloodstream, nor anything unusual with his metabolism – though it was particularly slow, which would make sense given his comatose state. Next, she probed the microbial flora on his external and internal surfaces. All she could do here, was to send focused vibrations on them and watch for their response. Something did seem to be off with his flora, but she couldn't say what was wrong exactly; she just knew the microbes in the guardian's guts responded to her probing with vibrations she had never felt before. But, given that she had not experienced all the various types of microbes that can exist on or in a person, she knew she might be mistaken. Still, she took a mental note of the finding and moved on to the guardian's brain, the last organ she had decided to probe.

Harlion watched with a preoccupied look on his still firm but aging face, a face which showed some alarm every time the Lux Baiula lingered over one part of the man's body or another.

Examining a person's brain had always been a much easier task for Elyana, than examining any other organ. Indeed, her senses were simply more attuned to the brain's vibrations, and this trait was perhaps what made her such a formidable political advisor; she could easily sense a person's state of mind and even without knowing their thoughts, she could determine their likely decision before they even voiced it.

As she probed the guardian's brain, Elyana's visual cortex painted an image upon which it displayed the vibrations she felt. And the image her brain now displayed was undoubtedly a confused one, with constantly shifting colors. She also perceived, in the soldier's brain, a subtle conflict between the regions controlling emotions and those controlling reasoning; this could be caused by a person fighting a compulsion of some sort. And then she felt something she did not expect to find in the man's brain: a set of vibrations which were strangely similar to those she had felt in the Zebulonian. But she couldn't be certain, given that she had only successfully probed the visitor once, and from a distance. So, she made another mental note to compare these vibrations to those of the Zebulonian when she had another chance.

Elyana lingered in the soldier's brain for a while, debating whether to probe his thoughts. But he was unconscious, and he had not given her permission to do that, so she rejected the idea. Watching the man's brain fight who knew what, Elyana wished she had better medical skills to help him; it bothered her to see him suffer. She thought *Perhaps, I can help him calm down – douse his mind with soothing vibrations which will clear the fog and help him recover his senses. After all, he is not ill. I could be wrong, but I don't think he is. I could calm him, the same way I calmed Aithen when he lost control in the Bind, though I won't need to rush this time.*

Just as Elyana prepared to still the guardian's mind, she felt a vibration indicative of consciousness reach her. Needless to say, that surprised her, but she focused, then sent a probing, gentle vibration to the brain's seat of consciousness and confirmed that the soldier was indeed awakening.

Elyana disconnected from the man at once, and when she opened her eyes, she saw him open his own eyes and look at her with a confused but pleased look.

Elyana said, "Well, it appears I wasn't needed after all, guardian."

Behind the Lux Baiula, the high captain asked, "What happened?"

Elyana looked from the soldier to the captain and raised her shoulders, uncertain what to say.

With both his captain and the Lux Baiula looking at him puzzled, the soldier sat-up abruptly and asked, "Captain, why are you here? Why is the Lux Baiula here?"

Harlion replied, "You mean to say you have no idea what happened to you, soldier? Why you wake only when First Light has come and gone?"

Neither Harlion nor Elyana could get a straight answer as to what had happened to the guardian. But the man did mention that he, his comrades, and their sergeant listened to the stranger's tales the night before, and that he and his comrades told him about the nightmares they'd been having since Horn's Pass, nightmares which the guardian suddenly realized had not visited him this past night. In fact, he felt good, really good, except for the slight feeling of confusion.

The other two soldiers both told the same story when they woke, which they did shortly after the first. Elyana probed them anyway, in case she was lucky and found a clue that might explain what happened to them, but alas. She did, however, sense those same vibrations she had felt in the Zebulonian. She took note again and decided that she would force the visitor to submit to a probe.

High Captain Harlion ordered his apprentice medic to keep an eye on the men, and to alert him if the guardians started exhibiting any unusual behaviors. He then departed with Elyana, shaking his head every so often, while the Lux Baiula decided on a strategy to obtain the Zebulonian's consent to be probed.

***

Elyana was pacing in her tent when she felt the Zebulonian approach. *He's coming, not very anxious; not anxious at all, in fact. I wish I had had another moment to prepare for this meeting, but this will have to do.*

A guardian cleared his throat at the tent's entrance. Elyana called him in. The soldier stepped in and said, "'m sorry Ma'am Lux Baiula. The man you asked to see –"

"Master Methrim? I know, Jonal. You may let him in."

The soldier was one who often did errands involving the Sister, and as he did every time, he realized the woman already knew what he was going to say, and reacted with the usual embarrassment as he turned to his comrade and motioned him to bring the man in.

Master Methrim's expression was neither expectant, nor curious as he entered the tent. Today, he was clad in a pale green tunic, tied with a red belt. He also wore high, black leathered shoes with pointed toes such as would be worn by nobility. Very strange, thought Elyana.

The man said with great formality, a slight nod and a small smile, "Lady Lux Baiula."

He certainly has a strangely pleasant figure, just as Aithen remarked. But why does it irritate me? And these vibrations I sense from him – why do they make me feel so...odd?

Elyana did not acknowledge the man's formality and simply said, "Master Methrim. Please sit down," pointing to the chair across from her desk. The man acquiesced with another smile and sat down with legs crossed and hands clasped on his lap.

Elyana said, "Master Methrim, I need your assistance with something," to which Lusk responded with what looked like genuine interest. "I need a healer to help me take care of the dozens of villagers who are still suffering as a result of the attack on Horn's Pass."

The man replied, "I would be honored to help, Lux Baiula," as he started to get up to thank her. But Elyana motioned him to sit back down, then moved to her desk, turned the chair around and stood against it with hands crossed in front of herself.

There they go again, these conflicting sensations. Why do I keep getting them, even though nothing else about him troubles me?

Elyana put her questions aside and continued with her plan. She asked, "What ointments do you have with you that may be useful to treat deep cuts and burns?"

"Oh, I have quite a variety of ointments in my saddlebag, many of which are unknown to Alvinorian healers, but are well regarded in Zebulonia."

"And one or more of them can treat deep cuts and wounds?"

"Yes, Lady Lux Baiula. I have a salve made from the salivary glands of an insect found only in the western part of Zebulonia, and which has incredibly strong regenerative properties. When applied to a day-old wound, it helps regenerate the lacerated skin without creating a single scar. It is known as *velnia*."

"Hmm, very interesting. And does it require the use of the Bind at all to maximize its effect?"

"No, not at all."

155

"That is a powerful extract indeed. It would be interesting to compare results with some of our own methods."

"Do you have such an ointment as well? I have not yet seen any since my arrival in Alvinor."

"Upper Alvinorian healers use a slug to heal the wound. The slug keeps scars from forming by continuously digesting the hardening tissues as the skin restores itself. After a day, the injury is healed without even a blemish. But I do not have any here, and I do not have the energy to heal every wound using the Bind. So, I would welcome other effective and *approvable* treatments – if you have them."

Lusk responded with an affirmative and eager nod, and went on to describe other ointments, poultices and treatments he thought might be useful.

Elyana questioned him every so often and appeared satisfied by the end of the exchange that Master Methrim was indeed a healer, and highly knowledgeable at that. She thought: *This is all good, but I still need to find out what really brought him here...and why I keep sensing these conflicting vibrations.* Elyana debated whether to start questioning him to ascertain the reason for his presence here or whether to find out about his abilities in the Bind. She looked at him, sitting there quietly, and decided to go for the latter. *I really wish we had a registry of all Alterintrants in the kingdom because I'm not the best at assessing another's connection to the Bind. But, hopefully my years of experience in politics will help me judge the truth of his answers.* Elyana said, "Tell me Master Methrim, I can tell you are an Alterintrant – unless I am mistaken."

But Lux Baiulae do not make mistakes, Lady Lux Baiula. So, you must hope that if I intend to be dishonest and do not know that Sisters are supposed to be infallible, I will lie about my skills. But I do not need to lie, Sister. And, in a tone mixing pride with intentional anxiety, Lusk replied, "I am."

Elyana nodded. He was being honest and that was good, though it was not sufficient. *Maybe you are a trustworthy man. Now, what skill do you have?* "Most healers are Sensors, while a smaller proportion are Binders, but I cannot tell which you are. I can sense the Bind's concentration in you, but it is of an unfamiliar signature which I cannot ascribe to either skill."

Lusk Methrim continued to reply with the same caution. "I assume it is because we harbor a very particular microbial flora; a flora which we also supplement with certain elements of K'Tara for their beneficial properties. This particular combination of microbes and inert matter operates to modulate our vibrations in a manner very different from the way it happens in Humans and Kynarians. It also makes Zebulonian healers impervious to almost any infection known on K'Tara. But in response to your question, Lady Lux Baiula, I am a Binder."

Elyana nodded thoughtfully. *A Binder, therefore one with the ability to harm or influence others if he chose to – yet, something makes me want to trust him. But don't I trust him already, to ask him to help heal the Horn's Passers?* "This particular combination of microbes and inert matter you mentioned; it would be very interesting to hear more about it, and to learn the ways in which Zebulonian Alterintrants use their microbial flora to access and use the Bind."

Lusk replied with some alarm, saying, "Please, pardon me my Lady, but that knowledge is something the Healers' Knowing Circle does not share."

"But you are a citizen of Alvinoria now. Surely, you do not owe allegiance to Zebulonia or to its institutions anymore, especially given the fact that you offered your services to the high prince – or was I misinformed?"

"You were not misinformed, Lady Lux Baiula – I did offer my services to the Crown. But the high prince has not yet accepted, and it is not certain the high king will. As for my allegiance, I still owe it to the guild that trained me."

Elyana grunted and finally asked the question she had been wanting to pose, "And why do you wish to serve the Alvinorian Crown, Master Methrim? You are a healer, not a diplomat."

"Honestly, Lady Lux Baiula, it *is* for a selfish reason. There is a very real possibility that Queen Zebula will march against Alvinoria, and I do *not* wish to see Zebulonian ways enacted here and lose what I have gained since I escaped the kingdom."

"The high prince has shared with me and the high captain what you have told him about the condition of men in Zebulonia, and I can see how you might choose to do as you have."

Elyana let the conversation stop for a moment and observed the visitor's gestures and expressions; nothing in his demeanor indicated that he was deceiving her. She tapped her fingers together for another

157

moment then said, "Going back to my earlier request; you must realize that before the king or prince accept your offer of services, you will need to share with us what you know about Zebulonia, which will include what you know about Zebulonian Alterintrants."

"I understand, Lady Lux Baiula, and I will consider your request."

Again, those odd vibrations, and now they seem to be causing the release of bonding hormones in my brain. "Very well, Master Methrim. Onto another topic, then. The High Lord Commander and I have noticed that the men seem to enjoy your company, and that some even trust you enough to take you along as they inspect the camp."

Master Methrim flinched a little at that hidden accusation, but said, "Indeed, they do enjoy my company, Lady Lux Baiula. All soldiers enjoy stories from far away, from places they have never seen. Some because they like to imagine the exotic, others because they like the sense of awe or fear they derive from the descriptions one may give of these places. As for trusting me, not as many do as enjoy my company, but when you can make a man laugh an honest laugh, he is likelier than not to want to trust you, as did Sergeant Ovris this morning."

"That is good; the men went through hell two days ago, and I am glad they have someone to distract them and to help them forget that infernal night."

With a nod and a smile, Lusk replied, "I am happy to be of service, Lady Lux Baiula."

Elyana thought: *I wish I could believe him. My reason tells me that I might not want to, but somehow, what feels like my instincts, tells me to trust him. Still, I must question him about the vibrations I felt in the guardians. If he caused their loss of consciousness, I must know it.* She said out loud with a serious look on her face, "There is one thing which concerns me, Master Methrim. Three guardians were found unconscious this morning, in the grip of some sort of coma." Elyana paused to watch for the stranger's reaction, and a reaction did manifest – Lusk looked mortified.

"My Lady Lux Baiula, were these three soldiers named Grael, Jurr, and Loke?"

Elyana nodded with a frown.

Lusk shook his head looking down, and said mostly to himself, "The Head Weave I gave them must have been too strong." Then, looking up at Elyana, he added with a contrite look, "I am sorry Lux Baiula. I have not performed such a Binding on Alvinorians before, and I fear I may have done more harm than good."

Elyana clenched her jaw, to keep herself from screaming at the man. How did Master Lusk manage to weasel out of her grip again and looking verily innocent while doing it?! And what was this *head weave* he mentioned? But Elyana dulled her anger, relaxed her jaw and said, "Well, fortunately for you, Master Methrim, they have awoken through no doing of mine just a little bit ago. But you should *not* have taken such liberties as you have."

Looking thoroughly regretful – and strangely attractive in his vulnerability – Lusk apologized again. Elyana expected some excuse from the man, but he did not give any, and this impressed her despite herself. So, she asked, "And what made you think you could take it upon yourself to treat our guardians?"

"Nothing, except my oath to care for and to protect sentient life."

"Yes, the Healer's Oath; it seems to be one of the few universal constants. Nevertheless, you were not given permission to treat members of the Royal Guard." Elyana thought: *This is my chance,* and she said, "If you wish to use your abilities in the Bind to heal our guardians, I will need to ascertain you are qualified to do so, which means that my Sisters will need to test your Binding abilities."

"My pardon my Lady Lux Baiula, but the fact that I was Master Healer in Lord Brando's court should be proof enough of my qualifications to practice the art."

"To treat plebeians, your position with Lord Brando certainly qualifies you, but none can treat the Royal Guardians unless permitted to do so by the Head Medica of our Order in Furan City. In extreme cases, High Captain Harlion, the high prince, or I may provide the release."

It appears I will have to submit to your probing after all. No matter, it might require some effort, but I can sustain it without giving away anything I do not wish to share. "Very well, then. If I must, I will submit to your testing."

"Thank you, Master Methrim. Of course, this means that you are *no longer* to treat any guardian until you are released to do so, regardless of your oath. You may, however, treat any civilian that requires medical care, if it is within your capacity to help."

"I understand, Lady Lux Baiula, and I will abide by your rules."

X AITHEN'S RETURN TO FURAN CITY

On the eleventh day of travel around noon, the caravan finally approached Alvinor's capital. They had made it to the city as planned, thanks to High Captain Harlion's efficient command. The journey *had* been hard, with the carts bouncing on the stony pavement all the days long, causing the adults' backs to ache, and children to complain and fight with each other as the excitement of the journey wore off.

But despite the fatigue, almost every Horn's Passer gaped as they laid eyes on the towers and walls of the great city – the oldest and grandest city of K'Tara. Some even believed it to be the birth site of the first humanoid, whose skull was enshrined in the Temple of Aiala and revered as a link to the Founders. In fact, some claimed the clerics actually conversed with the Founders via the First's skull.

Children, in particular, stared in awe, mesmerized by what they thought were gigantic Rattler[41] tails in the middle of the city, shooting toward the sky. Some asked their parents if those were indeed Rattlers tails, and they looked deeply disappointed when their parents told them that the things were in fact towers built to resemble the tails of the animals – just as the Rattle Formations, which they had come through on the third day of their journey though their resemblance with Rattler tails was the result of natural processes.

Other people were praying, thanking Aiala'Rhi for allowing them to reach the safety of the city. When a sweet smell – carried by a warm breeze blowing over the caravan – reached the kids, their voices and gestures became suddenly and newly excited, and the adults turned to each other and to their kids with smiles just as wide. It was the smell of the Sea of Tarkoth, located just beyond the capital, that had so enraptured them. Many, especially the children, had never smelled the sea, though the coast was only a day's march from

---

[41] Rattler: A large herbivore found throughout Lower Alvinor. The males of the species had very long tails made of a great number of empty, bony circular sections. The males rattled their tails to intimidate their predators, and when these continued to press them, they used their tails as whips to ward-off the attackers.

Horn's Pass; all they knew were the fragrance of the pines growing on the slopes of the Furan Peaks, and the dry, rocky smell of the Pass. Adults could be seen taking in deep, soothing breaths, while children screamed with excitement upon learning what was the cause of the wonderful breeze.

Sadly, the sweet smell of the Sea of Tarkoth did not excite Elyana as much as it did others. The Lux Baiula was exhausted and her mind filled with worries. Indeed, since that night in the Bind with Aithen, she had barely slept, and the Zebulonian, riding just behind her, did not cease to trouble her despite all appearances that he was a refined, well-educated and well-intentioned man, and despite some unexplainable compulsion she was moved by to trust him.

The civilians in the caravan had reacted with the usual fear and prejudices when they first saw the strange-looking healer, but most of them had eventually learned to ignore him. The soldiers, on the other hand, had happily welcomed him, perhaps through Aithen's and Elyana's own fault. Indeed, she and the prince had – for some reason she could not understand – removed the restrictions they had initially placed on the man's movements and on his fraternizing with the guardians. Every night, he had sat around the cooking fire of one group of soldiers or another, and told them stories of lands far away, and of the strange things he had seen during his travels. The guardians had obviously enjoyed his stories and company despite his strangeness and had even argued with each other when the sequence of his visits was disrupted by one night's storms.

Other soldiers, having heard that the Zebulonian had expelled the nightmares of three of their comrades, had hoped that he could do the same for them. But, to their great disappointment, they promptly learned that the healer had been forbidden from treating any more guardians until he was released to do so by the Sisterhood, and not a small number of guardians had been caught silently cursing the Lux Baiula. This had deeply disturbed Elyana as well as the prince and his captain.

Elyana had also spent much time mulling over the very unusual vibrations she had sensed in the Zebulonian, wondering why she could no longer sense them, and she was frustrated by the lack of answers. She worried too about the unwelcome attraction she felt for the man, and she had worked hard to crush it, but alas; the longer she interacted with the stranger, the more the attraction grew, albeit more

162

slowly than it might have in another woman. Still, it did, and Elyana was very concerned that the attraction was beginning to show outwardly, such as occurred one evening, when the Zebulonian had asked to join the prince and her around their fire. The man told them about the majesty of the Mountains of the Sagr, and his telling had been so vivid, that Elyana had felt her pulse speed up and her breath catch at one point. She was sure Aithen had noticed when she saw a question and veiled concern in his eyes, and she had nearly flogged herself for it in her tent, later that night.

But what preoccupied Elyana most of all, as they approached Furan City, was what they had heard the Serpent and its associate tell each other regarding the Lux Baiulae, the Kynarians and two Luxori. Regarding the two former, it was urgent that the Magna Mater warn everyone, both within the Order of Light and in Kynaria, as soon as she got confirmation of the threat.

Regarding the threat to the latter, all Elyana knew for certain was that there was a slight *possibility* that the king was indeed one of the two men the Serpent and Umbra had referred to. Indeed, Octavius was an Alterintrant, but he was no Luxor. And there was another – an outcast who had been banished long ago – who also had had some powers in the Bind. Aside from them, there was a third male Alterintrant serving as a medic apprentice in Urbs Lucis. But he had only the weakest Sensing abilities with no Binding skills at all. How could the Umbra be referring to any of them? Nevertheless, it *was* possible that the king was one of the enemy's targets, and so it was urgent that he be found and brought back to the capital.

Moreover, even without this possible threat against the king, one threat was very real and certain: if the king did not soon return to Furan City, rumors about his absence would start appearing, rumors which would spell trouble for Aithen, for the kingdom, and even for the Sisterhood. The patriciate would start accusing each other, the high prince or the Sisterhood of having removed him in a bid for power. Even the kingdom's subjects might become alarmed, thinking that perhaps their king had abandoned them for safer pastures, and with everything else happening, this was not the time for such turmoil.

Elyana's final worry was for herself. Indeed, she had not yet recovered her ability to sense the presence that other Sisters were sensing. She had hoped that being connected to the Magna Mater would enable her to regain her talent that night in the Bind, but it had not helped. Granted, she wasn't a Yellow, and she did not have their sensitivity to the varied biological and physical vibrations which existed. Yet, she remained worried because she did have many abilities beyond those of her own Sash, and it was because of it that a great number of Sisters believed she would be the next Magna Mater. What if the diminishment of her Sensing abilities was permanent? What if she began losing her Binding abilities as well? That had happened to other Sisters in the past – not often, but it had. This and her other worries rumbled in her mind as the caravan approached the capital.

All worries put aside, there *was* one thing which did bring Elyana some comfort. It was the fact that Krystiana – despite her puzzlement as to why Elyana had let her shield down inside the Serpent – had accepted Elyana's error as an error not to be explored any further, a potentially grave one for sure, but an error nonetheless. Had the Magna Mater insisted on a valid explanation, Elyana would have had to reveal to her superior that she had been shielding the high prince within herself, and face certain, unavoidable, and severe consequences. Yes, there was one thing to be relieved about.

As for Aithen, he felt himself smile as they approached the capital, his family's home, but the smile quickly faded as thoughts of the meetings and decisions to come invaded his mind, as did the memory of the communication he received two days back telling him that Toras's company was making a detour to defend a coastal village against a possible attack by the Serpent, and of a communication Elyana received from Merina Lux Baiula which told of a most ghastly discovery in said coastal village a few days after Toras's detour.

Merina had found a horrible scene of death in Galior, the kind of which neither she nor her Melinorian watchmen had ever before witnessed. Everything was burned or destroyed. Not a single building stood, no streets could be seen under the mass of rubble, and when Humans and animals were found, all that remained of them were corpses with faces locked in expressions of the worst fears and terror, and an oppressive stench of death.

The search party was apparently deeply unsettled by the scene, and they stood around, dumbfounded, for a while. Some had obviously had family or friends in the village, a fact which grated on

Merina who believed that guardians should never be posted in or near their places of birth. In any case, Merina eventually pulled the guardians out of their stupor and the party made their way to the village's safeplace in the hope that they would find at least one person alive there.

As luck would have it, the search party found the survivors and four Black Guardians sheltered in the safeplace, a well-hidden cave in the nearby woods.

One of the Black Guardians introduced Merina to the village's mayor-wife who told her of the arrival of a crazed rokon the night before, and of how it started killing every living thing in the village. Harima, the mayor-wife, said her husband quickly realized that he would not be able to keep his people safe, so he sent her to the safeplace with all the women, children and elders while the men tried to protect the village.

Harima told Merina how she heard the cries of a large number of furans approaching the village not long after reaching the safeplace. It meant that their messenger had been successful and had come back with help. The woman told Merina that she got out of the shelter after making certain no one would follow, and then ran to the edge of the woods to be sure help had come. As she approached the clearing she saw her village engulfed in flames. She wanted to cry, but by the light of the fire, she saw ten to twenty furanteams descending at once upon the wicked creature, and she regained some hope.

Harima told Merina how despair set back-in like a knife in her heart when the rokon brought down the first two furanteams, and then another…and another. Merina had watched the Black Guardians – who had been sitting not far from them while the mayor-wife told her story – grit their teeth and shake their heads every so often. The mayor-wife said that the battle did not last an hour, though she couldn't be sure with the town clock destroyed along with the rest of the village. She knew that the creature had won when the sky grew silent, except for the rokon's victorious screeches and the sound of its enormous, slow-beating wings over the trees under which she was hiding. Then she heard nothing more except for her own sobs, or the collapse of another home or barn in the distance.

Harima said she had wanted to run down at once, to look for her husband, but she remembered her people, and ran to them. The women and elders argued for a while about whether they should all go back to the village or just send the three oldest kids to see whether there were any survivors. The rokon had left anyway, and they could not think of a reason for it to come back. One woman argued that they could not think of a reason for it to have come here in the first place, either, so how could they be sure it wouldn't come back? But the majority chose to go back, and so they did, hoping against hope that they would find their loved ones alive.

When the group stepped into the fields that spread in front of what was once their village, they saw over a dozen furanteams take to the air and leave. They did not know whether to feel joy or distress at that. If soldiers lived, then perhaps their husbands and sons did too. But as they entered the destruction, desperation took them all, and mothers and children renewed their screams and cries. The dead they found in the streets were lying on the ground as if they had simply fallen over, their faces constricted in terror.

Harima too thought she had lost everything until, on the southern side of the village, she finally came upon some survivors: four soldiers, their furans, and a few of the village's men. The soldiers were tending to the wounded, as was one of the villagers. Incredibly, there was her husband, looking haggard and bruised but otherwise unharmed. The mayor told his wife that all were dead except these few here and the soldiers who left earlier, and that were it not for the guardians, none of the native defenders would have been left alive. He told her how ten soldiers and furans also died in the fight, and how these four had been left behind by their leader, Lord Toras himself, to help. The prince had also promised to send additional soldiers to help rebuild the village, along with a medic to make sure the injured received the care they needed.

This is what Aithen had read in Merina's letter, which was overly detailed, but all the more horrifying for the descriptiveness of the facts. Now, Aithen recalled the nausea he had felt upon reading the letter. Elyana had tried to give him courage, reminding him that Toras was one of the survivors, but Aithen had simply exploded in anger at reading of his brother's continued foolishness. Sure, he saved some people, but at what cost? What had made him believe he could confront the Serpent with the few men he had with him? Eventually, he realized he was being foolish, and that his brother had done the only thing he could have done, as a protector of the people.

Aithen shook the grim thoughts out of his mind and noticed that the caravan was now only a hundred meters or so from the city. He raised his right hand, and High Captain Harlion immediately roared a loud "All stop!" at the top of his lungs. His command was repeated all the way to the back, about two kilometers from the front of the caravan. The sound of all the people whoaing their vorans or bellowers to stop, along with the sound of the animals themselves and that of the furanteams landing, was truly deafening. The vorans trumpeted, and the bellowers bellowed, while the furans roared with the anticipation of returning to their comfortable stalls, and especially with that of seeing their mates.

For indeed, because furans had a fairly low reproductive rate, a large proportion of the Guard's steeds were allowed to mate to keep the Furanry replenished. And because, like the majority of K'Taran vertebrate species, furans were sequential hermaphrodites – meaning that individuals switched between the male and female form at periodic intervals or according to environmental conditions – the Guard had to keep twice as many furans as there were soldiers to ensure that there would always be sufficient males to serve as steeds given that partners did not convert in perfect synchrony, and a male could switch to the female form and prepare itself for pregnancy before its partner had switched to the male form. An individual could be prevented from becoming a female by removing an organ known as the verta, but to do so to the males of an entire herd was harmful to their mates who would be forced to remain in their female form indefinitely, a condition which brought them premature ageing and death. Therefore, only the royal family's steeds were deverted [42], as was case for Xyre and Scorch.

When the guardians' furans began roaring, their calls were heard far and wide, and in every corner of the large city people jumped at the sudden sound. Some Furanites became excited, remembering that the high prince was due back, while others mumbled curses, remembering that the high prince was returning with Horn's Pass' refugees.

Now, a young officer in charge of the guardians at Triumph's Gate came out of the city atop his voran, rubbing his ears with

---

[42] Deverted: An animal whose verta was removed to prevent the metamorphosis from male to female.

exaggerated motions and a grimace. A few meters from the prince, the officer stopped, saluted him as well as the high captain with a long nod, and welcomed them as well as Elyana back to the capital. He then gave a suspicious look to the man sitting atop a voran behind the prince, but he did not say anything, and turned his attention back to the prince.

"Leftenant Edrick."

"Yes, High Lord Commander?"

With a playful reprimand, the prince said, "I'm glad you weren't here when the furans roared, or I might have ended up with a deaf gate keeper."

Feeling a little embarrassed by his attempt at humor, the officer apologized to the prince, but Aithen replied with an honest smile and asked about the state of the capital.

The leftenant said, "It's well, my Prince, although the population became agitated after hearing of the rokon's attack on Horn's Pass. But the Senatorial Police were able to restore calm." With a sneer, the young officer added, "This, despite the claims by some preachers of the Order of Aiala that the attack on Horn's Pass is a sign of endtimes coming."

Aithen's and Elyana's brows knit themselves with deep annoyance. Aithen shook his head in frustration; yet another problem he might have to deal with. Where was his father?!

"Leftenant, please assist High Captain Harlion in taking care of the refugees."

The officer looked at the long caravan, straightened his back, and nodded.

Aithen then turned to Harlion and said, "High Captain, please see to it that everyone is lodged and fed, as needed. Also, please have someone take Master Methrim to the Senatorial Police so he may be registered there, and then have your soldiers take him to the Guest House."

Harlion made a simple nod and was about to motion his voran to step away when Elyana stayed him with a subtle motion of her hand.

Harlion stopped, and Elyana said aloud, "High Captain, I have a favor to ask of you." Then, stepping closer to him she added in a hushed voice, "I need you to assign someone discreet to keep an eye on the movements of our guest. Have your agent report to me first should he see anything unusual."

Harlion responded aloud and with an intentionally cheerful tone, "Certainly, Lux Baiula. It will be my pleasure."

Elyana smiled and the captain moved to do as ordered.

Aithen now turned to the Zebulonian who looked at him suspiciously. He said, "Master Methrim, you will need to be registered with the Senatorial Police; but do not worry, it is our customary procedure for foreigners. You will then be taken to the Guest House, and from there you will be free to do as you will until you are needed, so long as you inform posted guardians of your whereabouts."

The man still looked a little doubtful, but he nodded his understanding and thanked the prince for his courtesy.

Aithen shouted another command to his High Captain as the latter moved his voran toward the Gate Officer. "High Captain, go to your family once you are done taking care of the refugees, and give my salutations to your wife and son. I will see you in my rooms in the morning."

"Yes, my Lord. Till tomorrow then." Harlion signaled his voran to move with a determined tap and approached the young leftenant, anxious to get everyone inside and be back with his family.

Just as the two men started talking, Aithen called the young officer to give him one last order. "Leftenant, please send someone to advise First Senator Leo of my arrival, and to request that he assemble the elders for a meeting in the Senate Chamber around Four after Highsun this afternoon."

The man gave the prince a nod, and Aithen turned away from his High Captain and Gate Officer. He then got down from his voran and went to brush his wide muzzle with affection. The voran pulled his head back, and gave short, repeated trumpets marking his impatience to return to his stable. Aithen said in gentle tones, "Yes, yes. I know what you want, Magnus. Just be a little more patient; I will have Kil take you back because there is something else *I* want do to." The destrier responded with a short uncertain snort as Aithen called Kil.

Kil, who had been riding just a couple of rows back, was there at once. Aithen handed him the reins to his voran, and instructed him to give Magnus a bath before bringing him to his stall. Magnus gave another excited snort. Kil saluted the prince from atop his own voran, a mid-sized, tan animal, and then left with the beautiful Magnus, struggling a little to slow his pace.

Satisfied that things were being taken care of, Aithen gave a low, almost imperceptible whistle. Xyre came down but a moment later, landing just a few steps from Aithen, and lifting copious amounts of dust in the process, which brought fits of cough to everyone nearby, Aithen and Elyana included. Aithen let out a curse, but Xyre didn't seem to care and continued to approach his master with the purr typical of black furans – a deep, loud, and slow purr. When Xyre reached him, Aithen received him with a playful caress. He then turned to the Lux Baiula and said, "Elyana, I assume you will want to go to Domus Lucis to consult with the other Sisters?"

Elyana started patting down her dress with annoyed motions before she replied, "Indeed, after I change into something cleaner, my Prince." She then gave the furan and his master a stern look.

Aithen replied with a good-natured laugh, "Sorry for that, Elyana. I really *do* need to teach him to land further away."

A "*hrr*" was all the reply Elyana gave.

Aithen smiled and said, "Very well, I will see you around nine? So that we may dine and plan for tomorrow?"

Aithen got another "*hrr*", after which Elyana kicked her mare to a canter and quickly disappeared beyond the city gate.

Watching Elyana go, Aithen thought, *Founders! How I like it when she gets that way. Tonight...perhaps...at dinner, I can tell her how she makes me feel. But* – Aithen stopped himself right in his tracks, angry for continuously letting his thoughts stray in that manner.

He shook his head and looked up at the sky. Suddenly, he remembered what he wanted to do; it was a beautiful day, and he looked forward to spending some time alone by the sea, for an hour or two. But first, he would go to his quarters and see his little brother to reassure him. Then, he'd have some nice food and drink, something different from the bland root bread and halami [43] he had

---

[43] The halami was a drink made from the juices of a plump, sweet, round fruit, in which large, leather-winged insects were drowned. This process decomposed the internal flesh of the insect, extracting special nutrients from the insect, and protecting the drink from spoilage during long trips.

had the last few days, and finally be off to the sea to dive in its refreshing waters.

So, Aithen climbed on Xyre, tapped his flanks, and the animal took him to the north wing of the castle, the wing reserved to the high prince and Royal Guard.

***

"Aunt, have you heard the news that just arrived on carrierback from Elyana Lux Baiula?"

"I have, Aria. I meant to call you, but I'm glad you are here now. Our informants did tell us of something terrible happening in Aquinos a few days ago, but no more than that."

"What will you do? You can't leave Aithen on his own to take care of the hundreds from Horn's Pass, while he also worries about the king and Toras."

Darya repressed a desire to admonish her niece for her insinuations. "I know, Aria, I know. But before I can go, the situation must be discussed with the Grand Council."

Aria made a grimace. "You mean 'the situation must be discussed *by* the Grand Council, who will then decide what a mother may or may not do in the present situation.'"

Darya resisted the urge to glare at her niece and told herself the girl was still too young to see the truth of things beyond her senses. Instead, she said with the greatest patience, "You know that our rules are in place to aid us in making the best possible decisions, Aria, especially when matters of national or international importance are concerned."

"I know aunt, but in this case, the rules are just –" Aria paused, searching for the right word, and when she couldn't she simply blurted, "inappropriate!"

The high king's consort shook her head in despair. "Aria, you are almost ready for your Passage, and you cannot go on letting your emotions have the better of you. You will *not* convince me to change my mind by reacting this way, but you *will* cause the Council to question your readiness if they should hear of your cavalier rejection of the rules at this point of your training."

Aria did not look down as Lady Darya reprimanded her. Instead, she looked her aunt straight in the eye, gritting her teeth.

171

Darya sighed. "I *know* your reason can see the value of our rules, even if your sentiments whisper rebellious thoughts. And I understand your feelings for Aithen, although I disapprove of them. But even if I approved, I would still disapprove of your reaction. The greater good is what must drive a Kynarian priestess at all times, not personal motives." As she said that, Darya fought her own anxiety and fears, as well as her desire to do exactly as her young, foolish niece suggested.

Aria gave her aunt an exasperated look and said, "I do not have any such feelings for Aithen, anymore, Aunt. You must know that Larad, Lord Kilio's son, and I have been courting for a few months, now."

Darya blinked in surprise then said, "Very good. All the more reason, then, for your concern to be focused on your own family, so long as it does not conflict with your duty to the Order. You know your brothers and father depend on your gaining your first Ear Notch to ensure your family's continued prominence within the Union Council, and you are fully aware of what your father has done to gain your admittance to the school. Do you now reject your duty to them?"

Aria looked down, resignation plain in her posture. Her aunt was right. Her family's continued fortune, given her brothers' disinterest in politics, trade *or* finance did depend on her because *she* did have an interest in those things. But because "ordinary" women held little power in Terrae Regis, her father had recommended to his daughter – after negotiating her admittance with the Supreme Priestess – that she go to Kynaria to become a priestess of the Order. As a member of the Order, she would eventually be able to move into a position of authority given her interests in politics and finance, and this could be greatly advantageous to her family. Indeed, with her by his side, her father would have direct ties to the Kynarian Order which controlled all trade, finance, health and education in Kynaria – the Kynarian civilian government administering only civic works in the nation. This would open the doors to the commercial activities of the rich nation of Kynaria.

So it was that on her fifteenth birthday, Aria left her family to go to Kynaria to become a Kynarian priestess. She did have her aunt there, who – because of her status as a Highborn of Kynaria – was required to spend most of her time there rather than in Alvinor with her husband. But Aria was often unsure whether having her aunt there pleased her or not. Indeed, Darya always seemed more concerned with rules and propriety than with caring for those who relied or depended on her, even her own sons, though she did seem to really love her husband, High King Octavius who was Aria's blood uncle.

Darya took in a long, deep breath. She knew her niece too well, and worried about her readiness for Passage. Aria often reacted impulsively to events which affected those she cared about, and she was prone to show her anger no matter where she was. Her training as a Kynarian priestess should have taught her some measure of self-control, but Darya knew that whatever control the girl seemed to have, it was just an illusion. In a year, when she reached twenty, Aria would have to pass the test: a grueling ordeal meant to see what she had learned and determine her limits. If she passed, she would then be assigned a role within the Order of Kynaria.

Presently, there was a knock on the door. Darya said, "Who is it?"

"It's Lania, my Lady."

Lady Darya called the woman in. An old Kynarian entered. She had a round, plump face, and was dressed in the green robe of her class – a junior neo, despite her advanced age – with black lace around her right arm.

Lania made a deep curtsy and told the royal consort that the Supreme Priestess had just called an extraordinary meeting and requested her presence.

This obviously startled both aunt and niece and strengthened their belief that something horrible was happening on the continent. Lady Darya replied she would come presently and left her niece with instructions not to leave her chambers. Aria agreed begrudgingly, and her aunt followed the old student.

***

"Aithen!"

Aithen felt a wonderful sense of joy when he saw his little brother in the hallway. He truly loved Ori, perhaps because he saw himself in him so much. At thirteen, the young prince was already so aware of the world, so perceptive and logical, but he was also filled with joy and with a love of life that even he, Aithen, had never felt. In fact, this is what he loved the most about the boy. When Ori arrived, he opened his arms wide and hugged him for a good minute.

When Aithen released him, Ori rushed to explain how impatient he'd been. He said, "Tania Lux Baiula told me you'd be here soon. I've been going round and round my chamber all morning waiting for you – and for Elyana. Is she here too?"

He does like Elyana too, a lot actually. I wonder if he would be jealous or happy if he knew my feelings for her. "Yes, she is, Ori. She will be here later."

"And what about Toras, and Father?"

Aithen had expected the question, but he had found no good way to tell Ori how things were, and now, he berated himself for it. Still, he forced himself to give his little brother as honest an answer as he could give. He said, "Well, Toras is…on his way to Father. I'm sure they'll be here soon. But they'll be coming back from Spiritii, so it will take them a while."

"What's wrong, Aithen? Why do you have that look on your face?"

"Nothing. Well, something, but we don't know for certain yet, what may be happening. Hopefully nothing, but we don't know. I'm sorry, Ori. You were so excited to see me and now I've ruined it. But I'm certain Father and Toras will be here soon, so you can pester *them* with your questions when they return."

The diversion seemed to have worked and Aithen felt guilty for it. Ori said, "It's okay, Aithen. I *am* happy to see you. But you just look worried now. Are you going to tell me about everything that's happened in Horn's Pass, and why all the Horn's Passers came here?"

"I will. Promise. Later tonight, though?"

"Okay."

Aithen gave his young brother another hug, sent him away, and returned to his rooms.

***

When Elyana entered the city, she left her voran with the gate guard and promptly re-immersed herself in the daily buzz of the capital's streets, a buzz that got louder and louder as she moved away from the main artery. Here, people were going about their business of selling, haggling, and buying, with bleaters blaring and cacklers squawking in terror every time one was caught to be killed and handed over to a customer. All of this sounded like a cacophony to anyone unaccustomed to it. To others, it was the sound of the next good meal. The smells permeating the butchering lanes were sometimes overwhelming with their mix of manure, sweat, meat and blood. Fortunately, the Senate had decreed long ago already, that the blood spilled from animals should be captured and taken hourly to a factory outside the capital. The factory then processed the blood and sold blood pudding back to the capital as well as to the surrounding towns and villages. In addition, sweepers and washers came through twice daily to ensure the streets were clean and passable.

There were also more pleasant fragrances one could smell crossing the capital: those of the Kynarian and Yerlayan spices. These spices could fetch incredible prices, but the city's population was fairly well-to-do, and thus, the exotic, fragrant spices were found in almost every neighborhood. In the poorer neighborhoods – if they could be called poorer – more common spices were sold, which were nevertheless quite aromatic.

Just now, Elyana caught sight of her favorite shopkeeper, a fishmonger. As she approached, the man looked up a moment to acknowledge her with a broad smile and quickly returned to instructing his apprentice on the proper technique for extracting limpfish ink and pouring it into jars. Brak was the only provider of "live" ink in all of Terrae Regis. He had discovered the source of this beautiful liquid – the limpfish - some thirty years before, and he was still the only Alvinorian to hunt for the creature. Indeed, it took courage – madness some said – and very expensively outfitted vessels to reach the location where this animal was found, an area of the Sea of Tarkoth subject to the worst storms known to any humanoid, some two hundred nautical miles [44] east of Aquinos and north of Unumia. Because of the difficulties and cost, no other fisher had ever tried to reach that area, and that suited Brak just fine. The limpfish – considered a delicacy by most – earned a nice profit, and the live ink, which he supplied to various courts and administrations, made him a modestly wealthy man.

After Brak's apprentice had finished pouring the fluid into the last jar, the fisher turned to the Lux Baiula and welcomed her. The

---

[44] One nautical mile equals 1.8 kilometers or 1.15 miles.

man always had a smile on, but whenever he saw Elyana his smile widened further, and his eyes shone with delight. Indeed, he loved the woman; he loved her kind and he loved her conversation.

In his baritone voice, he said, "What can I do for you, my Great Lady?"

Elyana smiled in return and said, "Hello Brak. I am not sure, actually."

Brak blinked, surprised.

"I mean, I am not sure whether I want the ink or the limpfish. I did come for the ink, but my fare has been so dry and bland recently that the limpfish is making my mouth water as never before."

"Well, that can be easily fixed, my Lady. You can have both! I will have my son bring you the limpfish later. I can even have him cook it for you, if you wish it, although I know you do not lack for good cooks at Domus Lucis. But my son has just created a new recipe which combines limpfish and squash and it is absolutely divine. I would be honored to have you and your colleagues try it. As for the ink, I can have your usual five jars brought to you as well. We have a particularly vivid blue ink this time; it must be the best I've collected in years!"

Unable to resist the man's jovial nature, the Lux Baiula accepted his offer, but informed him that she would be having dinner with the prince tonight and asked him to send his son to the palace instead. The fisher replied with incredible excitement and an effusion of "My Lady will not be disappointed", and "The prince will thank you," and so on. When he was done, Elyana bade Brak good day, and resumed her walk toward Domus Lucis.

As she weaved her way through the throngs in the streets – which was not as difficult as it was for commoners – Elyana's mind went from one random thought to another. All the while, she took in the varied sights, smells and sounds that pervaded the city. Now, she was reminded of one extraordinary fact: that everyone in the capital had a job, trade or profession. Indeed, soon after the foundation of the city, then known as Alvinoria, the first Senate had ruled that all inhabitants, except the invalid, must have gainful employment and participate in the city's maintenance and development. If, for one reason or another, some could not find such employment, the administration would hire them to take care of the city's necessities, such as keeping it clean, tending to its gardens, repairing the roads, or processing its refuse. And the policy had been a success to this day, enabling all of the capital's inhabitants to contribute to its health – economic, structural, hygienic and otherwise – and conversely, the continued health of the city benefited its population by allowing everyone to feed themselves, and to live in clean, safe quarters. Only the rare fights and brawls that started when travelers came through with bad intentions or temperaments, or when residents simply took an argument too far, broke the general peace.

The layout of the capital had also been well planned. The main artery of the capital, Triumph Lane, led from the city's main gate to House Royal. The road, which was a good fifteen meters wide, was flanked by the city's main market on the north, and contained the Royal Plaza, located between the Temple of Aiala and House Royal, where festivities were held, and royal proclamations read. One of two major north-south roads was Imperial Lane, which crossed Furan City in front of the palace and met four other main roads running east to west. In case of need, the Guard could quickly reach any part of the city from these main roads.

Upon reaching Imperial Lane, Elyana saw the stunning walls which surrounded the city as well as the walls which enclosed the palace. Both were made of yellow ardamantis, a rock which was created by high pressure over thousands of years and came from an uninhabited island to the east of Aquinos. The walls of the city were three meters wide and had been built by the Order of Light at the end of the last age. Alterintrant masons had used a great deal of life-force to bind-fuse the blocks of ardamantis together, making the wall effectively unbreachable.

But the city's best protection assuredly derived from its surrounding landscape. Indeed, the capital was enclosed – together with the town of Antar to the west where the king had his summer palace – within what was known as the Rattle Formations. These were extensive rock formations which formed a semi-circle, a natural land barrier around the two cities. The only gaps were located to the west and to the south and were only wide enough for a couple of carts to pass side-by-side. The formations were made of thirty to forty-meter-high, closely-stacked columns of rock which resembled the tails of male Rattlers. The Rattle Formations made any land invasion impossible, allowing only for assassins and small surgical troops to attempt a strike, and these were rare events.

177

The capital was also protected from sea-based invasions or attack. Indeed, treacherous coral reefs, which spelled disaster for any ship that ventured too close, littered the northeastern coast of the continent, and only three easily defensible narrow passages led to the port of the capital.

There had been one major disadvantage to these natural barriers, however, and it was the fact that they made quick or massive sorties practically impossible. It was fine when battles were fought mainly in enemy territory, but by the fourteenth century, foreign forces had grown in size and had become a real threat, and the Coriolan kings had felt more and more constrained by the very landscape which had protected the heart of the kingdom until then. Indeed, enemy armies had posted themselves on the other side of the formations as well as beyond the coral reefs and laid easy sieges to the capital. The Alvinorians had spent the better part of the next century looking for ways to overcome that weakness. Then, in 1468, during the reign of High King Tarkian II, the secret to taming furans was discovered, and the game was completely changed for House Coriolis – and for its enemies. The discovery led to the creation of what became the most formidable armed force in all the known lands: The Coriolan Ten Thousand!

This was a force comprised of ten thousand black furans and their riders. With this force, House Coriolis achieved both defensive and offensive superiority: no one could lay siege to Alvinor any longer, and Alvinor could attack anyone it wished, whenever it wished it. As expected, House Coriolis quickly regained much of its former power and prestige. And it was at that time that the capital's name was changed from Alvinor to Furan City, and the form "Alvinoria" was coined to refer to Lower and Upper Alvinor.

But, given the relative peace in the kingdom since Tarkian the Second, the furan-mounted force had steadily shrunk in size with only three thousand teams remaining now. Notwithstanding this, it was still probably the most dangerous and effective force in all of Terrae Regis – at least Alvinorian military leaders hoped so.

A few minutes later, Elyana reached the Ministerial Road, the major north-south road crossing the city behind House Royal. The sea could be seen wide and open, and in all its beauty, from the top of the buildings that lined this road. Soon, in the middle of

Octavus [45], the citizens of Furan City would enjoy their yearly Sea Holiday, and spend a fourth going to the beach, reveling in dance and song, and swimming in the Sea of Tarkoth to celebrate its bounty.

Elyana snapped out of her reverie as she approached her destination: the impressive Domus Lucis – House of the Light, standing alone some one hundred meters to her left. With its five floors, Domus Lucis was the second tallest building in the city, taller even than the Senate building, though the latter was larger. The walls of the Sisterhood's Seat were a spectacular white, with red and blue suns at the center and top of each floor's wall, and brilliant red and blue flames streaking across each face of the structure. Ten magnificent columns adorned each side. The two innermost columns on the front of the building were fronted by statues representing the first two Special Advisors to House Coriolis. From the building's roof, one could look over the walls of the royal grounds, as well as over the city walls. Seats of the Lucis Sororum Societas were the only structures permitted to overlook the grounds of a castle within a city. The Sisterhood had been given this right by Emperor Flavius the Third, during a period of deep unrest, so that it might better help protect the Crown and its vassals.

"Hello Sister," said a young woman named Krpta as Elyana started on the wide front steps. She was one of the youngest Purples and would soon become one of the youngest administrators when her position as Secretary to Prime Lord Gorvald of West Amalor took effect. Elyana liked the girl; she was one who always smiled, no matter what, and the girl's grin put a similar smile on the faces of those she crossed, despite her strange foreign features. Indeed, Krpta was from Yerlah, a state to the southwest of Alvinoria. Like all Yerlayans, she had ash-white hair, dark eyebrows and deep blue eyes. But her jovial and confident attitude were sufficient to overcome the usual prejudice against southwestern Alvinorians, and Elyana was certain that because of it, many doors would open to the young woman that might otherwise be closed to others of her kind. Curiously, she did not smile today.

Elyana nodded and continued climbing the steps – wondering.

---

[45] Octavus: Eighth month.

"Ah! Sister, 'tis good to see you back," said another, older Lux Baiula, one whom Elyana would rather avoid now. The woman, a Yellow named Laranis, was always trying to get Elyana to join her and her followers in all kinds of idiotic psychological experiments. The woman tried to go toward Elyana, but Elyana saluted and sped up the steps as if in a hurry, causing the Yellow Sash's face to scrunch in disappointment. As Elyana reached the top of the steps, another dozen full and junior Sisters, as well as novices, came out of the main door, all frowning. Some saluted her with a deep bow, while others simply shook their heads when they saw her to warn her against what she would find inside.

What is happening here?

As she stepped onto the landing, the massive wooden doors opened on their own, retracting into the walls. She could now see inside the entrance hall, but not yet hear anything. Irania Lux Baiula was talking to several junior sisters standing around her in a semicircle, and they did not look happy – not at all. As Elyana passed through the opening, the sound of the Administrator's voice suddenly reached her ears.

"...probably don't realize how badly such mistakes can hurt us. We are supposed to be beyond reproach, *always*. Do. Not. Make. That. Mistake. Again!"

Carrain, Lopenia, Moradien, Lisandeka and Morla – all juniors – were standing around the Administrator, not looking mortified for their blunder, but rather, repressing their mutual accusations for having been caught. Elyana shook her head. *These five should never have been allowed in the Order*. Elyana stayed away, not wanting to create anymore discomfort, but Irania Lux Baiula, having felt her come in, waved her over. Elyana took a deep breath and approached the group.

"Elyana! Welcome back. Do you know what these five have done?"

Elyana shook her head.

"They were found drinking. Drinking! And not only drinking but drinking with men! Fortunately for them, they were not yet drunk, or I would have had them flogged right then and there."

The Juniors' faces flushed with resentment.

The Administrator continued, "I am sending them to my sister to learn what they should have learned a long time ago: self-respect and respect for the sash."

Elyana nodded in agreement and said, "Hum, yes, helping to purify the city's outflows will give them the time to consider the seriousness of their infractions."

The Juniors glowered at Elyana's comment, and the Lux Baiula stared back at them, her raised eyebrows seeming to ask "too low a task for you? " But the girls averted her look, except for Moradien: she never flinched, ever, and that self-confidence made her the de-facto leader of any group she joined. Last year, she became this group's leader. Given her talents, if she ever decided to take the rules seriously, she might very well become one of the most powerful Sisters.

I will need to speak to Krystiana about her – soon.

Just then, Moradien said, "This is not a fair punishment, Administrator. And do you really expect that we'll just submit to such a degrading penalty as the Field Purification [46]?"

"My dear, that statement just proves your immaturity. Acceptance of responsibility for one's mistakes is a trait of character central to our Order's stability and its continued existence. Women with such powers as ours would never be tolerated by the rulers of these lands if we did not adhere to the strictest code of conduct. Now go! Lucra Lux Baiula is waiting for you."

The Juniors' anger could be seen, seething just under the surface. It was a good thing for them that they were at least able to control their emotions; indeed, women of the Power who gave way to their anger or worse – used the Bind to hurt, received the most severe of all punishments: Unbinding. This procedure had not been developed for the treatment of women with violent emotional outbursts, but rather for women harboring dangerous microbes. But because no better treatment had been developed to treat Alterintrants with emotional excesses, the same procedure was used in their case. This treatment left the women dull, and in permanent internment at a facility known as the Observatory. Fortunately, only five Sisters were known to have suffered such a fate in the eleven-hundred years

---

[46] Purification Fields: Punishment handed-out to Sisterhood apprentices which consisted in the purification of a city's outflows.

since the Order was founded, a fact that spoke to the strength of the training and of the beliefs of the women that took on the sash.

The young women answered as one, with forced calm, "Yes, Administrator." They then bowed and, with Moradien in the lead, started toward the southeast corner of the building where Lucra's office was located, doing their best to avoid the Sister's eyes, except for Moradien who stared icily at anyone who dared look at her scornfully.

"I tell you, Elyana, I really don't understand what in Elande's name is wrong with the Committee. They don't seem to care anymore who they sash and who they don't."

Still looking at the girls, Elyana replied, "I often feel the same way, my friend." She then turned to the Administrator and said, "Well, there are some matters of high importance we need to talk about, Irania; can we have lunch in your chambers while we do so? I am starving."

"Yes, of course, Elyana, dear. I'll have the kitchen bring us something that'll restore you. This is bad business, Elyana."

"I know."

***

It was a delicious meal that Aithen's servants prepared for him, but despite that, he did not truly enjoy it. Too many thoughts kept running around in his mind. So, he ate quickly, and as soon as he was done, he got up and walked to the large balcony off his main chamber.

Xyre was there, waiting for him patiently. But when he saw the look in his master's eyes, he stood up, let out a short screech, shook his wings, and readied himself to be mounted, knowing exactly what Aithen wanted. That put an unexpected smile on Aithen's face. *I so love this animal.*

So, Aithen climbed on, put his feet in the stirrups, grabbed the reins with his left hand and the back strap with his right, and gave two quick taps under Xyre's belly. The furan extended his powerful hind legs and lifted-off at once.

It took ten minutes for Xyre to get to a section of the shore reserved to the royal family. It was wild and magnificent. The place was a large, secluded bay with a narrow pass. It had a wide beach on the southern side made of the purest white sand, while the northern

182

side of the bay was smashed with waves that sent the finest mist up the two hundred meters of the bluff, a mist which sustained a glistening colony of green, red, and purple algae, which covered the otherwise white stone.

As soon as the furan touched the ground, he let out a long, quiet purr, accompanied by an equally long and slow shiver.

"Yes, I know how much you love the sand and the water, Xyre. I know."

The furan nudged him.

"Hold on, let me remove my clothes first!"

The furan poked him again.

"All right…there! I'm ready." Aithen then went to Xyre's side and removed saddle and bridle. As soon as the tack hit the ground, Xyre sprinted for the water. Aithen roared and lunged himself forward with all his might to grab Xyre's hair and swing himself onto his back. After another few strides, the water had reached the animal's chest, and Aithen sprang off his mount and dove in headfirst, as Xyre began to swim.

The water must have been fourteen stones warm! It was never this warm this time of year; maybe eleven stones, at most. All around Aithen, there were fish and lizards. Most looked at Aithen and Xyre curiously, but others seemed to want to take a bite. The fishes' colors, which were utterly striking against the white bottom of the bay, always brought smiles to the prince.

Just now, a remarkable creature, about three meters across, swam toward Aithen. Its body was flat and shaped like a kite, with eyes on the dorsal side, but with the head bent down so that the animal might look forward. It had iridescent, dark blue skin with pitch black spots which shifted over its body in a hypnotic motion. It now looked at Aithen intently as it hovered in front of him.

Most humanoids would have frozen in place, terrorized, if they had come across such a creature. But the prince was not most humanoids, and he was not terrorized. In fact, he had always felt strangely safe in the creature's presence. Aithen had first met the Locari eleven years earlier on one of his rare escapades from his duties and studies. His explorations had taken him to the bay where he had hoped to find the mythical beings. It was then that the Locari noticed him, and brought him to their leader, the creature now swimming still in front of him. Aithen knew it as "Flowing Water" because his presence felt like a calm but strong current.

Several of the Locarus's conspecifics arrived now and placed themselves in a circle around Aithen. The Locari's leader acknowledged their presence with a rumble, after which all six of them inflated their gills to the point of tearing. They then opened their mouths and blew forth a rapidly expanding and shimmering bubble of *water within the water* around Aithen, until it enveloped him entirely.

The prince closed his eyes and entered a brief state of meditation to relax. A moment later, his eyelids separated, and he began to draw oxygen from the water. His first breath was still a little unnerving, but much less so than the first time he had experienced this.

The Locari's leader sent a thought now, or rather the image of a thought, *"Fins touch."* His lips did not move, except to maintain the flow of water within the water that allowed Aithen to breathe.

Aithen formed the response in his mind and sent, *"Fins touch, Flowing Water."*

The Locarus sent the image of a series of moons waxing and waning; it meant that many moons had passed since their last meeting.

Aithen tried to form his reply, but it was hard to find the right imagery to express his answer – even a 'yes' was difficult to form, as were most abstract concepts. Actions, on the other hand, were easier to communicate. Regardless, it always took the prince a while to relearn to communicate with the strange creatures given that he only encountered them a few times a year.

The Locarus waited patiently.

Aithen finally sent, *"There are great waves flowing against me,"* hoping to convey the idea that things had been happening in his life, which had kept him from coming back to the ocean, beginning with the revolt in Storm City eighteen months ago, and the attack on the fortress recently.

"A storm follows now," sent the Locarus.

Aithen took another longish moment before sending, *"Yes, a storm follows my people, and young and old are losing their color."* He hoped the Locarus would understand he meant to say that troubled times were coming and terrifying his people.

The Locarus's hue suddenly changed to a soft glowing orange. *"The suns will hide, and the waters cold will become. Then, to the bottom of the ocean, many will drift."*

It only took Aithen a moment to understand the Locarus's last Sending, and he tried to send back a disheartened, fear-laden *"Yes,"* though he did not know if his Sending properly conveyed his feelings.

The creature's skin shifted to a soothing dark red hue, and a soft ripple went past Aithen – perhaps the creature had understood. Just now, it sent an intense thought, *"Anew, fins will touch, Young of the Walking, when under the moon the farthest seas themselves first show."*

It meant that they would meet again, in twenty days, on the first night of the full moon, when it would be bright enough to light all the seas to the east of Aquinos. And just as quickly as he had appeared, the Locarus turned around and left with his companions, releasing the water within the water that surrounded Aithen.

The prince almost choked as he let himself start to take another breath of the now normal seawater; this still happened to him every so often. He quickly came to the surface and blew the salty water from his nose and throat. Once his airways were clear, the thought occurred to him that, even though he had come here to relax and forget about things for a while, and even though he should have enjoyed his meeting with the Locari, he now felt worse. But a large wave suddenly crashed into Aithen and pushed him back a few meters.

He looked in the direction of the source of the wave, and saw his furan break the surface with a gurgling screech – he had completely forgotten about him, but Xyre was a welcome distraction from the short, but disheartening conversation he had just had with the strange and wondrous creature. Before Aithen could say anything, another wave came crashing against him.

"All right, all right. Relax, Xyre. I'm coming."

Both turned and swam toward the narrow mouth of the bay, where Xyre liked to hunt for a particularly savory creature – according to Xyre anyways. The animal was shaped like a fish but had the soft body of a limpfish. It looked disgusting to Aithen.

Aithen alternated between underwater and surface swimming, while Xyre remained underwater the entire way, and only broke surface every so often to look back and make certain his master was still following.

Upon reaching the mouth of the bay, Aithen climbed on the rocky ledge and rested there, whereas Xyre went down again to hunt. Aithen closed his eyes and took in the smell and the sounds. They soothed him, despite his earlier troubled thoughts. When he opened his eyes to look at the vast expanse of the great ocean, they fell upon a vale breaching the surface of the water not too far off the coast, and he smiled. Vales were one of the largest leviathans – large, singing, marine animals. They usually travelled in groups, but this one seemed to be alone. Just now, it went down and disappeared for a moment, then breached again and plunged out of the water, spinning with incredible force, before it let itself fall flat onto the surface of the water, causing an incredible crashing sound.

At that moment, Xyre resurfaced, and Aithen watched him gulp down some of those repulsive creatures he enjoyed, making disgusting sounds when his beak broke through the animal's skin. But without warning, gloomy thoughts found their way back to the surface of Aithen's mind, and despite the fact this was his favorite spot in all of Terrae Regis, he dove back into the water, called Xyre, and returned to the beach.

There, Aithen sat down on the sand as he was, and went over everything once more, as Xyre continued to swim. He *needed* to understand what was going on but failed each time he tried. All he knew for certain was that things had been set in motion which would change his life – everyone's life – and his prospects for the future. Aithen punched the sand when the thought of the plans he had made, to begin wooing Elyana, broke through. He was fiercely attracted to the woman, more and more every day, and yet, how could he even think of courting her now? And in addition to his own, personal fears, Aithen needed to deal with everyone else's fears given his father's continued absence – another thing which troubled and angered him.

After a moment during which he simply stared at the variegated cliff on the other side of the bay, Aithen said aloud, "Damn it! What is the meaning of all this? Maintaining the order in the kingdom is one thing, and I can certainly manage it well; I have been doing it long enough assisting Father. But defending against things that should not exist anymore – how can I manage that? How can I even *begin* to plan our defenses?"

So went Aithen's thoughts for several minutes until something pulled him back to reality. He looked to his side, and saw Xyre standing there, looking at him with a questioning look.

"What? You're wondering why I am just staring, shaking my head and talking to myself?"

Xyre simply snorted back.

"All right," said Aithen, sighing. "Let us get back. My meeting with the Senate is coming up soon anyway."

Aithen walked over to the boulder where he had laid his clothes and put them back on. He then went to Xyre and saddled him up.

"I've been truly lucky up to now, you know. But I still have so much to learn and experience," and Elyana's beautiful face jumped at him as he said that. It made his heart skip a beat, and he shook his head to get her out of his mind.

"I just hope it doesn't all come to a premature end."

Xyre gave another snort and Aithen climbed on. After securing himself and taking the reins, he said, "All right Xyre. Fly home! I don't want the senators or landholders to wait for me, though I'd prefer not to have to meet with them at all."

The furan beat his powerful wings and was in the air a moment later. Aithen watched the bay disappear with a long sigh.

XI ON THE PLAIN

The journey since leaving Galior had been a very silent and long one. The men had no desire for pleasantries and their troubles they would not share, which meant that the only thing left to them was the silence that accompanied their permanent frowns. Several good soldiers and friends were lost during the battle against the Serpent in that forsaken village, and the memories of the Serpent's screeches and palpable foulness continued to trouble the minds of many, as well as to eat away at their courage and hope. And as if that were not enough, the weather was simply awful; it filled the days with naught else but drenching, chilly rain, a rain which brought out the biters at night and made everyone wish the whole place could just be set afire. Everyone ached from the long hours of flight each day, and some were also fighting the beginnings of a cold.

Toras only hoped that they would get out of these damned marshes soon, and that they could make it to Spiritii without any more losses. The swamps, which had already gone on for almost three-hundred and fifty kilometers along the southeastern edge of the Colossi's Peaks, and some fifty kilometers beyond the Peaks, were not known to be that extensive. The maps they had with them showed the marshes stretching for about a third of that distance and not at all beyond the mountains, but here they were, continuing on as if to purposefully add to the company's misery. Then, a couple of hours before sundown and a few kilometers from the Shadow Woods, on the fourth day of flight since Galior, the rain ceased, and the bog suddenly gave way to a beautiful, green grassy pasture splotched with all manner of brilliantly colored flowers. The men couldn't believe their eyes, and even the furans got excited at the sight of the lush grass which probably hid nibblers [47] and other small prey for them to hunt.

Toras, remembering the warnings about this place but thinking they still had a couple of hours before the suns set, decided to stop

---

[47] Nibbler: Animals ranging in size from a few centimeters to a meter long, with long, hard incisor which the animals used to eat from tough plant materials.

here an hour so the men and the furans could rest and eat something before continuing on to reach Spiritii, which was still a few hours to the southwest; he would just need to be careful and have everyone ready to take off again at the first sign of trouble. So, he lifted his arm to signal the men and directed Scorch to land with a little downward tug. As soon as the furan started to descend, the others followed. The flock, all fifteen of them, released chirpy sounds that told of their excitement.

However, as they got close to the ground, the furans became nervous and jerked. Scorch actually swerved up. Toras couldn't understand why he would do that. There did not seem to be anything to be concerned about in the grassy field which now surrounded them.

The prince knew he should trust his companion, but because he did not understand why Scorch was so nervous, he pushed him to land. The other men did the same and forced their own furans down. As soon as they touched the ground, the men stepped down from their mounts, and let out sighs of relief. The grass smelled good and the intensity of the green released their tension. But the furans wanted to take off again and pulled on the reins. Two young men got angry and yelled at their furans.

Suddenly, a man yelped. Jamir and Kendor turned to look, wondering what was happening. The man said something had just crawled on him. Then Jamir felt something on his own legs. He looked down and let out a yell as he tried to shake the insects, and screamed, "Commander, we need to leave, now!"

As soon as Secundus Jamir finished his sentence, hordes of wrigglers jumped up from the grass and latched onto the men and their mounts! The furans let out ear-shattering shrieks, and a few of them hurt their riders as they tried to shake off the insects. Scorch himself almost kicked Toras when he jumped and shook his body violently to keep off the wrigglers.

Toras, too, was assaulted by the insects, and he knew that unless they took off immediately, they would all be joining the Black Skies.

So, he calmed himself long enough to shout, "Kendor, Jamir! Order the men…aghrr." A wriggler had just about gotten into his mouth. He growled and slapped it with his hand, squishing it on his lip and chin. When he pulled it off, he released another yell as the thing's hooks tore his lip. Dozens of other wrigglers already covered his body. Every bite drew blood, and the warm fluid already covered his face, legs and arms.

Toras looked at Scorch and saw the poor animal's beak red with his own blood as he bit left and right to remove the wrigglers from his body – but they were unstoppable. Toras called to the captains again. They both looked at him with desperation in their eyes. Toras yelled, "We need to take off, now!"

Secundus Jamir did not respond – three wrigglers had attached themselves to his face and had just bitten him deeply; his eyes went wild. Kendor had several on his body and he had just ripped a handful from his scalp. He then turned toward Toras and acknowledged his command. He repeated it to his men with an angry, rough yell, but only a few soldiers heard him – the rest were in the grip of a terror greater even than the fear they had felt when facing the Serpent, and they were no longer receptive to anything other than the pain, the blood oozing from everywhere, and their terror.

When Toras, Kendor and a couple of the men finally remounted their furans and commanded them to take off, the furans responded with loud groans filled with pain, and found themselves unable to flap their wings. Toras felt his heart sink. He pulled on Scorch's reins and tried to encourage him to lift off, but his furan responded no better than the others. The steeds had even stopped fighting the insects.

Toras yelled and pleaded, "We can't die here, not like this! This is madness! Scorch, please lift off," as the realization came that he was the cause of this. Toras begged Scorch again, begged against hope. In response, the furan gave a deafening cry, and though his wings wouldn't work, he jumped up so hard that he threw Toras off his back. The prince was on the ground, and he knew his life had come to its end. He cursed at himself when he saw Scorch sway and fall to the ground.

Toras was now covered with wrigglers from head to toe, but by some miracle, he was still in control of his senses and actions. So, he got to his knees and looked up and around, wishing to know if any of his men had taken off. He did not see any furanteam in the air, but he did see three other furans falter and fall to the ground as Scorch had done, unconscious – or dead.

When another wriggler tried to pry open his lips, Toras panicked again, and just when he was about to give in to the certain knowledge that his life was at an end, a wave of intense heat blasted past him. Furans and men not already dead or unconscious were knocked out by the shock, including Toras, but not Scorch. Instead, the animal breathed a loud sigh of relief as the heat killed and desiccated the wrigglers which had bored inside his flesh. After a few minutes, the heat wave died, and an eerie calm returned to the field.

Scorch sat on the dried-up grass trying to pull out the dead wrigglers from his wounds. Every so often, he wiped his beak against the now yellowish grass. What had allowed Scorch to resist the intense heat that had knocked everyone else out was the result of a Healing he had received after being struck by lightning just a few months after Toras had first tamed him – the lightning strike that had scorched his back and drawn a permanently hairless pattern in the shape of the electric discharge amidst his thick back fur, and for which Toras had thus renamed him.

Just now, Scorch looked to the right and saw his master lying on the ground unconscious. He got up and groaned from the pain he felt in his muscles. He shook his entire body as vigorously as he could to try and dowse the pain. That seemed to have worked, for now, and he went to Toras and started licking his face with his raspy tongue.

The sustained licking woke Toras's wounds and reignited the pain, causing the prince to come to his senses abruptly and Scorch to pull back in response.

The prince felt dizzy and his vision was blurry and dark, but when his sight sharpened, and he saw Scorch above him, he shouted his name with the greatest relief.

Toras looked at himself urgently and realized that there were no more wrigglers crawling on him, and that those that had buried into his flesh had fallen off for the most part. The bleeding had also stopped. An urgent thought occurred to him, and he said to Scorch, "The men!" He feared that none might answer if he called their names, but he did anyway, starting with his first officer.

Primus Kendor responded with a hoarse voice, followed by Secundus Jamir who waved a hand. Two other soldiers did the same, and Toras shouted their names, elated to see that more than a few had survived and hopeful that all may have. Toras laughed with cautious relief, then got up despite the pain and went to check on the men, starting with Kendor.

When he reached his captain, he was comforted to see the man grin the way he always did after a good fight, though this hadn't been one. In fact, this was a tragedy, and it was Toras's own doing. But Kendor did not seem to resent him for it – at least, not yet. Toras helped him up.

Toras said, "Primus, I'm glad to see you don't look too bad." The man had three deep gouges running on the left side of his face, and smaller ones on the right, as well as wounds on his arms and legs, some of which contained dead wrigglers. Toras winced as he tried to imagine how he himself must look. These were not the typical battle wounds, for sure, and unless a medic could heal everyone completely, the scars would be a permanent reminder of his stupidity.

Kendor said, "You don't look so bad either, my Lord. But I have to say I'm surprised we're alive."

Toras looked down as he replied, "Yeah, I guess none of us will ever forget this day. I know I won't; I'm the cause of it."

Kendor frowned at that and put a hand on the prince's shoulder and called him by his name, a thing he had done only once before in the years since serving under the prince. He said, "Now, Toras. Don't go blaming yourself. I could have objected to the descent, as could have Secundus Jamir. But neither of us did because the heat and the exhaustion of the last fourth dulled all our senses." Kendor paused, considering a thought, then added, "And it also seems to me that the peace of the last few years has made us complacent, and that we are in fact no longer prepared for this type of intense, continued stress."

Kendor continued as another thought surfaced, "In fact, given the likelihood that things will only get worse – what with the Serpent and the Dark One, and who knows what else – it wouldn't be a bad idea to re-institute wartime training practices. You should speak to your brother about it."

Toras nodded reluctantly, knowing his captain was right about their unpreparedness, but he disagreed with relinquishing blame for his decisions; when he directed the company to land, his mind had been clear, and fully aware of the risk – or so he had thought.

Taking a deep breath to straighten his shoulders, Toras said, "Thank you Kendor. You are right – about some of it."

Kendor's frown deepened, but he did not say anything. He knew the prince, and understood it was pointless to argue with him about certain things.

Toras said, "Anyway, are you able to walk? I see you're favoring your left leg."

Kendor winced as he put his weight on it, but said, "Stepper did fall on me, but I'll be all right, Commander."

Toras nodded and said, "In that case, would you check on Jamir?" Then, pointing to a spot some twenty meters away from where groaning sounds were coming, "As well as on the men over there?"

"Be glad to, Commander."

And Toras went in the opposite direction. His heart sank when he came upon the three soldiers he had seen fall earlier. They were dead. Two were on their backs, both Royal Guardians, but he could not recognize them due to their disfiguration. Indeed, their lips and noses were eaten away. Toras's stomach lurched, and he forced the vomit back down. *Damn!*

The third man was lying face-down and wore the uniform of his own Guard. Toras turned him around, slowly, fearing to see who it was. This time, the chime reached into his mouth and burned his throat, as if angry at being pushed back down the first time. If he had been another man, no effort could have held down the vomit, but he was not any other man, and Toras swallowed his bile.

From Kendor's direction there came an angry, "Damned things, damned things!" Toras looked but knew he couldn't help and returned his attention to the body in front of him. Though the flesh on the right half of his face was gone, the left was miraculously intact, and Toras recognized the body as that of young Larad; he knew his parents. He was a good fellow and a good friend to his cousin. More really – or could have been but would no longer be. Larad had actually started courting Aria a few months back while she was on leave from her studies in Kynaria. Toras's chest contracted and he pushed back a tear with a groan. He was going to have to tell Aria of Larad's death, as well as his parents, and although he should normally secure the body's return as was customary for nobility, he decided that it was probably best not to do that this time.

Tears wanted to flow, and Toras had to fight to keep them back. A man in his position could not be weak, he always thought, although he did not yet realize that his constant rage was also a sign of weakness that made his men wonder at times whether they should be following him. Aloud, Toras said, "I can't leave him like this," and he got out his dagger, cut a long piece of cloth from the young man's shirt, and used it to wrap his face. Then, he pounded the ground with both fists – his jaw clenched so he wouldn't yell – and pulverized some desiccated wrigglers. At that moment, he wasn't sure whether he was angrier with the vile insects or with himself.

After striking the ground once more, Toras got up to continue his search, hoping to find more survivors. As he stood, he had a sudden, unexpected feeling, the feeling of a thing he knew, recognized. But he shook his head, thinking he must be hallucinating. It was the feeling he had when he thought of his father or when he "heard" his father call to him, even though the king might have been somewhere else entirely. Again, he felt the tug on his mind, and again he ignored it. The third time, however, he felt an irresistible need to turn his head. So, he did, and looked westward, and a scream of joy erupted from him! It *was* his father's presence he had felt!

The men turned around, and looked with fear, wondering if their commander had lost it. Kendor called his name, but Toras did not hear. Then he saw the prince run toward – toward a man standing next to a voran. Battle! What was the king doing there?

When Toras reached him, the king grabbed his son by the shoulders at once and embraced him.

The men shouted with one voice, "It's the king! The high king!" Those too wounded to get up and look responded with questions and shouts of joy, as well.

The king said, "Toras, I must admit that I have never been as afraid for your life as I was when I saw you here, assailed by wrigglers. They are merciless creatures and it doesn't take them long to bring down man or beast, no matter the size."

As if to confirm the king's words, Toras looked at his multiple wounds and felt the ones on his face. The scars these wounds would soon form would probably remain forever, he thought, as a constant reminder of his foolishness. *And it's just as well.* With some shock in his voice, he said to the king, "So I've gathered, Father." Then, after a swallow, he added, "We all have – those of us who survived."

And Toras shook his head grimly as he said, "I was sure this was it for me."

The king looked at him with a question but did not ask it now.

Toras said, "But, what are you doing here, and where is your guard?"

"My guard is on the other side of the forest."

Toras gave the king an incredulous look and asked, "Why aren't they with you?!"

"I had some business to attend to in which they could take no part, so I ordered them to wait for me at the camp."

Toras's eyes widened again. He did not say anything this time, but he did shake his head.

The king continued, "Anyway, after I concluded my business for the day, I decided to go look for a rare species of carnivorous plants which is supposed to grow by a stream not far from here, when I heard the distant shrieks of furans. Since there are no wild furans in these parts, I suspected the shrieks must be coming from Royal Furans and I turned Battle in this direction. It did not take long before I heard the first screams and I knew then that whoever had come must have raised the wrigglers. I had to help, and so I came."

"How would you have helped? They would have attacked you too."

"I know, but as I approached the edge of the forest, I was sure I heard your voice; you were yelling at Scorch, begging him to take off again. I knew your lives were in danger...so I pressed Battle on to reach you before it was too late, but the wrigglers began to assail us too – as you can see, we have our own scars – so I dropped down and did what I had to do."

"What do you mean you did what you had to do?"

"I mean, I did what I had to do to save us."

"Father, please!"

Octavius looked down and shook his head, knowing that he was going to have to tell his son something he should have told all of them a long time ago. "I am sorry Toras; I mean *I exterminated* those loathsome things."

"What?" Toras's expression was one of total confusion. He did not know if he should laugh or be shocked by such an absurd statement coming from his father – the king. "What do you mean you got rid of the wrigglers? There was an incredibly intense heat that came from this direction, and I thought that some Lux Baiula must have arrived and decided to help us. You're saying that heat came from…from you?"

The king waited a moment, as if considering his options, and then, appearing to have made a decision, laid it all out for his son. "The atomic constitution that enables Lux Baiulae and Kynarians to call the Bind is not exclusive to them, Toras. However, there are very few males, nowadays, who have the proper constitution to do so." Octavius took a short pause, breathed deeply, then said, "I am one of those very few."

Toras stood there utterly shocked, unable to say a word. He looked around, wondering if his father was taking credit for the workings of some hidden Lux Baiula. But no, the king was serious. How could it be? He was a Sensor, yes, Toras knew that, but a Binder?

"It is not something I have ever disclosed or made known before for the simple fact that most people see such abilities as unnatural, and if they knew I possess them, they would fear me rather than respect me or love me, as strange as that might seem. I, myself, have never felt comfortable with my Binding abilities. You see, the only things people want from their monarch are wisdom, goodness and leadership, or, as our forefathers put it, *"Magnus rex sapiens, bonus, et praestans dux esse.* [48]There is no room here for magic or what many consider unnatural abilities, despite the fact that these very powers have helped and continue to help people live healthier lives, and thwart dangers too great for swords or arrows to dispatch."

Toras was dumbstruck, and he continued to stand there, feeling numb. The soldiers, who were waiting for a sign from their commander to approach, watched and wondered what was happening, when finally, they heard the prince burst out in anger. "And you've never told me this?!" The king gave his son a look that immediately tempered his anger. Toras lowered his voice, but it was still filled with anger, and he said, "How could you? Really, Father, how could you hide this for over twenty years? Does anyone else know? Does Aithen know? Mother? Ori?!"

"Mother does, and Aithen suspects it. I am sorry son, but certain things were better left untold. I would have told you all but given

---

[48] A great king is wise, good, and an outstanding leader.

how I felt about such abilities in a king, I preferred to not encourage Aithen who will one day succeed me. As for you, your temperament and the difficulty you had in controlling yourself convinced me to keep the knowledge from you, to prevent you from even *trying* to develop these abilities for which…you in fact *have* the constitution."

Toras was bewildered beyond expression. He wanted to scream, to curse at his father, and looked up to do just that. And then he saw what looked like pain and shame in Octavius's eyes, and he stilled himself, exhaling loudly through his nose, and shaking his head. As his pulse slowed, he became aware of his men looking at them, and he said to his father, in a quieter voice, "You could have told –, you *should* have told Aithen and me, Father. You should have told all three of us."

"You may be right, Toras. I do not deny it. But! we are king and prince first, and we will therefore need to continue this discussion at a more appropriate time, because we must see to our men's needs now."

Toras agreed with a jerky nod, but not before the king promised to continue the discussion.

The crisis having passed, the king now asked, "But tell me, Toras, why are you here?"

"What? Father, a beast – apparently the Serpent of our myths – attacked Horn's Pass and is now attacking villages throughout Lower Alvinor! That is why we came to find you."

The king felt dazed, as if he had been hit on the head with the butt of a great sword. He put his hand to his forehead and said to himself, "So that is what I felt seven days ago. How is this possible?"

Octavius looked at his son and said, "Toras, I need you to tell me everything. But not now. First, we *must* see to your men."

Yes, my men and Aithen's men, thought Toras grimly. His jaw tightened with mounting anger when images of Larad's face popped in his mind.

The king said, "Kendor is approaching; I haven't seen the man in a long time." Toras didn't hear, wrapped up as he was in the deep disappointment he felt toward himself for his bad decisions.

Kendor walked toward them, doing his best to appear unaware of the earlier argument between father and son. Just now, Octavius looked at the old soldier and waved him forward, repressing an expression of disgust at the sight of the man's wounds.

"My King. It is good to see you; our quest is finally over."

"It is likewise good to see *you*, Primus Kendor."

That took Toras out of his stupor, and he nodded to his man. He exchanged a furtive look with him to ease his concerns, aware that he had been too loud and had probably alarmed the guardians, then said, "How many dead, Primus?"

"Six, my Lord."

Toras shook his head. His father gave a quiet curse, and Toras looked down momentarily. He felt ashamed, ashamed of another wrong-headed decision. *You were right not to trust me with knowledge of the Bind, seeing all the senseless mistakes I keep making.*

When Toras looked back up, he asked Kendor, "What about the rest of the men? Will they be able to fly back? In fact, how many furans survived?"

Kendor replied with a pessimistic look. "Four men are severally wounded, one being Secundus Jamir, and without the help of a medic or a healer, they won't survive long. The other four are well enough though scarred as badly as we are. Two of these are the Falirin brothers – two very strongly built fellows. I could send one of them to Spiritii to bring back a town healer or the Sisterhood's medic, if there is one. As for the furans, eight live, including Scorch."

Toras kicked the scorched grass and cursed a while, either castigating himself, or blaming the Founders for their predicament. Neither Kendor, nor Octavius disagreed with his sentiment, though they had different ideas about where the fault lay.

After his latest fit of rage had passed, Toras sent Kendor to order one of the brothers to Spiritii, to get help. He then turned to the king, deflated.

The king thought it best to avoid further talk of what happened here or why, and said, "Toras, let us help the wounded. As for the dead – men and furans alike – we will return their matter to the earth, unless there are any who need to be returned to their families."

Toras shook his head, thinking of Larad, then both he and his father marched toward the survivors whom Kendor had brought together, despite his injured leg. Toras glanced at his father every so often, wondering whether he would use the Bind to help heal the men. If he had the power, he should, shouldn't he? But would he, even if he could? Toras knew he was being silly; his father was an honorable man, and he would do what was necessary, even if it meant disguising his actions.

XII EVENTS IN KYNARIA

The meeting on the day of the arrival of the carrier had been quite frustrating. Nothing had been decided except that more talks needed to be had before making a final decision on whether to send a delegation to Furan City.

Lady Darya and Aria had spent the whole night talking and venting their frustration – yes, Darya too had felt frustrated on that day, despite all her "rationality".

Now, sitting cross-legged on her bed, Aria was re-reading a message she had just received from one of her friends in Furan City.

-*Dear Aria, I was quite pleased to receive your letter today. It had been too long since I last heard from you. You've certainly been too busy since you moved to Kynaria. In any case, things have been really tense over here, in the city, since the rokon attack on Horn's Pass eight days ago. A good many men died in that attack. I heard your cousin Loris was one of them – you do know, right? It's so sad. I can't imagine how you're feeling.*

People are wondering whether this rokon is a foreboding of bad times coming back; some say that maybe there's a drought in the Unknown lands and that rokons are coming to Aquinos to find food, and that no one will be safe anymore, not animals, not people. Others think that the Founders are angry and have sent this rokon to exact punishment, but no one agrees on the fault we might have committed. The priests of the Order of Aiala are scaring the peasants and city dwellers into observance, telling everyone to do away with their impure ways, to go to the Temple, and to pay homage to Aiala'Rhi if they want this evil to go away. The priests of the Order of Elando are doing the same with their own followers, but with less fanaticism.

And as if that weren't enough, we're also to host the whole of Horn's Pass here. Your cousin, High Prince Aithen, sent word of it a few days ago, and the Senate is expecting the caravan of a thousand or so men, women, and children any time now. I have no idea how we will absorb all these people and feed them all. What's for sure is the city's citizens won't be happy to be invaded by so many peasants – that's how they think of them, rather than as just people needing help.

Anyway, many are also wondering where the High King might be. They say your uncle must not care much for his people to stay away during such a time. As far as the Lux Baiulae are concerned, they are also wondering what is going on and are very angered by the King being so completely out of touch and out of sight. Some are suggesting that he should not be allowed to leave the City again unless accompanied by a Lux Baiula. I just hope he comes back soon. And if you hear from him, do let him know we need him back, urgently. I know he loves you very much and might listen to you.

Well, I need to get back to my studies now. I am reading a book on the Battle of the Sea of Irsis.

Love, Laren

Things are bad out there. And we're stuck here! As soon as I get my first ear notch, I'm leaving. I'll ask for an assignment in Furan City, and if not there then in Melinor, but I'm not staying here to rot, that's for sure, regardless of Father's wishes.

As the girl got up from the bed, remembering her appointment with Headmistress Delora, a tear came down her white cheek. *Loris...why did you have to be there? You didn't need to be there!*

Aria was pulled out of her thoughts by the sudden knock on the door. She wiped her tear and went to the door to open it. Carasina was standing there, with her hands on her hips. The young woman was a chubby, jovial creature, with bright blue, oval eyes and a complexion the color of pure, fresh brown cream. Carasina was slightly older than Aria, but nevertheless deferred to her friend in all things except when it came to her studies.

"Aria! I've been waiting for you for a few minutes now. If we don't go now, we'll be in serious trouble; you know Headmistress Delora does not tolerate tardiness, and she especially won't tolerate it today." Then, noticing the wetness on her friend's face, Carasina asked, "Are you okay?"

"What? Yes, I'm so sorry. I was just...oh, never mind, I'll tell you later. Let me put on my slippers."

Aria and Carasina started toward the school, walking as fast as they could without appearing to do so.

The trip from the private quarters to the school was not a very long one, but it did involve climbing a fairly steep staircase. The landscape here was just as breathtaking as anywhere else in Solinor. The whole capital was built on a series of five ridges, or hills, overlooking the fantastic Bay of Lardos, possibly the grandest place on K'Tara. The Kynarian Ruling Seat was located on the

202

northernmost ridge, known as First Seat Hill. This ridge comprised the private residence of the Ruler – Ylana Marin Dar'Muntake; the Civilian Council's Chamber; and Aiala'Rhi's Chamber. The School of Kynaria, along with the students' and the faculty's residences were situated on Second Seat Hill, clockwise from First Seat Hill. Various administrative offices were located on Third Seat Hill, and the fourth and fifth ridges were home to the civilians and were known as just that, Fourth and Fifth Ridges.

As they approached the school, they looked at the time disc on the left of the main building and saw that they were just on time. They took a moment to adjust their dresses and went in. The school's hall was majestic. There were statues all around, representing famous Headmasters and Headmistresses. The most striking one was that of Headmaster Adolphus. The eyes were large; the hair was long and wavy as that of a plebeian, to the contrary of the hair on all the other statues, which was short – the accepted style for Kynarians in high positions. But Adolphus had definitely not been the typical Headmaster.

The girls went up the large staircase to the second floor. Carasina's heart skipped several beats when she saw the door to Headmistress Delora's office already closed. She shot a desperate look to her friend, but Aria roller her eyes and proceeded to knock on the door.

The door responded with a loud echoing sound that projected through the hallway. People at both ends of the lobby turned around to look, wondering who was going to get a lesson in punctuality from the headmistress. When they saw the two girls, many shook their heads wondering why the girls insisted on finding trouble, while others – Arias's and Carasina's peers – snickered at the thought of the punishment that was coming to the two friends. Carasina fidgeted and shrunk, while Aria shot arrows at her peers.

The princess said, "I'm certain the door's wood has been intentionally selected for its echoing properties, just to embarrass people."

Carasina responded with an exasperated grunt.

After another long minute of irritating – or fretful – waiting, the door finally opened, and the girls were greeted by an annoyed headmistress's assistant.

"Come in," she said in a curt tone.

Aria and Carasina entered, one nervous, the other maintaining her appearance.

"Follow me."

Aria and Carasina looked at each other and went.

The Headmistress's office was awe-inspiring. Walls were painted with scenes depicting the various skills of Kynarian clerics: control of vegetation, control of sentient life, purification of water, and Beast Reading. In one scene, a priestess was portrayed causing a flock of flyers to execute the most unusual aerial dance; in another, a priest was directing thousands of aquilians at an invading army. There were also beautiful cages dispersed through the large office containing specimens of the most stunning flyers on K'Tara. Strangely, none sang or chirped, but simply groomed themselves or flitted around their cages to change position every so often.

"Headmistress, here are the girls."

Aria and Carasina bowed. The Headmistress was sitting at her desk – another beautiful piece of furniture in this striking room.

Without looking at them, the woman stated with a deceitfully beautiful southern Kynarian accent, "You girls are late." Aria and Carasina were about to reply but the Headmistress preempted them, adding, "I do not want explanations. You will know your punishment when we are done with our discussion." The headmistress stared at them with an unreadable look.

Carasina put her head down in a sign of acceptance and resignation. She hoped Aria would do likewise, but instead the girl kept her head high with only the slightest forward bend.

"Aria, your punishment will be double."

Aria was about to scream, but she repressed her anger and forced herself to show some humility this time, enough not to cause Headmistress Delora to quadruple her punishment.

"Much better," the woman added. Headmistress Delora was not a tall woman, but she was sturdily built, with legs like short and stocky posts, and arms equally thick; her square head was blanketed by straight thick hair, loosely tied on her nape; her clothes were starched to the point of looking like heavy tablecloth. She was the total opposite of the beauty which permeated the office, and her sternness and appearance were in complete contrast to her beautiful accent.

"Tomorrow will be the commencement of your final year of training as senior neos. This should be your most exciting year yet, but, know that it will be no easy journey. You will be tried like never before; you will be challenged with the most demanding works yet, and you will be pushed to face *all* your demons and fears – at least the ones we know of. If you overcome all the challenges presented to you, then and only then will you be allowed to test for your Passage to priesthood."

Aria and her friend didn't know what to make of this. They certainly had not expected such a declaration when they accepted the appointment with Headmistress Delora the day before. Now, they regarded each other with anxious looks. They knew that what the seniors said about the last year being an easy one wasn't true, but they did not expect it to be as demanding as Headmistress Delora was making it to be.

Aria asked herself how she was going to dedicate so much time to her final year of study with what was going on in her uncle's realm. And what if the rokon attacked her city next?

"...to the gardens where Magistera Annan will begin to train you in Beast Reading. Aria! Are you listening?"

Aria's hesitation was barely noticeable. She was good at hearing things even when focusing elsewhere or distracted. "Yes, of course, Headmistress. We will go to the gardens to begin our Beast Reading training."

The headmistress grunted. "Very well. Now, your punishments. Since it appears you have a problem with arriving on time, you will both report to the Great Hall at Five Hours after Highnight for the next month starting tomorrow. There, you will help prepare and serve the morning meal for the senior neos class."

The girls were horrified. *Serving their peers?!* They would be the laughing stock of the class. How could she do this to them?! But despite how humiliating this was even to her, Carasina prayed that her friend would not make things worse. And fortunately, for once, Aria controlled herself.

All the two girls gave in reply was a "Yes, Headmistress."

"That is good. As for you, Aria, you will also help clean-up the hall. And since that will make you late to your first class in the morning, I would expect another penalty from Magister Callain. But

I will speak with him this afternoon and ask that he be lenient given the circumstances."

Aria was seething inside. *I hate her! I hate this woman! How can she do this to me? I'm the niece of the Lady Darya and High King Octavius! And she knows very well that Magister Callain will not give a hoot about the reasons for my tardiness. This is not a double punishment, it's a triple punishment! But I will have my revenge someday, I don't care who she is.*

***

"Ah, Lady Darya, please sit down."

"Thank you, Honored One."

The Head of the Order of Kynaria was a tall woman, even when sitting. Supreme Priestess Ylana Maryn Dar'Muntake had brown skin and long graying hair with striking, orange-colored eyes. Her face was just as striking with sharp edges to her jaw and cheek bones, and a pointed chin. Overall, she was an imposing woman. She had also one of the sharpest minds in Kynaria.

Ylana asked, "How are you doing?"

"My health is good, but I am worried."

"Hum, I too am worried about a great many things and about one in particular."

"My husband," said Darya.

"Indeed. The king. He has been missing for many days now, too many, especially given the circumstances in his lands. I doubt anything untoward has happened to him or we would have known, but it is nevertheless worrisome that he should remain out of touch and out of sight at all. I should think you would know his whereabouts."

"I...I am uncertain," replied Darya. She was feeling extremely uncomfortable, sitting there to be questioned about her husband's doings by her Order's Head.

The king had told her he would be travelling incognito to Spiritii for a few fourths to attend to some business he had in the southern province, but he could tell her no more. Darya had asked several times to know the purpose of his trip, but the king had consistently refused to disclose his reasons for it. All he did say was that he needed to do this, that it was for the good of the kingdom and that he had to keep it secret because many would oppose his plans, and perhaps go as far as bar him from carrying them out, if they knew what they were. She, herself, might forbid him to go. By not telling her anything, she would not need to lie if she were questioned, and that was best for her. For all these reasons and especially for the latter, Darya agreed to remain in the dark, but not before Octavius agree to using Lord Valorian – the most discrete man in the kingdom – as an intermediary, in case anything urgent needed to be communicated between them.

What could she tell the Supreme Priestess? She had in fact sent a message to Lord Valorian after the events at Horn's Pass, but she had had no response yet. This worried her to no end. Not knowing where the high king was made her feel just as bad as the thought of lying about it.

Ylana said with a very discomforting tone, "Hmm, you mean you do not know where he is."

"Correct, Honored One…I know where he should be – at least his general location and I have sent a message for him, but I have not heard back yet. I am sorry, Honored One. This *is* embarrassing. I am worried, but not about his safety. I would have known if something unfortunate had happened to him."

"Yes, you do have this connection with him. Nevertheless, someone in his position should never travel without his inner circle knowing his precise itinerary, and doing so intentionally can only bring others to the worst conjectures."

Darya simply nodded, her features a mixture of frustration and embarrassment.

Ylana continued. "Tonight, you will go to Gharana to see if you can help her locate your husband and, if possible, send him a thoughtcall. All you need do is guide her; once she latches onto him, she will not let go until he responds or until she knows exactly where he is."

Darya nodded reluctantly. She wished she could give a reason to not comply, at least for another day or two. Yet, how could she refuse Ylana's demand?

This was beginning to give her a headache, and all she could do was hope that she and Gharana would not be able to locate the king, despite the fact that she, herself, very much wanted to know where he was.

Ylana continued, "Once all this is resolved, we will speak again about your husband's... practices." Ylana Maryn Dar'Muntake rarely called Octavius by his title – another thing that irked Darya. The Supreme Priestess had no real power over the high king of Alvinor, but the Alliance between the Coriolan Crown and the Order of Kynaria did create certain obligations for the monarch. The nature of these obligations was, however, a frequent matter of dispute between Ylana and Octavius.

Darya gave the only answer she could give. "I am at your service, Honored One."

"Very well. Now, about another of my worries. This is Aria's final year as a senior neo. She will then be able to test for Passage, *if* she is ready. This is what has me worried, however. Aria could be one of our greatest priestesses. She has the potential, but her potential has *yet* to be unleashed, and it won't until she fully accepts her path."

Her Path...is this her path? "I am aware, Honored One. It worries me as well, and it pains me every time she loses her temper for one reason or another, but most especially in reaction to what she considers are her magisteri's unreasonably high expectations."

Ylana got up and walked to the other side of her desk to sit next to Darya, her hands crossed on her lap. "I know about her temper. Headmistress Delora has kept me informed of Aria's progress and difficulties several times over the course of the past four years."

Darya made a small involuntary motion at that, and Ylana said, "My interest in her surprises you? She may not be a full-blooded Kynarian, but her potential is such that it cannot be ignored and should not be relinquished to Alvinoria so easily."

Darya's mind went in a frantic spin as she realized the implications of the Supreme Priestess's plans for her niece – Claudius would never consent to it. She took a deep breath and started to say, "Honored One, I understand your motives, but –"

"But her father may not agree to it. I am aware of his aims, and I do not oppose them. But the gains cannot be *his* alone. There are ways in which both Claudius and the Order can benefit from Aria's ordination."

Understanding of her role in this matter dawned on Darya, and she let her chest relax. She said, "I will do what I can, to see to it that Lord Claudius accepts the arrangement, Honored One. But I am afraid none of that will matter if Aria does not focus on her studies and is not permitted to test for Passage."

"Indeed, Darya. We must make every effort to ensure she does test. I will speak with her instructors this fourth. I will also take her on an...excursion with me. I wish to show her the beauty of things in a way she has probably never yet experienced. And most importantly, I will show her how a strong Kynarian priestess can not only protect this beauty, but can make it a hundred, a thousand-fold greater."

Ylana continued, "Of course, this favor could cause certain jealousies to develop, but I have no doubt she can put in her place any of her peers who might resent her such an honor."

Darya's mind was spinning as it rarely had. First the anxiety and embarrassment caused by her ignorance of her husband's whereabouts, then the Supreme Priestess's revelations regarding her designs for Aria, and now this? Claudius would be overjoyed, but why didn't she feel happy for her niece? *Because she doesn't want this. She has other dreams, other desires. But she does have the potential to be a great priestess and being received into the Order will be a greater achievement than anything else she has in mind. There must be a way to show her this, to convince her. She has shown some interest in what we can do, after all, such as during our semestrial Sensing contests. Maybe Dar'Muntake's plan will do it. Yes, it will.*

Having resolved her internal conflict, Darya replied with confidence, "I can promise you, Honored One, that she will be ready for Passage. I know my niece, and although she is sometimes confused about her future, this is what she needs, and if I can guess at what you will show her on this excursion you are planning, I am quite certain her doubts will vanish once she sees what a master of our art can do."

With a smile, the Supreme Priestess said, "Thank you, Darya. I hope we are both right, because it would be a great loss to our Order if your niece turned away from our society." The Supreme Priestess stood up.

Darya did the same, and after bowing to her superior, said, "I will see Gharana tonight as you instructed, Honored One, and I will inform you once we reach the high king. You also have my promise that Aria will be ready for Passage at year's end." Darya bowed again, deeper this time, and left.

XIII URBS LUCIS

As the Suns rose to wake Urbs Lucis, a city-state on the banks of the River Argon in Upper Alvinor, bothersome clouds interrupted the rays of the Red Sun, behind which the blue twin hid. Still, in the lower city, children came out hoping to play, and the adults started their morning chores or set-up benches with fruits, vegetables, and meats for sale. Others heated up their forges to fashion or mend tools, and others still got ready for whatever business they had on this not so glorious day.

The palace at the center of the city-state seemed to ache for the Suns' rays because, though it was one of the wonders of Terrae Regis when light illuminated it, its white ardamantis walls took on a depressing paleness on cloudy days, as if to enhance the gloominess of such times. Only the pinnacles of the lower towers, carved from blue ardamantis – a rare rock which reflected stored light on cloudy days and at night – gave the complex an otherworldly appearance.

Inside the palace, on the uppermost level, five women were talking, two of them with heated voices. They were sitting in a semicircle near one end of the large room. This was Krystiana's office.

"This is how it's been since Bilena first felt that presence ten days ago! The moment one of the Yellows feels like she's got it, she lets it slip away like a Bleaters' Bar[49]. No matter what they do, they cannot lock onto those vibrations. Why is that? I will tell you why. It is because this is not a problem the Yellow Sashate can solve. We need another solution, Mater, and we need it quickly!"

The woman was Larca Dax Amanis, a native of the coastal city of Bremin. She had the pale green complexion of her people, and a small, wiry frame, with a musculature which gave her a rather masculine aspect, especially when she was clad in her short-sleeved, tight breminese tunic during physical training. Her hair, which was short except for a longish braid in the back which pointed straight up

---

[49] A Bleater's Bar was a bar of soap made from bleater's milk.

and fanned like a fatock's [50] tail, gave her a most unwelcoming aspect. But then, she did not need to be welcoming as Praefecta Milites [51] and Leader of the Red Sashed Warriors' Assembly.

Bilena Mani listened patiently, patting her wide and richly weaved yellow sash, the mark of her status as Praefecta Philosophas [52] and Leader of the Seekers' Assembly. Bilena was from East Amalor, the Magna Mater's hometown, a fact that often irritated Larca. But Bilena had a strange mix of traits which the Red Sash was fond of pointing out when she had the occasion. Bilena was tall and pale as were most Amalorians, but with the short torso of Yerlayans and long nose of Pargahni.

When Larca quieted, Bilena replied without hiding her frustration with the woman, "Thank you for reminding me of our difficulties, Larca. You are right. Despite our best efforts, we have not been able to identify the source of this dark presence in the Bind. But the two Reds who have also felt the vibrations, they have done no better, might I remind you..."

That brought an ugly frown on the small woman's already disagreeable fatock face. It was a good thing Larca did not sit next to Bilena, as proximity might have caused the Red Sash to react with real gestural aggression, though all Lux Baiulae were expected to be in control at all times.

Krystiana decided to try and soothe Bilena's mood by ignoring Larca's comment, and asked, "So what do you suggest, Bilena?"

"At this point, I've run out of ideas Mater; no matter where we look or how we look, we fail to locate the cause of those strange and unsettling vibrations."

The woman sitting to the left of Larca cleared her throat to make a suggestion. This was Saara Rucius. Her wide, white sash marked her as Praefecta Medicas, that is Leader of the Medics' Assembly. Her ash-white hair also marked Saara as the oldest Lux Baiula, now one hundred and seventy-five years old, and yet – except for her raspy voice – she looked no older than sixty; she was in good health and had a mind as sharp as anyone else. She said, "Have you tried to

---

[50] Fatock: An animal of the Flyer's order, but unable to fly due to its highly modified tail, which was spread like a wind fan.

[51] Praefecta Milites: Military prefect, Head of the Warriors' Assembly.

[52] Praefecta Consuasores: Diplomatic Prefect, Head of the Public Servants and Advisors' Assembly.

locate the source by listening for conversations about our topic of interest? I know there is a slim chance of finding anything this way, with the myriads dreamers all entering in and out of the Bind, but all else failing, it might be worth a try."

Bilena replied, "We have, Saara. Two of our Sisters, they have spent several days and nights listening for anything that refers to the attack on Horn's Pass. But they've only heard the nightmares of the fortress's inhabitants."

Krystiana grunted and turned toward the woman sitting between Bilena and Larca, looking for her input. Ramela was Praefecta Consuasores [53] and Leader of the Public Servants' and Advisors' Assembly. She was a beautiful woman with a smoothly rounded oval face, and pale brown eyes. Her intense brown hair provided for a nice contrast to her purple sash. Ramela was a pure Jarahni, and was recognized for her straightforwardness, and level head. "Last fourth, I instructed our spies across Alvinoria to visit all major towns and cities, and to report any suspicious discussions about the Serpent or the Dark One, but they've had no better luck than Bilena's Sisters."

Bilena put her head in her hands and shook it.

Krystiana asked, "What is it Bilena?"

"I still cannot understand how any of this is possible!"

Saara was tapping her fingers rhythmically, as she always did when she considered unsettling things, and said, "Who knows what the Founders truly did, regardless of what is written in our books."

Larca, Bilena and Ramela glared at the old Lux Baiula as one, as if the woman had committed blasphemy. Attacking the truth of their books? No one did that! Saara looked back at them, unruffled; her age gave her some rights. Only Krystiana looked at Saara with eyes that said the old Sister might be right.

All sat in silence for a few minutes, frustrated thoughts rumbling through their minds. Then, Ramela made a suggestion she knew would displease Krystiana as well as the others, but it was the only idea that came to her mind. "What if we call on the Kynarians? Though I don't like it, it may be our only solution. They can enter the minds of animals, and if the Serpent has anything to do with the

---

[53] Praefecta Philosophas: Scientific Prefect, Head of the Seekers' Assembly.

vibrations and they can enter *its* mind, they might just be able to answer the question for us."

Bilena rejected the idea promptly but respectfully, "That won't work, Ramela. The Serpent, it is not an animal in the true sense of it. It is a creation of Noctiferus with a mind more advanced than that of a humanoid. No one will be able to enter its mind forcibly."

Krystiana suddenly felt an irrational fear of exposure; Elyana had done just that a few days earlier, and she herself, as well as Saara, would probably have been able to the same. Krystiana contained her reaction and didn't say anything – this was not the time for such a revelation.

Bilena continued, with a slight shade of irritation in her voice, as she looked around the table. "And frankly, I don't like the idea of looking incompetent." Bilena was always a very rational woman, except when it came to the Order of Light's reputation. In instances where that reputation was at risk, her pride took over and rejected any proposition, no matter how sensible or rational it might be.

Despite her own deep dislike of Ramela's suggestion, the Magna Mater remained calm. Krystiana was a woman very much in control of herself, and she rarely let her emotions show. She was an exemplar Lux Baiula – in most things. She mulled the suggestion for a moment and then her eyes sparkled, as they usually did when a solution appeared to her. There was some excitement in her voice when she spoke. "Your idea is not without merit, Ramela, but I also dislike the thought of asking the Kynarians for help. Yet, there is a way to have their skills without getting them involved." The other women waited expectantly as Krystiana took a pause, although Bilena had a good idea what the Magna Mater was thinking of. Krystiana continued, "Marena has been with the Kynarians for over seven years now, and as Bilena knows well, she has developed impressive Beast Reading skills. That, combined with her Mind Reading skills might very well do the job. Therefore, if we must call on the Kynarians, I will request that Marena return to us at once."

Krystiana thought to herself: *How did I not think of this earlier? Elyana and I would not have needed to endanger ourselves if there is indeed a safer, more animalistic back door into the Serpent's mind.*

Saara and Ramela seemed to like the solution. However, Larca – as was expected – objected and replied with visible disdain, "Bah!

Marena! She couldn't find a *nibbler* in a sack of grain. She's just a–
"

The Magna Mater – having had enough of the woman's unpleasant remarks – gave Larca a hammering look and stopped her comment short. As naturally defiant as she was, Larca could not hold the Magna Mater's stare and looked down with clenched teeth.

If Krystiana could punish the insufferable woman by putting her on Field Purification to relearn respect and self-control, she would do it in a heartbeat. But the woman was one of the leaders of the Order, and she could not be disciplined for such faults. Only if she broke an oath could she be punished, and severely so. All Krystiana could do was to talk to Larca to help her see that her ways were unjustified and unproductive.

I will speak to her...soon.

Bilena did not thank Krystiana for stopping Larca; she did not want to call attention to the Magna Mater's intervention. Instead, she brushed imaginary dirt from her robe. Saara, on the other hand, gave a short, satisfied snort, while Ramela watched impassively.

Finally, the Head of the Yellow Sashate turned to the Magna Mater and, in as neutral a tone as possible, said, "I am pleased by your suggestion, Magna Mater. But I am not certain Marena can do what you propose, despite her outstanding Beast and Mind Reading abilities."

Bilena darted a furtive glance toward Larca, and seeing her placated, relaxed a bit. That gave her a moment to think, and she became excited as understanding dawned on her. She added with some trepidation in her voice, "Actually, forget what I said. Indeed, it may be possible for Marena to bypass the Serpent's conscious mind and go straight for the seat of its more primitive memories; these would not contain records of spoken words, but they *would* contain visual, tactile and other auditory records!" Bilena smiled, excited by the thought that they might finally be able to figure out the source of the worrisome and vexing vibrations.

The Magna Mater replied with satisfaction, "Excellent. And using Marena will allow us to remain in control of whatever action might be required, should she find useful information."

Ramela and Saara looked at each other, exchanged some thoughts, then said as one, "We agree with the plan."

215

Krystiana turned to Larca and held her gaze until she too agreed. That done, Krystiana turned back to Bilena and said with genuine concern, "Of course, you know there is a serious risk of trauma, and even death to this plan. Do you think Marena will accept it?"

"She will, Mater."

"Very well, then. I will issue the request to Ylana Maryn Dar'Muntake today; Marena should be here by fourth's end."

The next few minutes were spent in silence as each woman considered what Marena might or might not be able to achieve, making soft, encouraging or dismissive noises every so often. Finally, Ramela cleared her throat and asked, "Mater, what of the high king? Has anyone been able to locate him yet?"

Krystiana frowned and shook her head when she answered, "No, and neither has Elyana."

To no one's surprise, Larca had another eruption, "It seems we can't do anything right anymore! There is a worrisome presence in the Bind that most of us cannot feel, and those who *can* feel it cannot tell where it comes from. And now we have a king – the high king no less – whom not even his assigned Lux Baiula can locate! Why is this happening? I will tell you why. It is because we have let ourselves become complacent!"

Larca, control yourself!

Larca reacted with such a sudden jerk that Bilena, Saara and Ramela wondered if the woman was losing her mind until they realized what had happened. Krystiana had put herself in a momentary trance and sent a pinching sensation to Larca. That was a rare feat, to be able to enter and return from the Bind in less time than it took one to utter a word, but it was a feat which the Magna Mater was capable of.

Larca, who was obviously shocked about being called to order in that manner, but mostly embarrassed by her own reaction which she knew had been noticed by the others, forced herself to quiet down and slowly relaxed her jaw muscles as well as the lines on her face. Krystiana's mental pinch seemed to have done the trick though, because the woman remained reasonably controlled for the remainder of the meeting.

Krystiana addressed the Red Sash's concerns in a plain, matter-of-fact tone, as if nothing unpleasant had just occurred, "The fact that we are unable to identify the source of the vibrations is troubling indeed, Larca, and hopefully Marena will be able to help with that. As for the high king, we know that he should be in or near Spiritii. I will therefore alert Juliana and Mara and ask them to begin a search for him. I will also ask them to get in touch with Lord Commander Toras who should be scouting the area with a company of Black and Royal guardians to look for Octavius. If we are lucky, the prince will have found his father by now."

Bilena asked, "And if he can't be found? Could it be that something has happened to him?"

Krystiana said, "That is unlikely, Bilena; if the high king had been captured by someone or harmed, we would have heard of it. I do not doubt we will find him soon, or that he will simply reappear. Once that happens, I intend to make sure he does not again disappear."

The Praefectae looked at each other curiously, and then turned their questioning eyes to their leader.

Krystiana said, "I heard Octavius actually started a search for a privy attendant now that he has reached the last third of his life. I intend to make certain this attendant is one our people."

The Praefectae gave the Magna Mater puzzled looks.

"You are probably wondering where in our ranks I would find a young man to send to the king? I am speaking of the only male Alterintrant we have, of course: Koricki Dar'Muntake."

This time, the first comment was not from Larca, but from Ramela. The Head of the Purple Sashate said, "I am sorry, Mater, but Koricki is a medic apprentice, and I do not believe he would enjoy serving as the high king's personal attendant. Moreover, isn't he related to Supreme Priestess Ylana?"

The Head of the White Sash Assembly responded for the Magna Mater, "Actually, Ramela, Koricki has always been ambivalent about his calling, and even though he is pursuing studies in medicine, he does have a passion for administration and politics, and he has often expressed his desire to eventually transfer to your Sashate. In any case, I think he will not mind serving the high king as his personal attendant."

Krystiana confirmed Saara's statement, saying "Indeed, I spoke with him yesterday, and he is in fact willing to serve in this capacity, if the high king will accept him. As an apprentice medic, the boy would not mind looking after the high king's physical needs, and as one who has a lingering passion for administrative activities, he would likely enjoy helping to keep the king organized. Most importantly, he is fiercely loyal to the Sisterhood – as strange as that may be to many – and yes, loyal to the Sisterhood despite a distant relation to the Supreme Priestess. Moreover, he understands the need for our Order to be aware of all that goes on in Alvinoria to help protect it from external as well as from internal threats. Koricki would therefore feel comfortable keeping me informed of the high king's doings should anything concern him."

Larca said with a darkly humorous tone, "Does *young* Koricki realize that what you are asking him to do is in effect to spy on the high king? And that if he were to be caught doing so, he would be banished at once and in perpetuity from the Crown's lands?"

Krystiana sighed in frustration before answering, "Koricki would only be acting as required by his duties to the Crown and to the *Societas*, duties which would be in keeping with the treaty between our two institutions."

Larca limited her response to a small, but satisfied nod this time, to show her agreement with the Magna Mater's game.

Krystiana continued, turning to the leader of the Purple Sashate, "Since we are all agreed, I will need your assistance, Ramela, to make this happen. I believe you and Elyana will be able to make the case for young Koricki after you yourself meet with him and find, as Saara and I did, that he is well-suited for the role."

Ramela nodded, and after a short pause, Krystiana added, "Of course, that means finding the king, and getting him back to the capital first."

More nods.

Krystiana continued, "One thing we have not considered is that he may be shielded or be in a *location* that is shielded."

Bilena replied, "The first could mean that he is being held captive, which, as you say, is unlikely, while the second can only mean two things, as far as we know. Either he is with the Colossi, or –" Bilena paused and said what followed with great reluctance, "or he is with the banished Marcus."

Larca barked, "Marcus the Reader? I hope not! The king will have much to explain if that is where he is. The terms of the Reader's banishment were very specific: he is to remain in perpetual exile and no one, not even one in authority, may seek contact with him. Any violation would result in the immediate punishment of the transgressor." When the other women looked at her with skeptical frowns, Larca added, "Yes, yes. I know the high king would not be punishable, but he would still be subject to our investigation, and Marcus would be expulsed from the continent."

Krystiana said, "Indeed. But there is no need to worry about that yet. Our first priority is to find the high king. If Elyana, the king's son, or our Sisters in the south do not find him by tomorrow, we will consider sending someone to the Colossi...and to the Shadow Woods."

The four Assembly Heads sat in their chairs with looks that spanned a range of emotions from simply disbelieving to frankly sour. Saara crossed her legs and tapped her fingers against each other, while Bilena tapped hers on her leg, and Ramela simply held her hands together and her head tilted downward, shrugging her shoulders every so often. Larca shook her head and snorted furiously.

Just now, Krystiana got up from her chair and started to walk around her office, pensive. The others watched her curiously, wondering what else she was going to reveal this morning.

Krystiana's office was large and beautifully furnished and decorated, but not ostentatious. The floors were made of dark bok. What's more, the bok was varnished, which was an especially-expensive treatment given that varnish was still quite uncommon in the kingdom. An expansive library covered the two side walls, whereas the back wall, which faced west, had wide sliding doors opening onto a large balcony, which overlooked the palace's plaza. Her desk was made of white ardamantis, and had maps, books and documents lying neatly on top of it. A sculpture representing the Order of Light sat on her desk. It had two spheres, one red and one blue, representing K'Tara's two suns. The blue sphere was set a little higher than the other, and the two stood freely atop a piece of marble from which blue flames emerged to surround the red sphere, and golden flames arose to envelop the blue one. Krystiana walked back toward her desk and felt the flames with her right hand. As she did so, she closed her eyes momentarily and breathed in, drawing the flames to her hand. The moment passed, and she turned to face the Praefectae.

"I have been wondering for a few days now, how to share some information with you, and I have come to the conclusion that there is no right way or right moment to do it other than to simply share it. Elyana and I met in the Bind a few nights ago to search for the source of the vibrations ourselves. We failed in that, but what we did learn was very disturbing in its own right."

Bilena replied with fierce incredulity, "Mater, you know that we trust your judgement in all things, but why did you not inform the Light's Assembly of your plans? Putting yourself in danger without first consulting with us is certainly against our rules."

"Ugh," replied Krystiana, letting her emotions show for the first time since the beginning of the painful meeting. "I know our rules very well, Bilena; I helped write many, myself. But I believed then, and still believe now that I made the right decision given the unusual circumstances in which we find ourselves. For indeed, while in the Bind, Elyana and I were lucky enough to find the Serpent." Now, the Magna Mater paused a moment to think of how to tell the truth without revealing that Elyana had entered the Serpent's mind, and that both the Serpent and its interlocutor had become aware of the two Lux Baiulae's presence. But the hesitation was only momentary, hopefully too short for the other four women to notice, and she continued, "We overheard the creature speaking with someone who had been known as "Umbra" during the Dark Battle." A mosaic of responses painted the four women's faces, depending on whether the name elicited a memory in them, or not. Krystiana paused to look for the right way to paraphrase the Umbra's words to lessen their impact – if it could be lessened. Finally, she said, "The gist of their conversation was that the Sisterhood and the Kynarian Order are an obstacle to their Master's plans, and they agreed that they must eliminate us both."

The four Praefectae stood stupefied for a long moment. Larca eventually broke the silence, embarking on a long tirade wondering why the Magna Mater had waited so long to inform them of what she and Elyana had done and discovered, especially something of this importance. She did it with restraint, however, given that she was addressing and questioning their leader.

Krystiana waited for the Praefecta Milites to be done, then addressed all four women, "I know you must be concerned by my actions, and by my decision to act without the Assembly's knowledge, but I can assure you that I took all the necessary precautions, and I am happy to say that the risk has been worth it. Now, however, I would like your help to determine what should be done next, and I will welcome any suggestion you might have regarding the manner in which this news should be shared with the rest of the Sisterhood."

Krystiana's overture and invitation did not immediately produce the effect she had hoped for. Her Praefectae were still trying to come to terms with what she had done and were doing so more or less successfully depending on how strongly they supported her. Krystiana gave them a few moments to process her revelation and when she saw their faces or jaws start to relax, she asked again for their help in determining the next steps. One by one, the women signified their agreement, starting with Larca as surprising as that was – perhaps because as a Red Sash, she understood and appreciated the value of risk-taking. Furthermore, Krystiana was the Magna Mater, and the Praefectae had no choice but to accept her decisions, unless they endangered the Sisterhood.

Saara spoke next and asked, "Mater, what you have shared with us will require some meditation to process before we can even begin to consider the next steps. May we reconvene in an hour to continue this discussion?"

"Very well, Saara. You are right. We will reconvene in one hour, at which time I will share the details of what Elyana and I have heard, and we will then decide on our next steps."

With that, the Praefectae got up to exit Krystiana's office. As they did, the Magna Mater asked Saara to stay another moment; the old Lux Baiula agreed and sat back down.

As the others walked toward the door, the Head of the Purple Sashate asked, "What if Noctiferus *has* returned, Mater? What if he *is* the one guiding the Serpent and its accomplice?"

Bilena's hair stiffened, and she responded to the question herself, a little more ardently that she should have, "You know that is not possible, Ramela. Aiala'Rhi herself took him, stripped him of his powers, and sent him to the furthest reaches of our universe ages ago, to die there a mere mortal. How could he be back?"

Krystiana looked at the Yellow Sash with surprise but decided to leave it at that. Bilena would be punishing herself the moment she got to her rooms for this irrational outburst. Krystiana had also considered the possibility of the fallen Founder's return and found that she was not yet ready to accept it, although she knew that whether or not one accepted a fact did not change its reality. So, she changed her mind about replying and said, "Unfortunately, Bilena, no one witnessed the mortalization of the one, or the destruction of the other, and Noctiferus's past absence from this world cannot be used as proof of the impossibility of his return. Just as the servant has returned, so could its master indeed. I am certain you will agree with this logic, as a Seeker of Knowledge."

Bilena did not reply, but everyone could see the self-reproach on her face. Indeed, she had forgotten one of the first laws of science: that negatives cannot be proven. She thought to herself: *I should ask Lucra to assign me to the farm to till soil or haul hay until my head is back on my shoulders. Either way, I'm going to spend this hour whipping myself,* and she shook her head dejectedly.

Krystiana tried to finish with an encouraging note and said, "No matter what the truth is, Bilena, or what the reality of things is, we will ready ourselves for it, and we will *be* ready. I will see you back here in an hour."

The three women nodded and left. As the door closed behind her, Larca could not help looking back, wondering what the Magna Mater might have to discuss with Saara.

XIV MEETINGS

The Senate Chamber was not a place Aithen visited often. Indeed, most matters of state that he attended were conducted in the Private Audience Chamber, where the high king heard and discussed matters with his closest advisors, the Senate's Eldest, or his sons. The king himself rarely went to the Chamber of the Senate, visiting it only when the First Senator was unable to secure the Senate's agreement on a matter of importance to the king or when the king needed to declare war upon a neighbor. Aithen wasn't going to declare war today, but what he had to say, he needed to say to all senators as the matters of the attack on Horn's Pass and of the Serpent itself were certainly ones which they needed to hear directly from him to avoid the story getting out of hand since the true identity of the Serpent could not be disclosed until its motives were known and a strategy to thwart its plans was decided. Furthermore, Aithen needed to make certain that the Senate was going to release the necessary funds to support the refugees he had brought back with him.

Later that day, he would speak to the assembled lords in the Grand Audience Hall, where the king had his throne, as they would need to prepare defenses against the Serpent in their own lands. He would deliver the same message to them as he did the senators. His final meeting of the day would be with First Cleric Galadrin. In the morning, he would meet with his top military aids to prepare the defense of the Capital in case the Serpent attacked here.

Aithen rubbed his temples as he thought of all the meetings he needed to have. Elyana had asked him again if he was certain he did not want her with him, to read the senators', the landholders' and the First Cleric's vibrations, and though the doubting part of him told him that he should accept her offer, he thanked her again and kept to his earlier decision to do this by himself.

As he approached the hall, Aithen felt his stomach flutter. This, combined with his spinning head, would make it very difficult to address the Senate, so he reached inside of himself and relaxed the way his father had taught him. He felt a warm breeze flow through him; it relaxed his muscles, cleared his mind, and slowed his pulse. It did not wash away his fatigue, but it helped. Now, he checked his uniform, made sure everything was in place. Ten meters from the Chamber, four guardians saluted him and pulled open the doors. As they did so, angry voices spilled over into the corridor. The sound reached the prince with minimal effect. One of the guardians went in and announced the prince.

As Aithen walked in, the elders quieted down at once, stood up and saluted him with their right arm across the chest. Most senators offered him genuine welcome backs, while a few were less than sincere, but the prince did not care much whether *they* welcomed him. First Senator Leo, flanked by the other two Eldest, was standing in front of a long oval table facing the rest of the assembled elders. The three Eldest also turned toward the doors and welcomed the high prince.

Aithen looked around the hall, acknowledging the men and women. *Hum, they must have redone the ceiling in here; it smells of fresh paint.* Aithen caught this odd thought and chided himself for it, but not before giving the stately room a long glance. The chamber had striking frescoes on the ceiling depicting some of the most important decisions the Senate had made over the centuries, and a new scene had indeed been recently painted on the ceiling. It showed a period between the end of the reign of Flavius the Third and the beginning of his father's reign when the Senate had ruled the city in the absence of a king. The white marbled walls were bare of any painting and made a nice contrast to the green granite benches. Busts of famous elders were displayed along three walls as well as on either side of the doors located on the fourth wall. The windows were wide and located at the top of the high walls. The light filtered through the glass of the windows and its rays pointed straight toward the Eldests' oblong table. *Right, time to begin.*

As Aithen approached the dais, First Senator Leo walked toward him, and said with a flourish, "High Prince, my seat is yours."

Aithen, as was expected, thanked the First Senator but did not take the chair and instead placed himself near the end of the table from whence he would more easily address the entire Senate, Eldest included. First Senator Leo officially gave him the floor, and the high prince gestured for everyone to sit.

After clearing his throat, Aithen began the first of two very important meetings of the day. "First Senator Leo, Eldest Amis, Eldest Paula, senators; thank you for receiving me today. As you

226

know, I have just this day come back with nearly eight hundred villagers from Horn's Pass." Many shifted in their seats and frowned at hearing that number, despite already knowing it, but Aithen continued unmoved. "I have had several exchanges with First Senator Leo since our departure from Horn's Pass regarding the matter of the refugees, and he has assured me that the city is ready to take care of them." First Senator Leo nodded to confirm the prince's statement. "He tells me that dwellings have been made available, and that farmers and artisans have been asked to start making available more of their products as well. He tells me also that some of you are concerned by this, and I say your concerns are not misplaced, but I had – and we have – no choice in the matter as there is no lodging available for the refugees outside of the City, and I do not wish for them to sleep in tents."

Many senators frowned again, but most nodded their heads in understanding. One of the elders, a man named Clovis, always the first to take the floor and give his opinion about one matter or another, stood and said with an overly unctuous tone, "High Lord Commander, it is nice to see you again. How long do you expect the refugees will stay in Furan City?"

Aithen noted the senator's use of his military title. He knew this was meant to say: "*I think you are acting as a general wishing to dispose of his burden as efficiently as possible, and not as a prince caring for his people.*" Aithen ignored this too, but noted it for the future, and answered simply and straightforwardly, "Two months, perhaps three, Senator."

Senator Clovis nodded but continued with his questions, "High Lord Commander, I believe most of us agree with your choice to extend our welcome to these people while they are in need, but what if they choose never to go back? What do we do then? Surely we cannot –"

This time, Aithen felt the need to put the man in his place, and he interrupted him to say with some force, "Firstly, Senator Clovis, bringing them here was not a choice, but a necessary decision, as I already stated. Secondly, I doubt a large number would choose to stay, but some may, and we *will* help those who have a valid reason for staying in the capital find themselves permanent living arrangements. They are hardworking people, Alvinorians as you and

I are, and as such, they have as much right living in the capital as does anyone else, Senator."

Senator Clovis's face paled slightly at that, and he decided to end his turn, saying, "Thank you my Prince. You are right, of course."

But the contrarians were not going to let the matter go so easily, and another senator, who had glared with disgust at Clovis for his bleatishness, took courage and spoke to express his concerns. "High Prince, I understand your sentiment, but I don't see how we can accept even a few dozen additional inhabitants. Surely you are aware that we are already to the walls of our city, and with our children now choosing to remain in the capital instead of venturing beyond, we will soon have no space for ourselves, let alone newcomers, as few as they may be."

Senator Luma Kraelion, a woman Aithen knew well, stood to reply. The high king often had her as a guest in their private residence in Antar. She was an intelligent and pleasant conversationalist and listened as well as she spoke. "My Prince, may I?" Aithen nodded and Senator Kraelion proceeded with her reply, "Sisipe, notwithstanding our present situation, I am certain it is our *duty* to welcome the refugees and give them the assistance they require until they can return to Horn's Pass, or to muster our collective ingenuity to help those who will choose to establish themselves within or without our city walls. Or is there a law that prohibits us from providing relief to those in need?"

Gritting his teeth, Senator Sisipe replied, "Of course there isn't, Luma."

"Are you then suggesting that if we assist the refugees, we will cause the capital irreparable harm?"

Again, the man gritted his teeth and said no.

"Then, you must perforce be suggesting that the inconvenience they will cause is sufficient grounds to deny the help we owe them, an obligation guaranteed by our beloved Coriolan Carta."

Senator Sisipe felt beaten at last, and he sat back down amid a flurry of applauds in favor of Senator Kraelion's argument, and the sound of other men and women shifting uncomfortably on the benches.

First Senator Leo rapped the First's Knuckles [54] to call the elders' attention and proclaimed that Senator Kraelion had won the case for the prince's plan, which meant that the Senate was now committed to support it.

After the First Senator rapped the First's Knuckles once more, Senator Kraelion took the floor again, and added proudly but without boasting, "My Prince, now that the Senate is generally ready to support you, I would like to announce how I, myself, plan to support the Horn's Passers: I propose to setup a work office to help them find jobs, so that they may feed their families while they are here, not as beggars, but as providers."

A large number of senators suddenly clapped hands on legs in support of Luma Kraelion's proposal, with only a few remaining quiet. There followed several minutes of one elder or another promising to help the refugees in his or her own way. This compounding wave of support verily and truly surprised Aithen, and he committed to memory the way in which this was achieved. After the last proposal – seven had been made in all by various senators – everyone quieted, exhausted from the unending clapping and cheering, and turned their head back toward the prince.

The prince said, "Thank you, senators, and thank *you*, Senator Kraelion. Your offers are most welcome and encouraging, and I invite any who made a proposal here to let the Crown know should you need its assistance in executing it."

Aithen waited a moment during which his expression became serious and grim, and then proceeded to address the other question everyone had. "Senators, as you know, this relocation of Horn's Pass's population comes as a result of the attack by a very unusual rokon. This one was much larger than any we have ever seen. Its attack was ferocious by all accounts, and we were fortunate that Elyana Lux Baiula was there with us for the Celebration of the Colossi because, without her, we would certainly have lost more men."

Just then, a young senator named Cronin Sur'Elando, who had strong religious tendencies, clapped his hands to ask for permission

---

[54] The First's Knuckles was an instrument made of black marble and shaped as a half-moon with four knuckles on the convex side. The knuckles were used to "rap" an aluminum base that made a loud popping sound as each knuckle depressed the metal.

to speak and said, "My Prince, pardon me, but some of us have heard that that beast was actually not a rokon, but something…bred by evil."

Two other senators uttered "yesses" in support of their colleague.

Damn! It seems Irania Lux Baiula was not able to prevent the rumors from starting. I am going to be forced to lie, now. Damn it! Unless…

"I wouldn't trust rumors, Senator, as they are often misleading."

"Pardon my insistence, my Prince, but we have even received accounts of people dying without any physical cause. If that is true, it can only mean that one of our founders has returned, namely Nocti–"

When Senator Sur'Elando started uttering the name of the fallen founder, an uproar of indignant voices arrested him mid-sentence. First Senator Leo rapped the First's Knuckles again, several times, until quiet returned to the Chamber.

I need to put an end to this here and now. "Senator… Sur'Elando, is it? A follower of the Church of Aiala. I understand why you would interpret things as you do. But interpreting rumors in ways that may very well agitate the population is not wise. Therefore, I urge you and everyone to refrain from doing so. But to be sure, whatever I *do* learn and confirm to be known, I will share with the Senate." *There, no lies, and hopefully, I've confused them enough to keep them mulling on that until we can tell them more.*

Senator Sur'Elando was indeed confused by the prince's statement, as was everyone else except Luma Kraelion. The senator seemed to want to ask the prince to repeat himself, but he thought better, and sat back down, and another elder stood to ask his own question.

This went on for a while, with elders asking about the prince's plans to protect Alvinoria from further attacks, or about his plans to help repair Horn's Pass's village and fortress, and of course, about the high king's prolonged absence which Aithen did not enjoy answering either. But, thankfully, there were no more questions regarding the nature of the rokon. The last question the prince was asked was from a short, slightly obese man who had seen the Zebulonian earlier that day. The elder wrung his hands nervously.

"My Prince…you have also brought someone else into the capital; a man who looks to be…" and the senator lowered voice as if speaking the stranger's origin out loud might bring ill luck to them, "...a Zebulonian."

The man to his left as well as a number of others asked, "What did you, say, Mimius?" While others simply blurted out 'Whats' or creased their faces with disbelief.

Aithen had fully expected the reaction and had known that someone would eventually ask him about the foreigner, so he answered as he had prepared to do, "That is correct, Senator Mimius. The man is named Lusk Methrim, and he is a healer from Zebulonia."

Senator Clovis was about to stand up to speak again, but Aithen raised his hand and motioned the man to stay seated. The elder did so with a silent growl. The prince said, "The man is here at my invitation. I therefore ask that everyone give him the courtesy due our guests. His appearance is startling; I'll give you that. But aside from his looks, he *is* a Human, and not some fantastic or nightmarish creature."

Eldest Amis stood up and asked, "My Prince, I am certain there is a reason for this...man's presence here. But given that our nations are enemies, and given that there has not been a Zebulonian here in ages, it is reasonable to wonder what this reason might be which led you to invite him here."

Another senator, Listus, stood and replied to that. "Actually, Eldest, I have heard rumors about a Zebulonian living in Shadin City for a while now."

The Chamber looked at Listus with surprise and turned to the prince with puzzled faces.

The prince said, "Eldest Amis, your question is a valid one. The man is a defector from Zebulonia. He is the selfsame Zebulonian Senator Listus just referred to, and he has indeed been living in Shadin City for the past three years as Master Healer to the Shadisha. His services to the Shadisha have been without reproach, but for reasons which are only ours to know, he now wishes to offer his services to the Crown, and I have brought him here to be tested by the Sisterhood to determine whether we can use him as a medic in the Royal Guard."

Eldest Amis did not appear to be completely satisfied with the answer, but it was an acceptable one, for now, and he thanked the prince for it. A flutter of whispers filled the chamber as elders opined or conjectured or shared their disbelief about a Zebulonian having served in Shadin City for three years with only one of their number having heard *rumors* about it, and about the same…man…now being the high prince's guest.

Aithen let the whispers be and turned to First Senator Leo to signify the end of his address to the Senate. The First Senator nodded and rapped the First's Knuckles three times to call the meeting to a close. Aithen thanked elders and eldest and walked out with the First Senator.

Once outside the Senate Chamber, Aithen thanked Leo and asked him to report any more rumors that might begin spreading within the Senate as a result of his announcements today. The aged man agreed, and then asked the prince whether he would clarify his statement regarding the rokon.

But Aithen would not. He could see the desire to insist in the man's eyes; the First Senator was not a fool, for sure. But Aithen truly could not share anything else about the Serpent at this point, so he took his leave of the First Senator, and walked to the courtyard where Kil awaited him with Magnus. As he walked, Aithen nodded and smiled to himself every so often and finally released a long-withheld breath.

When Kil saw his master, he thought he heard the prince praise someone, and said, "My Prince?"

It took Aithen but a fraction of a second to shift his focus back to the here and now. He said with a smile, "It went well, Kil. I was able to manage it."

"That is good my Prince."

"Indeed, Kil. Now, to the Lords!" And with one easy motion, Aithen climbed on the patient Magnus and made his way back to the palace accompanied by his squire, satisfied and thinking about how proud his father would be – he hoped.

***

The prince expected his meeting with the Alvinorian lords and ladies, and representatives of the vassal kingdoms of Jarah, Pargah and Yerlah to be difficult, but it was outright painful and almost ended in failure. There were many reasons for this, but perhaps the sheer number of members of the Union Council was the primary cause of the difficulty Aithen had faced. Indeed, the council was composed of twenty-eight lords and ladies and three kings, and each had his or her own needs, expectations and agendas. The shouting had threatened to tear his eardrums, worse than the Serpent's shrieks. The more powerful landholders were ready to ride back in their lacquered coaches to prepare their defenses, while the minor patricians – none of whom had defensive forces of their own – cried for help, and no one could agree on how to provide them any assistance. Some asked whether the Sisterhood could help. Others demanded that the high king's forces be dispatched to protect the minor patricians' lands.

If it hadn't been for two of the people in attendance, however, the meeting would have been much worse – if that were possible – and no agreement would have been reached. These two men were Aithen's uncles, Lord Gaius of Praeghe, and Lord Claudius of Bremin. They were not the most powerful of the high king's vassals, militarily-speaking that is, but they were nevertheless influential among their peers.

Lord Gaius was the youngest of the high king's brothers. He had just celebrated his 100th year of life. He was a jovial, boisterous fellow with fertile lands and prosperous affairs, beloved by his serfs and neighbors alike because of his generosity, and for the balls he gave regularly where both plebeians and patricians were welcome, though the former and the latter were obviously restricted from mingling. Gaius was also, to the surprise of many given his age and civilian life, the second-best archer in the land, right behind his nephew, Aithen, and he would oftentimes impress his guests by shooting an arrow through a wine pouch held between his sons' mouths. Another thing for which Gaius was particularly known was the talent he had for causing people to back down from their own demands and to accede to the demands of the side he supported. Sometimes he did it by the force of his infectious convictions, other times by embarrassing a lord or lady into relenting, with the lord or lady in question thinking they had done it to themself. Surely, these manipulations sometimes got him into trouble with the more powerful patricians, but Lord Gaius had enough supporters not to have to worry about that, and he was the high king's brother after all – fourth in line to the throne – so that no one therefore dared touch him lest they wished to bring Octavius's wrath upon themself.

233

Lord Gaius was widowed, having lost his Human wife twenty years earlier, and he had two sons, or rather, had had two sons: Ulvius, the foremost mining lord, and Loris who had been killed by the Serpent at Horn's Pass. Today, the prince's uncle was not his usual self, as he was still deeply troubled by the loss of his son. Gaius had even requested permission to decline the invitation to Furan City, but Aithen had impressed upon him the importance of his attendance, and so Gaius had come. Today, he did his best to mingle as he usually did, and the only signs he gave of his continued grieving were a less prompt smile and a quieter, forced laugh when one noble or another, who did not know of Loris's death, tried to elicit a laugh.

As for Lord Claudius, while he was as successful as Gaius, he could not have differed more from both Gaius and Octavius in nature. Claudius had an extremely serious disposition, bearing a quasi-permanent meditative look, laughing only when what was said was truly and genuinely funny and appropriate, and occasionally letting his lips and eyes form a smile when he felt real joy or pleasure because of someone's actions or words. To the contrary of Gaius's boisterous life and to Octavius's busy life as ruler of one of the largest and most populated lands, Claudius – now one hundred and thirty years old – lived a relatively quiet but comfortable life with his two sons and wife in a large and luxuriant villa on the shores of the Eastern Sea. Lord Claudius's daughter, Aria, was now in Kynaria, developing her Sensing skills to become a priestess. Indeed, Claudius needed Aria to ascend to the priesthood of Kynaria, which was the most powerful and influential institution of the wealthy nation, to help assure his family's future given that his sons had no interest in political, military or economic affairs.

Because of his preference for observation and reflection, Claudius had become a highly educated man with a mind for the law, and a particularly deep and thorough knowledge of the Coriolan Carta. His knowledge of the Carta was unsurpassed by even Octavius's own advocates, making him the most highly sought jurisconsult [55]. In fact, he was known to have helped resolve thousands of disputes between neighboring commoners and/or

---

[55] Jurisconsult: A person, an amateur, learned in law, whom anyone could consult on matters of law.

landholders, as well as to have aided in the resolution of many a dispute presented to the Royal Court itself over the decades. Claudius's jurisconsulting along with the revenues from one of the busiest ports in all of Alvinoria made him a wealthy man. But he was growing old and tired, and unless his daughter achieved priesthood and took over the landholdership when the time came, the wealth he had accumulated would eventually melt away.

After the squabbling had continued for about thirty minutes and the lords and ladies had decided to take a pause to breathe, Lord Claudius had stood up and seized the chance to address the high prince. He had said, "My Prince, Lords and Ladies, may I summarize the situation, as I see it?" Aithen nodded expectantly, while the others either sighed with exhaustion or begged the old thinker to speak, hoping that he would resolve things for them.

"My Prince, I believe that everyone agrees that if a village or minor town were to be threatened, its inhabitants should assemble in the nearest defended location, which would normally be the local landholder's fortress. The problem is the minor landholders' defensive forces are likely to be quickly overwhelmed by the rokon, given the destruction and death it brought to the much better defended fortress at Horn's Pass. I think that there are therefore only three options to address said problem: One, ordering that the populations of the affected communities relocate to the nearest major keep; Two, having the major landholders send small detachments to reinforce the guards of the minor landholders; Three, having the Royal Guard contribute said small detachments. Of course, regardless what is agreed to, assistance from Urbs Lucis will be required, despite many disliking the idea of a detachment of Red Sashes in their lands."

When Claudius re-seated himself, echoes of agreement coming from most of the minor landholders crossed the Hall. But these were rapidly followed by the sounds of disagreement voiced by various major, and a few minor landholders.

Aithen took note and replied appropriately. "Thank you, Lord Claudius; those do seem to be our only solutions, and although I cannot force anyone to accept the first or the second – or the fourth – I know that some combination of these solutions will need to be accepted. Indeed, the Royal Guard, though the largest force in the realm, is not large enough to send soldiers to every minor landhold.

A compromise is going to be needed to satisfy our common obligations, taking into account what each can and cannot do."

Claudius started to reply to agree with his nephew when Lord Arotek of Melinor interrupted him, shocking some and bringing unsurprised glances between others who knew Arotek well. Indeed, it was well known that he had a deep dislike of Octavius's intellectual brother, and that he had no care for propriety. The latter was glaringly demonstrated in permanence by the fact that Arotek styled his hair with an eight-centimeter tail, when – by convention – only the males of House Coriolis had the right to wear their hair tied in the back in that manner, with the heir to the throne allowed a ten-centimeter tail below the knot, the second in line a seven-centimeter tail, and all other males, a four-centimeter tail.

Lord Arotek said, "Thank you Lord Claudius, I appreciate you laying out the options for us. But my Prince, you must know that I cannot put the populations of my own lands at risk to lend support to landholders who chose to mismanage their resources and their forces. And though my stronghold is sizeable, it is only large enough to shelter and provide for my own land-dwellers. I am afraid Your Highness will need to consider sending contingents of the Royal Guard wherever additional protection is needed."

Aithen's nerves were about to snap in the face of such callousness and disrespect as were being displayed by Arotek, but he controlled his response nevertheless, and what he said surprised everyone and pleased many. With slightly squinting eyes and tight lips, Aithen said, "Lord Arotek. Firstly, I will remind you that although it is not written in laws, courtesy and respect are requirements of this body, whether my father presides it or not; I urge you to remember that."

Angry humiliation painted the lord's face, and many of his peers did their best to hide their pleasure.

The prince continued, "Now, Lord Arotek, I understand your concerns, but if my memory serves me well, every House has an obligation under the law to protect the people within the borders of its land. Moreover, the payments made to each landholder are a function of the size of the landholder's force, and a principle requirement for the maintenance of such a force is that it be used to protect the lord's or lady's land-dwellers. However, the payments that you, yourself, receive are quite substantial and disproportionately so relative to the size of your lands – a fact which often irritates many of your peers. But we are not here to discuss that. On the other hand, we do need to find a compromise which will ensure the safety of any community that may be threatened by the rokon in the coming days, and that compromise *will* require that we all participate in one manner or another, and that we put aside our dislikes and distrusts."

Feeling so utterly chastened and disgraced by the prince's remarks, as well as by his unexpectedly confident and authoritative demeanor, Arotek sat himself back down with a clenched jaw and a barely audible 'Yes, my Prince,' wanting only to steer everyone's looks away from himself.

As for Aithen, he wasn't certain how he felt about this score, and he wondered whether he had erred and created another enemy. Nonetheless, he needed to bring this debate to a conclusion, and it seemed to him that it should now be possible. So, he turned to his uncle and asked, "Lord Claudius, what is your recommendation?"

Claudius answered as if nothing had happened. "My Prince, I would recommend that the major Houses be primarily responsible for protecting their own land-dwellers as well those of the minor Houses which are unable to provide that protection, as is the law. When it is clear that a major House's resources will be insufficient, I recommend that your Highness send a detachment of the Royal Guard, for which the House in question will obviously compensate the Crown."

There were a variety of responses to Claudius's recommendations, but the law was the law, and most patricians knew that the Royal Guard would not be able to protect every minor landhold, no matter how large the Guard was, so most nodded their agreement.

After a moment, Claudius added, "I also recommend calling on Urbs Lucis to lend a hand, only where absolutely necessary."

Council members grumbled at that last suggestion, but Lord Arotek asked "Do you mean to send…Sisters, upon the request of a landholder or do you mean something else, Lord Claudius?"

"I mean, where it appears to be necessary to protect the high king's subjects."

Lord Arotek, his face red with anger, remained silent to keep himself from saying something which he might regret, but his supporters turned toward him with looks that said, 'Don't worry

Arotek, we will make the prince and his old hooter of an uncle regret this.'

Aithen noted it all and thought: *I really don't envy Father…and I do not like that man…in fact, I will need to beware of him and his supporters. The thing is, not even uncle knows how dangerous the* rokon *is, and that a Lux Baiula is the only thing that will prevent the otherwise unavoidable massacres – if Elyana can find or train more Sisters who can create that nebula.*

Even Arotek will see that, if the Serpent attacks his lands. There must be a Lux Baiula in every major fortress.

Having made his decision, the high prince looked over the entire Council and put his own recommendation forward: that Lux Baiulae be dispatched to all the major fortresses to help defend against the rokon. This was received with an uproar of opposition, and Aithen began to despair that he would ever find a way to get the major Houses to accept his proposal.

That is when Lord Gaius came to Aithen's rescue, berating the most vocal naysayers (all men) and doing it even more forcefully than usual, perhaps because of the loss he had just suffered as a result of the rokon's attack on Horn's Pass. He embarrassed the lords by reminding everyone that not a single case of usurpation of power by a Lux Baiula had been reported in decades, that not a single landholder who currently had a Lux Baiula for an advisor had attempted to seize land from a neighbor, and that Ladies Falco and Moradina – who were two of the most respected and befriended patricians of all – had two Sisters each in their service.

Several men sat back, embarrassed. Others, however, tried to argue with Lord Gaius on the basis of rumors that were all too common, such as rumors about Sisters fogging people's minds so that no one even realized what they had given up in exchange for their so-called assistance. Gaius exploded, and started to enumerate all the *recorded* instances where a Lux Baiula had helped resolve an issue between landholders in this very Council. Were they not satisfied with the result, he asked those concerned? Most gave a grumbled response, too embarrassed to use words. Seeing that the battle was nearly won, Gaius decided to give a final example of the Sisterhood's trustworthiness by reminding everyone that the high king himself, beloved across Alvinoria, also had a Lux Baiula in his service, a Lux Baiula who had argued for their very interest – the lords and ladies of Alvinoria – when the king had considered restricting access to the Crown's lands across the kingdom. This last reminder convinced the remaining opposition. Lord Gaius sat down under the clamorous applauses, satisfied with himself and feeling a strange sense of relief. He nodded toward his nephew to say, 'They are ready to compromise, Aithen.'

After two hours of negotiations the members of the Union Council had reached an agreement: Aithen would send some forces to the towns of minor patricians which the major Houses could not protect for one reason or another, except in the northern lands, where the kings of Jarah, Pargah and Yerlah – cherishing the little independence they had – preferred to see to their own defense. The most contentious part of Aithen's proposal, that Urbs Lucis send a Sister to every major fortress to support the local forces, was passed without conditions. Hands were shaken, and thanks were given – some grouchily and others in earnest – and everyone went to prepare for immediate departure. The representatives of the kingdoms of Jarah, Pargah and Yerlah thanked the Prince with gifts of precious stones and cartloads of the best swords and arrows on the continent, happy that no forces from House Coriolis would be sent to their territories; to them, it was a matter of pride, though they were vassals of the high king.

Aithen left the Grand Audience Hall, feeling exhausted but satisfied, and mulled on the last meeting he needed to have before the day was over.

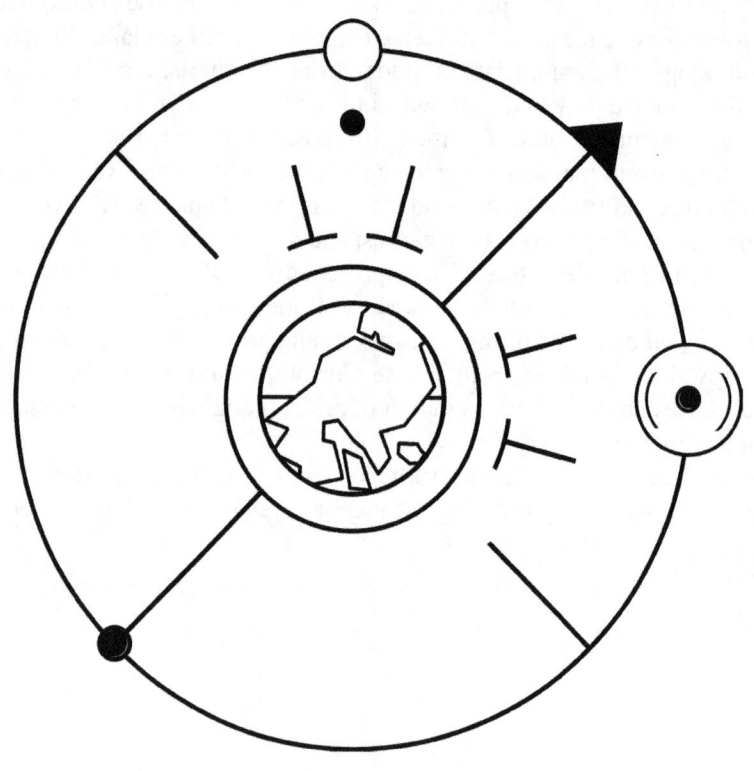

XV TROUBLESOME FEELINGS

Lady Darya reluctantly entered Priestess Tracker Gharana's large office. It was painted in blinding yellows and reds. *How can she stand this?* The priestess was sitting behind an overly large desk, polished to perfection, so much so that its wood shot glaring reflections into Darya's eyes. *This is going to give me a headache if I keep looking at it.*

Gharana welcomed Darya in a perfect Eastern Kynarian accent, that is, with long, exceedingly stretched vowels. "Lady Daaryaaa! Yeees, come in. Pleaase sit dowwne."

Darya had never gotten used to that accent from the East Territory of Kynaria, and to this day, she cringed every time she heard it. There were only two priestesses from that region of the small Kynarian continent. For some reason unknown, most men and women from that region did not possess the ability to sense or enter the Bind. Some believed it might be due to the mineral in the soil of the region which interfered with the ability of the mind to reach lower levels of consciousness, but even when natives of the East Territory were raised in the West, they did not develop the ability – this oiled the fire of those who believed in the inferiority of the easterners. For all their sophistication and advanced knowledge, the westerners were still prejudiced, Darya thought. But she wasn't such a one and considered any woman her equal if she had the education, although that didn't diminish her dislike of the eastern accent.

Darya said, "Thank you, Sister Gharana," as she sat down on a dark, polished chair.

"So, the Honored One asked me to help you locate the king, your husband."

Ahhr. That accent!

"Indeed. I have been unable to do it myself, though my connection with him is strong. I'm sure you realize how important it is we find him and call him back. My sons are capable of handling the situation for a while, but their authority as crown prince and protector of the Pass will only go so far. I am also concerned that Aithen will not be able to navigate the politics of the kingdom very long."

241

Again, stretching her vowels more than was necessary, Gharana said, "Yes, I am certain they will be in over their heads very soon. Well, let us get on with it then."

The woman stood and walked out of her room and onto the balcony. Kynarians believed that to be truly connected with the Bind, a Sensor must be out in the open to commune with the natural forces.

There was a small plush, cream-colored rug on the ground. Gharana kneeled and sat down on it, cross-legged. Her bottom hit the floor with a thump; the woman was definitely on the heavy side. Still, she was a proud and self-confident woman.

Darya kneeled and sat back-to-back with Gharana. The woman then leaned forward and picked up a conductive belt from a chair to her side. She tied one end on her right hand and gave the other end to Darya to tie to her left hand. With this, their electrical flows would be connected.

Darya had only performed the Flow Connection once before – indeed, she entered the Bind mostly on her own – but she knew the principle and the procedure. With a faint feeling of doubt in the back of her mind, she said, "I am ready, Sister Gharana."

"Very well, we will enter a Level Two meditative state. Once we are in trance, you will initiate the search for your husband as you are more familiar with his presence. I will be able to sense what *you* sense through the connection – I assume you know the procedure? Yes? That will make things a lot simpler."

Gharana continued and said, "Close your eyes, and descend into trance. Once we connect in the Bind, you may begin your search."

Darya did as Gharana instructed. When she reached Level Two, she entered the Bind and started listening for Gharana's heartbeat. It took her only a couple of minutes to find it and latch onto it. She now stood next to the other priestess in the bright, pure white light of the Bind, and its myriad colored tendrils. The experience should have given her joy, incredible joy, as it did most Alterintrants. But it was no longer as exhilarating as it had once been for Darya, and that saddened her deeply.

Gharana sent to Darya, *"Very well, Lady Darya. I am glad to see that political life has not debilitated you."*

Darya's form spun her head and gave the other woman a sharp incredulous look. Who did she think she was?!

"I have met many a woman in your position who let her skills in the Bind go wayside due to so-called higher priorities. But it has not happened to you, and that is good."

The furrowed brows on Darya's form relaxed a little, but *only* a little.

The Easterner continued in her awful accent, *"Now, do begin your search, Lady Darya. Once I sense what vibration you are looking for, I will be able to search for the high king myself and latch onto his vibration as soon as I find him."*

Darya felt her form cringe, and was annoyed that even here in the Bind, the woman's accent had to be so irritating. But she did need to get on with it and pulled her husband's image and vibration out of her memories to begin the search.

***

Their search was, unfortunately, unsuccessful. Sister Gharana was frustrated with Darya, and the king's consort silently cursed her husband for putting her in such an embarrassing position, though she knew that it was better that they had not found him no matter how much she wished she knew where he was and – more importantly – who he was meeting with. Indeed, he had assured her –that night before he left incognito with his guard – that if either the Kynarians or the Order of Light knew what he was planning, they would not have hesitated to bring an injunction against him. And, given that he could not let that happen, and that he did not want Darya to have to lie to her superiors to protect him, he had persuaded her that it was best she did not know the details of his trip.

Of course, this meant she would find herself in the exact position where she was now: embarrassed for not knowing where her husband was, and needing to bear the criticisms of the Supreme Priestess and of the Priestess Tracker. How she wished she could smack the latter; the woman was insulting her and questioning her abilities as she paced the room after their final trial and failure. Darya very much felt like giving the other priestess a piece of her own mind, but she knew that nothing good would come of it and decided to let Gharana vent her kettle. One pleasant realization popped into Darya's mind just now, however: Gharana had lost her accent – it appeared that anger did that.

Well, I guess good things can indeed come from bad ones.

"High Prince, I do not dispute the fact that you are responsible for the safety of the people, but what I am saying is that I am responsible for the safety of their *souls and of their divine bodies*. And what I know of this rokon tells me that both are indeed in danger."

Actually, it is their orbly bodies and minds *that are in danger...and your invocations will not save anyone. Nor will your flock's prayers or their atoning for their sins.*

Aithen did his best to hide his revulsion while looking the priest straight in the eyes. "What *do* you know of this rokon, First Cleric?"

"I have heard the reports about the rokon, and –"

Aithen interrupted the priest "You mean the rumors."

"I heard that many soldiers and villagers actually lost their souls at Horn's Pass, my Prince; that men witnessed these souls come out of their comrades' bodies as they fell, and that their bodies – the bodies they should have kept safe for the Day of Union – were contorted and deformed as a result of their vain struggle to hold on to their souls. These accounts are very disturbing, to say the least." The self-important man paused, as if to let his words sink into the prince's mind. "It is essential that I send some priests to the fortress and to any village that has been attacked to ascertain these facts, and..."

Aithen corrected the cleric again, "These rumors..."

"Yes, I understand no official statement has been issued by the Crown regarding this, my Prince. But you must admit that when numerous soldiers and peasants alike make the same claim, there must be some truth to it, and this is a possibility that I *cannot* ignore. It is therefore imperative that I send some of my priests out there to verify it. If the *rumors*, should turn out to be about false facts, we will quash them as it does not serve Faith to let false beliefs spread. But if they should prove to be as I suppose, then the Church will respond to safeguard the souls and divine bodies of our people – my Prince."

I'm going to strangle him here and now. Who does he think he is?! He is worse than that arrogant Arotek or foolish Sisipe. I wish Elyana were here; she would probably know how to handle him better than I.

244

"As I said, First Cleric, plans are already in place to protect towns and villages should the rokon continue its attacks. It is your right, of course, to visit the villages and give what support you can to those in need. But it would not be wise to paralyze the people by scaring them with stories of soul-taking, or even worse." Aithen gave the leader of the Order of Aiala a look which meant he was on notice. He was a powerful man, perhaps, but he would not be permitted to threaten the security of the kingdom by allowing his priests to spread crazy talk about the end of the world.

Galadrin's jaw tightened and then relaxed so he could respond, "Of course, High Prince. In the end, we have the same goals: to ensure freedom, peace and happiness for all. I will speak with my clerics at Communion tonight to ensure their message is consistent with the truth."

Yes, I am sure you will. The problem is, which truth? Yours, mine? And the fact is, you are right about the creature not being a mere rokon, Galadrin. But I can't let you take control of the situation. Father wouldn't, and I can't either.

"Very well, First Cleric. I expect that your followers will not cause any more unrest among the Crown's subjects."

Aithen could tell he had just offended the man, but he didn't care. He hated the cleric and what he represented: the continued enslavement of the Human mind for the *good of the gods*. It was wrong, whether these gods be true or false. Aithen waited for the First Cleric to give an angry response, but Galadrin obviously had a remarkable control of his emotions and only gave away his upset through a slight movement of his lips.

Just now, the man asked with false politeness whether there was anything else the prince wished to discuss. When Aithen answered that there wasn't and that the meeting was over, Galadrin thanked him for the audience, made a perfunctory bow, and turned to leave.

When Galadrin reached the door, Aithen added, "Ah, one more thing First Cleric. Should you or your people come across any more rumors that have the potential to cause disorder in the population, it is imperative that you not take any action or make any public statement before bringing said rumors to me."

"Certainly, my Prince, I understand." And the man stepped out, his face red with ire.

Exhausted, Aithen sat in a Lacora Leaf chair. It was nearly Eight thirty after Highsun. Whenever he was tired, and on hot days especially, he sat there to relax, supported by the living limbs and cooled by the transpiration of the leaves. The chair was formed by the branches and leaves of the lacora plant. Monks of the Order of Elande took months to shape the plants and sold the finished chairs to a select few. The leaves were thick and supple and had hooks along the edges which allowed them to connect to each other. Under pressure, such as when someone sat, the branches and leaves increased in turgidity, giving them enough resistance to sustain a man's weight; the surface could be hardened or softened by rubbing it slightly. When a person moved, the chair re-formed itself to maintain contact with the person's body.

Sitting in the living chair, the prince's thoughts wandered, shifting between the events at Horn's Pass, the night in the Bind with Elyana, the stranger, his brother, his father, his meetings – especially the last one he had had, and Elyana. And when his mind happened on the Lux Baiula, it lingered there, confused by the still disconcerting – or rather – troublesome feelings. Indeed, no matter the point of view from which he considered his sentiments for the Lux Baiula, he invariably concluded that pursuing a relationship with her would only burden him with worries he could not now afford.

A quiet knock on his chambers' door pulled the prince back to reality. It was followed by a young voice.

"High Lord Commander?"

"Yes, Kildare?"

"Elyana Lux Baiula is here to see you, my Prince."

"Let her in then, and have our dinner brought up."

Kildare acknowledged the prince's instructions but remained there, hesitating.

"What is it Kil?"

"We, have a… well, a… we have a *guest* cook in the kitchen. I have been told it is fishmonger Brak's son. He is here to prepare some limpfish at Elyana Lux Baiula's request."

"Limpfish!? At Elyana's request?"

"Do you wish me to send him away, my Prince, and have your cook prepare the meal?"

246

"Hrumph. No…no. I guess that if Elyana organized this, it must be because she suspects I will like the recipe – although I don't know how she can *know* that. Just make sure there is something I like with it, in case the limpfish does not suit me after all."

Aithen's squire nodded, bowed and exited.

A moment later, the Lux Baiula walked in. The prince sat up and as he did so, the lacora plant bounced back up. Aithen felt a stir at the sight of the woman. She looked even more stunning than usual. She had changed into something light and casual tonight – a white dress with purple sleeves, and of course, her purple sash with the piece of red sash on it – but the simple dress was nevertheless very well fitted, and Elyana's appearance, combined with the serene look on her face, made her irresistible, so much so that when his eyes met hers, he was overcome by a sudden onrush of feelings of joy and relief, and before he knew it, those feelings carried over through his voice as he welcomed her. Aithen hoped the Lux Baiula had not noticed, but she did, and he detected a very brief hesitation in the woman's step. *Aghrr. Why did I do that? What is wrong with me?!*

Elyana, quickly recovered, however, and continued to her usual place – a deep brown suede chair across from Aithen – stolid and intent on putting an end to the prince's emotional distractions. The problem was, deep down inside, she too was distracted by similar feelings. How she wished she could simply ignore them.

Aithen cleared his throat uncomfortably, sensing the awkwardness in the air. He knew it would be best if he jumped straight to their business, but instead, what came out was, "I'm happy you're finally here. My mind has been restless since we arrived in Furan City, and after all my meetings, I am in desperate need of some easy, friendly conversation."

"I hear. I assume your meetings were as challenging as we had expected?"

"Yes, especially my meeting with that blind idiot."

"First Cleric Galadrin?"

"*Uhu.* If I did not have as much control as I do over myself, I might have struck him where he stood and be done with him *hic et nunc* [56]. You should have heard him trying to convince me that he is

---

[56] Hic et nunc means 'here and now' [Note: This is an actual Latin expression, still in use today to describe those seeking immediate satisfaction of their desires].

equally responsible – if not more so – for the wellbeing of the kingdom's subjects."

Elyana replied, "From his perspective, he is the only one who can truly safeguard any of us. After all, when you fail to protect our physical forms, it is the very vessel which we are taught to keep and care for to give to the Founders at the Coming that we lose along with the soul that permeates it and cares for it. But, Galadrin safeguards the entirety of our persons."

Aithen shot her an irritated stare, said, "That is not helping, Elyana. I know you are not a believer."

"I am sorry, Aithen, but the fact is that as long as people believe in that nonsense, Galadrin and others like him will continue to be their only *true* protectors, and that gives the religious caste power."

"*Aghrr*! We should have eliminated the religious orders when we had the chance, years ago."

"That would not have helped. You cannot do away with religious belief by removing the religious caste or by suppressing religious rites. They tried it in the west and it didn't work. The only way to eliminate religion is by enlightening people and by giving them new means to defeat death."

"Are you referring to those tribes in Yerlah with that transmission ritual?"

"Yes."

"I have often wondered whether the rest of the kingdom could be made to adopt such rituals."

Elyana considered Aithen's question seriously and said, "Perhaps. And there may also be other ways to achieve the same ends…"

"What do you mean?"

"I am referring to Memory Transfer. Imagine a world in which everyone could transfer the most important part of themselves before they died – their memories; those of our Order have been doing it for centuries now. This would be better than the eternal life imagined by the religious which is a mere promise of things we cannot verify. Through Memory Transfer, one's mind is immediately and verifiably safeguarded, and remains forever accessible in the memories of the living."

"Yes, that's something to imagine, indeed," said Aithen, caught up in Elyana's excitement. But the ancient words on his family's

248

crest, which hung on his wall like a perpetual reminder of one of the royal family's most sacred duties, upset him for some reason and he growled. "*Aghrr*! This is all very nice, but it's also pointless when our very world's existence is being threatened!"

"Perhaps. In fact, you are right, Aithen. These musing are pointless now."

Elyana continued, "So, what was the conclusion of your meeting with Galadrin? And what about the elders and the landholders?"

Aithen was surprised by the transition-less change in topics, from their musings about a world in which everyone would be assured eternity via Memory Transfer, to his outburst at the thought that everything he knew might soon collapse, and to Elyana's question about his meetings.

Elyana noticed and said, "You know as well as I do that letting oneself be troubled by worry does nothing to solve a problem. On the contrary, it muddles the mind, and paralyzes the body."

Aithen gave a small grunt and said, "That is not what surprised me, Elyana. It's the fact that you accepted my outburst without comment, and that you then asked your question without so much as a change in tone. It's..it was like making exhilarating acrobatics on Xyre, then landing suddenly and just walking away without so much as a wavering step.

Elyana smiled and said, "In fact, I have seen you do just that."

"Ugh! It's pointless. Very well, then. In answer to your question: Galadrin promised to speak to his people tonight about not perpetuating rumors about an evil rokon roaming the land. But I wish we had someone on the inside to be sure he keeps his promise. Something tells me his message to his priests will be somewhat different." Elyana nodded in agreement but did not offer any suggestions.

Aithen continued. "As for the Senate, everyone accepted my story about the Serpent – more or less. However, there are many senators who remain concerned about the refugees. Senator Sisipe, for one, is convinced they will cause trouble, and would prefer they be relocated to a camp outside the city. I disagree; if we did that, they would immediately feel unwelcome and decide to see to their own interests rather than feel grateful and decide to participate in the city's life in a constructive manner. Fortunately, Senator Kraelion put him in his place."

Aithen added, "I am glad we have at least one ally in the Senate."

"Hmm. Your father actually has a large enough number of supporters in the Senate, and I do not doubt that if Elder Sisipe and his followers had tried to cause real trouble, the others would have spoken up too – eventually. But Senator Kraelion is not one to wait for the *right* time to defend what is just, or to oppose what is unjust regardless of whether or not others are ready to support her."

"Yes, father has told me that about her; she is a good woman. One thing does concern me though, about the villagers. I know they are honest people, and that they will work to earn food and shelter, but the city's infrastructure will be very tightly stretched, especially the medical services and the schools. Can the Sisterhood help?"

"I really doubt any of my White Sisters will accept the additional load for very long, but I will see if Urbs Lucis can send a few more medics – and teachers."

Just now there was a knock on the doors to the prince's chambers. Aithen recognized his squire's knock and called him in after thanking Elyana.

Kil announced, "The food, my Prince."

With a sarcastic glance at the Lux Baiula, Aithen said, "Ah, yes, the limpfish!"

"Well, bring it in, Kil. I *cannot* wait to try it!"

Unfortunately for Aithen, the Lux Baiula did not bite, and instead she said with the most congenial tone, "Fishmonger Brak promised that we *would* enjoy it, Aithen, assuring me that his son has created a dish that will suit the most *delicate* palates."

And unfortunately for Aithen, he did bite and was about to object when he thought better and decided instead to just 'land and walk away' – at least he tried, and succeeded to a degree, except for the slight edge in his tone. He said, "Well, let us hope the dish is as Fishmonger Brak promised, because I will not moderate my tongue when I am asked whether I enjoyed it or not, and I know I will be asked." The prince was right. Whenever non-palace cooks served new foods or recipes at the palace, they sent *news fetchers* in, the following day, to find out whether the food had been a success or not. If the royal family had enjoyed the food, the cook would let it be known throughout the city, hoping to receive invitations from noble families and rich merchants who wished to be among the first 'discoverers.' If, on the other hand, the royal family had disliked the food, the cook would kill the story if it were possible. If it were *not* possible, such as when a member of the royal family shared his or her displeasure with others, the poor cook either killed the recipe itself and retired from the culinary scene for a while or tried again if he had the courage.

Just now, Elyana decided to bring the conversation back to their business. "So, where were we? Ah, yes! The need for additional medics and teachers. I cannot promise we will get the medics, Aithen, because the White Sashate is already stretched to capacity, what with the declining medical candidates over the last ten years, but I will ask. On the other hand, I am confident the Yellow Sashate can send a few teachers."

"Thank you." Aithen paused a moment, unexpectedly surprised by the smell of the food being laid out on the balcony, where he and Elyana would be eating. He gave Elyana a guilty smile. She smiled in return, and Aithen said, "If the food tastes as good as it smells, I might actually enjoy it. Anyway, going back to my meetings: I am happy to say that after much squabbling, all the landholders left more-or-less satisfied knowing that military assistance would be provided – either by the local major houses or by the Royal Guard – to those needing it. They also accepted to have Lux Baiulae help defend all major centers; my secretary has the list. Can you discuss it with the Magna Mater?"

"Of course. She has been expecting the request. But remember that very few of us may have the skill to generate the required nebula; others will need to be trained, and it will take some time."

"I know, Elyana. I only ask that Urbs Lucis keep me informed of the progress, if it is the case that Sisters need to be trained, so that I may tell each landholder when he or she might expect one of you to arrive."

Just now a servant approached Aithen and announced that the table was ready. The prince invited Elyana to the table, still unsure about the limpfish, but he *did* like the smell. Aithen watched Elyana as she approached the table to sit, and he found himself hoping the conversation could move to something other than politics, evil things, or the security of the kingdom. And he chided himself again. How could anything happen between them? First of all, she was much older than he; she was also so much more knowledgeable about myriad topics *he* barely understood. How could she be interested in a romantic relationship with him, a mere mortal humanoid? Still, he felt like talking to her about his hopes and dreams; he felt like telling her about all the times when they were *supposed* to be meditating, but all he could do was stare at her beautiful, tranquil face. While all this collided in his mind, his eyes inadvertently set on Elyana. The Lux Baiula turned her eyes to the table to avoid the prince's stare.

They spent two hours eating slowly, suppressing groans and averting each other's eyes every time the conversation slowed, with Elyana keeping herself from feeling, and Aithen blind to the fact she desired the same thing he did. The prince couldn't tell whether the Lux Baiula noticed the strain in his face every time he suppressed a sigh, but he hoped she didn't. Or did he actually hope she *would* notice? In fact, he wasn't sure what he hoped; what he knew for certain was that his mind was becoming more and more troubled and foggy with every new day of this battle against his feelings.

XVI THINGS REVEALED

The woods were truly as foreboding as the stories told. Even with the suns approaching their apex, only the palest light filtered down to the ground. Shadows were everywhere and Toras kept turning his head one way and then another, certain he had seen something move. But the king just kept walking, seemingly uncaring about what might be lurking in this darkness.

The suffocating hot, humid air added to Toras's discomfort. Trees normally kept things cool – at least in the northeast – but here, they were of no help. Rivulets had formed on Toras's back and forehead. He wondered how his father could be so dry.

He said, "I'm going to need a bath soon. I am drenched to the bone."

"I am not surprised; you never did learn to breathe well. But we are almost at our destination."

After some forty minutes of walking through the ominous forest, the king finally stopped between two unremarkable trees. The ground between the trees seemed burned and the leaves of the few small plants still standing there were covered in some strange crystalline dust. Toras was about to question his father but the king now lowered his head and whispered some words too low for Toras to hear. Suddenly, a door appeared in front of them and stood there just above the ground, as if by magic. The trees behind the door seemed to be wavering in and out of existence and the ground in front of the door was crackling in reaction to some unseen energy field.

What in Aiala'Rhi's name is this? And this crackling, it reminds me of – what was it called? – an electric field *like the one the Lux Baiulae created at the Knowledge Academy, four years ago.*

Toras looked at his father quizzically, but the king put up his hand and motioned him to follow.

"Father, you know I trust you in all things, but I'm a little hesitant here. Firstly, I have no idea where we are going. Secondly, there's a door appears out of nowhere, and I'm supposed to just follow you through it? How can I protect you if something happens?"

Octavius raised an eyebrow and said, "There is no danger on the other side, Toras. But, yes, you are supposed to just follow me through it, and I promise that you will have answers soon." The king motioned his son forward and said, "Come." And with a slight push of his hand, the high king opened the door and stepped through. The prince followed, unsure and slightly unnerved when his father's body seemed to get out of focus.

What Toras beheld on the other side of the door was pure beauty and peace enclosed in what must be a large villa. Its grounds were striking with fruit trees, flowers and ponds, all around. Sculptured needle trees stood here and there representing various wonderful creatures. Multicolored cocks pecked at the ground alongside fancy white carriers and all manners of Chirpers, many of which the prince had never heard before. When he looked back at the door they had come through, Toras was surprised to see it encased in an unusually tall wall which likely surrounded the villa – whatever villa this was. The wall was some six to seven meters tall, and it was of the same unknown material as the door. They must be in some dangerous zone of the kingdom – if they were even still in Aquinos – for the owner to desire such a high enclosure.

Toras asked the king where they were. Were they still in the forest or in some other place? But just as his father was about to speak, two men came out of a house Toras had not noticed at first, some fifty to sixty meters ahead of them, nestled within the idyllic garden.

One of the two men walked slightly ahead of the other. He wore a broad smile on his cheery face as he welcomed his guests. The man was tall and lean, except for a slightly bulging belly. White hair and a neatly trimmed beard surrounded his face. On his cheeks were two conspicuous scars, angled from the outside corners of his eyes to the bottom of his ears. At first, Toras was merely intrigued, but something in the back of his mind clicked and he suddenly remembered what those scars were: the marks of a very rare punishment. They were in the presence of a banished man, the only banished man he knew of – Marcus the Reader!

Toras turned to his father and said to him as silently as he could manage, "Father, if this is who I think it is, we are breaking the laws of the land by being here! We *can't* be here!"

"Quiet, son! I brought you here for a reason, and you will control yourself and observe, and soon you will see the wisdom of my actions."

Toras churned inside, not understanding what reason might push his father to break the law. But he had enough sense not to make a scene now and he quieted himself as best he could. Their host and his follower – a short, strange-looking fellow with skin the color of white nut-milk, reddish hair, and slanted eyes – were now standing in front of them and bowing deeply.

Their host said in a jovial tone, "My King, welcome back."

The short man bowed uncertainly and said in a strangely hesitant tone, "Majesty."

Their host looked at Toras curiously, unsure what to think of him with his clothes in tatters and his face, arms, and legs still bruised and scarred despite the healing. Then he said, "And who is this young man, my King?" looking from one to the other.

"This is my son, Toras, Lord Commander of the fortress at Horn's Pass."

"Toras! Your father has told me much about you. I am Marcus Vrol."

Toras, still diffident, did not make any replies.

The man continued, "I understand your hesitation. But what has happened to you?"

The Halfling had no desire to strike a conversation with this man, although he knew he had no choice but to reply, and so he did, though he did say the man's name with a hint of disapproval. "I would rather not speak of it...*Master Vrol*."

Marcus noticed the tone in the prince's voice, but made nothing of it and said, "Fair enough."

Toras asked, "And who is your companion?"

The short man replied for himself, "I amma Methorr...of Zzebulonia."

Before Toras could reply anything, the king jumped in and said, "Methor is here to offer his friendship and request our help. There are many in Zebulonia who desire the end of the rule of Queen Zebula, as well as reconciliation with the rest of the continent. I am considering his request."

The prince turned toward the king but held back his question and thoughts. *What are you getting involved in, Father?*

Marcus the Reader said, "My King, my Prince, something tells me you might enjoy some refreshment. The woods are like a steam bath today; I had to go out there this morning to gather some herbs and although I was gone but thirty minutes, I returned drenched to the bone just as badly as the prince, and although the king appears untouched by the heat, I am certain he too will welcome something refreshing. As it happens, I have just harvested my first redmelons of the season, and they are an excellent remedy for an overheated body."

Octavius welcomed their host's invitation and the group followed Marcus the Reader back to his house. There, the men sat down under a canopy of vines that provided a comfortable shelter against the morning suns. Toras was surprised to see Marcus grab a melon from a wooden bucket and cut it up for his guests. He would have expected a man with such an impressive villa to own a servant or two, but he had none apparently. Marcus gave the first large fleshy slice to the king. It looked truly appetizing and made Toras's mouth water despite his misgivings. When Marcus offered him some melon in turn, Toras accepted with some reluctance, unwilling to open up to this man just yet, despite the complete trust his father seemed to place in him – a man known to all as a pariah.

"My Prince, please forgive me for being so direct, but I can see your discomfort. I assume the King, your father, did not tell you who you would be meeting?"

"Indeed, Master Vrol."

Marcus looked at the king, who nodded in return, giving him permission to explain the situation to Toras.

Marcus the Reader turned to the Zebulonian and asked him whether he would give them some time alone and return in fifteen minutes. The foreigner nodded, stood and left after bowing to the king and prince.

Once the man was gone, Marcus began, "My Prince, you probably wonder why the king would break the law by visiting a criminal, a man banished from society in perpetuity? A man who committed one of the worst possible crimes: the violation of a person's mind?"

"Yes, I do wonder."

"The truth is that I did *not* commit the crime for which I was punished, although I understand why I had to be banished, regardless."

Toras blinked and snorted in surprise. *What is this man trying to sell me?*

"You see, forty years ago, a group known as The Originator's Hand decided to unseat the king, believing that his religious and educational policies would doom the kingdom. They began by conducting high profile assassinations across the land targeting a number of the king's supporters. The palace's police – which I headed – together with Urbs Lucis spent months investigating the group without result; we had not a single clue and had not captured a single one of them. In Decimus of that year, we received a note from the group. It said: "The king dies this month." Given the fact that we had failed in preventing any of the earlier assassinations, we were very worried, terribly worried that their latest threat would also become a reality. So, at our wit's end, Elyana Lux Baiula and I decided to send the king into hiding while telling everyone else that he was going to his retreat in Antar. To make this work, we had to find a man who could impersonate your father, and luckily, we did. The man was aware of the great risk to his life, but he accepted the danger in exchange for a promise to support his family should something happen to him."

"Once all the preparations had been made and the king had been secreted away to Kynaria, Elyana Lux Baiula, High Captain Darius and I, along with a Guard of thirty men took the king's double to Antar. On nineteen Decimus, he was assassinated. That was not only unfortunate for the Originator's Hand and for the poor soul who accepted to impersonate your father, but for us as well as we again failed to prevent another murder and to capture the killer. One thing gave us hope, and it was that the assassin could not have come from the outside. But the realization that the assassin must be one of us or one of the guardians was also a moment of great horror. We decided to have Elyana Lux Baiula interrogate everyone, including the captain and me.

"The next day, while Elyana Lux Baiula interrogated High Captain Darius, I decided to go to the kitchens and find some food to relieve my tension. The cook was there preparing the Guard's meal, alone. Suddenly, the woman attacked me, but not to kill me, or I surely would have died. Instead, she pinned me down, placed her hand on my head and violated me. That is, she entered my mind by force. She was mad – raging really – unable to accept that she had been fooled by us and had gone on to kill an impersonator. She wanted to know where the king was and did her best to rip the information from my mind."

Marcus paused to take a sip of wine, and continued, "Fortunately, I am a Mind Reader as well, and I fought back. While doing so, I was lucky enough to learn the identity of the group's leader. The woman now felt *herself* violated, and she became even madder – if that were possible. She bombarded me with so much of the power that she would have literally fried my brain had I not been stronger than she in the Bind. The assassin's rage caused her nervous system to overload. The next moment, she released her hold of me, and dropped to the ground, dead."

Marcus could tell the prince was processing his account and trying to determine whether it changed anything.

Toras said, "So, you killed the would-be assassin. How is it that you came to be banished?"

Marcus Vrol now took in a deep breath filled with old, repressed resentment, and said, "The Sisterhood investigated the matter, as was its duty, and was convinced in the end that I *had* violated the woman; your father had strong doubts, but could not take the risk that I was indeed a violator, and he agreed with the Magna Mater's sentence: *permanent banishment*."

Toras sat silently and mulled over the story for a while. Marcus's tale was plausible, but that still did not explain why the king would now trust him. Toras asked, "Father, you have obviously changed your mind about Master Vrol, so what new evidence do you have that convinces you of his innocence?"

The king replied without hesitation, as if he were simply stating what he had had for lunch. "I entered his mind."

Toras, shocked, asked a little louder than he should have. "You did *what?!*"

"With Master Vrol's permission, I entered his mind the day I first arrived here. It was not an easy task given that the last time I had done something of the sort was before my ascension to the throne, when I commanded my father's secret service, before Master Vrol himself took command of it. In any case, no matter how deep I looked, I could not find any evidence of Master Vrol violating a woman's mind."

Toras noted Marcus's discomfort when his father mentioned looking deep inside him. He wondered why. Did the man have something else to hide?

"Do not mistake Marcus's reaction, my son. Though I did not uncover anything regarding the purported crime – or any other crime for that matter – entering a man's mind does reveal things any person would rather keep private."

Toras said, "Hum, right. I guess I wouldn't like that either. I am still puzzled by something, though. If you could enter his mind, why could a Sister not have done so forty years ago?"

"There did not seem to be a need; he was known to be a Mind Reader, and a woman was dead with bloodshot eyes." Seeing the question in Toras's eyes, Octavius added, "Those are the prime clues of mind violation."

Marcus added, "When a person's mind is violated, his or her blood rushes to the brain with the strain caused by the victim's resistance; the greater the resistance, the more blood rushes to the brain. If the victim dies, the blood remains there, and the eyes retain a dark red tint as a result. As far as my attacker was concerned, she ended up with the same symptoms upon her death because of the strain my resistance caused her."

Toras nodded a cautious understanding nod. "So, what made you decide to look into the matter again, Father?"

"Marcus contacted me to tell me of the Zebulonian rebels' request, rebels whom he knows for reasons we do not need to go into. I knew I could not ignore the request, so I came and did what I should have done so long ago." As he said that, Octavius looked at his friend with something that appeared like a remnant of deep guilt.

Everyone sat in silent thought for the next few minutes. Octavius and Marcus could see that Toras was processing the story in his mind, and that he was coming to some conclusion which caused him to finally relax his muscles and shoulders. Octavius also noted that – although he had relaxed – something still preoccupied his son. *Well, even if my transgression of the law is understandable, it is still a transgression, and Toras knows there will probably be consequences.*

Just as Octavius finished that thought, the Zebulonian came back. Toras looked at the time disc – a beautifully crafted instrument, sitting in an alcove in the side wall of the house – it said One Hour and Ten Minutes before Highsun. This was certainly a very punctual man. Marcus invited the rebel to sit down, which he did with a cautious look on his face, unsure whether he should discuss his request for support in front of Toras or not. Actually, he was still uncertain whether he should trust the high king, let alone this young military commander – whether he was the king's son or not. But their host's relaxed visage indicated to the Zebulonian that he could speak freely. So, he began.

***

"Saara. What do you know of the Temptatori?"

The ancient Lux Baiula blinked. "Why do you ask, Mater?"

"Because Elyana overheard the Serpent and its companion mention them. It appears the Serpent is to meet with their leader in Kartak."

Saara was so shocked, she almost fell into her chair as she exclaimed, "What?!"

Saara had never met a Temptator; the last of them had been destroyed nearly six hundred years ago during the Dark Battle. But she had the memories of a Lux Baiula that had been captured by them at the height of the war against the Dark One. The woman had been subjected to unsayable things for months, until she turned – almost. Seeing herself on the brink of giving in, she decided to take her own life by shutting down her kidneys and by releasing into her bloodstream all the toxins contained within her liver. Fate showed its ironical cruelty on that day, when a group of Red Sashes stormed into the compound to rescue the woman. They were shattered when they found their colleague with barely a thread of life left in her, but they were able to save something of her. Indeed, waiting outside the compound was Afanasiia Lux Baiula, a Sister who had just perfected the skill of Memory Transfer, and who would later go on to found the Yellow Sashate. Afanasiia decided to perform the first field attempt at mnemonic transfer on this occasion, and she was successful, capturing all of the dying woman's memories. Through successive transfers, the memories were now Saara's, and as old as they were, Saara could still feel the pain the Lux Baiula had suffered,

260

her doubts, her revulsion at her own weakness, her hate for the Dark One and its minions, and her resolve in ending her life before she broke.

Recovered from her shock, Saara said, "They were humanoids of the vilest kind. It is said they were created by Noctiferus himself, because he alone had the ability to penetrate one's mind and erase all inhibitions and traces of morals in them, whether they be commoners, nobles, philosophers, or soldiers. Once he controlled them, he sent them out to recruit their children, spouses, siblings, friends, colleagues and strangers. They tempted their victims by indulging their gluttony, lust, greed, sloth or any other of the known sins, as well as by stupefying them with some unknown Binding. Depending on their victims' strength of character, it took a few fourths to a couple of months to turn them but turn them they did. They did that to their own family members, Magna Mater!" The ancient Lux Baiula looked away and shook her head before adding, "And they corrupted some of us as well."

Saara's excitement took Krystiana aback. The woman rarely let her emotions show, but this evidently disturbed her deeply – and now it troubled Krystiana as well.

The White continued, "This horde of depravation had been more dangerous than all of Noctiferus's armed forces. They worked from the inside to tear down the very fabric of society throughout K'Tara. It was through pure luck we won the battle, back then, pure luck. And I am not just expressing an opinion; I *know* it was pure luck."

"You mean you know through mnemonic transfer?"

"Yes."

"The memories of Carla Lux Baiula? The one whom Afanasiia Lux Baiula and the others had tried to free…from the Temptatori?"

Saara nodded dejectedly.

Krystiana asked, "Saara, what could have brought them back? That is, what could have recreated these creatures now?"

The woman took a moment to respond, appearing to struggle with her answer, an answer which she did not want to be true.

"If our long-gone Sisters were right, the only thing that can have reestablished the Temptatori," Saara paused, looking straight at Krystiana, "is Noctiferus himself. Unless someone else has discovered how to wipe out all moral instincts in a humanoid's mind, which is very unlikely."

Krystiana was pacing across her room now, her muscles tense, her face paling with the realization.

"How fast can the Dark One build the Temptatori – if we assume he is the one doing it?"

"I believe he was able to corrupt one or two people a fourth, and each Temptator could turn another three or four humanoids every month. Quite mathematical. If he is the one doing this, or if someone from this Orb has developed the power he had, he could create as many as a hundred and four Temptatori in the first year, and in turn, they will recruit as many as two thousand, one hundred and twelve underlings. At the end of the second year, there could be as many as two hundred and eight Temptatori and nine thousand, two hundred and sixteen of their subordinates. These will be sent about to infiltrate every institution of society, here as well as in Kynaria and in the non-affiliated lands – meaning, our enemies' governments and other institutions, which will lead to global chaos."

Krystiana did not linger on the latter statement though she knew Saara was not exaggerating. Instead, she asked, "How easily did they infiltrate the Sisterhood back then, Saara?"

"Not easily, Mater, but they did, nevertheless. The Dark One actually had an easier time subverting Lux Baiulae than he did Luxori, but there are none to come to our aid this time."

Krystiana murmured the name of their male counterparts to herself, bemoaning their extinction. "What can we do to protect ourselves, Saara?"

"I am not certain, Mater."

Krystiana surprised Saara with the forcefulness of her reply, when she said, "Then, that is something you will need to investigate, Saara!"

The old Praefecta nodded, her face emotionless, though she felt the crushing weight of the responsibility her superior had just put on her. The only thing that betrayed her state of mind was the need for the Magna Mater to repeat her next question twice.

"Saara! How does one recognize a Temptator?"

Saara replied without a hint of the emotions she had just felt. "From what the books tell us, the Alterintrant ones – both the males and the females – had a very unusual signature, and a Lux Baiula could recognize it if she were paying attention and knew what to look for. Unfortunately, I haven't the faintest idea what that

262

vibrational signature might be. On the other hand, it is fortunate that there are very few male Alterintrants now, and that today's Temptatori are likely to be females, which were not as vile and not as powerful – according to Carla's memories."

Krystiana gave a tentative, hopeful nod.

"As for the Unsensing Temptatori, they could not be distinguished from any other humanoid, except for the fact that they had the ability to befriend anyone they chose to befriend."

Krystiana said, "Well, perhaps we can use that information about the Unsensing to search for both types since it seems logical to assume that even the Alterintrant Temptatori would have the same facility at taking up friendship with anyone."

Saara spread her hands, "Perhaps."

Krystiana tapped her fingers and said, "The Alterintrant Temptatori…don't Carla Lux Baiula's memories contain –"

Saara interrupted her leader. "I am sorry, Mater, but Carla's memories only give me faint feelings of repulsion and of…nausea, and because there are many people in the kingdom who repulse me, as well as some in Urbs Lucis who nauseate me, I am unable to distinguish the feelings I get from Carla's memories."

"I told you long ago that your inability to dampen those feelings would someday become a problem. And here we are now, possibly hindered by that problem."

Saara tightened her jaw and breathed in slowly to let the accusation wash over her. As she did so, she realized that the Magna Mater was, in fact, right. As old as she was, she still had not learned to dampen certain emotions. How long did a person need to live to become a true master of herself?

Meanwhile, Krystiana walked to her desk, stopped in front of it and fanned the blue flame licking the sphere representing the Red Sun. She picked up the sphere, causing the flame to grow momentarily, and then peered into the object's crystalline depth as if to find understanding and knowledge in it.

Saara watched her leader with what some might call mild jealousy. *I wonder if the rumors are true, about the spheres containing the knowledge of all past Magnae Matres in them. The disjointed memories we get from Memory Transfer would pale in comparison.*

At that moment, a worrisome piece of knowledge from Carla's memories surfaced to Saara's consciousness, and she said, "Mater, you do realize what the presence of a Temptatori cell in Kartak might mean? ...Mater?"

Krystiana snapped out of her reverie instantly and put the sphere back in its position above the marble base before answering the Praefecta Medicas. Krystiana continued watching the sphere as it bounced a few times before settling back into position, engulfed by the blue flame again. When it was done, she turned around and said, "Depending on how large that cell is, it could mean the Dark One – if it is him – has been at it for months – if not for years – already. It means that his minions may have infiltrated the whole of society already, just waiting for the right time to strike and hand this world to him. Is this what you are thinking?"

"That is my fear as well. We must send some Sisters to Kartak, as soon as possible."

"Yes, we must. I will speak with Bilena. If anyone can take on this task, it is the Yellows. But they will need preparation; you will have to tell them everything you know of the Temptatori, Saara. And they will need a way to infiltrate Kartak without putting themselves at risk. I want you to help them. You were once a Yellow Sash, and one of the best at that!"

Saara straightened her aged back and took a deep, heavy breath before replying, "I am here to serve, Mater."

"Thank you, old friend."

"As old as I am, and despite all the things I have heard and lived, I do not look forward to this task, Mater."

"I understand, Saara."

The Praefecta Medicas nodded, and then added with a certain urgency, "Mater, are you going to share this with the Ambassadors [57]?"

"I must think it over carefully, as we do not want to cause panic. But I will need to inform House Coriolis. I hope someone finds the high king soon, otherwise we will have to work with High Prince Aithen, and I do not know how ready he is to take on the

---

[57] Every kingdom and city of importance had an ambassador in Urbs Lucis.

responsibilities and the moral injuries a new Dark Battle would force upon him."

"Anyway, that will be all for now, Saara. I will let you know when I have spoken with Bilena."

Saara nodded, bowed and turned toward the door.

Krystiana said, "Do not share any of this with anyone for the moment."

"Of course, Mater. Anything else?"

"Yes, please ask Lupa Lux Baiula [58] to come in, in ten minutes, and put a smile on your face before you step out."

Saara frowned at that comment, but she knew what Krystiana meant. She left her leader's office and did her best to smoothen her face, thinking: *This is too much to just hide...I better just get to my chambers before anyone sees me and starts rumors about more bad news, though they wouldn't be wrong this time.*

The White almost forgot to stop by the Magna Mater's secretary as these thoughts occupied her mind. Worrying that Lupa might see the worry in her face, she decided to remain in the antechamber, give the woman her instructions through the half-opened door, and leave for her own chambers before any replies came.

As for Krystiana, she sat on the red and blue carpet near the back of her office, crossed her legs, closed her eyes, and descended into a shallow meditative state to chime Elyana for she was in great need of a friend's ear and words.

* * *

"High King, what I amma requesting is your intervention in support of the Organization for the Liberation of Zebulonian Males."

Toras could see the frustration in the foreigner's expression. The Zebulonian and the king had been discussing possible financial and tactical support for the group's planned rebellion for the past hour, but it was obvious his father had no interest in softening his conditions.

Octavius sighed and replied, "I understand, but why would I do that? Why support your group and not one of the other rebel factions? What of the civilian women in Zebulonia? Do they support you? You must understand that I will only intervene to support the

---

[58] Lupa Lux Baiula was the Magna Mater's personal secretary.

establishment of a free society, inclusive of all Zebulonians, and you have yet to convince me that that is your organization's intent."

"High King, our women cannot accept to live side by side with free men, especially the Janarae. Only one fate can be for Zebula's Guard."

"I am afraid that is not acceptable."

The Zebulonian stood from the table so suddenly that he caused the fruit bowls and wine cups to rattle. He said, "Do you understand that Queen Zebula will invade your kingdom!?"

Both Toras and Marcus shot incredulous looks at the Zebulonian. Though the king was not one to behead people for breach of protocol – as some rulers did in other places – he did end audiences with those who showed egregious lack of civility or respect without a second thought, whether they be locals or foreigners. But this time, the king simply gave the man a warning. With well-controlled irritation in his voice, meant to put the man back in his place and leave him with no doubt as to the consequences of further missteps, Octavius said, "Mind your tongue, Master Methor; our conversation is a hair away from being ended."

The short man appeared to be sincerely sorry and embarrassed for his behavior – exceedingly so even – and he lowered his head in a sign of contrition and submission which his short stature made almost comical. "My apologies, Majesty, I did not mean to disrespect. If you have suggestions for integrating women – and about integrating the Janarae especially – into a free Zebulonian society, for sure I will welcome them, because there is no Zebulonian male who exists who knows how that can be made. You see, the Janarae promise their lives, their bodies, and also their souls to the service of the queen; and for that, they are leaders, rich, and free. But we, the males, we are only servants, and have always to be servants for generations, and because of this, we do not have the experience…or…or the…the temper to achieve what you are requesting. But we are determined, and we are committed to changing things for to build a better society."

Octavius was thoroughly impressed by the man's sudden volubility and by his obvious sincerity. "Your apology is accepted Master Methor. It is rare to find a man who apologizes without giving any reason or excuse for his behavior; it takes great humility to do so, and that is a trait I admire. Had you tried to give me reasons,

I would have ended our meeting and never given you another audience. And your words do convince me of the honorability of your goals. But, to answer your question: I do understand your Queen's intentions and I am ready to defend my kingdom without any outside group's support. However, if I can prevent an attack on my lands in the first place by helping you achieve your goals – if they are honorable, which they do seem to be – then I will gladly assist you."

After a moment of reflection during which the foreigner considered the king's conditions, the man lowered his head, and offered his hands, face up, to the king. "Sire, I accept your conditions, even I do not see how the Janarae can be integrated in a free society, which is because of my ignorance. And I can promise that my brothers will also agree to your conditions."

"You will have my support then. As for the Janarae, simply know this: that the victors can impose whatever new order they desire on the defeated, so long as their victory is complete. If the victors are also honorable people, then the greater part of the defeated often ends up willingly submitting to the new ways. The unwilling minority, however – especially if it is vocal – usually needs to be removed from society to assure its peace, and their removal is something that must be planned just as carefully as everything else. We will help you plan for that, if it appears that such a measure will be necessary."

Methor looked at the king with utter amazement. How could a man be so confident? And his rationality and wisdom – qualities which Queen Zebula was totally deprived of, but which he had found in this foreign monarch – humbled Methor completely. In a sign of respect, he bowed deeply before the high king. Marcus nodded to himself, satisfied.

As for Toras, he wondered what his father meant by "the removal of the unwilling minority", but he had heard from his tutors that his father's consolidation of the kingdom had sometimes rested on the use of extreme measures. His tutors had not elaborated on the nature of those measures, and Toras still wondered if they meant the imprisonment, or the execution, of his father's opponents. But he also knew that the kingdom was stronger than it had been in a long time, and that the general sentiment in the lands was very favorable

267

to House Coriolis. So, whatever his father had done to consolidate his power, it could not have been that bad.

XVII PREPARATIONS

Having successfully concluded their meeting, High King Octavius and the Zebulonian agreed to target the following spring for the commencement of the rebellion, and made arrangements for their next encounter. In the meantime, Master Methor would obtain his organization's approval of the agreement and bring the confirmation back to the king at their next encounter, which they also agreed to before separating.

Marcus invited the king and his son to remain a little while longer, but Octavius, aware that he was needed in the capital, bade farewell to their host, and father and son returned to Toras's camp outside of the Shadow Woods.

Fortunately for Toras, the journey back was much more pleasant than it had been that morning. Indeed, the suns were now near the horizon and the earlier heat and humidity had dissipated. But the conversation was a tense one, nevertheless, with Toras questioning the king about his motives.

Octavius listened to his son's complaints and gave him what other explanations he could to assuage his doubts about the entire affair. But eventually, the king realized that Toras, being who he was, would only come around once he convinced himself, so Octavius ended the exchange to focus on what really concerned him at the moment: as king, the decision to raise an army was his alone. But to fight the Janarae, he would need the Sisterhood's support, and he had not discussed any of this with the Magna Mater before committing to something that would most definitely involve them. In the end, Krystiana would surely agree to support him, but she would not get there easily given that Octavius was going to her with a done deal, a deal achieved through the intervention of a certain banished person. Octavius wondered which of these would anger the Magna Mater more.

Well, what's done is done. She'll get over it, eventually. But it is Elyana, I feel the worst about. She is my advisor, and I should have told her – if no one else. When she learns I hid this from her, she will have a conniption.

"Father?"

"Hmm?"

"We've arrived."

"Indeed! Then, it is high time for a bath."

Toras looked at his father with a shocked expression. "A bath? How?"

"I had the men bring some water back from the nearby stream while we were away."

Toras was not pleased with that answer, finding the use of their men for such frivolities excessive. He said, with some sarcasm. "Oh. Well, I hope you enjoy it."

"You may have one too. Do not worry son, I gave the men leave to bathe themselves in the stream after bringing back some water for us – I am not as insensible as you seem to think. You should know me better."

"Should I? Do I?"

"Hum, I see. You are still upset about what you learned yesterday, and perhaps also about my dealing with Marcus Vrol and the Zebulonian. Well, I have explained my reasons, and it is now up to you to accept them."

Octavius continued, "If you do not wish to bathe, I would ask that you gather the officers to begin making preparations for our return to the capital, and that you come present your plans to me in an hour."

Toras gave a curt, "Very well, Father," and made his way to the Praetorian Guard's common tent, which had been transferred to him given that he had destroyed his own tent back at Mountain Lake.

As for the king, he continued his slow, pensive march toward his own tent.

An anxious looking man saluted the king. "Sire, it is good to see you; I have to say I've never awaited your return so impatiently."

Worried by the man's words and nervous hands, Octavius asked, "What is going on, Primus?"

Primus Julian was the captain of the king's personal guard. He was a tall, muscular, red-haired man, but his green eyes looked too soft for a soldier, and they often fooled his opponents.

"Sire…two Lux Baiulae arrived here around midday. They were sent by Urbs Lucis to find you, and they are in a sour mood. What's more, they've been questioning Primus Kendor, Secundus Jamir, and me all afternoon."

270

"Where are they now?"

"They are back in their tent over there, my King. They were going to question me again, until they decided to report to Urbs Lucis first."

"And what questions were they asking?"

"Sire, they wanted to know where you were, why you came here, and why you left Furan City without notifying anyone, not even Elyana Lux Baiula."

"Yes, I imagine they would want to know that. All right, I just need some time to refresh myself." Octavius pulled his pouch time disk from his tunic, looked at it and added, "You may inform the Sisters that I will see them at Eight Fifteen."

Julian – usually very prompt in acknowledging the king's orders – hesitated a moment before responding with a forced, "Yes, my King."

"Is something bothering you, Julian?"

The primus hesitated again, then said, "Yes, Sire. One of them is…well, my twin sister…Juliana Lux Baiula. She has been newly appointed to Lord Valorian, along with Mara Lux Baiula."

"Oh ho! That is certainly unexpected. I bet this is not how you envisioned meeting your sister again after – how long has it been? – three years?"

"Two years since she left for Urbs Lucis, my King."

"Well, I trust you told your sister and her companion nothing but the truth?"

"Sire, you were very wise in not telling me why you came here; therefore, there was no lie for me to tell. However, that did not keep my sister from braising me as much as – or perhaps more so – than her colleague did."

"I hear. If you prefer it, you can send someone else carry my message to the Lux Baiulae."

Primus Julian jerked back at that suggestion and said, "Sire, you know I have never shrunk from my duties. My discomfort is completely irrelevant. I will carry your message."

"Very well, Primus. I do know how committed you are to your duty."

Noticing that his captain was still hesitating, the king gave him a questioning look.

"Sire, are you aware that Juliana is a truthsayer?"

271

"*Ah!?* No, I was not, but it is good to know. Is there anything else, Primus?"

"No, Sire. That was all. I will go to the Lux Baiulae to inform them of your arrival and extend your invitation to them."

In his borrowed tent, Toras was listening to Kendor telling him of the Lux Baiulae's arrival, but the prince quickly dismissed the matter as one better dealt with by the king and moved the discussion to the returning of the king to the capital. But because the head of the Praetorian Guard would need to agree to whatever plan they came up with, Toras sent Secundus Jamir fetch him.

Secundus Jamir found Primus Julian walking about in circles, furiously stomping the ground, and looking strangely downtrodden. Indeed, Julian's last encounter with the Lux Baiulae had been the worst yet. His sister and her companion had been furious the king would choose to bathe before seeing them, and demanded explanations from him, none of which satisfied them, of course. In the end, the Sisters decided to thank him for the message, and dismissed the Primus. They had dismissed him! Primus Julian had made certain that his sister noticed the look of dismay on his face as he left their tent. He then called on one of his men, asked him to take the Sisters to the king by the appointed time, and walked to his voran, hoping that checking on the animal would help him cool off. Instead, he had made circles around the voran, stomping the ground all the while. When Secundus Jamir approached him, he shouted, "Now what?"

Jamir said, "My apologies, Primus. Lord Commander Toras sent me to get you. He wishes your assistance to plan the king's return to Furan City."

"Why would he –? No matter, let's go."

A moment later, Jamir and Julian entered the prince's tent. Julian made a small bow and asked, or rather said with some irritation in his voice, "My Prince, I hear you wish to discuss plans to take the king back to Furan City?"

"Indeed, Primus. I need to present our recommendations to my father in an hour."

272

The commander of the king's personal guard took a moment to consider the prince's statement. For some reason, he seemed to be utterly shocked by it – offended even. He said, "My Prince, with all due respect, that is *my* responsibility."

Toras blinked upon hearing Primus Julian's stern reply. *Well! What a nice start to the conversation. And who does he think I am? The fishmonger?* Toras gave Secundus Jamir a questioning look, to which the man answered with raised eyebrows and an expressive frown that meant that there were indeed extenuating reasons for the officer's behavior and the prince should simply ignore it for now.

Toras understood immediately and said, "I know, Primus, I know, but these are unusual circumstances. By now, I'm sure you have heard of the rokon's attack on Horn's Pass and on several villages along the coast. The few of you would not stand a chance against it, should you come across it, especially on voranback. I, myself, came with thirty men to find and bring back the king, and there are now only ten of us left. I understand the king's safety is your corps' personal responsibility and I will be very grateful to you and your men if you would ensure that my father remains alive and uninjured as we make our way back to the capital. However, given my experience with the rokon, I will be in command of this operation and you will follow my orders until we get the king back."

Primus Julian started objecting, but Toras cut him off, said, "Primus! I know your concerns, and I will not ask you to violate your life oath to my father. This means that while I am in command and expect you to obey what orders I may give, I will not, at any time, ask you to leave the king's side or do anything that might put his life at risk. He is my father after all, and I do not wish to see any harm come to him, either. Does this satisfy you?"

The officer reflected a moment and then answered with a definite "It does, my Prince."

"All right then. Let's get to work. Primus Kendor, the maps!"

***

Toras and the three officers spent the next hour discussing their options to get the king back to Furan City as quickly as possible, while ensuring his safety. Their main problem was not knowing where the rokon might strike next. Primus Julian suggested keeping to wooded areas as that should hide them from a flying creature, but

273

the furans did not do so well when forced to walk for long distances, and they scratched that idea. He also suggested getting vorans from Spiritii so that Toras's company may ride these instead of their furans, as that would increase the immediate protection around the king. But because numerous stretches of the itinerary would forcibly be on open ground, Toras and Kendor were adamant that their soldiers should ride furans to give them a better chance at keeping the rokon away from the king, should it attack then.

After taking everything into account, including the weather, availability of roads, and the proximity of villages and towns – their intent was to stay as far away from inhabited areas as possible given the rokon's attack pattern – they agreed to follow the foothills of the Colossi's Peaks all the way to Mountain Lake and from there cut across the plains toward Furan City.

Lord Commander Toras dismissed everyone to begin preparations for departure at first light, happy that they had reached an agreement without too much difficulty. But the possibility that they might encounter the Serpent continued to worry him. *Damn it! What does it want?!*

* * *

Back in the king's tent, a much tenser discussion was unfolding. The Lux Baiulae came at exactly Eight Fifteen. Lux Baiulae had an innate sense of time, and so when Kiron called on them, they paced themselves to be certain they arrived at the king's tent at the precise time, frustrating Kiron who found himself needing to slow his pace every so often.

The Sisters had spent the first twenty minutes of the meeting telling the king how irresponsible his secret escape had been. The king listened quietly to their accusations because, the truth was, they were right. They also tried, as best they could, to get him to disclose the purpose of his trip here. But the king would not tell and assured them instead that when he chose to do so, he would inform the Magna Mater directly. Not even Juliana Lux Baiula's familiarity with the king got him to reveal the motive of his presence here, though she tried hard and long.

Just now, Juliana said, "My King, I understand that as monarch, you need not justify your actions or decisions to anyone. But for the safety of the land, our alliance requires that – at a minimum – your

274

advisor be in your confidence always. However, even Elyana was unaware of your whereabouts in this instance, and the decisions and communications, which should have been made by you, were now made without the benefit of your input, support – or knowledge."

Juliana watched Octavius's reaction, trying to determine from his expression, a twitch of his eye or flicker of a finger whether he felt guilt or surprise or any concern at all. But trying to know a person's true thoughts from their physical signs was not always easy, especially with one such as the high king. She needed to get him to talk more. So, she continued, "Fortunately, High Lord Commander Aithen – under High Captain Harlion's and Elyana Lux Baiula's careful guidance – was able to take charge of the situation, beginning with the relocation of Horn's Pass's population to Furan City, and the calling of a meeting with the Senate and of another with the Union Council to inform them of what has passed and of what might come."

Hearing of what his eldest had done in his absence stirred the king's emotions more than the Sisters' ire. He had always been proud of Aithen, and just now that pride took hold of him and warmed him. But mixed with the pride was a certain amount of worry. Indeed, Aithen had only addressed the Senate and the Council once before, with the king at his side, to inform them of his plans to quell the revolt in Storm City, a year and half earlier.

I should have been there; they are right. Both bodies will try to take advantage of his inexperience. Hopefully, Luma and my brothers will be there to support him.

Juliana noticed the king's internal dialogue and took the opportunity to study his reactions a little more closely. He did seem to be feeling some guilt from that turn of his lips. And when he half-looked up toward her and Mara, he must have recognized they were right to question his actions. Juliana waited until the king looked up in her direction again and asked, "Sire, do you have reasons to distrust Elyana Lux Baiula?"

The king started and replied with some resentment, "No, I do not, Lux Baiula. Elyana has always had, and still has, my full confidence. However, I could not share my intentions with her in this particular case."

Juliana listened to the king's reply with her truthsense alert and primed to read the unsaid, but except for the same feeling of guilt she had sensed earlier, and for a heavier sentiment of frustration in the king's tone, she did not detect any falsehood in his reply. Still, the guilt was a meaningful piece of information, and she would need to report that to the Magna Mater.

The king added, "Now! I do not wish to keep discussing my actions with you, Lux Baiulae – not even with you, Juliana. But I will discuss them with the Magna Mater when I hear her."

The Sisters blinked, shocked by the king's statement. Not only was it terse, but it was on the verge of disrespectful. Actually, it *was* disrespectful! Never did anyone address Lux Baiulae so curtly. But then, High King Octavius was the most powerful man in the allied lands. Moreover, the heads of House Coriolis had always had a unique relationship with the Order, High King Octavius particularly so.

The king waited a moment while the Sisters processed his statement. When he was sure they understood he would no longer be questioned by them, he said, "Please tell me everything you know about the attack on Horn's Pass, and about this rokon that is not a rokon."

Juliana Lux Baiula, still recovering from the king's blunt rejection of their authority to question him, turned to her companion to let her tell what was known. Indeed, Mara Lux Baiula had received a report of the events at Horn's Pass, and it was therefore appropriate that she brief the king.

The woman, now Head Medic to Lord Valorian, was shorter than most but her attitude was nevertheless one of great self-confidence, which she used very effectively with plebeians as well as with patricians. Now, she turned to the king with a calm, self-assured demeanor, despite his earlier remarks.

The king tried to assess her character while she prepared her thoughts to brief him. Her thick black hair and white lock gave her a no-nonsense look, but her wide face and large oval eyes spoke of a soft, gentle woman. As hard as he tried, he could not tell what type of person she was, except that her spotless white sash and green robe – despite having come from Spiritii on voranback through dry and dusty roads – marked her as a person who cares perhaps too much about her appearance. Just now, Mara Lux Baiula looked the king in the eye, and began.

"Sire, we believe that the rokon that attacked Horn's Pass is actually the creature once known as the Serpent." Mara paused for a moment, during which Juliana studied the king's reaction.

But aside from taking a barely audible breath, the king maintained a stolid face. He asked, "What evidence do you have for that?"

"The thing spoke to Elyana Lux Baiula."

This time, the king's reaction was anything but calm as he blurted out a " *What?!* "

"Sire, the Serpent spoke to Elyana Lux Baiula during the attack and gave her a warning. It told her that "the end is here," and that we will either "follow or perish." It also spoke to her in the Ancient Tongue."

The king was obviously shaken by this news and plumped down in his chair. After he saved Toras and his men, Toras told him some of what happened at Horn's Pass and also told him about the attacks on Galior and other towns and villages across Lower Alvinor, but he had left out all the unnatural details except to say that the rokon was, well, un-natural.

Why didn't Toras tell me this? Aghhr! You are a fool Octavius. The king *was* upset with himself now, upset that he had put himself so completely out of sight and out of touch that not his sons nor his advisor had been able to reach him to alert him of such an ominous event.

As these thoughts ran through the king's mind, the Lux Baiulae exchanged looks, and told each other by way of the Bind what they thought was going on in the king's mind.

Finally, the king stood again, clasped his hands behind his back, and asked, "Have there been other signs of the rokon's identity, an explanation for the Serpent's return – if it *is* the Serpent?"

"None that Juliana Lux Baiula or I know of, Sire. As to how it may have returned, the possible answers are causing total consternation in the Sisterhood; as you might know, the Serpent was supposed to have been destroyed at the end of the Dark Battle, which –"

The king finished Mara's sentence, "Which means that either the books are incorrect, or the Serpent was resurrected, and if one extends the logic, one must also conclude that Noctiferus himself is not far behind – or away."

277

The Sisters acknowledged the king's conclusions with looks not nearly as blank as they typically were.

Feeling that the moment was now right to broach the topic of the king's return, Mara said, "Sire, it is imperative you go back to Furan City without any further delay. Decisions may be needed which only you can make, and although High Prince Aithen has done well to date, he has only done so under the guidance of his advisors. Fortunately for all, High Captain Harlion and Elyana Lux Baiula are two of the most loyal and disinterested people in the kingdom, but unless you return quickly, their influence may be forced to grow beyond simple counsel, and that would not be to anyone's benefit."

That last statement surprised the king. Lux Baiulae were known for their constant scheming to influence the decisions of rulers. One would have expected the Order to be quite happy with the opportunity to guide High Prince Aithen. But it was also true that, though many Sisters schemed for power in the land, Krystiana did not approve of such behavior, and if she was sometimes ignorant of what went on in the smaller courts, she was very much in control of her acolytes' doings in the high king's court.

"I appreciate your candor, Mara Lux Baiula. And, as luck would have it, I have already ordered my son to make preparations for my return to the –" The king suddenly tilted his head toward the front of his tent. "Ah! That must be Prince Toras. I can recognize even his grumbles, and his arrival is timely. You are welcome to remain and hear the plans for the return."

The two Lux Baiulae turned toward each other, nodded and replied as one, "Thank you, Sire. We will stay." That got a curious look from the king, after which Mara Lux Baiula added, "It is actually essential that we hear what those plans might be, because we have been ordered to accompany you on your way back, to ensure your safety."

The king's first reaction to that comment was one of annoyance. Indeed, the Magna Mater had no right to assign Sisters to him without first obtaining his consent. But Octavius's irritation evaporated quickly as he realized that, though they were not following proper form, he could not argue with the fact that they were probably his best defense if they were going to be attacked by the Serpent.

Still, Octavius grunted and stared at the Sisters with a look which he hoped would cause them a modicum of embarrassment. *Juliana is pulling at her dress. Good. She seems to understand that the mode of their assignment to my person was inappropriate. This Mara Lux Baiula, on the contrary, does not seem to care one bit about it. Still, something about her makes me want to trust her. Hopefully, I am right about that.*

And he stepped out to meet Toras.

***

When Aithen woke the morning after his dinner with Elyana, he made himself a promise: To put her out of his mind until things returned to normal – if they ever did.

Now, he read the Frumentarii's short report on the activities of the priests of the Order of Aiala since their Communion the night before.

Harlion sat silently across from the prince, studying his protégé's face as he read the report; not that he needed to, given that he had read the document himself as he did every police report marked with a stylized stinger's tail. Indeed, these identified all reports on activities or persons that posed a risk to the kingdom.

The prince's face, as the captain expected, went from worry to frustration, and from frustration to livid anger by the time he read the last sentence.

Here is what the report contained:

○   *Warrior kotors leaving nest, very excited*
○ ⌒   *Same heading across fields*
   ⌒   *Two observed in nearby nests, exciting workers there*

It meant that priests had been observed leaving the temple at Highnight. The same were seen heading toward towns and villages around three in the morning. Two were found in nearby villages after sunrise, spreading fear and urging people to rise-up.

Aithen exclaimed, "I knew the man couldn't be trusted! I knew it, and yet I took his word! I am an idiot."

"Don't be so hard on yourself, my Prince. We do not know whether he simply misunderstood you or whether he chose to ignore…your request."

"I know that if my father had dealt with First Cleric Galadrin, this would not have happened. Galadrin would have complied!"

"Perhaps, but that still does not tell us why your request was not enforced. If I know you well, and I am sure I do, you probably were not very explicit with him, and rather than forbidding him to raise fear among the populace in any manner, you intoned that such activities would not be tolerated."

"As I said, I'm an idiot. I don't have the required skills to manage adversaries like the First Cleric, and an adversary he is. I am a soldier, not a politician!"

"My Prince, may I make a suggestion?"

Aithen just shrugged his shoulders, his face a tragic mask of disappointment.

"You might want to ask Elyana Lux Baiula to meet with First Cleric Galadrin. She can make certain that there is no ambiguity whatsoever in his mind about the meaning of your instructions to him. If she meets with him, she can also tell us whether he willfully disobeyed you, or whether he simply did not understand what you meant."

"All right, I cannot say I disagree. I thought the same thing after the fact. And now, here we are."

Aithen went to his desk, wrote a note, then pulled on a rope on the wall. A moment later, a young man walked in. He was a short fellow, with wavy black hair, small eyes that seemed to want to look through things, a long, pointed nose, and a small mouth with lips forming a tight straight line from too much concentration.

"Master Trebloc, please take this note to Elyana Lux Baiula. Tell her that it is urgent."

Master Trebloc bowed to the prince, turned slightly to salute High Captain Harlion with a nod, completed his turn as if on a swivel, and stepped out to carry out his orders.

Harlion raised an eyebrow. "Where is Kil?"

"I gave him leave this morning to be with his family who are visiting the capital."

"Ah. Well, that is a strange young man just took your message."

"I know what you mean, but I have never met anyone as organized, diligent, and attentive to detail as he is, and I must admit that I rather like him. I thought I would miss Master Ramenic, but it is actually quite the opposite. I think Master Trebloc will go very far.

I have half a mind to make him my personal secretary if the king will let me have him." Then to himself, Aithen added, "If I will ever even need my father's approval again."

"What was that?"

"Nothing, Harlion, nothing. As I was saying, I am thinking of asking my father to let me have Master Trebloc. I realize he is young, but he has shown a lot of initiative since the king assigned him to the Royal Treasury three months ago, and he has uncovered some irregularities in the budget of the Upper Alvinor garrisons that make me question the capabilities of old Master Ramenic."

Harlion's brow furrowed. "Irregularities?"

"Yes. I do not know what to make of them yet. I was going to inform you tomorrow, but I might as well tell you what I know now, though the report I am waiting for from Master Trebloc may change things."

Harlion did not usually get involved in the army's financial or administrative matters; Aithen had made it clear a few years earlier that he wanted Harlion to focus on the men, their training, their development, and their good spirits. But there was something worrying in the prince's tone which meant this might concern him too.

Aithen walked to the front of his desk and sat on its edge, facing the captain, his hands crossed. His hesitation only increased the captain's worry.

"Master Trebloc's first report to me a month ago showed an unexplained decrease in the budget of the armories and an equal increase in personnel expenses. What was even stranger was that all the Upper Alvinorian forts had the same shift in expenses. Master Trebloc decided to look into things a little further, and he found that the blacksmiths of the concerned garrisons have all been replaced in the past six months – this, without Lord Warbender's [59] approval. Lastly, Master Trebloc noticed a change in the source of the metals used in the forging of the weapons. That is not strange in and of itself, as blacksmiths are allowed to select their sources as long as the metals are of the proper quality, but Master Trebloc believes the change to be suspicious, nevertheless. Taken all together – if he is correct – these events speak of some unethical goings on in our

---

[59] Lord Warbender was Lord of the Armory.

Upper Alvinorian forts. Not a good thing ever, but especially not now if we are soon to be engaging in another Dark Battle."

Harlion rubbed his chin doubtfully. "My Prince, I doubt young Master Trebloc could have come to such a conclusion by studying our financial books. They do not show whether monies shift between accounts at the garrison level."

"Actually, they now do. If you recall, Lord Kaffin [60] recently instituted the use of what he calls *ledgers*, and with the establishment of the mail service earlier this year, he can now track the expenditures and revenues of all our operations across the kingdom on a quarterly basis."

Harlion made a small grunt and said with some irritation, "I had forgotten about that. But if what Master Trebloc uncovered is correct, why did you not inform me immediately? The irregularities you speak of could seriously affect my men's capabilities!"

"I know, Harlion, I know. But I did not wish to alarm anyone on the basis of the young man's findings; he could have misinterpreted the journals and reports from the garrisons. I asked Lord Warbender and Lord Kaffin to look at their records this morning and send their assessments back with Master Trebloc later today. Hopefully, he will return with better news, and tell me that his suspicions were wrong. That would not be good for him, but it would be welcome news regardless."

"*Ghrr*. Well, let us hope it was all just smoke, and that no fire is burning."

"Indeed. If you wish it, you may attend my meeting with Master Trebloc this afternoon."

"Thank you, my Prince, but as you know, I must meet with my officers this afternoon. But I can certainly come back toward the evening."

Harlion continued after a short pause, "I will not share any of this with my officers until it is confirmed."

"It is probably wise. Very well. Now, onto another topic…how are the refugees settling in?"

"I must say things are going surprisingly well, my Prince. Dwellings have been found for all without trouble."

---

[60] Lord Kaffin was Royal Treasurer.

"And what about the animals? I cannot imagine they are in the city."

"Most Horn's Passers were able to board their animals with the local peasants and landholders for a reasonable fee or other arrangement. Others simply decided to sell their beasts and have the money instead."

Aithen nodded in satisfaction. "And the food situation?"

"We have already distributed half of what food we had in our stores to the refugees. It should last them a few fourths, but other arrangements will have to be made soon."

Aithen replied, "That should not be a problem; Senator Kraelion is looking to find work for all the abled men so they may put food on their families' tables with their own sweat. She is also working with the local farms to increase the production of reds [61], fruits and eggs."

The captain's lips turned up in a smile. He knew the senator – had known her for years – and he expected no less from the woman.

Aithen said, "It feels good to know there exist persons who will do the right thing, doesn't it? And that they do it not because they are told to do it – or even asked to do it – but because of an internal compulsion to do what is good and right."

"It does, indeed."

After a moment of silence during which the prince and his captain considered how lucky the Horn's Passers were to have a woman such as Senator Kraelion on their side, Aithen changed the conversation again, and in a grim tone that clashed with that of the moment before, said, "So, on to more serious matters. As you know, the Serpent has attacked other villages and towns since Horn's Pass, and there are no indications it will stop any time soon. From what Elyana and I heard while in the Bind, its goal is to sow terror, and it is a fair guess it will continue to do so until the whole land is a mess as it searches for…for the two Luxori."

Every time the prince mentioned anything related to his mad and foolish adventure in the Bind, the captain frowned. How could the prince expose himself to such unknowable dangers?

---

[61] Reds: K'Taran vegetables. Most plant life on K'Tara was reddish in color due to them absorbing mostly blue light. Tropical plants, however, appeared blue as their leaves reflected the too-intense blue light at that latitude.

Aithen continued without acknowledging the man's disapproval; he knew Harlion's thoughts on the matter, but Aithen's reasons had convinced Elyana, after all, and that should be all anyone needed. So, ignoring Harlion's frown, Aithen said, "Anyway, because we do not have enough troops to defend every last village, we will concentrate the peasants and inhabitants of said villages in the more easily defensible towns across the kingdom. Major landholders have agreed to defend their own lands and towns, as well as to provide protection to some of the minor towns on the adjoining lands. As far as our forces are concerned, we will deploy a portion of them to the undefended minor towns whose populations cannot be absorbed by the major landholders. Everyone had also agreed to receive the help of the Sisterhood to help defend against the creature."

Harlion rubbed his chin and said, "Hum, I don't know that any of this will be of much help, but there is nothing else we *can* do. I assume you have a list of the towns where our men are to be sent?"

"I do." Aithen reached on his desk, grabbed the list and gave it to his captain.

Harlion said, "This is a long list, my Prince. You know we can't afford to send troops of any consequence to each one of these towns."

Aithen's reply went from discouraged to a rationally-motivated refusal to yield, "Yes, I know. But we *cannot* not act, and we cannot concentrate the population any further; it will be chaos otherwise." After a short pause he added, "If only we could predict the Serpent's targets; we could better manage our troops that way."

The high captain bobbed his head in agreement, took a moment to reflect and then suggested, "Our furan force is not great anymore, counting only three-thousand furanteams [62], but perhaps – in lieu of knowing our foe's path – we can dispatch what we have to a few strategically-located towns across the kingdom. We could also place watchers across the land and near the undefended towns and villages to give the alert should they spot the Serpent; we could have a response in most places within one to three hours."

Aithen rubbed the thin hair on his chin as he considered his captain's idea, his eyes moving but not looking at anything. It was a good idea, but insufficient.

---

[62] Furanteam: A furan and its rider.

"I like your plan, Harlion. But the help will be of no use if, in addition to the time it will take the furanteams to arrive, there is also a delay in communicating the Serpent's approach to any particular location."

"True. But all we have *are* the fire towers."

Aithen walked around his office, his mind racing through options. He shook his head every so often, and finally hit his left hand with his right fist. "I will convince Urbs Lucis to dispatch Lux Baiulae throughout the kingdom, as well as with our troops. We will use *them* as watchers, that way, they will be able to relay any sighting of the Serpent to each other and to our troops the moment it happens."

"I have never heard of the Sisterhood providing such a…service. But if they have the capacity and you can convince the Magna Mater, then we have a plan! I will put things into motion then, as there is much to be done to get the force ready for departure. It will probably take a few fourths or so to get everything organized."

"High Captain, let me inform the Senate first, as placing the army on active duty will cause great commotion; especially because it's been a long time since three thousand furanteams have been assembled. Speak with your officers if you must but wait until after I have informed the Senate to begin the preparations. My meeting with them should occur within the next couple of hours."

The old captain looked at his mentee with a strange combination of excitement and reluctance.

"What is it Harlion?"

"It's nothing my Prince, but somehow, I feel eager…excited at the thought of assembling the entire Furanry [63] again."

"I know what you mean. I feel it too, though there is nothing to be excited about."

"No, there isn't." Then, getting up from the Lacora Leaf chair, which had been getting a little too snug around him, Harlion added "I will await your news in my quarters, my Prince."

"It goes. I will send for you if I need you later, otherwise, you are free to begin preparations as soon as you receive confirmation of my meeting with the Senate."

---

[63] Furanry: Furan-mounted force.

***

Young Lady Aria was rubbing her temples. She was sitting back-to-back with Carasina, trying to read the mind of a Red Locarian situated in the next room. There, a junior neo interacted with the locarian, and it was Aria's and Carasina's task to determine what the junior was doing. They were then supposed to communicate to each other what they had read in the locarian's [64] mind.

Their initial lessons had been in the gardens, where Magistera Annan had demonstrated the techniques to enter the mind and read the thoughts of a variety of animals, as well as to see what the animals saw. Those lessons in the gardens, especially while linked to Magistera Annan, had seemed easy to the two girls. But trying to do it by themselves, locked here in a room and not being able to see even a hair of the object of their reading, was a lot more difficult.

Without turning around and without seeming to be speaking to anyone, the young Halfling whispered to her friend, "My head is starting to hurt. We've been at this for over three hours now. When's she going to come back?"

Carasina groaned. "My temples have been throbbing for a while already. It's like someone put a helmet on my head, tightened it until it hurt, and then just left it like that."

"How would you know how a helmet feels?"

"My brothers used to let me play swords with them, and they would insist that I wear a helmet, even if they were always too large for me. Once, though, they made a helmet out of a large racanut shell, which they said would fit me better. It didn't, and I was in pain for days after that. Well, the present pain is worse!"

Still whispering, Aria asked, "Have you been able to read anything from that stupid Red Locarian?"

"Actually, I think I *have* read it. But I just can't find a way to then send the feelings or images to you."

"Same here. Every time I think I've read something and try to send it to you, I fail, *and* I lose my connection with the locarian."

Carasina, being an eternal optimist, replied that they probably just needed more time to practice. Aria doubted it.

---

[64] Red Locarian: One of the most evolved lower Locarians, the group of species from which the Locari evolved.

286

Changing topic, the princess asked, "So when do you think our *oh-so-helpful* magistera will be back?"

With alarm in her voice, her friend whispered, "I would say right now!"

Magistera Annan entered the beast-reading room with pinched lips and raised brows, the wooden soles of her shoes resonating softly on the marble floor. She was one of the most eccentric women in Solinor [65], with graying hair which looked as if she had not brushed it in days, a violent array of reds and yellows on her otherwise cream-colored dress, and earrings of all sorts hanging from her ears. The only thing that marked her as a Kynarian priestess was the high collar of her dress and the rounded nick in the top ridge of her ears. This notch in the ears of a Kynarian represented the strength of their Sensing abilities. The deeper the groove was, the greater the priest's or priestess's strength in the Bind was. Magistera Annan's groove was quite deep, though not as deep as that of the Supreme Priestess's notch, which was the deepest.

Standing in front of Carasina with her hands clasped, the priestess said, "Carasina, Aria, I know you're aware of my presence. You were probably venting each other's frustration when I got here."

Carasina opened her eyes with an honest look of embarrassment on her face. Aria, instead, put on a fake look of indignation.

With a smile, Magistera Annan said, "As I suspected. I would have been surprised if you had not felt frustration and discouragement by this point. I have never seen anyone learn this skill in fewer than five or six months. It takes even longer to master. So, don't despair. You will learn."

Aria did not seem convinced and she grunted.

Carasina tried to encourage her friend. "I think Magistera Annan is right, Aria. We can already read the emotions of animals better than anyone else; I'm sure we can learn to read their thoughts too." Then, looking at their instructor with pleading eyes, "And I am sure Magistera Annan won't mind giving us more lessons, given that we are the only two senior neos who will be tested for Passage this year."

The priestess-instructor smiled.

---

[65] Solinor: Capital of Kynaria.

Aria didn't. Actually, she felt like hitting her friend on the head. What was she thinking? They barely had the time to sleep with all the coursework this year. Older neos had told them that the last year was the easiest. This was anything but! And on top of it, she had to work in the dining hall every morning, getting dirty cooking, serving and cleaning, and getting laughed at by her peers all the while. Carasina might not mind *serving* the others, but she didn't have to clean-up after them too!

Well, maybe it is your fault, what happens to you. You do have a bad temper, and bad habits like being late everywhere, all the time.

Aria realized that Carasina and Magistera Annan were looking at her, wondering what was happening to cause her to lower her head and drop her shoulders. If they could have read her thoughts, they would have been stunned. This was the first time Aria had ever recognized her faults to herself.

Suddenly grasping the importance of what had just happened to her, Aria surprised herself by saying, "I would like to practice more, too, Magistera Annan. I just don't know where to find the time, though."

At that, Carasina smiled a big smile, and her eyes shone with relief.

Magistera Annan looked puzzled but said, "We can look at your schedules after dinner, when you come back to discuss today's Beast Reading session. I am sure we can find an arrangement that works for all of us, and I will be happy to speak with your other instructors to lighten your load, if necessary."

Aria stared at her instructor with shock. What was happening here? Since when had anyone cared about her workload?

Magistera Annan added, "Well, go on, I will see you in an hour. As for me, I am going to go ask Priestess Veterinarian Loma to probe Brutus. Sometimes, when students develop a headache from trying to read an animal, the locarians develop one too."

The girls got up, brushed and straightened their dresses, then bowed slightly and thanked Magistera Annan before leaving the room. Carasina still grinned widely, and Aria still bore a look of total confusion in the face of the unexpected changes in and around her.

288

XVIII ON THE WAY BACK TO FURAN CITY

Toras turned on his saddle, looked back at the men, thinking to himself: *I've lost so many. Please don't make any more stupid mistakes.* Then, as he turned to his father, he asked, "Father, are you ready?"

The king nodded.

Toras yelled, "All right! Let's go!"

Primus Kendor and the other furan-mounted men took to the air, furans screeching, just as happy to leave this place as the men were. Indeed, though Mara Lux Baiula had cured their wounds, the memory of the wrigglers' attack remained and had kept the furans tense, day and night. In fact, they had been difficult to handle since the attack; the animals were reluctant to return to camp after their hunting trips, and the men had been forced to use their Sagr Bleater horns to call them back. These horns, obtained from the males of the bleaters living on the Mountains of the Sagr, produced an ultrasonic sound which carried for dozens of kilometers and which furans abhorred. Through training, the animals quickly learned that the best way to stop the sound was to return to their riders.

The furanteams, which included Kendor, Secundus Jamir and several guardians, kept an eye out for danger, ready to sound the alert should any of them see the Serpent. The rest of the company traveled on voranback.

The prince, too, was going to travel on voranback so that he might ride next to the king, and exchanged his winged steed for the voran of one of his father's men. Scorch had not been too happy about the arrangement at first, but Merr was a good rider, and the furan seemed to have accepted the stranger. Toras, on the other hand, had had no trouble with Merr's voran; the castrate was a very well-trained war animal and was used to being ridden by different people.

The king had a strange – if ominous – feeling, surrounded as he was by a most eclectic guard, having on his right his son in tattered clothes, on his left his fierce Primus in his impeccable tabard and cloak, behind him the two Lux Baiulae in their spotless robes and stern looks on their ageless faces, and forming a triangle around them all, three more of his men with Jashan in the lead who, as a native of Spiritii, knew these parts of the country very well.

Astride Merr's voran, the prince thought about how taxing the first stage of their journey was going to be: indeed, to avoid the possibility of another wriggler attack, the company needed to reach the foot of the Colossi's Peaks before sunset, which meant they needed to cover some two-hundred and thirty kilometers in fifteen hours. For sure, that was nothing for the winged furans – they could cover five hundred kilometers in a day – but even the best voran could only manage a hundred and eighty kilometers if the day was reasonably cool and dry. He knew that the Royal vorans were well trained and would be able to take the punishment, but the two Lux Baiulae's vorans – though they were good animals – were not trained for hard, long distance riding. That meant they were going to have to stop every few hours to let them rest, as well as – and more importantly – to let them be restored by Mara Lux Baiula at great cost to her own energy levels and health.

But everyone was prepared for the difficult ride, and Toras simply hoped that Jashan would be able to pick a safe path through the bogs which lay ahead of the mountains, despite not having traveled these parts in more than three years.

Around mid-morning, the company came by a stream fed by the mountains. Jashan slowed his voran and suggested to the prince that they stop for a short rest. Toras looked at the Lux Baiulae who nodded in agreement as they pointed to the lather their vorans had already worked up. The prince informed the king then lifted his hand to call everyone to a halt while Jashan blew his horn to alert the furan riders.

Jashan had maintained a fairly intense canter for the first three hours, wishing to cover as much ground as possible while the temperature was still bearable. He guessed they must have traveled a good seventy-five kilometers in this first stretch. Not bad. But it wouldn't be long before the heat became oppressive, and they were forced to slow their pace lest they caused *all* the vorans to overheat, regardless of the fact that they were now in the first In-Between fourth, with the more intense Blue Sun hidden behind its larger, but duller red counterpart.

So, vorans, furans and Humans quenched their thirst at the stream. While their own vorans drank, the Lux Baiulae wet some rags and rinsed the animals down to help them cool off. But because the water itself was quite warm already, Mara was forced to use the Bind to draw heat from the water so that it might in turn draw heat from the vorans as it evaporated.

Toras took the opportunity to go see Scorch who greeted his master with a loud screech and a bump on the chest, which almost toppled him over.

Merr was checking the straps on the other side. Toras liked the man. Perhaps because he was Kynarian or perhaps because, though he had faced Toras and Aithen in the last three yearly Aquinian Games and had nearly won each time, he remained quite unassuming.

Upon noticing the prince, Merr said, "He is quite the devil this one, Lord Commander."

"Ha-ha! Yes, he is. I bet he made your heart race on the descent."

"Well, I won't deny it. He is definitely not made for the faint of heart."

"No, that he's not. But he's also very aware of his rider, and he will adjust his position if he feels the rider is losing his grip on him."

"Yes, I noticed that, and it allowed me to relax and enjoy the last stretch of the descent."

"I'm glad. Your voran is not bad either. But it was strange to be on the back of one again. The last time I rode my voran, or any voran for that matter, was last winter after an enormous icicle fell on Scorch's head and he was locked in the healer's stable for a few days while he recovered."

Merr's eyes opened wide with surprise. He had never heard of an icicle so big that it caused an injury. There certainly weren't any in Kynaria where temperatures rarely went below the freezing point, and although he did accompany the king on his visits to the coldest parts of the Aquinian continent during the winter season, the largest icicle he had ever seen had been about a foot long, but it was thin and could hardly have seriously hurt anyone if it had fallen on them.

Toras noticed the guardian's questioning look. He said, "We were hunting belwohrs near the top of Furan Peaks. We had stopped on a ledge for a moment to catch our breath when a belwohr appeared on a shelf above us and caused the ice to crack. The belwohr and everything else came down. The animal missed us, but an ice spear hit Scorch straight on. After he lost consciousness, I was so angry I would have gone after the belwohr on foot, but there had been no way for me to get off the ledge without breaking my neck, so I sat there and nursed Scorch instead. For a while, I thought for sure I was doomed. But he finally came back to, and though he was in pain and wobbly, he still let me climb on him, and then simply dropped off the ledge and flew back down to the fortress. I have never met a furan as tough and determined as he is."

"Have you ever thought of breeding him, Lord Commander?"

"Others have suggested it, but I haven't decided yet." Then, looking at his pocket watch, Toras noticed that thirty minutes had already passed. He petted Scorch and reminded him to be nice to his rider. Scorch replied with a snort. Merr saluted the prince, and Toras walked over to the king to let him know it was time to go. When the signal was given, everyone remounted, and the company resumed its journey.

The temperature began climbing very quickly over the next two to three hours. By midday, the temperature had become unbearable. Juliana Lux Baiula figured it must have been over eleven stones warm. Her mount, a five-year-old gray voran named Petal and presently in the female phase, was breathing heavily by now, and was lathered in frothy sweat. Her companion's voran, an older roan castrate named Star, was doing even worse. The Royal Guard's vorans did not seem to be suffering as much yet, but they were definitely beginning to slow down. Only Battle, the king's mount, appeared unaffected by the heat and hard riding.

Suddenly, the sound of a horn came from above. The furan riders had just spotted the lake Jashan had been looking for to make their next halt. Jashan stopped to look in the direction indicated by the furan riders, and after confirming that it was indeed the lake he knew – one of the few safe ones in the area – he informed the king and prince, and the company made for their next resting point.

A few minutes later, everyone dismounted, and Toras called a meeting to discuss their progress.

He asked, "Jashan, how are we doing? Will we reach the mountains before nightfall?"

The guardian rubbed his blond, neatly trimmed chin for a moment, looking at the vorans with the keen eye of a man used to this kind of trek.

"Hum, well, we still have a little more than half the distance to cover, and only eight hours or so before the wrigglers surface, m'Lord Commander. That's, hmmm, some fourteen to fifteen kilometers per hour. It's going to be hard to keep up that pace, especially if the temperature goes beyond seventeen stones – as you know, even the best vorans start foundering beyond that – and the Founders burn me! it looks like it will get that hot today." Realizing he had cursed near women – Lux Baiulae no less – Jashan turned toward them and apologized with a "Sorry m'Ladies." The Lux Baiulae did their best to increase his embarrassment with frowns and snorts.

Jashan continued, "And it seems like the Sisters' vorans are already near collapse despite Mara Lux Baiula's healings." Jashan turned to the woman and apologized again.

Mara responded, addressing herself to Toras, "As difficult as it is to admit, Guardian Jashan is right. I am exhausted, and I do not think I will be able to continue healing our vorans."

Toras asked, "Any suggestions, Jashan, anyone?"

Primus Julian put an idea forth, and said, "Lord Commander, I recommend we have the Sisters ride with two of the men on furanback. Their vorans should be able to cover the distance if they don't have to carry them. As for the rest of the vorans, we'll just have to keep an eye on them. We can reassess the situation in a few hours and if need be, we'll all double-up on the furans."

The two Lux Baiulae looked at each other hesitantly; they didn't like the thought of riding behind the men as little children behind their fathers. But neither would they accept having the guardians sitting behind them. But how ridiculous they were, they then sent each other; they did not even *know* how to ride furans. So, it would be as it would be.

The prince responded with a growl. "All right then. Let's make it so. We have no time to waste. Hopefully the rest of us will make it with the vorans all the way to the mountains because the king would be highly exposed on furanback, and we know nothing of the whereabouts of the Serpent or rokon, or whatever it is. But if we have to double-up on the furans, let's wait until the last possible moment." Toras turned to his father for his agreement.

Octavius said, "That is probably the most sensible thing to do at this point, Toras. But I must admit that I wouldn't have minded being on furanback on such a hot day as this." And the king wiped some sweat from his forehead.

Toras was surprised to see his father sweat when he had been totally dry in the woods, a few days earlier. Toras still nodded with an understanding grin and gave the order to remount. Juliana Lux Baiula climbed behind Secundus Jamir, and Mara Lux Baiula behind Primus Kendor. Within a few moments, wings flapped, and toes clopped on the drying ground.

The next four hours were the most difficult yet; Juliana Lux Baiula put the temperature at fourteen stones by mid-afternoon. All the mounted vorans were breathing hard, with heavy froth at the corners of their mouths, and bodies sweating profusely. Only the Lux Baiulae's vorans, their reins tied to Kiron's saddle and carrying only a couple of light sacks each on their backs, fared better.

By Five Hours after Highsun, the temperature was so high that Toras started to worry about Scorch who might very well get dehydrated. He thought: *Damned weather! Like this whole thing is not difficult enough already.* That is when Jashan decided to call for another halt.

Indeed, the guardian had already slowed the company's pace to around 10 Km/hour, and he knew that at that speed, they would never get to the mountains before nightfall. So, he called for another halt and everyone, except Jashan himself, doubled-up behind a furan rider. Jashan was going to ride Battle and continue with the other vorans to the foot of the mountain.

There had been a moment of awkwardness when considering with whom the king should ride and whether he should be in front or in the back – the last time the king had ridden with someone else was when Toras was five. To think that the king, the high king, should ride with someone else, especially behind them, was embarrassing to everyone except to the Lux Baiulae – they thought it might do him good. In the end, it was decided the king should ride with the prince who would have his bow and arrows at the ready in case there should be danger.

The king himself did not feel any embarrassment at having to ride with someone else, but he did have a momentary hesitation when he decided to be the front man. Indeed, he was a little out of practice now, given that he had not been on a furan since the death of his own furan a few years earlier. Normally, the king would have hunted for a new mount, but he was already one-hundred and thirty-eight at the time and decided against replacing his furan. Moreover, he had looked forward to having only one animal to take care of. Indeed, the king had always taken personal care of his mounts, grooming and spending time with them daily, and only failing to do so if he was ill. But as he was no longer a young man overfull with energy, he enjoyed having only a voran to ride and to care for. So, he now felt a little nervous riding a furan again, especially Scorch. Indeed, when Octavius had captured him to give to his son on his tenth birthday, the animal was already sexually mature, which meant that he was bold and daring, and would most likely remain forever so. But that is what Toras had wanted and the king – being the father he was – had obliged him.

Now, he looked at Scorch with a gauging eye and said "So, are you still as wild as you were, Scorch?"

Scorch said "no" with a shake of his head in response.

Toras laughed at the furan's reply, and said, "I know for a fact he's as wild as he has ever been, Father. I hope you know what you're doing."

The king raised an eyebrow and replied, "I am not that old yet, son."

"Ha! No, you're not, Father. No, you're not."

After checking the cinches and breast collar, Octavius mounted Scorch with one spry motion. Toras climbed behind.

When all were mounted, Toras signaled Primus Kendor who gave the order to take off. Dust lifted from the ground as the furans beat their powerful wings, choking everyone and causing Juliana Lux Baiula to curse out loud, shocking the soldiers. Only the king and prince chuckled. Within a moment all furans were airborne and lined-up behind Primus Kendor in two nested "V" formations, with Kendor at the point of the outer formation and the king at the point of the inner one.

Meanwhile, Jashan picked up speed on the ground, and engaged the vorans through the dangerous bogs that lay ahead of the mountains. Here, the wrigglers were less of a problem, but quick sands lay in wait for anyone foolish enough to try to cross the area. Jashan had done it before – and survived – but he had never had seven vorans trailing behind him. He simply had to trust them to follow in line, because he wouldn't be able to take his eyes off the ground until they reached the mountain. And he prayed to Aiala'Rhi because he was going to need all the help he could get to take himself and the vorans out of the bogs before nightfall.

After two hours of flight, during which the riders' backs were burned by the red sun, Kendor sighted the mountains ahead. He shouted, "Lord Commander, my King! The Peaks!"

Toras would have seen the mountains first, but he had been looking to the West, toward the setting sun for the past ten minutes, as if transfixed by its slow descent. Upon hearing his officer, he shook his head and yelled back, "I hear you, Primus!" Then a little more quietly, though still loud enough to overcome the double-deafening effect of the wind and beating wings, he said to the king, "Father, do you see?"

Octavius turned his head back slightly and responded that he did.

Ten minutes later, the company was above the foot of the Colossi's Peaks. Kendor signaled the trumpeter, and the young man blared a slow, long toot with his horn. Furans shrieked, and riders readied themselves for the descent by checking their back straps.

Juliana Lux Baiula caused a little stir when she didn't find the strap latched onto her belt. Had she been another person, she might have panicked, but all she did was create a Binding to send her voice to Secundus Jamir without needing to yell, asking him to wait before descending. The man started when the voice reached him, and he caused his furan to veer unexpectedly. Jamir became even more alarmed when he saw that the Lux Baiula was not secured, but the woman calmly reached behind herself, grabbed the strap, and re-attached it. That done, Jamir relaxed and returned his attention to the forthcoming descent.

As Toras and Octavius prepared to descend, Toras shouted, "Father, do you remember how to land Scorch?"

"Do I…!?" The king stopped himself short, realizing his son was probably being serious. "I certainly do, son. The question is, does your furan remember how *I* like to descend?"

"Father, I'm sorry, but you hesitated to get on Scorch earlier, and now you want to perform a dive?!"

"It is called muscle memory, Toras, and it has already retaught my muscles all that they knew to do on a furan."

Toras turned around carefully, grabbed the strap behind him and latched it to his belt. He was going to tell Octavius to do the same, but the king had already taken care of it. Toras nodded to himself and took a heavy breath. As soon as Kendor gave the signal to drop, the king broke formation and initiated the heart-stopping descent for which he had been known in his younger years. Toras and Aithen were well known for their own furanback stunts, but neither had yet succeeded in matching Octavius's brutal descent.

It had been a long time since Octavius had completed a drop with Scorch, but the furan had not forgotten the signals. As soon the king lowered himself onto the furan's neck and pushed his heels forward, Scorch closed his wings on the riders' legs, straightened his body and dropped.

The pull of the strap on Toras's belt suddenly squeezed his guts, and almost caused his stomach to empty itself. *Damned him! I'll never get used to this.* The last time Toras had sat behind his father on furanback, he had been much younger. But he could clearly remember the vomit that had made its way into his throat and then into his mouth, as well as remember desperately forcing the bile back down lest he puke on the king's back and became the laughing stock of the court.

The gushing wind now flayed Toras's face, causing his eyes to water and his eyelashes to stick to his eyeballs. He felt like telling his father to slow the descent, but he didn't – he couldn't. The king, on the other hand, did not seem to be bothered at all, his eyes mere slits, focused on the approaching ground.

Just now, Octavius spied a clearing and tugged on Scorch's reins to direct him to it. The furan decreased his pitch, adjusted his course, and the moment he felt Octavius's heels come forward again, he dropped. Behind, atop the other furans, heads shook, and all manners of curses were exchanged between the guardians while the Sisters watched the king's descent with unimpressed, stony faces.

Within a minute, everyone was landed, and Primus Julian walked toward the king looking frankly upset.

"My King…"

"Yes, Primus?"

"…you should have let someone else land first. I cannot pr –"

The king raised his hand and stopped his officer mid-sentence, "I know Primus, I know. But my eyesight is still superior to that of any officer here, and I could tell the area was clear of any danger, so I descended and enjoyed something I have not enjoyed in a long time."

"Of course, Sire, but even your eyes could not have penetrated the thick woods which surround this clearing..."

"Primus! No more on this. Or, do you wish to rob me of this small pleasure I have given myself?"

"Of course not, Sire. My apologies."

Octavius grunted his acceptance of his officer's apology and turned to Toras to ask, "Lord Commander, I assume this is an acceptable place to set-up camp while we wait for Jashan?"

Toras did not reply, but instead shouted, "Primus Kendor, Secundus Jamir! Is the area secure?"

When the officers replied that it was, Primus Julian excused himself, and went to take care of his furan. Octavius turned to his son with a smile of complete satisfaction and joy – an almost childish grin.

Toras said, "I can tell you really enjoyed the drop, Father. I wish I could say the same, though."

The king gave a big, joyous laugh, "I know you never developed the stomach for it, son. Aithen alone has been able to do it. But no need to worry, I will not hold it against you...ahhh! What a grand day this has been!"

Toras did not respond to that. *Really, he's lost his mind! A great day?*

***

The next couple of hours were spent relaxing, singing and eating. In the beginning, much of the conversation steered toward the king's dramatic descent. The Lux Baiulae alone were not impressed – on the contrary, they thought his stunt immature and irresponsible, especially for a centenarian, but they kept their comments for each other, knowing that they would find no support among these men. Indeed, even the officers seemed to gape in awe as the king recounted the thrill of the earlier drop and of drops he used to do with his own furan, the great Thunder, Scorch's sire.

Thunder had been the high king's favorite furan. He had had two in his lifetime, Lumos, his first, who died in battle some seventy years earlier, and Thunder, who died a natural death just four years ago. Lumos had certainly been a great steed, but Octavius had never been able to completely trust him. Thunder, on the other hand, the king had trusted with his life, and the beast had trusted his master equally; the king had needed but lay his hand on the furan's neck to stay his pounding heart in the face of battle. He had also been a furan of unparalleled skill.

Scorch, one of the fureens Thunder had sired, was very much like him, and that is why the king had decided to perform a drop with him on this day; he knew the furan would still remember how to perform the descent and do it safely.

While his father entertained the men, Toras wondered about the Lux Baiulae who were sitting slightly to the side. There was just something about them which he found unsettling. Although he trusted Elyana with his life, he distrusted the Sisterhood. Indeed, though they were supposed to work only for the good of Humankind, he had witnessed many of their decisions and actions have the contrary effect. During his late teens, when nights were spent debating one thing or another with his friends and cousins, he had tried to figure out the reasons for these contradictions, to understand what motivated Sisters, but he had failed every time; the study of political and social interactions was not his strength, much less when it involved the Sisterhood, and so, he watched Mara and Juliana suspiciously, wondering what they were discussing, and wondering why they even bothered to sit nearby if they were not going to participate in the conversation.

When the suns had almost set, Primus Julian approached Toras. He was beginning to worry about Jashan and wished to send out a scout to see if he might spot the man. Toras agreed, understanding that if Jashan was not already at the foot of the mountains, he and the vorans were likely being assailed by a new wave of wrigglers.

Toras said, "Send two furanteams, one with Mara Lux Baiula, in case they find Jashan injured – or worse."

Primus Julian nodded and went to dispatch Kiron and Almiar, along with Mara Lux Baiula, to look for their missing comrade.

The activity worried the others too, and the revelry quickly ended. When twenty minutes had passed, the red sun's last rays had vanished, and the scouts had not yet returned, sparking a heated debate between Toras, the king, Juliana Lux Baiula, and the officers. Toras wished to take to the sky in the hope that he might see the others come back from above the tree line. Secundus Jamir suggested sending another man, while Juliana Lux Baiula suggested that she try to connect with Mara, through the Bind.

The prince was throwing his hands up in desperation when the dying screeches of furans suddenly tore through the camp causing shock and panic. Kendor, Jamir and their guardians picked up weapons and burning sticks and ran to the trees along the northern edge of the clearing where their mounts were tied. Scorch, who had been laying down next to his master, got up in alarm upon hearing his companions' distressed shrieks and would have run toward them as well if Toras had not held him back. The prince did not know why, but he knew he shouldn't let his furan go, so he tied him to a picket in the ground and ran after the others, accompanied by Juliana.

The darkness made it difficult to see what was happening to the mounts, but three of them were on their sides, releasing cries of deep distress, while the other two stood panicking, frantically pulling at their ropes, trying to get away. Toras, Kendor, and Jamir looked at each other and approached the dying furans. The combined light from the torches they carried, lit up a tragic scene: the furans had long, red quills sticking out of their bodies. Blood oozed from every pore, and the acrid smell of it sickened the air itself. It was a miracle that no one vomited; perhaps it was their state of alarm that kept them from doing so.

The king wanted to walk over to the others, but Primus Julian held him back. "I'm sorry, Sire, but we have no idea what has happened over there, and the risk is too high to let you approach."

The king, however, seemed intent on going to see for himself.

"Sire, please! Do not force me to hold you."

"All right, Primus. But I need to know what is happening."

"The prince and Lux Baiula are coming back, Sire."

Not a moment later, Toras approached the king, with strictly contained fear apparent on his face.

"Father! You need to leave, now."

"What?"

Juliana Lux Baiula, with the reflection of the nearby flames giving her eyes a wild look though she only felt the controlled concern of a Lux Baiula, replied in Toras's stead. "My King, the prince is right. You need to leave this place now. There are…things out there. They shot poisoned darts at the furans, and three of them are now as good as dead. I have no idea what sort of poison can do

302

this to an animal, and I fear for your safety…we need to leave while there are still some furans to carry us."

The hesitation and concern in the Lux Baiula's voice should have given the king second thoughts about remaining, but he seemed undeterred. "Juliana Lux Baiula, I appreciate your concern, but I will not–"

Just then, the agonizing scream of a man rang through the camp, cutting off the king's reply. The cry was followed by Kendor's voice. "Lord Commander! We are being attacked! The king must go!"

Toras turned to his father, imploringly. The king looked toward the forest and shook his head.

Primus Julian now added his own demand to the others. "My King, I agree with them. You have no armor to fight, and we have no idea what is coming. The only sensible thing is to take you to safety, now."

The realization that everyone was probably right now hit the king, and he growled in frustration. "Very well, Primus. I will…come."

The moment the king said that, Falor and Gabel arrived with the two surviving furans. Primus Julian grabbed one and urged the king to mount.

The king said, "There are not enough furans to take all of us."

"Father, you must still go. Primus Julian, Juliana Lux Baiula and Merr can accompany you. The rest of us will stay and fight as we can."

From the edge of the clearing a shout came. It was Secundus Jamir. "Lord Commander! We need help! And shield yourselves!"

Toras was torn between seeing his father off and running to the men. He was about to urge the king to go, one last time, when two furans arrived from above and landed next to them. The men and Lux Baiula had returned with Jashan.

Mara Lux Baiula, sitting behind Kiron, asked in a weak voice, "Juliana, what is happening here?"

It was Primus Julian who replied, "There is no time for explanations, Lux Baiula. We are leaving, now."

Mara reacted with surprise, but she had no chance to say or ask anything else. Primus Julian gave the order to his men and his sister to mount. Julian mounted a furan with the king, and seated himself in front of Octavius, rather than behind him as the prince had done on their way here. Indeed, the king could not, per protocol, have any man behind him that might decide to draw a knife and plunge it into his back, as had happened to two of his ancestors, both of whom had been killed by the captains of their personal guards. Having someone else at the reins annoyed Octavius, but rules were rules, even for him.

Juliana, who had climbed behind Merr, now looked at her companion, her face filled with questions and worry. Mara simply shook her head and made a sign which meant that they had narrowly escaped a tragedy as she pointed toward Jashan. The man sat, or rather, slumped behind Almiar, looking weak and scarred, but he was alive. No one asked about the vorans. If they had, Kiron would have told them that most had fallen prey to the wrigglers, and that two or three seemed to have escaped, including the king's mount.

When all were ready for departure, the king called his son. "Lord Commander!"

"My King?"

"Please take care."

"I will, father. Now, go!"

And the furans took off, and as they did, the newcomers' eyes showed confusion and questions, while the others' eyes, including the king's, were creased with guilt.

Frightening sounds shattered the forest anew, sounds none here had ever heard before. The prince did not hesitate this time. Remembering Secundus Jamir's words, he ran toward the saddles. There he took one to use as a shield, and after quickly removing the stirrups and grabbing the specially-designed hold underneath the saddle, he ran toward the fighting men, ready to face whatever was there.

As he approached, what looked like arrows jammed into his saddle. He took a deep breath and lunged forward to help the embattled guardians. As he shot forward, Toras looked quickly to the sky, wondering whether he would see his father again.

Already some ten meters above ground, the king looked down and asked himself a similar question as he watched his son plunge into the melee. *By the Founders, I already feel the guilt of a coward! And yet... they are right. Even if I used my Binding skills, I would not be able to prevent those quills from landing in my belly.*

Poisoned quills suddenly whizzed by the furans and their riders. Fortunately for them, none hit. But Octavius heard a quill plant itself into the ground next to Scorch, who was still tied to his post.

The king yelled an order to Merr. Without a moment's hesitation, the guardian shot an arrow straight through the rope holding Scorch, despite the distance and the darkness, and released the furan. The king was not surprised, and he praised the Kynarian blood.

Down below, a contented Scorch released a ferocious growl. The king saw him turn toward the forest with an angry roar, which became louder and louder.

He knows Toras is over there, fighting. Go! Go to him, Scorch, and keep my son alive; I couldn't forgive myself if he died here.

***

Standing atop a dead furan, the creature looked at Toras viciously. It had a claw, almost as long as its forearm, sticking out of its left hand's knuckles. The claw was red with the blood of the furan it had just stabbed for good measure, perhaps to scare the prince. It must have succeeded, because Toras now just stood there, paralyzed by the thing's appearance. The thing made a gnarling sound and looked at Toras with eyes red like fire and a crimson tongue which the creature seemed to use to transfix its adversaries.

Suddenly, the creature lunged toward the prince with an ugly growl which pulled the prince out of his stupor. The prince tried to back away from his attacker, but his boot caught on a branch and he fell backward. As he did so, his feet kicked up, accidentally smashing the thing's jaw. The creature let out a strange yelp and doubled over. Just then, a hand pulled Toras to his feet. The prince looked back with some confusion but was relieved to see Rulok, one of his brother's men. As he nodded to thank the man, a claw came through the guardian's belly. Rulok looked at Toras with indescribable pain contorting his expression, but his eyes were wetted with the certain knowledge of death. Still, he used one last breath to yell, "Behind you!"

Responding with the automatism of a trained soldier, Toras turned and deflected his attacker's unnatural claw. But in doing so, he caused the talon to slide upward and cut his right arm. The prince felt a burning, painful sensation. That angered him, and he brought his sword arm back down with such force, despite the pain or perhaps because of it, that he cracked the creature's skull. But he did not gloat over it, and instead turned around from sheer instinct just in time to parry the claw that had pierced his brother's officer. Its stinking owner began dancing around the prince, making gnarling sounds, and alternately retracting and thrusting its claw in an apparent desire to confuse Toras.

The creature's trick seemed to work because twice Toras swung his sword to stop the claw, found nothing, almost lost his balance, and nearly impaled himself on the suddenly reappearing talon. By now, Toras was beginning to feel exhausted, and his brow was sweating so profusely that he risked being blinded by it. Fortunately for him, the creature was not attacking him, but continued to toy with him instead, so he forced himself to focus a moment and consider his options. After a few more of the creature's dancing steps, the prince made his decision. He now set his jaw and threw himself against the thing. His sword caught his opponent's clawed arm, and with his left hand and all the rage he had, he thrust a dagger into its throat. No sound came from the creature, but its blood sprayed the prince who recoiled in horror despite several years of military experience.

Before he could take in two breaths, another cry came to Toras's ears. "Lord Commander!"

Kendor! Where is he?

"Lord Commander!"

Toras wiped the blood and sweat from his eyes and, in the dim twilight of this young but mortal night, saw men and creatures fighting some thirty meters to his right. The men were surrounded by a good dozen of the nameless things.

The prince ran toward the men without replying to his captain, wishing to avoid alerting the creatures of his approach. Just a few meters from the group stood a large bok; the prince stopped behind it to think on how best to help the men. He needed to think fast; he could see the men – Kendor, Jamir, Gabel, and the twins – still fighting, but barely so, and he understood that adding his strength to the fight would only delay their inevitable death. He needed something else, another way to fight the things. But what?

As if to answer his question, Scorch had just come up behind Toras, almost causing him to gasp and give alert to the creatures. In whispers, the prince asked, "Scorch where are you coming from?"

Scorch indicated the deep of the woods with a motion of his beaked, crested head, then motioned toward the creatures attacking the other men.

"You went after the things?! But who freed you? Forget it. It doesn't matter now. I am going to need you to help push back those foul things, Scorch. It should be ok, as I've not seen any of them project any more of their quills for a while now. It seems they've somehow run out, though the projectiles appear to grow out of their hands. Can you help?"

Scorch reassured Toras with an emphatic nod. So, the prince pointed toward the farthest creatures which were assailing Primus Kendor and two other men, and not a moment later, Scorch attacked.

Toras smiled a small smile when he noticed the confusion and fear Scorch's attack was causing, and he took advantage of it to come around the tree and decapitate the thing closest to him with a swift motion. Its neighbor turned around and flicked its angry crimson tongue at Toras. The thing lunged at the prince with vicious ferocity, but he did not give it a chance to get close; he threw his dagger at it with such precision that the blade went right into the creature's open jaw, causing the vertebrae in its neck to separate. The head fell back, held onto the shoulders only by the foul gray skin.

Meanwhile, Scorch took down three creatures, crushing their skulls with his beak. The men took courage from the reinforcement and tried to push the attackers back. But they were even more exhausted than the prince, and in the space of a moment, both Felor and Gabel were transpierced by claws.

Falor cried out in anger at the sight of his falling twin; he wished to run to him, but he was engaged in a fight for life against an enormous version of the creatures, and he could not evade it. This one's claw had a deep curve at its end, so it couldn't thrust to kill, but the monster used the curled claw to try and hook Falor. At first, Falor thought this might work to his advantage and that if he got hooked and the creature pulled him close, he would simply jab his dagger into its belly. But he had noticed a shorter, straight claw sticking out of the thing's right arm, so he decided to change tactic and simply tried to tire the thing, doing his best to avoid being hooked, while looking for an opening, which came after what seemed like a very short time. Indeed, after seeing his brother fall, Falor's senses and mind became sharp as a blade and fast as lighting, and he knew now how to dispatch the thing; it was so simple – the thing's right arm was short, and it always swung its left arm from the top. He knew he could make use of that!

Presently, Falor slowed down and opened himself to the creature. The moment it began lifting its left arm, he slid down and between the creature's legs. The creature made an angry hissing sound, and it tried to reach down with its right claw, but as large as it was, it couldn't, and Falor jabbed his sword into its belly. The thing screamed a high-pitched yelp – such a silly sound for such an evil creature, he thought. Now, Falor turned around on his knees and pulled on his sword to dislodge it from the creature, but as he did so, foul blood and intestinal materials gushed all over him, burning his skin. Shockingly, the substance solidified and encased Falor in a vile, solid shell, except in his mouth and nose where the material remained viscous and blocked his airways. The soldier screamed in panic, but no sound went out. He tried to break the chitinous coffin by causing himself to bounce-off the ground. But nothing worked, and the panic and lack of air had nearly depleted his energy when luck came, and he heard the material start to crack, loosen and splinter off.

Falor stayed there a moment, breathing hard and thanking Aiala'Rhi for her help. Suddenly, he remembered the others and heard them still fighting. He forced himself up and looked around. He was surprised to see that only three creatures remained standing, each one facing a man: a tall one stood in front of Lord Commander Toras, a short one in front of Primus Kendor, and another large and fat-looking one in front of Secundus Jamir. The two officers seemed to be in bad shape and on the defensive, but the Lord Commander continued to attack. He knew he needed to go, but he hesitated a moment when the memory of his brother surfaced. So, he pushed the thought deep down with a growl, scooped up some dirt to remove the remaining foulness from his face, grabbed his sword, and ran to help the others.

Falor ran toward the prince first. His approach distracted the prince's opponent, and Toras took advantage of it to plunge his sword into the creature and retrieving it and stepping back quickly. Indeed, Toras had learned that a hardening substance frequently spewed out of the creatures' bellies and that it was better to avoid being covered by it. That done, Toras gave Falor a nod of appreciation, and turned to decide on their next target.

Having assessed the situation, Toras sent Falor to aid Secundus Jamir, who had just been stabbed in the side, while he himself ran to Primus Kendor's aid.

Falor tried to attack the creature from behind, but it noticed Secundus Jamir's eye movement, and it turned around to slash Falor across the face before doing the same to Jamir. The men dropped to the ground, screaming in pain.

The large, fat creature now turned and made its way toward its shorter, beleaguered companion. Toras noticed the approaching creature and alerted Kendor. The two men repositioned themselves to protect against the two monstrosities. They looked at each other with grim faces, fully aware that neither would last much longer. But hope returned when they caught sight of Scorch coming back from the forest after chasing and killing two other creatures. The two men looked at each other and determined their next move. They then took a deep breath through burning lungs and lunged toward the creatures with frightful growls.

That unnerved the creatures, and they backed away, if only slightly. As they did, a deafening screech came from behind them, and they turned around, frightened. Feeling caught between the men and the large, devilish furan, they placed themselves back-to-back and waited for the assault. A ferocious grin painted the prince's face when Scorch looked his way, and at once, soldiers and furan attacked.

The things lashed out in all directions, full of the fear of predators become prey. One succeeded in slashing Kendor's chest, and the man dropped to his knees. But Toras and Scorch closed in on the two creatures and crushed their skulls with sword and beak.

It took Toras a while to stand down, unsure whether there were any more of the creatures around, ready to pounce on them. When he realized that nothing more was coming from the woods, and he saw Scorch just sitting there near him, resting, Toras released the tension that had kept him going, and plumped on his behind, exhausted.

The combat was over, but Toras knew he still had work to do; he needed to take an account of the dead and the survivors, and then tend to each according to their needs. He first went to Kendor, and was relieved to find him alive, and able to stand. So, the two of them surveyed the camp, becoming grimmer and grimmer as they went 'round. Out of ten men, only Jamir and Falor remained alive in addition to themselves. No furan remained alive aside from Scorch: one furan for four men; this meant they would not be able to leave this place together.

Toras and Kendor spent the little energy they had left to tend to the guardians' wounds as well as to their own, all the while praying that nothing else would come this night.

XIX TWO MORE RETURNS TO FURAN CITY

It took the high king's company three days to make the trip from the southern tip of the Colossi's Peaks to the capital. The trip was spent in sometimes-heated discussions about what was happening, and about what should be done to protect the king's subjects. Octavius had also spent some time wondering how he had gotten himself into a situation where everyone was looking to place new restrictions on him to protect him from himself and to ensure the kingdom's stability during these uncertain days.

It was near Three Hours after Highsun when the company first sighted the city. All were exhausted: men, women, and furans, especially the latter. And some still carried feelings of guilt, especially the king.

Juliana Lux Baiula poked Merr in the back and asked him to approach the king. The man pulled on the furan's reins and the animal swerved to align itself with the furan carrying the king and the captain of the Praetorian Guard.

Juliana shouted to overcome the wind, "Sire, I suggest we land soon, so we may clean up a bit before entering the city."

The king looked at the Lux Baiula with annoyance, because though he had agreed with her and with Primus Julian to enter the capital through Victory Gate, he still did not look forward to smiling to his subjects today, or to being assailed by members of the Senate who might be walking the streets at this time of day. But Juliana Lux Baiula had convinced him that, despite the irritation that encountering some political enemies might cause him, showing himself to the population – especially to the Horn's Passers – was very important. As a Purple Sash, she knew this to be the right action for the king to take, and she was certain Elyana Lux Baiula would have given him the same advice. So, Octavius had agreed.

The king gave the order to descend, and the small company landed near a copse of gigantic shading trees that stood just beyond the Rattle Formations. Once on the ground, everyone hurried to unruffle their clothes and pat the dust off.

Mara Lux Baiula, though she hadn't totally recovered from her ordeal in the swamps, was well enough to make herself look as stately as any Lux Baiula – if one did not look too closely – after calling a Binding to mend her robe and lift the blood the wrigglers had drawn from her arms and legs. The procedure was not perfect as it destroyed the fabric's pattern along the mended edges, and the bloodstains – if they were less intense – were still there, but no one would know from afar. She then took out a small mirror she carried in her robe's pouch and straightened her hair as well as wiped her face clean.

As for Juliana Lux Baiula, she thought she looked well enough after patting the dust off her dress, so she went to take a look at Jashan to make sure he could sit straight and not give the onlookers any reason for concern as the company crossed the busy streets of the city on their way to the palace. Once satisfied, she went to the king who was also shaking off dust and grumbling about the sweat-stained clothes.

Octavius noticed the approaching Lux Baiula from the corner of his eyes and looked up. "What is it, Juliana?"

"I can help you with your clothing, Sire, given that you do not have a squire or servant with you now."

Octavius pulled his head back in surprise and said, "You are a strange woman, Juliana. I did not think that a Lux Baiula would find it acceptable to act…as a valet. But I accept."

"I have known you for a long time, Sire, and I have not forgotten how generous you were to my family, when I was growing up."

The king nodded and let the Lux Baiula straighten the collar of his shirt and the back of his doublet, as well as use some Bindings to efface the sweat stains.

As Juliana made the finishing touches to his clothes, the king thought about something which had been tying his stomach ever since their departure from the Colossi's Peaks; he would soon have to tell various people what happened on those peaks, including why the prince and his men were not with him, and he was not looking forward to it, especially not to telling Aithen. Indeed, his eldest would not react well to the news. But he would do what needed to be done, as he had done for fifty years already as ruler of the Greatest Kingdom of Alvinoria.

Once everyone felt they looked as good as they could look given the circumstances, Primus Julian ordered Merr to fly on ahead of them with Juliana Lux Baiula to inform the high prince that his father would be in the capital within the hour, and to request that he have two furans saddled and waiting outside the main gate. Merr was also to tell the Gate Guard as well as the palace staff that the high king was on his way and would arrive within the next *two* hours.

Ten minutes after Merr and Juliana left, the rest of the company prepared to follow. But while tightening the cinch on his mount, Julian noted that the animal's wing muscles were sore. He asked Kiron and Almiar to check their own mounts, and the two men found that they too were just as sore. So, the company agreed to cover the rest of the way by ground. As they ordered their furans forward, Octavius was reminded of his voran, Battle, and he let out a quiet curse, wondering whether the animal still lived or whether he, too, had fallen to the wrigglers.

**

Aithen was wiping his mouth when Kildare entered to announce Merr. He was just finishing a meal with Elyana, Harlion, Leo, and Luma Kraelion. It was now near Three Hours Thirty Minutes after Highsun.

Kildare approached his master quietly. "High Prince, one of the high king's guardians is outside waiting to deliver a message to you."

The prince's heart skipped a beat, and his stomach tied itself in a knot. Not wishing to question his squire here, he pulled his chair back, placed his hands on the table, and said to his guests, "I apologize for leaving you so suddenly, but I have something to attend to urgently. I will be back shortly."

The prince turned to Rovali, his majordomo, and asked him to have some bitters [66] brought in for his guests. Harlion and Elyana gave the prince a questioning look, and he replied with hand signs that he would share anything of importance with them as soon as possible, but that in the meantime they should stay with the senators to prevent any unwanted speculation. And without further ado, Aithen followed his squire.

Outside the dining hall, he met an impatient Merr. The man bowed deeply and began.

"High Prince, I have a message from the king, your father."

---

[66] A digestive drink.

In his excitement, Aithen replied more abruptly than he would have liked, "What is it man? Speak!"

"The king will be here in some thirty minutes, that is, at Four after Highsun. However, he had me inform the guardians at Victory Gate that he will be here within the next two hours."

This means he doesn't want to be received with a big fanfare.

"Is he all right? Is my brother with him?"

"The king is well, my Prince, but Lord Commander Toras…"

"What is it man?"

"We had to leave him and a few other men at the foot of the Colossi's Peaks three days ago; there was an attack, too few furans left and no vorans to carry us all back, so they stayed behind while we brought the king to safety. Two Lux Baiulae also accompanied us, one of whom came here with me, and took a carriage to Domus Lucis."

"What attack? Who attacked?"

"I have no idea who or what attacked us, my Prince; I didn't see them. But Lord Commander Toras and the officers were adamant that the king should leave immediately seeing that we had no vorans, and that the creatures had killed half our furans and one of our men already…they felt the risk was too high for the king to remain there."

Merr watched the prince as his face and jaw tensed and twitched, alternating between worry and anger.

"Was there a flying creature accompanying those that attacked your party?"

"No, my Prince. Not that I know. If you are referring to the creature that attacked Horn's Pass, we didn't see it."

After a moment, the prince replied with a simple "Very well." Then, turning to his squire, he said, "Kildare, call High Captain Harlion, and give my apologies to the senators; I will call on them later."

"And have Elyana Lux Baiula meet me in my chambers."

Turning to Merr again, he added, "Merr, you will give exact coordinates of that location where you left my brother to High Captain Harlion, so he may send a rescue team."

"Of course, my Prince. You should know that the Lord Commander did still have his furan when we left, so there is a chance he might be making his way back here now to get help for the others."

314

Aithen was about to reply to that, but he heard his captain's footstep coming behind. It was quicker than usual and had a tone of worry in it. Then it paused. Harlion must have recognized Merr. Aithen turned around.

Harlion stopped in front of the prince, nodded to Merr with a visage full of urgent questions and said, "High Lord Commander, you called me."

"Yes. Merr has just arrived to inform me that the king will be here shortly. But my brother is not with him; he was left somewhere at the foot of the Colossi's Peaks fighting who knows what. I need you to dispatch a rescue team immediately. Send our best fliers along with a medic from Domus Lucis. I want them there by end of the day tomorrow, at the latest. Also," Aithen hesitated here, and looked at Merr as if to request a confirmation which the man would not be able to give, "my brother may be making his way back here already, so have our fliers keep an eye out for anyone coming in this direction."

Harlion nodded, and Aithen continued, "Merr, please give the high captain what other details he may need. I am returning to my chambers now....and Captain, please make the preparations for my father's return. You know what to do?"

"I do."

Merr looked like he had something else to say; Aithen prompted him to speak.

"I'm sorry, my prince. Primus Julian wishes to have two furans saddled and posted in front of Victory Gate."

Aithen and Harlion frowned at that strange request. Merr explained. "My Prince, that is because the high king and the others are doubling up on three furans."

"Ah, right. High Captain, please have the furans readied."

Harlion nodded.

"Is that all, Merr?"

"It is, my Prince."

"Very well then. Thank you, Merr. Captain."

Harlion and Merr saluted, Merr deeply and Harlion with a nod, and Aithen left.

* * *

A few minutes later, Aithen was in his chambers with Elyana.

"Elyana, my father is on his way here and should arrive within twenty minutes."

Elyana's expression showed real relief at hearing this news. She asked, "And your brother?"

"That has me worried. He is not with them. My father, his men, and two of your Sisters had to leave *him* and a few men behind because there weren't enough mounts to carry them all, and the company was being attacked by some unknown creatures."

That caused a veil of concern to replace the sense of relief Elyana had on her face. She said, "Unknown creatures. And signs of the –"

"The Serpent? No."

"Hmm. I assume you are sending help?"

"I am."

"Well, let us hope they are safe."

"Yes, let's. Anyway, we need to prepare for my father's arrival. I think we should give him some time to settle in, but we'll need to meet with him tonight to brief him on the events at Horn's Pass, as well as to tell him what we learned when…when we entered the Bind."

Elyana noted Aithen's hesitation at the mention of their unsanctioned excursion into the Bind. She, herself, was not looking forward to disclosing that fact to the king. *Oh well, what is done is done.*

"I agree, Aithen; and I also have a need to question him. In fact, I am certain the entire world will wish to question him, though those who can do so are few. Still, something tells me the next few days will not be pleasant for him, especially if he is unwilling to give satisfactory answers to the Magna Mater and to the First Senator."

"You believe he has something to hide?"

"I do."

"Why? Sorry, forget it. There's no time for that now, but I want to know what it is you're thinking later. What we do need to do now, is get ready for his arrival."

He is using too many contractions. He only does that when he is really edgy. Well, who could blame him? Everyone has been worried about the king, and I am sure Aithen most of all. "Of course, Aithen. What do you need from me?"

"Would you put healers and medics on the alert, in case they should be needed? Merr told me the king is well, but I suspect others in the party may need healing."

"I will. Anything else?"

The prince scratched his right thumb with the nails of his index and middle finger nervously, then said, "No. That is all."

"And when do you wish to brief and debrief the king?"

"At Six Hours after Highsun?"

Elyana thought for a moment and answered. "That should be fine."

"I assume you'll inform Urbs Lucis of my father's return?"

"Yes. I will do that as soon as I have informed our Head Medic of your request."

"Thank you."

"You are welcome." Then, with a tone of concern in her voice, the Lux Baiula added, "Try to relax, Aithen. You *are* a little tense."

"I'm tense? Why ever would I be?!"

"You just proved it again, just now; you know that you only use contractions when you are nervous or excited, right? And you have been doing it a lot in the past five minutes."

The prince replied with a small, embarrassed laugh. "Really?"

Elyana replied with a kind smile, "Yes, really."

"I had not noticed. Anyway, I guess you're –, you *are* right. But I will relax once I hear my father, and once my brother is safely back."

With a smile, Elyana said, "There, much better already."

"Ha-ha! Yes…well, forcing myself to calm down does not mean I am."

"Hmm. Anyways, I will go now…and may the air sing [67] when you hear your father."

"See you later, Elyana."

The Lux Baiula's dress swished gently on the floor as she turned to go. Even when there were urgent or important things to do, she went calmly, always in control – except at Horn's Pass, the night of the attack. She had walked fast that night, getting from Toras's dining hall to the courtyard. Aithen followed the Lux Baiula

---

[67] "May the air sing" was an Alvinorian well-wish given to another before a long-awaited reunion, an expression which meant "may your reunion be joyful."

317

longingly as she exited his office and then the anteroom. *How I like her company, even when it's to talk about affairs of state. And how I love her smell; I could hear her all the day long. Soon…soon, I'll reveal my feelings to her, but –*

The prince did not finish his thought. Instead, he looked at the clock: still ten minutes or so before his father arrived. He wondered whether he should have Leo and Kraelion informed of the king's arrival. But his father did not want the Senate to know. Still, he couldn't just leave the senator and First Senator like that.

I will send Kil to ask them to come back at Seven Hours after Highsun today, and to come in their formal attire. That way, when they hear that father has come back, they won't be too upset that I didn't inform them of his imminent return, since they will understand, once they see him, that I was planning for them to meet with him anyway, given my particular request.

And Aithen called Kildare to give him his instructions regarding the senators, as well as to send him to inform Ori of their father's imminent arrival. Then, he rushed to the stables to saddle his voran, and joined the guard along Triumph Lane.

***

Aria had never felt this hopeful in her young life. Magistera Annan had done as she had told them she would. She had spoken with her and Carasina's instructors and got them to lighten the girls' workload for a few fourths so that they may spend more time practicing Beast Reading. Magistera Annan had also agreed to spend half that additional practice time demonstrating the techniques. And today, after months of learning, and all the supplemental practice, Aria finally had a breakthrough.

"I did it! I did it! *We* did it!"

Carasina, just as excited and surprised, said "Yes, I can't believe how easily it happened, all of a sudden! It was as if it were the most natural thing for me to do…like, like walking!"

"Like walking? Like flying!"

"Like flying? Flying is not natural."

Aria retorted, "I know, but to me, it felt as though I had suddenly learned to fly and was doing it as naturally as a flyer. It was just so incredible!"

"Carasina, I want to do it again!"

318

"Well, sure. But Brutus may not want to. We've been working with him for hours already."

"Let's find out." And Aria walked to the specimen room where the locarian was being kept during the Beast Reading sessions. She knocked on the door and a middle-aged, short, plump woman opened the door; she was Priestess Veterinarian Loma.

"Are you done, Mistress Aria?"

"Actually, Veterinarian Loma, I was wondering how Brutus is doing. I know we've been at it all day long, but Carasina and I would like to try reading his mind just once more."

"Hmm, normally, I would say no, but he has been in a good mood all day, and his vital signs have been normal. I would say you have succeeded in establishing a stable connection with him."

Excitedly, Aria replied, "I think so too. Can we try once more, then?"

"All right. Once more, and we will let him rest afterward. Give me five minutes."

"Thank you, Veterinarian."

The priestess yelled instructions to an assistant, telling her to change the objects in the room where the locarian was, and the door shut behind her.

Aria looked back at her friend with such excitement that Carasina could not help but be excited too.

"Let's do this Cari. And then, we go find Magistera Annan!"

"I can't wait to see her reaction. And your aunt's – she will be pleased too. Everyone will be!"

And the girls sat back-to-back on the ground in the middle of the Mind Reading room and got ready to read the Red Locarian's mind one more time before announcing to the world they were ready for Passage. At least, that is how they felt just now, though they had many more things to master before they could test for Passage at the end of the year.

***

High Captain Harlion had timed the arrival of the guardians on Triumph Lane well. He understood the king would not want to be bothered by officials pestering him as he entered the city, and he made certain that whatever he did to clear the way for the king's entry into the capital, it didn't raise the alarm in the Senate, and that if it did, it would be too late for the elders to arrive *en masse*.

To begin, he had sent some guardians to Triumph Lane to quietly ask peddlers and others who might have tables or carts along the way to move them. The guardians were instructed to reply with a simple "High Prince's orders" if anyone asked why they should move their things. Harlion also instructed the Gate Sergeant to alert him when the king's party was a kilometer from the city. That would give him and twenty mounted Royal Guardians just enough time to get to Triumph Lane and form a cordon for the king's passage as he and his party made their way to the palace, leaving no time for the elders to be alerted and come to meet the king. Of course, that might not keep senators strolling about on private business from learning of the king's arrival, but there was nothing Harlion could do about that. As for First Cleric Galadrin, he would cause no trouble today given that he was in the country, trying to recruit peasants of the neighboring villages to his views.

At exactly Four Hours after Highsun, the king's party arrived at the gate, looking fresh and dignified. Octavius would need to thank Juliana and Mara who had done a remarkable job at removing any trace of battle or injury from everyone. Mara had also had to confuse some men who had passed them on their way to the Capital, and that was not something she had done happily, as Sisters were only allowed to use Confusion in extreme cases. But the king had asked, and given that she did not consider the Order's rule against Confusion to be necessarily warranted anyways, Mara had consented; the procedure was a fairly innocuous one after all, and at most, it left people with a small, short-lived headache.

Just now, High Captain Harlion – sitting straight-backed atop his chestnut voran, Rufus – approached his king.

"My King! Welcome back."

"Thank you, High Captain. It is good to be back."

Primus Julian saluted the high captain. Harlion nodded back.

"Where is my son, Captain?"

"He will arrive soon, Sire."

The king nodded and then, pointing to the furans behind Harlion, said to Julian who was sitting in front of him, "Primus, you may dismount and take one of those two furans. I will remain on Runner; he is a good animal."

"Certainly, Sire."

After he got off, Julian added, "I will have Almiar and Jashan take separate furans as well and leave Mara Lux Baiula to ride in with Kiron."

While Julian and Jashan got themselves on their respective furans, Harlion informed Octavius about Aithen's orders to send a rescue team to Toras and his men. That news lifted the king's heart, and it brought a smile to his lips to know his son could make needed decisions on his own.

Primus Julian took the king out of his reverie, saying, "Sire, we are ready."

Octavius turned to look at the troupe and, seeing everyone on a furan, said in a voice filled with excitement – but an excitement which hid the anxiety he felt at the thought of the questions he would soon be assailed with – he said, then, "Very well, to the palace!"

And Octavius entered the city, surrounded by his personal guard, Mara Lux Baiula, and the captain of the Royal Guard.

The king's subjects reacted with the expected surprise and excitement when they sighted their monarch. Men took off their hats and bowed, and women curtsied. Everyone wondered, too, how it was that the king and his party were riding furans for they knew that the king only went by voran now. The king responded to the cheers and salutes of respect with a wave of the hand.

Mara Lux Baiula's reaction, was one of surprise. She knew the king's subjects respected and liked him, but she had had no idea how deeply they loved him.

Kids were running in the street alongside the party, excited by the sight of the king, but even more so by the sight of the furans which rarely paraded through the city.

At one point, a young lad who was running alongside the furans shouted to his friend that one of them had blood on its cinch. An adult heard him, and a rumor began spreading that perhaps the king and his party had come back from a secret mission to kidnap the woman, whom they did not recognize, and that their furans had gotten injured in the ensuing fight; or perhaps the king and his party were attacked by the rokon which destroyed Horn's pass, and the woman was a Lux Baiula the king had called upon to help fight the creature. One courageous kid decided to ask the king whether one of the rumors – the one he preferred – was true.

321

The king replied with a smile. "No, no, we were not attacked by a rokon, son." The kid was evidently disappointed, but the king had called him "son", and that was enough to take his mind off the rumors and onto something else even more exciting: telling his friends how the king had addressed him.

To the king's delight, there were only two senators in attendance, only two senators to talk in whispers to each other as they put on smiles to greet him, and to then spread their favorite rumors. These two had probably come to the market to meet the people as senators did in turns, once a fourth. And First Cleric Galadrin was nowhere to be seen. That pleased the king greatly.

But the one thing which comforted Octavius most of all, and lit up his face, was Aithen's arrival. His children's company always gave him immense pleasure, unless they had done something wrong of course, and this was a rare occurrence with his eldest. As he watched his heir approach, he thought that even if Galadrin were to suddenly appear, it would merely annoy him, without taking away any of the joy he felt at this moment.

To his surprise – whether it was from relief or pride, he did not know – his son looked splendid and more relaxed than he would have expected him to be.

As Aithen turned to put Magnus alongside the king's furan, some in the crowd cheered. Men bowed, and women curtsied. Girls blushed, and then sighed from the knowledge they would never get to know the prince personally, feel his sinewy arms around their hips or his lips on theirs. Some did their best to lock eyes with the prince – without luck. Aithen ignored it all; he had never been one to respond one way or another to all this adulation, and at the moment, his thoughts were only on his father, and they battled a multitude of feelings: feelings of relief at seeing him, feelings of apprehension in the face of the news about his brother, and feelings of nervousness as he wondered what the king would think of his performance at the reins of the kingdom.

"Aithen. It is nice to see you again, and it is nice to find you in such great form." Octavius paused and smiled for a moment before he continued, "I must say I was a little concerned that the responsibilities, which were forced upon you in my absence, might have greyed your hair and given you a sour look, but I was wrong."

Aithen smiled a jokingly cynical smile in return and said, "I am doing well enough indeed, Father, considering the circumstances, and it is probably because you prepared me so well for just such a situation. But it is nice to find you well too. You did have everyone worried these past few fourths, Toras and me included. And, speaking of Toras, why isn't he with you? Merr said you had to leave him behind, that you were attacked?"

"I will tell you everything once we reach the palace, son, because I would not be able to keep a smile on for the public otherwise."

"Now you *are* worrying me, Father. But I understand. We are almost there anyway."

And indeed, the party reached the palace five minutes later. The king found his staff assembled in the central plaza to welcome him back. He fought back an oncoming frown when he did not see his youngest at the front so as not to appear unappreciative to his staff.

Their cheers were more subdued than those he had endured along Triumph Lane, though not because his staff felt any less excited than the rest of the population, but because they knew their master, and they knew he did not enjoy boisterous demonstrations. So, rather than rowdy cheers, his staff gave him warm, genuine welcomes filled with smiles, bows and curtsies. The king showed his appreciation by nodding toward each and every person present.

Once that was done, all returned to their duties. The king dismissed his guard for the evening and nodded back to High Captain Harlion who saluted him with a promise to hear him later. Mara Lux Baiula gave him a nod, got off the furan, thanked Kiron with a grunt, and climbed into the carriage waiting to take her to Domus Lucis.

With everyone gone except for his son, Octavius asked, "Where is Ori? Why isn't he here?"

Aithen was going to answer he did not know when his little brother appeared at the top of the palace's steps along with Master Rackeli, the king's majordomo. Pointing with his head, Aithen said, "He is coming, Father."

At that, the king turned, and a large smile appeared on his face. As soon as the young prince saw the smile on his father's face, he ran to him, leaving Master Rackeli behind.

Octavius spent a few precious minutes with Ori, as Aithen and Rackeli waited. He listened to Ori "brief" him on everything that had happened during his absence, and he asked Ori about his studies, and Ori told him what he had learned about the biological basis of the Sensing and Binding powers of various Alterintrants. Finally, Ori asked his father if the capital was in danger, and after Octavius reassured him that things would be alright, he gave him another warm embrace and sent him back to Master Rackeli who took the young prince to Magister Setarcos for his next lesson.

Octavius let a sigh escape him as he watched Ori leave. He loved the boy very much, and it pained him to think he, too, would be endangered by what was coming. When Ori disappeared from view, Octavius turned to Aithen and said, "Let us talk, son."

Aithen nodded, and the two of them walked to the bench that stood underneath the great bok tree which dominated the north side of the palace's plaza. The king and prince often went there to have private conversations rather than go to their chambers. Indeed, Lux Baiulae of the Yellow Sash had inserted resonant minerals within the bark of the tree, minerals which created a sound barrier within a three-meter radius of the tree.

Father and son sat themselves on the white marble bench located there, Aithen with legs extended in front of the bench, and Octavius with arms resting on his legs and hands tapping each other.

Octavius took a deep breath and proceeded to explain what had happened at the southern tip of the Colossi's Peaks. He knew he would also need to explain to his son what he had done in the Shadow Woods, but he decided to leave that part of the account for the evening.

"After your brother and what was left of his company found me near Spiritii – or rather, after I found them – we headed for the southern tip of the Colossi's Peaks. Indeed, everyone had agreed that travelling along the foot of the mountains all the way to Mountain Lake, and then cutting through the plains to reach the capital would be the fastest and safest way back. The journey to the Peaks was not an easy one, however, with the heat climbing to nearly seventeen stones by the afternoon, and the vorans in worse and worse shape as the hours passed, even with Mara Lux Baiula's Healings. Fearing that the vorans would falter before we reached the mountains, we decided to leave the vorans with Jashan, while the rest of us, including the two Lux Baiulae, doubled-up on the furans to make our way to the mountains. We got there without trouble, but as the suns set, the screeches of dying furans erupted from the clearing's edge. Your brother and some of the men picked up their weapons and ran to the furan line to see what was happening. I do not know what they saw, but it shocked them. Given that no one knew what had so gruesomely killed the furans, Toras and Juliana Lux Baiula demanded that I leave, especially since there were only four furans left, aside from Scorch. I did not wish to go, but given the situation and everyone's insistence, I left with my men, and the Lux Baiulae. The last I saw of Toras, he was running back to the edge of the clearing to assist the others."

Aithen was clearly alarmed by this account. He understood that the threat must have seemed great indeed, especially if it had caused even the Lux Baiulae to suggest what looked like a cowardly escape. But couldn't they have stayed? Couldn't Juliana and Mara have protected them? Aithen asked the question, trying to keep the edge off his voice.

"Father, I do not know that I can disagree with your decision, but I need to understand why even the Lux Baiulae felt so powerless as to suggest an escape and abandoning Toras – second in line to the throne – and the rest of the men."

The king, a very perceptive man, perhaps one of the most perceptive in all the kingdom – a quality which probably accounted for much of his ability to negotiate with the minor kings and lords of the land – had noted his son's restraint and appreciated that in him, but he also felt embarrassment and decided to let it show to his son. He shook his head and said, "Mara Lux Baiula was actually not there when the suggestion was made; she had been out to the marshes with two of my men to find Jashan. The party returned just as we were preparing to leave, with Mara and Jashan both needing urgent healing. Given this, given Juliana's intense fear of what she had sensed, and given the fact that only five furans remained for over a dozen of us, everyone urged me to go. So, we did."

Octavius paused, then added "I know how you feel, Aithen; I feel the same way."

Aithen was about to respond when he heard the flapping wings of several furans. He looked up.

"Well, I believe that's the rescue team; let us hope they find Toras and the others alive."

"Yes, let us. Anyway, that is what I wanted to tell you."

325

After a moment of uncomfortable silence, Octavius asked, "How is Elyana, by the way?"

Aithen was surprised by the sudden change of topic, but he let it be and answered his father's question with a slightly troubled edge, "She is well, although quite exhausted, despite not looking it." He paused, then with more urgency, added, "I do not know what I would have done without her since Horn's Pass." Aithen paused again, and added almost as an afterthought, "Or without Harlion. But Elyana will join us later."

An imperceptible twitch crossed Octavius's lips upon noticing the varying tones in his son's voice. *Hmm, I could swear something has changed in Aithen's attitude toward Elyana. His tone seemed laden with admiration, comfort and, something else.* He decided that he would pay attention to their interaction during the meeting to see whether there was anything to what he had sensed or not.

Octavius said, "I assume she has been tiring herself looking for me in the Bind?"

Aithen gave the king a resentful look. "Yes, she has, Father. She has indeed tired herself to find you – and to look for that creature from hell, as well."

The king's mouth drew itself into a slant, perhaps because he felt some guilt for the worry he had caused, and for not being immediately available in a time such as this.

With a now somber tone, Octavius said, "Your brother told me what happened in Horn's Pass; it seems he doesn't want to believe that the rokon that attacked you was the Serpent, but from everything I, myself, have sensed, and from what Mara and Juliana Lux Baiulae have told me, it must be."

"It *was* the Serpent, Father. Elyana and I have confirmed it. And there is more."

"More?"

"It is not alone. There is at least another working with it, one who is definitely intent on conquest."

"Who? And how did you come by this information?"

The prince hesitated a moment. He wasn't sure this was the time or place to disclose this fact to the king, but he decided he would, perhaps for a purely selfish reason; he was an adult and he had made the decision he thought was right. He said, "Elyana took me into the Bind…into the Serpent's mind."

326

"She did what?! Urbs Lucis has known for a long time my stance relative to roaming the Bind, and Elyana should not have taken you there without discussing it with me."

With an accusatory tone, Aithen replied, "You were not there to be asked, Father, and it was necessary for me to join her in her search so that I might learn what we were dealing with."

The king continued to stare at his son with clenched teeth.

"You have always told me to learn for myself all things critical to me, to my function, to my tasks. Knowing who our enemy is, is one such critical piece of knowledge…and our mission was successful."

The king shook his head in disbelief. But a moment later, his eyes changed.

Aithen asked, "What?"

"Though what you did was extremely dangerous, there's a …very…strong feeling of pride swelling in me right now."

The prince drew a breath of air, a breath of relief.

Octavius felt like brushing his son's hair, as he used to do when Aithen was younger, but he resisted the temptation now, and instead asked, "So what did you learn…in the Serpent's Mind?"

The dismay in Aithen's response surprised Octavius with its intensity, "It is working with a humanoid Elyana calls 'Umbra.' This man seems intent on conquering K'Tara to deliver it to the Dark One, who is apparently returning from wherever he was."

"As for the Serpent, it is so full of hatred for us – for the Sisterhood – that I still feel it inside me like some foulness invading my mind every time I think of it."

The king's expression changed from the earlier prideful one to one of incredulity and consternation. Octavius clasped his hands, his mind racing to make sense of this small, but ominous revelation. *How is it possible?* he thought.

He said, "Tell me that is all, son."

"Ohh, no. There is more, Father, there is more." Aithen hesitated to continue. He wanted to but thought it might be better to reveal the rest of what they had learned with Elyana present, and he proposed just that to Octavius.

Octavius replied, "Very well. Perhaps it is best." He then stood up and said in a tone that belied his true feelings, "I will go to my chambers now to refresh myself; this has been a tiring journey after all. I will see you at Six Hours after Highsun?"

"Yes, Six after Highsun, in your Private Audience Chamber. I hope that when you get a chance, you will also tell me why you went to Spiritii in the first place, Father. In fact, there are many who will want to know that, and though you will likely not tell everyone, I hope you will tell me."

"I will, Aithen, before the day's end."

Octavius turned around and made his way to the palace's South Wing where he had his quarters. Every so often, he shook his head, and then sighed.

Aithen watched his father go. He had a lot of respect for him and had always admired his strength of character, his courage, his integrity in all things, his dedication to his family and to his subjects. But today, he was disappointed in his father, and wasn't so certain about his good judgement any longer. How could he have agreed to leave Toras and the few men that remained with him to face an unknown danger on their own? He, himself, would not have agreed to that if he had been in his father's position. In fact –

Aithen stopped his train of thought when he heard Elyana's voice.

"Aithen!"

The prince turned to his right and saw Elyana with her hands on her hips.

"I am sorry Elyana, I hadn't heard you."

"Right. What were you doing here?"

"I was discussing things with my father under the bok tree; he left just a short while ago."

"And how did it go?"

In response, Aithen just shrugged his shoulders and frowned.

"I hear. Or rather I don't since you are mute. But I can imagine you did not learn what you hoped to learn; I am sure the king will open up and reveal what secrets he may before long."

Aithen shook his head and said, "It isn't that, Elyana. It is his decision to abandon Toras and the other men in the face of an unknown enemy that upsets me."

"Well, I am sure there is a good explanation for it, and it is likely my associates, Mara and Juliana Lux Baiulae, will confirm it to be so. I am on my way to go meet with them just now."

"I don't know that it will help. My father has already told me that Juliana Lux Baiula and the officers suggested the escape, and that Mara and Jashan were in need of immediate medical attention."

"Hum, regardless, I will still speak with them. But, Aithen, you know your father is not a coward, and you know he is not one to make decisions lightly – or to agree to any ill-conceived recommendation. Why do you doubt him now?"

"Because this is so unlike him. It was wrong of him to leave my brother to face who knows what, without a minimum of confidence that Toras and his men would survive. They could have tried to triple-up on the furans. True, they might not have gotten far, but far enough to get them all out of danger, they certainly would have gone!"

A blanket of silence fell around the two while Aithen regained control of himself, and Elyana considered how she might help him have the answer he really needed.

After pacing back and forth along a short hedge which lined the walkway that led to the bok tree, the prince stopped and looked at Elyana with eyes crying for help and filled with embarrassment.

Elyana broke the silence, saying, "Tonight, I will go into the Bind and try to locate your brother. If he is in there dreaming, I will find him, and if I find him, we will know he is all right. I can tell that your mind will not be at ease until you know he is well, and we cannot afford to have you unfocused with everything that is happening here."

"Thank you, Elyana. But I can't ask that of you. I know you, yourself, have been strained with entering the Bind so frequently these last fifteen days to look for my father as well as for the Serpent and its associate. You need to rest."

"I know my limits, Aithen. Do not concern yourself with my health."

"But –"

"Aithen, let me do this. I must admit that I too am slightly concerned about your brother."

Hesitatingly, Aithen said, "All right…thank you…"

The Lux Baiula made a simple nod, and nothing else. That simple gesture drew a silent sigh from the prince, a sigh carrying with it the undisclosed desires within him. But as ever before, the moment of longing passed, and Aithen shook his head and asked, "So, why are you here, anyway? I thought you had gone to Domus Lucis."

"I needed to obtain a dispensation to allow Mara and Juliana Lux Baiulae to remain here, both. As you know, the Sisterhood is only allowed seven Lux Baiulae in the capital at any one time, and we would be eight with the two of them."

"A silly rule. And were you granted the dispensation?"

"I was, and I am on my way back to Domus Lucis with it."

"Good. Hear you later then?"

"Yes. I will hear you later." And the Lux Baiula walked away, her walk that of a confident woman, confident in her skills, confident in her place in society.

But Aithen wondered, as he watched her go, whether she could love. He knew of very few wed Lux Baiulae; in fact, he knew of only two.

You fool, there you go again! Aghrr. Why do I even bother? And why shouldn't I? What would be wrong with me pursuing her? I am a man, she a woman – a good and amazing woman! The prince shook his head again, sighed and made his way to his chambers after giving Elyana one last glance, and after shooting an icy stare at two strangers who were leaving the palace and had observed his soliloquy.

XX EXPLANATIONS

At exactly Six Hours after Highsun, High Prince Aithen, Elyana Lux Baiula, and High Captain Harlion awaited the high king in the Private Audience Chamber, dressed in their formal attire; the king was never late, but neither did he arrive before any others.

Aithen sat at the right end of the marbled table, straight, hands down, and deep in thought. Elyana sat on the long side, facing the door, with hands on her lap and receiving updates on Master Methrim from the high captain. Harlion did not sit, but stood by the table, looking at Elyana, and turned slightly toward the front of the room so that his back would not be to the king when he entered.

Finally, the wooden door swiveled on its well-oiled hinges and the king entered. He did not have his crown on – he usually reserved that for formal meetings with foreign dignitaries or the Senate, and for hearings in the Grand Audience Hall, but he looked regal, nevertheless.

Harlion took a step back and bowed, naming the king. Octavius replied with a simple "Harlion" and a nod.

Aithen and Elyana stood, as was the custom upon entrance of the monarch. Aithen greeted his father with his title, and the king replied with a simple nod. Finally, Elyana followed with a shallow bow and said, "Sire." She then paused a moment, and added, "It is good to see you."

The king did not immediately return his advisor's greeting. Instead he looked down for a very brief moment, tapped the table and sat himself. "Likewise, Elyana," he said, inviting the others to sit also.

Octavius started promptly, saying, "I must begin with an apology."

Aithen, Harlion, and Elyana reacted with the expected surprise and confusion. They knew the king was not too proud to apologize when he was wrong or had acted wrongly – he had done it before – but a monarch did not *need* to apologize to his subjects, so on the rare occasions where Octavius did, most people reacted more with a sense of embarrassment than one of vindication.

"I should have made certain I could be reached in the event of urgent need; I thought I had, but it seems the measures I put in place weren't adequate in this instance. It may be that something is interfering with the Bind and prevented those who knew of my location to relay the information when it was needed."

Elyana nodded in agreement with the king's assumptions, though she had no evidence of forces interfering with the Bind – except for something interfering with her own abilities – that is.

The king continued. "You probably wonder why I left Furan City with such secrecy in the first place."

Harlion spoke for the first time since the king's entrance. "Indeed, we do, Sire, and so does everyone else, including my officers, the elders, and the leaders among your subjects as well as the common folk. And as Elyana will attest to, so does Urbs Lucis. I can only assume that the Supreme Priestess of Kynaria, and the Lady Darya have the same question too. At the very least, those closest to you should have been informed of the object of your trip. I have known you long enough, Sire, to gather that it is not a matter of trust which kept you from telling any of us where you were going. Therefore, it was either to protect us or to protect yourself from actions which we would have had to take, had we known of your destination."

Aithen looked mortified. Harlion was a bright and wise man and he had always been highly regarded by the king, serving as his advisor in matters of security and war before becoming the high prince's own advisor and first officer, and Commander of the Frumentarii – the king's secret service. Harlion had also been a friend to the king for over thirty years now, and that gave him certain rights which very few others had. But to accuse Octavius so plainly?!

As for Elyana, she merely looked surprised, but not shocked by Harlion's directness. She would have confronted the king with a similar statement if Harlion had not done it. Now she waited patiently for the king's reply.

"My dear friend, that is exactly why I chose not to tell you anything, as to tell you even one thing would have been as bad as to tell you everything and force an action on your part which I could not risk."

This time, Elyana did react and raised a worried eyebrow. Aithen turned his eyes toward her and they exchanged a flitting nervous look. Octavius caught that but returned his attention to Harlion.

"The reason I kept the *object* of my voyage secret is that I went to meet with a Zebulonian, and the reason I kept the *destination* secret is that the place where I met with this man is forbidden, even to me."

Harlion said, "I do not like the sound of that, Sire. Who is this Zebulonian you met with? Where? And why?" Harlion turned to Aithen and Elyana, certain that they must be having the same questions.

The king sighed as he realized that this was going to be just as he had feared. With another sigh, he replied, "I did not imagine you would like this, Captain. The Zebulonian's name is Lub Methor." The king noted the others' surprised reaction, and asked, "Do you know the name?"

Aithen replied, "No, we do not, Father. But it sounds strangely similar to that of *another* Zebulonian we met recently. In fact, Elyana and I need to discuss him with you."

The king nodded and noticed his son exchanging another secretive, puzzled look with the Lux Baiula. He said, mostly to himself, "Another Zebulonian; strange coincidence." Then, addressing the others, he continued, "Anyway, this Lub Methor is the representative of a rebel group that was formed some five years ago in Zebulonia, and he came to ask for my assistance."

Aithen asked, "Your assistance in doing what?"

"He came to ask whether I might intervene in support of his group's rebellion against Zebula! The group is – strange as it may sound – the *Organization for the Liberation of Zebulonian Males*. Very odd name, I know, but so is the Zebulonian society."

Aithen, Harlion and Elyana gave the king a knowing look.

"This rebel group is only one of many, but apparently it is also the largest, and acceding to their request may serve our purposes."

Harlion and Aithen were wide-eyed, disbelieving what they were hearing.

"Father, you know we trust your judgement in all things, but to discuss military matters without High Captain Harlion or me present was unwise."

"As I said, to inform and involve any of you would have made it quite impossible for me to attend this meeting at all."

Elyana spoke for the first time. "Because of the location of the meeting?"

The king nodded and stated plainly and without hesitation, "Yes, the meeting took place at Marcus Vrol's villa."

Shock and consternation painted Aithen's and Harlion's faces, while troubling confirmation of her doubts darkened Elyana's normally cool face.

Elyana said, "Sire...you put me in a very bad position. I am certain you are aware that I will need to report this to the Magna Mater."

"I am."

"And that you will be called to answer for this transgression in front of the Light's Assembly."

"I understand. But perhaps, I can convince you to take your time."

Elyana replied with a voice tight with restraint, "Sire..."

Octavius raised his hand and said, "Elyana. Let me explain how I came to be in this situation and what is at stake here."

After a tense moment during which the worst possible scenarios sent everyone's thoughts running wildly, Elyana finally nodded.

Octavius spent the next fifteen minutes explaining to his Privy Council why he had gotten back in touch with Marcus the Reader, how and why he had decided to accept his invitation to meet with the Zebulonian, and why he now believed he had made a good decision.

When the king was done, Aithen said with a sigh, "Well, what Master Methor has told you corroborates what Lusk Methrim has told us. It may be that having a way to keep Zebula's focus on her own territory was worth the risk you took. And yet, you have broken the law, Father, and though king you are, you are not above...above our laws. You have often said so yourself, *publicly*, that no one in Alvinoria should have the freedom to make a mockery of our laws, laws that our own ancestors wrote into our very fibers, and twice now, you have –."

Octavius raised his hand again and said, "Son, I *will* face the consequences when the time comes, I promise. But do *not* presume to understand my actions."

That brought a chill into the king's Private Audience Chamber, and everyone sat in silence for a while. But to one who could read it, Aithen's face spoke volumes; his emotions seemed to shift from embarrassment, to self-pity, to anger, to understanding, and finally to some sort of acceptance when his face and jaw relaxed, and his shoulders fell.

Aithen knew his father was an honest man, and what he did, he did for the good, always. His father was also an honorable man, and never shirked from the consequences of his decisions or actions, so the prince also knew that the king would pay the price for his errors – whatever that might be.

But what convinced Aithen that he was perhaps misjudging his father's actions was the recall of a thing the king had said to him once: "'Human laws are not physical laws, Aithen; they are imperfect, created by men and women who are neither perfect nor constant , and one should therefore not ever be bound to them to such a degree as to be liable to commit a grave injustice or error in their blind, dogmatic application.'"

**

"Alia, tell me why we persist in wanting to continue living? What keeps pushing us to live one more day even after two thousand years of life? It certainly can't be our biological impulses..." Genghis did not finish his thought. Alia did not like to be reminded that she had very little of the Human left in her – perhaps only her thoughts, if that.

In a voice more perfectly modulated than her general's, the Empress of Earth and its Colonies, and Savior of Humankind replied once more to this question Genghis had often asked over the centuries, though it seemed he did not remember it – it was possible; his brain was a biological organ after all. She said, "It *is* imprinted in our minds, Genghis. For those with biological tissues, it is imprinted there by the genes which encoded their bodies when they were first conceived, forever unchanging – so long as they take care. For the few who, like me, have transferred their minds to positronic brains, the drive to continue is written in *those* circuits."

The proconsul tapped his finger on the low wall of the Empress's spacious balcony which overlooked the capital. He saw the solid metal structures, the living bacrete walls, the people everywhere, the enormity of it all, but he did not look at any of it, his mind was elsewhere. He said, "And yet, I don't think that is sufficient. Without a goal, without wants or desire, there is no reason for those impulses to maintain themselves."

"Genghis, it is not the first time you ask me this question, you realize, but it *is* the first time you make this argument."

"Are you certain?" Genghis was remembering another time, a time long ago, when he had questioned their reasons for continuing to live.

"I am. I have a very long memory, unbroken for two thousand four hundred and sixty years, to be precise."

To be precise, you have *forgotten. But it does not appear you realize it. It is as if certain events had never been. How much longer can you continue functioning, Alia? Even positronic brains degrade with time, no matter how perfect the circuits and their self-repair procedures.*

Genghis made a conscious decision to point out Alia's declining condition, an Inhuman condition, hoping that it would not set her against him, but just further degrade her self-confidence. He knew it was a dangerous game. He said, "Alia, I *have* made this argument at least once before, many centuries ago as we were to embark on our conquest of Sirius One. You recall that, don't you?" Alia's eyes flickered for a fraction of a second, but a fraction long-enough for Genghis to notice her alarm. He took courage and continued, "And, what I mean is that the mere continued existence of neural networks or pathways or circuits, or whatever else they may be, their mere integrity is not sufficient to drive a Human being forward. One needs more, something to want to live *for*, and I, in particular, need one thing which I am forbidden to have – you know what I am talking about, Alia."

The Empress's perfect features took on a look of annoyance, "I do know what you are talking about, Genghis. And this thing is your weakness, a weakness made possible by the organic parts of your body. I am convinced you would fare much better if you accepted to undergo the transformation because *my* brain, though positronic it is, does continue to drive *me* forward despite the lack of desires. I am humanity at its purest; I am its thoughts, its soul, devoid of any organic influence, an influence which only serves to drag Humans down to their animalistic motivations. I do not fault you for what you are, Genghis, but I do require you to be more."

Genghis turned away from the Empress and ground his zirconium teeth. He wondered why he even bothered; she would never understand. He wondered, too, whether she was still a Human at all. Had her memories, transferred into her positronic brain from the living tissues she had discarded so long ago, ever sufficed to retain her humanity? He did not think so. No. He would do what he had set out to do, with or without her.

* * *

Just now, the time disc on the back wall of the Private Audience Chamber rang. It indicated fifteen minutes to Seven Hours after Highsun. The time disc was composed of a main disc, which told the time, and a smaller one set in the bottom half, which was set to produce a soft ringing sound after a certain amount of time.

"Father, First Senator Leo and Senator Kraelion will be here soon, but there is still what Elyana and I have learned in the Bind which we must inform you about, and fifteen minutes are not enough."

"From the little you have told me, it is certainly more urgent than my meeting with the senators and I would rather hear it first."

Aithen nodded and pulled on a cord behind him. Kildare entered the room.

The young man was not unused to being in the presence of the king or of the powerful – his master was the heir to the throne after all. But he was a shy young man, and he very firmly believed that the high king and High Prince were the representatives of the Founders on K'Tara, and this, above all, prevented him from ever growing too comfortable around either. So, he made the deepest bow for the king, a slightly shallower one for the prince, and a normal one for Harlion and Elyana, before facing his master again to take his orders.

"Kil, please give my apologies to the senators and inform them that we must postpone their audience with the king until Seven Hours and Thirty after Highsun."

"Yes, my Prince." Aithen's squire exited the room with as much reverence as he had employed coming in.

337

After the doors had closed again, the king said, "That is a strange kid, Aithen. You must tell him that there is no need to be so unsettled in our presence."

Aithen sighed. "I have told him before, Father, but I have been unable to change him, despite my best efforts."

The king shrugged his shoulders and said, "Anyway, what exactly *did* you hear in the Bind?"

"As I told you earlier, when Elyana and I entered the Serpent's mind, it was talking with the one Elyana calls 'Umbra.'"

Harlion watched his king's reactions, hoping that he would have some idea on how to fight these enemies, though why he should hope that, he did not know; the king had never had to fight such foes either. Indeed, the king's reign had been a mostly peaceful one, and things of evil had not been seen on K'Tara in centuries. Still, Octavius was wise; he had extensive knowledge of ancient history; he even had abilities in the Bind; and he was a formidable leader. Surely, having him back increased the odds of their survival, if not of victory against a fallen Founder and his minions.

Aithen continued, his tone even graver now. "It appears that the goal of the Serpent's attacks on Human settlements is to spread terror, which means that the attacks will continue, and more innocent people will die." Aithen paused to let the king process the information.

"While spying on them, we also heard the Umbra refer to the existence of…Temptatori…in Kartak. Do you know what those are, Father?"

The king shook his head, rubbed his right temple and shook his head again, disbelieving what he was hearing. He said, "Of course, I do!" Aithen and Harlion blinked in surprise. The king sighed, embarrassed by his reaction. "Do you know how long they may have been at work? – recruiting humanoids?"

Elyana answered, "No, we do not Sire, but Urbs Lucis is looking into it."

"Good. I want to be kept informed of everything the Sisterhood may learn relating to Kartak. Please ensure the Magna Mater is aware, Lux Baiula."

"Yes, Sire."

"A nest of Temptatori! In my kingdom? How is that possible?!"

"Father, there is another thing we learned while listening to their conversation. They are searching for two Luxori…but the last of them disappeared over two hundred years ago! You are an Alterintrant, but not a Luxor, and there are only two other male Alterintrants in the kingdom. So, either our enemy is mistaken or there are indeed Luxori somewhere."

In a half joking tone and with a heavy sigh, the king replied, "I could very well be one of these two Luxori they are searching for."

Aithen and Harlion snorted incredulously.

Elyana intervened now and said, "That may be true, Majesty; to them, any Sensing male must be a Luxor. But the question remains: why would they be looking for you?" After a short pause during which Aithen and Harlion wondered about the answer to that question, and during which Elyana wondered whether the king had hidden from her – from everyone – much more than his dealings with a banished man, Elyana said, "Perhaps they wish to make you pay for your ancestor's part in bringing down Noctiferus…in fact, this makes the most sense…"

The king said, "Whatever do you mean, Elyana?"

"I mean, both your ancestor, Emperor Flavius the First, and Marcus Vrol's ancestor, Nogarin Vrollis, worked together to bring about the Founder's final and most humiliating defeat. The Umbra and Serpent may actually not want to eliminate you to exact revenge, but rather because they fear what you and Marcus might do to their plans."

Octavius got up suddenly and started pacing. He spoke aloud, but mostly to himself, saying, "This is madness. Madness! How is any of it possible? I thought I had an easy reign, boring at times, even, and often hoped for something more, something different, and so I was – well – excited when Marcus contacted me about a Zebulonian rebel wishing to speak with me. But *this?!*"

Elyana tapped her fingers together, looking down at the table. The king noticed and said, "What is it you wish to say, Elyana?"

"Sire, the Serpent and the Umbra may or may not be looking for you, though it is likely they are, and though we have not yet positively established that the Dark One is behind all this, the existence of Temptatori…"

The king finished his advisor's sentence, his face a grim mask, "…means that Noctiferus is most likely directing all this, given that he was the only one able to create Temptatori through his Umbra."

"Indeed, Sire."

Octavius heaved a heavy sigh, then asked, "What do you suggest, Lux Baiula?"

"Temptatori are a serious threat to the kingdom, Sire, even more serious than the Serpent, because they will infiltrate *every* institution of our society, including the Court, and that will bring Alvinoria down more surely than the killings of the Serpent will."

All stood in silence while they tried to come to grips with Elyana's conclusions.

Elyana continued, "Majesty, we do not yet know what all the pieces of the game are, and so cannot form a proper plan to protect our world or you. But one thing we can and should do immediately is to increase security around you. I suggest Lux Baiulae be assigned to your protection, in addition to the Praetorian Guard."

Elyana seemed to hesitate again, and the king prompted her to say her piece. "Given the high likelihood that Temptatori will try to get to you, I would recommend that no unknown beseechers be allowed near you anymore unless one of my Sisters is with you. The problem, unfortunately, is that we do not yet know how to identify a Temptator." The king and captain dropped and shook their heads, wondering how many more pieces of bad news they were going to get. Elyana tried to give them some hope, adding, "But a well-trained Lux Baiula would still know if a beseecher were directing some unnatural vibration toward you, or if they were unnaturally influencing you, Sire."

Octavius bit his lips and made small circles near his seat, his hands clasped behind his back, until he reached a decision and said, "All right, then. I assume a White or a Purple Sash would be assigned then?"

"Yes, a Purple Sash. We are better trained at recognizing unusual brain patterns, unexpected changes in attitude or temperament, all symptoms of a Temptator's influence – if our records from the Dark Battle are to be trusted."

The king nodded and grunted, then said, "I only see one problem with that: how would we justify attaching another Purple Sash to me?"

"We will find a good reason, Sire."

Octavius sighed and said, "So, my personal guard is to be augmented by Sisters – of the Red Sash, I assume – and I am to have another Sister attend all my audiences." With evident sarcasm, Octavius added, "That will be pleasant."

"I know how much you value your privacy, Sire, but I do not see, at the moment, other means to protect you."

Octavius nodded and started pacing again, deep in thought.

Harlion, who had been silent all this time, said, "Sire, I believe we should post members of that augmented Guard to your balconies. As you know, they are rather easy to reach by way of the trees."

"Hgrr. Fine! I will speak with Primus Julian about it. But I will ask him to have the guardians and Sisters use furans to get on and off the balconies, as I will not have them cross my chambers."

Harlion nodded.

Turning to Elyana with a look that left no room for debate, the king said, "And the Sisters will answer to Primus Julian!"

Elyana searched for a truthful reply, and said, "That will be arranged, my King."

Just now, Aithen looked up at the time disc, and realizing what time it was, said, "Father, the senators will be here in a few minutes and we cannot delay our meeting with them any longer; we should get ready."

"Yes, let us. High Captain, Lux Baiula, if I do not call on you later tonight, I will see you in the morrow. And High Captain, please resume the guarding of the Gaps. It won't help against the Serpent, but it *will* help against the ground-bound creatures that are certain to come soon."

Harlion blinked at the unexpected request, but he nodded and as he started to go, said, "Sire, may Alba keep your path clear." Elyana did the same, and the two exited.

Octavius sighed, and looked at his son, his eyes filled with uncertainty at the thought of the coming darkness, wondering how he was going to get his family and his subjects through it all. How could he fight both Zebula and Noctiferus's hordes, he wondered? Perhaps, he thought, Zebula's plans were not so coincidental. But whether or not it was pure coincidence that Zebula was planning an invasion of his kingdom, the Dark One's attack would most certainly prompt other rulers, rulers jealous of his kingdom's wealth, to try to

341

take advantage of the mayhem. Pandemonium was coming; the king felt a shiver course through his body.

I am looking too far ahead. No one knows for certain exactly who is behind this yet. And there is a plan in motion to keep Zebula in her own territory. Calm yourself, Octavius. Calm yourself.

The king turned to his son and said, "All, right. Where are the senators, Aithen?"

Just then, a guardian knocked at the door, came in, and announced the elders.

***

When First Senator Leo and Senator Kraelion entered the room, the king forced himself to clear his mind, and the sight of his old friend Kraelion helped him do that. He had always enjoyed the senator's company: she was funny and jovial, but also highly intelligent, and that always made for equally useful, constructive, and pleasant conversations. First Senator Leo, on the other hand, disappointed him often, but he had very little power over the election of the First Senator, and so he learned to tolerate the man, listen to him when he had to, and use him as best he could when it was necessary to achieve his own goals. This time, as it happened, the senators were not here to make demands or share the Senate's complaints about taxes or administrative policies, but only to discuss the refugees, and that was a topic Octavius was very keen to discuss.

After a quick glance toward Aithen to thank him for arranging the meeting, First Senator Leo took the lead in welcoming king and thanking him for his time, as was customary; the king responded as warmly as he could. Kraelion followed with her own, more sincere, welcoming words, and in response the king took the woman's hands between his and held them warmly for a moment, causing an all-too obvious jig in the First Senator.

This casualness between the two had always displeased the Senate's leaders, and there had been a few given Octavius's already long reign. First Senator Leo did not feel any differently from his predecessors – in fact, he often felt threatened by Kraelion's friendship with the king, and he did his best to always be one step ahead of Kraelion, and when he couldn't, he tried just as hard – though more slyly – to take credit for the woman's achievements.

Once the pleasantries were over, Leo proceeded to give the king a detailed account of the refugees' situation. He also informed the king about the discontent expressed by many elders, as well as by a small but vocal number of residents and merchants, in the face of such a large influx of peasants whom they deemed uncivil, uncouth, smelly, and even lazy.

Noticing the king's displeasure at hearing such news, the First Senator did note that Senator Kraelion's proposal to help the refugees – a proposal he had approved of – seemed to have paid-off and most Horn's Passers had now found themselves living quarters as well as work. This was comforting news to the king, even though it paled in comparison to the other news he had been given earlier in the day.

One thing which pleased the king even more was Senator Kraelion's praise of Aithen's handling of the elders who had opposed the entry of the refugees. "He handled them masterfully," she said, and she even got the First Senator to add an "indeed," despite himself. That brought a smile to Octavius's face, along with the feeling of deep pride he felt every time his sons exceeded expectations.

When the senators were done with their report, the king shared with them what he could of the attack on his party and gave them his thoughts on what this attack by an unknown foe, as well as the attack by the rokon, might mean. He resented having to hide things from Luma; perhaps he would speak with her in private later – if he had the time.

The recounting of the attack on his party at the foot of the Colossi's Peaks obviously shocked the senators who wondered what could possibly be so dangerous as to cause the king to retreat when he was guarded by the best soldiers in all the allied lands, as well as by two women with powers drawn from the Bind. The retelling soured Aithen's mood quite visibly, though only Octavius understood the true cause of it. The king shrugged it off – for now.

When everything that needed to be said had been told, the king thanked the two senators and got a promise from them to keep what they had heard here in confidence until further notice. In return, the king promised to keep both informed of what they learned about these new threats. Kraelion shook hands with the king then bowed and walked toward the doors. First Senator Leo did the same, though his bow was a little shallower.

After the doors closed behind the senators, Octavius turned to his son, said "You are still disturbed by my having left your brother behind?"

"Father, you know how I feel."

"Aithen, my son. I believe we are done with all official matters today. Let us sit and talk; it will be good that we do so to mend whatever tendrils got frayed between us as a result of this particular matter."

***

Octavius and his son spoke for nearly three hours, interspersing their discussion with some food and drink, Aithen swallowing his morsels without much pleasure at first, and Octavius eating slowly as he considered his son's emotions, replies and silences until they finally indicated the first signs of real understanding. Then, father and son dipped their bread into the stew – though it was now cold – with an appetite they had not felt before.

When the stew was finished, and the bowls had been wiped clean with the day's bread, father and son embraced and wished each other a good night and returned to their respective chambers. Aithen still wished that a different decision *could* have been made, but he now knew that the only reasonable decision had been made, given the circumstances. Said differently, the *least bad decision* had been made, and he hoped that he would never have to make such a one himself.

***

When the king finally readied himself for bed, the Highnight had come. He spent an hour after his conversation with Aithen reviewing all manner of missives from around the kingdom, as well as a variety of reports from Harlion and Master Trebloc. One report worried him. It detailed highly unusual transactions in the garrisons' budgets, as well as in the sourcing of the metals used for the forging of blades. Fortunately, it seemed the changes had been the result of a Blacksmith's Guild decision earlier in the year, which had thus affected all garrisons' budgets and sourcing practices. The report was signed by Neaj Trebloc and countersigned by Lords Kaffin and

Warbender. This young man was proving quite capable, thought the king, and he wondered at how much the boy seemed to have learned of late. He would have to consider giving Master Trebloc greater responsibilities; perhaps he could transfer him to the Royal Guard to help manage all the army's budget.

By One after Highnight, Octavius realized he could no longer remember what he had just read, so he covered the Living Lamps [68] in his office with a Quieting Cloth and walked to his bedroom. As he prepared to lay down, he felt a sudden tug on his mind. He paused a moment, wondering what might have caused that, but not finding any reason for it he laid himself down.

A moment later, the noise of men running and of people shouting in surprise reached his ears. It seemed they said…the door to his antechamber opened and he heard Kiron and Merr welcome someone in surprise, but he failed to hear the name of this late visitor. The king rose from his bed, and readied himself for he knew not what, when he heard a voice he could never mistake accompany the excited knock on his bedchamber's door, "Father! It's me!"

* * *

Prince Toras's arrival had caused quite a commotion in the palace, especially because the late hour meant that many people were dragged from their beds to go meet the prince, prepare his chambers, or simply to be told the news by an overexcited spouse or mate.

Octavius and Aithen, as well as Elyana – who had been fetched from Domus Lucis - were now in the king's quarters listening to Toras's retelling of the events since the king's departure from the Colossi's Peaks.

Octavius and Aithen both felt great relief at seeing Toras alive; the former because he was relieved from the guilt which had plagued him since that awful night, and the latter because he would not need to hate his father for his brother's death, though he understood why the decision had been made.

Aithen spoke. "Hopefully, the furanteams I sent to look for you will find your officer and the other two guardians alive. But the

---

[68] Living Lamps were lamps containing luminescent micro-organisms used to light-up a space. Quieting Cloths were placed on the lamps at night to block the light and arrest the luminescence so that the micro-organisms' energy stores could be restored.

needless loss of all the other men is hard to accept, Toras. I am not upset about those men of mine you lost when you went to Galior; you did the right thing there. But stopping in the fields beyond the Colossi's Peaks at night was reckless, especially because Elyana had warned you against them!"

"I've already said I did not stop there at night! There were still two –"

Elyana interrupted the argument. "Aithen, Toras, it is useless to dwell on that. What has happened has happened, and I am certain that Toras has learned a lesson which he will not soon forget. It is a tragedy, though, that it had to be learned at the cost of other men's lives. But I believe Toras is telling the truth and that when he and his men landed, there were still a couple of hours before sundown. Indeed, my Sisters of the Yellow Sashate have recently become aware of a few nocturnal species that have advanced their active hours. It appears the wrigglers have made a similar shift. I would have advised Toras differently if I had suspected."

Aithen's anger was not quelled, however, and he said, "Still, he should not have stopped there at all, Elyana, knowing what he knew. Larad was one of those who died there! How do you plan on telling Aria he died, Toras?!"

Realizing that this exchange would not lead to anything good so late at night, the king intervened and said, "Aithen! That is enough! Toras and I will speak of this in the morrow. There is no need for you to become so agitated again."

Aithen stood down, shaking his head. He felt like putting his *hands* on his head in frustration, but he simply turned around and distanced himself a little.

Octavius rolled his eyes, then turned to the younger prince and said, "I am happy you are here safe and sound, son, but I need my sleep now. Come and break fast with me; we will speak more then. Elyana, please have one of your medics attend Toras in his chambers."

"I will, Sire."

"Aithen, I will see you in my offices at Ten Hours after Highnight."

With that, everyone understood they had been dismissed, and left the king's chambers. Aithen felt conflicted, anger and relief battling each other, while Toras felt only anger at the reception he had gotten after everything he had been through. As for Elyana, she silently calculated the probability that Aithen might turn on his family when the skies turned red, and she did not like the result, though she knew Aithen to be a rational man. As the three split at the end of the South Wing – each focused on his or her own thoughts – Elyana made a small grunt. Aithen turned toward her, wondering what had caused it, but Elyana was already walking toward the palace's exit.

The king went back to his bed chamber, sat on his bed and – putting his head in his hands – spent the next hour thinking about his sons, unable to sleep. *At least, I don't have to worry about Darya*, he thought.

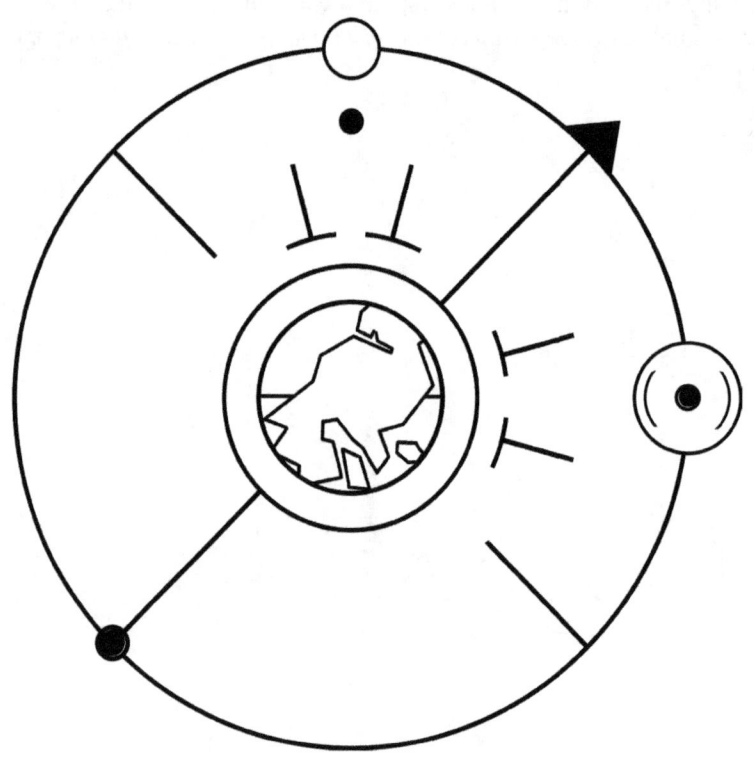

XXI TESTINGGE

Elyana did not sleep much after returning to her quarters. For one, she had spent a good hour thinking about Aithen, trying to convince herself that she was being irrational, that he would never turn on his family, especially not on his father. Perhaps, she thought, these irrational scenarios were sneaking into her mind because of her feelings for him.

In the end, she concluded that she was just being foolish, and turned her mind onto something else which worried her too: Toras's continued impulsivity. She had tried for many years during the prince's adolescence to convince the king to send his son to a military school in Kynaria. Indeed, the school was known for teaching self-discipline to the most recalcitrant youngsters, but the king had always refused to even consider the suggestion. She wondered whether he regretted that now. So went Elyana's thoughts for another little while. When she finally felt the fatigue assail her, she made a motion to dim the Living Lamps, but she must have sent the wrong vibrations because they all lit up brighter instead. That drew a rare, low growl from her. But she repeated the motion, and this time got the lamps' micro-organisms to dim their emissions. That done, Elyana laid down on her bed, dressed as she was, and quickly drifted into sleep.

When she woke, she felt rested despite having slept only three hours. But then, Lux Baiulae were able to control their metabolism and, by adjusting the levels of various hormones, they could bring about a deep and restful sleep almost at will, only unable to do so when their cells were depleted of sweet salts as a result of acute, prolonged stress or severe malnourishment. This was something the Order had discovered in its early days, before it placed an interdiction upon experimenting with eyed organisms.

In the year 1568, the year following the death of the last Luxor, which had also been the year that ended a decade-long famine on Aquinos, a curious, creative and unscrupulous Lux Baiula had decided to investigate what in their food, if anything, enabled Lux Baiulae to make use of the Bind, after noticing that Lux Baiulae in different parts of the continent were less affected than others by the famine. For this, she was authorized to take thirty Sisters, and conduct an experiment with them. She split the women into three groups, one receiving almost exclusively meats and sweets, another mostly fatty and sweet foods, and the last mostly meats and fatty foods for ten days. She noted that those women who lacked sweet salts had a harder time entering the Bind, while those who lacked fats had difficulty staying in the Bind for more than thirty minutes. Those who lacked proteins, on the other hand, presented symptoms similar to the other two groups in addition to wasting altogether away. Needless to say, none of the women were in a happy, healthy state at the end of the experiment, and several had had to be removed from the research entirely after collapsing from inanition. It was after this experiment that laws were established to prohibit harmful testing on eyed organisms.

With her worries about Aithen and Toras safely tucked away somewhere in the back of her mind, the beautiful yellowish glow of the Red Sun warmly suffusing her room – this being the second Bolingar Fourth, when the Red Sun rose first – and tree flyers beginning to sing joyfully, Elyana's mood was hopeful, even optimistic this morning. So, she decided that today was a good day to do something she had been putting off for too long: she was going to call Lusk Methrim and have his healing abilities tested.

As she thought about it, she had an internal conversation with herself: *Is that really what you wish to find out about him? Or is it that you suspect him of some dark purpose?*

Perhaps. And there is also the fact that males with the ability to use the Bind are rare, and we need to find out how he *does it, find out what part or process of the Zebulonian male's atomic constitution protected them from the same fate as our Luxori centuries ago. If we discover nothing else about him or from him, this would be good knowledge to have.*

Elyana pulled on the cord next to her bed and her attendant, a Junior studying for the Purple Sash, came in to take her orders.

"Good morning Lux Baiula, did you call?"

"Good morning Claren. Yes, I will go eat with Administrator Irania shortly. In the meantime, please have a message delivered to Master Methrim requesting his presence here at ten. I will receive

350

him in the Insulated Chamber [69]. I also need you to carry this to Mara and Tania Lux Baiulae. Let them know that we will test Master Methrim's healing abilities today."

The girl bowed and exited to carry out her orders.

* * *

The king was looking at the Frumentarii's morning reports, which High Captain Harlion had forwarded to him. The bundle contained a report on the Order of Aiala's activities, the details of which bothered him but no more than usual, a second report on Border issues – this was a report about illegal traffic across the Zebulonian border, and a third on abnormally suspicious activities in Kartak. It was this report the king was reading – fingers tapping his desk nervously, and deep furrows creasing his forehead – when Toras entered.

"Toras! Come in," said the king as he put away the reports.

The prince was still slightly miffed by last night's less than cheerful welcome when he answered, "Good morning, Father."

"What do you know about Kartak?"

The sudden and unexpected question surprised Toras a little, but he did have a strong opinion about Kartak, and he did not hesitate long before replying. He said, "What do I know? That it should be wiped clean of all the wretched rabble living there. But then, we can't simply execute them all, and we would only cause them to move their filth and troubles elsewhere if we kicked them out of the town and region. Why do you ask, Father?"

"Because it appears that the seeds of the troubles to come are being planted there."

"What do you mean?"

"That someone or something is raising an army of subversives in Kartak. These subversives were known as Temptatori during the days of the Dark Battle, and though they did not use the Bind to conjure fire or split the ground, they were more dangerous to humanity than all of Noctiferus's hordes."

---

[69] The Insulated Chamber was a room constructed of materials which did not allow the Bind to flow through. One could make use of the Bind by drawing on the matter and energy within the room, but since that was limited, the resulting actions were also limited.

351

"Surely, there must be something we can do then, if it is only a matter of flushing and capturing Humans!"

"Ha! Yes, one would think so, but it is not so easily done, Toras. You should read the histories of the period; it will help you to understand what we are facing. Still, we must try. But I have no idea how we might ferret them out; hopefully, their numbers are not so large yet."

"Can't the Sisterhood find these – what do you call them? – Temptatori?"

"I do not know whether today's Lux Baiulae have the ability to do that anymore; and they did not do it easily during the Dark Battle either. Still, Urbs Lucis will be sending their Eyes and Ears to Kartak, as will we – Harlion is already at work, trying to identify our best agents to send there. Hopefully, one of them will succeed in infiltrating Kartak, and return with usable information. That is, if they do not get captured, killed, or – worse – turned."

Octavius now took a silent breath, and looked his son straight in the eye, his lips inauspiciously slanted, the same expression he always took when he had unpleasant things to discuss, things he would rather be able to ignore.

"Now, onto something else, son. I know you explained some things to me when I saved you on the plains near Spiritii, but I think it is time we spoke frankly about your command."

The sting was plainly visible on Toras's face, but instead of an objection to the implications of the king's statement, it was an avalanche of words that rushed forth. "Father, I know you saved us on the plain, and that if it weren't for my error, you would not have needed to do that. I don't know why I keep making reckless decisions, and I know I can't continue this way and still retain my command, I know it!"

Toras turned his head a moment, biting his lips, then continued, "Kendor is loyal to me, and I know he will not turn on me even if I send him to his death for no good reason, but I can see how the rest may become unwilling to follow me any longer…and I wouldn't be able to blame them for it."

The king looked at his son, surprised by the admission. Because of the pause, the king thought Toras might be done now, but as soon as he made a sound to give the prince his opinion on the matter, Toras started again.

"It's as if I have this spirit telling me to do one thing when I know I should be doing another. It's always been this way, but it has become more frequent these days, and it frustrates me to no end! I know I tended to overreact and disobey when I was younger, but it was never this bad or you would never have given me my command in the first place."

"That is correct."

"And I don't *want* to lose my command. I do a good job at it, at least in terms of managing the daily operations and keeping the Pass safe."

The king lifted his eyebrows in response to that, not wanting to say to his son that that was an exaggeration given that Rokothians had not attempted to invade their land since their last attempt fifteen years earlier. There had therefore been no opportunity for Toras to truly test his capabilities in this matter.

Toras continued, "It seems that my emotions get the better of me when my men or the ones I care about are in danger. I..." Toras finally sighed and looked at his father with pleading eyes.

The king was not one to be drawn into emotional debates, and his responses always remained rational, which sometimes still frustrated his wife. But that was Octavius's style and approach to all things, and it had proven to be a good trait for him as well as for the kingdom. He said, "And that is when it matters the most that you control your impulses, take time to think, and make rational decisions, Toras."

Octavius got up from his desk, and sat himself on its edge, facing Toras. He said, "Toras, the days that are coming will be *dark* days if what the Lux Baiulae fear is true, and there will be no room for errors of the sort you have made, as it will not be your life or that of a few men alone which you will be throwing to the shadows, but the life of countless numbers. You must realize that our enemies will look for- and try to make use of every weakness they can find, and at the moment, this impulsivity of yours is a major weakness."

This last statement had the potential to destroy his son – Octavius knew it. But something told him he had to make things clear to Toras, once and for all. So, he waited, hopeful. And his heart was lifted when he heard Toras say with a strong voice and his pupils dark and small, indicating a powerful resolution, a resolution reached not under the pressure of imminent threats, but through the calm assessment of the truth: "I understand, Father. I only wish I knew how to help myself!"

"I believe that only life itself can be your teacher now, Toras. What I mean is that you are past the time to be educated by others telling you and showing you what to do and what to say, teaching you how to think. The only worthwhile teachers to you now are the consequences of your actions and words."

Octavius paced a while, with his arms crossed and one hand brushing his neatly trimmed beard, the prince following him with worrying eyes. Finally, Octavius nodded to himself and said, "I have been pondering this for a long time now, and I believe that the only solution, aside from immediately removing your command, is to assign you a new first officer, one who will not be forced into unreasonable actions, but most particularly, one who will have the nerve to remove you from command should she believe that you are being irrational."

Toras's face had never been paler in his life, not when he took the scariest dive of his life atop Scorch, nor when he was pitched against the late Trevok, the Royal Guard's own colossus, three years earlier during the yearly games. He felt his world come down, and he felt humiliated. And did Octavius say *'she'*?

"I will have High Captain Harlion call Kendor back next month, and request from Krystiana – who has already agreed with my plan – that she send a Red Sash to Horn's Pass to take Kendor's place as your second in command."

Octavius gave his son some space and returned to sit on the edge of his desk, looking at Toras with eyes that alternated between hope and worry.

As for the prince, his mind felt ablaze with a torrent of sentiments, which – if they overwhelmed him – would surely bring about the end of all his aspirations, if not his imprisonment. But the prince's reason did prevail, and after several, long minutes, he looked up at the king and said, "I understand, Father…and I accept your decision. Thank you for trusting in me."

Octavius found himself smiling, relieved. Relieved that his son had succeeded in maintaining control over the raging emotions he knew Toras had felt, relieved that Toras had understood the truth behind his decision. He answered Toras with sincerity and emotion in his voice, "I am…very proud of you, just now, Toras. This – your reaction, your words – is precisely what is required of a man in your position, and it comforts me to know that you understand that this challenge I put before you is a sign of the consequential nature of any further errors in judgement, but that it is also a sign of confidence, and not one of distrust."

With that, Toras made an affirmative nod and straightened his shoulders, his expression one of calm resolution.

Octavius understood from his son's expression that he was ready to move on, and he said, "So, are you ready to hear of an assignment I have for your Guard?"

What?! He's changing topics? Just like that? But of course. That's what he does. "An assignment?"

"Indeed."

"Yes…of course. What is it?"

"I need your assistance with the Kartak problem. It is not too risky, and it is the type of thing you might do as commander of the fortress, so it will not look too suspicious. I need you to return to Horn's Pass as soon as you are rested and restored and monitor the eastern edge of the Furan Peaks – up to and including the Argon Pass – and pay special attention to any increased or unusual movements of people to or from Kartak."

Toras said, "We do not regularly patrol that zone, but following the Serpent's attack, it should not be too difficult to make people believe that the creature is the reason for our increased patrols."

"Good. To be sure, though, it is imperative you not question anyone about –"

"Yes, I know. We cannot confront anyone about their knowledge of, or association with these *Temptatori.*"

"Correct." The king smiled and added with a rubbing of his hands and an eager tone, "Now, let us break fast, and talk about lighter things!"

Surprisingly, Toras did not immediately accept his father's invitation. He looked to be considering whether he *could* talk about lighter things with his father, after what had just happened. After a moment's reflection, he said, "I would like that, Father."

And Octavius rang Rackeli to have their breakfast brought up. As father and son walked to the lounge, Octavius prayed that Toras's resolution would hold, while Toras prayed that his father's decisions were indeed meant to help him learn – by force – what he had not been able to learn through discussion and debate.

***

In Domus Lucis's Insulated Chamber, three women were seated in a semicircle, the usual seating arrangement for Lux Baiulae. One of them was speaking in her strange accent which emphasized the last syllable of every word, adding an "e" to each, especially to the words "not" and "testing."

"Frankly, I do notte think that he should be allowed to practice the Healing arts if even one of us has any doubts. And even if Mara and I found him acceptable, I would oppose his release given that you have doubts, Elyana dear."

The woman was Tania Lux Baiula, a Yerlayan, and Head Medic in Furan City. Women educated in Urbs Lucis normally lost their accent after a few years and spoke Alvinorian almost as perfectly as a native of Lower Alvinor, but Tania had long ago made it a point to retain her Yerlayan accent. The medic was also one of the best healers in Urbs Lucis, and this had earned her the post she now held in Furan City – a post she was very proud of and took very seriously, as seriously as her need to ensure the continued respectability of the Medics' Assembly through the maintenance and enforcement of very strict requirements both for the elevation of Juniors to the White Sash, as well as for the release of commoners to practice the Healing Arts.

Indeed, though healers did not need to be trained by Urbs Lucis or be authorized by Urbs Lucis to practice on plebeians, they did need a release to practice on any member of the Royal household, including the servants, the administrators, and anyone else attached to House Coriolis. Many noble families also required that their healers be released by Urbs Lucis, a service the Sisterhood was happy to provide for a fee. And healers of the commoners often sought the Sisterhood's release because of the higher standing it afforded them back in their native communities.

Elyana replied to her colleague, said, "I understand Tania, but even the elevation of Sisters to the Sash is not always a unanimous decision. And it is the same here; even if I have doubts, but you and Mara find him acceptable, you would be authorized to release him to practice the Art. After all, I am not a medic and it is possible I am misinterpreting the vibrations I sensed in him. One thing that gives me comfort is that Lord Brando *has* verified that Master Methrim was in his service the past few years, and that aside from the Zebulonian's dealings with smugglers, which the Shadisha could not tolerate, he had no problem recommending Master Methrim as a healer. So, I will recommend his release to serve as Healer to the Royal Guard *if* we find that he is what he says he is, and that his use of the Bind is free of harmful vibrations."

Tania shook her head, raised on her hands in exasperation and continued in her slow, emphatic accent. "But why? Is it because he is a man? I know, you have always been curious about male Alterintrants."

Elyana was about to reply when a voice came through and interrupted the discussion. The voice was channeled across the wall through a long, metallic rod, known as Communicator. The voice rendered at the receiving end was not un-distorted, but one learned to recognize the distorted voice of different persons. "Elyana Lux Baiula, your guest is here."

Elyana turned to the others to force their agreement, and when they finally nodded their consent – albeit with a promise from Tania to get an answer from Elyana about her interest in male Alterintrants – Elyana channeled her own voice through the Communicator and asked that Lusk be brought in.

A moment later, an opening appeared in the wall to let the Zebulonian in, followed by Junior Claren. Contrary to Elyana's expectations, the man entered and stood in front of the women perfectly calm and confident, despite the surprise he must certainly be feeling at finding himself before three Lux Baiulae when he expected to be meeting with her alone.

Well, he either has nothing to hide and he is looking forward to proving his worth, or someone forewarned him.

"You may leave us, Claren. Please inform the attending Sisters that the testing will begin soon and that we are not to be disturbed anymore."

"Yes, Lux Baiula," replied the junior. Once outside the room, Claren turned and touched the Chamber's outer wall. The door rematerialized at once, and the wall returned to a solid, unbroken state.

357

Elyana's colleagues both looked at the man with deeply curious eyes.

Mara scanned him from top to bottom, as if assessing a voran's value, but she also felt an unexpected attraction for the Zebulonian, and she had to repress a rush of blood to her skin, which she was able to operate by dampening her adrenal gland and constricting her superficial vessels. This took her a mere moment.

Tania's reaction was more tempered, perhaps because she was older and less prone to the influences of her female biology. But she did lock eyes with the man and was fascinated by his intense gaze and self-assurance.

The Zebulonian took advantage of the women's silent assessments of him to inspect the room. He had faint memories of being in a room such as this a long time ago, although these were not his memories, but Umbra's. He could tell this was an Insulated Chamber from the materials used in the construction of the structure.

Insulated Chambers were built of materials known as insulators; these were only to be found in the depths of the Unnamed Island. The materials had two unique properties: they shifted in color depending on the nature of the energy that hit them, but they were otherwise impervious to vibrations of the Bind, preventing the flow of any and all vibrations *across* them. Were it not for the metallic Communicator, Insulated Chambers would effectively and completely isolate those inside from the outside world, and a person locked in an Insulated Chamber without a Communicator very rapidly lost all sense of time, of reality, and of themselves.

This chamber, however, had a roof made of a slightly different material which allowed sunlight through. This was needed to sustain the plants located inside the room, which were sometimes used to test hopeful healers.

Elyana began. "Master Methrim, these are Tania and Mara Lux Baiulae, respectively Head Medics of our Order in Furan City and in Spiritii. They will test your healing skills today. If you pass, you will be released to practice the Healing Arts – under supervision – as well as to enter High Prince Aithen's service, should he still have need of you."

"I am here to serve, Lux Baiulae."

Hmm. This is a very different attitude than that which he displayed two fourths ago; he wasn't as unconcerned and happy to submit to our testing then.

Elyana indicated a chair placed across from them and asked Master Methrim to sit.

The Zebulonian took the chair, and sat, straight backed, head high, hands crossed on his lap and an expectant look on his face. The man looked perfectly calm and confident, and waited for one of the Lux Baiulae to speak again.

After a moment, Elyana turned to Tania and the Head Medic began in her accented speech: "Firstly, you must understand that we will need to look at nearly every aspect of your anatomy and physiology – that includes your microbial flora. Elyana Lux Baiula did inform me that you did notte wish to share information about your microbial flora. If that is still the case, then we cannot proceed, and we will send you back to Shadin City without delay."

"I understand... Tania Lux Baiula. I wish to serve the Coriolan Crown, and I will therefore submit to any testing you require."

Tania exchanged a brief look with Elyana, and said to Lusk Methrim, "Good. You will likely find the testingge long and exhausting. But we will notte harm you. We will ask that you be completely open, and that you notte resist us in any way. We will study your physiology and analyze the vibrations which will be emitted by your body as we touch it with the Bind. If you pass these tests, we will then ask you to perform certain tasks to test your Healing abilities. *If* you pass all assessments, and...we are all satisfied with the results," Tania gave a quick glance toward Elyana, signifying her intent to keep to their agreement here, "you may be released to practice the Healing Arts for the Royal Guard under supervision."

"As I indicated earlier, I am ready and willing, Lux Baiulae. But may I ask why you say *"may be released"*?"

"Certainly. It is simply because we have not yet received all the information we have requested from those who knew you before you came here, and that some may present evidence against your release to practice."

"I understand. But I can assure you that you will find no such evidence, Lux Baiula. I am a healer, and that is all I am."

"Very well; hopefully, that is the case. So! For the first and second tests, you will keep your eyes closed, but you must remain awake. These two tests may last an hour. For the third test, we will need you to disconnect from reality while we continue touching you with the Bind. This may be shorter. Once we are done with the first three assessments, you will be allowed thirty minutes of rest, after which we will proceed with the fourth and final test. For this, we will assign you a number of tasks to assess your healing abilities; you will have one hour to complete them."

Lusk nodded.

Tania looked toward Mara who responded with a simple nod; the two women were going to take turns probing Master Methrim, starting with Mara. Tania then turned to Elyana who also nodded, and all three created a soft version of the mind-tie, known as a mind-link. The mind-link was easy to establish and only connected thoughts, and none of the senses of the so-tied Alterintrants. This would allow Mara and Tania to send mental notes to Elyana who was acting as the scribe. Now, the mind-link was normally established through a remarkably wondrous ritual, but given the foreigner's presence, the women took their time to create the link in complete silence, and only their staticky hair and a faint, short-lived bluish spark gave any indication that the women were using the Bind.

The younger medic stood with what one would almost have called excitement and went to fetch a pair of gloves which rested on a shelf on the back wall. After putting the leathered gloves on, she went to get a strange-looking table at the back of the room. Using the Bind, Mara moved the table easily across the floor. As she did so, the floor gave off an orangish glow. She placed the table in front of Lusk. She then removed the gloves, put them back on the shelf where she had gotten them, and sat herself across from the Zebulonian.

The table was small and made of a translucent material known as an Amplifier, and it augmented the various vibrations emitted by all living things, giving off different colors of varying intensities, depending upon the nature and properties of the energy that it absorbed from its surroundings. One of the table's most peculiar properties was that when hands were laid on it, it grew extensions which jutted out from its edge and came to wrap the person's hands and forearms, causing great anxiety in uninitiated testees.

Mara said, "The table is partially made of a living material which will amplify all our vibrations, common and uncommon. The table will surround your hands and forearms, but do not be alarmed; you will be able to remove your hands, should you panic."

Lusk reacted with feigned indignation at that, but the Lux Baiula merely raised her brows in response. In truth, Lusk felt curious, as he did not recognize the table. In fact, he had no memories of it, which meant that this type of table must have been created after the memories he had obtained from Umbra.

If the Lux Baiulae could have read his thoughts, they would have sensed a question, but also a dismissive reply. Indeed, regardless of the properties of the table, the Lux Baiulae would not penetrate him unless he wished it; he was sure of that.

Now, Mara Lux Baiula said, "Very well, place your hands on the table and close your eyes, Master Methrim, but do not enter the Bind. Your mind must remain connected to the Outer World."

Lusk did as requested, silently enjoining them to do their best.

As soon as their hands touched the Amplifying table, the slight vibrations intentionally sent by Mara along with the unintentional ones sent by Lusk triggered the extension of the table's surface, which continued to expand until it had completely enveloped their hands and forearms. The table now emitted a faint bluish glow, which was a little more intense around Mara's hands. The Lux Baiula closed her eyes and entered the Bind.

Mara was going to probe Lusk Methrim's outer and inner surfaces to determine the composition of his microbial flora. Later she would probe certain organs to determine their mitochondrial density. Knowing these facts was important given that the strength of a person in the Bind depended in large part on three things, two of which she was going to test: firstly, on the kinds and quantity of microbes one harbored, secondly on the abundance of mitochondria in the cells of various organs involved in the execution of Bindings, and thirdly on the ability of one's nervous system to harness and channel the vibrations of either a specific kind of organism or of the entirety of the flora colonizing him or her.

Mara's specialization being the study of *Vita Invisibilis* [70], she could recognize a thousand distinct kinds of microbes through the vibrations that they emitted and the chemicals that they secreted into the body. Of course, one single microbe's vibrations were so faint – or secretions so limited – as to be practically impossible to sense, but when you had a colony of them, their sheer number made the vibrations and secretions easy to detect. Based on the composition of a person's microbial flora, Mara could predict with fair accuracy his or her potential strength and skills in the Bind.

Mara could also tell whether the person harbored any dangerous kinds of microbes – the type which made the person's use of the Bind uncontrollable – and this was one thing she would be looking for, while probing Lusk Methrim. Indeed, the Sisterhood probed all Alterintrants for dangerous microbes, whether they wished to join the Order or not. When a woman was found to harbor such microbes, a medic would attempt to permanently remove them. If the procedure were successful, the woman would be released or received as an apprentice. If it failed, the woman would be sent to an observational facility for the rest of her natural life. There, she would be washed daily in antimicrobials, and forced to drink noxious concoctions every night to keep the harmful germs in a suppressed state. Unfortunately for the patient, these medications also repressed beneficial microbes, leaving the woman weak and miserable, and with a much-shortened lifespan. The internment of Soiled women at the Observatory was something Urbs Lucis did with great reluctance but it was currently the only way to keep society safe from potentially dangerous Alterintrants, and the White and Yellow Sashates continued to investigate means to eliminate dangerous micro-organisms in the hope that someday the Order would not need to intern anyone anymore.

Probing a person's microbial flora was a slow process which usually took a medic twenty to thirty minutes. Mara did it better than anyone, and faster as well. To begin with Lusk Methrim, she sent out vibrations of different frequencies along the surfaces of his body and watched for the organisms' responses. If she sensed anything in the purple frequencies, she would need to slow her scanning and test that

---

[70] Vita Invisibilis: Invisible Life, which included the study of all beings too small for the naked eye, namely microbes.

area of tissue more thoroughly as these were the frequencies emitted by the known prohibited microbes. If she confirmed their presence, she would need to exit the Bind and have Master Methrim transferred to a holding Insulated Chamber at once, while she informed the Head of the White Sash Assembly of the finding. The Praefecta Medicas would inform the Magna Mater and request the Removal procedure be performed. If successful, Master Methrim's testing would continue. If the removal of the unwanted microbes failed, the Praefecta Medicas would inform the Magna Mater who would commit Master Lusk Methrim to the Observatory without further testing or consideration. Mara hoped that Lusk Methrim was clean so that none of this would need happen to him.

After fifteen minutes of probing, Mara had not found anything of concern outside or inside of Lusk, not on his external integuments, not on those lining his digestive tract, and not on those lining his respiratory tract. All the vibrations she had sensed had given off frequencies in the reds, yellows, and blues. No purples. The Lux Baiula release a silent sigh of relief, opened her eyes and spoke to the Zebulonian.

"Master Methrim, you may open your eyes and rest a moment."

As the Zebulonian complied, the table retracted its extensions and released both Mara and Lusk. Lusk rubbed his arms to release a strange sensation he felt upon being let go, but he did not complain. He now looked at the Lux Baiula with a smug grin. He asked, "I assume this first test was a success, Sister?"

Mara replied with a matter-of-fact tone, "You pass the first test, Master Methrim," although her eyes had a very faint luminescence in them. The Lux Baiula berated herself silently as soon as she became aware of it. Part of her mind seemed to want to sink into the man's eyes, while the other part told her a Lux Baiula should not react this way. After Mara had reasserted control over her thoughts, a moment passed in uncomfortable silence, she instructed Lusk to place his hands on the table again, and their hands and forearms were once more enveloped by the warm, radiant material.

A minute later, Mara sent out vibrations toward Lusk Methrim to test the mitochondrial content of his cells. Indeed, the White Sash had discovered a century earlier that the more mitochondria a Lux Baiula had inside her cells, the more energy she could generate. They later also found that Alterintrants had a higher concentration of mitochondria in the cells of their brains, guts and hands compared to Nonsensing women.

As Mara's vibrations reached Lusk's skin, the table responded by emitting some low frequency light (dull reds and oranges). This was as expected as the skin had very low concentrations of mitochondria, except in the hand, where the intensity of the returning vibrations was much higher. In fact, the returning vibrations from Lusk's hands were unusually intense, appearing as a vibrant blue. Mara sent a mental note to Elyana. The medic then moved on to the internal organs, beginning with the lungs and the heart. Those gave off low-intensity red light, as in a Nonsensing person. She continued to probe other organs, finding nothing of concern.

Now, Mara took a deep breath and slowed her metabolism before probing Lusk's guts and finally his brain. Indeed, because of the potential for very high concentrations of the power generating structures in these two organs, she needed to use very low intensity vibrations lest she fry Lusk's body by accidentally activating billions of mitochondria. In Nonsensing humanoids, this was not an issue, but in an Alterintrant, especially a powerful one, the sheer number of mitochondria could cause such a great release of energy that it effectively cooked the subject from the inside out, and there was also the potential for harm to the tester – both very bad outcomes. This had happened twice in the history of the Sisterhood, two very sad events following which very strict protocols had been established to prevent such accidents from ever happening again. One of the requirements of the protocol was that only specially-trained Lux Baiulae should perform the test. Mara was one such specialized White Sash. She would not fry the handsome Lusk, and she would not harm herself or her Sisters through carelessness.

Why did I just think that? He is just a man, a Zebulonian. What is wrong with me?!

Elyana received the other woman's accidental thought, and she promptly sent back an urgent, *"Focus, Mara."*

The woman sent back *"I know. Thank you, Sister. But –"* But she couldn't lie, *"I know."*

Elyana sent a nod through the Bind. Mara immediately sent another thought to both Sisters, to warn them of the next test, *"Tania, Elyana, I am going to begin probing the mitochondria in his guts and brain."*

They responded as one, *"We are ready."*

Mara began by sending vibrations over Lusk's guts. The vibrations she sensed in return were intense and concentrated in the blues and violets. The intensity of the response certainly signified that Lusk was a powerful Alterintrant, and a male at that! but it was no cause for concern, in-and-of itself. Still, when she probed the small intestine, there was a large and unexpected surge of energy; Lusk Methrim flinched and groaned, and Mara was hit with an intense backflow, nearly causing her to faint. Her Sisters became alarmed and were about to intervene, when Mara sent a *"No, I am fine."*

Master Methrim's guts were laden with mitochondria. In fact, Mara had never before met anyone with such concentrations of the little organelles in their guts. Lusk must be able to discharge an enormous amount of energy when he called the Bind. Mara sent another mental note to Elyana and continued her probing.

Mara did not come across any more unusual concentrations of mitochondria in Master Methrim's organs. Having completed this other test, she sent her final notes to Elyana and said, "Master Methrim, this is done. I will disengage myself from the table, but I ask you to remain as you are. Tania Lux Baiula will take over now."

Tania and Mara switched seats. As they passed each other, Mara gave the other woman a look that seemed to say, "This was the most disconcerting probing, I've ever conducted." The older Sister simply narrowed her eyes in response.

"Master Methrimme, I will conduct the third test. For this, I will need you to enter the Bind and repeat a verse or two from a song of your choice. Do you have a song?"

Lusk did not respond right away, and thought: *Ha! We used that method as well, when we wanted to look into a subject's mind while their attention was focused elsewhere.*

"Yes, I do, Lux Baiula. Do you wish me to tell you it?"

"Please do, as I will need to look for it in the Bind."

And Lusk sang, in a mournful voice, "From mountain top to valley, there are only empty alleys. In this long-forgotten place, there are only ghostly faces."

This song troubled the Lux Baiula. Why would he choose such a gloomy air? Or was it the man's voice which troubled her?

Regaining control of herself, she quelled her emotions and quashed her questions.

"Very well, Master Methrimme, you may enter the Bind and keep repeating that verse until I find you." Tania continued, "Once I do, I will probe your mind to – among other things – verify the authenticity of your replies to a number of questions, which I will ask you." Tania did not tell him that she would also be sending out vibrations to probe him for signs of violence or immorality.

"I understand, Lux Baiula; I have nothing to hide."

That said, Lusk entered the Bind and began repeating the verse in his mind. In the Outer World, his lips moved but uttered no sound.

Tania took a deep breath, entered the Bind and began listening for Lusk Methrim. She did not need to search the Bind long before finding him. Indeed, she latched onto the hypnotic verse he was singing almost the moment she entered that inner world, recognizing it among a million other songs, sung by a million-other people in a thousand different places, and uttered in a hundred different languages. It was then only a matter of following it to its source. She found Lusk at the top of a mountain, which overlooked an empty city with narrow streets, covered in moss and vines and old trees. He was dressed quite elegantly, but with his hood covering his head; he had a mysterious air to him, mysterious and attractive.

This man will doom us all, she thought to herself.

Tania approached his form, and he acknowledged her.

"I will now question you, Master Methrimme. You must answer each question promptly."

"Of course, Lux Baiula."

Tania proceeded to question the Zebulonian. This required that she first establish the firing patterns associated with truthful answers by asking the man questions to which she knew the responses. That done, she asked the Zebulonian the test questions. She asked him about his past experiences and whether he had ever harmed or wished to harm another, whether he had ever lost a patient, and all sorts of other questions to determine whether he could be trusted to heal another.

Each time the man answered, Tania scanned his prefrontal cortex to compare the firing pattern to the truthful ones she had established earlier. If a pattern were to deviate significantly, she would know he was lying. The method was not an absolute one, of course, and she could never be totally sure she had properly interpreted his responses, but if she had the slightest doubt, she would fail him without further ado.

After what might have felt like an eternity or an instant, the old Sister ended her questioning. The man had passed this other test, but she did not tell him. Instead, she told Lusk that she was now going to poke various areas of his mind to test his involuntary responses. She would also send him images of various situations, which might be pleasant, violent or neutral. If the man was prone to acting violently or immorally, she would know. Indeed, the White Sashate had discovered that humanoids (Alterintrant and Nonsensing alike) who perpetrated violent or immoral acts had abnormally firing neurons in two regions of the brain: the prefrontal cortex (also involved in truthfulness), which was abnormally quiet in violent individuals; and the amygdala, which was abnormally active in individuals with violent tendencies.

Tania started sending rapidly changing images to Lusk, not so fast that he would not have the time to perceive them, but fast enough that he would not have the time to consciously temper his reactions. A quick succession of images assaulted Lusk: Children playing in a field – *no firing;* vorans running – *no firing*; an old man crying – *firing in the prefrontal cortex*; a parent spanking a child – *amygdala not firing. Did he smile at that?* She sent a note to Elyana and continued shooting images. Next, came a soldier at attention – *amygdala not firing, prefrontal cortex firing quietly;* and finally a man hitting another man's wife and the husband putting a dagger in the assailant's belly – *prefrontal cortex* – The Lux Baiula did not complete this note.

Tania now exited the Bind and opened her eyes. She felt strange, as if she had been unconscious for a moment. But she did not feel the need to question the sensation. Instead, she turned toward Lusk Methrim who had also just come out of the Bind and reentered the Outer World, and smiled at him, saying, "Thank you, Master Methrimme. You may now rest for thirty minutes and we will then test your healing abilities. That will be the final test."

Lusk nodded, and the Lux Baiula caused the table to release its grip. The Zebulonian rubbed the skin of his hands and forearms again; he definitely disliked this device.

Pointing to a table to the right side of the Insulated Chamber, Tania said to him, "You may have some water and biscuits, if you wish it." She then turned to her fellow Sisters looking for their agreement to prepare for the final test. Mara and Elyana responded with a nod, after which Tania walked to the Communicator and called for an attending Sister. A moment later, the wall shimmered, and the door re-appeared and opened to let in a young Red Sash, looking no more than twenty. Tania asked her to have the Healing samples prepared and brought in in thirty minutes. The woman left to do as requested, and the opening disappeared once again behind her.

At the end of exactly thirty minutes, a voice came through from the outside, startling Mara a little, who had been deep in her thoughts, eyeing Lusk. Tania responded, and the same Red Sash who had come to take her orders walked in, followed by two young men in white liveries. The males took out the Amplifying table with some effort – the object being a lot heavier without the Bind – and then brought in a wooden table with various live non-eyed specimens as well as numerous dead, eyed specimens in jars or small aquariums.

Lusk looked curiously but did not show his surprise as he thought: *Hum, another innovation, of these Lux Baiulae.*

Tania said, "Master Methrimme, you will now have one hour to complete the Healing test. Your task is to first restore the health of the injured or ill non-eyed organisms. You will then perform the procedure described on the note in front of each brain-dead, eyed-organism."

Lusk nodded, completely unconcerned.

"Do you have any questions?"

"No, Lux Baiula."

"Very well, your test begins now. My colleagues and I will return in one hour."

"Don't you want to see how I use the Bind to heal and repair?"

Mara replied instead of Tania, saying, "No, no need, Master Methrim. The plants will record the energy flows you generate to perform the repairs and healings, and this, combined with what we learned by probing you earlier, will give us a fairly good idea how you do what you do."

Lusk seated himself in front the table, a small snickering grin on his face, and the Sisters left the room.

When they came back, an hour later, they found the Zebulonian standing by the back wall, studying the plants. He had a highly satisfied look on his face.

Tania spoke first, "Master Methrimme, you are done."

"Yes, Lux Baiula. I have been done for ten minutes. I trust you will find that I have completed each task satisfactorily."

"We will let you know if we are satisfied once Mara Lux Baiula and I are done reviewing each specimen. You will now be escorted back out, and we will call on you once we have a decision."

"May I know when that might be?"

"We will inform you of our decision tomorrow, Master Methrimme."

"Excellent! I will be looking forward to it."

Tania called the attendant Sisters and asked them to accompany Master Methrim out of the building. The Zebulonian promptly thanked the Lux Baiulae, and fell in behind his escort, a satisfied expression on his face.

After watching the Zebulonian go, Tania turned to her colleagues and said, "Well, Mara, we should begin our review of the specimens. It is probably going to take us a few hours, and I would like to be done before supper."

Mara nodded and Elyana said, "I will leave you to your work, then. I assume we will meet after supper to review all his results, ahead of our decision tomorrow?"

Tania replied with slight annoyance, "Yes, Elyana, after supper. I know you are anxious to make a decision on Master Methrimme."

Elyana was about to reply, but decided to limit herself to a simple snort, and left with a promise to return later.

* * *

The next day, Elyana and the two White Sashes approved Lusk Methrim's release to practice the Healing Arts. Indeed, the two medics had been very positive about Lusk's results, although they were still disconcerted by the extremely high density of mitochondria in his guts. But, he had passed all the tests, and had properly healed or repaired all the creatures presented to him.

Furthermore, they had not found anything pointing to the man having done harm in the past or being prone to do harm, and they had just received their Eyes and Ears' report stating that they had not found anything of concern in their investigation of his past. Elyana agreed with their assessment, despite the intermittent sense of confusion she felt when she thought about the man.

When Elyana informed Lusk, he thanked her with a disarmingly charming smile. *Why do I get the sense he knew he would pass our tests? There is still something troubling about him. But why can't I act on this feeling? The suns be burned!* Elyana smiled in return and invited Lusk to come to her office in the morrow so that she may prepare him for his new duties.

XXII SPARRING

The Zebulonian's first fourth serving as a Healer to the Royal Guard was an eventful one, to say the least. To begin, there was the murder of a soldier by another, in which Lusk was suspected – if briefly. High Captain Harlion had received the news on the morning of nineteenth Sextus [71], while discussing military resources with his officers.

The murderer was a recent recruit and had had an unusually tough time dealing with the trauma from the attack at Horn's Pass. He was also one of those who had been treated by Lusk after the latter was released to practice. Suspicion naturally fell on the Zebulonian, but Dalima Lux Baiula, another medic in the capital, had attended the healings and had not sensed anything wrong with Lusk's procedures. When she informed Elyana Lux Baiula of the facts, Elyana was relieved, but she still asked Tania to probe the victims' rigid body to see if she would pick up any unusual signatures. As it turned out, the Head Medic did not detect any odd vibrations, nor anything she could ascribe to Lusk. When she gave her report to Elyana, the latter felt doubly relieved.

The next day, questioning of the accused's comrades and of his superior only reinforced the leading opinion that the young man had simply lost his mind following the attack on Horn's Pass. The conclusion was noted in the soldier's files, and a missive sent to the victim's family, along with a letter to inform them of the circumstances of the unfortunate event, compensation for their loss, and an invitation to Furan City two fourths from then. Another letter was also sent to the murderer's family to inform them of the same, and to request that they attend the Passing ceremonies during which the ashes of the victim, along with what was known about him, would be passed on to both families by the priestesses of Elande.

To try to prevent additional tragedies, Elyana Lux Baiula requested that additional medics be called in to probe all the guardians that had been at Horn's Pass, and to preventively soothe their minds. As for Lusk, he had been barred from probing or healing

---

[71] Sextus: Sixth month.

anyone's mind for the moment and was restricted to treating physical injuries until further notice – this had irritated him greatly, but he had agreed to comply.

On twenty-third Sextus, Aithen finally introduced Lusk to the high king. Octavius's initial reaction to the Zebulonian's account was surprise. Did he know Master Methor? Was Master Methrim a member of the Organization for the Liberation of Zebulonian Males? At least, his account was in line with what Master Methor had told him back in Marcus's villa.

A few minutes into their discussion, Octavius decided to be direct and asked the Zebulonian if he knew of the OLZM. It was Lusk's turn to be surprised.

The king noticed and said, "I know many things, Master Methrim; it is my duty to know. Are you familiar with the organization, then?"

Lusk responded with diffidence. "Yes, I am, Majesty."

"Hum, you were not a supporter of it?"

"No, I was not, Majesty."

"Why not? You cannot have disagreed with their aims, surely."

"The organization's leaders were an indecisive bunch who would never achieve the freedom they sought without direction."

Hmm, this is important to my negotiations with Master Methor.

"I assume you speak from experience, Master Methrim. You were once a member of this organization?"

"I was, Majesty, but I parted with them a short few months after joining. That was four years ago. But, may I ask why the interest?"

"It is simply that I have recently become aware of the group and thought it curious that such an organization would even exist."

"The Zebulonian society is unlike any other, Majesty, and it has led to a great many things which would baffle any non-native."

"Indeed, I do not doubt it. Now then, my son has told me, of course, that you wish to offer your services to me. But I will have you make your case for yourself. Why would I need your services?"

"Because, Sire, as you may have heard, Queen Zebula intends to march on Alvinoria, and as one who knows Zebula and her court, I may be able to advise you to better protect your land."

"And how did you come to know Zebula and her court as well as you claim?"

With an undeniably sarcastic tone, Lusk replied, "I was Private Healer to Her *Greatness's* Vessel."

Aithen, sitting behind and to the left of Lusk, made a frown and thought to himself: *That is not what he told me. I swear he told me he took care of the Queen's children.* Aithen was about to question Master Methrim, but the king spoke.

"I am unfamiliar with that expression. A *vessel* in Alvinorian is a ship or a container."

"Sire, *this* Vessel is the female who carries Queen Zebula's children."

"Carries?"

"Yes, the Zebulonian society has highly advanced medical skills, Majesty, especially in the field of reproduction. The queen's children are carried by another woman, known as the Vessel, who takes them into her womb as embryos after one month of gestation in the Queen. The Janarae also use this horrible reproductive method. It was my responsibility to see to the health of her Greatness's Vessel as well as to that of the developing fetuses. But that is not the most fantastic feat of Zebulonian medicine, Sire. The children of the queens have all been, what we call clones – that is copies, of Zebula I – produced without a male, via a process known as virgocreatio [72]."

Aithen still had a slightly confused look on his face, which his father, just as shocked as his son, took as incredulity in the face of such revolting practices, but Aithen still wondered whether Lusk's earlier statements to him about his function in Zebula's court were in agreement with what he told the king now. He said, "Those are certainly strange practices, Master Methrim, and I cannot imagine how they are medically feasible, but it is irrelevant now. However, I do need to confirm something. Tell me, did your being the Vessel's Private Healer mean that you were also responsible for the *children's* health?"

"Yes, my Prince. That is, in fact, the main task of the Private Healer to Her *Greatness's* Vessel."

"I hear. Thank you." Aithen looked at his father and signed that he was done.

---

[72] Virgocreatio: A mode of reproduction by which a female produced offspring without a male's genetic contribution.

Octavius said, "So, going back to your petition, Master Methrim, you wish to offer your services to me *because...*"

"Because I hate everything about Zebulonia and do not wish to go back to my former life, which would surely happen if *she* were to march here and conquer."

"That is a reasonable motivation. And how would I benefit from your service?"

"I am very familiar with Zebula VI, her motivations, and her weaknesses and strengths, having served her for many long years. I am familiar with Zebulonian society, and with most of Zebula's court. It is true that some players may have changed since my departure, but my knowledge will still prove useful when Zebula attacks, Majesty."

"Your offer is not without merit, Master Methrim. I will consider it over the next few days and give you my answer thereafter. In the meantime, you may continue to provide the benefit of your healing skills to our medics, although I understand that your duties have been restricted until the matter of the violence committed by one of your patients is fully resolved."

The Zebulonian's expression was not one of shame – or guilt, but rather one of irritation. Still, he replied evenly and respectfully, "Indeed, Majesty, that is so."

"The loss of a sentient life, when it is the result of someone else's carelessness – or worse, intentional killing – is never a pleasant affair, Master Methrim, and laws were established long-ago to ensure that those responsible are found and punished as befits their actions, so that order may be maintained within the kingdom. But given the facts, I would not concern myself overly much." Octavius turned to his son to signal the end of the meeting.

Aithen walked to the Chamber's doors and knocked. A guardian promptly entered the room to escort Master Methrim back out of the palace. The Zebulonian thanked the high king and his son and then left with the guardian.

King and prince remained in the Audience Chamber a while to share their thoughts on the Zebulonian. Aithen told his father how it surprised him that Octavius had not felt the same strange emotions in the presence of the Zebulonian as he himself had felt during the journey from Horn's Pass. And now that he mentioned it, it surprised Aithen even more to realize that he had not felt those emotions anymore, not since being back in Furan City; perhaps the mistrust he had felt during their journey to the capital had merely been a result of the attack on Horn's Pass. Elyana and the medics had released him to practice after all, which meant that Elyana too must have changed her mind about him.

As for Octavius, he thought the man honest; his story made sense, and Elyana had verified his employment with Lord Brando of Shadin City who, aside from not wanting to be associated with a man who had dealings with Zebulonian smugglers, did not have any complaints about his former Healer. Given these facts, Octavius told Aithen he would accept the Zebulonian's offer of service on the morrow, after receiving confirmation from Master Trebloc that the Crown could afford employing another medic and receiving confirmation from Harlion's Frumentarii that Master Methrim had no writs against him anywhere in the kingdom.

***

The sound of a double-handed longsword on armor reverberated in the palace court. Indeed, after a few days' rest, his wounds healed and effaced by Tania and Dalima Lux Baiulae for the most part – indeed, he had insisted on keeping a scar on his left cheek–Toras had decided to resume his martial exercises. These were an important ritual for the prince, and back at Horn's Pass he never let a day go by without handling a blade of one form or another, except on festive days.

Today, he had found two guardians to spar with him and he had been at it for nearly two and a half hours already, showing no desire to quit yet, despite the heat. One of the two men was a hulking guardian – a colossus really, and the other a lean but furiously fast fellow. They were among the elite of the Royal Guard.

In attendance there were Elyana, who happened to pass by, several off-duty guardians, some plebeians, and a number of young patrician folk – sons and daughters of the capital's noble families. These young lords and ladies came to the palace every fourth, from First Day through Fourth Day, to learn from Magister Setarcos. The scholarly Magister Setarcos had been in the high king's employ for thirty years now, first to educate his sons, and then to educate the children of the capital's patricians in the arts of grammar, rhetoric, and logic. Magister Setarcos also taught the sciences, but most families preferred to have Elia Lux Baiula – a Yellow Sash – provide that education to their children, and old Setarcos had made his peace with it. These students visited Domus Lucis on Fifth and Sixth Days to receive Elia's instruction.

Magister Setarcos's students typically spent their mornings observing the practitioners of the various arts, such as poets and writers reading the creations of their minds, or senators debating legislation, or Yellow Sashes from Domus Lucis conducting scientific experiments, such as Laranis Lux Baiula's psychological experiments. They then spent their afternoons learning the hows and the whys about each art from Magister Setarcos, himself, before returning home. But this morning, they had decided to observe the prince dance with the sword instead, to study what makes a good fighter, and they were gifted with an amazing display of skill by the prince and his opponents, though the former only sweated streams while the latter two sweated rivers.

The prince owed his lighter perspiration – despite the fact he was engaging two strong opponents at once – to the light Kynarian chainmail he was fortunate to possess, whereas his opponents were wearing the typical, thick varagoth leather vest guardians wore. This leather was almost as impenetrable as chainmail, but it was heavier and hot.

The spectators marveled at Toras's motions, which were beautiful, not because they were elegant but because they flowed, swift and confident. His maneuvers surprised Rior, the quick one, while his blows surprised Gorus, the larger of the two guardians, and his constant motion surprised both. They had expected that the prince would tire within an hour given that he had to defend against two very different and skilled opponents, requiring constant movement and adjustment of his parries and attacks – this would be taxing, both physically and mentally, to even the best of them. However, Lord Commander Toras continued to dance like a Founder, and he irritated the guardians with his childish grins and constant taunting with remarks of "Ha! Ha!"; "Missed!"; or "Oops, too slow!"

Just now, the time disc sounded the start of the second half of the third hour. The prince paused and said with a wild grin, "All right, men, let's end this."

The guardians looked at each other with determined and hopeful eyes and, with only a nod, agreed on their finishing tactic; Gorus pulled back and took a waiting position while his nimbler companion redoubled his efforts.

Toras found this suspicious, but after three minutes of parrying Rior's frenetic and incessant thrusts he forgot about Gorus. *Where is he finding the energy to fight like this, now!? I must put an end to it before I crumble.* Distracted as he was, Toras did not see the larger guardian attack him from behind. Gorus slammed the side of his sword into the prince's flank and Toras groaned as he backed away from both men. *How could I just forget about him?! I must be losing my wits, and if I don't end this soon, they will be the ones laughing.* Gorus and Rior looked at each other with devilish grins, ecstatic to have finally found a way to give the prince some of his own medicine back.

The prince's groans had been loud enough to be heard by the audience, and they released cries of surprise and imagined pain, causing his adversaries to slow down, if only slightly. Some students asked if Gorus's attack from behind was legal. A guardian standing next to them replied that it was indeed. Training was meant to prepare someone for real battles, and in real battles, one's opponents were not all honorable and might very well attack from behind to dispatch an enemy fighter.

During the few seconds that the pause lasted, Toras decided on his tactic, and what happened next remained forever impressed upon the memories of all in attendance that morning. The crowd, seeing the prince reposition himself with unwavering determination, held its breath.

As the prince watched his adversaries, he thought: *Ok, this is it.*

Gorus and Rior, standing next to each other, swung their blades, waiting for the Lord Commander to make a move, and wondering what he would do. But the prince remained there nimble and focused, focused on them both. After another moment of tense inaction, Gorus decided to advance toward the prince, his thick arms glistening with sweat and a wicked smirk twisting his square face. The crowd, which had suddenly been enlarged by the arrival of a group of curious guardians, waited silently, expectantly.

Gorus was now within striking distance. He feigned a lunge, and still Toras did not move – nor did he grin or make any comments this time. That seemed to unsettle the colossus. But Gorus decided to taunt him again, wanting to be done with this unending sparring session, and still, the prince continued to stand there, nimble.

The spectators became nervous, wondering what the prince's tactic might be. Only Elyana seemed to know. She said quietly to the two guardians standing next to her, "The prince is focused on both men, and he is waiting for the signs."

One of the two guardians, a dark-haired, small-mustached, noble-looking fellow said, "Waiting for signs? He is getting them already, and if he doesn't move, he'll be struck before he knows it."

Elyana retorted, "You are wrong," and left it at that, as if she knew the final act was imminent.

Toras finally made his move when he noticed that his opponent had stopped breathing. The prince slid sideways just a fraction of a second before Gorus lunged to strike with incredible speed, despite his large mass. With one swift motion, Toras smacked Gorus's blade, and he did so with such force that the man, despite his musculature, lost his grip on the sword. As the blade fell, the colossus uttered a cry of pain; the spectators watched in awe as the man rubbed his aching sword arm.

Unable to resist the temptation, Toras said, "Missed!" Gorus simply shook his head.

The next moment, Toras spun away from Gorus, and stepped back as Rior lunged at him from his right, causing the limber man to lose his balance and fall on Toras's blade. But Toras pulled back his sword to prevent seriously injuring the soldier. He then spun again and smacked Rior on his back, flattening him on the ground. The young man let out an aching growl and surrendered.

Toras shouted another "And missed!" and the crowd erupted in cheers. Elyana turned to the too-pretty guardian, and with raised eyebrows and a barely perceptible smile, awaited an admission from the man.

In a croaky voice, he responded, "You were right, Lux Baiula. I stand corrected."

Behind them, one of Magister Setarcos's students yelled, "By Horin! The prince may be strange, but he knows how to fight, and I would not want to face him in battle!"

Hearing this, Lord Merlo, Elyana's neighbor, grunted in annoyance and promptly followed the other guardians to go cheer up their defeated comrades who were shaking hands with the prince.

Toras practiced this way another two days, during which he continued to surprise many in the Royal Guard who had only heard of him but had never seen him fight. On the First Day of the last fourth of Sextus, feeling fully restored, Toras returned to Horn's Pass, eager to see how the restorations were going, and to initiate the patrolling of the Kartak region. But one thing he did not look forward to: the replacement of his first officer by a Lux Baiula; and having to welcome Kendor with this news, when the man made his own way back to the fortress – whenever that might be.

XXIII BAD NEWS ARRIVE

Aithen was in his bed chamber, getting dressed in his riding uniform: a short blue tunic embroidered with the two-headed furan of House Coriolis, black-leather half-breeches to protect his legs from chafing, and a white shirt loosely tied at the front to keep him cool on this already warm day. He was putting on his riding uniform because he had decided to ride to the Royal Bay to go meet with the Locari. Indeed, he had been having nightmares for the past three nights, and in each of them, he saw the Locari's leader, distant, trying to communicate with him but never succeeding.

What was more, a report had arrived the day before informing the high king that the rokon – the truth of its identity was still being kept secret – had attacked a village not very far to the south. The report was accompanied by a bitter letter from Lord Arotek decrying the agreement reached two fourths earlier, stating that it was ludicrous to expect his forces – though not small – to protect the people against such a creature. What he did not mention, was his refusal to receive the help of any Lux Baiula with ties to neighboring landholders – a refusal which had made any assignment as yet impossible.

Octavius had called a meeting with Aithen, Elyana and Harlion to discuss Arotek's situation, and after much debate, the king had decided to request from Krystiana that she immediately dispatch a medic to the lord's landhold. To stave off any refusal by Arotek, the high king would provide the Lux Baiula with a royal passport granting her direct access to any of the king's subjects who might be in need of Healing. The passport would also note that the medic was being sent thanks to Lord Arotek's goodwill. As for military reinforcements, the king informed Arotek that he simply did not have sufficient troops to dispatch any to Melinor, but that quick strike units were being organized, to lend support anywhere across the kingdom, when an attack was imminent.

True, Harlion had begun rebuilding the Furanry, but only two thousand of the three thousand teams had been assembled as of yet, and they required much training still – fourths of training, if not months – before they were all ready. And in any case, Octavius was not going to assist Arotek shirk his responsibilities toward his land-dwellers. The king had smiled proudly when he was told Aithen had also refused the Lord's request.

So, a Lux Baiula was what Lord Arotek would get. It was unlikely anyway, that the Serpent would return to his lands. On the other hand, there was the slight chance that the Lux Baiula might start changing Arotek's attitude toward the Sisterhood if she helped heal the injured, and, if his land-dwellers thanked *him* for it – that would be a good result, and it was therefore easy for Octavius to convince Krystiana to dispatch someone immediately. But they had also agreed that sending "any" medic was probably not wise, and that it would be best for the success of the mission to send one of the Sisterhood's top medics, though it rankled Krystiana to have to honor such a distasteful, unpleasant man with one of her best. Thus, Fausta Lux Baiula, a high-ranking medic and former Advisor to King Juur no'Duur of Yerlah, was now being flown to Melinor.

Thinking back on all this, Aithen wondered if he would have made the same decision his father had. Octavius's plan was bright and would kill two flyers of a stone. Aithen hoped that when his turn came to take the throne, he would be as wise and insightful, though there were things he would do differently, such as…but before his thoughts could sink deeper into the unpleasant memory of the king's decision to leave Toras and the other men behind when they were attacked by those fell creatures, Aithen stopped himself and returned to his previous worries – his nightmares. He had the distinct feeling that Flowing Water was using Aithen's dreams to call him. He wasn't sure the Locarus could do that, but Lux Baiulae could, so why not the Locari?

Just as he was putting his breeches on, his hairless chest still bare – most Kynarians had very little body hair, and this was a trait the Halflings retained – a knock sounded. It was Kildare's knock. Aithen frowned, slightly annoyed, but said, "Come in, Kil."

The young man entered, and he lowered his head when he saw the prince in his breeches. Squires usually helped their masters get dressed and therefore became quickly comfortable with seeing them half-dressed or even completely nude, but Aithen preferred to dress himself, and Kildare had therefore never become habituated to seeing his master anything but fully clothed.

"My Prince, Elyana Lux Baiula is here. She says she would like a moment with you…should I ask her to return later?"

Now, it was Aithen's turn to feel awkward. His first impulse was to instruct Kil to have Elyana wait in his office while he finished getting dressed, but he really wanted to get to the shore, and he felt a sudden, deep desire to – well – provoke Elyana, so he said to Kildare, "No, let her in."

The poor boy blushed as he nodded and stepped out of the bedchamber to go fetch the Lux Baiula, hoping that his master would be dressed by the time he came back with the woman.

When Kil returned and saw the prince had still not covered himself, he asked again whether he should have the Lux Baiula wait outside the bedchamber, but Aithen said irritatingly, "Kil! Why –? Ugh. Just let her in please."

The poor Kildare backed out of the room, mortified, and fetched Elyana at once. She stepped in just as Aithen was tying the laces of his riding boots, his slender but muscular and nervous chest still bare. It was not the first time Elyana had seen him bare-chested – Aithen often trained with the guardians with only his boots and breeches on – but it was the first time she had seen him so in his bedchamber and, somehow, this caused an unexpected flutter in her chest. Her training quickly took over, however, and she prevented a breath of surprise from escaping her throat.

Aithen felt a fire light-up in his chest the moment he saw Elyana. His welcome was warm and urgent at the same time, as he said, "Elyana, come in. Kil said you wish to speak with me?"

"Aithen. I would have waited in your office, if I had known you were…"

"Don't be silly, Elyana, I –"

"I am *not* silly, Aithen. Anyway –"

"I'm sorry, Elyana, you know what I , you know I didn't –, aghrr. I don't mind Elyana." Then, with a diminuendo in his voice, Aithen added, "Your presence always soothes me."

Elyana did not respond to the prince's admission, but she felt her blood vessels dilate without warning, and she repressed the reaction at once, though her voice still betrayed her state of mind when she said, "Aanyway, as I had started saying, I wanted to give you some news I have just received from Tania. She informed me that Mela Lux Baiula – the medic we dispatched with the rescue team – sent a thoughtcall to her last night, informing her that they found the survivors from your brother's party."

Aithen's visage brightened suddenly, and just as suddenly, it took on a worried look, but he did not speak, waiting for more. Elyana continued, "The team arrived at the southeastern edge of the Colossi's Peaks by the end of the day on seventeen Sextus, as you had instructed them to, but it took them another two days to actually locate the men. They found Primus Kendor, one of Toras's guardians, as well as one of your officers – Secundus Jamir – alive. The men waited there a couple of days while Mela Lux Baiula stabilized the guardian and your officer who had both been severely injured. They then made their way to the Mountain Lake outpost, where they spent another two days while the young soldier, whose condition had somehow worsened, was properly healed by Mela Lux Baiula. They are now in flight and should be back here by tomorrow."

Aithen looked about ready to erupt again. He could feel anger well-up from deep within when he said, "All of my men, *dead*, except for an officer."

Elyana replied with a simple nod, not daring to use words to either condone or condemn his emotions.

The prince, who had been buttoning his shirt, stopped his fingers, which turned dead white as he pressed them against a button. A moment later, he resumed the fastening but ripped off one of the buttons in anger and cursed.

Elyana tried to calm him by diverting his mind, remarking in all seriousness, "The buttons had nothing to do with it, Aithen. But if you still feel so strongly about what happened, perhaps you should speak to someone about it, seek their counsel – your uncle Claudius, for instance."

The prince turned to the woman, ready to quash the suggestion, until he realized she was only trying to help. He shook his head, took a deep breath and said, "I just hate the loss of life, and though I understand why my father and his men left as they did, I still find it hard to accept."

"Aithen, it appears to me that you are purposefully *not* letting go of those emotions, and it is not good."

"Perhaps…perhaps. But I need to go now." The prince looked at his time disc and yelled "Kil!"

Why must so many things have to sour my mood every time I am with Elyana? I was looking forward to seeing her before leaving, and now, I'm yelling!

The squire came into the room, alarmed.

"Yes, my Prince?"

"Is Xyre ready?"

"He is, my Prince. He is being brought to your balcony as we speak."

Aithen calmed himself, said with a forced smile, "Thank you, Kil."

The young man retired, a relieved expression on his face.

Elyana said, "We should speak of this more, Aithen. I am concerned."

Aithen's immediate reaction was a frown and a grunt, but he thought better and said, "I know I have been too angry recently, Elyana. I know, and I appreciate your concern. I really do...very much so. It's just..."

Surprisingly, Elyana smiled and the warmth of it, the very definite impression it gave Aithen that she cared for him perhaps as deeply as he did for her, caused him to very nearly admit his feelings. He said, "I truly wish things were different, Elyana. I wish none of this were happening so that –"

Elyana fought back another dilation of her blood vessels, then forced herself to say, "So that?"

"Sorry, nothing. I'm just rambling."

"There you go again, contracting your words." Then, with an uncharacteristically soft voice and intense look, she added, "I wish things were different too."

It was Aithen's turn to start as his heart went into a sudden gallop. But Elyana did not give him a chance to reply or ask a question as she realized that she would have difficulty keeping her own reactions in check if she let him. Hoping to interrupt any further uncomfortable exchanges and reactions, she quickly said, "Anyway, where are you going, if I may ask?"

The question had the intended effect, and Aithen's pulse slowed as he answered, "Where am I going? Where am I going...well, I have something to do at the shore."

"Hmm, I know this has been a ritual of yours, going to the shore at certain times of the month and almost always with great urgency, for years now. And that has made me think that there is something else, aside from the beach and water, that brings you to it. Perhaps you can enlighten me another time?"

"I actually would love to. Someday. Perhaps soon."

Elyana smile again, relieved by his answer, and replied, "Very well, then. Enjoy your escapade, Aithen."

"Thank you, Elyana. And thanks for giving me the news about the rescue team. Have you informed my father and brother yet?"

"I am going to see your father shortly, and then send a thoughtcall to my Sisters in Horn's Pass to relay the news to your brother."

"Until later then."

Elyana smiled another warm smile and left before the prince had a chance to react. Better to not see his pleading eyes, or hear his quickening heart, or feel his intensifying vibrations.

Aithen followed her form as she walked to the chamber's door, paused, opened it, and stepped out. A diffuse heat spread across his entire body as he watched her go. He very much desired her, more than anything he had ever before desired, and in that moment, he decided that he would no longer resist this need.

Then Kildare appeared, seemingly out of nowhere, and snapped him out of his strange reverie, saying, "My Prince, Xyre is on the balcony waiting for you."

The prince blinked and said, "Thank you, Kil. Please have a good lunch ready for me when I return." Aithen rarely had heavy lunches, but on the days he met with the Locari, he invariably came back with a voracious appetite. Perhaps it was the swimming more than the Locari which depleted his energy – he wasn't sure. But given that he rarely went to the shore just to swim, he had no way to know the true cause of his hunger. But what did it matter anyway?

Kil replied, "As always, my Prince. I hear fishmonger Brak's son is coming back to cook for the palace today."

Aithen gave a strange look, "He is? I do not recall inviting him back."

"Elyana Lux Baiula did after your dinner two fourths back. Apparently, you had enjoyed the meal."

"So I did. But–"

A loud, impatient snort came from the balcony, interrupting Aithen's sentence. The prince turned from his squire and said as he walked to the balcony, "Just make certain that Master Brak's son prepares me a satisfying meal for lunch today, Kil! You know how hungry my trips to the shore make me. Here I come, Xyre. Ahhh, finally."

His steed greeted him joyfully and nudged him to get him into the saddle, which Aithen did as soon as he had checked the saddle bags for water, as well as for the cake he liked to take on his "escapades" – as Elyana had called them. He also checked that his hunting knife was in the scabbard on the right of the saddle. As expected, all was in order, and the only reason he still verified was that his father had drilled the practice into him ever since he had started giving orders. But his men – from stable boys to guardians – had never given him reason to check their work. Indeed, the men and women attached to the royal house were the most trustworthy in the kingdom thanks to highly selective recruitment practices enabled by the size of Alvinoria's population (totaling nearly two million men, and two and a half million women, as of the last census). Of course, there were times when both the Crown and a vassal desired to have the same man or woman, and in such instances, the Crown relied on a practice instituted long ago which authorized the Royal Treasury to purchase the right to acquire such a person's services. For this right, the Treasury paid a yearly Advantage Fee to said vassal for as long as the man or woman remained in the Crown's service, and the system had made it possible for the Royal Guard, in particular, to be composed of the finest men in the kingdom.

But Aithen wondered, now, if he and Harlion would be able to keep recruiting such excellent men with the coming darkness. Indeed, when an army's needs grew beyond a certain percentage of a population, such as in times of war, it was known that the quality of the recruits inevitably dropped.

Out loud, Aithen asked his furan, "But do I really have the best of men, Xyre? It seems that ever since Horn's Pass – or is it since the Zebulonian's arrival? – many of my men have exhibited strange behaviors."

Xyre snorted uncertainly and then bobbed his head impatiently. That reminded Aithen of the reason for his trip today. So, he shook that last question out of his mind, and without further delay climbed onto the furan, saying, "All right, my friend, you know where we are going!" And under the slight pressure of both heels, Xyre took-off.

The furan launched himself with a loud screech which reverberated through the capital and was then echoed by the other two thousand furans stabled nearby. The screeches probably woke some still-sleeping people, many of whom walked out onto their balconies to curse. But Xyre had already passed the city limits and Aithen did not hear the cussing.

As Xyre flew toward the royal cove, anticipation built in him as much as in Aithen, though they had different reasons for it. Aithen was anxious to find out whether the Locarus had really been calling him, and if so, why. Xyre looked forward to cooling-off in the bay's waters, and to hunting for his favorite snack.

**

Standing at the water line, after hopping off his steed, Aithen said, "How I love this place! Isn't it beautiful, Xyre?" The furan responding to his master's good mood with a jolly cry.

"Look! The algae growing on the cliff are now a vibrant yellow, whereas they had been green, red, and purple the last time we came. I read in a book in Elia Lux Baiula's library that it is due to the salinity of the water increasing as the temperatures rise throughout the summer."

Xyre bobbed his head, not in response to Aithen, but rather due to the excitement he felt at hearing things zipping through the water. Indeed, the fish had obviously spawned since their last visit, and their myriad fry swarmed the shallows along the shore. There, they sought refuge among the grasses from the predators prowling the deeper waters. Their movements caused tiny vibrations to spread through the water, and from the water across the air until they reached the sensitive microhairs Xyre had on his beak. The furan searched the purple grasses for the source of the vibrations, turning his head one way and then the other. But the 'source' kept changing location, maddening the furan who couldn't pinpoint it.

The females of several lizardine species could be seen either swimming about a little further off or basking in the suns some distance from the two interlopers. The creatures were now gravid and about to birth their younglings, which would then take advantage of the plentiful fish fry to sustain their rapid growth.

Aithen looked down at the water and said, "You prefer the moving fish to sessile algae, do you? Well, I don't disagree with you that they are exciting."

"Look! Those are the fry of the razor-tooth. You can tell by their flattened body. Ha! ha! It's a good thing they're harmless while small, or we'd have to turn back."

Xyre, who was impatient to get into the water, released an annoyed cry and nudged Aithen.

The prince gave him an annoyed look in return; perhaps Xyre didn't like the view, but he did. So, he took one last look at the glittering cliff, then undressed, and unsaddled his impatient furan.

"Ok, race you to it!"

And man and beast plunged into the water with a splash which scared all the fish and lizards away. The water was indeed warmer than it had been just a couple of fourths ago, as Aithen had predicted from the coloration of the algae. It comforted him to be able to make sense of some things in life, even if they were insignificant compared to everything else going on.

Aithen swam alongside Xyre, that is, three meters to his right to avoid being hit by the furan's wings which now had taken the role of fins. The furan's hair and the lamellae of his wings had also transformed as soon as he immersed himself: the lamellae were now fused to each other, and the hair to his skin, forming a smooth surface for swimming. Aithen thought it made the furan look quite ugly, actually, but it was still an impressive adaptation.

Aithen did not have any remarkable adaptations for swimming, but he did learn a long time ago to hold his breath just about as long as his furan, which was impressive in and of itself given that furans could hold their breath for over ten minutes. Aithen had learned to do that when he and his father had started coming here as part of the king's mental and physical trials for his son. Aithen had been twelve then. Learning to swim underwater for extended periods was only one of the many trials Octavius challenged his son with, to help him develop his mind as well as his body. Octavius had later done the same for Toras. The swimming feat had involved Octavius throwing a disc into the water, some ten meters from the shore and asking Aithen to retrieve it before his furan did. After several years of this, Aithen had not only become a very good swimmer, but he had also learned to breathe for maximum oxygenation of his lungs, to control

389

his most minute movements to maximize the amount of oxygen available for swimming as well as for his brain, and to master his fear of dying – something which had already served him well and would continue to do so in the days to come.

Now, Aithen remembered how he met the Locari, ten years ago, and he thanked his father's training for it. Growing up, he had often heard of creatures saving drowning humanoids, but no survivor had ever been able to recall anything useful about them. So, on that day, on his fourteenth birthday, he had come to the bay, and decided to try and catch one of the creatures in the act. To begin, he had sent Xyre off to hunt for some land game, so he would not interfere with his plans. He then entered the water, and once far enough from the shore, pretended to drown, with screams and all. After a few minutes of that, he slowed his movements and heartrate to a minimum, to pretend he was unconscious. His scheme had succeeded, and he was rewarded grandly for it when he felt the water being displaced around him by something very large. He did his best then to keep his eyes shut and to maintain a slow, quiet heartbeat until the mythical creatures approached him.

Aithen had just about run out of oxygen when it finally happened, and something touched him. He opened his eyes to set them on a creature even more fantastic than he had ever imagined. The creature swam back, surprised to find this humanoid fully conscious. As it did so, it moved closer to a conspecific swimming behind it. The two seemed to be communicating. Then, something amazing happened – Aithen felt a sudden flow of water envelop him. The water within this 'bubble' felt lighter, and he sank within it. Then the fluid surged into his lungs, and Aithen had started to panic. But he relaxed when he realized he could breathe! Astounded and amazed, he looked at the creatures in front of him; they watched him intently for a while, then turned around and started swimming. Aithen thought they were leaving him, and he screamed, but then, some type of thick filament came from the creatures to surround the bubble, and it started to move, dragged by the creatures.

A few minutes later – minutes which had seemed like an eternity of wonder, and during which Aithen had stared in complete amazement at the creatures gliding in front of him – the bubble stopped, jerking him slightly inside. The creatures had taken him to what looked to be their colony. After a few moments, a creature even more awe-inspiring than the first two approached him. It was the one he now knew as their leader, Flowing Water. Aithen was initially confused and dazed by a stream of thoughts and images which suddenly appeared in his mind, and which seemed to be sent by the creature facing him. Eventually, the flow slowed, and Aithen understood that the creature had welcomed him, and invited him to come again.

Since that time, Aithen had returned regularly to the bay to meet with the Locari, and under their leader's wing, had learned their language as well as things only *they* knew about the history of K'Tara. For one reason or another, his visits had been less frequent these past two years, though, and the last time he had met with them, Aithen had labored to communicate with the Locarus. How easy it was to forget a language, and how frustrating the forgetting was.

As before, when the Locari arrived, water moved past Aithen as if pushed forth by a large vessel. Flowing Water and his congeners formed a circle around Aithen, with Flowing Water facing him. They then created the usual shimmering bubble of *water within the water* around Aithen, which allowed him to breathe. Flowing Water's form still looked surreal to the prince, even after all these years. Once Aithen began breathing, the Locarus sent *"Fins touch."*

Aithen formed the reply *"Fins touch,"* which he sent with his mind, probably through the Bind, though he wasn't sure about it, but he would ask Elyana when he told her about the creatures – soon.

The Locarus sent an image of the moon waning, followed by that of roiling water. It meant that a full moon cycle had passed since their last meeting, and that the world had become a troubled place.

Surprisingly, Aithen did not struggle as much to form his thoughts this time. He formed images to reply, *"Yes, and these waters trouble me as well."* Aithen wanted to add a "but" to his thought, however he still had not learned how to form it, so he continued his Sending by adding an "also" to the image, *"My sibling and my genitor also trouble my waters."* He hoped that would work.

Flowing Water seemed to have understood and sent, *"Over your mind a shadow I see. Dissipate soon this shadow must, for harm you it will."*

Aithen sent, *"There is one who helps to clear my mind,"* following which he shook his head, wondering why he had said that.

"This one, one of your kind who can link the living and nonliving she is."

Aithen thought for a moment about the meaning of the imagery, and answered, *"Yes."*

"This one, good for you she is."

Aithen reacted with alarm and tried to hide his thoughts from the Locarus as Elyana's image and her smell came to his mind and roused his senses.

The Locarus noticed and said, *"Fear not, Young of the Walking."*

But Aithen wasn't sure he could accept the Locarus knowing his private thoughts, and he sent an image of himself covering a thought with his hand, representing the thought as a little ball of bright white light.

The Locarus sent a nod and continued, *"Your genitor's wisdom you know, and with him swim you must."* He then sent a thought which seemed to show clear, pristine waters in the distance, flowing to the *here*, where Aithen was, and continuing on ahead. It was a metaphor for something which had always been, was and would continue to be in Aithen's life.

As the Locarus sent these thoughts, images – generated by the prince's own mind – appeared in him; images of his father by his side at every important moment of his life; of his father standing in front of an angry crowd and appeasing it; of his father delivering on his promises to his family and to his subjects, always and without fail…so long as he promised things which were in his total control, which meant he made few promises, despite being the most powerful man in the land. This last thought saddened Aithen, and the sadness was replaced by resurging anger when images of his father leaving Toras and the other men on the Colossi's Peaks resurfaced. That had been wrong! And the decision, though he understood it, continued to revolt him.

"Young of the Walking, a dark cloud in your mind I see, covering your genitor's decision. But necessary, this one's decision was."

Aithen started and thought to himself: *How does he know that?*

"Open to me your thoughts are, Young of the Walking, and there I sense the hidden truth, which to yourself you deny." He then sent the thought of a river splitting in two, the left branch murky and dark, the right one clear. An image of his father was at the fork, and there was an image of the king downstream of each branch as well. The

upstream image of the king was clear, as was the image at the end of the right branch. But the image at the bottom of the left branch was dark. And Aithen sensed a wind – which felt like him – blowing past and pushing his father one way and then the other.

For a moment, Aithen remained with that thought in his mind, confused, not understanding it. But the Locarus sent another thought to Aithen, which he interpreted properly. *"These doubts about your genitor, cause you to push him into dark flows they may."* Aithen was suddenly overwhelmed by a sense of shame. How could he mistrust his father so?

Aithen sent the thought of himself facing down in front of the Locarus – the thought used to say thank you.

A sentiment of peace passed from the Locarus to the prince, which was subsequently replaced by one of concern. He sent, *"Young of the Walking, called you I have, because other currents there are which warn you against I must. Among those who can link the living and nonliving, some who will poison your waters there are."*

The prince's stomach lurched, and he felt a sudden access of nausea; had Flowing Water just warned him against the Lux Baiulae? Aithen sent an urgent question.

Flowing Water replied, *"Some, there are among them who are…treacherous. Your waters, they will trouble, then foul them and poison them. Prepare against that, you must."*

Aithen felt his heart sink. How were they going to get through whatever was coming if even the Sisterhood couldn't be trusted anymore? With some reluctance, Aithen asked, *"Flowing Water, do you know who these…"* Aithen did not know how to form the image "traitors." Maybe the image of a friend stabbing him? That did not work, and Flowing Water sent an image of shock back at him. Aithen tried again and sent the image of a friend in the company of an enemy, both men laughing at him. That worked, and Aithen converted the Sending into a question about the identity of the supposed friend who represented the traitors.

"These, I cannot see, Young of the Walking, but throughout the place your kind calls…Urbs Lucis… their vibrations are dispersed."

Did he send that? The feeling was different from that of his usual Sendings, and the name of the Sisterhood's seat seemed to have been sent in Aithen's own language. The prince rubbed his temples. The rubbing felt strange in the light watery fluid that sustained his breathing. He thought of the Sisterhood's base being infested with traitors and felt a shiver.

The Locarus sent another thought, *"This, these Walking ones will do: foul and poison your waters, because* weak *they are. And join the waters of those you call...Temptatori, they will."*

Aithen felt his mind begin to spin wildly as he tried to make sense of all he was learning from the Locarus. He felt the need to take a deep breath to calm himself, but he panicked as he started to inflate his lungs, thinking for a moment that he would drown.

"Young of the Walking." No response.

"Young of the Walking, breathe you may."

Upon receiving Flowing Water's second Sending, Aithen relaxed, took another, more controlled breath, and relaxed further. After a moment, he sent the image of himself facing down in front of the Locarus, to thank him again. Then he sent the imagery for his question, *"Flowing Water, do you know who the Temptatori are?"*

The Locarus sent a frustrated thought.

"Ones I cannot know, unless with the Locari they are connected or in your mind they reside already. But their vibrations I sense in the mountains, in the place where the river which flows to the south of your city begins."

The prince made the connection: Kartak.

Flowing Water continued. *"There, plans they make for the evil which He wishes to bring upon our orb."*

Aithen sent urgently, *"Flowing Water, you know of the one we call Bringer of Darkness?!"*

"The Locari do not know of him. *The Locari know* Him*!"*

Surprise and myriad questions painted the prince's face, wet and wrinkling as it was in the bubble within the water. Aithen also thought he felt the water around him pulse.

He sent two questions, *"Flowing Water, how do you know Him? And why do you care for me, my kin, and my kind?"*

"A child to us your kind is. And among your kind, you and your kin our care the most deserve. But the Locari do not wish to see your kin or *your kind to the racked mole! fall prey."*

The water around Aithen and the Locari vibrated and bubbled fiercely when Flowing Water sent that last thought.

Aithen asked, *"Are you saying, are you sending...and what is a... racked mole?"*

It seemed to Aithen that the Locarus had laughed when he received the image of a rodent which Aithen had sent with his question. But soon after, Flowing Water sent the thought of a Founder swimming in his own foulness. The thought which accompanied the image still sounded like "racked mole," however. So, Aithen coined a Human-sounding – and meaningless – word for the Locarus's Sending.

Aithen sent, *""Rackmole"?"*

"Hrackmol!"

Aithen suddenly felt like laughing, though the topic was anything but funny. He shook his head instead, and felt his heart skip a beat as the water vibrated again around him.

Flowing Water continued, but his thoughts seemed different, somehow; Aithen interpreted them more easily now. *"Locari were* here before *humanoids; we are not* of *the Founders, because we are of this* orb. *Over twenty-four thousand solar cycles ago, before even I was brought forth, the one you revere as the Originator to us came."*

At that, Aithen arched his eyebrows; he did *not* revere the Originator.

Flowing Water did not seem to notice and continued. *"Permission she asked to place on our orb the unborn from which you came; an imperative need it was for her and for her kind, because of the ailing of their world. Permission she also asked to bring here the seeds of a few plants and creatures from her world. To persuade us, the potential of all these, the beauty they could create, she showed us."*

"But we feared that this new life might compete with K'Tara's own inhabitants –with us. Your Originator promised us that would not happen, that sufficient raw materials to support what existed and what would be, was present on our orb. She said that that which existed, the new life would complement. To ensure that it would be so, another she promised to send, one whom she trusted, to see to your needs and education, and to ensure that your kind developed respectful of our orb. We agreed."

"The Originator's promise came to pass and with new beauty, our orb was filled. Supremely adapted to life on K'Tara, the

Afterkind [73] *were. For a long time, we roamed the world in awe, grateful to Aiala'Rhi.*

Aithen felt dazed. This was the second time now in recent days that someone had revealed to him things beyond his imagination, things which made him question the very truths he had learned. *And how is it that his Sendings are so much more fluid than just a few minutes ago? I could swear someone else is sending for him every so often.* He wanted to ask but the Locarus resumed his fabulous account, though he did it with a certain grimness in his strange face.

"The bliss did not forever last, however, because humanoids quickly became unruly, and insatiable, sowing chaos where they stepped, and for the first time, K'Tara knew strife."

"And when the Hrackmol! came, he began to corrupt the weak, and with the help of the one you call Umbra, he established chaos so that he might take this orb for his home. Fortunately for your kind, the Hrackmol! you defeated eventually, but K'Tara was not our orb anymore."

"When the Originator placed your kind here, still on land we walked, over K'Tara we flew, and in its waters we swam. But humanoids changed it and corrupted it, and to the seas we retreated where the Hrackmol!'s creatures and your kind still had little influence. It may be that a day will come when even the seas despoiled will be."

Aithen felt disgust in the face of what he knew to be true, the humanoids' – well not all humanoids, just Humans and Zebulonians, as far as he knew – their perpetual need to always acquire more land, transform it, and fit it to themselves rather than fit themselves to it. *And why are we not taught this history!? Why are our history books, our art, silent about the Locari? Surely the Lux Baiulae must know of them, of this history. And shouldn't those of the Yellow Sash know that not all species on K'Tara have the same origin? That might explain so many things!*

Flowing Water's facial expression changed again, and a smile seemed to reappear on his inhuman lips. He said, *"During the Black Years, the –"*

"The black years?"

---

[73] Afterkind, the-: A Loracan term referring to the lifeforms which evolved from the seeds placed on K'Tara by the Founders.

"During the Dark Battle, as your kind knows it, under cloak to the land the Locari returned to fight alongside your kind. Then, we discovered the courage and loyalty of your kin. To your ancestors my forebears owed their lives, Young of the Walking. It is why many cycles ago you were brought to me."

Father has never told me of this relationship between our family and the Locari. Does he know of it? Aithen turned his thoughts back to the Locarus, and sent, *"Flowing Water, I give you my thanks. I have learned much today, and I am...grateful, although what I learned...blankets my waters with concern and confusion. I will return to the land, now, and visit you again when the moon lights all the sea."*

The great beast – should he think of it as a beast? It was wiser than any humanoid he knew, though it had the shape of a sea beast – the creature sent a nod followed by a thought which was structured more like his earlier Sendings, *"Young of the Walking, as a branch being swept by a waterfall you may feel. This knowledge with you I shared, so that the* true *waterfall which lies still ahead you may avoid."*

Aithen scratched his head, perplexed, upon hearing the Locarus switch again to the highly inverted sentence structure he typically used. Perhaps Flowing Water was learning to organize his thoughts the way Alvinorians did. Regardless, Aithen sent the thought of himself facing down in front of the Locarus to communicate his gratitude.

But Flowing Water was not done, and sent, *"This truth, I have sent already: that to the Locari your survival matters. For this reason, we must help. It is why another of my kind there is who will begin sending to you."* As Flowing Water's Sending finished, another Locarus approached from behind him. This one was colored in hues of bright orange. It was smaller than Flowing Water, but still enormous compared to a Human. It was the first time any of the other Locari had approached Aithen since that time when they saved him and took him to Flowing Water, many years ago.

This one's Sendings were more melodious and much more easily interpretable than Flowing Water's. Something made him wonder whether it had somehow helped Flowing Water make his recent Sendings. And was this Locarus a female?

"Aithen," it sent, which startled the prince as their leader had never used his Human name, *"I am Current. Fins touch."*

"Fins...I...fins touch. Your thoughts are different...Current."

The Locarus sent a smile, and it seemed to Aithen that even its mouth formed a smile now. Its eyes seemed to shine brighter as it sent the thought of the smile.

"I am she."

Aithen sent a surprised thought.

The creature sent again, her vibrations somehow more intense, *"I came to rescue you many cycles ago."*

"You, you are the one I met when I..." He did not know how to form the thought for "I tricked you", so he just ended it there.

"Yes. I am one of two you met when we captured you."

The prince was about to object to that, when Flowing Water cut in and sent, *"Skilled in your language Current is, more than I am. And learn more she must. You and she must connect, Young of the Walking."*

"Connect?"

Current said, *"To the Locari it is important to...fully relearn your language. Torrent wishes me to connect with you...through what you call...the Bind, so that during the coming storms we may be ready to help you and your kind."*

"Torrent?"

"Yes, you think of him as Flowing Water. It is close, but not...sufficient. Torrent *is how K'Tara has known him for over three thousand solar cycles."*

"Oh. Three hundred years?!"

The Locara did not seem to like the conversion, and repeated, *"Solar cycles."* She added, *"I will connect to your thoughts, and what passes through your mind while you wake, I will know."*

Aithen's *"What the!"* translated into a high-pitched, uncertain rumble which confused the Locarus – or rather the Locara.

She sent, *"I do not recognize your Sending."*

"I am, sorry...I cannot permit you to be connected with me permanently."

The Locara sent another thought of confusion.

Aithen sent, *"I cannot permit you to be connected with me from suns up to suns down."*

The Locara seemed to understand, this time, and her colors shifted, switching from her metallic orange to an arrangement of intense blues and violets. She seemed irate. Now, she sent an overly powerful, demanding thought, *"But I must fully learn the Sendings of your kind!"*

Boy! Are all females this demanding? Aithen did not know how to argue with a Locara, so he turned to Flowing Water, or Torrent, and reiterated his objection. The Locari's leader seemed to understand the inappropriateness of the request and asked Aithen to excuse the young Locara, and to state what duration of connection he would accept.

After a few minutes spent considering the risks of being connected with the Locara while engaged in important conferences, or while interacting with Alterintrants who might detect her presence, Aithen made a decision. He only hoped it was not a mistake, and started sending his proposal to Flowing Water, *"Torrent, I can..."* But he could not find the appropriate imagery for "agree", and he let out a quiet growl, proving their point, about the need for them to learn his language. After another moment of frustrating brain-racking in search of the right metaphors, Aithen had an idea: two people at a road-crossing, looking at each other, nodding, and then moving as one in the selected direction. He went with this image and sent, *"Torrent, I can...agree to connect with Current one hour every day after the suns are down, and once again, if possible, at Highsun."*

"Thank you, Young of the Walking. To discuss this with Current, I will leave you. Fins again will touch, when all the sea the moon lights." And the majestic creature departed with most of his retinue except the young Locara, and another – a male? who took hold of the bubble within the water.

The young Locara faced him now. He had the darndest time telling male Locari from their females, but then, if they were like most other K'Taran species, they probably alternated between the forms, so what did it matter? *Well, it matters because gender is part a person's identity, even if it is only temporary; it can tell about a person's motivations, status of mind, and – but what am I rambling about?*

Just now, Aithen received a Sending from the Locara. She was irate again, *"So, females have all the same attitude when angry, they do?"*

"W –, what?"

"That is what I received earlier, Young of the Walking!"

The Locara did not call him by his name this time. Aithen decided he had better relax and try to work this out with the creature. The Locarus or Locara next to Current appeared to be amused.

Aithen sent, *"I apologize, Current. That was not...proper. Please tell me what we need to do to help you learn our language."*

The Locara made an actual snorting sound which rumbled quietly in the bubble within the water. *"I will connect with you now and leave a...a part of a thought as a signal. When ready...when you are ready to share with me, think of the...part, and we will be connected."*

Aithen sent a nod. *"A part of a thought, as a signal. That is like what we call a beacon."*

"Yes, a beacon."

"Current, will Lux Baiulae – those of us who can link the living and nonliving – will Lux Baiulae be able to sense this beacon?"

"I do not think so. Our knowledge of the Bind is older...of, older...as. What is the thought for this comparison?!"

"Older than."

"Yes, our knowledge of the Bind is older than...humanoids."

"Older than that of humanoids."

"Yes. Thank you, Aithen."

Aithen smiled, and then, thinking that perhaps the Locari might not understand humanoid facial expressions given that their own expressions were not as plastic, he also sent the thought of a smile, which he represented as the Blue Sun's rays caressing someone's face early in the morning. *"All right, I will contact you tomorrow, at Highsun – perhaps. If not, then after sunsdown."*

The Locara thanked him with what seemed like a sense of anticipation. She then sent the usual salutation marking the end of the meeting, released the bubbles and left with her companion, who – it seemed to Aithen – was greatly amused by the entire thing.

***

As he swam back toward the shore, Aithen tried to reconcile himself with what was probably a necessary risk. He would just need to make certain Elyana did not find the Locara in his mind by accident. But she would understand, would she, if she did find the creature there? If he told her? He should tell her. *Oh boy!* was the final thought which escaped his mind before he exited the water. Shockingly, Current was able to pick it up, and she responded with a Sending that seemed to indicate amusement, causing Aithen to growl. *It is obviously not going to be easy managing this connection between us. I need to be careful. Founders!* As he walked out of the water, Aithen saw his furan who was waiting for him impatiently. He wondered how long Xyre had waited for him there. He looked up and saw that both suns were now slightly past their crest and said, "I guess it is high time to return home, isn't it, Xyre?"

A loud, complaining screech was the furan's only response.

***

When Xyre landed on Aithen's balcony, a pleasant smell reached for the prince from across the doors and invited him in, to come and satiate his now ravenous hunger. That surprised Aithen because Kil had said that Brakis, Fishmonger Brak's son, would be preparing the meal, and though he had enjoyed the limpfish, he wasn't certain such delicate foods could satisfy his rumbling stomach today. But Kil must have advised Brakis, who had obviously consented to his request because on the table there was a plate with braised wild karsh in a red fruit sauce, served with stuffed lizard eggs and a salad of reds. As he sat down to eat, Aithen thought of how much he liked Kil, despite his strangeness. Then, as he put the first bit of meat in his mouth, his mind strayed, and he wondered whether lizards and karsh were descended from K'Taran native species, or whether they were *Afterkinds*. But there was no way for him to know this – he wasn't a Seeker after all – so he decided to simply enjoy the food. Strangely, he did not think of Flowing Water's worrisome revelations and warnings. Instead, he started to think about…Elyana – he wanted to see her. That is when the memory of his deal with the Locara raced back to his mind, along with all the things her leader had told him.

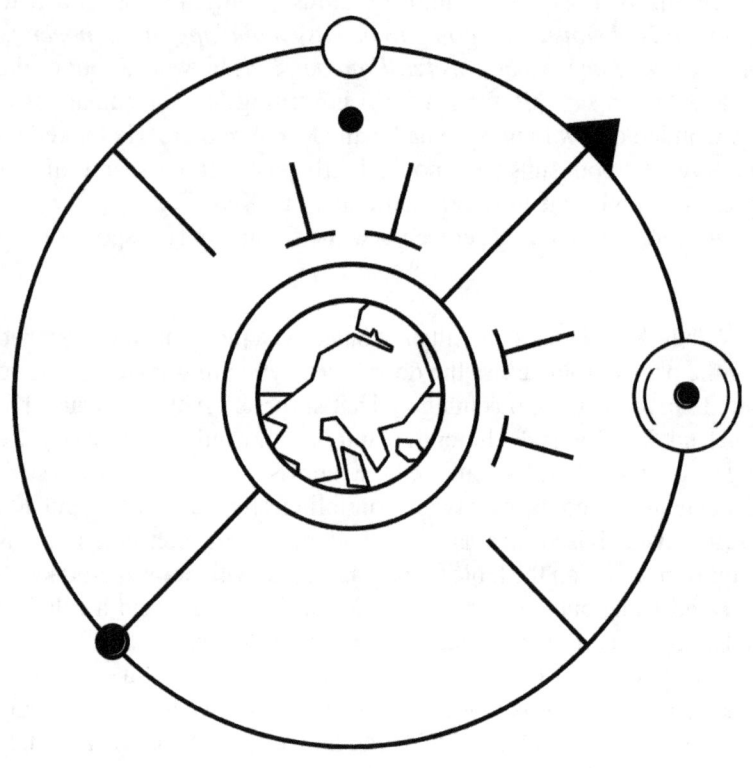

XXIV MORE THINGS REVEALED

The day following Aithen's unsettling meeting with the Locari, the news everyone dreaded arrived in the capital: The Serpent had just attacked two nearby villages, and it looked like it was now on its way to the city.

Octavius, Aithen, Harlion and Elyana were on high alert, fearing that the Serpent might be coming to hunt for the king, if Octavius was indeed one of the two Luxori the Serpent and its companion were looking for, a thing which they had not yet ascertained. In any event, they all agreed to keep this potential threat quiet for the time being.

The Small Council was now meeting in the Private Audience Chamber to consider the options in the face of the imminent threat to the capital. The council normally included Octavius's sons, the High Captain of the Royal Guard and Commander of the Frumentarii, the Senate's Eldest, the king's Special Advisor, as well as Lord Kaffin. However, the latter was not present today given that the decisions that needed to be made did not involve the treasury, nor was Prince Toras who had flown back to Horn's Pass a few days earlier.

The mood was sour and filled with palpable concern, concern that the capital would suffer the same fate as the fortress at Horn's Pass – and concern, for some, that the king's own life would be in danger. First Senator Leo was especially anxious, having just learned the truth about the rokon, and he sat there, shaking his head and rubbing his temples as he wondered how in the Founders' names he was going to maintain order in the capital after the king made the public announcement he was intending to make regarding the rokon.

Octavius, hands laid tensely on the table was speaking, "This city has never fallen, and it will not fall now, not to one single, lone opponent, no matter how dangerous and destructive he is. All we need to do is be ready for it, and ready we *will* be." The king turned to Harlion and to Elyana for confirmation.

The high captain said, "The Royal Guard will be ready, Sire. But it cannot fight the rokon's mental powers."

The mention of the rokon's psychic powers caused First Senator Leo to redouble the rubbing of his temples.

Elyana jumped in to address the high captain's concern. "I have already requested that two Red Sashes be immediately dispatched to the capital, Sire; they should arrive tonight. With them and the other eight of us already here, we *should* be able to defend against the Serpent's attacks, whether physical or psychic."

Aithen said with the utmost sincerity, "Well, you did manage to fend-off the rokon at Horn's Pass by yourself. With your Sisters' support, who knows, you might even be able to bring it down."

Elyana raised an eyebrow and replied, "As far as bringing the Serpent down, my Prince, I cannot say whether we can or cannot; it seems to have unnatural regenerative abilities, beyond what the best medic can do for herself. Then, there is the matter of the Serpent's psychic abilities from which we can only hope to protect ourselves but cannot fight back with similar attacks…" Elyana added in a near whisper speaking to herself, "…at least, not yet."

The men looked at each other, wondering what she had said. Harlion asked, but the Lux Baiula's only reply was "I am sorry, it was nothing."

Aithen thought to himself: *Did she mean what I think she meant? Is she looking for a way to re-enter the thing's mind and do harm to it?* Aithen looked at her, trying to read her face, and his concern about what she might be planning to do was quite plain to her.

Elyana tightened her lips and continued. "Based on what I learned during the attack at Horn's Pass, I believe there are only three of us in the Sisterhood with the ability to establish a proper nebula against the rokon's psychic attacks, myself included. The Sisters I have requested from Urbs Lucis are the other two. But the three of us will still not be able to cover the entire capital and protect all its citizens from these attacks. Our best defense, then, will be to strike at the Serpent and harass it to prevent it from using its psychic abilities in the first place."

The king said, "Hum, all right. We *will* have the advantage of greater numbers than the fortress had, and that will help, I suppose?"

"It seems logical to assume so, Sire. As for the nebulae to protect against the Serpent's psychic attacks, the two Red Sashes and I will take care of that while the others aid your forces in repelling the Serpent."

That caused a reaction of surprise from the king, the prince, and the captain.

The king said, "I would have thought that the Red Sashes would be best used in attacking the creature. Do you mean to say that the only other women with the ability to establish a nebula are Red Sashes?"

"It's what I said earlier, Sire. That is quite unfortunate, as you understand. But it does appear that the ability to create a nebula is tied to a Sister's offensive skills, somehow, though the sample is too small to establish a definite link."

The king replied with a grunt, "Well, if it must be. As Aithen said, you were able to fend-off the Serpent nearly on your own at Horn's Pass. Please continue, Lux Baiula."

"Yes, Sire. As I was saying, the three of us will each establish a nebula. I will create one over the palace to protect the defenders, but the palace's civilian staff, along with all visiting officials, Master Methrim – and Ori – should go into the cellars; I am certain they will be safe there. Indeed, none of the Horn's Passers who took refuge in the fortress's caves were harmed, and they were beyond the reach of my nebula. It might have something to do with interference by the rock's minerals, I am not certain. But again, they will be safe – in fact safer – there, since it is possible I will become incapacitated at some point, and accidentally release the nebula. The rest of the population should ideally be assembled indoors somewhere, but there is not a single structure large enough to contain one hundred thousand people. So, they will need to be concentrated in one or two outdoor areas which will be defended from mental attacks by Xena and Ulva Lux Baiulae, and from physical attacks by a detachment of guardians." Elyana turned to Harlion, seeking his advice and support.

Shaking his head, the high captain replied, "As far as support from our guardians is concerned, your Sisters may, of course, have what they need. But as for a location to assemble the entire population, the only place large enough to do so is in the old Imperial Park between the temple and House Royal. However, it is highly exposed and would not easily be defended by my guardians."

Aithen asked, "High Captain, could we assemble half the population in Domus Lucis plaza and the other half in the Senate plaza?"

405

Harlion turned his eyes to Elyana and First Senator Leo. Elyana replied affirmatively, simply adding that she would need to inform Irania Lux Baiula. First Senator Leo, however, was not as forthcoming with his agreement and hesitated, causing the others to frown, the king included.

"My Prince...I believe the Senate would...not be against it, but–"

The king interrupted the Eldest, asking, "What is the reason for your hesitation, Leo?"

"I am sorry, Sire, how should I put it? The Senate will not disagree with assembling part of the population in the plaza, of course, but...they will likely not want to be in the streets with the population."

The king's frown widened visibly, but the First Senator continued, "Elyana Lux Baiula, would it be possible to center the...nebula, on the Senate House. So that senators may remain within its walls...for additional protection?"

Elyana asked, "Isn't the Senate House over two hundred meters wide, First Senator?"

"I am not certain, Lux Baiula. Why do you...?"

Harlion interrupted the Eldest and said, "It is exactly three hundred meters wide, First Senator, which means that if a nebula were to be established from within Senate House, a radius of at most one hundred and fifty meters outside of the building would be left for the citizens to assemble in. That cannot be done."

Elyana said, "In that case, I am afraid the only way to establish the nebula from within the Senate House, First Senator, will be for the Senate to agree to let as many citizens into the building as can fit; the rest can then remain in the plaza, close to the building."

"Letting tens of thousands of comm –"

The king interrupted the Eldest again, his jaw muscles tight, and said with a voice like ice, "First Senator, I advise you to *not* finish that sentence. The elders and their families may remain within the Senate House and benefit from the physical protection it affords as well as from the presence of a Lux Baiula. But whatever number of citizens can fit must be let in, lest you and the rest of the Senate prefer to go into the streets with everyone else."

The man shrank as he apologized for what he had been about to say.

The king accepted the apology even while trying – unsuccessfully – to hide his frustration in the face of such callousness from a public servant. *Why did I not prevent this man from ascending to his post? Why?!*

Once he recovered his calm, Octavius asked, "Now, how do we ensure order after I make my announcement to the public?"

Leo replied with an anxious look on his face, his voice shaky and his hands restless, "Sire, I urge you to reconsider your decision. Telling anyone outside this room the true nature of the rokon is, well, it is a risky…a very risky proposition. Our constables are ready to serve, as you well know, but they will be powerless to control the crowd if people believe darkness has finally come to claim them. And many will believe just that, if not most, especially if the clerics of Aiala learn of it too – which obviously they will, if you make a public announcement."

"First Senator, rumors already abound about the rokon and about the meaning of its presence in Alvinoria. If it attacks the capital, the rumors will become facts, and if I should lie to the population about the creature's nature, they will never trust in me again, and with what we know is coming, I *will* need their trust and their willing sacrifice when they are called upon to help defend the kingdom."

Aithen understood his father's argument, and knew it to be right, but he also agreed with the Eldest's assessment of the risk. He said, "Sire, First Senator Leo is right in this matter. Making this announcement now would be a bad idea, a very bad idea."

The king's face tightened as he listened to his son oppose his plan. But he did not reply, and instead took a deep breath and turned to Harlion.

Harlion sat back, took a deep breath of his own and said, "Sire, I must agree with the High Lord Commander and the First Senator." The old soldier paused, then took courage and continued, "Without disrespect, Sire, I believe that this revelation would be both unnecessary and dangerous: unnecessary because whether or not the citizens know of the rokon's psychic abilities, they may still die as a result of its attacks; dangerous because it may cause the population to become unresponsive – or worse, to riot if certain religious orders should find it in their best interest to push them to it. As for risking their trust in you as their protector; that could be handled by feigning ignorance a little while longer."

"You make some good points, High Captain, but I disagree with your suggestion that we feign ignorance. How will we – how will I – feign ignorance when the population learns that ten Lux Baiulae were needed to defend the capital against a rokon? Even if only a handful of the city's citizens have ever faced a rokon before, they surely all know someone who has, or they have heard stories of rokon attacks in the western provinces or may even have studied them in school. Regardless, most know that such actions as we are planning to protect the capital and its inhabitants are not needed against a rokon."

Aithen added with a sense of unavoidability, "And if we don't tell them and the Serpent does succeed in killing civilians with its psychic abilities, there will be panic and chaos as soon as people see their mothers, daughters, sons, or husbands die inexplicably while their *souls* escape the victims' bodies."

Harlion grumbled, recognizing the truth of the king's and the prince's statements. The king awaited a response from him, but it did not come. He just shook his head, unable to determine the best course; Elyana replied instead.

"Sire, it may be best to do as you wish. But going back to your original question, there may be ways to control the reaction. If we can prevent the clerics and other fearmongers from spreading terror, we will stand a better chance at controlling the population."

Aithen asked with a suspicious frown, "What are you suggesting, Elyana?"

"Firstly, before making the announcement, I suggest that an officer and guardians be sent to each of the temples, simultaneously, to instruct the clerics to retire into their caves until the morrow. For this, your officers will need to present orders from you, Sire."

Octavius asked, "And what reasons would I give for this unusual order?"

"A truth, Sire. That we are expecting an imminent attack from the rokon and that you do not wish to put them at risk and that as soon as the danger has passed, they may come back to the surface."

Octavius considered the Lux Baiula's cunning suggestion; he did not dislike it – he often spoke in half-truths himself, but he was concerned about the clerics and asked, "And they will be protected, in their caves, from the Serpent's psychic powers?"

"Indeed, Sire."

"Hmm. Very well. And your second suggestion?"

Elyana looked at the First Senator to determine his current state of mind. She noted his relentless grimacing and the nervous tapping of his feet on the floor, and she knew he would not welcome her next recommendation. So, she said, "I realize this will not be a welcome suggestion to the First Senator, but I am making it because it is necessary, and I am confident he will recognize its soundness." Everyone looked from the Lux Baiula to the First Senator, wondering what it was that Elyana was thinking of, while the Eldest got a very wary look on his already gloomy face.

Elyana said, "We should fetch Senator Sur'Elando and find a reason to hold him in the palace's cellars with your civilian staff and your son."

First Senator Leo shouted incredulously, "What? Why?!"

The king's angry stare was immediate, and the First Senator's contrition just as rapid. Indeed, outbursts of anger were strictly forbidden in the high king's presence. The king thought: *I don't know if I should appreciate his quick apology or be discouraged by his spinelessness.*

Elyana waited for the king's shoulders to relax, and then answered Leo's question. "First Senator, you know as well as I do that as soon as we gather commoners in the Senate House, Senator Sur'Elando will want to address them to warn them against the coming evil."

"But —"

"He may even go as far as ask them to repent for their sins by, perhaps, sacrificing themselves to the creature to appease it."

Leo, having been called to order by the king once already, forced himself to contain his anger when he replied that the senator would "do no such thing."

Elyana maintained her position, however, and said, "He will, and you *know it,* First Senator. He has done such things in the past, such as during the Storm City revolt last year. I am surprised, in fact, that he did not join one of the religious orders rather than the Senate, for he is quite the mystic."

The king added, "And a bad influence too. But we digress. First Senator, unless you have solid counterarguments, it will be as Elyana Lux Baiula suggests."

First Senator Leo did his best to hide the feeling of defeat he now felt; nothing had gone right for him, this night. But Elyana was correct, and the young senator was going to cause trouble if left to his own devices. He said, "My only argument, Sire, is that Senator Sur'Elando will not respond well to his sequestration, and the rest of the Senate will demand an explanation, if not now, surely when this is all over."

Octavius replied, "I am sure they will, First Senator. And I am certain we can find a perfectly sensible reason for bringing Senator Sur'Elando to the palace. It will need to be a clever reason, High Captain, one that will give the senator neither a sense of importance, nor reasons to feel slighted. Frankly, I am more concerned with the first. Perhaps the Lux Baiulae will be able to help in this matter." And the king gave Elyana a knowing look which made her sigh. She knew he was thinking of using Confusion on the man.

Harlion nodded.

Octavius said, "Very well. Is there anything else we should consider before adjourning?"

Harlion nodded again and suggested that most of the two thousand furans be relocated to their stables near Antar, reminding the king that the Serpent had taken pleasure in razing the village outside Horn's Pass, and that it was likely it would do the same to the extensive stables which adjoined the House of the Guard outside the capital's walls. First Senator Leo asked why the furanteams could not be used to defend the capital, to which Harlion responded with annoyance that the teams were unfortunately not ready and would not be for another few months. So, the king agreed to the captain's recommendation, and gave his final orders.

"High Captain, Lux Baiula, First Senator, please see to it that all decisions are enacted; we must be ready by nightfall. Aithen, please stay a moment."

At once, Harlion and Elyana left with a determined stride to put the agreed plans into action, while Leo made his way to the chamber's doors with a slow, uncertain pace, trying hard not to shake his head as he thought about the decisions – the king's decisions.

He did not like them one bit and thought it unfair that he would be forced to deal with their consequences. Didn't the man have any qualms about treating senators as he did? Leo also disliked the fact that he had such a weak position in the Small Council. He led the

Senate which was responsible for the administration of the city and of its police, as well as responsible for the passage of laws presented by the high king – given all that, he certainly deserved a better position in the Small Council, better than that of the high captain, better than that of the Lux Baiula! Not that the others did not deserve the high king's trust; he knew Harlion was a good man and a good officer, but he was too loyal to the royal family and often let his judgement be clouded by his loyalty. As for the Lux Baiula, she *was* a good advisor and had gotten the high king out of quite a few pickles over the years, but Lux Baiulae often had their own agendas in doing what they did, and there was no reason to believe Elyana Lux Baiula was any different. Actually, it seemed to Leo that even the king himself had his doubts about her, if what he heard yesterday about the king leaving the capital without informing his advisor was true. Well, if there was anything for him to exploit here, he would. For now, though, he needed to deal with the king's orders.

***

Once all were gone, the high king turned to his son who was standing next to him.

"Aithen, I would like you to prepare a note for your mother. She should hear from us what is happening here, before she hears it from others."

"By carrier or by furan?"

"I think we can spare a furan now. But do not send a Royal Messenger as I do not wish to alarm all of Kynaria. Send your squire. It will be more personal."

"Very well, Father. Anything else?"

"Indeed, you told me earlier that the rescue team is on its way back with Primus Kendor, Secundus Jamir, and another of Toras's guardians?"

"Yes."

"We should send a furanteam to intercept them and bring them in from the north, just to be certain they will not arrive and be met by the Serpent."

"I had the same thought, Father."

"Excellent. Then, there is nothing else. Let's us get to work, son. I, myself, need to prepare my announcement regarding the Serpent."

The prince responded with a sigh followed by a nod of understanding. He then saluted his father, arms on chest and head slightly bowed, and left the chamber with urgent steps.

***

"I have tried this procedure multiple times, Saara, and it does not work."

The Praefecta Medicas responded in her raspy and old, but insistent voice, "Well, you will need to try again, Kelysia. It *must* be possible to entangle these objects. Although I am not certain of it, this property of matter must be similar to that which allows two persons to be connected at a distance, as when we perform a mind-tie or mind-link. There must be some physical process which, when it occurs, binds the particles of two objects – whether animate or inanimate – together."

Kelysia was an unusually tall woman, with short blonde hair, and hazel eyes. She had been elevated to the Yellow Sash five years earlier and was now a leader in the study and advancement of mind-tying, though she was only forty.

Kelysia said, "Hum, I don't know. It seems to me that if that were the case, we would also feel what the other person feels…physically, I mean. And our movements would be tied to the other person's movements."

"That is because we tie only certain assemblages of particles, such as those that form the reasoning part of the brain. I say that it must be possible to entangle any two sets of particles, as well as entangle two bodies entirely, if the proper methods are used."

Kelysia gave a hesitant grunt in response.

The old Sister said, "We will do it together, Kelysia."

"Really? Whites rarely get involved in the discovery of knowledge and prefer to simply apply what the Yellows discover to the practice of Healing."

"Really. And because you are a friend, I will not take offense at your comment." Saara would have pointed to her Yellow stipe if it had still been attached to her White Sash, but Praefectae did not typically keep reminders of their old Sashate, so she said, "But you know well that I was a Yellow Sash a long time before joining the White Sashate, and that I miss the thrill of scientific work."

412

Kelysia grinned at that; she couldn't agree more about the excitement of scientific research, though it was often equally frustrating.

Saara added, "In any case, Krystiana asked me to help your Sashate infiltrate Kartak, and it is not for my medic's skills that she asked me to help. It is for *this*, for my experience with entanglement, a subject I studied long ago, but still master, nevertheless. I think that finding a way to entangle objects may be just what we need to do in order to have eyes and ears in Kartak without putting any Sister at risk."

Feeling convinced, Kelysia said, "All right. Let's get to it, then."

XXV ATTACK AND A THREAT

As the suns descended below the horizon, only the sounds of weapons being readied, or commands being given breached the silence within the walls of the city. The population had been divided as planned between the Senate plaza to be shielded by Ulva Lux Baiula, and Domus Lucis plaza to be shielded by her twin, Xena. The Red Sashes had arrived an hour earlier, and Elyana had explained to them the method she had used to shield the defenders at Horn's Pass, as well as described what she had learned from the experience in the hope that they might be able to avoid the mistakes she had made.

In the Senate House, some of the elders could be seen crossly eying the plebeians who had entered, especially any who tried to climb the steps toward the upper floors, where the senatorial living quarters were located. For the most part, however, the elders were welcoming, and many of them – including, of course, Senator Kraelion – walked among the commoners to reassure them as best they could, or to answer what few questions they had answers to. But they were politicians, and they were therefore familiar with the art of speaking without saying.

Surprisingly, the "relocation" of Senator Sur'Elando to the palace had been carried out without any ruckus. Harlion had gone to the Senate House with a secundus and three guardians and asked to speak with him and with First Senator Leo. There he told Leo that he had credible evidence of an imminent threat against the two men's lives, and that he was sent by the high king to bring them to the palace where they could be kept under the protection of the guard as was customarily done for members of the Senate. When Sur'Elando asked where the threat came from, Harlion replied that he did not know, not wanting to take the lie too far.

Seeing that the First Senator made no objection to the high captain's request, Senator Sur'Elando had fetched a few things and gone with the officer, having been told that Leo would follow shortly. Once at the palace, Harlion "accidentally" knocked the senator's head against a ladder, giving the man a minor cut on the forehead for which he received the ministrations of Tania Lux Baiula. In reality, Tania had used Confusion on the man – at the king's request – to erase his memory of the fabricated story Harlion had given him, and then administered a soporific which would keep the man unconscious for the next twenty-eight hours, hoping that by the time he came to, the Serpent would have come and gone. Tania questioned the wisdom of this plan, and Harlion replied that it was better to deal with the man's anger once the danger had passed, than to deal with him while defending the capital against the rokon.

In the plazas, the Senatorial Police kept watch on the citizens that had been assembled there, and they waited anxiously for the high king's announcement, which – they had been told – was likely to cause the populace to erupt in riots. But what he might say, they had not been told. So, they watched the people warily, the majority of whom were simply praying on their knees, while others huddled and waited for the world to end, and others still gesticulated nervously and shook their heads as they tried to make sense of what was happening and asked their neighbors what they knew. As it was, no one knew much, and what they did know was mostly myth and did not quiet the questioners' worries.

Many also wondered why the clerics were not there with them, to give them courage against this evil thing making its way to Furan City, and to pray for their salvation or, perhaps, even to ward-off the creature with their prayers. No one had answers to this question either.

The clerics of the temples of Aiala and of Elande were in fact being forced to retire into their underground shelters. A secundus had been sent to the leaders of the latter. High Priest To'kahr and High Priestess To'kahra, having no political ambitions whatsoever, were more than happy to comply and retired at once to the bosom of their temple to pray for the people – and for themselves. But it was High Captain Harlion who went to the leader of the former with a guard of ten. For, First Cleric Galadrin was a different creature altogether, and he *did* have political aspirations as well as what the king and prince considered dangerous religious delusions.

As Harlion had expected, Galadrin was resisting the king's orders; he insisted that he and his clerics should be allowed to be with the people, to give them courage, and save their souls in case death came to claim them.

Galadrin, of course, suspected the true reason for the strange orders, and he harangued the high captain for ten long minutes, after

416

which his vociferous indignation left the officer with two bad choices: use physical force to get the First Cleric and his followers into the basement of their temple, or tell another lie, a better lie, to get the cleric to do as requested. But Harlion hated lies more than war, and necessity – the mother of creation – provided him a third choice: a bluff and a truth; he told Galadrin that either he and his clerics retreated to their cave of their own accord or they would be physically forced to do it, and that either way, he was welcome to lodge a formal complaint with the high king once the danger was passed.

Seeing the resolve in the high captain's attitude and believing in his readiness to act on his threat, the First Cleric relented, and asked only that he be allowed to let his civilian acolyte join his family above ground. Harlion did not see the harm in it, and relieved as he was that he was not going to have to use force against the priests, he approved the request. Galadrin thanked him with a deceptive smile, and after giving some inaudible parting words to his attendant, descended into the temple's cave with his people on his tail.

Every one of them shot disapproving, disappointed looks at the king's men as they passed. Once the last cleric had crossed the threshold, Harlion nodded to Secundus Krptus who closed the heavy metallic door.

The men gave Harlion loud sighs of relief, and remarked on his patience, saying that they would have knocked the man unconscious if they had been in the captain's position. Harlion gave an uncomfortable smile in response, relaxed his hands, and turned to his secundus to ask if he had brought the timed lock.

The secundus replied in his native accent which emphasized the last syllable of nearly every word and added a letter "e" to many, "I did, captain. Do you really want to lock the priests in their cave?"

"No, I don't, Secundus, but you know as well as I that Galadrin cannot be trusted to remain there. Please lock the door."

Krptus was a thirty-year old Yerlayan, and brother to Krpta Lux Baiula. Their parents had sent them to Furan City as teenagers so that they might improve their lot in life – and that, they did. The two had been taken in by Tania Lux Baiula, a Yerlayan herself. When the woman discovered that Krpta had the atomic and microbial constitution of an Alterintrant, she immediately requested permission to send her to Urbs Lucis for testing and possible admittance as a novice. The girl was now on her way to becoming the youngest political advisor ever, and she deserved it, having developed and honed her mind-reading and influencing skills to a truly impressive degree.

Krptus, on the other hand, was sent to the Royal Guard, given that he appeared to have the attitude and physique that High Prince Aithen sought in guardians. Krptus had done well in the guard and had been promoted several times. But his beginnings in the capital had not been easy. Indeed, his thick Yerlayan accent, which he had never lost to the contrary of his sister, and his strange looks had made him the target of relentless and hurtful jokes, and only the status afforded him by the Guard, and the interest shown him by the clerics of Elande, had eventually saved him. It was this connection with the clerics that made him question his commanding officer just now. But he was a bright and rational, young man, and he understood, despite his misgivings, the reason for their orders, so he locked the door.

The deed done, Harlion left with his company and with the worse headache he had had in a very long time. While rubbing his forehead, he spotted the First Cleric's attending boy scurrying away in the distance, and he had a sudden suspicion. Not wanting to take any chances after what they had just done, he halted and said to Krptus, "Secundus, please have this message delivered to Frumentarius Parok immediately: "*Keep an eye on the queen's fetcher.*""

Secundus Krptus gave a quizzical look to his commanding officer, but he did as ordered, and sent one of the soldiers deliver the message.

*****

The departure of nearly two thousand furans, following three furanteams at their head, occurred shortly before Harlion and his men returned to the palace. The officer turned his head to the sky and smiled at the beauty of the sight despite the lingering headache, and then sighed as he thought of how much he still had to do to get the Furanry ready for combat. However, to most of the people lucky enough to witness the departure of the furans during the fifteen minutes that it lasted, the view was simply a marvelous spectacle. For the children, the sight was a wondrous one, which fed their imaginations and their hopes, and excited them to endless screams until the last furans disappeared. But, as is often the case, there were

418

those among the gaping civilians who saw the departure as a bad omen, and these men and women could be seen shaking their heads with resignation. Only thirty furans, including Xyre, were being kept in the capital in case it became necessary to evacuate the king, the princes, and critical personnel. To facilitate a potential escape, as well to protect the furans from the Serpent, the animals had been moved into the palace grounds' old stables.

As for the guardians, two-thirds had been assigned to the defense of the plazas while the other third had been assigned to the defense of the palace. The latter were now in position, or getting in position, along the walls surrounding the grounds. Fortunately for everyone, that was as far as Elyana's nebula extended.

Octavius looked on from the top of the palace steps with a grim expression. It pained him to see the palace grounds so transformed; this was where he took his daily walks, or where he came when he needed to think, or relax.

One thought did comfort Octavius, though. It was the knowledge that he had the best force, assisted by ten gifted women, to defend the capital. It was the knowledge too, that the capital's and palace's walls had been twice bind-fused when built, giving them at least thrice the strength of Horn's Pass's walls and structures. With such protection, what should he fear?

Octavius now turned his attention to the nervous chatter and fidgeting which took hold of those who had fought the Serpent at Horn's Pass. Fortunately, the presence of *eight* Lux Baiulae among them reassured the soldiers to a degree.

Octavius finally turned to watch his son discuss the placement of four arbalests with his officers when the first bone-chilling cry reached the city. Aithen looked up at his father, and then turned to Harlion who yelled the command to raise the arbalests at the top of his lungs.

The shrieks and the order gave the primi and the eight men they had with them the boost they needed to hoist the four arbalests to the top of the palace's walls – an arduous task, even with the use of cranes. One of the men hoisting the weapons was Mekiir himself, who had lost his twin to the Serpent at Horn's Pass. Harlion had been hesitant to let the man join the arbalesters this time, but Mekiir had recovered better than some other soldiers who had faced the Serpent, and the young man wanted nothing more than to avenge his brother.

419

So, here he was. Harlion watched the man flex his ropy, taut muscles to help hoist the heavy weapon onto the parapet. Satisfied, the high captain nodded to himself and left to attend to other urgent tasks.

The king, who was now walking toward his son with a brisk step, saw Harlion leave and intercepted him to ask if Ori was safe. The high captain replied that he was, safe from physical and psychic attacks in the palace's cellars, along with the rest of the civilian staff.

Octavius nodded uneasily then decided to walk to Irania Lux Baiula who was discussing final preparations with Elyana and the rest of her Sisters. He asked if they were ready. Irania nodded that they were. He then indicated that he was ready to speak to the capital's population as well as to the guardians. Irania therefore called Elia Lux Baiula, a Yellow Sash skilled in increasing the vibrations of particles to enhance the transmission of sound.

Tonight, Elia was going to enhance the high king's voice, so it could carry across the palace grounds as well as across the entire capital. To achieve the latter, three other Lux Baiulae were going to create a sound shield over the capital using the metallic flag poles planted at each corner of the palace grounds; the sound shield would in turn reflect the king's voice back into the city. This contraption resulted in a strangely resonating sound, but it did its job.

"High King, I am ready when you are. Just speak normally, without yelling, but with a clear voice, and I will project your words around the palace."

Octavius made a slight frown at the Sister's comment; he always spoke clearly! The woman flinched, and the king grunted. He then turned to Harlion and said, "Ready."

Harlion signaled a young soldier with a strange contraption of an instrument next to him, and the guardian hit the Sound Carrier, with his mallet. The sound was repeated all around the palace grounds as well as across the capital within seconds as it was picked up by other such instruments positioned at regular intervals. The instruments picked up the sound on their windward faces and, through an ingenious mechanism, sent it forward by way of their leeward faces. A second, even cleverer invention prevented the sound from being repeated by the preceding instruments or from being repeated by the initiating instrument when a loop was closed; without this, sounds would soon become confused, cancel each other out, or amplify themselves to unbearable intensity rendering the instruments useless

420

to carry orders. Indeed, the instrument, also known as a tabellarius [74], had been developed several centuries earlier to facilitate the communication of orders across a large army. Various commands could be transmitted in this manner, and the codes could be changed as necessary to prevent the enemy from learning them.

Upon hearing the sound, all the soldiers within the palace grounds stood at attention. In the plazas, too, the guardians stood at attention, but the civilians started, unused as they were to the abrupt, cadenced roll of the tabellari.

Octavius breathed in deeply, nodded to the Lux Baiula again, and then said what he needed to say. "Citizens of Furan City! This thing approaching our city, this creature we believed to be a rokon, we now know is no such thing, for it is in fact the creature the ancients called the Serpent. We do not know why it is here, but we do know how to survive it. Horn's Pass has! True, there was much destruction there, and the lizard has destroyed many other places since. But our guardians, as well as ten of the best Sisters of the Order of Light, are here to defend you. Trust in them as I do, and trust in me and in your prince, no matter what happens. Tomorrow, though rock and limb may have shattered, and though death may have visited us, this city will still stand, and we, its people, will still be here. Thus, fear not, and may your bodies prove worthy!"

With that, the citizens of Furan City did their best to calm their fears and to believe this king whom they trusted above even their own parents, or children, or friends. And the senatorial police looked on suspiciously, ready to quash any disturbance which might still come, especially from the foreigners who were not persuaded by the king's words.

Octavius now addressed his soldiers, "Guardians! Though this beast may be supremely dangerous, we can repel it; it was done at Horn's Pass with fewer defenders. Do as you have been trained to do; remain calm and focused at all times and follow your superiors' orders. Remember, as well, that fear will cause many more deaths among us than resolve will. Therefore, steel yourselves, prepare to defend your city and your people, and may your bodies too be worthy!"

---

[74] Tabellarius: This referred both to the sound device which carried orders, as well as to the person using the instrument [Note: A tabellarius was in fact a roman letter carrier].

That last injunction was met with a ruckus as feet were replanted firmly on the ground and bows and lances were knocked against the pavement in a sign of determined resolution. The casting of these sounds to the citizens helped to steel their own resolve.

When quiet returned, Elyana, who was standing by the front steps of the palace, called to herself the other nine Lux Baiulae. She then proceeded to link them all in a strange ritual which sent shivers through the spines of the onlooking guardians. The Sisters placed themselves in a circle around Elyana – now their acting leader. Each Sister then closed her eyes and crossed her hands, maintaining a straight head, pointed toward their leader.

Noticing the turning of heads toward a common point, Aithen did the same and saw Elyana standing there, in the center of a circle, confident, and…beautiful. This time, however, he did not grumble upon realizing that his thoughts were straying. Instead, he let himself feel the sentiments – and the fear – he had for Elyana, a fear that she might be hurt again – or worse. Then, he exhaled loudly and made a wish – for *what* he did not even know, but it gave him hope. Octavius – always aware of what his son was doing – eyed the prince questioningly. But Aithen did not respond and turned back to look at the Lux Baiulae.

Octavius was now certain he knew what his son was hiding. *Hum, this I had not expected. I can see why, but it is not what I had planned for. If we are all here when this is over, I will need to speak with him about it.*

Encircled by her Sisters, Elyana closed her own eyes and with a supremely powerful voice established a mind-tie between the Sisters, "Sorores, nostris mentibus nunc nos ligare [75]."

A short moment later, Elyana's hair stretched out in all directions, while her Sisters' hair stuck out pointing toward her. Scarves of blue light stretched between the women and converged on Elyana. Guardians and officers alike gaped at the spectacle. Even Octavius and Aithen were awed by the sight, which they had only seen once before from another group of Lux Baiulae. The ethereal ribbons continued to connect the women, zapping and crackling, and giving rise to a minute-long spectacle of wonder. Then, the sparks ended, the ribbons dissolved, the women opened their eyes and fixed their

---

[75] Sisters, let us now bind our minds.

hair, and without a word moved to their respective positions, ready for whatever was coming. Just then, what sounded like a dismissive, contemptuous cry reached the capital; the Serpent was not very far anymore. Hearing that, Ulva and Xena climbed atop the vorans that had been brought for them, nodded to Elyana and to each other, then galloped away to reach their respective plazas.

Aithen turned his head toward Octavius and said, "Well, Father, let us hope our guardians' nerves are indeed steeled and their courage greater from having just witnessed the use of the Bind in such a spectacular way, because it will not happen once the Serpent gets here, and from the increasing loudness of its screeches, I guess it will be here in a few minutes at most."

Octavius grunted and nodded gravely, then said, more to himself than to his son, "Yes, let us hope…"

* * *

The appearance of the Serpent in the distance shook the high king, who was unable to believe that this creature still existed, though he was not one to question his senses.

The high prince felt a tremor pass through his body, as he remembered the destruction and death the thing had caused when he last encountered it. A groan escaped him despite his efforts to display confidence.

Worse moans and groans rose along the walls from the smaller number of men who had already fought the creature, as well as from the greater numbers who reacted with shock at the sight of what they believed to be a thing of myth only.

Just now, the king turned toward Elyana, who was standing at the top of the palace staircase and nodded a command. The king then tapped his son's shoulder, and both men stepped away from each other as well as from surrounding people and objects. A moment later, the air surrounding Octavius and Aithen shimmered, and their clothes inflated momentarily, as Elyana established the Bound Shield around them.

The shield was a discovery of the Luxori, five hundred years before, when they too had been involved in the development of the Binding Sciences. The Bound Shield protected the bearer from fire as well as from any oncoming object containing metals. The more metal the object contained, the more resistance the shield offered.

423

But the Bound Shield also had its disadvantages: it could be maintained at most three to four hours, and some of its effects could kill the shielded person.

Having been shielded by Elyana, the king and the prince – followed by the Praetorian Guard, High Captain Harlion, Elia Lux Baiula, *and* the Tabellarius – now climbed the winding staircase leading to the top of the tower to the south of the palace gate. Once there, the prince gave the king a respectful nod accompanied by the traditional "May nothing nor anyone take you," and separated from his father, making his way to the north tower by way of an aerial passageway. He was followed by his officer and the Tabellarius. This was a centuries-old practice, meant to reduce the risk that the kingdom might lose both its king and crown prince at once, while at war or under attack.

The Lux Baiula remained with the king to serve as his transmitter of orders, as well as – and more importantly – to shield the king's mind from the Serpent's probing vibrations by laying an Inhibition field on him. This meant that the king would be hidden from Elyana as well, but it was an acceptable trade-off, should the king indeed be one of the Luxori that the creature was hunting for.

***

In front of Domus Lucis and Senate House, the civilians had begun to panic, and their screams had started to agitate the soldiers.

The high prince, with his mind now on high alert, realized that an order was needed at that moment to stay the soldiers, lest one of them strike before the time. So, he instructed the Tabellarius to transmit a staying command.

As the command was transmitted across the palace grounds, and all the way to the plazas, the Serpent's terrible wings flapped once more and positioned it some eighty meters above the palace walls. There it stood in midair, merely scanning the Humans amassed along the ramparts for what seemed like an eternity. The Serpent's sheer size and fierce appearance – its fierceness increased by the glow of the tall lanterns which gave it a blood-red hue – transfixed everyone, but fortunately not the king, the prince, their senior officers or the Lux Baiulae.

Octavius raised his voice to reach his son across the walkway and asked, "Is this what it did when it came to Horn's Pass? Standing in midair, as if searching for someone?"

The prince responded without turning to look at his father, his gaze fixed upon the Serpent through the tower's fenestration, "No, not when it arrived, but it did display some similar behavior later on, when it caused Elyana's unfortunate accident."

"Yes, she told me about that."

From the prince's right, now came Harlion's voice, "High Lord Commander, we should release."

"No, hold Captain." Aithen continued to watch the Serpent, as if trying to determine its intent. As he did so, he walked over to his father in the next tower, alarming everyone.

When his son reached him, the king asked with a quiet but urgent tone, "Son, what are you doing here and what are you waiting for?"

The prince responded in the same tone, "I want to know what it wants, why it's here."

"Aithen, I doubt that finding that answer will change the outcome; it will kill, and we must prevent it if we can."

When no response came from his son, Octavius shouted, "Aithen!"

But Aithen did not respond to the king. Instead, his head was twitching, and he appeared to be experiencing some acute and sudden pain.

Octavius became alarmed. He grabbed Aithen by the shoulders and asked, "Aithen, what is happening?" Nothing. Octavius shook his son's shoulders again and, still getting no response, yelled for the Lux Baiulae's help.

Aithen finally opened his eyes, and looked up at his father, embarrassed and angry. The pain had been caused by the beacon Current had placed in his mind. She was concerned that he had not communicated with her since the day before and had activated the beacon herself. Aithen replied with an angry Sending, prohibiting her from reaching out to him again. The Locara apologized but asked to know when he might communicate with her. He responded he would do so in two days, if he was still alive, and then shut the Locara out of his mind. At least, he prayed that what he sensed as a block was indeed one. Aithen brushed his hair back and said, "I'm sorry, Father. I...I was having a really bad headache. But I'm okay now."

"Aithen, you worry me. But our men need your order to attack, now."

"Yes, of course, Father, you are right." And the prince shouted the awaited order, which was transmitted by Elia Lux Baiula to her Sisters through the Bind, and by Harlion to the men via the Tabellarius.

Not a moment later, the first arrows and firewhorls hit the Serpent, causing the creature to release a shriek which reached even the priests in their caves. As had happened at Horn's Pass, however, the Serpent was barely hurt by this first volley, despite the much greater quantity of both conventional and bound projectiles. The Serpent now plunged toward the wall, to the north of the prince's tower, its eyes flaring.

Harlion shouted, "Shields!" and the soldiers' oval shields went up in one swift motion a mere second later in response to the command received via the tabellari. Harlion and Aithen had decided to try this defensive tactic when the Serpent descended upon them, rather than keep launching arrows at it; they hoped that this might prevent so many soldiers from being picked up by the creature to be crushed by its claws or beak, or to be dropped to their deaths. The Lux Baiulae, on the other hand, protected themselves with Bound Shields more or less successfully, given that none here – except for Elyana, and the two Red Sashes in the plazas – had any military experience.

The shields did their job and prevented the Serpent from grabbing anyone on its first sweep, but it came right back down and one poor soldier, who had forgotten to let go of his shield when the Serpent clutched it, was taken away and tossed toward the ground, a short moment later.

The first man had died in this new encounter. His secundus, a burly man named Telpornion, spat and muttered a harsh "fool!" Aithen, who had heard through the skylight on the side of the tower, wondered if his fears of diminishing quality as numbers increased were already coming true; he hoped not. He hoped this was an unfortunate accident, and that perhaps the soldier's glove had gotten stuck in the shield's handle, and that he had therefore been unable to let go when the beast grabbed onto the armament...he would have to

426

look into it when this was over…if he, himself, survived this new battle.

Irania Lux Baiula, standing atop the walkway to the north of the North Gate-tower, sent a concerned thought to Elyana, who broadcast it to all Sisters, *"Elyana, our firewhorls have no effect."*

"I know, Irania. As I said earlier, the creature has incredible regenerative powers. But as long as we resist and keep attacking, it will eventually tire, and when it does – if we cannot kill it – we can at least chase it away."

"Understood," was the only response Irania gave, though she felt like adding a 'I hope you are right.'

One realization quickly frustrated everyone: the fact that their opponent was not restricted to one side of the walls, and that it could fly over the palace grounds. This meant that their use of conventional weapons was greatly limited given that an arrow, bolt, or lance shot toward the Serpent while it was on this side of the walls might very well fall back down on a defender. Most of the defending was therefore being done by the Lux Baiulae whose bound projectiles vanished in mid-air if they did not hit their target. And only when the Sisters succeeded in pushing the Serpent away and back to the other side of the walls were the soldiers able to use their weapons.

Every so often, Ulva and Xena, who could see the battle from their respective vantage point, sent each other a private thought, complaining about the ineffectiveness of their Sisters' attacks. Ulva was especially irritated by her inability to use her warrior skills, *"If we survive this, Xena, we will need to find a way to teach our Sisters of the other Sashates to establish nebulae so that –"*

Xena finished her twin's thought, *"So that we may do what we do best, fight! I know, Ulva, it maddens me too that we cannot help. They've been launching the same weapons over and over, with no effect."*

Ulva said, *"Firewhorls are the only bound projectiles Sisters of the other Sashes are taught to form, as you well know."*

Xena finally said, *"I wish it were easier to transfect a Sister with the microbial flora of other Sisters…it would make us all so much more powerful…"*

All this while, the Serpent had ignored the civilians assembled in the two city blocks defended by the twins. But after about thirty minutes of battle at the palace, the Serpent suddenly and without warning flew toward the Senate House and launched itself into the crowd clustered in its plaza – and tragedy befell the civilians and soldiers assembled there. The guardians posted there immediately launched arrows at its wings, but without effect. Ulva Lux Baiula, who had been itching to attack since the Serpent first struck the palace, let her instincts take control, releasing the nebula and projecting a firebolt at the creature.

Ulva grunted proudly when she saw the Serpent swerve back up. Unfortunately, the Lux Baiula's pride lasted but a moment because the creature – suddenly aware of the release of the nebula – launched its cerebral attacks, and two dozen Furanites, including guardians and senators, died in agony as their brains started to fry.

Most unfortunate of all, the bolt of a guardian who had been aiming at the Serpent when it launched its mental attack, fell on two children instead, piercing them through and through right in front of their parents. Sheer panic erupted in the crowd and Ulva called to Elyana through a private thoughtcall, shamed and angry with herself.

Elyana wanted to whip her. She had told the twins not to attack. But she also remembered her own reaction at Horn's Pass, and her anger dissipated. She replied to the Red Sash, *"There is no need to feel shame, Ulva. I made the same mistake at the fortress, but do not make it again. I will send a Sister to you, as well as one to Xena to provide you both with offensive support."*

After an awkward silence, during which Ulva battled with her costly mistake, she thanked Elyana and returned her attention to the Serpent.

Elyana now sent a message to Irania but decided to broadcast it through the mind-tie so everyone might know of it, *"Irania, we need to send a Sister to each of the twins."*

"It will be dangerous, Elyana. They will be outside the range of any nebula while they get there."

Elyana replied through a private thoughtcall, *"I am aware, Irania, but we have no choice. The Serpent just killed two dozen civilians after Ulva released her nebula to keep the creature from descending upon them."*

"How could she...?! Well, regardless, so be it." And Irania sent the order to two Sisters, broadcasting it to everyone in case the two intended Sisters did not receive it, or were incapacitated, *"Dalima, please take yourself to Ulva now. She needs offensive support while*

she maintains the nebula. Krpta, you are to go to Xena. Be careful, both, as you will be beyond the nebulae until you reach the plazas."

Just now, an urgent broadcast communication arrived from Ulva, *"Elyana, the Serpent is descending on us again, and we now have no way to stop it!"*

Horror at the thought of what was about to happen spread through the Sisters' link. Elyana's mind raced for a solution.

Xena, having heard the communications, sent a private question to her twin, and received a response filled with a sense of helplessness, which was highly unusual for a Red Sash; her sister, like her, was a warrior! *What is happening to Ulva?*

Xena was about to send another question when Elyana sent an urgent request to all, *"Sisters, we need an idea to assist Ulva, now!"*

Several ideas did make their way to Elyana in quick succession, but none satisfied her. She urged her Sisters for more, and when none came, and she received another broadcast message from Ulva informing her Sisters that the Serpent had just taken three more civilians, and that she herself had barely escaped, Elyana decided on the only course of action left to her. She sent, *"Sisters, I will break our link to call the Serpent to myself."*

Nine objecting voices reached her at once urging her against such a bold and dangerous tactic, but Elyana ignored them all and broke the link with the words, *"Rumpo vinculum nostrum!* [76]*"*

Irania was furious. But all she or anyone could do now was to watch and support Elyana as best she could, and use the slower, and less effective private thoughtcalls to communicate.

Elyana, her mind focused on the Serpent, began calling to it, summoning it to herself to talk.

"Bestia! Volo tecum loqui. [77]*"*

Nothing.

"Bestia! Volo tecum loqui."

Still nothing.

"Bestia!"

This time, the Serpent received Elyana's call, and it replied with a painful Sending which shook the Lux Baiula. The creature thought about ignoring the call, but something about it made it curious.

---

[76] I break our bond
[77] Beast! I wish to speak with you.

Having decided to find out who the caller was, it dropped the child it had just snatched off its mother's arms and made its way back toward the palace. Fortunately for the babe, it fell right back into loving and caring arms – injured by the squeeze of the Serpent's beak – but alive nonetheless.

As the Serpent flew over Ministerial Road, it noticed a woman running along the buildings, trying to hide herself from view. A malicious smile stretched its scaly face as it wondered curiously who it was, scurrying in the dark.

Hic jucundus est. Quid hic? [78]

Dalima was about to cross the road between the Treasury building and Senate House, when she became aware of something dangerous above her and she stopped to look up – it was the Serpent, and it stared at her with lips drawn and a growing, roaring laugh. Dalima's heart skipped, but she recovered quickly and immediately tried to shield her mind from the Serpent.

Regrettably for her, that was not a skill she had studied much, and her attempts at blocking the Serpent resulted in nothing more than a weak dampening of the oncoming vibrations.

So, when – after a few minutes of toying with her – the Serpent intensified its attack, Dalima screamed a horrible scream of agony, and writhed on her knees. The woman fought with the one part –the only part – of her mind that still had a will. And she fought valiantly. But after a few more of the Serpent's lashings, the Lux Baiula was ready to surrender, ready to give in, stop resisting. That is when a thought – a small, but strong sentiment of indignation – appeared in her mind, a thought that urged her to resist for she *was* a White Sash, and she *had* ways to dampen the pain, if not block the creature's attacks. So, she expelled all her fears until she was able to focus, and then imagined a cooling, soothing flow of water over her head, and the pain receded – sufficiently so for her to think again. And at that moment, she understood that unless she reached the safety of a nebula soon, it was the Black Skies she would see next.

With no time to waste, she commanded herself to run to the Senate House, which was but a road, a lawn, and a wall away. However, in doing so, she inadvertently relaxed the dampening field, and the pain returned more excruciating than before.

---

[78] This is interesting. What have we here?

Just then, the Serpent spoke to the Sister to let her know she would not escape, *"Tu non effugies me, Soror!* [79] *"*

And the pain and throbbing were so great that Dalima dropped to the ground and cried in agony. Yet, that small part of her brain that still had a will sent an urgent, pleading thoughtcall to both Irania and Elyana, *"Sorores, adiuva me!* [80] *"*

Unfortunately, because Elyana had severed the link between the Sisters, and because private thoughtcalls were less efficient than those sent through a mind-tie, it took a while before *this* message reached its intended target, as urgent as it was. But both Elyana and Irania heard it eventually, and they looked at each other, horrified.

Irania yelled out loud, creating a near panic, "Elyana, do something! Now!"

Elyana did the only thing she could do. She sent another thoughtcall to the Serpent. However, this thoughtcall was not a mere Sending, it was a summons which few K'Tarans would have been able to resist, *"Bestia, veni huc!* [81] *"* Elyana doubted it would have the same effect on Noctiferus's creature, but she hoped it would be sufficient to draw its attention to her – and away from Dalima.

When the Serpent received Elyana's summons, it got momentarily distracted, surprised by the daring nature of the thoughtcall. As it turned its attention to the summoner, Dalima's pain subsided. But by this time, her brain had suffered too much damage already: her motor cortex had been destroyed, and only some of her cognitive centers remained functional, along with the pain processing regions. Perhaps, if the cerebral attack had ended now, Dalima might have been saved, and with the careful ministrations of Urbs Lucis's best medics, she might have recovered some, or most, of her motor and mental capabilities. But despite its strength, Elyana's call failed to stop the Serpent, so intent it was on killing the woman, and after a short pause, the creature resumed its assault on the White Sash and put an end to her. Dalima let out a final scream as her weak mental shield dissolved completely, and the rest of her brain fried like meat on a hot stove. When steam escaped through her orbits, past her shrinking eyes, a believer might have thought that her spirit was passing, but alas.

---

[79] You will not escape me, Sister.

[80] Sisters, help me!

[81] Beast, come here!

Back on the palace grounds, Irania sent a troubled thoughtcall to Elyana, *"I do not hear Dalima anymore. Can you sense her?"*

A response tinged with a terrible sense of failure returned to Irania, *"Our Sister no longer lives,"* to which Irania replied, *"And with no one to transfer her memory – the Sisterhood is diminished."*

Elyana replied as matter-of-factly as she could, trying hard not to let her sense of guilt, which she knew was misplaced, transpire through the thoughtcall, *"It is diminished."*

Shortly after Elyana and Irania completed their exchange, the Serpent returned to the palace. It stopped some distance from the walls and began scanning the defenders, as it did when it first arrived at Furan City. Aithen was about to give an order to shoot when he noticed that the creature was looking straight at – Elyana!

He yelled, "Oh Founders! I hope the same thing doesn't happen here! Elyana!"

The Lux Baiula nodded toward him, calmly, as if to say that all was alright. Her Sisters turned toward her anxiously, eyeing each other, waiting for orders.

But instead of giving orders, Elyana shook convulsively and a gasp shot through the on-looking defenders.

Tania Lux Baiula climbed down from the ramparts as fast as she could and ran toward Elyana. When she got to the Sister, she found her frozen in place, her face contorted with pain. Tania palpated her to ascertain her condition; they could *not* lose another Sister tonight, and *not* Elyana. Tania tried to shake Elyana out of whatever was holding her, but it was a futile attempt; the woman was locked in placed like a statue, unmoving and barely breathing. Finally, Tania placed her hands on her Sister and knew then that the woman was linked with the Serpent. The medic whispered a desperate injunction to her Sister, not knowing whether the woman could hear her, "Elyana, you had better pull yourself out of this, because I would notte like to lose you."

The only response she got from Elyana was another violent shaking episode. Elyana had just received a Sending from the Serpent; it was pleasantly surprised to meet her again, and wondered why she had called it but its sarcasm was conveyed by the painful, aching vibrations that accompanied its words.

It said in the Ancient tongue, *"Soror! Quam feliciter iterum te invenio! Cur ergo vocatis me?* [82]*"*

Despite the throbbing, Elyana was in control of her senses, and replied in the same language, *"Do you not seek someone?"*

"Of course, I do. I know that my quarry is here. I can feel his presence. Where is he?"

"Stop killing, and I will tell you."

"You cannot coerce me, Sister, and you should not try because it insults me. On the other hand, I can and will *hurt you so that you may understand that* I *am the one in control."*

And the Serpent did just that, sending another painful vibration to Elyana. Elyana fell to her knees and let out a scream that made Tania shudder. The medic laid her hands on her Sister again, to try and pry her from the beast's clutches, but when she did that, the medic experienced such excruciating pain, that she pulled her hands back lest she faint then and there. Not knowing what else to do, she called to Irania, urging her to do something, anything, or lose Elyana too.

The Purple Sash's decision was immediate; the creature was on the outside of the wall, which meant that the guardians could loose their arrows and bolts without fear. Irania sent a thoughtcall to Elia to instruct her to transmit the order to fire to all the Sisters. She then yelled the same instructions directly to the Tabellarius, bypassing both Aithen and Harlion – there was *no time* for long command chains now.

Harlion was about to delay the order, when Aithen put his hand on the man's arm and shook his head, pointing at Elyana who sat on her knees in front of the palace. Harlion grunted his understanding and let Irania's order stand. Aithen now instructed Harlion to order the launch of the burdened arrows and bolts, which had been prepared earlier in the day. These had little sacs of oil attached to them, which Aithen hoped would burst upon contact with the Serpent to splash flammable liquid all over it, a liquid which would then be ignited by the Lux Baiulae's firewhorls.

While the burdened projectiles were being fetched, Elyana continued her ethereal battle with the Serpent, who did not release its hold on her despite being targeted with an interminable barrage

---

[82] Sister! How wonderful it is to find you again! Why do you call me?

of missiles of all sorts. Suddenly, Elyana screamed aloud, "Exit my head, Serpent!"

The Serpent sent its reply through the Bind, *"I will exit when I wish it, Sister."*

Elyana repeated her injunction, again and again, with a voice laden with the pain of the unending torture, "Exit!!"

A moment later, everyone began experiencing a deep, sharp headache, and doubled over or clutched their heads. The Sisters, also in the throes of pain, realized that Elyana was losing her battle, that the nebula was weakening, and that if it failed completely – and it surely would if the creature's hold on Elyana did not end soon – they would all die, as Dalima had already.

So, they mustered all the strength they could, and slowly resumed their attacks until five of them were launching any and all manner of fire at the beast, as they were capable of generating.

Their efforts paid-off, and as the Serpent switched its attention from Elyana to its attackers, the nebula regained its strength and the defenders their ability to fight – including the guardians, who began launching their burdened projectiles at the beast.

In the tower, the king straightened, rubbing his temples, and after making certain everyone around him was well, approached Elia Lux Baiula. When the woman launched her next firewhorl, she noticed a strange shimmering around the king. *I could swear this happens every time I launch fire at the Serpent. Perhaps it is some interference with the Bound Shield covering the king. I will need to mention it to Elyana once this is over – if we are all still alive.*

In fact, the king – who could not bear to simply stand there without helping – had been secretly reinforcing Elia's bound projectiles, hoping that she would not suspect anything with the stress of the battle. The members of his personal guard might notice what he was doing, but he was not worried about them saying anything.

The creature released a deafening shriek as its oil-splattered skin started burning away when it was hit with Elia's fourth firewhorl.

Tania wondered whether the Serpent's reaction might cause it to release Elyana completely, but the woman still appeared to be fighting it in her mind. The White Sash turned toward Irania and shook her head gloomily. Irania nodded and ordered the exhausted Sisters to redouble their efforts.

But despite everything, the Serpent neither fell nor retreated. Instead, the thing seemed to have let its flesh burn until the oil was gone, and then regenerated its skin. Irania wondered how Elyana and the fewer soldiers at Horn's Pass had managed to resist the creature and eventually cause it to retreat. Was this the same creature? She dared not consider the possibility that there were others of its kind.

The beast now shook itself and grayish flakes fell toward the defenders, revealing shiny, bright new skin that glowed in the fading suns. The defenders either stood there in shock or brushed themselves frantically to rid their hair and clothes of the evil matter.

The ineffectiveness of their weapons, and the exceedingly rapid recovery of the creature baffled everyone. It seemed that the Serpent did not respond to K'Tara's physical *or* biological laws, because instead of weakening as the battle went on, the creature got stronger and fiercer.

With its healing completed, the Serpent turned its thoughts to Elyana again and said threateningly, *"These Humans and all your Sisters will die tonight if you do not tell me where my quarry is."*

The beast tightened its mental grip on Elyana and she trembled again, violently. She thought that she was going to crumble and die this time. She wanted to ask for help, but her mouth would not speak, and her brain would not send, except in response to the Serpent. She could see Tania trying to help, but to no avail; Elyana was in a mental dungeon from which only the beast could release her. Still, she resisted. But the Serpent's vibrations were so much stronger than they had been at Horn's Pass. How was it possible? And the pain! The excruciating pain! Yet, Elyana managed to send a stout response to the creature, saying, *"But I will not, Beast!"*

Just then, Elia shot at the creature, but instead of a firewhorl, it was a firebolt she had generated! And it flew with such force! *How is this possible?* The bolt hit true, blackening the beast's body, and pushed it to just a few dozen meters from Mekiir's position.

The man, who had been standing next to his massive arbalest, cursing and kicking at its uselessness for the past hour, finally saw an opportunity and yelled at his assistants to load the varagoth net onto the machine. The soldiers struggled, though they were no scraggly youths, and Mekiir yelled again, to speed them up. Once the net was in place, he swiveled the bulky weapon on its axis with one swift motion, aimed and launched, and shouts of pure joy erupted when the net entrapped the creature.

Unable to beat its wings any longer, the Serpent started falling, but it forced its body into a furious twisting motion, which shredded the net and allowed the creature to reopen its wings just before hitting the ground.

Mekiir growled and kicked at the arbalest again, shoved it in anger, and punched it. Then, he turned and shook his aching fist in the beast's direction.

The rokon which was not a rokon cried-out in frustration and looked from tower to rampart, trying to decide on its next target. A moment later, it set its sights on the South Gate-tower and launched itself toward it, hoping to crush the Lux Baiula that had dared blacken its body again – he could take care of the gesticulating soldier later.

As the Serpent descended toward its new target – focused on it – its hold on Elyana weakened, and the Lux Baiula suddenly became aware of the danger to the king in the tower. She wanted to warn Elia, tell her to create a Bound Shield around the tower, or to barrage the creature with sufficient bound projectiles to stop it, but she still could not send; all she could do was listen for the inevitable with horrified, disheartened, and disbelieving anticipation.

Elyana felt herself crumble at the thought of her Sister and Octavius being crushed to death. But instead of the sounds of shattering stone or toppling tower she had expected, what Elyana heard brought a smile to her face despite the pain that the creature's hold caused her.

Indeed, when the Serpent collided with the tower, it was thrown to the side as if it were a magnet hitting an oppositely charged surface. Elia had shielded the tower! Inside the structure, a strange reverberation deafened everyone.

Aithen called to his father to ask if he was well, but he could not hear himself or anyone else, nor could anyone else in either tower hear him. It took another twenty seconds before the dampening effect dissipated and the king heard the prince's question.

The king said, "I am well Aithen, thanks to Elia Lux Baiula, though I do not like the side effects of this shield."

The Lux Baiula snorted at the king's comment, and then felt her body being drained of whatever energy remained in her.

Primus Julian, who was looking out the window searching for their foe, noticed the beast turning back around and making for the tower again, at a furious speed. He turned to the king and said urgently, "Majesty, it may be wise to retreat to the lower level. I know these walls are strong, as is the Lux Baiula's shield, but the Serpent is coming back, and it seems intent on destroying the tower – and I don't wish to experience the thing we just did again, especially since it leaves us incapacitated for a while."

The king looked out the window and agreed with his primus. He then yelled an order for everyone to get down to the lower level.

As the last of them descended, the Serpent hit both the South and North Gate-towers. The twice-bound fused stone responded with a strange stretching and returning sound, and the whole structure shook a few times. But it remained whole.

Seeing that the towers had resisted its second assault infuriated the Serpent, and it flew to an incredible height before starting down again like some gigantic bolt. Juliana Lux Baiula, who was standing on the parapet walk south of the South Gate-tower, decided to try a different weapon she remembered and shot an electric bolt at the Serpent, while the guardians continued their mostly ineffective barrage of steel arrows and bolts. But the discharge did not produce any effect whatsoever, and Juliana's eyes widened when she realized that the Serpent was now descending straight toward her. Sweat trickled down her face as she continued to exert herself, trying to stop the thing.

From her vantage, next to Elyana, Tania saw what was about to happen, and she shouted, "Juliana, get away from there!"

But Juliana did not hear, and when the creature was but a few meters above her, it released the loudest screech yet. Juliana closed her eyes and froze. She was a Purple Sash, after all, not a Red; none of them were, except for the twins who were stuck shielding the capital's citizens. How could any of them be expected to face the breath of such a creature with cold, unwavering eyes? When she felt the wind of the Serpent's beating wings, Juliana froze. Nearby guardians took courage and attacked the beast with their swords to try and keep it away from the Lux Baiula. But the creature snatched her just the same, uncaring that the soldiers had cut tears into its leathery wings, and then flew away, releasing a strange barking sound – almost a laugh – as it did so.

The king ordered everyone to desist at once. Elia, who had been expecting the order, enhanced the sound, to be sure that no one unintentionally hit Juliana.

Upon hearing the king's command, a numbing, dispiriting wave spread through the defenders' ranks. The king looked at the retreating creature and released a disheartened sigh. His son, who had run to him, asked in a voice filled with fear and anger, "Father, what do we do?"

"I am thinking, son, I am thinking!" The king turned toward his primus, Julian – the poor woman's brother. He knew something had to be done to save her from whatever end awaited her. But what could they do? What could *he* do? Still, he had to do something. He tried to reassure Julian with a confident expression.

Julian looked back with a look of absolute desperation in his eyes.

The king straightened himself with a snap, having made a decision, and said, "We need to call it, draw its attention, and stop it from doing whatever it is intending to do to Juliana. We need to give it what it wants. Lux Baiula, transmit this to the Serpent: "Creature! I am –""

Before the king could finish giving his message to Elia, Aithen objected, "Father, you cannot –, you cannot…reveal yourself to the Serpent. It may not be safe. It *is* not safe! And though we must do everything we can to save Juliana," and Aithen gave the primus a pointed look to show him he meant what he said, "you cannot endanger yourself in this way!"

Surprisingly, the king did not argue, and responded with a growl, "Damn these shackles! All right then. Lux Baiula, ask the Serpent what it wants, and then ask Irania Lux Baiula to get here at once so she can help negotiate Juliana's release!"

Octavius expected the Lux Baiula to execute the order instantly, but instead, he noted a blank stare on her face and asked, "What are you waiting for, woman?!"

The appellation drew shocked stares from everyone, except from the Lux Baiula who replied, "Sire, I am deciding how to address the thing."

"How to –?! Say "Serpent!"; what else would you call it?"

And without any further delay, Elia projected her voice so that it reached the beast loudly and clearly.

The Serpent, who was now near the Temple of Aiala, stopped and turned, standing in midair and slowly flapping its black leathery wings as it held onto its now unconscious hostage – or perhaps soon-to-be victim if their tactic failed. It searched the palace wall for the one who might wish to confront him. But it did not see any such person, and it growled and shouted aloud, for the first time, "Who calls me and faces me not?"

The Serpent's hateful, unnatural voice made everyone's skin crawl, whether they be civilians, guardians, Lux Baiulae or royals. The creature repeated its question, irritated that no one had answered yet.

Inside the tower, Elia said to Octavius, "Majesty, I need to go out into the open."

Octavius did not respond but paced furiously in the small space of the tower's lower level, debating whether to go face the Serpent himself, let the Lux Baiula do it, or wait for Irania when the Purple Sash finally arrived.

As another angry and threatening shout came from the Serpent, Elia said urgently, "Sire, one of us needs to go out there, now."

Turning toward Irania, Octavius said, "Indeed. Lux Baiula?"

"I will go, Sire. Elia, follow me."

And everyone in the tower waited anxiously for a new battle, a psychological battle, to begin. Aithen and Octavius looked at each other apprehensively. They knew Irania was a good negotiator; she was Urbs Lucis's chief representative in the capital, and they had frequently seen her build agreement between diametrically opposed parties. But the parties had always been humanoids, beings imbued with some rationality. Could anyone reason with this abomination?

Irania and Elia arrived at the top of the tower puffing. They stepped out; Irania looked at Elia, seeking confirmation that the Yellow Sash was ready to project her voice, and when the woman nodded, Irania began. She said, "Creature, I am Irania Lux Baiula, responsible for the well-being of my Sisters here, and I wish to discuss the release of the woman you are holding."

The Serpent projected its response with unmistakable scorn, "You are another Alterintrant."

"Yes, I am."

"It matters not. And know that I am not a creature, but the *Alis Domini* [83]."

Irania replied, "My apologies…Alis Domini."

The Serpent accepted the apology begrudgingly and proceeded to make its demand, "Now, I wish to speak with the Luxor among you."

"I do not understand, Alis Domini. The Luxor?"

"Yes! One of them is here, among you. Do not attempt to deceive me, witch!"

"I need a moment to consider your request, Alis Domini. But first, I need you to release my associate."

The Serpent's bellowed response caused cries to rise from the civilians, and jaws to tighten among the defenders, "You are in no position to dictate my actions, witch! If I release her now, it will be only to send her to her death below. Therefore, bring me the *Luxor*!"

Irania had a feeling that this conversation was not going to go well, and that it should therefore no longer be projected for everyone to hear, so she told Elia to stop enhancing her voice, and turned to the king – who was watching from the fenestrations down below – to tell him that she was going to continue her negotiations through the Bind.

Octavius replied he understood, but said, "Irania, you must insist again. The Serpent has been looking for…for this Luxor for many fourths now, and if it thinks he is here, we have the advantage. Do confirm that it is right about a Luxor being here, but then ask it to deposit Juliana in front of the palace gates. I will have three guardians wait for her there."

Irania took a deep breath and tried again, sending the request through the Bind, *"Alis Domini, we are willing to discuss the matter of the Luxor, but first, I ask that you bring back my associate and safely deposit her in front of the gates, here. You obviously outmatch us, and we will have no choice but to discuss your request, but we will not do so if you kill our Sister. Three guardians will…"*

While Irania discussed terms with the Serpent, Elyana suddenly moaned, and rubbed her head. Tania looked at her with an uncertain smile. Somehow, the Serpent's exchange with Irania had caused it to release its hold on Elyana.

"Elyana, can you hear me? Elyana?"

---

[83] Alis Domini: Lord's Wings.

Elyana's voice was weak, but she replied, "Yes. What is happening?"

Tania replied, "Sister, the Serpent has captured Juliana and Irania is negotiating her release; the Serpent wishes to speak with the…Luxor. I am notte sure what it means."

"We…cannot…negotiate."

"You must be mad!"

"High King Octavius is –. We…cannot negotiate. Please tell Irania."

Tania felt her head spin. "Elyana, you cannotte be serious?!"

With sudden and surprising strength, Elyana yelled, "Tania, now!"

Without further argument, Tania relayed Elyana's directive to Irania and Elia both, in case the Purple Sash should not receive her thoughtcall promptly.

As a matter of fact, Irania did not receive the thoughtcall, but Elia did, and – unable to believe the orders – she sent a stinging reply, back to Tania.

Tania repeated Elyana's orders, and this time, they did reach Irania who turned to Elia with incredulous eyes and all sorts of expletives unbecoming of a Lux Baiula. But the Serpent was sending to her again, and she returned to her negotiation with the creature after shooting an icy stare in Elyana's direction.

Elia, unsure what to do, turned toward the tower and shouted, "Majesty! You must speak with Elyana! She just had Tania instruct Administrator Irania to *not* negotiate the release of our Sister!"

Primus Julian shot a disbelieving, stunned look at the king, while Jashan, Almiar, Kiron and Merr looked at their commanding officer with consternation on their faces. Julian yelled, "What does she mean, we cannot negotiate? It is my sister that thing holds in its talons!"

Octavius interjected, "Primus, calm yourself. You know Elyana's reasons."

"I know, Sire. But there must be something we can do."

Elia continued, without answering Julian's question, "Sire, Elyana also wishes me to tell you that you *cannot* reveal yourself to the Serpent, let alone surrender yourself to it."

Octavius growled his frustration and kicked at a stool. Just then, Elyana released a frightening cry, which was loud enough to be

441

heard even by those in the tower. Aithen became alarmed and ran to the fenestration to ask Elia what was happening to Elyana.

Elia replied, "My Prince, it appears that whatever had distracted the Serpent from her, no longer does."

Just as Elia finished her sentence, Irania turned toward the tower and called the king. She said, "Sire, the Serpent will not release our Sister unless we...unless we let it speak with you. It believes you are one of the Luxori it has been searching for. But as Elia has told you, Elyana has instructed me, actually *demanded*, that I not let you interact with it. And I must admit...that I agree with her."

A dreadful silence crushed everyone as the king considered the situation. And everyone hoped against logic, that he would decide what was right.

When the king finally came to a decision, he straightened his back and spoke with a commanding, resolute tone. "I will not let anyone die for me in this way, and it is certain that Juliana will if we refuse the Serpent's request. If we accept, she will live, while my fate is uncertain. But I am ready to bet that it will *not* kill me, and if it should take me, you can always come res–"

Before the king could finish his sentence, the most awful "No!" rose from five Lux Baiulae.

The Serpent was now above the grounds, and after releasing another angry cry, it hurled Juliana onto the marbled ground in front of the palace. Laranis Lux Baiula, who was on the northern side of the North-Gate tower, tried to form a shield around the woman, but reacted too late, and Juliana hit the ground with the sickening sound of crushed bones and splattering blood.

A gut-wrenching howl rose from Primus Julian when he saw what had happened. Incredibly, he jumped out the skylight of the lower level, which was still several meters from the ground, and – ignoring the sound of fracturing bone in his tibia – got up and ran toward his sister. There, he kneeled by her limp body, which was disfigured by awkwardly bent legs and a crushed skull. At first, he did not seem to notice the condition of his sister's face, and he caressed it, unaware of the blood and splinters of bone sticking out through the flesh. Then, something happened, and he cried out in abject rage, turning a face contorted by hate toward Elyana, and by incomprehension toward the king. Elyana did not see – could not see – but the king did, and he repressed the feelings of guilt and anger which risked overwhelming him as he took in the scene and turned a tortured face toward Elyana.

As for the Serpent, it shrieked in response, then spoke again, addressing itself to both Irania and Elyana, in its strange echoing voice, "Sisters! Know that the next time I return, you will all fall should you try to resist me! You have witnessed my strength; it has grown in the short time since I first met the one of you, and it will continue to do so with every village and town I dispatch, until we meet again. The next time, you *will* give me what I want!"

With that, it turned around and with one final shriek, flew away, heading west.

With the Serpent gone, the king, his men and Elia ran to Julian and his sister. When they approached and saw Juliana's condition, the horrified looks on their faces lifted the veil shielding Julian's mind, and the realization that he could no longer recognize his sister's once beautiful face hit him like a varagoth. The next moment, he retched and emptied his stomach on the ground, then he took his sister's hand and remained there sitting, with his mind closed to the outside world for a long while.

* * *

The night, in Furan City, was spent taking care of the dead and wounded, as well as releasing the clerics from their caves and Senator Sur'Elando from the palace. Officers and guardians had been instructed to not answer any questions anyone might have that night, but to reassure everyone that the king would address the capital's citizens soon.

The Lux Baiulae's first task, however, had been to see to the prompt transfer of Juliana's memories. So, after electing Krpta Lux Baiula as the Receiver, and delicately prying the woman's body from her catatonic brother, Tania Lux Baiula performed the sacred Memory Transfer ritual. Krpta spent the next two days in isolation, integrating the other woman's memories, and trying to come to terms with those that Juliana had of her, from the time when the two of them were in training at Urbs Lucis. Indeed, memories charged with feelings toward the Receiver were especially difficult to deal with, whether positive or negative, but some of Juliana's memories were particularly uncomfortable to Krpta.

Dalima's memories were unfortunately lost to all and forever due to the horrific fate of her brain, but her remains as well as those of Juliana would be preserved and brought back to Urbs Lucis where they would be honored following the Order's ancient Ascension Ceremony.

**

The days following the attack on Furan City were very difficult ones, and everyone, from king to guardian to commoner suffered from doubt, and anger, and fear for one reason or another. The king was furious with Elyana for taking the decision to negotiate or not away from him, while Primus Julian wished that Elyana had been the one in the Serpent's claws, and Aithen strained to look her in the eyes.

What revolted everyone even more was learning that while Irania, the king, and the others were discussing the Serpent's request, it had communicated with Elyana and told her to convince her friends to accede to its demand lest it begin slowly crushing every bone of its hostage's body, and that Elyana had taken it upon herself to send a categorical, final refusal to the Serpent, the refusal which had incensed it and caused it to pitch the poor Juliana toward the ground, there to meet her death.

Irania, and a few others, understood what Elyana had done and the necessity of it, despite its horrible consequence. The king himself, understood it, though he hated the principles upon which the decision was based, principles which bound him more surely than shackles would, and which had now twice caused the death of others when they might have otherwise been saved.

Aithen too understood. But that understanding was of little comfort to Elyana in the face of the disgust they all felt, despite their better judgements.

Aside from that, Octavius and Harlion had to contend with an infuriated First Cleric, who had been told by his little spy that the king had sacrificed large numbers of civilians to the Serpent by assembling them in the plazas in front of Domus Lucis and the Senate House. This was obviously untrue, but the cleric was going to use it against him, regardless. And so he did, and an unfortunate vocal minority of the capital's citizens – encouraged by the clerics of Aiala – made endless petitions in the king's court, demanding to know why the king had sacrificed his subjects to the creature. This same minority was also spied assembling in the Temple of Aiala in the night. Harlion's man did not know what the meetings were about, but the captain knew they could only bode ill, and this, most of all – aside from the disappearance of Frumentarius Parok – gave Harlion and the entire Secret Service a great, big jolt and sense of failure – and a new worry.

But on the third day following the attack, after shock, denial and anger had begun to turn into reconstruction and acceptance, a semblance of calm returned to the capital. In the Private Audience Chamber, the king, his advisors, and Irania finally agreed that Elyana could not have done anything else: the king's life – a leader's life – could not and would not ever be traded for another, as terrible as the immediate consequence might be. For indeed, if they began doing that, the kingdom would soon find itself leaderless, and no better off as vicious and immoral enemies subjugated the entire population.

The king and his advisors also agreed that the kingdom needed to be put on high alert, and that the Furanry's training needed to be completed in very short time – or else.

As for Irania and Elyana, they realized that unless the Yellow Sashate found a way to train Sisters of other Sashes in the generation of nebulae, the Order would be effectively crippled given that those of the Red Sash would be unable to use their most effective powers against the Serpent. The women therefore decided to leave for Urbs Lucis to make the case to the Magna Mater, ahead of the Gathering scheduled for the Fourth of Septimus [84].

On the First of Septimus, then, the two women left on furanback with two Royal Guardians to carry the bodies of the deceased, as well as with Krpta Lux Baiula and the Zebulonian.

Krpta Lux Baiula would be taking part in the Ascension Ceremony as the receiver of Juliana's knowledge, while the Zebulonian was there at Elyana's invitation so that her Sisters of the Yellow and White Sashates might further investigate his vibrations. Indeed, because of the continued rumors of the planned invasion by Zebulonia, Elyana felt that it was necessary for the Order to learn all it could about the way in which Zebulonians accessed and used the Bind, so that they might then be better prepared to defend against the

---

[84] Septimus: Seventh month.

445

Janarae whom Lusk Methrim had painted as the most frightful humanoids he knew – aside from Zebula herself.

Lusk Methrim had objected to Elyana's request, of course, saying that he had sworn his service to the king, and not to the Sisterhood. But Octavius – who naturally agreed with Elyana – reminded the Zebulonian that he had indeed come to serve him, and in particular to help him prepare against Queen Zebula, which now meant going to Urbs Lucis.

Octavius and Aithen watched the departing party, their minds conflicted with uncertainty and hope. As the furans started to take off, Aithen caught Elyana's glance and felt his heart skip as it did each time she looked at him. He had been hoping she would look toward him, but now that she had, he could only give her a small smile, but he put as much hope in it as he could manage. Elyana made a small nod in his direction, then kicked her furan and a moment later, she was following the others across the sky, heading toward Urbs Lucis. Aithen felt his heart sink as he wondered how long it would be before he would see her again, even as he fought back conflicted thoughts.

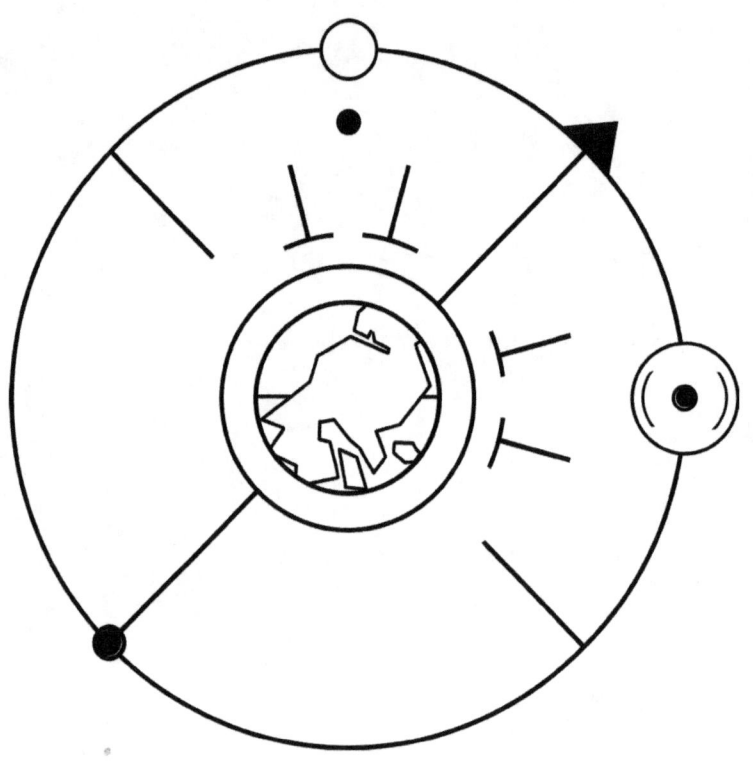

XXVI THE ASCENSION

The party's arrival in the busy, but typically quiet inner-sanctum of the capital of the Light caused a stir. The sight of the two furanteams carrying a bundle each covered with the Flaming Suns of the Order, as well as that of a most intriguing, dazzling male advancing atop another furan, caused everyone to drop whatever they were doing and give inquiring looks at the three Sisters, hoping to learn something from their grave expressions or perhaps from a Sending. But the women did not say anything, either verbally, through the Bind, or with any meaningful gesture or expression as they continued their slow advance toward the palace.

In the center of the courtyard there stood two immense spinning spheres representing the Flaming Suns. A Junior of the Purple Sash stood by the sphere representing the Blue Sun, while a girl of the Red Sash stood by the other sphere, each with her head down, eyes closed, and hands facing the sphere whose flames they were sustaining. Junior Sisters of the four Sashes took turns nourishing the blue flames and the golden flames, day and night.

When the party reached the staircase in front of the magnificent gold and blue palace, a startling woman, First Barrier Laiella, approached Irania and saluted her with a stern nod.

The First Barrier was the officer in charge of security at Urbs Lucis. Barriers were raised from the Red Sash and were among the deadliest of the Sisterhood. To the contrary of their other Sisters, they were armed and wore tight-fitting clothes, suited for physical combat, though they used the Bind whenever appropriate. Their uniform was composed of long, fine-plated red breeches, a deep red tunic constructed of narrow, interlocking plates, a black baldric atop that, which contained a short sword known as a gladius, and black leather vambraces and rerebraces, which were embroidered with the Flaming Suns. Laiella's rank was marked by the golden embroidery surrounding the Flaming Suns on her rerebraces. But the flamboyance of her uniform was nothing next to her own disquieting natural appearance. A native Bremin Islander, the woman looked fierce indeed with the thick red hair, pale green skin, and slate gray eyes typical of her people.

With the short side of her right fist on her abdomen, the officer said, "Welcome home, Sisters. We have been awaiting you."

Irania replied, "Thank you, First Barrier. The bodies of those who were taken from us lie beneath our cloak. Would you see to it that they are taken to the Elevation Chapel and given to Zilla Lux Baiula?"

After a very short moment of silence during which the officer seemed to consider the meaning of the violent death of two Sisters, she replied, "I will, Administrator." Then, nodding toward the Zebulonian, "And what will you do with the man?"

"Elyana Lux Baiula will take him to the White Sashate. I, on the other hand, must go to the Magna Mater immediately."

Laiella grunted, then turned to Krpta and asked, "And you Sister?"

Krpta replied with an almost perfect northeastern Alvinorian accent, that she was going to visit her Sisters in the Purple Sashate, ever emphasizing only the last syllable of the word "Sashate."

"Very well. You are free to enter, Sisters."

And with that, Irania exchanged a few parting words with her companions and quickly climbed up the ornate staircase to go to Krystiana.

The First Barrier approached Elyana and gave her an acknowledging nod. She knew Elyana, of course, given that the woman had been the most powerful Red Sash before transferring to the Purple Sashate, and given that she remained one of the most powerful, if not *the* most powerful Lux Baiula in existence.

"Sister, it is an honor to have you in Urbs Lucis again."

"Thank you, First Barrier, although I wish it were under different circumstances."

The woman gave Elyana an understanding nod, after which she ordered a male attendant in black liveries to take the furans to the stables, and finally left with the Royal Guardians to take the bodies of the deceased to the Elevation Chapel, where Sisters of the White Sashate would prepare them for the ceremony.

The guardians followed from a distance. Laiella suspected why: she was one of the most dangerous women in Alvinoria. But she did not care what they thought.

Elyana and Krpta glanced once more at the cloak-covered bodies, and then started up the long staircase, with Lusk following a few steps behind. It had been months since the last time Elyana had been here, and climbing the staircase brought back all sorts of welcome memories to her. She loved Urbs Lucis and all it represented; she loved its atmosphere; and she still relished the unending opportunities for learning – even after nearly fifty years of her Elevation – afforded by both the presence of so many other Lux Baiulae, as well as by the city's library, the largest in all the kingdom.

In fact, the library was probably what she loved the most about Urbs Lucis, and up until she had left for Furan City to become Octavius's advisor, she had sat nightly in the soft lacora chairs of the paper-filled, leather-smelling building, reading one book after another. Upon arriving in the capital, she had been a little saddened by the much smaller library though it was the third largest in the kingdom – that of the Magisteri's College in Antar being the second largest. But Elyana had requested and received permission to return to her Alma Mater for a month every year, and that had brought her a modicum of happiness back, for indeed the yearly pilgrimage enabled her to re-immerse herself in the City of Lights' vast collection, as well as learn what new things she could by assisting one Sister or another in her research. She wondered now, as she climbed and thought about these things, what drove a person to continue learning. Someday, she would have to investigate *this*.

When the three visitors reached the top of the stairs, a spectacular atrium met their gaze. It had a high, intricately carved and beautifully painted vaulted ceiling representing the evolution of the Order, as well as Living Lamps on every wall. The grand staircase at the far end of the atrium led to the second floor where the Magna Mater's offices were located. Four stone-looking Barriers guarded that staircase. The entrance to each of the Sashates was located in one of the four corners of the atrium. The Sashates were identified by the statue of the founder of each respective Assembly.

Krpta took leave of Elyana and walked toward the entrance to the Offices of the Purple Sash Assembly, which was located in the near right corner of the building. Elyana, on the other hand, turned left to go to the White Sashate. Indeed, before leaving Furan City, she and Irania had decided to deliver Lusk Methrim to Saara Lux Baiula, Head of the White Sash Assembly, because her age – and the particular skills she had – made her the least vulnerable of them all to Lusk's discomforting ways. This in turn, would give her the best chances to learn from him all the things they needed to know.

Upon entering the White Sashate, Elyana was greeted by Praefecta Saara's personal aid. The woman was a plump, Nonsensing, low-ranking Shadiner with a bubbly temperament, and heavy earrings stretching her ear lobes, as was typical of Shadiner men and women. She knew Elyana, of course, and welcomed her effusively, eyeing her male companion every so often. Elyana introduced him as Master Methrim of Zebulonia, causing the woman to utter a little grunt of surprise, immediately followed by an involuntary swooning stare at the man.

"Dame Nila, would you inform the Praefecta Medicas that I am here to see her?"

Dame Nila snapped her stare away from the Zebulonian, and turned to Elyana, embarrassed. "Certainly, Lux Baiula. I will be back in a moment." And the plump woman left with slightly more hurry than was appropriate, almost brushing Lusk Methrim as she passed him.

I really hope Saara will be able to resist whatever it is Master Methrim exudes – Dame Nila surely can't.

Elyana started when she heard Lusk, who had been quiet since arriving in Urbs Lucis, "She seems like a very jovial woman. From Shadin City, I suppose – unless there are others in Alvinoria with such ear lobes?"

Elyana was irritated by the man's lack of propriety and replied with a curt whisper. "No, there are not. She is indeed Shadiner."

As soon as Elyana finished her sentence, Dame Nila returned and announced, "Lux Baiula, the Praefecta will receive you." And, indicating the thick red wooden door, she added, "You may enter."

The Praefecta's office was filled with an exquisite tapestry of drawings of the Human body, as well as with an array of petri dishes adorning every shelf and desk, and containing preserved microbial colonies of all kinds, colors and textures. The woman was sitting behind her desk, tapping her fingers in frustration as she reviewed notes in a thick book. Her eyes lit up when she heard Elyana enter.

She gave Elyana a raspy but warm welcome, walking toward her and taking her arms to embrace her, "Elyana! It is good to see you!"

"Likewise, Praefecta."

452

"Will you ever lose that formality, Elyana?"

"I have too much respect for you to ever lose it...Praefecta."

"Hmm, indeed." Then, turning her attention to Lusk, she said, "Your companion *looks* to be a...Zebulonian."

Lusk gave Saara a respectful nod and said, "I am *indeed*, Zebulonian, Praefecta. I am Lusk Methrim, recently appointed as a Healer to the Royal Guard."

"Ah, you are the one Tania Lux Baiula informed me about."

Elyana said, "The selfsame man."

With an honest smile, the ancient Lux Baiula said, "So, please tell me what it is that you wish of me, Elyana." With a grimmer tone, the praefecta added, "Once this is taken care of, I will want you to remain to speak to me about what happened in Furan City."

It took fifteen minutes for Elyana to explain what she desired of the White Sashes, and particularly of Saara, speaking in carefully coded terms when referring to his discomforting ways. In the end, Saara agreed to take charge of Lusk and to probe him further. As for the foreigner, he agreed to share what information he had about Zebulonian Binding skills in general, and about the Janarae's skills, in particular.

It seemed to Elyana that Lusk had been frustrated at times during those fifteen minutes, that he appeared to be irritated when the older Lux Baiula did not respond to him in the same way that other people did, such as by dropping their guard or giving in to his requests. Elyana herself had made two perplexing comments in response to statements by Lusk, causing Saara to stare at her with surprise. Elyana hid her embarrassment when she realized what she had said, but she was relieved to see that Saara was unaffected by the man. *Irania and I have made one good decision, at least, by bringing Lusk to her.*

After releasing Lusk into the care of two Barriers with orders to quarter him in the guest house, the Praefecta took Elyana by the arm and invited her for a stroll through the palace's gardens. There, she asked Elyana to recount what happened in Furan City, which the Purple Sash did in great detail, save for the parts involving her. The Praefecta listened with grave, genuine concern, worried about the Medics' Assembly's readiness to deal with the mental injuries the Serpent was inflicting upon its victims. When Elyana finished her

453

account, Saara took a deep breath and nodded to herself, having determined what she must do to ready the White Sashate.

After the two of them strolled quietly for a moment, Elyana turned to the old Praefecta and voiced a hesitant, "Saara."

Saara turned to Elyana, with her hands crossed in front of her white robe, and said, "What is it my child? I can tell something else is bothering you."

Elyana sighed and said, "I am worried that my Sensing ability is weakening – or that something is affecting it."

"Why do you think this?"

With unusual self-consciousness and candor – her concern visible in the lines of her face – Elyana told the Praefecta of her inability to sense the malevolent vibrations which others had been feeling, and of the sudden loss of her ability to sense vibrations she had initially felt in Master Methrim. Saara listened and nodded, her own expression neither worried nor dismissive.

When Elyana was done, Saara crossed her arms on her chest and brought her right hand to her lips while she considered the "young" Lux Baiula's concerns. Elyana waited with slightly fidgeting hands. Finally, the Praefecta said, "May I probe you, Elyana?"

Elyana nodded and the Praefecta Medicas proceeded with her test. Elyana did not close her eyes but watched the woman anxiously, trying to decipher the meaning of the varying expressions on the Praefecta's face. *Why did she frown just now? Did she find something wrong? And now? Why are her lips turning down?* So went Elyana thoughts until Saara opened her eyes and spoke again.

"I do not believe the two problems are related, Elyana. I have probed your brain's telesensory cortex and found nothing amiss there. You are, after all, neither a Yellow Sash nor a White Sash, and though you do have strong Sensing and Binding skills, your ability to sense vibrations outside the normal range *is* limited. This means that your inability to sense the unknown vibrations others have sensed is nothing to be concerned with. As for why you cannot sense the vibrations you first received from Master Methrim, I cannot say. It is possible that you misinterpreted what you felt when you first saw him –" Saara paused when her former student gave her an offended look, "I am not trying to insult you, Elyana. I simply mean that your exhausted mind may have erred." The Praefecta Medicas regarded the younger Lux Baiula with caring eyes, as Elyana's facial expressions went from irked, to uncertain, and finally to accepting.

Saara grabbed Elyana's hands and said, "If you wish me to probe you further, stop by later – I will take another look."

Elyana shook her head and replied, "No, thank you Praefecta; you may be right. I still have not fully recovered from the exhaustion of the last battle against the Serpent, so trying to evaluate my Sensing skills now is probably futile. But if I still have any concerns once I am fully restored, I *will* let you know."

Saara chuckled and the two women parted ways to prepare for the afternoon's meetings.

***

What the Magna Mater and the Praefectae learned on that day from their Sisters from Furan City stunned everyone. They realized that unless they unraveled very soon the true nature of the threat facing them, and unless they promptly put in place the required response, the world was doomed.

The White Sashes who had prepared the bodies of their deceased Sisters for the Ascension Ceremony told their leader that they had confirmed at least one thing during their autopsy of Dalima's brain: the type of injury her brain had suffered was exactly as described in the medical books from the time of the Dark Battle, an injury which had been caused by the Serpent as well as by Noctiferus's elite assassins using a vibration known then as the *Quatiô* but now referred to as Dark Energy Brain Surge Attack, or DEBSA.

Elyana spoke now, her tone most serious. "Mater, it is critical that we immediately begin exploring the skill required to generate nebulae with the goal to dissociate it from the offensive skills, so that we may then train Sisters of all Sashes in its use..." Elyana thought of what the White Sash coroners had reported, and added, "...especially if we are going to have to defend ourselves against the possible emergence of *assassins* capable of using the Quatiô."

Ramela said, "That is not something that can be easily achieved, Elyana, if at all. It might be easier to simply train more Red Sashes."

Larca replied with her usual acidic tone, "You forget *Ramela* that women with the atomic constitution to become Red Sashes are quite rare to begin with, and if we are to increase our *offensive* capabilities, we cannot cripple my Sisters with this shielding skill."

Ramela, not letting the other Praefecta's remark upset her, retorted, "But as far as I know, you have not recruited a new Red Sash in many years, and not because you cannot find women with the proper constitution but simply because you have not needed to increase your ranks in a long time. This means that you might actually be able to find quite a large number of good candidates for your Sash, now."

Krystiana tapped her fingers and said, "You may be right, Ramela, but I actually agree with Larca and Elyana in this case. We need to increase the Red Sash ranks *and* find a way to develop the skill to shield against the Quatiô in all Sisters. But such an effort will require time and funds, neither of which we may have much of."

As Head of the Purple Sash Assembly, Ramela was also responsible for the Sisterhood's Treasury. She said, "Well, as of last month, our Treasury had sufficient funds to support Urbs Lucis as well as our Sisters abroad through the rest of the summer and fall, but I am afraid that with the need now to send Sisters across the kingdom to help defend towns and villages against the Serpent, there are not enough funds to support a recruitment effort such as the one we are discussing."

Krystiana did not respond to that but continued to tap her fingers pensively. "Saara, Bilena, how long do you think you will need to figure out a way to isolate this shielding skill?"

Saara looked at her colleague, and replied for both, "A month, perhaps, Magna Mater."

"Very well, a month – earlier if you can, because you will then be needed to help test the new recruits for the Red Sashate."

Saara's and Bilena's chests heaved with unexpressed pessimism, but they nonetheless replied with assenting nods; they understood what was at stake here, or at least they understood as much as anyone did at this point.

Krystiana continued, turning back to the Praefecta Consuasores, "Ramela, I want you to call back all non-essential Sisters from abroad; that will be a start to save us some coin." Ramela's face twisted itself with the significance of such a recall. But Krystiana continued, "You will also demand immediate payment from any and all debtors for the Bind-wrought products [85] we provide them, and I want you to bring me options to dramatically increase our revenues – any options."

Ramela held back a shudder but accepted her instructions, and then glanced at the other Praefectae who looked back with stony or worried faces.

Although Krystiana was aware of the agitation the women felt at this moment, whether they expressed it or not, she merely nodded in satisfaction and looked at the time disc on the wall. It indicated Seven Hours after Highsun. She said, "Sisters, sundown is only three hours away; it is time we prepare for the ceremony. We will resume our deliberations in two days, on the day of the Gathering."

The women stood, nodded respectfully and exited Krystiana's office to go and prepare themselves for the ceremony. Larca exited by herself, ahead of everyone; Irania and Krpta went with Ramela, and Saara left with Bilena. When Elyana passed in front of her long-time friend, Krystiana put a hand on her and held her back a moment.

She asked quietly, "Do you think Saara and Bilena stand a chance at resolving the problem with the nebula?"

"I do not know, Krystiana, but if someone can, it is Saara…so long as she can get Larca's cooperation given that they will need to probe the twins. I will also submit to the testing, of course."

"Well, finding ways to develop the skill in other women is what Larca wants Saara to do anyway, isn't it? But I know that she is likely to tell Saara and Bilena to solve the problem without interfering with her acolytes' duties."

Elyana nodded, and Krystiana added, "I will make certain Larca cooperates and gives leave to the twins and any others who may be needed, to assist Saara and Bilena in their investigations."

Elyana nodded and waited for Krystiana to speak again. But her friend simply looked at her with wishful eyes, making her a little uncomfortable. She asked, "What is it, Krystiana?"

The Magna Mater gave a little sigh and replied, "I find myself wishing that I could appoint a Manu Dextra [86] to assist me, and counsel me."

---

[85] Bind-wrought products were objects created by Sisters of the Yellow Sash, and sold to those who could afford them, such as reinforced walls, reinforced doors, poison detectors, Living Lamps, etc.

[86] Manu Dextra: Right Hand

Elyana felt her stomach tighten, and she said with a similar tightness in her voice, "And you would like that person to be me…"

"I would, Elyana, because I trust none more than you. You are rational and have a broader understanding of the capabilities and weaknesses of our Order than most other women. You also hold in your mind some of the most valuable memories any of us have, and they may prove critical as we prepare to face what is likely to be the greatest challenge of our era."

Elyana's face betrayed her reservations about that, but she nodded, if reluctantly.

Krystiana continued. "I know that your oath to serve the high king must be respected. I should be very grateful to you if you would, nevertheless, consider my request and let me know by tomorrow what your decision is. Do not worry if you decide to decline; I know that whatever decision you make, it will be the best and perhaps the only decision you can make."

Feeling the weight of the Magna Mater's request on her, Elyana replied, "I will contact Tania, and ask that she meet me in the Bind with the king present so that I may discuss this with him, Mater. I will give you my decision by the morning."

"Thank you, Elyana." Then, rubbing her hands together, she added, "Best we get ready for the Ceremony. I will see you later, Elyana." And with that, Elyana left her friend, while Krystiana walked to the spheres on her desk, pensive and troubled.

***

"Greatness, I understand your desires, and that is why I continue to advise you, though others might have discarded me a long time ago."

"Yes, you do understand me, Nihildrina [87]," replied the woman as she passed the chaise upon which her lover was sleeping half naked. She turned to look at the boy, and added distractedly, "That you do."

"I do, Greatness, and this too I understand: that you must prepare to invade Alvinoria as soon as Quartus [88] has passed. We need their men because the cloning of women can no longer be sustained, and

---

[87] Nihildrina: Zebulonian for 'daughter of none.'
[88] Quartus: The fourth month.

Zebulonian males are unfit to restore our creatic [89] balance; centuries of delegating their production to the lower classes have seen to that."

"Hmm, and I still wonder how and why my ancestor was put upon this path. Wasn't it the first of your line who convinced her of the wisdom of the practice?"

An imperceptible tremor rushed through Nihildrina. This was not the time to lose her position in Zebula's court. She said, "The practice of virgocreatio was and remains sound, Greatness, but it is the rejuvenation of our lines that has suffered, and that we must –"

"That?"

"Which – which we must now correct."

Zebula regarded her advisor with an uncomfortably scrutinizing look. After a moment, she said, "You know Nihildrina, you have been making these types of mistakes more and more frequently. In fact, ever since you began spending more time in your sanctuary than in court. You should really have a healer probe you. But please finish your thought."

The accusation sent another tremor through Nihildrina's body, a tremor quickly replaced by the irritation she felt every time she heard Zebula make an illogical statement. Indeed, her grammatical errors were not caused *by* her more frequent seclusion, but her seclusion was a consequence of these errors, errors which she needed to address urgently, and not because it was imperative she maintain perfect grammar, but because of the underlying defect those errors pointed to. Nihildrina said, "Thank you, Greatness. You are right, of course, and I will have Zeron probe me."

"Perhaps you should have my Private Healer probe you this time."

Nihildrina repressed another alarm and said, "Thank you, Greatness, but that will not be necessary. Zeron is capable of finding and treating whatever ill is affecting me, and I promise my condition will be resolved."

Zebula nodded uncertainly, but accepted her advisor's assurances nevertheless, and Nihildrina breathed a silent sigh of relief, after which she returned to her earlier remark. "As I was saying, Greatness, it is essential we take a new approach to rejuvenating our

---

[89] Creatic: Refers to the molecular instructions which determine the development of an organism.

lines and doing so will require that we obtain males from compatible race – from *a* compatible race." Nihildrina silently cursed herself, but continued before the queen, who had just made a small frown, interrupted her again. "As you know, the Alvinorians are the only other race close enough to ours to ensure a successful infusion of new creatics into our bloodlines. Of course, as you already suspect, the conquest of Alvinoria will not be without cost, but all the data I have, and all the scenarios I have run, lead me to the same conclusion: that we will be successful."

Zebula nodded slowly and smiled, said, "I like your confidence, Nihildrina, and you may be right about the need for new blood. You may assemble my generals to begin the planning in true. But please ensure that you quickly resolve this issue you have, or I may be forced to replace you with your daughter sooner than at the Great Succession."

Myriad alarms rang inside Nihildrina, but she remained composed, as before, though her sense of self-preservation wanted her to run – or fight. But the latter was not an option she was allowed.

Having thus concluded their audience, Zebula sent her Royal Surgeon and Eternal Advisor away, and went to sit by her lover. As she sat near him and looked at his form, a shadow of disappointment and resentment covered her face. She had really hoped to use *him* to rejuvenate her own bloodline.

***

The solemnity of the Ascension Ceremony that night quieted even the Chirpers. Four Yellow Sashes, one in each corner of the plaza, banished the winds and kept all insects and other animals at bay and silent. The leaves of trees and other plants still fluttered outside the inner sanctum, but their rustling was not heard here.

In the center of the courtyard stood the Magna Mater, the four Praefectae, and Krpta Lux Baiula, forming a semi-circle around the bodies of Dalima and Juliana Lux Baiulae. The latter were laid atop lacora beds placed in front of the Flaming Suns, and were wrapped in translucent dresses with interwoven white, yellow, purple, and red threads representing the loss that the entire Sisterhood had suffered as a result of their death.

The bodies seemed almost alive thanks to the treatment they had received in the Elevation Chapel. Indeed, the medics had warmed

460

the bodies sufficiently to cause the blood to flow back into the skin, enabling them to erase the signs of torture from Dalima's visage, and the signs of the fall from Juliana's face. They had also reoxygenated their blood to give it a red color. None of this brought the women back to life of course, but it certainly improved their appearance, which helped the living deal with the deaths.

All around the courtyard, Novices, Juniors and full Sisters, as well as the city's two thousand inhabitants looked on, in silence, waiting for the Ascension of the two dead Sisters' bodies.

Krystiana signaled the Juniors attending the Flaming Suns, and suddenly the spheres began to accelerate, while the blue and golden flames grew in intensity around them, giving rise to faint crackling sounds – the first sounds of the Ceremony. The onlookers released quiet gasps.

Krystiana began, her powerful voice resonating through the plaza with a sad note. "Magna K'Tara, congregamur ut dare tibi sororibus nostris, eos qui mortui sunt tibi servandum. Sorores, nostris mentibus nunc nos ligare! [90]"

The six women now began entering the Bind, while all the Alterintrants in attendance connected themselves to their leaders so that they might witness the Ascension from within the Bind. The Magna Mater's, the Praefectae's and Krpta's hearts slowed to the prescribed beat as they searched for each other in the ethereal world. The lub of the pumping muscles became louder and louder within the Bind as the women found each other and their pulses synchronized themselves until, suddenly, the sound exploded through the plaza, as one single, repeating heartbeat. The auditory spectacle was augmented by a visual one just as wondrous, with the crackling and zapping of undulating scarves of blue light connecting Krystiana to all the other Alterintrants, their hair stretching toward her, and hers toward them.

Gasps of pure astonishment and wonder spread through the courtyard, among even the Sisters. The shimmering from within the Bind began to manifest itself around the Flaming Suns and a wondrous pattern of a myriad colors appeared around the spinning spheres. The filaments of light now stretched toward the Magna

---

[90] Great K'Tara, we are assembled to give you our Sisters, those who have died in your service. Sisters, let us now join our minds!

Mater, the Assembly Heads and Krpta, and from them onward to the bodies of the fallen. Everyone looked on in anticipation of the Ascension – a rare event, given the long lives of Lux Baiulae, and the infrequency of violent deaths – when the Magna Mater started slowly spreading her arms open, followed by Saara and Ramela Lux Baiulae, the Heads of the Sashates to which the deceased belonged.

As the three women continued to open their arms, Dalima's and Juliana's bodies began to shimmer, and the most amazing song arose suddenly from the throats of a group of Juniors standing on the steps of the Elevation Chapel. The guttural chant moved from sustained graves to gut-wrenching, unending crescendos, all in synchrony with the golden and blue flames surrounding the spheres, and with the shimmering light which rose from the bodies of the dead.

When the song reached its apex, the dead disintegrated themselves with an explosion of light which flowed into the spheres behind them at an ever-increasing rate. Just then, Krystiana, Saara and Ramela began shouting, "Dalima Lux Baiula, intrâ junctionem! Juliana Lux Baiula, intrâ junctionem! [91]" They repeated the incantation – which was picked up by the onlookers – until the bodies completed their transformation and the last particles of light left the lacora beds to enter the Bind through the Flaming Suns. The Juniors now brought their song to a sudden end, thus marking the completion of the Sisters' transmutation.

Around the plaza, some twenty-five hundred flushed faces tried to regain their composure. Krystiana gave the Praefectae as well as Krpta a nod filled with sorrow as well as with pride, sorrow for the loss, and pride for the traditions which held the Order strong and united. The women responded with similar nods, after which the Magna Mater turned to Krpta Lux Baiula to thank her for receiving Juliana's memories, and invited her to her office in the morning so that the young Lux Baiula may share anything which Juliana knew, and which might be of importance to the Sisterhood in the present situation.

Finally, the Magna Mater addressed all in attendance with a voice filled with conviction and certainty – despite her misgivings – and ended the Ascension Ceremony with the thousand-year-old formula:

---

[91] Dalima Lux Baiula, enter the Bind! Juliana Lux Baiula, enter the Bind!

"Those who have left us have arrived. May we continue as strongly in their absence."

This done, the crowd dispersed, most civilians returning to the Lower City while the Lux Baiulae and their attendants walked to their private chambers. And as the plaza emptied, except for the Juniors who would be tending to the Flaming Spheres that night, the breeze returned, and the insects of the night reclaimed their voices.

***

The day of the Gathering was greeted by the largest congregation of Lux Baiulae in years. Sisters from across Alvinoria and Kynaria were here today to discuss the threat facing K'Tara, and to agree on the required response to defend its peoples from what was already here, as well as from whatever else might follow.

The Lower City was abuzz with excitement due to the arrival of so many Sisters and their retinues, either on voranback or in coaches. The civilians, rightly or wrongly, had not been told the reason for the Gathering, and so they welcomed the arriving Sisters as they would on Feast Day. The fact that the Sisters remained expressionless as children, women, and men greeted them, did not dampen the populace's joy – after all, Lucians were familiar with the ways of Lux Baiulae, and they knew that behind the stoic faces there was joy – if joy was to be felt, and sadness – if sadness was to be felt. And, for the Lucians, today was a joyful day because of the spectacle it provided, because of the increased business for the tradesmen and tradeswomen, and perhaps most importantly because of the pride they felt at the homecoming of so many powerful women.

In the plaza of the Inner Sanctum, a festival of colors took place, though the mood there was quite different. Sisters of the different Assemblies gathered in front of the steps to the palace, some with purple, some with white, and others with yellow sashes tied around dresses of contrasting colors. Red Sashes were not among them, given that most resided in Urbs Lucis, and those who had been dispatched across the kingdom to help defend against the Serpent could not return. Whispers and questions abounded, and the Lux Baiulae's faces, typically unreadable, showed their emotions now that they were amongst their own. The First Barrier and her guards greeted each in turn, and then sent them on to see Dame Falca,

Praefecta Ramela's assistant, who stood at a nearby table and gave to each woman her calendar and room assignment.

From his room in a building to the north side of the plaza, Lusk observed the arrival of the Sisters. The smile he had had was quickly replaced by a gloomy frown. He then walked to the smaller room in his apartments, a room the Sisters called a Contemplation Room. There, he sat himself on the carpeted floor and descended into a deep meditative state to enter the Bind. It did not take him long to find the vibrations of the one he was looking for.

The vibrations came from what looked like a castle overlooking a most magnificent lake surrounded by a forest of purple, red, and yellow-leaved trees. Not a place he was familiar with, but perhaps it was a construction of the Umbra's mind. The Umbra presented himself in what looked like a military uniform, but unlike any Lusk had ever seen before. It was tight-fitting and elegant, and accentuated the man's slim musculature. As Lusk approached, he had a moment of doubt: the vibrations were the Umbra's but the face was…androgynous. Umbra noted the reaction and immediately shifted his appearance to the one Lusk recognized. Lusk hesitated a moment then sent, *"Umbra, I am here at your call."*

"What have you to report, Vaedrin [92]?" The Umbra preferred to call Lusk by his given name – a name Lusk hated – to remind him of where he came from, and of the reasons why he should continue to serve faithfully.

"I have been brought to the seat of the Sisterhood to be further tested by the Lux Baiulae, as well as to tell them what I know of Zebulonian Binding and Sensing skills."

The Umbra seemed excited instead of being upset. He sent, *"This is excellent news, Vaedrin. Infiltrating the high king's court certainly remains important, but undermining the Sisterhood is an unexpected opportunity which we dare not forgo given our Master's desire to see them, along with the Kynarians, destroyed first. You will therefore take advantage of this situation and infiltrate their*

---

[92] Vaedrin: Lusk Methrim's given name, formed by combining his genetic mother's name 'Vae' with the term 'drin' meaning 'progeny of'.

organization, gain their trust, and start corrupting them as soon as feasible. Once you have begun, I will send others to assist you."

The Umbra rubbed his lips a moment. *"The Lux Baiulae were certainly not an easy group to tempt during the Dark Battle, but I am confident that you can do it, especially given the state of degeneration of today's Sisterhood."*

Lusk wanted to ask what evidence the Umbra had of this degeneration. But he knew better, and simply said, *"I will do as you command, Umbra. Will you inform our master of the changing plans?"*

"Hum, you may actually be able to do so yourself when he appears again three months hence."

Lusk's face tightened with worry. He asked, *"Does he wish to speak with me?"*

"Indeed! He wishes to learn directly from you how your infiltration of our enemies is proceeding." The Umbra continued with intense, threatening eyes, *"It will be good to have some results by then, Vaedrin."*

Lusk nodded, resigned to his condition. What else could he do? He could neither escape, nor oppose the Umbra.

The Shadow-Maker now moved the conversation to another topic. *"And how did your infiltration of the high king's Guard proceed, in any case?"*

Lusk's form in the Bind shifted momentarily as he thought about his answer. *"It went well, Umbra. My story grabbed the high prince's attention, and I was able to gain his confidence as well as that of the king, his father, as you had predicted. I made a mistake, however, when I stupefied some of the high prince's guardians with the result that the others became suspicious. Bad luck struck next when a soldier I had healed and stupefied murdered another."*

"I hear. Does this mean you will no longer able to serve me there?"

Lusk felt the threat deeply this time, and gave the Umbra the answer he desired, *"I will be able to continue to serve the high king and High Prince, once I am released from Urbs Lucis."*

"Excellent. I did not doubt the sacrifices you made in Zebulonia would prove worthwhile, Vaedrin, and your reward will be commensurate with said and continued sacrifices."

Lusk did not respond to that, though the virtual furrows on his usually handsome face told of his persistent resentment. His fall from Zebula's good graces had scarred him both physically and psychologically. But at least, his birth mother – one of the Janarae's countless birthing vessels; the one who had raised him and taken care of him – was safe.

Realizing the Umbra was watching him curiously, he dismissed his stray thoughts and returned his attention to Noctiferus's lieutenant who asked if he had something to add. *"Yes, Umbra. Although the king and prince should not cause any trouble, I am concerned that the king's advisor – a Lux Baiula by the name of Elyana Marina – will eventually see beneath my veil given the difficulty I have in keeping her stupefied."*

The Umbra raised his eyebrows questioningly.

Lusk explained, *"Every so often, her suspicions reawaken – for a short time only, but reawaken nevertheless. This has caused her to restrict my freedom to operate one way or another, more than once."*

"Hmm. She seems to be a powerful one. But since she has never met a Temptator before, it is highly unlikely she recognizes your true nature, and she cannot doubt your story either. The Sisterhood does have a vast library, however, and she may have read a few things about the nature of the vibrations of Temptatori, and accidentally sensed something similar in you. I suggest you mask your vibrations every time you use the Bind, whether or not you are close to her; I know that will be difficult to sustain very long, but again, the stakes here are great."

"I will do as you ask, Umbra, and I will be more careful. But there is another who will be even more difficult to tempt: the head of their Healer's Guild, named Saara Lucius. She is an old, emotionless woman. I have not yet been able to stupefy her."

"Hmm, well, you have tempted all sorts of males and females while in Zebulonia, no? Old and young alike. Surely you can tempt this Human. You may need to use more invasive techniques. But if you do that, take care that you do not raise more suspicions on yourself."

Lusk nodded.

"And what of their Great Mother?"

"I have not met her yet."

"Let me know once you have. For now, do as I have instructed you to do. I, myself, need to go meet with our Lord's Wings to discuss...its attack on Furan City."

"You mean its failed attack on Furan City? That lizard is too full of itself; I doubt it will succeed in bringing you the Luxori."

"Perhaps. But know that if the creature fails, capturing the Luxori will become your responsibility. I therefore urge you to help it along."

"I...I understand, Umbra."

"Very well, now go. And report back to me in a fourth's time. I expect great things from you, Vaedrin. And remember that you will also be reporting to our Master in a few fou –, in a few months."

Lusk nodded deeply and left the Bind. He did not show his surprise at the Umbra's error, nor did he show his anxiety at the thought of having to meet with their master again.

Once back in his body, Lusk stood and started pacing, thinking about Noctiferus. He had only met him once before, the year the Dark One sent him to Shadin City to learn the ways of Alvinorians by serving Shadin City's governor – one of the kindliest men Lusk had ever met.

The vibrations he had received from the Dark One during that conversation four years ago were horrendous, and he had felt all his will vanish, while an ugliness overtook him and buried itself deep within him. Lusk still remembered waking the morning following that meeting with a fierce sense of having been violated. He remembered wanting to escape, flee, get as far from Zeblinia as possible, but knowing that he must comply, nevertheless, or else – or else see his birth mother suffer. And comply he did, and in doing so he had reneged his values and principles to such an extent that he had begun to not recognize himself anymore.

Lusk had often wondered since then, how he could on the one hand serve such vile creatures as Noctiferus and the Umbra – violating every moral principle he held – and on the other hand continue to treat those who sought his healing services. Somehow, it seemed, he had succeeded in compartmentalizing the two aspects of his person.

Well, the present situation was no different; he would heal guardians that needed healing, then stupefy them, or tempt them, or worse, as would be necessary in his service to Noctiferus and obedience to the Umbra. And he would do the same to the Lux Baiulae, the prince and the king. He would continue to tear holes in his soul each time he betrayed his principles until there was nothing left to betray anymore, until he finally made his way to the Dark Halls to spend the rest of eternity there – alone, lost, destroyed.

Sometimes, when he was paralyzed by the thought of the horrors that awaited him, Lusk reminded himself of the reason he had sold his soul to these creatures: to free his birth mother from the Janarae's shackles. And the Umbra had kept his promise: Oolviana Methrim was safe, living in a small Yerlayan hamlet to the north of the Mountains of the Sagr. It was for this that he served as he did and continued to corrupt himself.

* * *

The Hall of the Light was very quiet as Krystiana opened the session at mid-morning. Concern was visible on every woman's face – if one could read them.

The Magna Mater stood in front of her cathedra at the center of the dais. The Praefectae were seated in a semi-circle behind her, with Saara, the longest serving Praefecta, furthest to her right, followed by Larca, Ramela, and Bilena furthest to her left. Ordinary Sisters [93] were all seated in short rows in front of the dais, with Elyana, Irania and Krpta in the first row.

Krystiana swept everyone with her gaze and stopped, when it landed on the Sisters who had fought in Furan City, to make her opening statement. "Sisters, thank you for gathering here today so that we may discuss a very real threat, one unlike any threat any of us has ever experienced before."

"For a while though, we have been sensing some unknown and deeply disturbing vibrations. I asked Marena, a skilled Yellow Sash, to try and uncover their source, and I believe that she will reveal this morning what she has found."

All the faces turned toward the Praefecta Philosophas, looking for her confirmation, but not even *her Sisters* could read Bilena's expression, which possibly indicated the worst news.

---

[93] The term 'Ordinary Sisters' referred to all Sisters below the rank of Administrators.

Krystiana proceeded to give an overview of all that was known to date, starting with the vibrations many of them – especially the Sisters of the Yellow Sashate – first sensed many fourths ago, followed by a short account of what she and Elyana had learned from their venture into the Bind – a revelation which raised many eyebrows, though some, who knew the Magna Mater well, simply nodded to themselves. She then told the Sisters of the Serpent's attacks on Horn's Pass, on small villages throughout Lower Alvinor, and finally on Furan City, where two Sisters were lost. She concluded her overview by telling the gathered Sisters of the creatures that attacked the high king, the prince, and their company on their way back from Spiritii.

When the Magna Mater was finished, a White Sash raised her hand to ask a question. Krystiana would have preferred to silence the woman, as she tended to ask the most inappropriate questions, but she gave her leave to do so, anyway, and Alina Lux Baiula said, "Thank you, Magna Mater." She then turned to look at Elyana and Irania, and said, "Sisters, Juliana – may her mind enlighten us – had a brother. Do you know how Primus Julian is doing? I cannot imagine that he is faring well, as he must surely have witnessed what happened to his sister that fateful night."

Irania stood, turned toward the back, and responded after giving Elyana a quick look, "Primus Julian did indeed witness his sister's death, Alina, and his shock was terrible, as you rightly imagine. And it only got worse after the fog from the initial shock lifted from his eyes." Irania paused to bury the memory of Juliana's crushed skull deeper into her mind, lest it overwhelm her, then added, "Primus Julian is now in Tania Lux Baiula's care. With her help, he should make a full recovery, but it may take a while, unless he decides to have his memories wiped."

Alina said, "Hum. Thank you for sharing that, Administrator."

The Purple Sash was about to make a final comment, but Krystiana was eager to be done with this somber digression and said, "And thank you, Alina. If there are no other questions about the Serpent's attack on Furan City, I will now have Marena report on her findings."

No other questions came, but Alina did add with a sincere tone, "I have no other question, myself, Magna Mater, but I do find it important to bring some humanity into our deliberations every so often. So, I thank you too for allowing my question."

Krystiana did not say anything but nodded and turned her lips inward. Alina was right, but she still wished she had stopped the woman from asking her question. She could hear the Praefectae fidget in their seats, tap their fingers or grind their teeth. Lux Baiulae were said to be impervious to emotions, and to be able to discuss any topic rationally, but the truth was somewhat more complex, and they very much preferred to ignore uncomfortable topics rather than be forced to repress the feelings they *would* elicit if discussed.

Elyana caught Krystiana's eye and gave her an understanding look, forming the word "later" with her lips, meaning that she would go to her office later to speak more fully about what happened in Furan City, and more importantly, about preparing the Lucis Sororum Societas for the deaths – the horrible deaths – they could expect to keep coming. The Magna Mater acknowledged Elyana's facial signals then turned to Marena to give her the sign to begin her report.

Marena stood and cleared her throat several times before approaching the large Living Screen by the wall. This was a gel-containing screen which harbored various pressure-sensitive, pigment-producing microbes. Drawings were created by pressing one's finger on the screen with more or less force to cause the microbes to release various pigments. In the present case, a map of Aquinos had been drawn, with green for continental outlines, red for plant life, cream for arid areas, and brown for mountains, while towns and cities were represented by black pigment.

After one more "ahem", Marena began. "In order to pinpoint the source of the vibrations that many of us – and especially the Sisters of my Sashate – have felt in the past month, I spent the first few days of my assignment trying to follow the vibrations through the Bind. But that was a failure. I then searched for…the Serpent, being careful not to reveal myself, and once I found it, I was able to confirm that it is not the source. Not knowing what else to do, I spent another two days brainstorming with my Sisters, and we decided to try a new method we recently developed to help us locate Alterintrants anywhere on K'Tara."

That caused blinks and frowns among the audience. An older Sister asked, "Can't we already do that by entering and searching the Bind?"

Marena responded with a meek "Not always, Sister," not wishing to offend the elder. She then uncovered a fist-sized, purple-colored crystal encased in a golden ring set at the top of a tripod sitting on a marble table near the dais, and said "This is called an AAD, or Amplifying Alterintrant Detector." Marena then walked to the Living Screen and said, "I sent three of my colleagues across Alvinoria with an AAD each," and when she touched the screen at three points across the map of Alvinoria, the pressure-sensitive microbes lit up with a bright yellow light which promptly turned to a bright orange. The glow lasted several minutes, allowing Marena to complete her presentation. "We placed these devices far from populated areas so as to maximize their sensitivity. We had to make several adjustments to it last fourth, but once that was done, we were able to estimate the source of the vibrations."

Everyone waited anxiously, the hall so quiet that one would have heard a dust grain fall. And yet, Marena remained silent, her nervousness apparent in the way she pressed her hands one against the other.

Larca broke the silence, asking loudly "Well, what did you calculate to be the source, Marena?"

Taking a deep breath, the Yellow Sash replied, "The vibrations come… from…the Sol System."

Dozens of incredulous "whats?" rose among the Sisters. Some asked, "What did she say? Solstice?"

Praefecta Ramela, who had been listening very carefully all this time, asked with an incredulous tone, "Marena, did you say, Sol? The star system in the eastern night sky?"

"Yes, Praefecta. There is no doubt about it."

Ursula Lux Baiula, a Purple Sash from Kirgad, asked in her chopping accent, "And how d'you know t'at, Marena?"

"The AADs are able to pick up virtually any Binding vibration. And because they are spherical, and because their surfaces will light up only in the direction from which they receive the strongest signal, they are able to triangulate the source of the vibrations they pick up. The three of them together point to the general vicinity of Sol.

Modified versions of the AADs were then installed on a celestial machine [94], which confirmed the source to be Sol."

The Sisters threw myriad suppositions at each other. Ursula Lux Baiula, sitting next to Elyana, asked her in her grating accent, "What d'*you* think lies in Sol, Sister?"

Elyana sighed heavily and said, "I would rather not speculate, Ursula. But I believe that Marena may have an idea."

Finally, Krystiana asked, "Marena, please share with everyone the conclusion you have reached as to what is generating the vibrations."

"Mater, as I have already reported to you, the vibrations are without a doubt generated by a sentient being, and my Sisters and I believe that being to be…Noctiferus himself."

Shouts of disbelief and curses brought about by the gloomy realization that another Dark Battle was at hand, broke out in the Hall of the Light.

Krystiana waited a moment and then enhanced her voice to call the Ordinary Sisters to order. Little by little, quiet returned, and when the last peep vanished, Ramela turned to the Head of the Yellow Assembly, sitting to her left, and asked, "Bilena, do you agree with your acolyte's conclusion?"

The tall, pale woman rose and with hands crossed in front of herself, answered "I do, Ramela. The vibrations are definitely similar to what those of us with memories of the Dark Battle can remember; this conclusion also helps to explain two other facts: the presence of Noctiferus's Wings on K'Tara, as well as the re-emergence of the loathed Temptatori, whose presence has now been confirmed in Kartak," Bilena paused a moment, as if considering something else before completing her sentence, "by our Eyes and Ears."

A renewed commotion swept over the Ordinary Sisters, giving rise to a cacophony of questions and atypically coarse curses as the significance of what they were hearing settled in. Krystiana let the moment pass, knowing that order would soon return, and with it, a more rational discussion.

---

[94] A celestial machine was an optical instrument used to look at celestial objects.

When the assembly finally quieted, Krystiana heaved a heavy sigh and asked, "Bilena, why the pause before mentioning your Eyes and Ears?"

"Hrhhm. Yes, well, my Eyes and Ears, they came across two of High Captain Harlion's spies in Kartak, Mater, spies he sent there to try and ferret out the Temptatori, himself. My Eyes and Ears, they witnessed the capture of the royal spies by a large group of thugs, and their subsequent release – a few days later – apparently unharmed. This made my spies curious, and they decided to confront High Captain Harlion's men. When they did, they thought they sensed unusual vibrations emanating from them. But the worst was when the men tried to…well… abuse our Sisters. Fortunately, my operatives, they were able to lift the fog which had blinded the two men. It is obvious now that these men had been…altered in some way."

Perceiving the coming question from a few Sisters, Saara clarified her colleague's statement. "I believe the proper expression is *turned*, Bilena." Bilena nodded in appreciation of the correction; a Yellow Sash never resented a correction and cared only for the truth. Saara continued, "What concerns me more, Mater, is what should be done with the two royal spies given that they may have been turned to the service of the Dark One. I, for one, do not believe they should be allowed to return to Furan City."

Krystiana said, "Obviously – *if* they have been turned. Can you ascertain their condition, Saara?"

"The White Sashate has been working diligently since we last spoke of the Temptatori, Mater, to learn everything there is to know about them and those they turn, the *Converts*. Bilena's Eyes and Ears have now started applying what we have learned, to try and confirm the condition of the two royal spies, as well as to hunt for other Converts, and for the Temptatori."

That last statement alarmed Krystiana, and she said urgently, "Saara, surely it is too dangerous, yet, even for Bilena's best to go hunting for *any Temptatori*! How could you authorize this?"

Saara started. It seemed she had not expected this reaction from the Magna Mater. She was about to respond when Bilena stood and answered, "Mater, I agreed to have my operatives use the newly learned skills, but you are right, they do not yet master them, and they might very well endanger themselves if they were too rash in

474

their search. I have therefore given them strict orders to work in pairs, always, and to only have one of the two open her senses to the vibrations that might be released by those they encounter, and finally, to *not* connect with or probe anyone they suspect of being a Temptator, but to try for the Converts if they otherwise seem inoffensive enough."

"Humm, all right then. You may continue as you plan to do. But please ensure that there are proper procedures in place for the "watcher" to be able to stop the "receiver" if need be, and that they immediately inform Urbs Lucis if anything goes wrong."

Bilena said, "I understand, Mater. Know that we *are* also continuing to explore technical means by which we may safely infiltrate Kartak, and we may have found just what we need. Indeed, Kelysia and Saara, they are working on an entangled device which might allow us to hear things at a distance."

Looks of incredulity and amazement popped up across the hall.

Krystiana asked, "Did you say *hear things at a distance*, Bilena?"

"I did, Mater. Saara can tell you more about it, if you wish it."

"Saara?"

The old Praefecta stood and replied, "Bilena is right, Mater. The device Kelysia and I are working on should allow us to transmit sound from one place to another. But it is still early to tell whether it will work or not. We will run our definitive experiments soon, and if it *does* work, we can place the devices around Kartak to listen in on conversations of suspected individuals, eliminating the need for Bilena's Eyes and Ears – our Sisters – to put themselves in harm's way."

The original surprise and wonder on the Sisters' faces was quickly replaced by either eagerness or concern. Even Krystiana raised an eyebrow. A device was now going to possibly do what they did through the Bind?

The Magna Mater said, "That is not exactly what I had expected of your explorations, Saara, but it is certainly interesting. Please continue and come to us once you have conclusive results. The Light's Assembly will need to consider and approve the use of this new technology, of course – if it will indeed do what you claim it might."

"Of course, Mater."

Krystiana's face relaxed and Saara breathed a quiet sigh of relief. The Magna Mater took a moment to consider Bilena's plan to uncover Temptatori and Converts in Kartak, as well as Saara's plan regarding this new device she was working on with the Yellow Sashate. "I suppose your plans are an acceptable compromise, Praefectae, given our urgent needs."

Bilena and Saara thanked her in turn.

The Magna Mater continued, looking at the two Praefectae, "But please continue to work together to fill in our gaps in knowledge, and to find ways to give us the advantage we need. It is imperative we learn of our enemies' plan to infiltrate Alvinoria, and that we learn to detect both the Temptatori and the Converts." And with palpable fear in her tone, Krystiana added, "It is especially critical we find ways to protect our organization quickly lest we soon find ourselves surrounded and powerless."

Saara, as the senior Praefecta, responded for both, "Yes, Mater. We understand our tasks. And we will deliver what is needed."

Satisfied, Krystiana now glanced at Elyana and Bilena and asked, "Now, what should we do about the royal spies while you verify or disprove their...*turning*, if that is a word?"

Elyana replied in Bilena's stead, "Mater, I would like to speak with the high king and High Captain about this, given the sensitivity of the issue. I will suggest to them that their men be sent to us and kept here until we are able to ascertain that they have *not* been turned."

"Very well. You must also warn the high king against sending anymore of his people there. Kartak should be off-limits to anyone except to a few of us from now on."

"As you command, Mater."

That taken care of, Krystiana moved the discussion to the final topic. She called on Elyana and Bilena to report their findings on Zebulonia.

Elyana stood and began. "Thank you, Mater. Sisters, some of you may have heard that a Zebulonian came to the high prince during our journey from Horn's Pass to Furan City. Some of you may also have seen him here, in Urbs Lucis, where he is now undergoing testing by the White Sashate." Looks of surprise creased the faces of the majority of the women who looked at their neighbors, wondering if they knew. Elyana went on. "The man, Lusk Methrim, told the prince that Queen Zebula intends to invade Alvinoria."

The Hall of the Light erupted once again, more furiously than it had earlier when the Sisters heard of the possible presence of Temptatori in Kartak. Elyana let the dismay subside, thought to herself: *This Gathering will surely be one to remember, but compared to what Aithen said happened when he addressed the Union Council and the Senate, this is a mild response. Still, I wish Sisters had a little more decorum if not complete mastery of their emotions.*

When a few women finally asked Elyana whether she had verified this claim, she resumed her communication. "I, myself, could not verify the man's claim, but logic and the results of my own probing tell me that he is not lying. Still, Praefecta Bilena has sent Eyes and Ears to the southern border to confirm or disprove what Master Methrim told the high prince, and I believe she has information to share in this regard."

Though she did not need to, Bilena thanked Elyana for giving her the floor; Elyana had a special position in the Sisterhood, as advisor to the high king and close friend to the Magna Mater. Bilena stood and said, "Sisters, what this Lusk Methrim communicated to the high prince is, likely and unfortunately, true." At that moment, a crushing wave of discouragement swept through the gathered Sisters. "My agents, they have been able to confirm that there exists a genuine belief among the Zebulonian smugglers that Zebula is in fact planning the invasion of Alvinoria."

A Sister in the back of the hall asked if a timetable of this invasion had also been communicated by the Yellow Sashate's sources. Bilena replied, "That is perhaps the one piece of good news, Mariana: all sources, they agree that this invasion is many months, if not a year or more, away. Our sources' only disagreement has to do with Zebula's motives. But we will try to determine what those motives are when we ourselves attempt to obtain information from within Zebulonia to confirm what we have heard."

Larca, who had been chewing her lips all this time, couldn't hold her tongue any longer and said, "From within Zebulonia? How do you plan to do that, Bilena? I am not aware that we have anyone who speaks Zebulonian. It might be better to simply enter your smugglers' minds to get the truth out of *them*! Or out of this Lusk Mer –, Methrim."

With unusual calm and assurance, Bilena replied, "Larca, you know we no longer have those capabilities. And even if we did, aside from the fact that our laws prohibit the practice, I could not, and would not authorize the violation of another's mind."

Krystiana listened quietly, and thought: *I wonder how Bilena would react if she knew Elyana and I have those forbidden capabilities.*

Larca released a sarcastic grunt and continued. "*How* do you propose to obtain information from inside Zebulonia then?"

"Well, as you may or may not know, there is a little isolated enclave deep within the Mountains of the Sagr – but on this side of the border – a place known as Razeb…it stood for Rakilah Zebulonia, meaning 'Little Zebulonia', but today it is just Razeb. It is populated by descendants of Zebulonians who immigrated here some – well, we are not exactly sure – but perhaps a hundred years ago. Until we discovered them in 1798, they had had little to no contact with the rest of Alvinoria. We've been visiting them since then to study their culture, and we have been able to establish some level of trust between us. Interestingly, they still speak a Zebulonian dialect, and though we cannot be sure how closely it resembles the current Zebulonian language or any of its present dialects, we may be able to take advantage of it."

Larca barked, "Take advantage of it?" How?"

Bilena sighed and continued "We just recently discovered two girls with burgeoning Sensing skills there."

"Girls?!"

"They are eighteen years of age. Technically, adults, Larca."

Again, Larca barked her question, "And why did you not discover them before? Surely they must have developed their Sensing skills a few years ago already."

"It is possible that Zebulonians, they reach puberty later, or that they reach puberty at the same age as Alvinorians and Kynarians, but that they develop their Sensing skills later for some reason. Either way, we will bring them here soon to teach them to control their newfound skills as we do with all girls. And, because these two are adults, we will be able to use them to infiltrate Zebula's court once we have trained them."

478

To Bilena's and everyone else's surprise, Larca had no insulting remark this time. Instead, she said, "That is a very bold plan, Praefecta."

Krystiana gave a satisfied nod upon hearing Larca address Bilena by her title. The change in Larca's attitude was a welcome one, and it comforted her as she thought of what she was planning to say to the gathered Sisters as soon as Bilena was done with her communication.

Ramela now asked, "Bilena, your plan seems reasonable, but wouldn't it be better to send someone to Zebula who is sure to know the current language, and who does not need all the training the girls will need? Like this Lusk Methrim?"

Bilena turned to Elyana who stood and replied in her stead. "From what we have learned, Praefecta, Zebulonian males are not free to move as they please. We have been told by Master Methrim that they are in fact, all slaves, and for that reason, he would be of no use to us there. Furthermore, he is...*persona non grata* in Zebula's court. What Praefecta Bilena proposes is our best chance to get someone inside Zebulonia to either confirm or refute what he has told us, and what our Eyes and Ears have heard regarding Zebula's intentions. *But!* we can certainly use Master Methrim to verify the girls' skills in the current Zebulonian language."

Ramela thanked Elyana, followed by Larca who said, "Hum. Thank you, Elyana. And thank you, Praefecta. Given all these facts, I suppose I might have pursued the same course."

Another satisfied look crossed Krystiana's face. *This is good, very good. And it is time to conclude the morning session and for me to make my announcement.*

The Magna Mater stood from her cathedra and thanked both Bilena and Elyana. She then took a deep breath, crossed her hands and said, "Praefectae, Sisters, you now know everything that is known by our Sisterhood, everything we have been able to gather since those first worrisome vibrations many of us felt several fourths ago, as well as what the White and Yellow Sashes have done to date to try and find answers to some of our most pressing questions, or to prepare us against our enemy. We will spend the rest of the day, after we have had our mid-day meal, considering our defensive and offensive options. But before we do that," and as Krystiana pronounced these words, the golden time disc at the back of the room proclaimed Highsun, "there are two announcements I must make."

After a tense few moments during which women shuffled on their seats, sitting straighter or tugging at their robes, in anticipation of some momentous communication – Elyana alone sitting still, though she knew that the Sisterhood was about to be turned over on its head by the few sentences Krystiana was going to pronounce – the Magna Mater began.

"The danger we already face is clear; the Serpent is attacking one place after another and killing indiscriminately in its search for these two *Luxori* it is intent on finding. There are also vile and dangerous creatures suddenly reemerging from the recesses of our orb, creatures which had been hidden there for the past six hundred years, all of which we will need to learn or relearn to defend against. It is also clear that the Temptatori and their Converts will penetrate us soon – if they are not already among us – to dismember our entire society from within. We must prevent this at all costs."

"Finally, with respect to the source – and cause – of all this disturbance, I find myself forced by the evidence to agree with the Yellow Sashes: Noctiferus, as unlikely and far-fetched as it sounds, must be the one behind it all, and we all know what that means. Of course, we *cannot* let his plans come to fruition, though how we will thwart them, I do not know. Sadly, our Sisterhood is only a fifth of what it was during the Dark Battle, and there are no Luxori now to fight alongside us either."

"But fight and resist, we will. And prepare we must. In order to achieve this, I appoint Praefectae Saara, Ramela, and Bilena Defensive Advisors, to ensure that decisions made in our offensive efforts do not weaken the Sisterhood. And because I must retain my neutrality and my capacity to see to the good of the entire Sisterhood as well as to the good of all people, I name Praefecta Larca, General Supreme of our war efforts."

"Furthermore, I name Elyana Lux Baiula my Manu Dextra. She will therefore resign her post with the high king, a post which I will transfer, immediately thereupon, to Irania Lux Baiula."

EPILOGUE

"Aithen, why are we so afraid of Noctiferus?"

"What do you mean, Ori?"

"Magister Setarcos said that Noctiferus is probably just like us, a being of flesh and blood. So why should we be so afraid of him, then?"

"Magister Setarcos believes that he is of flesh of blood, but we actually *don't* know if he is one like us, one who can be hurt, or stopped, or even reasoned with. So, even skeptics *must* remain afraid of him. And if he is a Founder like most people believe – one of the creators of our world – then we *are* but insects to him."

Ori said, "I, myself, don't think he can be anything else but of flesh and blood. No matter where he is, or what he looks like; he belongs to this universe, so he's made of the same things *we* are made of, even if he *is* a Founder and helped create us."

"You know, Ori, that is in fact what I believe too. But the thing is, even if he is as you say, we are still…but insects to him."

"You're not very encouraging, Aithen."

"I am sorry, Ori. Sometimes, I think I should probably lie to you when you ask me these questions, to keep you from being scared. But that would be wrong; Father has taught us that truth is best, and I agree with him."

"But Ori, there is one positive thing to *this* truth – if it is the truth – and it is that if he is a being like us, *of flesh and blood*, then we need not revere him, which would force us to abdicate our reason as well as our senses. Instead, we can look at him with open eyes when we meet, and then we can judge him, weigh him, and…and think of the best way to defeat him. Just like you did with Senator Clovis's son, when you realized that even if he was bigger and stronger, he was still a kid – like you – and you took courage, fought back and defeated him."

Ori smiled. *This* was a better way to look at the world.

END OF BOOK 1

481

If you enjoyed the book, please place a review on Amazon.com, and share it on your social media. Your honest feedback is very important – to other potential readers, as well as to me. You may also visit https://ladipaolo.net/ to find information about the series, as well as about me, and subscribe to my mailing list.

APPENDIX I – MAPS

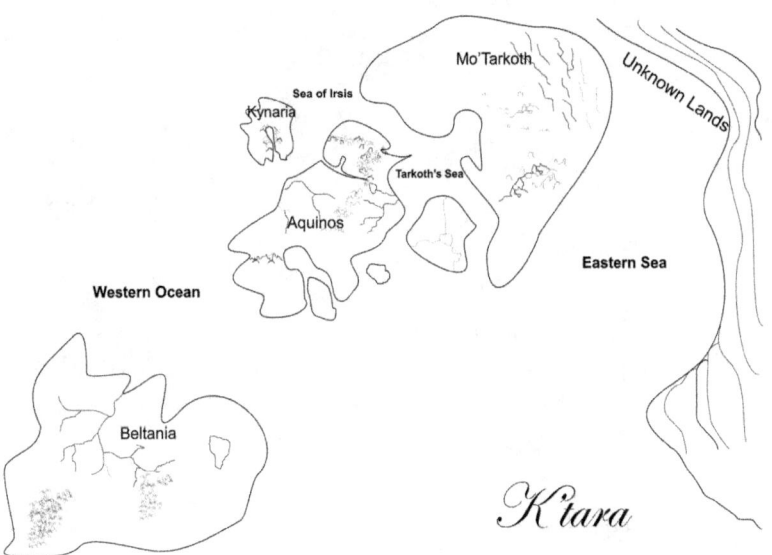

Rokoth • Summit

✚ Morkor

Mounts of Rokoth

Horn's Pass

✚ Antar

Furan City

East Amalor

West Amalor

River Argon

Urbs Lucis

Kartak

Argon Pass

Rattle Formations

Furan Peaks

Upper Alvinor

• Melinor

• Galior

Jarah

• Jarad

Pargad •

Praeghe

Peaks of the Giants

Pargah

• Kirgad

Lower Alvinor

Alvinoria

Yerlah

• Yerlaya

• Spiritii

• Storm City

Great Lake of Shadows

• Shadin City

Mountains of the Sagr

Zeblinia

• Karlinyia

Unnamed Island

Zebulonia

• Bremin City

Worm •

Bremin Island

Aquinos

Scale: Worm to Summit = 5000 Km

485

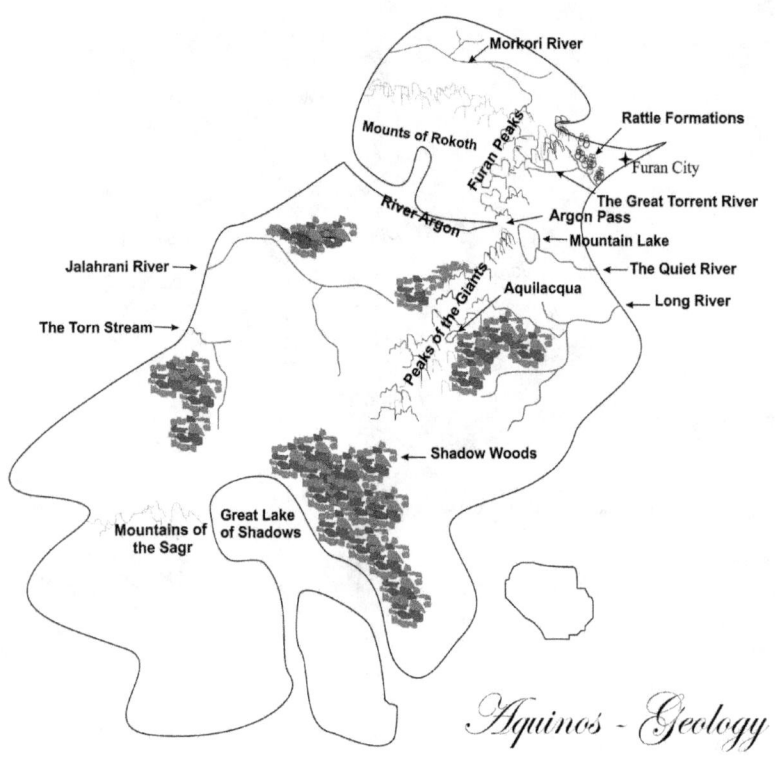

Morkori River

Mounts of Rokoth

Furan Peaks

Rattle Formations

Furan City

River Argon

The Great Torrent River

Argon Pass

Mountain Lake

Jalahrani River

The Quiet River

The Torn Stream

Peaks of the Giants

Aquilacqua

Long River

Shadow Woods

Mountains of
the Sagr

Great Lake
of Shadows

Aquinos - Geology

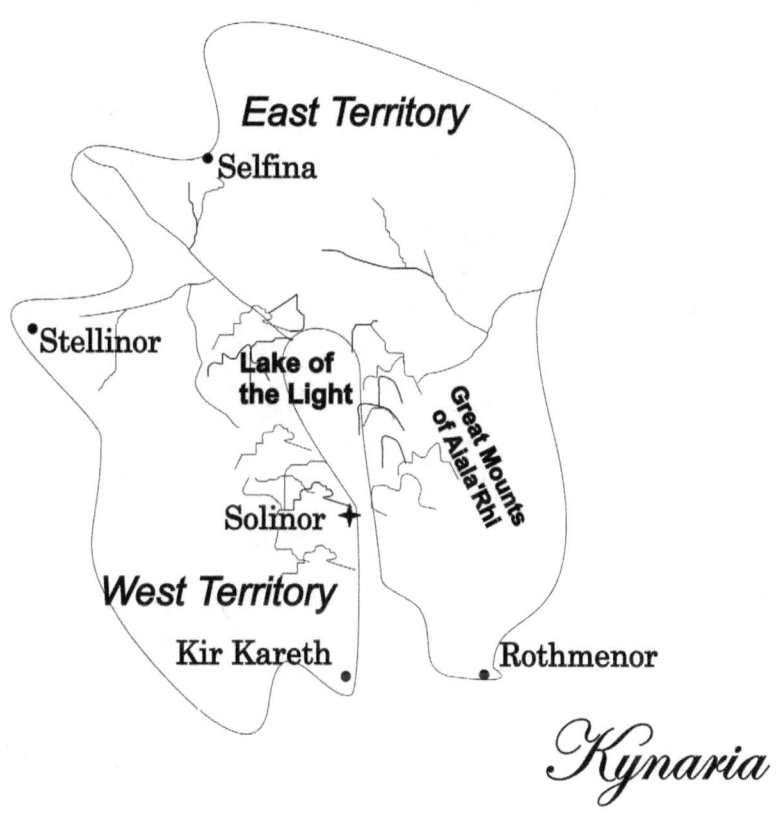

East Territory

•Selfina

•Stellinor

**Lake of
the Light**

Great Mounts
of Alala'Rhi

Solinor +

West Territory

Kir Kareth

Rothmenor

Kynaria

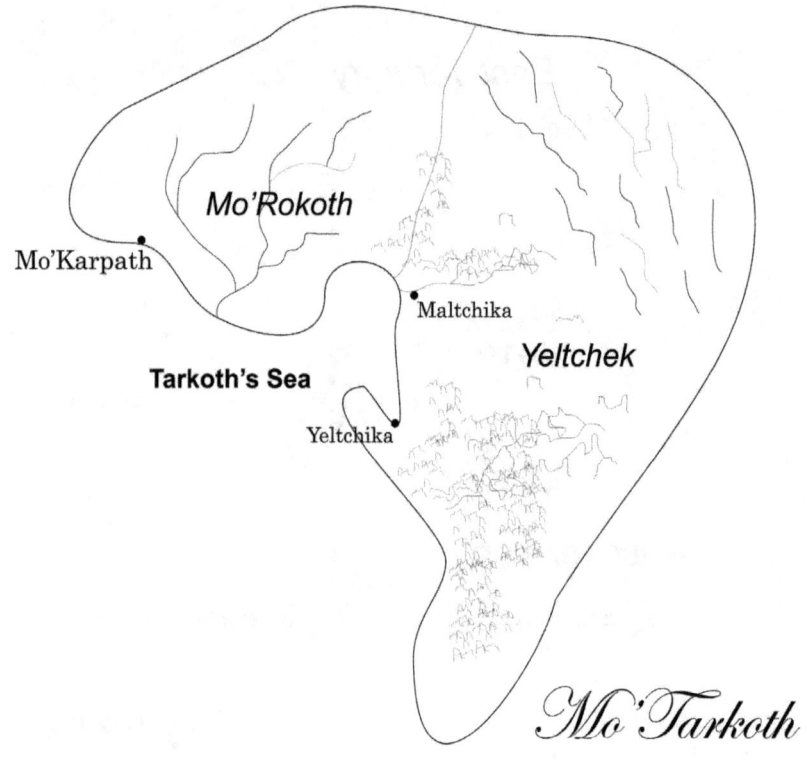

Mo'Rokoth

Mo'Karpath

Maltchika

Tarkoth's Sea

Yeltchek

Yeltchika

Mo'Tarkoth

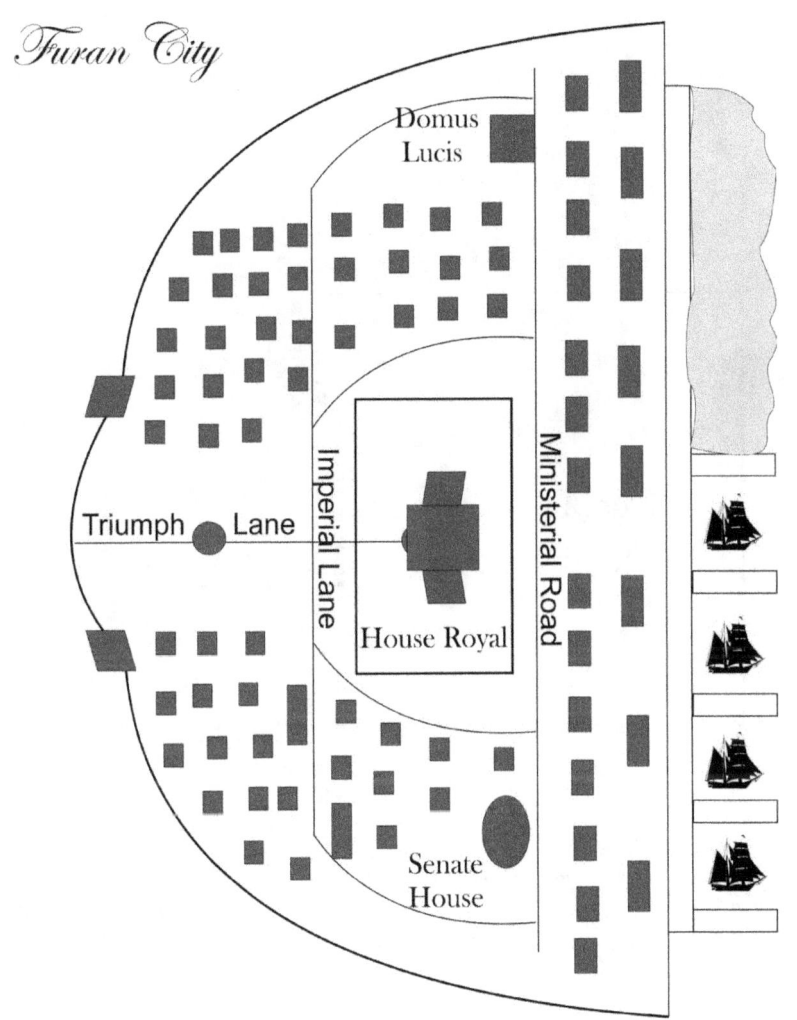

Furan City

Domus
Lucis

Imperial Lane

Ministerial Road

Triumph Lane

House Royal

Senate
House

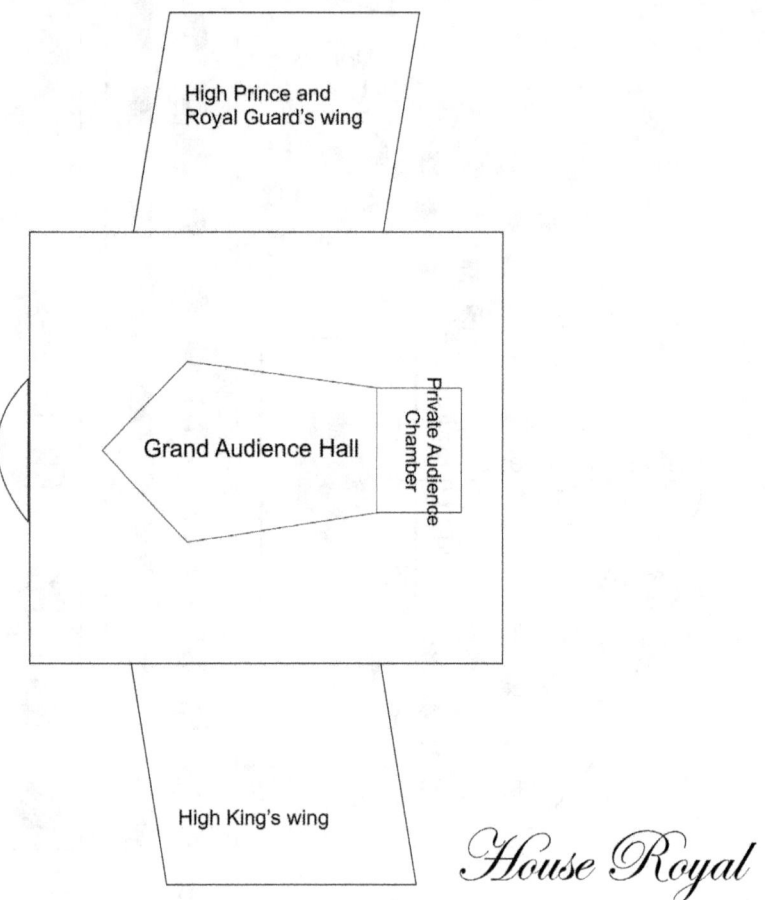

High Prince and
Royal Guard's wing

Grand Audience Hall

Private Audience
Chamber

High King's wing

House Royal

1.   **Adagnitius:** Oldest of the Lonem trees. It was revered by the Tree-Dwellers. The Living Branch, leader of the sect, lived within the tree.

2.   **Adid, King:** Ruler of Jarah, vassal to High King Octavius.

3.   **Afanasiia Volkov Lux Baiula**: Discovered and developed the power of Memory Transfer during the Dark Battle as a means to safeguard the Sisterhood's knowledge. Founder of the Yellow Sashes.

4.   **Aithen of House Coriolis, High Prince and High Lord Commander:** A Halfling, eldest son of Lady Darya and High King Octavius. He was Overseer of the Royal Guard and of the Army of the Union. He was 26 years old. He had the height, thin nose, and thin build of a Kynarian, but a Human's pitch-black hair, along with the green eyes and eyebrows of House Coriolis, and pale brown skin. Aithen had a furan named Xyre, and a voran named Magnus.

5.   **Alina Lux Baiula**: A White Sash from Antar. She was a short, blond-haired woman of thirty-five, a contrarian.

6.   **Almiar ("al_me_r"):** The youngest member of the high king's personal guard; he was 18, but brave, skilled with the sword and stealthy.

7.   **Amis, Senator:** One of the three eldest, along with Senator Paula and First Senator Leo.

8.   **Annan, Magistera:** A Kynarian priestess and Beast Reading instructor.

9.   **Aria**: A Halfling, daughter to Lord Claudius and cousin to Aithen and Toras. Aria was highly skilled in pattern recognition. She had a fierce and rebellious temperament. She was 19 years old.

10.   **Arotek, Lord**: Lord of Melinor. He had a deep dislike of Claudius Coriolis.

11.   **Battle:** High King Octavius's voran.

12.   **Bilena (bee_lay_na) Lux Baiula**: Praefecta Philosophas and Leader of the Seekers' Assembly. She was from East Amalor. She was tall and pale as were most Amalorians, but with the short torso of Yerlayans and long nose of a Pargahni. Bilena was always a very rational woman, except when it came to the Order of Light's reputation.

13. **Brak:** Fishmonger, discoverer of "live" ink, and later spy for the Order of Light.

14. **Brathan, King: Had ruled** over what was once called Trionia. He was murdered by an assassin of Emperor Flavius the Third at the beginning of the Third Age, 267 years before present, in the year 1333.

15. **Brando, Lord:** Governor of Shadin City, also known as Shadisha.

16. **Brokk, Big Fist**: Leader of the Colossi nation.

17. **Callain, Magister**: Instructor in mathematics.

18. **Carasina (a.k.a. Cari)**: A Kynarian, Senior Neo, friend to Aria. She was a chubby, jovial creature, with bright, oval blue eyes, and a complexion the color of pure, fresh brown cream.

19. **Carla Lux Baiula:** A Lux Baiula who had been captured by the Temptatori during the Dark Battle. She had been Afanasiia Lux Baiula's first Memory Transfer subject.

20. **Carrain:** Junior Sister. Part of a circle of friends with Lopenia, Moradien, Lisandeka and Morla.

21. **Claren:** A Junior attendant to Elyana Lux Baiula. Claren intended to join the Purple Sash.

22. **Claudius of House Coriolis, Lord of Bremin**: Brother to Octavius I. Claudius was a learned man, a jurisconsult, and lord of one of the busiest ports in Alvinoria. He was married to Lord Brando's sister, Lady Brandea. They had two sons and a daughter. Claudius was 130 y.o.

23. **Clovis, Senator:** Always the first to take the floor to give his opinion about one matter or another, and always the first to ask questions.

24. **Coris**: Guardian, one of four assigned to guard Aithen.

25. **Crassius, Primus**: Officer of the Royal Guard.

26. **Curos:** One of the soldiers at the outpost of Mountain Lake.

27. **Dalima Lux Baiula:** A White Sash in Furan City, in charge of Juniors. Killed by the Serpent.

28. **Darius:** High Captain of the Royal Guard; predecessor to Harlion. He was poisoned.

29. **Darya of Laranir, Lady**: A Kynarian noblewoman and priestess, wife to High King Octavius I and mother to his children. She was a woman of great beauty and character, with soft brown skin and blue eyes.

30.   **Delora, Headmistress**: Head of the School of Kynaria. She had a beautiful southern Kynarian accent. The woman was not a tall woman, but she was sturdily built, with legs like short and stocky posts, and arms equally thick.

31.   **Elia Lux Baiula**: A Yellow Sash from Furan City, able to enhance voice.

32.   **Elmanon:** Soldier of the Lake Mountain Outpost.

33.   **Elyana Lux Baiula**: A Purple Sash and former Red Sash. Elyana was perhaps the greatest Lux Baiula since ages past, and a loyal friend to High King Octavius I to whom she was assigned as Special Advisor thirty-three years before present. She was a beautiful woman from West Amalor, tall, but not as pale as most Amalorians. She had long, wavy reddish hair, and deep blue eyes. She was 65 years old but looked no older than a 24-year-old woman.

34.   **Falca, Dame:** Praefecta Ramela's assistant.

35.   **Falco, Lady:** Lady of West Amalor.

36.   **Fausta Lux Baiula**: A high-raking medic and former Advisor to King Juur no'Duur of Yerlah.

37.   **Falor Falirin:** Soldier in Toras' guard; brother to Felor.

38.   **Felor Falirin:** Soldier in Toras' guard; brother to Falor.

39.   **Flavius the First, Emperor: Had** ruled over the continent of Aquinos at the beginning of the Third Age, five hundred and eighty years ago, from year 1210-1252. He was a Luxor.

40.   **Flowing Water:** Leader of the Locari, known as Torrent by them. The Locari were a sentient aquatic species belonging to the Higher Locarian clade whose members could quickly metamorphose to switch from terrestrial to aerial and to aquatic lifeforms.

41.   **Frelina**: Aid Healer at Horn's Pass.

42.   **Gabel:** Soldier in Toras's guard; a member of the search party.

43.   **Gaius of House Coriolis, Lord of Praeghe**: Youngest brother to High King Octavius I. Gaius was a jovial, boisterous man, owner of the one of the most fertile lands in Alvinoria. Gaius was 100 y.o.

44.   **Galadrin, First Cleric of Aiala:** Galadrin was the leader of the Order of Aiala.

45.   **Genghis (pronounced chin-kiss):** Proconsul of Earth Force from Earth year 2261 (two thousand three hundred and seventy years before present time, or year 570 BCE on the K'Taran calendar). Genghis was 2409 y.o.

46.   **Gharana, Priestess:** A plump Eastern Kynarian. She was a Priestess Tracker. She had an Eastern Kynarian accent with long, exceedingly stretched vowels.

47.   **Gorvald:** Prime Lord of West Amalor.

48.   **Grael**: Guardian who had been affected by Lusk Methrim.

49.   **Grom:** Messenger from Galior.

50.   **Hanne**: A guardian posted at Mountain Lake. He was slender but ropy, dark-eyed and dark-haired, in his mid-twenties.

51.   **Harlion Stormbreaker:** High Captain of the Royal Guard, Commander of Alvinoria's secret police, and mentor to Aithen. He had a chestnut voran named Rufus. Harlion was 60 y.o.

52.   **Irania Lux Baiula**: Head of the Order's Chamber in Furan City, a Purple.

53.   **Jamir, Secundus:** One of the captains of the Royal Guard.

54.   **Jashan:** Personal guardian of High King Octavius, native of Spiritii.

55.   **Jonal:** Royal Guardian assigned to Elyana's needs.

56.   **Julian, Primus:** Head of the Praetorian Guard. He was a tall, muscular, red-haired and green-eyed Human, around 30 y.o.

57.   **Juliana Lux Baiula**: Purple Sash, Advisor to Lord Valorian of Spiritii, younger sister of Primus Julian. She had a five-year-old gray voran named Petal.

58.   **Juur no'Duur, King**: Ruler of Yerlah, vassal to High King Octavius.

59.   **Kaffin, Lord**: Royal Treasurer.

60.   **Karista**: First Healer at Horn's Pass. She was a tall, large and intimidating woman.

61.   **Kendor, Primus**: Lord Commander Toras's first officer. Kendor had short gray hair, a square face atop a blocky neck from years of sword fighting, and no mustaches or beard except for thick grazer chops for sideburns. Kendor was 65 and had fought alongside Harlion in his earlier years.

62.   **Keresina Lux Baiula**: A Furan City Red Sash. She was 21 y.o.

63.   **Kelysia Lux Baiula**: A Yellow Sash, elevated to the Order five years earlier, and a leader in the study and advancement of mind-tying. Kelysia was an unusually tall woman, with short blonde hair, and hazel eyes. She was 40 years old.

64. **Kildare:** Aithen's squire, a young man of 18, the son of a minor lord to the northwest of the capital. He had wild blond hair, the beginning of a mix of blond and black facial hair on his face, and a slender body with strong legs. Kil had a bay voran named Wind.

65. **Kilio, Lord:** Landholder of a territory to the northwest of Bremin near the southern tip of the Shadow Woods. His son, Larad, was courting Aria.

66. **Kiron:** Personal guardian of High King Octavius.

67. **Krpta Lux Baiula**: A Yerlayan, one of the youngest Purple Sashes, and soon to become one of the youngest administrators as Secretary to Prime Lord Gorvald of West Amalor. Sister to Secundus Krptus. She was 32 y.o.

68. **Krptus, Secundus**: A Yerlayan, officer of the Royal Guard. Brother to Krpta Lux Baiula. He was 30 y.o.

69. **Krystiana Lux Baiula**: Magna Mater, Leader of the Order of the Light for fifty-five years. From East Amalor, tall and pale, but still beautiful, though she was near 100 years old, she looked no older than a 40-year-old woman.

70. **Kynaria Moro:** Priestess who lived 1200 years before and founded the Order of Kynaria, known at the time as Order of the Sisters of Aiala'Rhi.

71. **Laiella Lux Baiula:** First Barrier. She was a tall, stern warrior with deadly skills. A native of Bremin Island, she had their pale green complexion, and red hair.

72. **Lania:** An old Kynarian, recently admitted to the Kynarian Order as a junior neo.

73. **Laranis Lux Baiula:** A Yellow Sash, in Furan City, who specialized in psychological studies.

74. **Laren:** Aria's friend from Furan City.

75. **Larca Lux Baiula**: Praefecta Milites, Head of the Red Sashate, or Warriors' Assembly, for twenty-six years. A Breminese of mixed origins. She was a small, wiry woman. Her red hair was short, except in the back, where it was tied to point straight up and fanned like a fatock's tail. Her complexion was a pale green.

76. **Lenion:** Toras's servant.

77. **Leo, First Senator**: Head of the Senate of Furan City.

78. **Leon**: Sergeant in the Royal Guard, whose men Gael and Loke had been affected by Lusk Methrim.

79.   **Liolwyn, Lady**: Priestess, the first Kynarian to marry a Human.

80.   **Lisandeka:** Junior Sister, part of a circle of friends with Carrain, Lopenia, Moradien, and Morla.

81.   **Loke**: Guardian that had been affected by Lusk Methrim.

82.   **Loma**: Kynarian Priestess Veterinarian.

83.   **Londo**: Friend of Toras.

84.   **Longbrows:** Horn's Pass librarian.

85.   **Lopenia:** Junior Sister, part of a circle of friends with Carrain, Moradien, Lisandeka and Morla.

86.   **Loris of Bremin, Prince**: Cousin to Aithen and Toras, died during the attack at Horn's Pass.

87.   **Lub Methor:** A Zebulonian, representative of the male rebels, short-statured, light-skinned with slanted eyes.

88.   **Lucius the First, King, then High King:** The first ruler of Aquinos who had initially tamed furans, created the Union, and published the Coriolan Carta.

89.   **Lucius the Third, High King:** Grandfather to Aithen and Toras.

90.   **Lucra Lux Baiula:** Sister to Irania Lux Baiula, Head of Restoration.

91.   **Luma Kraelion:** Female senator, friend to High King Octavius, funny and jovial, but also highly intelligent.

92.   **Lupa Lux Baiula:** Secretary to Krystiana Lux Baiula.

93.   **Lusk Methrim (a.k.a. Galdrin, Vaedrin Unus):** One of the Dark One's most powerful Temptatori. Lusk Methrim was his assumed name since arriving in Alvinoria; Vaedrin was his Zebulonian given name. Lusk had skin the color of white nutmilk, slanted eyes, a narrow nose, and charcoal hair with streaks of red, shaven on the sides and braided in the back. His facial hair was completely red, including his eyebrows.

94.   **Magnus**: Aithen's voran. He was a magnificent destrier. He had a dark black-red coat with dark red mane and fetlock hair. His tail had strands of black and dark red hair. His shoulders stood at seventeen hands.

95.   **Mara Lux Baiula:** Head Medic for Lord Valorian of Spiritii. She was shorter than most, but with an authoritative presence, nevertheless. She had thick black hair with a white lock in front, and

a wide face with large oval eyes. She had an older castrated voran named Star. Mara was 48 y.o.

96. **Marcus Vrol, The Reader:** A Halfling Sensor and Binder, the only male that had been granted membership into the Sisterhood in recognition of his great skills. Marcus had been Head of the king's police force and Octavius's friend. He was banished four decades earlier for entering a woman's mind against her will. Marcus was 127 y.o. He was tall, pale-skinned, with scars on either side of his face.

97. **Marena Lux Baiula**: Sister of the Yellow Sash, sent to Kynaria to learn to beast-read.

98. **Martius:** Ten-year-old boy healed by Elyana.

99. **Mela Lux Baiula:** A medic, she was part of the rescue team that went to look for Prince Toras and others.

100. **Menn:** Soldier in Toras's guard; a member of the search party.

101. **Mekiir:** Soldier in the Royal Guard. Mekiir and twin brother Kemiir, were from Upper Alvinor. They were of average height, but with a frightening musculature. Mekiir lost his brother in the first attack by the Serpent on Horn's Pass.

102. **Merina Lux Baiula**: Yellow Sash stationed in Melinor.

103. **Merr (mer as in "her"):** Personal guardian of High King Octavius; a Kynarian, one of the best archers on Aquinos.

104. **Moradien:** Junior Sister, part of a circle of friends with Carrain, Lopenia, Lisandeka and Morla. She was daughter to Lady Moradina.

105. **Moradina, Lady**: Lady of Antar, mother to Junior Sister Moradien.

106. **Morla:** Junior Sister, part of a circle of friends with Carrain, Lopenia, Moradien, and Lisandeka.

107. **Natalia Do'Manis:** Former Lux Baiula, in exile in Unumia. She had the ability to enter other humanoids' minds and was exiled sixty years earlier for apparently forcing her thoughts into the mind of a student.

108. **Nihildrina**: Eternal Surgeon and Advisor to Queen Zebula. .

109. **Nila**: The woman was a plump, Nonsensing, low-ranking Shadinian with a bubbly temperament, personal aid to Krystian Lux Baiula.

110. **Noctiferus**: See description in Appendix V

111. **Nogarin Vrollis**: Lord and Royal Marshal of Flavius the First's army.

112. **Octavius I of House Coriolis, High King**: Ruler of Upper and Lower Alvinor and Overlord of the lands of Jarah, Pargah, and Yerlah; also called "the Wise". Octavius was 142 y.o. He was married to Lady Darya.

113. **Ones – The**: They were a communal humanoid race, acting more like a single organism than as individuals. Individuals were difficult to distinguish, and their language extremely difficult for any other humanoid to understand.

114. **Oolviana Methrim**: Birth mother to Lusk Methrim.

115. **Ori of House Coriolis, prince**: Ori was the youngest of High King Octavius's children. He was 13 y.o.

116. **Parok Vrol, Frumentarius**: In charge of the secret service under High Captain Harlion.

117. **Parthos**: Young guardian at the fortress, assigned to standing guard in front of Toras's chambers.

118. **Paula, Eldest**: One of the three Eldest, along with Senator Amis, and First Senator Leo.

119. **Peter**: Royal Guardian, apprentice medicus militus.

120. **Piros**: Guardian assigned to guarding Aithen.

121. **Rackeli**: High King Octavius's majordomo.

122. **Ramela Lux Baiula**: Praefecta Consuasores, Head of the Purple Sashate, or Advisors' Assembly. She was a beautiful woman, with brown hair, smoothly rounded oval face, and pale brown eyes. She was a pure Jarahni. She was a straightforward, level-headed and smart woman.

123. **Rathos**: Guardian at the fortress, assigned to standing guard in front of Toras's chambers.

124. **Rinius, Primus**: Officer of the Royal Guard.

125. **Rovali**: Aithen's majordomo. Rovali oversaw the prince's household.

126. **Rufus**: Harlion's voran.

127. **Rulok**: Royal Guardian, died killed by a gnarler.

128. **Saara Lux Baiula**: Praefecta Medicas, Leader of the White Sashate, or Medics' Assembly for thirty-three years. Former Yellow Sash. The oldest Lux Baiula, she was 175 years old.

129. **Saborin**: Friend of Mekiir, soldier in the Royal Guard.

130. **Sarrinia Lux Baiula:** A White Sash; Healer of Bearers, responsible for the health of other Lux Baiulae.

131. **Scorch:** Prince Toras's furan. He was the same age as his master, 22 y.o. He was the son of Thunder, one of the high king's furans.

132. **Serpent, The - :** Also known as *Alis Domini* or the Master's Wings. It was a mutated rokon. It resembled the species physically, but its mutations had given it incredible powers, including the ability to fry its victim's brain with an unknown form of energy similar to the Quatiô or DEBSA (see definition in Appendix IV).

133. **Sharan:** Horn's Passer, mother of the young boy healed by Elyana.

134. **Sheffar of Amalor:** A secundus of the Black Guard at Horn's Pass.

135. **Sur'Elando Cronin:** Young mystical senator.

136. **Tamas, Sergeant:** Commander of the outpost on Mountain Lake.

137. **Tania Lux Baiula:** A White Sash from Yerlah. Head Medic in Furan City. She was 95 y.o.

138. **Tarchus the Great, Emperor:** During the beginning of the First Age, ruled over the continent of Aquinos, and the islands of Kynaria and Unumia. The Alvinorian calendar marked Tarchus the Great's ascent to the throne as Year 0 CE (current era).

139. **Tarkian the Second, High King:** Developed what became the most formidable airborne force in all the known lands in 1468 CE: at its peak, the force comprised ten thousand Black Furans and twenty thousand riders.

140. **Telpornion, Secundus:** Officer of the Royal Guard.

141. **Thabo:** Minister of science; collaborator of Genghis.

142. **To'kahr:** High Priest of the Temple of Elando, brother to To'kahra, of Rokothian origin.

143. **To'kahra:** High Priestess of the Temple of Elande, sister to To'kahr, of Rokothian origin.

144. **Toras of House Coriolis, Prince and Lord Commander:** A Halfling, middle son to Darya and Octavius. He was commander of the Black Guard. He was 22 years old, of average height, and had a strong build. Toras had a furan named Scorch.

145. **Trebloc, Neaj:** He was a young attendant in the Royal Treasury. A short fellow, with wavy black hair, and small eyes that seemed to want to look through things.

146. **Ulva Lux Baiula:** Red Sash from Urbs Lucis, twin to Xena Lux Baiula.

147. **Ulvius Coriolis, Lord:** Son to Lord Gaius Coriolis, and owner of the Great Mining Company which owned all rights to the exploitation of ardamantis.

148. **Umbra:** Umbra was Noctiferus's lieutenant on K'Tara. Also known as Shadow, or Shadow-Maker.

149. **Urlis:** Royal Guardian, originally from Shadin City. He was tall and boasted a frightening musculature. He had grown up on fishing ships, helping his father hunt sea leviathans.

150.

151. **Ursula Lux Baiula**: A Purple Sash from Kirgad, with a word-chopping accent.

152. **Valorian, Lord:** Ruler of Spiritii, friend to High King Octavius.

153. **Warbender, Lord**: Lord of the Armory.

154. **Wasil, King**: Ruler of Pargah, vassal to High King Octavius.

155. **Xena Lux Baiula**: Red Sash from Urbs Lucis, sister to Ulva Lux Baiula.

156. **Xyre**: Aithen's furan. He was 27 y.o.

157. **Ylana Maryn Dar'Muntake, Honored One**: Supreme Priestess of the Order of Kynaria. She was a tall woman, standing at a little more than 2 meters. She had brown skin, long graying hair, and striking orange-colored eyes. Her ears had very deep grooves at the top, indicating her great strength in the Bind.

158. **Zebula the Sixth, Queen of Zebulonia**: Current ruler of Zebulonia, descendent of Zebula the Repressor.

Administrator: The rank of Lux Baiulae in charge of local seats of the Sisterhood, such as Domus Lucis in Furan City. Administrators were typically of the Purple Sash but may be of the White Sash in small towns, or of the Yellow Sash in collegiate cities such as Antar. There were no Administrators of the Red Sash.

Ages: The first age spanned from year 0 to year 687 and was known as the First Imperial Age; the second spanned from years 688 to 1034 and was known as Second Imperial Age; the third and current age was known as the Aquinian Age.

Afterkind: A Loracan term referring to the lifeforms which evolved from the seeds placed on K'Tara by the Founders. Humanoids were among them, as well as most other non-sequential hermaphroditic creatures. Afterkind species are opposed to Firstkind species (see below).

Alnoor: A tree found only in the woods adjoining the Colossi's forest. Its wood was made of long and resilient, but highly resistant fibers.

Alnoor longbows: These were the most prized bows in all of Terrae Regis. They were made from the branches of the Alnoor tree and could project arrows at distances well over one thousand meters.

Alterintrant: People who were able to connect with the Bind were known as Alterintrants. Those who developed Sensing skills alone were known as Sensors whereas those who could both feel and make use of the Bind were known as Binders. An Alterintrant "called" the Bind and used various "Bindings" to effect the intended action (such as telekinesis, healing, etc.).

Attending Sisters: Lux Baiulae posted as guardians outside of meeting rooms.

Barrier: Barrier was the title given to the Sisters responsible for security at Urbs Lucis. Barriers were raised from the Red Sash and were among the deadliest of the Sisterhood. The First Barrier was the commander of this guard.

Bind, The: Dimension of space and time where the energies of livings things were reflected. Nonliving things could also be reflected there if a humanoid interacted with them.

Bind-wrought products: Objects created by Sisters of the Yellow Sash, and sold to those who could afford them, such as reinforced walls, reinforced doors, poison detectors, Living Lamps, etc.

Birthing vessel: A low-class Zebulonian woman used by the Janarae to carry their progeny.

Bitters: A herbal infusion used after a meal. These infusions had digestive as well as medicinal properties.

Black Skies: Used in the expression "Join the Black Skies", meaning to join those that died a tragic death.

Bok tree: A large, red-leafed tree, which provided shade and privacy.

Bolingars: The Bolingars were the hottest hours of the K'Taran day, when the two suns stood side-by-side at their apex. During those hours, land animals either went into hiding or deployed one adaptation or another to protect themselves from the burning rays. Flowering plants withdrew their flowers into protective, waxy casings. The term was an Alvinorian deformation of "Boiling Hours." A Bolingar Fourth was a fourth during which the two suns were side-by-side. Bolingar Fourths alternated with the In-Between Fourths during which the suns overlapped, with the smaller Blue sun or the larger Red sun in front; these fourths were cooler than the Bolingar Fourths.

Caves of Death: A series of caves in Zebulonia, used by the Queen to imprison thieves, murderers, and political opponents where they were left to die if they were not executed.

Captain: "Captain" was a general title for any officer in charge.

Cleaning up: The removal of all "disruptive" males from a city.

Coonay: A sweet spread made from the caramelization of the cocoon produced by bellowers against the Bolingars.

Coriolan Tomb: A cave beneath the palace which contained the remains of Coriolan rulers.

Dark Battle: It lasted from the years 1220 to 1226. It was a battle against Noctiferus and his forces. It ended when High King Flavius the Third succeeded in assembling the remaining Human and Kynarian forces to eradicate the Dark One's forces after Noctiferus was captured by the Luxori and Lux Baiulae.

Elevation Chapel: Chapel of the Order of the Light in Urbs Lucis where various ceremonies were held such as the Elevation of Juniors to full Sisterhood, or the Ascension of deceased Sisters to the Bind.

Field Purification: This was a punishment handed to Juniors and Novices for disobeying the Sisterhood's rules and laws. It consisted in using the Bind to sterilize a city's outflows, then restoring beneficial microbes, and hastening the decomposition of the detritus into simpler organic and inorganic matter.

Firstkind: Firstkind species were those that originated on K'Tara. Most Firstkind species were sequential hermaphrodites which alternated between male and female anatomy and physiology.

First's Knuckles: The First's Knuckles was an instrument made of black marble and shaped as a half-moon with four knuckles on the convex side. The knuckles were used to "rap" an aluminum base that made a loud popping sound as each knuckle depressed the metal.

Fourth: A fourth was an 8-day period. The Alvinorian calendar had four fourths in a month, and sixteen months in a year. The fourths were based on the suns' cycle of rotation around each other, which lasted 32 days

Frumentarius: A member of the secret service of the kingdom.

Furan Bonding: The art of raising captured furans and bonding them to their masters. A Bound furan would be allowed to return to the wild once it reached the age of 50. There, it would usually find a mate and reproduce. Once bonded, a furan would waste away if its master died, unless a Lux Baiula released the bond.

Furanry: The furan-mounted force of the Alvinorian army, rebuilt to 3000 teams at the start of the story.

Gnarler: Also known as Night Terror by Lux Baiulae of old. It was a beast of the ugliest kind; it was of a Human form, but walked mostly in a crouched position; it was able to produce quills which it ejected through its knuckles at great distances to kill its prey; it did not have a proper language, and so it gnarled most of the time.

Grand Council: Council of Kynaria. Among other things, they determined the passage of neos to priesthood.

Guard: The Alvinorian Guard was split into the Royal Guard, the Army of the Union, and the Black Guard. The Black Guard numbered one thousand men, of which 100 were furan-mounted. The Royal Guard was headed by High Captain Harlion and overseen by High Lord Commander Aithen. It was comprised of 20,000 soldiers, stationed in five bases around Alvinoria, of which 3000 were furan-mounted, and of which 1000 were stationed at House of the Guard outside the walls of the capital. The Army of the Union, also under the high prince's oversight, included the soldiers maintained by each of the major landholders, numbering 105,000 in total. The Black Guard protected the pass between Lower Alvinor and Rokoth. The king's Praetorian Guard, an elite unit of the Royal Guard, was composed of four men under Primus Julian.

Halami: A drink made from the juices of a plump, sweet, round fruit, in which large, leather-winged insects were drowned. This process decomposed the internal flesh of the insect, extracting special nutrients from the insect, and protecting the drink from spoilage during long trips.

Halflings: Half Kynarian and half Human.

Highsun: Two to three hours surrounding the noon period during which the suns were at their apex.

Honored One, The: Head of the Order of Kynaria.

Howler-night: A howler-night was the number of howlers needed to keep one warm. The more howlers were needed, the colder the temperature was.

Insulated Chamber: The Insulated Chamber was a room constructed of materials which did not allow the Bind to flow through.

Janarae: Sorceresses and soldiers of the queens of Zebulonia. Queen Zebula the 3rd instituted the Janarae as a secret society soon as she rose to power, while Zebula the 4th made them into an army.

Knowing Circles: These were Zebulonian guilds and included healers, instructors, philosophers, and stone masons, all working to provide the Queen and her subjects with things they needed.

Kynarian: One of the humanoid races on K'Tara. They were typically intellectuals, artists, and politicians and were very strong Sensors. They also had a powerful priestly class. Physically, Kynarians averaged 1.8 m (5'10") tall; they had tapered noses and thin lips, brown skin, and eyes ranging from grey to deep blue. They also had higher hips for their height, compared to Humans. Kynarian lifespan averaged 180 years.

Kynarian Priests and Priestesses: Members of the Order of Kynaria, founded by Kynaria in the 200 CE. Kynarian clerics graduated from junior neos to senior neos, also known as "advanced", and then achieved priesthood through the ritual of Passage. Junior neos had green robes, with a black lace around the right arm. Kynarian clerics were recognized by the high collar of their dresses or robes and the rounded nick in the top ridge of the ears. The deeper the groove, the greater their connection to the Bind was.

Lacora Leaf objects: Objects such as chairs, litters and beds were formed by the branches and leaves of the lacora plant. Monks of the Order of Elando took years to shape the plants and sold the finished products to a select few. Chairs and beds were the favorite such objects. When a person moved, the chair or bed re-formed itself to maintain full contact with the person's body at any angle the person desired. The angle was determined by the placement of the two lead branches of the plant. In a chair, one lead branch would be set horizontally for the seat, and the other vertically for the back.

Locari: An aquatic sentient species as highly evolved as any humanoid. Their bodies were flat and shaped like a kite. They had iridescent skin which could shift in colors. The Locari, similarly to many other native species of K'Tara, could move between water, land and air, after a short metamorphosis.

Lonem: A fragrant tree; inhabitants of the east coast made themselves homes inside of the trees which could reach heights of one hundred meters and boast trunks nine meters wide.

Lucis Sororum Societas: See "Order of the Sisters of the Light".

Lux Baiulae: Bearers of Light. Lux ("u" as in "Luke") Baiula (ba as in "latte" + "ee" + you + "la" as in "latte." Members of the Order of Light.

- **Progression**: Women were admitted into the Sisterhood as novices, who could then progress to become Junior Sisters. Both novices and juniors were considered Apprentices. Junior Sisters reached Full Sisterhood through a ritual known as Elevation.

- **Divisions**: The Sisterhood was divided into four functions, each represented by a differently colored sash, and each organized into an Assembly. These were: red sash for the Warriors, yellow sash for the Seekers of Truth, purple sash for the Public Servants and Advisors, and white sash for the Medics. Each Assembly was led by a Praefecta. A woman might be elevated to more than one Sash, in sequence, but not at the same time. In such a case, a short section of her old sash would be sewed onto the new one. Novice Sisters did not wear any sash. Junior Sisters wore the sash representing the Assembly they had chosen, but with a white stipe sewn vertically across the sash.

- **Ruling**: The leader of the Sisterhood was elected by the Praefectae and was known as Magna Mater. The Magna Mater was advised by the Praefectae, and together they composed the Light's Assembly, or Ruling Council. Beneath the Praefectae there were Administrators who represented the Sisterhood in local seats across Alvinoria as well as in Kynaria.
- **Symbol**: The two suns, the Blue and the Red, represented the Order of Light.
- **Miscellaneous**: Only 7 Lux Baiulae were allowed in Furan City at any one time.
- **Size of the Sisterhood**: As of the start of the story, the Sisterhood comprised 681 Sisters, including the Magna Mater. There were a total of 200 White Sashes (of which 20 inside Urbs Lucis), 180 Yellow Sashes (of which 110 inside Urbs Lucis), 149 Purple Sashes (of which 18 inside Urbs Lucis), and 151 Red Sashes (all within Urbs Lucis). There were also 200 Apprentices (111 novices and 89 juniors).

Luxor: Member of the male branch of the Order of Light; Luxori disappeared in the year 1567, following an epidemic which wiped them all out in a few months.

Manu Dextra: The Magna Mater's personal advisor or Right Hand.

News Fetcher: A man who gathered news for paying parties.

Order of the Sisters of the Light or Lucis Sororum Societas, ak.a. Sisterhood: The Order had been in existence since the beginning of the Second Age, nearly twelve-hundred years earlier. Its members were special Human females who could sense and make use of the energies stored within the Bind – but this – only after years of strenuous training, although there were those who progressed much faster toward Elevation. One of the Order's responsibilities was to protect K'Tarans, a purpose for which they swore an unbreakable oath. Its members were known as Lux Baiulae.

Organization for the Liberation of Zebulonian Males (OLZM): An organization founded in the year 1796, the year following a failed uprising, by the leaders of a number of male guilds who aimed to overthrow Queen Zebula and her government.

Originator's Hand, - The: A group of religious fanatics who carried out assassinations to remove atheists throughout the Union. The group was thought to have been eliminated in the year 1760, forty years before present.

Pargahnese and Kirgahnese Peace Treaty: A treaty signed between the two cities twenty years earlier.

Praefecta Consuasores: Leader of the Public Servants and Advisors' Assembly.

Praefecta Medicas: Leader of the Medics' Assembly.

Praefecta Milites: Leader of the Warriors' Assembly.

Praefecta Philosophas: Leader of the Seekers' Assembly.

Praetorian Guard: The guard was an elite unit of the Royal Guard. Its members served as bodyguards to the high king. High King Octavius's personal guard was composed of Primus Julian, and guardians Jashan, Almiar, Kiron, and Merr.

Racanut: A large seed, the size of a Human's head.

Sabara: Small, fleshy, dark purple sweet fruit that grew in clusters on the main branches of the tree.

Safeplace: This was a hidden shelter that each village, town and city in the kingdom was required to have. The locations of these shelters were kept by the Royal Guard and the Sisterhood

Sashate: Offices of a Sash of the Order of the Light at Urbs Lucis. Each Sashate occupied one of the four angles of the palace: the White Sashate occupied the southwest angle, the Yellow the northwest angle, the Purple the southeast and the Red the northeast angle. The term was also used to denote the Sash Assembly.

Secret police: A secret corps that had first been created under High King Lucius III. Octavius was its first commander under his father's rule, followed by Master Vrol, then Harlion. Its members were known as Frumentarii.

Selection Council: Kynarian and Alvinorian body whose role it was to approve the unions between the Alvinorian ruler and his chosen Kynarian or Human consort.

Senate: Comprised of elder members of the Alvinorian patriciate.

Senatorial Police: A policing corps responsible for maintaining order in the capital.

Sending: As a noun, referred to the non-verbal, concept-based communication used by the Locari or to the telepathic communications of Alterintrants. As a verb, referred to the act of communicating in this manner.

Soiled man or woman: Soiled men or women were individuals with dangerous microbes which could cause them to harm others when using the Bind. Such individuals were interned at Urbs Lucis's

Observatory for the rest of their lives, to be washed daily in antimicrobials, and forced to drink noxious concoctions, every night, to keep the harmful microbial flora in a suppressed state. Unfortunately for the patients, these medications also repressed beneficial microbes, leaving them weak and miserable, and with a much-shortened lifespan.

Stinger's tail: Symbol used on communications to the high king regarding activities or persons that posed a risk to the Alvinorian kingdom.

Stones: One stone was the temperature reached by a liter of near-frozen water in one minute when one burning, 10g (0.3 oz) stone was added to it.

- 1 stone was equivalent to 2°C (35.6°F)
- 10 stones was equivalent to 20°C (68°F)
- 25 stones was equivalent to 50°C (122°F)

Sunshield: The word referred to the physical coverings or chemical mechanisms that animals, which could not hide from the suns at midday, deployed over their bodies in order to protect themselves.

Tabellarius: See definition in Appendix VI.

Temptator: A Temptator was a humanoid turned by Noctiferus to infiltrate K'Taran societies and recruit their leaders and members to do Noctiferus's bidding by indulging their every wants and needs. Alterintrant Temptatori could use the Bind to influence their targets, while Nonsensing Temptatori used only their charm and wiles to do so.

Time disc: The time disc was composed of a main disk, which told the time, and a smaller one set in the bottom half, which could be set to sound an alarm after a certain amount of time. Each turn of the alarm disk equated to 15 minutes. When it was unwound all the way, the unwinding occurring at a known speed, a mechanism hit the disk and produced a soft ringing sound.

Trionian War: In 1333 CE, Emperor Flavius the Third had King Brathan of Trionia assassinated which led to a war between the Trionian and their allies' (Rokothian) forces and the Emperor's forces. At the end of the war, a treaty was signed, giving Trionia and Rokoth their independence.

Union – The: It was comprised of all the lands under the rule of Octavius I, including the Kingdoms of Upper and Lower Alvinor, and the lands of Jarah, Pargah and Yerlah. The Union was forged at the beginning of the Third Age, four hundred and sixty-seven years earlier, by High King Lucius the First.

Union Council: Composed of the thirty-two landholders (twenty-eight lords and ladies and three kings) of the Union.

Velnia: A Zebulonian medicinal plant from the western part of that country, which had incredibly strong regenerative properties, helping to heal day-old lacerated skin without creating a single scar.

Works, The: Being put to the works was a punishment handed to soldiers guilty of disobedience or disorder. It meant several fourths of cleaning vorans' muck, digging and covering refuse holes, and repairing carts and doing all sorts of other backbreaking or very unpleasant tasks.

APPENDIX IV – ANIMALIA

Aquilian: Large predatory flyer.

Belwohrs: These were huge carnivorous animals of the Furan Peaks, the size of a battle voran, which often tried to feed on young furans.

Biters: Insect which could tear pieces of flesh from under Human and furan hair, leaving holes the size of a pinhead that bled for a while. These wounds oftentimes became infected afterwards, and certain infections were fatal. They lived at the foot of the Furan Peaks and Colossi's Peaks.

Bleaters: These were milk-producing land flyers, having lost the ability to fly during the course of their evolution.

Bograms: These were squat, elongated herbivorous amphibians, about two meters long. They had iridescent skin. They were loved by Alvinorians their flavorful meat

Carrier: A small flying animal used to carry messages between cities.

Chirpers: One of a hundred species of singing flyers.

Fatock: An animal of the Flyer's order, but unable to fly due to its highly modified tail, which was spread like a wind fan.

Furan: An animal with a beaked head, furry body, and two pairs of leathery wings. It had long powerful legs it used to launch itself into the air or to run, though because of the wings, the running was not as elegant as that of other animals.

Furans lived in structured societies, used an intricate vocabulary of screeches and grunts to communicate complex thoughts to each other which they used to organize their hunts, and understood humanoid languages as well as sign language. Unfortunately, their squawks and purrs were not easily understood by humanoids, though soldiers learned to recognize some of their vocalizations as well as the motions furans made with their heads and paws, and Kynarians were able to read their thoughts through the Bind. The young of furans were known as fureens.

There were three species of furans:

- The **Green Furan** was the smallest species. It had an average wingspan of 2m, and with its mild character it made a good pet when Humans were able to capture a young one. The species had a lifespan of 40 years. Its range was centered on Unumia and extended toward the southwestern coast of the Yeltchek to the east of Unumia, and the eastern coast of Lower Alvinor to the west of the large island.
- The **White Furan** had a 2.5m wingspan and a lifespan of about 50 years. A territorial species, whose males often fought each other to the death, it could not be tamed. Its range included Mo'Rokoth and Kynaria.
- The **Black Furan** was endemic to the Furan Peaks. The largest of the three-known species, it had a 4m wingspan, making it a formidable war animal. It could live well over 90 years. The Black Furan, which lived in large prides, established strong, monogamous bonds. It was the species from which the Royal Furans were selected. Its bonding to humanoids was performed by specialized Lux Baiulae. Its purr was a sound deeper, louder, and slower than that of domestic cats. As did all furans, the Black Furan was capable of hearing ultrasounds and riders used Sagr Bleater horns to call their mounts back. These horns produced an ultrasonic sound which carried for dozens of kilometers.

Honkers: Flyers with a honking call. These flyers were one of the few families of large flyers without Sunshields and therefore needed to find shade at midday.

Howler: A large, domesticated predatory flyer; at its shoulders, it stood about waist-high; it provided Humans with company, and protection from other beasts, often larger than itself, and it also assisted Humans in hunting.

Lemma: These hip-high grazers lived in small groups, feeding mostly in the evening.

Leviathan: Large sea animals ranging in size from 15 to 50 meters (45 to 150 feet). Leviathans were mostly peaceful creatures despite their size and were also known for their beautiful songs.

Limpfish: An invertebrate animal living in the Sea of Tarkoth, hunted for its black ink.

Nibbler: Animals ranging in size from a few centimeters to a meter long, with long, hard incisor which the animals used to eat from tough plant materials.

Red Locarian: An advanced Lower Locarian.

Rokon: A large reptilian flying predator from Mo'Tarkoth. The male rokon had a wingspan of around five meters, while the female's wingspan neared six meters. The rokon killed its prey, typically a bleater, by knocking it over with full force to break its spine. It would then fly over it to tear its flesh with the teeth that covered its wings and body, tenderizing the meat with the enzymes that flowed from the teeth.

Shellie: Small invertebrate creature with a thin shell on its back

Tarkan: A Tarkan was a creature of the underground which would open a gaping hole in the ground to swallow its prey. Tarkans lived on Bremin Island.

Vale: One of the largest species of leviathan. Their songs were not the most beautiful, but could still enrapture anyone. Vales usually travelled in groups.

Varagoths: They were large beasts, some seven meters long from head to tail, and three meters high at the shoulder. They had six long, straight horns on the forehead as well as two long curved tusks. Their body was muscular with a hump on the back of the neck, and their leather thick and golden in color. Because they were extremely dangerous, Alvinoria had undertaken an eradication campaign some 20 years earlier, and they were no-longer to be found in the northeast of the kingdom.

Voran: A tall, domesticated trumpeter used for pulling or riding. Trumpeters were three-toed herbivores, recognized by their trumpet-like calls; vorans, in particular, had beautiful calls. Many breeds of vorans existed, each with varied coloration of the fur and eyes, as well as varied calls.

Allied Lands: Included Upper and Lower Alvinor, as well as Rokoth.

Alvinor, Upper and Lower: Known together as Alvinoria, these lands were now ruled by High King Octavius I.

Alvinoria: Its population totaled nearly four million.

Argon Pass: Pass between the Colossi's Peaks and Furan Peaks. Named after the river that had its source there on the slopes of the Furan Peaks.

Bremin City: A city founded by a splinter group of **Breminese.** The city came under Coriolan rule in the year 1350. It was ruled by Claudius of House Coriolis, brother to High King Octavius I at the time of these events.

Bremin Island: Large island at the entrance of the Great Lake, home to the Independent Nation of Bremin. The Breminese were a humanoid species with red hair, pale green skin, and gray eyes.

Grand Audience Hall: Hall which contained High King Octavius's throne.

Furan City: It was a city of 90,000, flanked by the House of the Guard, just outside the northern wall of the city. The House of the Guard was home to 1000 men and their furans. The royal palace was situated to the east of the city.

Hall of the Light: Audience chamber on the second floor of the palace at Urbs Lucis. It was oval shaped, with a dais, a lectern and seats behind it for the Praefectae. Bilena was seated left-most of the Magna Mater, followed by Ramela, and then Larca and Saara to her right, Larca being in the right-most seat.

Horn's Pass: Name of the pass to the north of the Furan Peaks between Rokoth and Lower Alvinor and of the Fortress protecting it. The guard at Horn's Pass, known as the Black Guard, numbered one thousand men. It had been built in the years after the secession of Rokoth from the Coriolan empire, between 1334 and 1338.

Kynaria: Land of the Kynarians. The Kynarian civilian government only administered education and civic works. The priesthood administered – controlled – trade, finances, health and national defense.

Private Audience Chamber: Chamber where High King Octavius held important meetings when problems needed to be discussed and decisions made.

Solinor: The capital of Kynaria was built on a series of five ridges, or hills, overlooking the fantastic Bay of Lardos, possibly the grandest place on K'Tara. The Kynarian Ruling Seat was located on the northernmost ridge, known as First Seat Hill. This ridge comprised the Ruler's private residence, the Senate's Chamber and Aiala'Rhi's Chamber. The school, known as School of Kynaria, was situated on Second Seat Hill, east of First Seat Hill, while various administrative offices were located on Third Seat Hill, to the west of the first, and the fourth and fifth ridges were home to the civilians.

Urbs Lucis: A.k.a. City of Lights. Capital of the Order of the Light. It was divided into a Lower City, inhabited by a civilian population of 2000 which provided the Sisterhood with various products and services, and an Upper City, or Inner Sanctum, which was populated by the nearly 500 Lux Baiulae, Juniors and novices, along with their civilian attendants and any other civilian employed by the Sisterhood. The Order's palace was in the center of the Inner Sanctum. The city was an autonomous city of the kingdom of Alvinoria, and as such owed only taxes and the provision of free medical care to the kingdom's subjects as payment for their autonomy.

Yerlah: Vassal kingdom from the southwest of Aquinos. Yerlayans had ash-white hair, dark eyebrows and deep blue eyes. Their accent emphasized the last syllables of words and added a letter "e" to most.

Zebulonia: Land to the south of the Mountains of Sagr, formerly known as Trionia. Zebula the First changed the name when she took the throne at the end of the Trionian War which led to Trionia's secession from Aquinos in the Year 1333, a war which was caused by Emperor Flavius the Third's murder by an assassin sent by King Brathan of Trionia.

APPENDIX VI – THE POWERS & K'TARAN TECHNOLOGY

POWERS

Individuals who could connect with the Bind were known as Alterintrants. Accessing the Bind depended, in general, on one's microbial flora and atomic predisposition, as well as on one's ability to approach near subconscious levels of the mind. In this state, a sensing person, a Sensor, could enter the Bind, and perceive various forms of energy not sensed by the Unsensing. He or she might also be able channel various vibrations of the Bind to a point or area of focus to cause some effect. Such an Alterintrant was known as a Binder. Depending on the combination of microbial floras, as well as on a person's atomic predisposition, diverse types of Binding capabilities emerged.

Bind-fusion: The ability to harden mineral matter and fuse mineral objects.

Black melding: Taking control of another's thoughts.

Bound Shield: An electromagnetic shield placed around a person's body or object. The shield was a discovery of the Luxori, five hundred years before, when they too had been involved in the development of the Binding Sciences. Shields placed around a person depended on them being previously treated with certain microbes. The shield protected the bearer from fire as well as from any oncoming object containing metals. Objects had to be similarly pretreated.

Chime: A vibration which was used to call or alert another Lux Baiula through the Bind. The vibration was sensed by the recipient in a way similar to the sound of wind chimes.

Confusion: A safe procedure by which a Lux Baiula erased a person's short-term memory; Urbs Lucis prohibited using this on non-threatening humanoids.

Dark Energy Brain Surge Attack, or DEBSA: This power allowed its wielder to kill from a distance by causing massive static discharges in the victim's brain. The power had been known as Quatiô in the previous era and was subdivided into Quatiô Major which referred to the brain-frying power used by the Serpent, and Quatiô Minor which referred to the brain-arresting power used by Noctiferus's assassins.

Firebolt: Javelin-like projection of fire formed with the use a small, dense stone held at a distance, serving as the fuel. A Lux Baiula formed a cone-shaped Bound-shield around the stones; the shield was closed in the back and pointed toward the target. Spinning the shield ignited the stone, and the fire was then projected forward

Firewhorl: Ball of fire ignited around a target by projecting flammable material at it.

Inhibition field: A field established around a person's mind to hide their presence or prevent them from exchanging thoughtcalls.

Linking: In Kynarians, linking enabled two persons to speak to each other telepathically.

Memory Transfer: To capture a dying person's memories. This transfer of memories could lead to greater knowledge, as well as to greater understanding of the world and its workings. But Transferred Memory could also lead to greater confusion and madness. The Lux Baiula receiving the memories was known as a Receiver. The procedure was discovered and developed by Afanasiia Lux Baiula in the year 1225, during the Dark Battle.

Mind-link: This simple procedure allowed two or more willing Alterintrants to connect their thoughts.

Mind-tying: This procedure allowed the minds of two willing Alterintrants to share their sensory signals as well as their thoughts, if so desired. The sharing of thoughts was not necessarily bidirectional. A mind-tie also allowed a Lux Baiula to shield the other person's mind from discovery. Its establishment was quite violent.

Nebula: A field of energy generated by some Lux Baiulae which could shield people from certain harmful cerebral waves; also known as a disruption field.

Roaming: Ability to travel within the Bind.

Sound Shield: Created by increasing the density of particles along the surfaces of a room, causing said particles to vibrate in a distortive manner.

Sound-barrier: Created by placing resonant minerals within certain structures, such as stone, metal, and the bark of hardwood trees. The more the minerals, the larger the diameter of the barrier created. Only tree flyer songs (or other similar high-pitched sounds) could cross such fields.

Telekinesis: Ability to affect objects at a distance.

Thunder-strike: A powerful weapon of the Bind but rarely used in battle because of the difficulty one had in aiming it accurately.

Thoughtcalls: Communication achieved through either a Mind-link, or Mind-tie between two Sisters or while Roaming the Bind between any Sister. Thoughtcalls were nearly impossible to overhear.

Transfection: Transfer of one Sister's microbial flora to another to give the recipient powers equivalent to those of the giver. But these were only equivalent and not the same, given that a Sister's powers depended both on her microbial flora as well as on her atomic constitution.

K'TARAN TECHNOLOGY

Most K'Taran technology was based on the ability to use and control microbes. Other technologies relied on the use of minerals or stones that interacted with the forces in the Bind.

Amplifying Alterintrant Detector (AAD): A fist-sized, purple-colored crystal encased in a golden ring sitting atop three long legs which was created to find Alterintrants anywhere on K'Tara

Communicator: This device allowed sound to cross from one side of a wall to the other. To communicate, a Sister would simply channel her voice toward it.

Living Lamps: Lamps containing luminescent micro-organisms used to light-up a space. Quieting Cloths were placed on the lamps at night to block the light and arrest the luminescence so that the micro-organisms' energy stores could be restored.

Living Screen: This was a gel-containing screen which harbored various pressure-sensitive, pigment-producing microbes. Drawings were created by pressing one's finger on the screen with more or less force to cause the microbes to release various pigments.

Tabellarius: An instrument, also known as Sound Carrier, which carried orders in the Royal Guard. A person, also called Tabellarius, hit the device with a mallet. The instrument transmitted the resulting sound through the air. The sound was then picked up on the windward face of the next tabellarius and, through an ingenious mechanism, automatically repeated by way of its leeward face to be received by the next instrument in the chain, and so on. A second invention prevented the sound from being repeated by the preceding instruments, an event which would result in canceling out the sounds, scrambling them or rendering them otherwise incomprehensible.

APPENDIX VII – THE FOUNDERS & K'TARAN CREATION MYTH

Aiala'Rhi: Principle of Order; known as the Originator of all things by Humans, Kynarians and Zebulonians alike. Aiala'Rhi meant 'Aiala the Great'.

Noctiferus: Bringer of the Night in the ancient tongue, also known as Hrackmol! by the Locari. He was formerly known by the K'Tarans as Aiala'Rho, Principle of Change and husband to Aiala'Rhi. He was considered to be the First Founder.

Horin: Horin was known as the Principle of Truth. He was the Second Founder.

Elande: Elande was known as the Principle of Balance, created by Aiala'Rhi to contain the effects of Aiala'Rho. She was the Third Founder according to scriptures.

APPENDIX VIII – RITUALS

Applauds: Given by clapping the hand to the leg.

Greetings to the royals: To greet a royal, hands were joined while the head was slowly tipped forward.

Passing ceremonies: These were held one to two fourths after a death by murder. During the ceremony, the ashes of the victim along with what was known about him or her were passed on to both the victim's and the murderer's families by the clerics of Elande.

Well-wishing:

- "May your body be worthy" was a form used to wish others well upon parting. It originated from the belief of the main Terrae Regian religion, Rhiism, that on the Day of Union, the Founders and other gods would come to K'Tara and grant eternal life to the bodies of the worthiest Humans. They would do so by merging their own spirits with the bodies of the worthy, whether the bodies be those of the deceased or of the living.

- "May the air sing" was an Alvinorian well-wish given to another before they reached a long-awaited reunion, an expression which meant "may your reunion be joyful.

- "May Alba keep your path clear" was an Alvinorian and Kynarian well-wish given to one who had a difficult road, and tough decisions, ahead.

 L.A. Di Paolo is a tri-lingual, Canadian-born Italian-American who lives in Pottstown, Pennsylvania. By day, because of his background in science and business, he manages drug development projects. By night, he rides and writes, but his horse is not the source of his inspiration. Rather, the constant questions in his mind are; questions about evolution, nature, and the human condition. And he has been writing to explore them and their answers, first in student newspapers, then in a magazine he authored and published, and now in this – his first novel.

If you are interested in learning more about L.A. Di Paolo or about this novel, you can visit his author web site at https://ladipaolo.net. or with your phone by scanning the code below.

www.ingramcontent.com/pod-product-compliance
Lightning Source LLC
Chambersburg PA
CBHW070926100726
47908CB00001B/110